PATH OF THE ELDAR

The ancient eldar are a mysterious race, each devoting their life to a chosen path which will guide their actions and decide their fate. On Craftworld Alaitoc, three friends – Korlandril, Thirianna and Aradryan – each follow their paths, their lives intertwining as they all play their parts in a great war that engulfs the craftworld and threatens the existence of everything that they hold dear.

PATH OF THE WARRIOR

Korlandril abandons peace for the Path of the Warrior. He becomes a Striking Scorpion, a deadly fighter skilled in the art of close-quarter combat. But the further Korlandril travels down this path, the closer he gets to losing his identity and becoming an avatar of war.

PATH OF THE SEER

Thirianna eschews her simple existence to embark upon the mysterious Path of the Seer. She will tread a dark and dangerous road that leads her to the other realm of the warp, where daemons are made flesh and nightmares are manifest, for only there can she realise her psychic abilities.

PATH OF THE OUTCAST

Aradryan has chosen to leave his sheltered life on Craftworld Alaitoc and walk the Path of the Outcast, seeking the myriad pleasures and threats the wider galaxy has to offer. Still unfulfilled as a ranger, he is lured into the life of a star pirate, bringing him into conflict with the Imperium of Man.

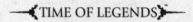

PATH OF THE ELDAR

GAV THORPE

BLACK LIBRARY

A Black Library Publication

Path of the Warrior copyright © 2010, Games Workshop Ltd.
Path of the Seer copyright © 2011, Games Workshop Ltd.
Path of the Outcast copyright © 2012, Games Workshop Ltd.
'The Curse of the Shaa-Dom' first published in the Games Day Anthology 2011/12
copyright © 2011, Games Workshop Ltd.
'The Rewards of Tolerance' first published in Victories of the Space Marines
copyright © 2011, Games Workshop Ltd.
'Dark Son' has not appeared before in print.
All rights reserved.

This omnibus edition published in Great Britain in 2014 by
Black Library,
Games Workshop Ltd.,
Willow Road,
Nottingham, NG7 2WS, UK.

10 9 8 7 6 5 4 3 2

Cover illustration by Neil Roberts.

A CIP record for this book is available from the British Library.

UK ISBN 13: 978 1 84970 576 9
US ISBN 13: 978 1 84970 577 6

See Black Library on the internet at

www.blacklibrary.com

Find out more about Games Workshop
and the world of Warhammer 40,000 at

www.games-workshop.com

Printed and bound by CPI Group (UK) Ltd, Croydon, CR0 4YY

It is the 41st millennium. For more than a hundred centuries
the Emperor has sat immobile on the Golden Throne of Earth.
He is the master of mankind by the will of the gods, and master
of a million worlds by the might of his inexhaustible armies. He
is a rotting carcass writhing invisibly with power from the Dark
Age of Technology. He is the Carrion Lord of the Imperium for
whom a thousand souls are sacrificed every day, so that he may
never truly die.

Yet even in his deathless state, the Emperor continues his
eternal vigilance. Mighty battlefleets cross the daemon-infested
miasma of the warp, the only route between distant stars, their
way lit by the Astronomican, the psychic manifestation of the
Emperor's will. Vast armies give battle in His name on uncounted
worlds. Greatest amongst his soldiers are the Adeptus Astartes,
the Space Marines, bio-engineered super-warriors. Their comrades
in arms are legion: the Imperial Guard and countless planetary
defence forces, the ever-vigilant Inquisition and the tech-priests of
the Adeptus Mechanicus to name only a few. But for all their
multitudes, they are barely enough to hold off the ever-present
threat from aliens, heretics, mutants — and worse.

To be a man in such times is to be one amongst untold
billions. It is to live in the cruellest and most bloody
regime imaginable. These are the tales of those times.
Forget the power of technology and science, for so much has
been forgotten, never to be re-learned. Forget the promise of
progress and understanding, for in the grim dark future
there is only war. There is no peace amongst the stars,
only an eternity of carnage and slaughter, and the
laughter of thirsting gods.

CONTENTS

INTRODUCTION

It's a well-documented fact that I have been a fan of the eldar in War-hammer 40,000 for a long time. In fact, I've been a fan since *Rogue Trader* came out, with its wonderful double-page (almost) piece of art with armoured fairies descending on a moon-like landscape. But my real passion for the eldar started with the Jes Goodwin-designed relaunch in *White Dwarf* 127. It was here that farseers, avatars, aspect warriors and exarchs first made their appearance, both in beautiful 3D and Jes's enchanting concept sketches and notes. It was also in that issue of the magazine that we learned so much more about eldar myths and psyche, and most importantly the eldar path.

I find the concept of the eldar path fascinating – the idea that life experience for the eldar is so intense that they have to shut off parts of themselves in order not to be driven mad by it. Sensation and emotion so overwhelming that it drove their entire civilisation slowly insane and birthed a ravenous Chaos god, and the solution is a form of self-selective mental lobotomy. Amongst the organic lines, clean technology and hippy juice, the eldar are certainly just as messed up as anything else in the Warhammer 40,000 universe!

I love the psychology of characters. That idea of transition, the char-acter journey in fiction, is the source of the best narrative in my eyes. The thought of creating a narrative in which the main characters not only undergo character development, but fundamentally shift from one person to another over the course of the story was a siren call to me. The *Path of the Eldar* gave me a chance to show, to explore, just what it is

9

like to wake up one morning as a poet and realise that you're done with that and it's time to psychologically and psychically metamorphose into someone else…

I wanted to make sure these novels were *eldar* novels first and foremost. Everything had to be from the eldar perspective, which brought with it some issues. The first was language. The eldar have a highly complex vocal and visual language, full of nuance and reliant on huge amounts of current and cultural context. It is, frankly, impossible to convey that in English in a way that would have any meaning for a reader. It was tempting to layer the text with eldar words and phrases, the exact sort of thing that I found so appealing all those years ago. However, every word and phrase would have required explanation and that would have cluttered up the prose. In the end, with the exception of names and a handful of already established words and phrases, I decided to present everything as if in translation. This means a lot of *portmanteau* words like 'silverscale' and 'wishbringer' and so forth, and if ever these strike readers as awkward I hope they can imagine that the eldar version is laden with far more gravitas and meaning!

There is also an issue of length. The eldar live a very long time, a thousand years and more by human standards, and they do not change quickly. I could have tackled this by writing a trilogy on each of the three feature characters, charting their lives with a narrative of battles and relationships over several books, but that was never my aim. From the outset I wanted to show a couple of things.

Firstly, I wanted to show different ways eldar interact with the path: getting trapped by it, moving along it and leaving it altogether. Secondly, I wanted to view the craftworlds (and Alaitoc in particular) through three lenses: in war, psychically and from the outside. Nine books to do that seems indulgent, and so I settled on the format of this trilogy, with three overlapping story arcs that allow us to watch as the transformation of the path (or lack of it in Aradryan's case) changes our characters and the way they interact with each other.

It is a forced perspective, I admit. Much like a movie crams as much story as possible into ninety minutes, these tales are a deliberately 'heightened reality' of the eldar experience. In order to cover the ground I wanted within a trilogy, this was unavoidable, and though for some background purists it may seem convenient, it's a narrative indulgence I'm prepared to accept so that the tale can be told in some reasonably consumable fashion. I dislike overly-long (one might say padded, but that would be rude) narratives that meander and go nowhere, and in order for our eldar characters' lives not to seem too indolent and introspective I upped the pace.

The structure of the trilogy itself was also a challenge I set myself from the outset. I had started toying with the idea of concurrent storylines in *The Sundering* for the Time of Legends series. With The *Path of the Eldar*

I took it one step further, with not only portions of the three books sharing the same timeframe, but all of them taking place over exactly the same tumultuous period in Alaitoc's history, with only the ending teasing out until volume three (because, why not?).

This presented a number of issues but in the end I think the story moves on enough with each telling – each fresh perspective sheds sufficient new light on previous events – that the narrative continues to be engaging. In all, it took quite a bit of planning, but I think it pays off.

Lastly, a quick word about exarchs and Harlequins and the way they talk. Because I seemingly cannot bring myself to do things the easy way, I decided exarchs would have haiku-style speech patterns and I am dreading someone finding a line of dialogue that doesn't match the correct word or syllable count, but that is a good exchange for the odd, archaic style it gives them. Similarly, I backed away from the Harlequins always talking in rhyming couplets (an approximation of their lyric style not meant to be literal) but you might find there is a certain... *rhythm* to the way they speak.

I've loved eldar for a long, long time and I hope this trilogy does justice to them in the eyes of other fans. And rest assured that there will be more to come...

Gav Thorpe,
Nottingham, July 2013

PATH OF THE WARRIOR

'Life is to us as the Maze of Linnian was to Ulthanesh, its mysterious corridors leading to wondrous vistas and nightmarish encounters in equal measure. Each of us must walk the maze alone, treading in the footsteps of those that came before but also forging new routes through the labyrinth of existence.

In times past we were drawn to the darkest secrets and ran wild about the maze, seeking to experience all that it had to offer. As individuals and as a civilisation we lost our way and in doing so created the means for our doom; unfettered exploration leading to the darkness of the Fall.

In the emptiness that followed, a new way was revealed to us: the Path. Through the wisdom of the Path we spend our lives exploring the meaning of existence, moving from one part of the maze to another with discipline and guidance so that we never become lost again. On the Path we experience the full potential of love and hate, joy and woe, lust and purity, filling our lives with experience and fulfilment but never succumbing to the shadows that lurk within our thoughts.

But like all journeys, the Path is different for each of us. Some wander for a long while in one place; some spread their travels wide and visit many places for a short time while others remain for a long time to explore every nook and turn; some of us lose our way and leave the Path for a time or forever; and some of us find dead-ends and become trapped.'

— Kysaduras the Anchorite,
foreword to Introspections upon Perfection

PROLOGUE

A blue sun reflected from the still waters of the lake while its yellow companion peeked just above the red-leaved trees that surrounded the edge of the water. Red and black birds skimmed above the lake with wings buzzing, their long beaks snapping at insects, their chattering calls the only sound to break the quiet.

A white stone building bordered the water, its long colonnaded veranda stretching over the lake on thick piles. Beyond the portico, it reared up amongst the trees, square in shape, turreted towers at each corner. Thin smoke seeped lazily from vents in the wall, the breeze carrying it away across the forests. Narrow windows shuttered with red-painted wood broke the upper storeys, small balconies jutting from the wall beneath each one.

Armed figures stood guard at the high doorways and patrolled walkways running along the red-tiled roofs. The men were dressed in loose black trousers tucked into knee-high boots, with bulky red jackets buttoned and braided with gold. Their heads were covered by black hoods, with tinted goggles to protect their eyes from the strange light of the local stars. They walked their rounds and chatted with each other, thinking nothing was amiss.

Causing barely a ripple, five green-armoured figures slid from the water, silvery droplets falling from the overlapping curved plates of their suits. They carried pistols and saw-toothed chainswords. Making no sound, the eldar warriors pulled themselves up to the veranda and stopped in the shadows of the pillars, invisible to the group of guards at the doorway.

Patiently, they crouched in the darkness and waited.

There was a flash of light through the sky and a massive explosion rocked the front of the manor house, shards of stone and cracked tiles thrown high into the air by the impact. A moment later, another blast seared down through the clouds and detonated, destroying one of the turrets in a cloud of dust, spilling mangled bodies to the close-cut lawn beside the mansion.

At the far end of the gardens, black-armoured figures appeared at the tree line, long missile launchers underslung from their arms. A rippling burst of fire sent a volley of projectiles towards the roof of the house while other warriors dashed across flower-filled beds and vaulted over stone benches and ran through bubbling fountains.

Kenainath, exarch of the Deadly Shadow shrine motioned for his Striking Scorpions to stay in the shadows of the lakeside porch, his eyes fixed on the soldiers at the door. As predicted, the men unslung their rifles and dashed from their post, heading towards the attack across the gardens. Kenainath pounced as they passed, his energy-covered power claw ripping through the back of the skull of the closest human.

His warriors followed him, pistols spitting hails of molecule-thin discs, their chainswords purring. Caught by surprise, the soldiers stood no chance and were cut down in moments, dismembered, disembowelled or beheaded by the blades of the Striking Scorpions.

Kenainath crouched amongst the dead soldiers, red-lensed eyes scanning for signs of danger. Other eldar warriors – Dire Avengers in armour of blue and gold – leapt over the veranda and joined the squad. Together they headed towards the back doors.

A creak and a small movement in one of the ground floor shutters alerted Kenainath to danger. He dived towards the cover of a plant holder as the shutters swung open, his warriors reacting instantly to follow him.

The wide barrel of an automatic weapon crashed through the windowpanes and muzzle flare bathed the portico. Bullets whined and ricocheted around the Striking Scorpions sending up shards of stone and ripping splinters from the plant container. There was a shout of pain from Iniatherin just behind the exarch. The Dire Avengers returned fire, unleashing a storm from their shuriken catapults through the window. His body shredded by the fusillade, the man within fell back with a long shriek.

Kenainath glanced over his shoulder to see Iniatherin sprawled across the white stone, armour pierced by a long shard of broken wood, bright blood pumping from a gash to his throat. In moments the warrior was dead, his twitching body falling still as the pool of red spread around him.

More explosions rattled the windows as the eldar forced their way into the building to Kenainath's right. Through the shattered window the exarch saw lithe, bone-coloured figures bounding across a hallway, the air split with piercing wails from the Howling Banshees' masks.

Signalling for his squad to move towards the door again, Kenainath spared another glance for his fallen warrior. He felt no sorrow; it was impossible for him to feel guilt or remorse. Death was no stranger to those that trod the Path of the Warrior. Kenainath's squad was lessened by the loss, but as he looked down at the awkwardly splayed body he knew that the diminishing of the Deadly Shadow's strength would not be for long.

The universe strained for harmony and balance and, as the philosophers claimed, abhorred a vacuum. Another would take Iniatherin's place.

Part One

Artist

FRIENDSHIP

In the time before the War in Heaven, Eldanesh, spear-carrier, hawk-friend, lord of the eldar, faced the armies of the Hresh-selain. Eldanesh was the greatest of the eldar, his spear the finest weapon forged by mortals, yet the king of the Hresh-selain had many warriors. Though he was lord of the eldar and knew it to be his burden alone to protect them, Eldanesh knew also he could not gain victory by himself. He turned to Ulthanesh, second greatest warrior of the eldar, sword-bearer, raven-friend, and asked for his aid in battling the Hresh-selain. Together Eldanesh and Ulthanesh fought, and against their skill and strength the Hresh-selain had no defence. 'Ever shall it be thus', said Eldanesh, 'that when we are most sorely tested, our friends shall stand by our side'.

A star was dying.

To the eldar she was Mirianathir, Mother of the Desert Winds. She hung in the dark firmament, a deep orange, her surface tortured by frenetic bursts of fusion and rampaging electromagnetic winds. Particles streamed from her body and fronds of energy lapped at the closest planets, scourging Mirianathir's children with their deadly touch. They hung barren around her. For a million years she had been dying and for a million more she would continue to die.

Yet in her death there was life for others.

For the eldar.

Bathed in the radioactive glow of Mirianathir's death throes, a craft-world floated upon the stellar winds; an artificial, disc-like continent of glowing domes and silvery energy sails, arcing bridges and glittering towers. Wings unfurled, the craftworld soaked in life-giving energy, an inorganic plant with mirrored leaves a hundred kilometres long. Surrounded by the ruddy light of the dying star, Craftworld Alaitoc absorbed all that Mirianathir had to offer, capturing every particle and stellar breeze, feeding it through the spirits of its infinity circuit to sustain the craftworld for a thousand more years.

The space around Alaitoc was as full of movement and energy as the star upon which it fed. Ships whirled and swerved, tacking across the stellar winds, refuelling their own energy stores. The webway gate behind the craftworld swirled and ebbed, a shimmering portal into the space between the material and immaterial. Trade ships with long fluted hulls slipped into and out of the gate; sleek destroyers with night-blue hulls prowled through the traffic, weapons batteries armed, torpedoes loaded; slender yachts darted amongst the shoal of vessels; majestic battleships eased along stately paths through the ordered commotion.

With a fluctuation of golden light, the webway portal dilated for a moment and where there had been vacuum now drifted *Lacontiran*, a bird-like trading schooner just returned from her long voyage to the stars of the Endless Valley. Trimming her solar sails, she turned easily along the starside rim of the craftworld and followed a course that led her to the Tower of Eternal Welcomes.

The dock tower stretched five kilometres out from the plane of the craftworld, encased in a bluish aura that kept at bay the ravening emptiness of space. Like a narwhal's horn, the tower spiralled into the darkness, hundreds of figures along its length, lining the elegant gantries and curving walkways. Eldar of all Paths had come to greet their long-travelled ship: poets, engineers, autarchs, gardeners, farseers, Aspect Warriors, stylists and chartmakers. Any and all walks of life were there, dressed in the fineries of heavy robes, or glittering skin-tight suits, or flowing tunics in a riot of colours. Scarves spilled like yellow and red waves and high-crested helms rose above a sea of delicately coiffured heads. Jewels of every colour shone in the glow of the craftworld alongside sparkling bands and rings and necklaces of silver and gold and platinum.

Without conscious thought, the eldar made their way around each other: embracing old friends; exchanging pleasantries with new acquaintances; steering a private course, never encroaching upon the private space of another. Their voices rose together, in a symphony of sound as like to the babbling of a crowd as a full orchestra is to the murmurings of a child. They talked to and around and over each other, their voices lyric, every intonation a note perfected, every gesture measured and precise. Some did not talk at all, their posture conveying their thoughts; the slightest raising of a brow, the quiver of a lip or trembling of a finger displaying agitation or excitement, happiness or anxiety.

In the midst of this kaleidoscope of craftworld life stood Korlandril. His slender frame was draped in an open-fronted robe of shining silk-like gold, his neck and wrists adorned with hundreds of molecule-thin chains in every colour of the spectrum so that it seemed his hands and face were wound with miniature rainbows. His long black hair was bound into a complicated braid that hung across his left shoulder, kept in place with holo-bands that constantly changed from sapphires to diamonds to emeralds and every other beautiful stone known to the eldar. He had taken much time to style himself upon the aesthetics of Arestheina, and had considered long the results in a mirrorfield, know-ing that his companion was partial to the ancient artist's works.

She, Thirianna, was dressed in more simple attire: a white ankle-length dress pleated below the knee, delicately embroidered with thread just the slightest shade greyer than the cloth, like the shadows of a cloud; sleeveless to reveal pale arms painted with waving patterns of henna. She wore a diaphanous scarf about her shoulders, its red and white gossamer coils lapping across her arms and chest. Her white hair, dyed to match her dress, was coloured with two azure streaks that framed her narrow face, accentuating the dark blue of her eyes. Her waystone was also a deep blue, ensconced in a surround of white meresilver, hung upon a fine chain of the same metal.

Korlandril looked at Thirianna, while all other eyes were turned towards the starship now gracefully sliding into place beside the uncoil-ing walkway of the quay. It had been fifteen cycles since he had last seen her. Fifteen cycles too many – too long to be away from her beauty and her passion, her smile that stirred the soul. He nurtured the hope that she would notice the attention he had laboured upon his appearance, but as yet she had made no remark upon it.

He saw the intensity in her eyes as she looked upon the approaching starship, the faintest glisten of moisture there, and detected an excited tremble throughout her body. He did not know whether it was simply the occasion that generated such anticipation – the gala atmosphere was very infectious – or whether there was some more personal, deeper joy that stirred Thirianna's heart. Perhaps her feelings for Aradryan's return were more than Korlandril would like. The notion stirred something within Korlandril's breast, a serpent uncoiling. He knew his jealousy was unjustified, and that he had made no claim to keep Thirianna for himself, but still the precision of his thoughts failed to quell the emo-tions that loitered within.

Set within a golden surround, the opal oval of Korlandril's waystone grew warm upon his chest, its heat passing through the material of his robe. Like a warning light upon a craft's display the waystone's agitation caused Korlandril to pause for a moment. His jealousy was not only misplaced, it was dangerous. He allowed the sensation to drift into the recesses of his mind, closed within a mental vault to be removed later when it was safe to do so.

Thoughts of Aradryan reminded Korlandril why he was at the tower: to welcome back an old friend. If Thirianna had wanted to be with Aradryan she would have travelled with him. Korlandril dismissed his fears concerning Thirianna's affections, finding himself equally eager to greet their returning companion. The serpent within lowered its head and slept again, biding its time.

A dozen gateways along the hull of *Lacontiran* opened, releasing a wave of iridescent light and a honey-scented breeze along the curving length of the dock. From the high archways passengers and crew disembarked in winding lines. Thirianna stretched to her full height, poised effortlessly on the tips of her boots, to look over the heads of the eldar in front, one hand slightly to one side to maintain her balance.

It was Korlandril's sharp eyes that caught sight of Aradryan first, which gave him a small thrill of pleasure; a victory won though no competition had been agreed between them.

'There he is, our wanderer returned to us like Anthemion with the Golden Harp,' said Korlandril, pointing to a walkway to their left, letting his fingers rest upon Thirianna's bare arm for the slightest of moments to attract her attention.

Though Korlandril had recognised him immediately, Aradryan looked very different from when he had left. Only by his sharp cheeks and thin lips had Korlandril known him. His hair was cut barbarically short on the left side, almost to the scalp, and hung in unkempt waves to the right, neither bound nor styled. He had dark make-up upon his eyelids, giving him a skull-like, sunken glare, and he was dressed in deep blues and black, wrapped in long ribbons of twilight. His bright yellow waystone was worn as a brooch, mostly hidden by the folds of his robe. Aradryan's forbidding eyes fell upon Korlandril and then Thirianna, their sinister edge disappearing with a glint of happiness. Aradryan waved a hand in greeting and wove his way effortlessly through the throng to stand in front of the pair.

'A felicitous return!' declared Korlandril, opening his arms in welcome, palms angled towards Aradryan's face. 'And a happy reunion.'

Thirianna dispensed with words altogether, brushing the back of her hand across Aradryan's cheek for a moment, before laying her slender fingers upon his shoulder. Aradryan returned the gesture, sparking a flare of jealous annoyance in Korlandril, which he fought hard not to show. The serpent in his gut opened one interested eye, but Korlandril forced it back into subservience. The moment passed and Aradryan stepped away from Thirianna, laying his hands onto those of Korlandril, a wry smile on his lips.

'Well met, and many thanks for the welcome,' said Aradryan. Korlandril searched his friend's face, seeking the impish delight that had once lurked behind the eyes, the ready, contagious smirk that had nestled in every movement of his lips. They were no longer there. Aradryan radiated solemnity and sincerity, warmth even, but Korlandril detected a barrier; Aradryan's face was turned ever so slightly towards Thirianna, his back arched just the merest fraction away from Korlandril.

Even amongst the eldar such subtle differences might have been missed, but Korlandril was dedicated to the Path of the Artist and had honed his observation and attention to detail to a level bordering on the microscopic. He noticed everything, remembered every nuance and facet, and he knew from his deep studies that everything had a meaning, whether intended or not. There was no such thing as an innocent smile, or a meaningless blink. Every motion betrayed a motive, and it was Aradryan's subtle reticence that now nagged at Korlandril's thoughts.

Korlandril held Aradryan's hands for a moment longer than was necessary, hoping that the extended physicality of the greeting might remind his friend of their bond. If it did, Aradryan gave no sign. With the same slight smile, he withdrew his grasp and clasped his hands behind his back, raising his eyebrows inquisitively.

'Tell me, dearest and most happily-met of my friends, what have I missed?'

The trio walked along the Avenue of Dreams, a silver passageway that passed beneath a thousand crystal archways into the heart of Alaitoc. The dim light of Mirianathir was caught in the vaulted roof, captured and radiated by the intricately faceted crystal to shine down upon the pedestrians below, glowing with delicate oranges and pinks.

Korlandril had offered to drive Aradryan to his quarters, but his friend had declined, preferring to savour the sensation of his return and the casual crowds of eldar; Korlandril guessed from the little Aradryan said that his had been a mostly solitary journey aboard the *Lacontiran*. Korlandril glanced with a little envy as slender anti-grav craft slipped by effortlessly, carrying their passengers quickly to their destinations. A younger Korlandril would have been horrified by the indolence that held sway over Korlandril the Sculptor, his abstract thoughts distracted by mundane labour of physical activity. Such introspection was impossible though; he had put aside self-consciousness in his desire to embrace every outside influence, every experience not of his own body and mind. Such were the thoughts of the artist, elevated beyond the practical, dancing upon the starlight of pure observation and imagination.

It was this drive for sensation that led Korlandril to conduct most of the talking. He spoke at length of his works, and of the comings-and-goings of the craftworld since Aradryan had left. For his part, Aradryan kept his comments and answers direct and without flourish, starving Korlandril of inspiration, frustrating his artistic thirst.

When Thirianna spoke, Korlandril noted, Aradryan became more eloquent, and seemed keener to speak about her than himself.

'I sense that you no longer walk in the shadow of Khaine,' said Aradryan, nodding in approval as he looked at Thirianna.

'It is true that the Path of the Warrior has ended for me,' she replied, thoughtful, her eyes never straying from Aradryan. 'The aspect of the Dire Avenger has sated my anger, enough for a hundred lifetimes. I write poetry, influenced by the Uriathillin school of verse. I find it has complexities that stimulate both the intellectual and the emotional in equal measure.'

'I would like to know Thirianna the Poet, and perhaps your verse will introduce me,' said Aradryan. 'I would very much like to see a performance, as you see fit.'

'As would I,' said Korlandril. 'Thirianna refuses to share her work with me, though many times I have suggested that we collaborate on a piece that combines her words with my sculpture.'

'My verse is for myself, and no other,' Thirianna said quietly. 'It is not for performance, nor for eyes that are not mine.'

She cast a glance of annoyance towards Korlandril.

'While some create their art to express themselves to the world, my poems are inner secrets, for me to understand their meaning, to divine my own fears and wishes.'

Admonished, Korlandril fell silent for a moment, but he was quickly uncomfortable with the quiet and gave voice to a question that had scratched at his subconscious since he had heard that Aradryan was returning.

'Have you come back to Alaitoc to stay?' he asked. 'Is your time as a steersman complete, or will you be returning to *Lacontiran*?'

'I have only just arrived, are you so eager that I should leave once more?' replied Aradryan.

Korlandril opened his mouth to protest but the words drifted away as he caught, just for a moment, a hint of the old wit of Aradryan. Korlandril smiled in appreciation of the joke and bowed his head in acknowledgement of his own part as the foil for Aradryan's humour.

'I do not yet know,' Aradryan continued with a thoughtful expression. 'I have learned all that I can learn as a steersman and I feel complete. Gone is the turbulence that once plagued my thoughts. There is nothing like guiding a ship along the buffeting waves of a nebula or along the swirling channels of the webway to foster control and focus. I have seen many great, many wondrous things out in the stars, but I feel that there is so much more out there to find, to touch and hear and experience. I may return to the starships, I may not. And, of course, I would like to spend a little time with my friends and family, to know again the life of Alaitoc, to see whether I wish to wander again or can be content here.'

Thirianna nodded in agreement at this wise course of action, and even Korlandril, who occasionally succumbed to rash impulse, could see the merits of weighing such a decision well.

'Your return is most timely, Aradryan,' he said, again feeling the need to fill the vacuum of conversation. 'My latest piece is nearing completion. In a few cycles' time I am hosting an unveiling. It would be a pleasure and an honour if both of you could attend.'

'I would have come even if you had not invited me!' laughed Thirianna, her enthusiasm sending a thrill of excitement through Korlandril. 'I hear your name mentioned quite often, and with much praise attached, and there are high expectations for this new work. It would not be seemly at all to miss such an event if one is to be considered as a person possessing any degree of taste.'

Aradryan did not reply for a moment, and Korlandril could discern nothing of his friend's thoughts from his expression. It was as if a blank mask had been placed upon his face.

'Yes, I too would be delighted to attend,' Aradryan said eventually, animation returning. 'I am afraid that my tastes may have been left behind compared to yours, but I look forward to seeing what Korlandril the Sculptor has created in my absence.'

MASTERPIECE

In the first days of the eldar, Asuryan granted Eldanesh and his followers the gift of life. He breathed into their bodies all that they were to become. Yet there was no other thing upon the world. All was barren and not a leaf nor fish nor bird nor animal grew or swam or flew or walked beside them. Eldanesh was forlorn at the infertility of his home, and its emptiness made in him a greater emptiness. Seeing his distress, Isha was overcome with a grief of her own. Isha shed a tear for the eldar and let it drop upon the world. Where it fell, there came new life. From her sorrow came joy, for the world of the eldar was filled with wondrous things and Eldanesh's emptiness was no more, and he gave thanks to Isha for her love.

A snarl of frustration rose in Korlandril's throat and he fought to stifle it before it came into being. He glared at the droplet of blood welling up from the tiny puncture in his thumb, seeing a miniscule red reflection of his own angry features. He smeared the blood between thumb and finger and turned his ire upon the small barb that had appeared in the ghost stone, tipped with a fleck of crimson.

It was an affront to every sensibility he had developed, that tiny splinter. It broke the precise line of the arcing arm of his sculpture, an aberration in the otherwise perfect flow of organic and inorganic. It was not meant to be and Korlandril did not know how it had come to be.

It had been like this for the last two cycles. Whenever he laid his fingers upon the ghost stone, to tease it into the forms so real in his mind, it refused to be held sway by his thoughts. It had taken him all of the last cycle just to get three fingers perfect, and at this pace the piece would be far from ready when the unveiling was to be held in just two more cycles.

The pale ochre of the ghost stone sat unmoving, dormant without his caress, but to Korlandril it had developed a life of its own. It rebelled against his desires, twisting away from the shapes he wanted, forming hard edges where soft curves should be, growing diminutive thorns and spikes whenever his mind strayed even the slightest.

He knew the ghost stone was not at fault. It was possessed of no will, no spirit. It merely reacted to his input, shaping itself under his gentle psychic manipulation. It was inert now, but Korlandril sensed a certain smugness in its unwillingness to cooperate, even as another part of his mind told him that he was simply projecting his frustrations onto an inanimate object.

His mind divided, all concentration now gone, Korlandril stepped back and looked away, ashamed at his failing. The shimmering of the holofield around him, erected to conceal the work from admirers until it was unveiled in its finished glory, played a corona of colours into Korlandril's eyes. For a moment he was lost gazing at the undulating view of the forest dome beyond the shimmering holofield, the distorted vista sending a flurry of inspiration through his mind.

'I almost dare not ask,' said a voice behind Korlandril. He turned to see his mentor, Abrahasil, gazing intently at the statue.

'You need not ask anything,' said Korlandril. 'It is Aradryan's return that perturbs me, but I know not why. I am happy that my friend is once again with us.'

'And what of your thoughts of Aradryan in relation to your work?'

'I have none,' replied Korlandril. 'This piece was started long before I knew of his return.'

'And yet progress has been slow since you learnt of it, and almost nonexistent since it happened,' said Abrahasil. 'The effect is clear, though the cause remains obscured to you. Perhaps I might help?'

Korlandril shrugged his indifference and then felt a stab of contrition at Abrahasil's disappointed sigh.

'Of course, I would appreciate any guidance you can give me,' said Korlandril, forcing himself to look at the statue. 'I see it clearly, all of it, every line and arc, as you taught me. I allow the peace and the piece to become one within me, as you taught me. I direct my thoughts and my motion towards its creation, as you taught me. Nothing I do has changed, and yet the ghost stone is rebellious to my demands.'

Abrahasil raised a narrow finger at this last comment.

'Demands, Korlandril? It is desire not demand that shapes the ghost stone. A demand is an act of aggression. A desire is an act of submission. The thought shapes the act which shapes the form. Why has desire changed to demand?'

Korlandril did not answer at first, startled that he had not been aware of such a simple distinction, subtle as it was. He repeated the question to himself, searching his thoughts, sifting through his mental processes until he could locate the point at which desire had become demand.

'I wish to impress others with my work, and I feel the pressure of expectation,' Korlandril said eventually, pleased that he found an answer.

'That is not what is wrong,' said Abrahasil with the slightest pursing of his lips, spearing through Korlandril's bubble of self-congratulation. 'Always has your work been expressive, intended to impose your insight upon others. That has not changed. Remember something more specific. Something related to Aradryan.'

Again Korlandril drifted within his own memories and emotions, massaging his thoughts into order just as he manipulated the ghost stone into its flowing shapes. He found what he was looking for, visualised the moment of transition and gave a quiet gasp of realisation.

He looked at Abrahasil and hesitated, reluctant to share his discovery with another. Abrahasil waited patiently, eyes fixed not on Korlandril but on the statue. Korlandril knew that if he asked his mentor to leave, he would do so without complaint, but until then Abrahasil would await a reply. Abrahasil did not need to remind Korlandril that he could be trusted, that the bond between mentor and student was inviolate; that in order to explore and engage the passions and fears Korlandril needed to express himself as an artist, anything he told Abrahasil was in the strictest confidence. Abrahasil had no need to say such things, his patient waiting and the understanding between the two of them was all the communication needed.

'I wish to impress Thirianna out of competition with Aradryan,' Korlandril said eventually, relieved at unburdening himself of sole knowledge of this revelation. He had never spoken of his feeling towards Thirianna, not even with Abrahasil, though he suspected his mentor saw much of Korlandril's thoughts that he did not comment on. After all, Abrahasil had observed them both together on many occasions and Korlandril knew he would not have been able to conceal every sign of affection from his mentor's studied gaze. 'There is a fear within me, and anger that I feel such a fear. Aradryan is a friend. Not a rival.'

Abrahasil turned his head and smiled. Korlandril felt another layer of connection falling into place between them, as if he had stepped across a threshold that he had been poised upon for a long time.

'That is good,' said the mentor. 'And how will you control that fear, that anger?'

Now it was Korlandril's turn to smile.

'That is simple,' he said. 'This sculpture is not for Thirianna, but for me. My next piece... that will be for her. These thoughts have no place in this creation, but they will be the inspiration for another. I can put them aside until then.'

Abrahasil laid a hand upon Korlandril's arm in reassurance and Korlandril gave him a look that conveyed his deep appreciation. Abrahasil stepped out of the holofield without further word and Korlandril watched his wavering form disappear into the miasmic vista of trees.

Feeling refreshed and invigorated, Korlandril approached the sculpture. He laid his hand upon the raised arm he had been working on, delicately running his fingertips along the accentuated flow of muscle tone and joint, rebuilding his mental vision of the piece.

Under his touch, the barb flowed back into the ghost stone and was no more.

There was an air of excitement and anticipation in the Dome of the Midnight Forests. Across meadows of blue grass and between the pale silver trunks of lianderin trees, many eldar gathered to await the unveiling of Korlandril's latest creation. Through the invisible force field enclosing the ordered gardens, the ruddy twilight of Mirianathir glowed. The lilt of laughter and the chime of crystal goblets drifted on an artificial breeze that set the jade leaves of the trees rustling; a perfect accompaniment to the swish of grass and the soft conversation of Korlandril's guests.

Some three hundred eldar had gathered for the unveiling, dressed for the occasion in their most fashionable attire. Korlandril mingled with the crowd, remarking upon an elegant brooch or particularly pleasing cut of skirt or robe. For his grand moment, he had decided to dress himself in an outfit that was elegant but austere, out of a desire not to upstage his sculpture. He wore a plain blue robe, fastened from waist to throat with silver buckles, and his hair was swept back with a silver band ornamented with a single blue skystone at his brow. He kept his conversation short, eluding any questions concerning the nature of the piece until he was ready to reveal all.

As he wandered amongst the guests, Korlandril felt a thrill running through him. With each beat of his heart his waystone reciprocated, the double-pulse quivering in his chest. He absorbed excitement from the guests and projected it back to them. He was pleased with the attention, a salve to his pride after the tribulations he had faced completing the sculpture.

Exchanging pleasantries, Korlandril scanned the crowd for Thirianna and spied her with a group of three other eldar in one of the lianderin groves not far from where the shimmering holofield concealed Korlandril's exhibit.

Korlandril allowed himself a moment to admire her beauty from a distance, delighting intellectually and emotionally in the close-fitting suit of red and black she wore. The curves of her arms and legs mirrored those of the branches above her, a natural elegance accentuated by her delicate poise and precise posture. Her hair, pigmented a deep yellow, fell in a tumble of coils down her back, woven through with red ribbons that hung to her waist.

As she stepped to one side, Korlandril saw Aradryan. He was smiling, in the deliberate way maintained by those not entirely comfortable with their surrounds. Korlandril felt the serpent of envy quiver ever so slightly within him, which disturbed him. He thought he had put aside that haunting doubt, that fear lingering at the very edge of his awareness. Seeing Aradryan with Thirianna brought his concerns into stark view and Korlandril's pulse quickened and his thoughts raced for a moment.

Korlandril directed his gaze away as he walked across the meadow, allowing the calm of the garden dome to still the turbulence in his thoughts. Lianderin blossom was just beginning to bud, like golden stars in a deep green night, and the scent of the grass rose up from beneath his tread, cleansing and pure. By the time he reached the group, Korlandril was composed once more, genuinely happy to see his friends in attendance.

Aradryan extended a palm in greeting and Korlandril laid his hand upon his friend's in return. The welcome was repeated with Thirianna, her touch cool and reassuring. As he pulled back his hand, Korlandril allowed his fingertips to brush gently over those of Thirianna, and he allowed his eyes to meet hers for a heartbeat longer than was normal.

'We are all quivering with anticipation,' said one of the group, another sculptor called Ydraethir. He wore a half-gown of deep purple across his waist and left shoulder, cut short on the thighs, exposing skin that had been bleached almost pure white. Ydraethir followed the school of Hithrinair, which saw the sculptor as much a part of the work as the sculpture itself. Korlandril had dabbled with its aesthetic for a few cycles but had quickly found himself to be a dull subject and preferred to express himself through his work at a distance. Korlandril searched for a hint of irony or rivalry in his companion's comment and pose, but concluded that Ydraethir was being sincere.

'It is my hope that such expectation is warranted,' replied Korlandril with a grateful bow of the head. He turned and greeted the fourth eldar, the renowned bonesinger Kirandrin. 'I am very grateful for the interest and enthusiasm you have all shown in my work.'

'I have watched your development closely since I first came upon one of your early works,' Kirandrin said. 'I believe it was *The Blessing of Asurmen*, a life-size piece displayed in the atrium of the Tower of the Evening Melodies.'

'My second ever piece,' said Korlandril with a warm smile of remembrance. 'I am still privileged that Abrahasil saw fit to show my works so early on in my time upon the Path. I have kind regard for that particular sculpture, though my work has moved so far beyond such simplistic formulae now, it feels as if it might have been created by someone else!'

'Is not that the purpose of the Path?' said Ydraethir. 'That we change and grow, and shed that which was before and transform into something new and better?'

'Indeed it is,' said Korlandril. 'To strive for the perfection of body and spirit, craft and mind, that is what we all desire.'

'But is it not the case that we also lose some of who we are?' said Aradryan, his tone one of mild dissent. 'If we are forever moving forward on the Path, when do we stop to admire the view? I think that sometimes we are too keen to discard that which made us as we are.'

Silence greeted Aradryan's remarks. He looked at the other eldar, his face betraying a small measure of confusion.

'Forgive me if I have said something out of place,' Aradryan said quietly. 'It was not my intent to question your opinions, but to merely voice my own. Perhaps my manners have strayed a little while I was away from Alaitoc and the niceties of civil society.'

'Not at all,' Kirandrin said smoothly, laying a hand upon Aradryan's arm in a gesture of reassurance. 'It is simply that such questions are… rare.'

'And the answers far too long to be addressed here,' Korlandril added quickly. 'We shall continue this discussion at a later time. At this moment, I must make my grand unveiling.'

'Of course,' said Kirandrin. Aradryan gave a slow, shallow nod and dipped his eyelids in a gesture of apology.

Korlandril smiled his appreciation before crossing quickly to the holo-field and stepping within. Obscured from view, he let out a long breath, releasing the tension that had unexpectedly built up within. There had been something about Aradryan's manner that had unnerved Korlandril. He had again felt that otherness he had encountered when Aradryan had first returned – a subtle desire to be elsewhere. Sheltered within the holofield, Korlandril's waystone was again warm to the touch, reflecting inner assurance rather than anger or embarrassment.

The distraction had taxed Korlandril and with a stab of guilt he realised he had said nothing to Thirianna. He had all but ignored her. He wondered for a moment if he should apologise for his offhand behaviour but quickly dismissed the idea. Thirianna probably had not noticed any deficiencies in his attention and it might be unwise to highlight them to her. If she had recognised any affront at all, she would surely understand the many demands conflicting for his attention on an occasion such as this. Korlandril resolved that he would seek out Thirianna after the unveiling and lavish as much attention as possible upon her.

His mind upon Thirianna, Korlandril's thoughts were awhirl in many different directions, his heart racing, his skin tingling. Ideas flashed across his mind, crashing against the excitement he felt at the unveiling, blending with the disturbance caused by Aradryan, colliding with the apprehension that had been building since he had completed the sculpture.

Korlandril whispered a few calming mantras. As he did so, he ordered his thoughts, pushing some aside for later reflection, drawing on others to reassure himself, focussing on his confidence and experiences to steady his worries. He stood in silent repose for some time, until he was sure he was ready to address the crowd.

When the mental maelstrom had become a still pool, Korlandril stepped out of the holofield to find that his guests had gathered in the clearing outside. Most of the faces were familiar, a few were not. All seemed eager to see what Korlandril had created.

'I am deeply honoured that you have all come to witness the unveiling of my latest piece,' Korlandril began, keeping his voice steady, projecting his words to the back of the crowd without effort. 'Many know that I draw great inspiration from the time before the War in Heaven. I look to our golden age not with regret of a paradise lost, nor with sadness that such times have passed. In the first age of our people I see a world, a universe, that we can all aspire to recreate. Though the gods are gone, it is up to us to make real their works, and through our desire to rebuild heaven bring about the peace that we all deserve. Our civilisation is not lost whilst we still sing and paint – and sculpt – of those times that none of us now remember save in myth. We all know that legend can become truth; that the line between myth and reality is not clearly defined. I would take myth and make it reality.'

Korlandril continued at some length, citing his influences and dreams, expounding upon the schools of thought and aesthetic that had led him to create his sculpture. He spoke smoothly and with passion, giving words to the thoughts that had been streamlined and refined through the long process of sculpting. He talked of the complexities of the organic and the inorganic, the juxtaposition of line and curve, the contrast of solid and liquid.

His eyes roved freely over the crowd as he spoke, gauging their reaction and mood. Most were held rapt by his oration, their eyes fixed upon Korlandril, their minds devouring every syllable. A few stood with expressions of polite attendance, and Korlandril felt a moment of dismay when he realised that one such viewer was Aradryan. Korlandril did not falter in his delivery, sweeping away his concern with his enthusiasm even as he searched for Thirianna. He saw her at the front of the crowd, eager and expectant, her eyes constantly flicking between Aradryan and the holofield that shielded his work.

When he was finished, Korlandril allowed himself a dramatic pause, savouring the anticipation than he had created in his audience. He walked to a small table that had been set to one side, circular and stood upon a spiralled leg, a single crystal goblet of deep red wine set in its centre. He sipped at the drink, relishing its warmth on his lips, the spice on his tongue and a sweet note of aftertaste in his throat, even as he relished the hushed calm that had descended in the wake of his speech.

As he placed the glass back upon the table, Korlandril slipped a thin wafer from his belt and let his thumb run over the rune upon its silvery surface. At his touch, the holofield disappeared, revealing the statue in all of its glory.

'I present *The Gifts of Loving Isha*,' he announced with a smile.

There were a few gasps of enjoyment and a spontaneous ripple of applause from all present. Korlandril turned to look at his creation and allowed himself to admire his work fully since its completion.

The statue was bathed in a golden glow and tinged with sunset reds and purples from the dying star above. It depicted an impressionistic Isha in abstract, her body and limbs flowing from the trunk of a lianderin tree, her wave-like tresses entwined within dark green leaves in its upreaching branches. Her face was bowed, hidden in the shadow cast by tree and hair. From the darkness a slow trickle of silver liquid spilled from her eyes into a golden cup held aloft by an ancient eldar warrior kneeling at her feet: Eldanesh. Light glittered from the chalice on his alabaster face, his armour a stylised arrangement of organic geometry, his face blank except for a slender nose and the merest depression of eye sockets. From beneath him, a black-petalled rose coiled up Isha's legs and connected the two together in its thorny embrace.

It was – Korlandril believed – breathtaking.

Most of the guests moved forward to examine the piece more closely, while Kirandrin and a few others surrounded Korlandril, offering praise and congratulations. Amongst them was Abrahasil, who must have remained out of sight during Korlandril's address. Mentor and student embraced warmly.

'You have nurtured a fine talent,' said Kirandrin. 'It is a masterly work, and one that graces the dome with its existence.'

'It is my privilege to guide such a hand in its work,' said Abrahasil. 'I am very proud of Korlandril.'

His mentor's words brought a flush of happiness to Korlandril and a concomitant throb from his waystone, and he accepted the plaudits of his peers with a gracious bow.

'If my hands have created wonders, it is because others have opened my eyes to see them,' he said. 'Please excuse me. I must attend to my other guests. I am sure we will have many cycles to further discuss my work.'

Receiving smiles of assent, Korlandril sought out Aradryan and Thirianna. They were stood side-by-side in a knot of eldar admiring the statue from a short distance away, the majestic Isha towering above them.

'She is so serene,' Thirianna was saying. 'Such calm and beauty.'

Aradryan made a small gesture of dissent and Korlandril stopped, staying a little distance away from the pair to listen to what they said.

'It is self-referential,' Aradryan explained and at his words the serpent within Korlandril coiled around his heart and gripped it tight. 'It is a work of remarkable skill and delicacy, certainly. Yet I find it somewhat... staid. It adds nothing to my experience of the myth, merely represents physically something that is felt. It is a metaphor in its most direct form. Beautiful, but merely reflecting back upon its maker rather than a wider truth.'

'But is not that the point of art, to create representations for those thoughts, memories and emotions that cannot be conveyed directly?'

'Perhaps I am being unfair,' said Aradryan. 'Out in the stars, I have seen such wondrous creations of nature that the artifices of mortals seem petty, even those that explore such momentous themes such as this.'

'Staid?' snapped Korlandril, stepping forward. 'Self-referential?'

Thirianna looked in horror at Korlandril's appearance, but Aradryan seemed unperturbed.

'My words were not intended to cause offence, Korlandril,' he said, offering a placating palm. 'They are but my opinion, and an ill-educated one at that. Perhaps you find my sentimentality gauche.'

In the face of such honesty and self-deprecation, Korlandril's anger wavered. A rare moment of humility fluttered in his breast, but then the serpent tightened its coils and the sensation disappeared.

'You are right to think your opinion ill-informed,' said Korlandril, his words as venomous as the snake laying siege to his heart. 'While you gazed naively at glittering stars and swirling nebulae, I studied the works of Aethyril and Ildrintharir, learnt the disciplines of ghost stone weaving and inorganic symbiosis. If you have not the wit to extract the meaning from that which I have presented to you, perhaps you should consider your words more carefully.'

'And if you have not the skill to convey your meaning from your work, perhaps you need to continue studying,' Aradryan snarled back. 'It is not from the past masters that you should learn your art, but from the heavens and your heart. Your technique is flawless, but your message is parochial. How many statues of Isha might I see if I travelled across the craftworld? A dozen? More? How many more statues of Isha exist on other craftworlds? You have taken nothing from the Path save the ability to indulge yourself in this spectacle. You have learnt nothing of yourself, of the darkness and the light that battles within you. There is intellect alone in your work, and nothing of yourself. It might be that you should expand your terms of reference.'

'What do you mean by that?'

'Get away from this place, from Alaitoc,' Aradryan said patiently, his anger dissipated by his outburst. Now he was the picture of sincerity, his hand half-reaching towards Korlandril. 'Why stifle your art by seeking inspiration only from the halls and domes you have seen since childhood? Rather than trying to look upon old sights with fresh eyes, why not turn your old eyes upon fresh sights?'

Korlandril wanted to argue, to snatch words from the air that would mock Aradryan's opinion, but just as the serpent within stifled his heart, it strangled his throat. He satisfied himself with a fierce glare at Aradryan, conveying all the contempt and anger he felt in that simple look, and stormed away through the blue grass, scattering guests in his flight.

FATE

At the start of the War in Heaven, all-seeing Asuryan asked the crone goddess Morai-heg what would be the fate of the gods. The crone told Asuryan that she would look across the tangled skein of the future to discern what would become of the gods. Long she followed the overlapping threads, following each one on its course to the ending of the universe, and yet she could find no answer for the lord of lords. All paths took the crow lady into a place of fire and death where she could not venture further. To find the answer she sought, the crone followed Khaine the bloody-handed killer who would wage war on the other gods and the mortals, and took from him a thimbleful of his fiery blood. Returning to her lair, Morai-heg set the burning blood of the war god upon her balance. Upon the other side of her scales she coiled up the thread of fate belonging to Eldanesh. All was equal. The crone returned to Asuryan and he demanded the answer to his question. Morai-heg told the lord of lords that the fate of the gods was not his to know. The mortal Eldanesh and his people would decide if the gods survived or not.

Rose-coloured water lapped at the white sands, each ripple leaving a sweeping curve along the shoreline. Korlandril followed the ebb and flow, mesmerised; every part of his mind was directed towards memorising every sparkle, every splash, every grain. Sunwings flashed above the waters, darts of yellow skimming the surface, bobbing and weaving around each other. Korlandril absorbed every flight path, every dipped wing, every extended feather and snapping blue beak.

A sound disturbed his concentration. A voice. He allowed part of his consciousness to depart the scene and recall what had been said. He remembered himself at the same time, sitting crossed-legged on the golden grass of the lawns in the Gardens of Tranquil Reflection, listening to his companion.

'I am leaving Alaitoc,' Aradryan said.

Shocked, Korlandril turned all of his attention upon his friend; sea, sand, sunwings all put aside in a moment. Aradryan was sat just an arm's length away from Korlandril, lounging on the grass in a loose-fitting robe of jade green. He lay on his back, arms behind his head, while his bare toes, seeming possessed of a life of their own, drew circular designs in the air just out of reach of the lake's pale waters.

'You are leaving Alaitoc?' said Korlandril. 'Whatever for?'

'To become a steersman,' replied Aradryan. He did not look at Korlandril, his gaze directed over the waters to the shining silver towers of their homes, and beyond even that, to some vista that only he could see. 'It is time that I moved onwards. I am filled with a curiosity that Alaitoc cannot satisfy. It is like a hunger growing within me, that no sight or sound of this place can sate. I have taken my fill of Alaitoc, and many splendid feasts she has offered me, but I find my plate now empty. I wish to go further than the force shields and domes that have protected me. I feel coddled not safe, stifled not enriched.'

'How soon will you leave?' said Korlandril, standing up.

'Soon,' said Aradryan, his eyes still distant. '*Lacontiran* leaves for the Endless Valley in two cycles' time.'

'*Lacontiran* will be gone for more than twenty passes,' said Korlandril, alarmed. 'Why must you leave for so long?'

'She sails on her own, far from Alaitoc,' replied Aradryan. 'I wish for solitude so that I might reflect on my choices so far, and perhaps divine something of where I should head next.'

'What of our friendship? I am at a loss without your companionship,' said Korlandril, crouching beside Aradryan, an imploring hand reaching out. 'You know that I would be adrift without you to steer me.'

'You will need to find another to guide you,' Aradryan said softly. 'My mind wanders all of the time. I cannot be trusted to watch over you while you dream any more. I cannot walk the Path of Dreaming with you any longer. I am tired of living within myself.'

Korlandril could say nothing, lost as he was in his thoughts. As he dreamt, as he wandered the paths of his subconscious, it was Aradryan that provided his anchor; a reassuring presence at the edge of his mind, a warmth to which he could return when he came upon the chill and dark places in the corners of his spirit.

'You will find another dream-watcher,' Aradryan assured him, noticing his distress. He stood and took Korlandril's arm, pulling him upright.

Now he directed his eyes upon his friend, filled with concern. 'Perhaps Thirianna will join you on the Path of Dreaming?'

'Thirianna the Warrior?' replied Korlandril, aghast at the thought.

'I spoke to her yesterday,' said Aradryan. 'She feels the time is approaching when she will change Paths. You should speak to her.'

A gentle chime broke Korlandril's reverie and he opened his eyes to see a winding road of silver far below him, cutting through gently sculpted terraces. The softest of breezes brushed across his skin and teased his hair. For a moment he thought he was floating far above the landscape. Sliding completely from memedream to reality, he recognised himself on the balcony outside his chambers, bathed in the dying glow of a constructed twilight. He was leaning on a fluted balustrade, looking down at the vineyards that surrounded the Tower of Starlight Majesty.

It took him a little longer to fully recover his bodily control; blinking rapidly, stretching his limbs, quickening his pulse to ease blood back into numbed fingers and toes. He felt a lingering stiffness and wondered how long he had spent exploring his memories, walking back along the Path of Dreaming. He felt an edge of thirst and licked his lips instinctively though there was no moisture in his mouth.

Recalling the alert chime that had roused him, Korlandril turned slowly and reached out his fingertips to a grey, slate-like panel on the wall beside the archway that led into his home. At the moment of contact with the chill slab he felt the presence of Abrahasil outside his chambers and with a brief psychic impulse bid him to enter.

Breaking contact with the infinity link, Korlandril stepped into the shadowy lounge area inside the archway. It was very much like being inside an egg. The wall was a bluish-white, gently speckled with pale green. Curving couches with high backs were arranged facing the centre of the room, and under his feet he felt the thick ply of a heavily woven mat. Sculptures, by Korlandril's hand and others, stood on plinths around the wall. As he looked at each in turn Korlandril felt a flicker of recognition, his mind still tied to the processes of his memedreaming: memories of how they were made or acquired; of conversations concerning them; of moods he had felt whilst looking at them. As each thought bobbed to the surface of his mind he pushed them back, away from direct contemplation. Moving to another infinity terminal, he thought the lights into a soft blue and raised the temperature a little; he felt strangely chilled.

'Perhaps some clothes would warm you quicker,' said Abrahasil, entering the room through the arch from the main foyer.

It was only Abrahasil's observation that allowed Korlandril to realise that he was naked. His nudity caused him no self-consciousness; in his current state of internal awareness – or rather his utter lack of it – such thoughts were impossible.

'Yes, that would probably be for the best,' said Korlandril with a nod.

He gestured through another arch to the dining area. 'Please take whatever refreshments you desire, I shall return swiftly.'

Korlandril strode into his robing chamber, still somewhat out-of-synch with himself following his long dreaming. He absent-mindedly touched a hand to a panel on the wall. A door slid aside, revealing a wide selection of attire, from skin-tight bodysuits with glittering metallic sheens to voluminous shirts and long gowns. Korlandril chose a green robe, tight at the waist and flared at the shoulders. He selected a broad belt without thought, his aesthetic instinct guiding his hands to a choice that matched his robe. As he cinched it around his waist, he walked barefoot across the rugs of the lounge area and joined Abrahasil in the dining quarters.

'Six cycles,' Abrahasil said as Korlandril entered. The room was dominated by a long, narrow table extruding from one wall, between eight single-legged stools in a row on either side. Abrahasil sat at the far end. Korlandril saw that he had taken nothing to eat or drink.

'Six cycles of what?' asked Korlandril, opening a crystal-windowed cabinet door. From within he pulled out a blue bottle and two silvered goblets.

'No drink for me, thank you,' said Abrahasil. Korlandril brought both cups to the table nonetheless, in case his mentor had a change of mind. He poured himself a generous helping of icevine juice, keenly aware of the dryness of his mouth and throat.

'Six cycles have passed since the unveiling,' Abrahasil explained. 'I was worried. You left in a hurry. Thirianna explained that you had a disagreement with Aradryan.'

Korlandril sipped his drink, his thoughts of Aradryan fixed on distant memory, another part of him savouring the taste of the icevine with its immediate tang and warm afterglow, while yet another part of his consciousness watched Abrahasil carefully. Korlandril shifted the focus of his memory, replaying events from when Aradryan had returned, reminding himself of what had occurred. After remembering the argument, Korlandril felt the serpent in his gut writhing with anger, hissing and spitting at Aradryan's words.

'Calm yourself!' warned Abrahasil.

'It was to calm myself that I went into my dreams,' Korlandril replied with annoyance. 'Dreams you have disrupted.'

'Six cycles is too long to wander in your mind,' said Abrahasil. 'It is dangerous to indulge in such self-contemplation when treading the Path of the Artist. It can lead to clashes within your spirit – over-analysis of self, confliction between real observation and imagined memory. I have told you this before.'

'I could not think of any other means to hold back the pain, except to return to those times with Aradryan that were more pleasant.'

'You are an artist now, you must express your thoughts, not conceal them!' said Abrahasil. He leaned along the table and poured himself a drink. 'What is the point of creating such great works as you are capable of if you are not going to learn the lessons that underpin them. The Path of the Artist is not about painting or sculpting, it is about controlling your means of expression, of filtering your influences and observations so that you can avoid falling prey to unfortunate stimuli. This argument with Aradryan is a fine example of what you must learn to deal with. You cannot just wander into your dreams and forget the real universe.'

'You think I am juvenile?' said Korlandril, dispensing with all memories of Aradryan as he finished the cup of icevine juice.

'Not juvenile, just rash,' said Abrahasil. 'I have not trod the Path of Dreaming, so I do not know what solace it brings to you. I know that in retreating from your observations you are stepping back from the Path of the Artist. That cannot be healthy by any consideration.'

Korlandril contemplated Abrahasil's warning as he poured himself more drink. The agitated snake within writhed and clamoured for Korlandril's attention and he washed away its nagging with more icevine, for a moment tuning every fibre of his spirit towards savouring the drink, driving away his darker thoughts with a tide of stimuli.

'I need to engage myself in another work,' said Korlandril. 'If I must expunge these feelings with expression, it is best that I not allow myself to dwell on them for long.'

'That would be good,' said Abrahasil.

'I should seek out Aradryan, and listen to him so that I might extract what it is that continues to plague me about his presence.'

'Be careful, Korlandril,' said the mentor. 'You may find Aradryan in an uncertain state, a destabilising influence on your psyche. I sense that you are at a critical stage upon the Path of the Artist. It is my joy to guide you further, but these next steps must be taken with caution. You are on the cusp of realising the full potential of expression, but you must choose wisely those emotions you choose to put on display.'

Korlandril smiled, calmed by Abrahasil's gentle tone. A surety settled in his mind, as if a light had sprung into life to show him the way forward. Under the glare of that light, the devious serpent of his jealousy shrank back into the shadows, cowed for the time being.

Now fully recovered from his dreaming session, Korlandril was filled with purpose once more, his thoughts fixed firmly upon what was to be, the past hidden away where it could do no more damage. Choosing to forget his disagreement with Aradryan, Korlandril lingered for a moment on the happier memories and then allowed those to drift into shadow as well, leaving him nothing but the present and the future.

Korlandril took a skyrunner across the dome, delighting in the rush of air against his skin, the flash of terrace and tree beneath the one-pilot craft as it soared upon the winds, its wings angling and curving in tune with his thoughts. For a short while he allowed himself free rein, forgetting his intent to see Aradryan. Powered by his psychic urging, the dart-like vehicle climbed rapidly, wings tilted back, Korlandril laughing with exhilaration. In his mind his path sculpted a complex web of interleaving arcs and loops and the skyrunner responded, twirling and swooping at his whim.

As the sensation receded and he returned the skyrunner to a stable flight, Korlandril captured the essence of his experience and stored it away. He briefly imagined creating a work of art out of air and fluid, a piece of constant motion illuminated from within, held in slowly uncoiling stasis.

Thinking of his art brought Korlandril back to his current errand. The thoughtwave sculpture was a fine idea, but it could wait. He needed to unburden his spirit of the passion roused by Aradryan's return, and so he angled the skyrunner down towards the silver ribbon of the road, swerving down between the red-leafed icevines on the terraces, darting beneath other craft that zipped to and fro across the dome's artificial sky.

Anticipation grew within Korlandril as he sped through the connecting hub between the Dome of New Suns and out into the Avenue of Starlight Secrets. Here there was more traffic. It was one of the main thoroughfares of Alaitoc where hundreds of eldar moved between the many domes and plateaus that made up the bulk of the craftworld. Some strolled languidly by themselves or with friends, others on skyrunners like Korlandril, many on drifting platforms that eased serenely from one place to the next guided by the group desires of those on board.

Korlandril allowed himself a little amazement at the scene. Rather, not at the scene itself, but at Aradryan's incomprehension of the inherent beauty and intricacy of the craftworld. Aradryan did not look upon the same things as Korlandril with the eyes of the artist, and so perhaps missed the precision of geometry at subtle odds with the inherent anarchy of a living system. He had not developed the senses to appreciate the cadence of life, the ebb and flow of the living and the immaterial and those things that lay in-between.

A hope sprang to mind and Korlandril studied it for a moment, slowing the skyrunner slightly so that its navigation demanded less of his attention. It occurred to the sculptor that he might persuade Aradryan to join him on the Path of the Artist. If Aradryan sought new vistas of experience, then none compared with opening up one's mind to every sensation without hindrance. It bordered on intoxication for Korlandril, and the thought of sharing such delights with Aradryan filled him with energy.

Engines pitching to a constant note that sang in Korlandril's heart, the skyrunner sped onwards. Veering left, Korlandril cut into the Midnight Dome, plunging into near-blackness. His eyes immediately adjusted to the lack of light, seeing shades of dark purple and blue amongst the deep grey. The laughter of lovers lilted above the song of the skyrunner but he ignored them, fearing that to contemplate their meaning would lead him towards thoughts of Thirianna; thoughts he did not want to explore at that moment. He allowed the whisper of the wind to carry away the treacherous sound and instead dwelt on the sensation of motion and the blur of dark trees washing past.

Exiting the Midnight Dome into the twilight of the Dome of Sighing Whispers, Korlandril slowed once more, the engine of the skyrunner falling to a pleasant hum. In respectful quiet he skimmed between the columns that soared up towards the dome roof. While he banked left and right without effort, he pondered how he might broach the subject of Aradryan joining him as an artist.

Slowing further still, Korlandril allowed the skyrunner to drop to ground level and swerved down a tunnelway that led deeper into Alaitoc. Here all pretence of the natural was set aside as he followed the long passage that led towards the docking towers. Oval in cross-section, the tunnel glowed with a warm orange light, flutters of energy pulsing along infinity circuit conduits embedded within the material of the wall. Korlandril felt their ghostly presence all around him as he dived deeper into the craftworld's interior, the psychic energy of the craftworld's spirits merging and dividing around him, whispering at his subconscious.

It was with some relief that Korlandril exited the passageway into the Tower of Infinite Patience, where Aradryan had taken quarters since his return. Leaving behind the psychic susurrance of the infinity circuit, Korlandril brought the skyrunner to a halt not far from a spiralling ramp that led up into the tower.

Dismounting, he allowed the craft to slip away towards an empty mooring niche and with considerable effort focussed on himself. He smoothed crumples in his robe and adjusted his belt, and with a flick of his fingers tamed his wind-tossed hair into something less unruly. Satisfied that he was presentable, he ascended the tower ramp, his long legs carrying him swiftly up to the eighth storey, momentarily revelling in the physical effort after so much recent inactivity.

Finding the Opal Suites, Korlandril touched the infinity plate to announce his presence. He waited for a moment and no response came. Allowing his fingers to linger longer on the psychically conductive slate, he sought for the presence of Aradryan but could not detect it. Only a residual impression of Aradryan remained in this place.

Adjusting his thoughts, Korlandril found that the adjoining apartment was occupied and he made an inquiry to the eldar within. She appeared at the archway a little later. She was of considerable antiquity, surrounded by an aura of wisdom and solemnity. From the brief contact he had shared with her on the infinity circuit, he knew that she was Herisianith, a shuttle pilot.

'How might I help you, Korlandril?' she asked, leaning a shoulder against the archway. Her eyes roved quickly up and down Korlandril, looking at him the same way he looked at others. At some point in her long life, Herisianith had been an artist.

'I am seeking my friend, your neighbour, Aradryan,' said Korlandril. 'He came back aboard *Lacontiran* nine cycles ago.'

'Your *friend* has not returned in two cycles,' Herisianith told him. Korlandril did not know why she had used the past-sarcastic form of 'friend', though perhaps she had seen some tiny reflection of doubt in his manner. 'He departed with a companion, Thirianna. Since then I have not seen him or felt him.'

'Did you have any sense of where they were going?'

Herisianith flicked a finger in dismissal, her turn of wrist indicating that she considered such inquiry importune. Not wishing to impose upon her longer, Korlandril gave a nod of departing and turned away. He walked slowly down the ramp, wondering what could have occupied Aradryan for two cycles. Had he spent all of that time with Thirianna?

Korlandril was drawn into a memedream, a small part of his mind guiding his body to a curving bench not far from Aradryan's quarters while the waking vision occupied the rest of his thoughts. His waystone throbbed dully, but he ignored its nagging and delved deeper into the dream.

Sineflower perfume mingled with merecherry blossom. Chatter and laughter. Thirianna standing next to her father, resplendent in a long dress of gold and black, her bronze hair caught up in a floating net of sapphire-blue air-jewels. Her eyes were green with flecks of gold and fell upon Korlandril as soon as he entered the domed chamber. Korlandril felt the warmth of Aradryan by his side: physically and emotionally. His friend had been correct, the daughter of Wishseer Aurentiun was beautiful, a radiant star in a galaxy of light.

Aradryan introduced them. Thirianna smiled and Korlandril melted under her gaze. She complimented him on his moontiger patterned cloak. He muttered a reply, something stupid he had chosen to forget. They danced, exchanging partners, to the skirl of Aradryan's scythe-harp. Korlandril played his light-flute, dazzling the party with the sound and colours conjured by his nimble fingers and playful mind.

A hot cycle followed, the three of them enjoying the artificial sun and lilac beaches of the Dome of Rising Hope. Korlandril revelled in their innocence, reliving the unabashed joy they had shared. Each of them musicians, delighting and teasing each other with their melodies, coming together upon the rhythm of their thoughts and feelings.

The serpent intruded once more, tearing Korlandril from his reverie. Had Thirianna and Aradryan ever been more than just good companions? Quivering slightly from the shock of departing the memedream so suddenly, Korlandril reapplied himself to his current purpose. It would be easier to find Thirianna than Aradryan, and if his wayward friend was not actually with her she might have some better idea where he might be found.

Korlandril found an infinity terminal in a small grove of whisper-leaf not far from the apartments. He made a gentle inquiry, seeking Thirianna. She had been on the craftworld longer than Aradryan and her presence in the psychic matrix that powered Alaitoc was stronger. Korlandril concentrated on Thirianna and felt the after-shadow of her spirit moving around the craftworld over the previous two cycles: here, where she met Aradryan, his spirit also registering strongly; the Boulevard of Split Moons, along the arcades of the fashion-sellers and jewelsmiths; her own quarters – alone, Korlandril noted with some satisfaction – for half a cycle; then to the Bay of Departing Sorrows, where Aradryan was present again, his presence lingering alongside hers for just the shortest time. Now she was back in her quarters, silent, perhaps meditating or composing.

Korlandril voiced thoughts of companionship and directed them towards Thirianna. He waited for her to respond. He allowed the background vibrations of the infinity circuit to occupy him: celebration in the Dome of the Last Sunrise, a disturbing darkness emanating from the Shrine of the Ending Veil.

At this Korlandril withdrew, repelled by the taste left in his mouth from the Aspect Warrior shrine. He had little to do with warmakers, but the Ending Veil was home to one of the Dark Reaper sects; his friends Arthuis and Maerthuin counted amongst their number. He did not pay much attention to military matters, finding it a disagreeable influence on his creations. There was no place for bloody-handed Kaela Mensha Khaine in his work. That his friends might be involved did interest him and he passed on his observations to the dormant Thirianna.

She roused almost immediately, sending him a vision of his Isha statue. The scene was an imagination of the two of them standing beneath it: an invitation. Korlandril reflected the vision back to Thirianna, with a slight adjustment. The night shields were active, dimming the light of the dying star to the twilight of early evening. Thirianna responded in kind and the rendezvous was agreed.

Korlandril broke from the infinity circuit, satisfied with himself. He returned to the Opal Suites and took another skyrunner back to his chambers. His exuberance was muted on his return journey, the lack of Aradryan's touch upon the infinity circuit preying on his thoughts.

Thirianna was at the statue, sitting at one end of a curving bench, her eyes directed to the dim glow beyond the dome. Korlandril crossed the grass quickly and Thirianna turned at his approach, a smile hovering on her lips for just a moment.

'Aradryan has left Alaitoc,' Thirianna said quietly when Korlandril was seated beside her.

Korlandril was taken aback and it took him a moment to readjust his thoughts; he had been ready to open the conversation with an inquiry about Thirianna's wellbeing. A flurry of emotions warred within Korlandril: shock, disappointment and, worryingly, a small degree of satisfaction.

'I do not understand,' said the sculptor. 'I know that we had a disagreement, but I thought that he planned to remain on Alaitoc for some time yet.'

'He did not depart on your account,' said Thirianna, though an unconscious asymmetric blink betrayed conflict in her thoughts. She was not lying, but neither was she wholly convinced that she spoke the truth.

'Why would he not come to see me before he left?' Korlandril asked. 'It is obvious that some distance had grown between us, but I did not think his opinion of me had sunk so low.'

'It was not you,' Thirianna said, her tone and half-closed eyes indicating that she believed it was her fault their friend had fled the craftworld.

'What happened?' asked Korlandril, trying hard to keep any tone of accusation from his voice. 'When did Aradryan leave?'

'He took aboard *Irdiris* last cycle, after we spent some time together.'

Korlandril had heard the name of the ship in passing but could not place it immediately. Thirianna read the look of questioning on his face.

'*Irdiris* is a far-runner, destined for the Exodites on Elan-Shemaresh and then to the Wintervoid of Meios,' she explained.

'Aradryan wishes to become a... *ranger*?' Incredulity and distaste vied with each other in Korlandril's thoughts. He stroked his bottom lip with a slender finger, stilling his thoughts. 'I had no idea he was so dissatisfied with Alaitoc.'

'Neither did I, and perhaps that is why he left so soon,' confessed Thirianna. 'I believe I spoke hastily and with insensitivity and drove him to a swifter departure than he might otherwise have considered.'

'I am sure that you are no–' began Korlandril but Thirianna cut him off with an agitated twitch of her finger.

'I do not wish to speak of it,' was all the explanation she would offer.

That sat in silence for a while longer, while littlewings darted amongst the branches of the trees above them, trilling to one another. Deep within the woods a breezemaker stirred into life and the leaves began to rustle gently: a calming backdrop.

'There was something else about which I wish to speak to you,' said Korlandril, having put aside his thoughts on Aradryan. 'I have a proposal to make.'

Interest flared in Thirianna's jade eyes. She indicated with a raising of her chin that they should stand.

'We should discuss this in my chambers, with something to drink, perhaps?'

'That would be most agreeable,' said Korlandril as the two them made their way towards the dome entrance.

Neither spoke as they crossed the dome. They walked a little way apart, the distance a compromise between companionship and decency. Korlandril's heart beat a little bit faster than usual. He tried to contend with a mounting excitement, having not expected such an accommodating response from Thirianna.

It took some time to reach the dome entrance on foot and the night cycle was midway through when they came upon the silvered archway that led into the main thoroughfare around the rim of the craftworld. Here twilight was also in effect, the darkness broken only by a faint red reflection from the dying star and the will-o'-the-wisps of the infinity circuit around them.

The wide passage was quiet; they passed perhaps a dozen other eldar before they reached the turning towards Thirianna's apartments. She had taken up rooms in a poet's commune in the Tower of Dormant Witnesses. It was a place noted for its contemplative atmosphere, with views out to the stars and back across the whole of Alaitoc.

They were about to step onto the sliding walkway up to the towers when a large group appeared from the gloom ahead. Sensing something dark, Thirianna strayed closer to Korlandril, who put a protective hand upon her shoulder even as his own mood dropped, filled with foreboding.

The group were Aspect Warriors, and an aura of death hung about them as palpable as a stench. They were clad in plates of overlapping armour of purple and black, their heavy tread thunderous in the still twilight. Korlandril could feel their menace growing stronger as they approached, waystones glowing like eyes of blood. They had taken off their war-helms and carried them hooked upon their belts, leaving their hands free to carry slender missile launchers.

Dark Reapers: possessed of the War God in his Aspect of Destroyer.

Though their helmets were removed, they still bore the rune of the Dark Reaper painted in blood upon their faces. Thirianna and Korlandril shrank closer to the edge of the passageway as the Aspect Warriors passed, seeking the faces of their friends. Korlandril realised he had inadvertently pulled Thirianna in front of him a little and the realisation brought a small wound to his pride. For her part, Thirianna was calm but apprehensive. Korlandril could feel her trembling under his palm. It was not fear, it was something thrilling. She had walked the Path of the Warrior, did Khaine even now call out to her? Did the presence of the Aspect Warriors resonate with some part of her buried beneath the layers of civilisation the eldar worked so hard to maintain?

Thirianna pointed, directing Korlandril's attention to Maerthuin. Arthuis walked a little way behind. The brothers stopped and turned their eyes upon Thirianna and Korlandril. Their gazes were empty, devoid of anything but the remotest recognition. Korlandril repressed a

51

shudder as he smelt the blood upon their faces.

'You are well?' asked Thirianna, her voice quiet and respectful.

Arthuis nodded slowly.

'Victory was ours,' intoned Maerthuin.

'We will meet you at the Crescent of the Dawning Ages,' said Arthuis.

'At the start of the next cycle,' added Maerthuin.

Korlandril and Thirianna both nodded their agreement and the two warriors moved on. Thirianna relaxed and Korlandril gave a sigh of relief, glad to be free of their friends' blank yet strangely penetrating gazes.

'It is inconceivable to me that one should indulge in such horror,' said Korlandril as the two of them stepped upon the moving walkway, still feeling a small aftercurrent of fear from the encounter.

They made a spiralling ascent, languidly turning upon itself as the sliding ramp rose around the Tower of Dormant Witnesses. Korlandril felt a thrill as they emerged into the starlight-bathed sky, nothing more between him and the void than an invisible shield of energy. For a moment he thought he understood something of the lure of the stars that so enamoured Aradryan.

'It is not an indulgence,' said Thirianna.

'What is not an indulgence?'

'The Path of the Warrior is not an indulgence,' she repeated. 'One cannot simply leave anger in the darkness, to fester and grow unseen. Sooner or later it might find vent.'

'What is there to be so angry about?' laughed Korlandril. 'Perhaps if we were Biel-Tan, with all their talk of reclaiming the old empire, then we might have a use for all of this sword-waving and gunfire. It is an uncivilised way to behave.'

'You ignore the passions that rule you,' snapped Thirianna.

Korlandril felt a spear of guilt and embarrassment.

'I meant no offence,' he said.

'The intention is not important,' said Thirianna, her eyes narrowed, lips thin. 'Perhaps you would care to ridicule the other Paths on which I have trodden?'

'I did not mean…' Korlandril trailed off, unsure what he did actually mean, his glibness burned away by Thirianna's sudden scorn. 'I am sorry.'

'The Path of Dreaming, the Path of Awakening, the Path of the Artist,' said Thirianna. 'Always self-indulgent, always about your needs, no sense of duty or dedication to others.'

Korlandril shrugged, a fulsome gesture employing the full use of both arms.

'I simply do not understand this desire some of us feel to sate a blood-lust I do not feel,' he said.

'And that is what is dangerous about you,' said Thirianna. 'Where do you put that rage you feel when someone angers you? What do you do with the hatred that burns inside when you think upon all that we have lost? You have not learnt to control these feelings, merely ignore them. Becoming one with Khaine, assuming one of His Aspects is not about confronting an enemy, it is about confronting ourselves. We should all do it at some time in our lives.'

Korlandril shook his head.

'Only those that desire war, make it,' he said.

'Findrueir's *Prophecies of Interrogation*,' said Thirianna, lips twisted in a sneer, brow furrowed. 'Yes, I've read it too, do not look so surprised. However, I read it after treading the Path of the Warrior. An aesthete who wrote about matters she had never experienced. Hypocrisy at its worst.'

'And also one of Iyanden's foremost philosophers.'

'A radical windbag with no true cause and a gyrinx fetish.'

Korlandril laughed and received a frown in reply.

'Forgive me,' he said. 'I hope that is not an example of your poetry!'

Thirianna vacillated between annoyance and humour before breaking into a smile.

'Listen to us! Gallery philosophers, the pair! What do we know?'

'Little enough,' agreed Korlandril with a nod. 'And I suppose that can be a dangerous thing.'

Korlandril stood attentively beside Thirianna while she mixed her preferred cocktail of juices and ground ice. She passed a slender glass to Korlandril and waved him towards one of the cushions that served as seats in her reception chamber. She had rearranged and recoloured her rooms since Korlandril had last visited. Gone was the holographic representation of Illuduran's *Monument to the Glories of Impudence* and the pastel blue scheme. All was white and light grey, with only the hard cushions as furniture. Korlandril looked pointedly around the room.

'It's a trifle post-Herethiun minimalist, is it not?' he said, reclining as best he could.

'You had a proposal?' said Thirianna, ignoring the implied accusation.

Korlandril hesitated. The mood did not feel right. Though they had made up their differences before arriving at the chambers, the comfort he had shared with Thirianna in the garden dome had all but gone. He needed her to be receptive to his idea. He would start by finding some common ground: Aradryan's departure.

'I am sorry that Aradryan has left us again,' he said, meaning it sincerely. 'I had hoped that I could have persuaded him to join me on the Path of the Artist. Perhaps we might have rekindled something of what we shared on the Path of Dreaming.'

Thirianna gave a flick of her hair, a momentary gesture of annoyance.

'What is so wrong with that?' Korlandril asked.

'It was not for Aradryan's benefit that you wished,' said Thirianna, sitting opposite the sculptor. 'As ever, it was because *you* want him to become an artist, not because it would be the best thing for him.'

'He is directionless and lonely,' argued Korlandril. 'I thought that if he could learn to see the universe as I do, with the eyes of the Artist, he might learn to appreciate what the craftworld has to offer him.'

'You are still annoyed that he didn't like your sculpture!' Thirianna was half-amused and half-scornful. She sighed in exasperation. 'You think that if he learnt to "see" things the proper way he would appreciate your genius all the better. You think his criticisms are invalid simply because he has not shared the same education as you.'

'Perhaps that is the case,' Korlandril said in a conciliatory tone, realising he had chosen the wrong tack. 'I do not want us to be divided by Aradryan's absence. He will return one day, of that I am sure. We have both coped without him, and we will do so again. If we stay close to each other, that is.'

'Your friendship has been important to me,' said Thirianna, warming Korlandril's hopes. He pressed on.

'I have a new piece of sculpture in mind, something very different from my previous works,' he announced.

'That is good to hear. I think that if you can find something to occupy your mind, you will dwell less on the situation with Aradryan.'

'Yes, that is very true! I'm going to delve into portraiture. A sculptural testament to devotion, in fact.'

'Sounds intriguing,' said Thirianna. 'Perhaps something a little more grounded in reality would be good for your development.'

'Let us not get too carried away,' said Korlandril with a smile. 'I think there may be some abstract elements incorporated into the design. After all, how does one truly replicate love and companionship in features alone?'

'I am surprised. I understand if you do not wish to tell me, but what inspires such a piece of work?'

Korlandril thought she was being coy for a moment, but a quick reading of her expression confirmed that she had not the slightest idea that she was to be the subject. That serpent in Korlandril's gut, hissing with annoyance, uncoiled itself. What had been the point of all of his overtures? He had not been obvious in his affections, but neither had he been too subtle in his intent. Was she playing some game with him, wanting him to say aloud what they both understood to be true?

'You are my inspiration,' Korlandril said quietly, eyes fixed on Thirianna. 'It is you that I wish to fashion as a likeness of dedication and ardour.'

Thirianna blinked, and then blinked again. Her eyebrows rose in shock.

'I… You…' She looked away. 'I do not think that is warranted.'

'Warranted? It is an expression of my feelings, there is nothing that needs warranting other than to visualise my desires and dreams. You are my desire and a dream.'

Thirianna did not reply. She stood and took a couple of paces away before turning to face Korlandril, her face serious.

'This is not a good idea, my friend,' she said gently. 'I do appreciate the sentiment, and perhaps some time ago I would not only be flattered but I would be delighted.'

The serpent sank its fangs into Korlandril's heart.

'But not now?' he asked, hesitant, scared of the answer.

She shook her head.

'Aradryan's arrival and departure have made me realise something that has been amiss with my life for several passes now,' she said. Korlandril reached out a hand in a half-hearted gesture, beckoning her to come closer. Thirianna sat next to him and took his hand in hers. 'I am changing again. The Path of the Poet is spent for me. I have grieved and I have rejoiced through my verse, and I feel expunged of the burdens I felt. I feel another calling is growing inside me.'

Korlandril snatched his hand away.

'You are going to join Aradryan!' he snapped. 'I knew the two of you were keeping something from me.'

'Don't be ridiculous,' Thirianna rasped in return. 'It is because I told him what I am telling you that he left.'

'So, he did make advances on you!' Korlandril stood and angrily wiped a hand across his brow and pointed accusingly at his friend. 'It is true! Deny it if you dare!'

She slapped away his hand.

'What right do you have to make any claim on me? If you must know, I have never entertained any thoughts of being with Aradryan, even before he left, and certainly not since his return. I am simply not ready for a life-companion. In fact, that is why I cannot be your inspiration.'

Thirianna took a step closer, hands open in friendship.

'It is to save you from a future heartache that I decline your attentions now,' she continued. 'I have spoken to Farseer Alaiteir and he agrees that I am ready to begin the Path of the Seer.'

'A seer?' scoffed Korlandril. 'You completely fail to divine my romantic intents and yet think you might become a seer?'

'I divined your intent and ignored it,' said Thirianna, laying a hand on his arm. 'I did not wish to encourage you. To admit your feelings for me would be to bring them to the light and that was something I wished to avoid, for the sake of both of us.'

Korlandril waved away her arguments, pulling his arm from her grasp.

'If you have not the same feelings for me, then simply say so. Do not spare my pride for your comfort. Do not hide behind this excuse of changing Paths.'

'It is true, it is not an excuse! You love Thirianna the Poet. We are alike enough at the moment, our Paths different yet moving in the same general direction. When I become a Seer, I will not be Thirianna the Poet. You will not love that person.'

'Why deny me the right to find out? Who are you to judge what will or will not be? You are not even on the Path and now you think you can claim the powers of the Seer?'

'If it is true that you feel the same when I have become a Seer, and I feel the same too, then whatever will happen will come to pass.'

Korlandril caught an angry reply before it emerged, his mind catching up with Thirianna's words. Hope blossomed, bright flowers stifling the angry serpent.

'If you feel the same? You admit that you have feelings for me.'

'Thirianna the Poet has feelings for you, she always has,' Thirianna admitted.

'Then why do we not embrace this shared feeling?' Korlandril asked, stepping forward and taking Thirianna's hands in his. Now it was her turn to pull away. She could not bring herself to look at him when she spoke.

'If I indulge this passion with you, it would hold me back, perhaps trap me here as the Poet, forever writing my verses of love in secret.'

'Then we stay together, Poet and Artist! What is so wrong with that?'

'It is not healthy! You know that it is unwise to become trapped in ourselves. Our lives must be in constant motion, moving from one Path to the next, developing our senses of self and the universe. To over-indulge leads to the darkness that came before. It attracts the attention of... Her. She Who Thirsts.'

Korlandril shuddered at the mention of the Eldar's Bane, even by euphemism. His waystone quivered with him, becoming chill to the touch. All that Thirianna said was true, enshrined in the teachings of the craftworlds; the whole structure of their society created to avoid a return to the debauchery and excesses that led to the Fall.

But Korlandril did not care. It was stupid that he and Thirianna should be denied their happiness.

'What we feel is not *wrong*! Since the founding of the craftworlds our people have loved and survived. Why should we be any different?'

'You use the same arguments as Aradryan,' Thirianna admitted, turning on Korlandril. 'He asked me to forget the Path and join him. Even if I had loved him I could not do that. I *cannot* do that with you. Though I have deep feelings for you, I would no more risk my eternal spirit for you than I would step out into the void of space and hope to breathe.'

There were tears in her eyes, kept in check until now.

'Please leave.'

Korlandril's anguish was all-consuming. Fear and wrath in equal measure tore through him, burning along his veins, churning in his mind. Dropping beneath it all was a deep pit of shadow and despair, down which he felt himself falling. Korlandril wanted to faint but held himself upright, forcing himself to breathe deeply. The serpent inside him wound itself tight around every organ and bone, crushing the life from him, filling him with a physical pain.

'I cannot help you,' Thirianna said, staring with misery at the anguish being played out in Korlandril's actions. 'I know you are in pain, but it will pass.'

'Pain?' spat Korlandril. 'What do you know of my pain?'

His whole psyche screamed in torment, honed by his practice as an Artist, thrashing for expression. There was no outlet for all of the pent-up frustration; passes upon passes of suppressing his emotions for Thirianna threatened to erupt. Korlandril was simply not mentally equipped to unleash the torrent of rage that whirled inside him. There was no dream he could go to for solace; no sculpture he could create to excise the pain; no physical sensation he could indulge to replace the agony that wracked his spirit. Incandescent, his waystone was white hot on his chest.

Violence welled up inside Korlandril. He wanted to strike Thirianna for being so selfish and shortsighted. He wanted to draw blood, to let his pain flow out of deep wounds and wash away the anger. Most of all he wanted something else to feel the agony, to share in the devastation.

Wordless, Korlandril fled, his anger swept around by a vortex of fear at what he had unleashed within himself. He stumbled out onto the walkway and stared up into the endless heavens, tears streaming down his face, his heart thundering.

He needed help. Help to quench the fire that was now raging in his mind.

REJECTION

In the time before the War in Heaven, before even the coming of the eldar, the gods schemed their schemes and planned their plans, engaging in an eternal game of deceit and love, treachery and teasing. Kurnous, Lord of the Hunt, was the lover of Lileath of the Moon, and they enjoyed both the blessing of Almighty Asuryan and the friendship of the other gods; save for Kaela Mensha Khaine, the Bloody-Handed One, who desired Lileath for himself. He craved her not for her beauty, which was immortal, nor for her playful wit, which made friends of all the other gods. Khaine desired the Moon Goddess simply because she had chosen Kurnous. Khaine endeavoured to impress her with his martial skills, but Lileath was unimpressed. He composed odes to woo her but his poems were ever crude, filled with the desire to conquer and possess. Lileath would not be owned by any other. Frustrated, Khaine went to Asuryan and demanded that Lileath be given to him. Asuryan told Khaine that he could not take Lileath by force, and that if he could not win her heart he could not have her. Enraged, Khaine vowed that if he could not possess Lileath then no other would. Khaine took up his sword, the Widowmaker, the Slayer of Worlds, and cut a rent in the void. He snatched up Lileath by the ankle and cast her into the rift in the stars, where her light could no longer shine. For a thousand days the heavens were dark until Kurnous, brave and resourceful, dared the blackness of the rift and rescued Lileath so that her light would return to the universe.

It took some time for Korlandril to restore a small measure of equilibrium. Ashamed and desperate, he hid himself amongst the trees of the Dome of Midnight Forests, no longer weeping or growling. Korlandril detached himself from his physical processes, allowing them to continue without his intervention, losing all sense of sight and touch, smell and hearing. To isolate himself in such a way was a legacy of the Path of Dreaming, shut off entirely from outside stimuli. He was locked up with his own thoughts with no distraction, but resisted the urge to plunge into a memedream and forget everything. On the Path of Awakening he had learnt to divide his attention in the opposite direction, locking away conscious thought, concentrating purely on sensation and response.

The two Paths had complemented well his choice to become an Artist, but now they left him vulnerable. His experience as an adult had been directed towards compartmentalising and controlling his interaction with the world; later, as Korlandril the Sculptor, he had been a conduit for creative expression, turning thought into deed. Now his thoughts were bleak, bloody even, and he could not express them.

Sorting through his impressions and memories, Korlandril tried to make sense of what had happened. He did not understand what had broken the emotional dam that had kept his darker feelings in check. He could not find an answer. Disturbed, he was not sure what questions needed answering. He knew that he could not let these thoughts run rampant, nor could he act upon them. That would be to embrace the mayhem and indulgence that had brought about the Fall.

Korlandril thought for a moment of finding an infinity terminal and contacting Abrahasil. He dismissed the notion. He was in no state to be interacting with the infinity circuit. His emotional instability would be sure to attract attention of the wrong kind, if it didn't do any actual harm to him or the circuit. Even if he could muster enough self-control to navigate the circuit properly, Abrahasil would not be able to help him. This was not some dilemma of form or sensation, or even one of expression. Korlandril simply could not comprehend why he had become so distressed, and why that distress was manifesting itself in such a destructive manner.

Amidst the maelstrom of his thoughts, Korlandril's attention was brought to a small matter that needed resolving. A thought-cycle demanded his attention, a future-memory yet to be experienced. Korlandril analysed it and was reminded of the appointment he had made with Arthuis and Maerthuin. He linked the reminder with a memory and cycled them together with his current feelings. He encountered a shock of recognition, drawing on what he had seen, or rather not seen, in the blank stares of his friends while they had been wearing their warmasks. The deadness that was there, an expression devoid of shock, guilt, shame or remorse.

If anybody could help him understand the turbulence that so unbalanced him now, it would be the Aspect Warriors.

The Crescent of the Dawning Ages curved out from the starward rim of Alaitoc, bathed in the glow of Mirianathir. The kilometres-long balcony was covered by an arching vault of subtly mirrored material that dimly reflected the patrons below, blending their visual simulacra with the ruddy light of the star to paint an ever-moving scene across the heavens.

The new cycle was just beginning and there were many eldar sat at the tables along the balcony or moving between them and the food bars on the inward side. They ate fruits from the orchards and breakfasted on spiced meats brought back by traders with the Exodite worlds. Drinks of all colours, some luminescent, others effervescent, were dispensed from tall, slender urns or arranged in rows of glittering bottles, regularly replenished by those walking the Path of Service. A dampening field kept the conversation quiet, though there were thousands of voices raised in greeting and debate, departure and conciliation.

One area was sparsely populated, the other eldar leaving an indistinct but noticeable gap between themselves and the patrons that sat at the long benches there. Here were the Aspect Warriors, shorn of their warpaint, together in quiet contemplation.

Korlandril approached cautiously. Even after much meditation and calming mantras, he was still jittery from his recent experience. His nervousness was not helped by the stares of the other eldar as he crossed the pale blue floor, heading towards the Aspect Warriors.

He stopped and poured himself a glass of dawnwater and leaned against the curving counter top as he scanned the assembled Aspect Warriors looking for his friends.

A hand was raised in welcome and Korlandril recognised Arthuis. On his left sat Maerthuin. Around them were several other eldar that Korlandril did not know. They sat with thin platters on their laps, picking at finger food, their voices quiet. Space was made on the bench opposite his friends and Korlandril sat down, agitated by the presence of so many warriors.

'Greetings of the new cycle to you,' said Maerthuin. 'Are you not hungry?'

'I'd skin and eat a narboar if I could,' said Arthuis. His plate was heaped with food and he broke off speaking to cram a handful of scented grains into his mouth.

'This is Elissanadrin,' said Maerthuin, indicating the female eldar sat to his left. She was perhaps eighty or ninety passes old, almost twice Korlandril's age. Her cheeks were prominent, angular, and her nose thin and pointed. When she turned and smiled at Korlandril, her movements were precise, every gesture clearly defined and a little abrupt. She paused as she sensed the identity of the newcomer.

'Pleased to make your acquaintance, Korlandril the Sculptor,' Elissanadrin said. Her tone was as clipped as her motion.

Korlandril opened a palm in greeting. Other introductions were made: Fiarithin, a male just out of puberty; Sellisarin, a tall, older eldar male; others whose names and features Korlandril stored away for future reference.

'There is something different about you, Korlandril,' said Arthuis, placing his empty plate on a shelf underneath the bench. 'I sense something aggrieves you.'

'It is hard not to feel your agitation,' added Maerthuin. 'Perhaps you are uncomfortable with your company.'

Korlandril looked around at the Aspect Warriors. On the face of it, they appeared no different to any other eldar. Without their war-masks on, they were each individual. Some were obviously distressed, others animated, most thoughtful.

'I do not wish to intrude,' said Korlandril. His eyes strayed to one of the warriors, an old female who sat weeping, comforted by her companions. 'I know that recently there was a battle.'

Arthuis followed Korlandril's gaze and shook his head disconsolately.

'Several of us were lost. We mourn their passing, but their spirits were saved,' said Elissanadrin. There were approving nods from others at the benches.

'I shall compose a verse to commemorate their time with us,' said Arthuis.

'I wept like a babe when I unmasked,' Maerthuin admitted with a lopsided smile. 'I think I shall miss Neamoriun the most. He was a good friend and a gifted singer.'

The name flickered with recognition and Korlandril remembered attending a concert in the Dome of Enchanting Echoes.

'I saw him perform,' said Korlandril, wishing to add something to the conversation. 'He sang the *Lay of Ulthanesh*.'

'That was his favourite,' Arthuis chuckled. 'It is no surprise that he joined the Fire Dragons, so full of energy and excitable of temperament.'

'It was only last pass that I saw him, I did not realise he was a Fire Dragon,' said Korlandril.

'One cannot fight all of the time,' said Maerthuin. This appeared to remind him of something and he looked at Korlandril. 'I am sorry that I missed the unveiling of your statue. I will visit it later this cycle.'

A flicker of agitation disturbed Korlandril as he recalled his memories of the event, his disagreement with Aradryan marring an otherwise perfect evening. The others sensed his disquiet.

'I was right, something is amiss,' said Arthuis. 'I cannot think that your work was anything other than spectacular.'

'I had a friend who thought otherwise.'

There were whispers of concern and Korlandril realised he had used not only the past form of friend, but one used to refer to those that were dead. It was a slip of the tongue, but betrayed something deeper. Korlandril was quick to correct himself.

'He has left Alaitoc to become a ranger,' he said, making a reassuring gesture. 'It has been difficult, I saw him only briefly. He is still with us, though I do not think our friendship has survived.'

'It is Aradryan of whom you speak?' asked Maerthuin. Korlandril nodded.

'I always thought Aradryan was a bit strange,' confided Arthuis. 'I half-expected to wake each cycle and discover that he had taken the starwalk.'

Korlandril was shocked. To suggest that another eldar would take their life was one of the crudest notions he had heard. Arthuis laughed at Korlandril's distaste.

'I know that he was your friend, but he was always far too distant,' said Arthuis. 'It does not surprise me at all that he's become a ranger. I have always sensed something of the radical about him.'

'I knew him well and sensed no such thing,' argued Korlandril.

'Sometimes the things that are closest to us are the hardest to see,' said Maerthuin. 'I can sense that you would prefer not to talk about it, so we will change the subject. How is Thirianna, I see she has not come with you?'

The glass shattered into splinters in Korlandril's hand. As one, many of the Aspect Warriors turned their attention to him, a sudden silence descending as they sensed a wave of anger flowing from the sculptor. There was concern in the eyes of several.

'Have you hurt yourself?' asked Elissanadrin, leaning forward to look at Korlandril's hand. He examined his fingers and palm and found no blood.

'I am unhurt,' he said stiffly and made to stand. Arthuis gently but insistently grabbed his wrist and pulled him back down.

'You are trembling,' said the Aspect Warrior and Korlandril realised it was true. He felt a tic under his right eye and his hands were clenched in fists.

'I am...' Korlandril began, but he could not finish the sentence. He did not know what he was. He was frustrated. He was saddened. Most of all, he was angry.

'Our friend is irritable, it would seem,' said Maerthuin. 'Is there a problem with Thirianna?'

Korlandril could not reply. Every time he turned his mind to Thirianna his thoughts folded in on themselves, sending him crashing back into the pit of anger that had swallowed him. The snake within had coiled itself through every part of his body and would not let go, no matter how hard he tried to push it back.

'It is Khaine's curse,' said Sellisarin, intrigued. He reached out a hand towards Korlandril's brow, but the sculptor pulled back.

'Don't touch me!' Korlandril snarled.

Sellisarin made soothing sounds and moved closer, meeting Korlandril's gaze.

'There is nothing to be afraid of,' said the Aspect Warrior, again reaching out his hand.

Korlandril writhed as the serpent whipped and wriggled inside, urging him to lash out. He raised his hands defensively instead, warding away Sellisarin's attention.

'Leave me in peace,' he sobbed. 'I'll… I'll deal with this in my own way.'

'You cannot find peace on your own,' said Elissanadrin, sitting next to Korlandril. 'The hand of Khaine has reached into you and awoken that which dwells within all of us. You cannot ignore this. If it does not destroy you, it could harm others.'

Korlandril looked pleadingly at Maerthuin. His friend nodded silently, affirming what Elissanadrin had said.

'This is part of you, part of every eldar,' said Arthuis. 'It is not a judgement, not something that brings you shame.'

'Why now?' moaned Korlandril. 'Why has this happened now?'

'You must learn to understand your fear and your anger before you can control them,' said Maerthuin. 'Always they have been with you, but we hide them so well. Now you must bring them into the light and confront them. Your rage is growing in power over you. It is not something you can fight, for such desires fuel themselves. Nor can you expunge them from your spirit, no more than you can stop breathing. It is part of you and always will be. All you can do now is find the means by which you can contain it, turn its energy elsewhere.'

'And keep it contained when it is not needed,' added Arthuis.

Shuddering, Korlandril took a deep breath and looked at the faces around him. They showed concern, not fear. He was surrounded by bloody-handed murderers, who not more than a few cycles ago had slain and mutilated other creatures. Yet he was the one that was weighed down by his anger; he was the one who felt a bottomless hatred. How was it that they could indulge that dark part of their nature and yet stay sane?

'I do not know what to do,' said Korlandril, slumping forwards with his head in his hands.

'Yes you do, but you are afraid to admit it,' said Arthuis. Korlandril looked at his friend, not daring to speak. 'You must come to terms with Khaine's legacy.'

'I cannot become a warrior,' said Korlandril. 'I am an Artist. I create, I do not destroy.'

'And that is good,' said Sellisarin. 'It is the division of creation and destruction that you need, the split between peace and war, life and death. Look around you. Are we not peaceful now, we who have killed so many? The Path of the Warrior is the path of outer war and inner peace.'

'The alternative is exile,' said Maerthuin. A sly smirk twisted his lips. 'You could always follow Aradryan, flee from Alaitoc.'

The thought appalled Korlandril. To abandon Alaitoc was to abandon all civilization. He needed stability and guidance, not unfettered freedom. His spirit could no more survive without the protection of Alaitoc than could his body. Another thought came to him. To leave the craftworld would mean parting from Thirianna – in shame, his last act towards her one of anger.

'What must I do?' he asked quietly, resigning himself to his fate. He looked at the warriors. Each had chosen a specific aspect of the Bloody-Handed God to become: Dark Reaper, Howling Banshee, Shining Spear. How did one know which Aspect thrived within? 'I do not know where to go.'

It was Elissanadrin that spoke. She crouched in front of Korlandril and held his hand in hers.

'What do you feel, at this moment?' she asked.

'I just want to hide, to be away from all of this,' Korlandril replied, eyes closed. 'I am scared of what I have become.'

The Aspect Warriors exchanged glances and Elissanadrin nodded.

'Then it is in hiding, in secrecy, in the shadows that you will find your way,' she said, pulling Korlandril to his feet. 'Come with me.'

Korlandril followed her mutely as the other eldar parted for them. He could feel their stares upon his back and cringed at their attention. So much had changed so quickly. A cycle ago he had craved the interest of others, now he could not bear their scrutiny.

'Where are we going?' he asked Elissanadrin when they had passed out of the Crescent of the Dawning Ages.

'In the darkness you will find strength. In the aspect of the Striking Scorpion you will turn fear from enemy to ally. We go to the place where I also learnt to hide: the Shrine of the Deadly Shadow.'

Quiet but agitated, Korlandril allowed Elissanadrin to lead him to the shuttle vault beneath the Crescent of the Dawning Ages. The wide platform was almost empty, only a handful of other eldar waiting for the cross-hub transport. Korlandril sat on a bench next to Elissanadrin but the two said nothing as they waited for the shuttle.

A soft hum heralded its arrival, pulsing from the tunnelway to the left a moment before the shuttle whispered alongside the platform and came to a standstill, a chain of bullet-shaped compartments hovering just above the anti-grav rail.

The pair found an empty carriage towards the front of the shuttle and sat opposite each other.

'It is not wrong to be afraid,' said Elissanadrin. 'We must learn to live with our fears as much as our hopes and dreams and talents.'

Korlandril said nothing as the shuttle accelerated, plunging into a blue-lit tunnel. For a moment the swiftly-passed lights dappled through the windows until they became a constant stream of colour, blurred together by the speed of the shuttle.

Korlandril tried to relax, to find a dream to take him away from what was happening, but his fists gripped the moulded arms of the chair and every muscle in his body was tense. Closing his eyes did not help. The only memory that came to him was a real dream, a nightmare battle that had plagued his sleep the night-cycle before Aradryan's return.

'Do you dream of war?' he asked suddenly.

Elissanadrin shook her head.

'It is so that we do not dream that we learn to don our war-masks,' she replied. 'Combat is an immediate, visceral act and should not be remembered.'

Her answer only increased Korlandril's anxiety, while the shuttle raced on, heading for the Vale of Khaine, speeding him towards his fate.

Korlandril stood in front of the last of the three gates that led to the shrine. He could see nothing beyond the white portal and was alone. Elissanadrin had left him between the first and second gates and taken another route. The entranceway was physically unassuming, identified by a solitary rune above the outer door. They had passed several such Aspect shrines on the short walk from the shuttle station, along deserted corridors and through empty passageways.

Though the Vale of Khaine looked little different to any other part of Alaitoc – visually bland in Korlandril's opinion – it certainly had its own feel. As soon as he had stepped off the transport, Korlandril had felt it, an oppressive air that filled the space between the curved walls with a pressure that nagged at one's mind.

Fear fluttered in Korlandril's heart as he stood there, not knowing what lay beyond the doorway. The Aspect Warriors never spoke of their shrines and no eldar went to them unless they were destined to join. He could barely feel the infinity circuit in the walls around him, subdued and distant. The spirits within its crystalline matrix avoided this place.

Taking a deep breath, Korlandril stepped forward and the door peeled apart in front of him.

The first sensation was cloying heat and humidity. It washed over Korlandril, sweeping around him with a wet embrace. His skin was slick within moments, a sheen of droplets on his bare arms and legs. The plain white tunic he wore was sodden before he had taken a step forwards.

Dim mist drifted out, swallowing him within its gloom. He could barely see the contorted trunks and drooping branches of trees, over-hanging a path ahead. Stepping across the threshold his booted foot came upon spongy ground, his feet sinking slightly into the soft mire. After three more paces the doors silently shut behind him. Korlandril felt closed off. Suddenly panicked, he wheeled around and stepped towards the portal, but the gate would not open.

There was no turning back.

The path itself wound a meandering track between dark pools of thick liquid that gleamed with an oily sheen. Creepers hung down from the branches overhead, sometimes so many of them that Korlandril had to paw his way forwards, their wet tendrils slapping at his face and shoulders.

Not only vines populated the trees. Serpents with glistening green bodies slithered between the large fronds, their red eyes dead of all expression. Insects with wings as large as his hands burred and buzzed around him, skimming over the pools or clinging to the smooth tree trunks, gently fanning their brightly-patterned wings.

The only sounds were the patter of drips on the leaves and the trickle of water through the mangrove roots; and the hammering of his heart. No breeze stirred the trees and the heat grew more oppressive as he followed the snaking path around moss-covered boles. Looking back, all was obscured by heavy mist, the only sign of his passing the coiling wisps left in the air.

He had no sense of how far the chamber stretched. Though he had been walking for some time his route had never been straight and he wondered if he had been circling aimlessly, one stretch of path looking much like any other. He could not feel the pulse of Alaitoc; the inorganic had given way to this artificial wilderness. There was no echo and above him the sky was a distant ochre haze.

For a while Korlandril found himself at peace with this place. Its sombre atmosphere soothed his turbulent thoughts. There was a melancholy air, a primordial stillness that made his anger seem irrelevant. The twisted trees grew larger and larger, almost as old as the craftworld itself. He had no idea how many others had passed along this path before him; hundreds of the Alaitocii had come this way seeking the answers held within the shrine.

A doubt crept into Korlandril's thoughts. Perhaps they had not come this way at all? Perhaps he was lost? His fear returned. Every flitting shadow startled him, every hanging vine a snake in disguise waiting to strike. He quickened his pace, eager to push on to whatever awaited his journey's end. In his haste his foot caught a twining root and he stumbled to a knee. Korlandril thought the root had moved, deliberately tripping him. With fresh dread he stared around at the trees, feeling them coming closer.

He broke into a run. The faster he went, the more the path wound to and fro, the slicker underfoot it became. He thrashed through the creepers, panting wildly, eyes wide, alert for any sign of his destination.

All his other thoughts were put aside, all of his considerable mental powers concentrated on escaping this morass. He flinched at every movement in the shadows, recoiled whenever he strayed from the path and his foot sank into the mire. Whirling, he fell back against a tree, his hand coming against something soft and wet. Looking down, he saw a large-eyed toad leap away, dropping into a pool with a heavy plop. He wiped his hand on his tunic, which was now not only much stained but also tattered in places.

He felt ragged and alone, his mind fraying like his clothes. His boots felt far too tight and he ripped them off, casting them into the mist. Barefoot he squelched along the path again, this time more deliberately, scanning the ground for any sign that he was going in the right direction.

He felt the ground dipping and he pressed onwards, moving down a tree-shrouded slope. The path straightened in front of him and he came upon two thin pillars carved from a grey stone flanking his route, crusted with dark blue lichen. Stopping, he swept aside a patch and saw runes inscribed into the columns, so age-worn he could barely see them. He ran his hands over the rough surface of the left-hand pillar, using his artist's fingertips to read what was written there.

The shadows call and those who answer come here.

On the other column he found more engraving:

Even the deepest shadows cannot hide us from ourselves.

Korlandril stood between the pillars and looked ahead. He saw something concealed in the mists, half-hidden by moss and creepers. Approaching closer he could make out the rough outline of a large zig-gurat, made of the same grey stone as the pillars. Trees grew upon its levels, masking it with their leaves. Lichen and vines criss-crossed its blocks, a natural camouflage that had grown over an age.

The path led into a dark opening. Korlandril could see nothing of the interior. Beyond the portal was utter blackness. He stopped just before stepping across the threshold. The darkness was not just the absence of light, it was something else. There was no gradual dimming from the gloom to total blackness, a stark plane of utter shadow marked the boundary. Hands held out in front of him, Korlandril plunged in.

In the darkness it was cool. Compared to the heat outside, the inside of the shrine was icy cold and Korlandril's skin prickled. Stretching to either side, Korlandril ran his fingertips across a smooth surface. It was also cold and he snatched back his fingers. He was in a passageway just a little narrower than his outstretched hands. Pressing on, occasionally he would come to an opening on the left or right. There was no sight or sound that guided him and so he kept moving straight ahead. His footfalls were muffled, bare feet padding on a hard surface.

Korlandril felt himself step into a larger chamber. There was no less-ening in the intensity of the shadow but he could sense the walls were more distant, his fingers stroking nothing but air. He stood motionless, head turning left and right, seeking something to fix upon.

There was a soft rustle to his left and Korlandril turned his head sharply. He could see nothing.

Then a sound came from the right, a rapid but barely audible drum that lasted for a few heartbeats and then fell silent. He could see nothing in that direction either.

Two lights flared into life ahead of him, pinpricks of yellow that grew quickly in brightness to reveal golden eye-shapes. They illuminated nothing, casting no shadow.

A voice came to him, from behind those glowing eyes. It was quiet, a deep whisper.

'What is this I see, a wanderer perhaps, lost and all alone?'

'I am Korlandril. I seek the Shrine of the Deadly Shadow.'

'And you have found it, seeker of the dark answer, child touched by Khaine's hand.'

Korlandril was not sure what to say and an unnerving silence descended. He dropped his hands to his side and looked at the yellow eyes. They were lenses, of that he was sure.

'Whom do I address?' he asked.

'I am Kenainath, the Deadly Shadow Exarch, keeper of this shrine.'

'I wish you to teach me the ways of the Striking Scorpion. My fear and anger eats at me from within, I must find release for it.'

'What makes you afraid, darkness and shadows perhaps, that which is hidden? What makes you angry, a friend's death or lover's scorn, that drives you to hate?'

Korlandril did not answer, ashamed. Now that he was stood here, in this dark place, it seemed such a trivial thing.

'You give no answer, perhaps you do not know it, that which destroys you.'

'I have been spurned, by one I called friend and one that I loved.'

A sinister laugh came in reply.

'Do not mock me!' snarled Korlandril, taking a pace towards those unmoving eyes. 'My pain is real!'

'We all have our pain, which eats away at our hearts, turns our love to hate. But where is pain now, when anger comes so easy, that you would strike me?'

Korlandril gritted his teeth, sensing that he was being teased. He took several deep breaths and stilled his whirling thoughts, preferring to say nothing.

'Do not fight this urge, the need to unleash your ire, embrace it instead.'

'I do not wish to hurt you,' Korlandril said, and was again laughed at.

'You do not scare me, I am the master of fear, Striking Scorpion. It is you that fears, that which consumes you inside, feeding your desire. You cannot harm me, you have not the skill or strength, nor the will to hurt.'

At that, the shadows receded slightly, revealing an armoured figure crouched upon a step. Its face was a heavy mask, with a serrated grille for a mouth, flanked by bulbous pods, framed with segmented finger-thick black cables for hair, which moved with a life of their own. Green and golden plates slid across each other as it stood, fully a head taller than Korlandril. The ring of its armoured boot echoed around Korlandril as the exarch took a step forward. It lifted its right hand, gloved in a heavy claw that shimmered with an energy field.

'I could break you now, tear you limb from limb with ease, a work of moments,' said Kenainath, his tone low and menacing.

Korlandril shrank back and took a step away from the exarch as he strode forward, those glowing eyes unwavering. Terror gripped Korlandril, flooding through him like a chill. He fell to his knees, eyes fixed on the mask of the exarch, unable to break from that lifeless gaze.

'I am sorry, I am not worthy,' Korlandril sobbed. Self-loathing mixed with his dread; he had failed, he could not control his fear or master his anger. Kenainath loomed over him, his deadly eyes implacable. 'I do not wish to die, but I cannot live like this!'

The exarch straightened and took a step back, extending his other hand towards Korlandril.

'Then you are welcome. A warrior should fear death, but cannot crave life. Stand up Korlandril, Striking Scorpion at heart, Khaine's deadly shadow.'

Part Two

Warrior

FOCUS

In the time before the War in Heaven, it came to pass that the ambitions of Ulthanesh and the will of Eldanesh were at odds. Eldanesh was greatest of the eldar, and would brook no discord. Ulthanesh could not keep his desires bound within and Eldanesh banished his friend, sending him out into the desert. Ulthanesh was weary from his arguments with Eldanesh and sat upon a rock. He sat for a long time contemplating the wrongs of the universe and the dishonour visited upon him by Eldanesh. Seeing Ulthanesh so distraught the war god Khaine sensed an opportunity for strife. He broke the tip from one of his iron fingers and cast it into the shadows beneath the rock, where the fingertip became a scorpion. The scorpion stole out of the darkness and stung Ulthanesh on the hand. The poison consumed Ulthanesh and for countless days and nights he writhed in the sands burning with fever. Yet Ulthanesh was strong and in time the venom was conquered and the fever passed. When he awoke from his poison-tormented dreams, Ulthanesh found himself at peace. He had survived on his own with no aid from Eldanesh. Ulthanesh realised he had strength enough in himself and no longer needed Eldanesh's protection. Thus was the House of Ulthanesh founded and the strife of the eldar began.

Korlandril again reminded himself that treading the Path of the Warrior would ease his torment. He was, he admitted, at a loss to work out quite how standing on one leg in a swamp would bring about this change.

Kenainath squatted on a branch above him, divested of his armour and clad in a close-fitting bodysuit of pale green and golden yellow. Or at least Korlandril thought the exarch was still watching him; the last time he had glanced up to check he had been on the end of a stern admonishment from the master of the shrine. Korlandril kept his gaze firmly ahead, focussed on a knot in the hunched bole of a tree on the far side of the pool.

The warrior-to-be controlled his posture with precision, carefully controlling every muscle so as not to lose balance for a moment. He stood on his left foot, toes sinking into the mud, leaning forward as far as possible without falling, one hand raised in front of his throat in a guard position, the other stretched behind him to offset his forward lean.

It was the seventh cycle since his training had begun and the only other eldar he had seen in that time had been Kenainath. Of Elissanadrin and the other Striking Scorpions, there had been no sign. For seven cycles – and Korlandril was convinced the duration of the cycles were longer here than in the rest of Alaitoc – Kenainath had woken his pupil early and brought him out into the mire surrounding the shrine. The first cycle had been spent learning to breathe – long and low breaths that barely stirred the air. That was all, a whole cycle spent breathing. For the second cycle, Kenainath had commanded Korlandril to hang from a branch by his knees, until he was quite dizzy from the blood in his head, and then led him on a run along the twisting mangrove paths that left the former artist panting and dishevelled. And so on had it continued, each cycle bringing some new yet facile torture to be visited upon him.

'I have no doubt that your methods have been successful in bringing many on to the path of the Striking Scorpion, exarch,' Korlandril said quietly, barely moving his lips for fear of upsetting his delicate state of balance. 'Yet I have not yet seen a weapon nor a scrap of armour. I am quite sure I have no idea how this teaches me how to control my anger.'

'Are you angry now, my young warrior-to-be, standing in the mud?' the exarch replied, his voice a slight relief to Korlandril who thought that perhaps he had been left alone as some kind of mockery. 'Are you frustrated, to be treated in this way, dirty and downcast?'

Korlandril thought about this for a moment and realised that he wasn't angry, nor was he particularly frustrated; not in the same way that thoughts of Aradryan and Thirianna frustrated him. If anything, he was bored. The physical exertion was considerable – a reminder that even the eldar body had its limits of endurance, speed and strength – but the mental occupation was non-existent. Kenainath had forbidden his student from entering a memedream or any other distraction, insisting that Korlandril be fully attentive to every part of his body and surroundings.

'You wish to have peace, to escape the rage and hate, yet also crave it,' said Kenainath, without waiting for an answer from Korlandril. 'You must learn two ways, the paths to both war and peace, in equal measure.

That which we unleash, the face of battle we wear, is as a war-mask. You must put it on, within your spirit alone, and then take it off. Peace must be the goal, war helps us achieve this peace, and then balance comes. It must be a choice, shunning war and death and blood, choosing life and hope. You must make that choice, in every part of life, so that you are free. War is a not a state, it is an absence of peace, a passing nightmare. We awake from it, not remembering its curse, divorced from its taint. We must become death, to protect and to survive, but do not love death.'

Korlandril allowed the words to resonate through his thoughts, glad of something to occupy himself. Something occurred to him, a question, but he was hesitant to ask. The exarch must have sensed something of Korlandril's unease.

'We are here for truth, to find the answer you seek, no question is wrong.'

'You speak of peace, yet you are an exarch. What can you know of peace, who cannot leave Khaine's embrace?'

There was a slight creak and a subtle swish of leaves as Kenainath shifted his weight on the branch above. Korlandril wondered if his question had been inappropriate.

'Freedom is not mine, to wander from this temple, out with the others,' the exarch said quietly. 'You do not see me, singing and dancing outside, writing poetry. I stay in this shrine, where my curse cannot harm you, forever trapped here. Though I wear no paint, my war-mask remains inside, clouding all my thoughts. Had you angered me, that first day you came to me, I might have killed you. Even now I hate, filled with my anger always, but I do not strike. It is not madness, not uncontrollable ire, which my war-mask brings. It is an urging, to release what is inside, fighting to get out. I struggle with it, but I am its true master, exerting my will. It is no frenzy, no bloodlust that would swamp me, but a perspective. I see things unseen, pain and misery beneath, which others hide from. It is my duty, the covenant of exarchs, to prepare your mind. You will see horror, witness death and agony, and must confront it. This is my calling, to lead you on that dark path, where others recoil.'

Korlandril's limbs were trembling from fatigue and he fought to remain balanced. The thought of falling into the mud, humiliated in front of Kenainath, stiffened his resolve and he dug deeper into his spirit for strength.

'It is very good, my young but keen disciple, that you do not fall. Look into yourself, tell me what it is you see, what you used to see.'

Korlandril sifted his thoughts, parting a section of his consciousness to keep himself balanced while he danced through his mind. He set aside the physical discomfort and examined his emotional state. He was calm. He hadn't been this calm since...

As soon as Korlandril's thoughts turned to Thirianna, the serpent of jealousy reared, spitting and hissing. For an instant Korlandril's whole body was on fire. Every nerve tingled with vibrant life. He saw the colours of the swamp with a clarity he had not witnessed even as an Artist. Every ripple shone in his mind; every chirrup, scratch and burr of insect sounded distinct in his ears. The faintest breeze on his flesh, the feel of the mud between his toes and the coolness of the water on his skin. His waystone was like a white-hot coal over his heart. Everything stood out in sharp contrast and for that moment Korlandril felt an urge to destroy it all. The need to wreak havoc, shed blood, take life, was overwhelming. He could not take another breath without striking out.

He fell splashing into the muddy pool, his loss of balance so unexpected that he landed face first, unable to break his fall. Spluttering, he rose from the murk, filth dripping from hair, brow and chin.

'A trick?' he snarled, whirling around, still awash with after-eddies from the wave of perfect anger that had swept across him.

The exarch was no longer on the branch. Korlandril cast around for a sign of him but saw nothing, heard nothing. But he could sense the exarch's presence close at hand, subtly mingled with the essence of the swamp. With a shock, Korlandril realised how attuned he had become to his surroundings, unconsciously absorbing its presence, analysing every smell and sound and sight without effort. There was the slightest of disturbances to his left and he turned sharply.

There was nothing; no movement, not even a flicker of shadow.

'Where is your anger, where is the rage from within, which you felt just now?' Kenainath's voice was a distant, echoing whisper, seeming to come from every direction and none, like several voices speaking at once. Korlandril calmed, every fibre relaxing, even his heart quietening as he made himself silent in an effort to attain the sensory state he had briefly achieved.

'It was your anger, bringing heightened awareness, which you felt just now. Our hate is our strength, not some weakness to be purged, if we use it well.'

Korlandril understood the exarch and tried to bring back the moment of pure rage he had experienced after falling, but all he felt was frustration.

'Do not have outbursts, letting your anger fly wild, an unfettered beast. You must learn control, to strike like the scorpion, not the fire dragon. When you can do that, when your anger serves your will, you have your war-mask.'

Slowly, cycle-by-cycle, Korlandril exerted ever greater control over his mind and body. The two became as one; the physical effort of maintaining the strenuous Striking Scorpion fighting poses narrowed his focus, concentrating his thoughts to a single point. Whenever he deviated from the routines set for him by Kenainath, Korlandril struggled and lost his balance, physically and mentally.

For all that he understood Kenainath's teachings, Korlandril became ever more frustrated by his inability to unleash that moment of primal rage he had felt earlier. He feared that all he was doing was suppressing further and further the anger that had first propelled him towards the shrine.

For forty cycles Kenainath kept Korlandril apart from the other Striking Scorpions, training him alone within the gloom of the shrine and its dismal surrounds. Korlandril longed to see the rest of Alaitoc again. Though it pained him every time he thought of Thirianna, he could not suppress his curiosity and longed to know how she fared. Had she started upon the Path of the Seer? Did she even know what had become of him? How did she feel about her part in his decision to take the Path of Khaine?

As the first glimmer of the forty-first cycle crept through the narrow windows of the upper levels of the shrine, Kenainath appeared as usual. The exarch was clad in his dark green robe, sleeveless, open at the front, a deep yellow bodysuit beneath, his dark red waystone fixed to the centre of his chest. Korlandril looked at the oval of the waystone, noticing the shimmering of its colour, a flickering in its depths as of many lights far away.

'It is time again, to learn the Falling Storm pose, come outside with me,' said Kenainath.

'No.' Korlandril crossed his arms, legs braced apart. 'I do not want to train today. I'm sick of this gloomy swamp. I want to see Thirianna.'

Moving so swiftly that Korlandril barely saw him, Kenainath stepped forward and flicked a hand towards Korlandril's ear. The blow was light enough, but stung quickly. Korlandril lunged, aiming the tips of his fingers knife-like towards the exarch's throat, finishing in the stance known as Sting From Shadow. Kenainath swayed away and retreated with several quick steps.

'It will not be safe, you cannot yet control the hate, and could blindly strike out.'

Korlandril shuddered with the shock of realisation. He had tried to harm Kenainath. He had wanted to cause him injury. Even kill him. He had acted without conscious thought, but he could feel the desire to inflict hurt that had driven the reflex. If he had done such a thing to anyone but another warrior, he would have murdered them.

'Now you understand, that which we are creating, safe here in the shrine,' Kenainath said softly.

'Why would you do this to me?' demanded Korlandril. 'Why turn me into this before I can control it?'

'This is your war-mask, expanding from within you, consuming your mind.' The exarch's tone was unforgiving, with no hint of shame or comfort. 'It is for battle, where you cannot hesitate, but act or react. Do not be worried, you will learn to remove the mask, I will teach you how.'

'You have done this to trap me here, because you cannot leave,' said Korlandril.

'Until you wear it, you cannot remove the mask, it is still hidden. In time you will learn, be free of the mask's control, and then you can leave.' There was no sympathy in Kenainath's voice, but his determined tone eased Korlandril's fears a little. 'Now you have a goal, to leave behind your war-mask, to gain your freedom.'

Korlandril did not know whether it was the mental forces being unleashed by the exarch's training, or the exarch himself, but he despised Kenainath even more. He allowed his anger to simmer inside as he followed the exarch out into the swamp once again. The prospect of finishing his training seemed a distant dream. Yet the exarch's words had struck a chord. If Korlandril truly wanted to be free of this place, he had to rid himself of the cause for his being here – his anger. Kenainath's methods seemed counterproductive, but he had trained many Striking Scorpions and Korlandril had to put his trust in that.

Resigned more than hopeful, Korlandril trailed after Kenainath into the gloom.

'Peace is as it is, unwavering and endless, a constant of life.' The exarch's words were hushed. 'Anger is fleeting, a momentary relapse, when will slips away.'

Korlandril barely heard Kenainath, a whisper on the edge of consciousness. He stood upon a branch of a stooping tree, a greenish pool below him mottled with leaves and algae. A moment's loss of concentration and he would fall into the water.

'The Whisper of Death, and then into Surging Wave, end with Rising Claw,' instructed Kenainath.

Korlandril shifted position with controlled slowness, bending almost double while he eased his left foot forward yet kept his weight on his back leg, left arm raised above his head, right arm crooked by his side. Taking a pace forward, he shifted his balance, thrusting forward with his right arm, sweeping outwards with the left hand. To finish, he straightened, left arm curving up in front of him, right arm held back.

The exarch continued and Korlandril obeyed, moving forwards and backwards along the branch as dictated by Kenainath, making mock strikes and defences as he did so. The motions were effortless, remembered by instinct rather than conscious thought. Korlandril moved gracefully through all twenty-seven basic poses. The branch buckled and swayed beneath him, but his balance remained perfect.

Even as his body moved, Korlandril's mind was still. Seventy cycles now had passed and Korlandril could barely recall his life before coming to the shrine. He knew there were memories inside somewhere, but no longer knew where to look for them. He was little more than a physical vessel moving along a branch, waiting to be filled by something else.

When the exercise was complete, Kenainath signalled for Korlandril to follow him. Korlandril hid his surprise as he leapt lithely down to the path beside the pool. It was early yet in the cycle and it was unexpected to take a break so early.

Kenainath offered no explanation as he turned back up the creeper-crossed path and headed towards the shrine. Korlandril followed close behind, intrigued by this change of routine. The pair plunged into the cool shadows of the temple and then took a turn to the left, down a passage Korlandril had never trod before. It brought them into a long gallery, high and narrow. Along each wall stood five suits of aspect armour, fashioned from many overlapping plates of deep green edged with gold, the red lenses of the helmets dull and lifeless.

Beside four of the suits stood the other warriors of the shrine.

Korlandril recognised Elissanadrin and she smiled in reply to his quizzical glance. The others he had seen around the craftworld, but did not know their names.

'Now to make your choice, to meet your companions, Striking Scorpion,' Kenainath intoned solemnly, taking his place at the far end of the gallery in front of the much heavier exarch armour he had been wearing when Korlandril had first arrived.

Korlandril looked around, wondering which suit to pick. At first they seemed identical, but there were subtle differences; in the placement of gems, the hang of the hair-like sensory antenna-crests of the helmets, the brightly coloured ribbons tied about the armoured limbs.

His first instinct was to stand beside Elissanadrin, seeking the familiar, but he dismissed the urge. It was change and renewal that he needed, not the comfortable. Out of the corner of his eye, Korlandril thought he saw a momentary glitter in the eyes of one suit. He turned towards it. There was nothing to distinguish it from the others, but something about it tugged at Korlandril.

'This one,' he said, striding towards the armour. He stood beside it and turned to face the exarch.

'That is a wise choice, a noble suit you have picked, which has served us well,' said Kenainath. 'You are now ready, in body if not in mind, to don your armour.'

A thrill of elation shivered through Korlandril. For the first time since coming to the shrine he sensed a moment of achievement. He had been dimly aware of the progress he had been making, so subtle had been the changes wrought in him by Kenainath. Now that he was stood beside his armour, Korlandril looked on what had passed with fresh eyes. Just as he had learned to control the ghost stone as a sculptor, now he controlled every muscle and fibre of his body. It was an instrument wholly subservient to his will and whim.

The donning of his armour was not as straightforward as Korlandril had imagined it might be. Just as with the fighting poses, every stage of armouring was precise, each stance and movement strictly defined by Kenainath. With each stage came a mantra from the exarch, which resounded in Korlandril's mind as the Striking Scorpions repeated the words.

First he stripped naked, casting his robe aside as if throwing away a part of himself. He took his waystone on its silver chain and placed it carefully in a niche in the wall. He felt a quiver of fear at being separated from his spirit-saviour. It was perhaps his imagining, but Korlandril felt a moment of scrutiny, as if detecting eyes suddenly upon him, regarding him from a great distance. He dismissed his unease, knowing that nothing could befall him in the shrine.

'The peace is broken, harmony falls to discord, only war remains.'

Korlandril followed the lead of the others, taking the bodysuit that was folded on a small ledge behind the armour.

'Now we clothe ourselves, with bloody Khaine's own raiment, as a warrior.'

Korlandril stepped into the legs of the bodysuit. It was large and sagged on his limbs and gathered in unsightly bulges between his legs and under his arms, its fingertips dangling uselessly.

'In Khaine's iron skin, we clad ourselves for battle, while fire burns within.'

Korlandril's heart quickened. In his gut, the serpent of his anger stretched slowly. He placed his palms together in front of his face, copying the movements of the other Aspect Warriors. In response, the body suit tightened. As the fabric of the suit shrank against his taut muscles, dormant pads began to thicken, forming rigid areas across his chest and stomach and along the bulge of his thighs, stiffening along his spine.

'The spirit of Khaine, from which we draw our resolve, strengthens within us.'

Korlandril kept his eye on Elissanadrin, following her motions. Reaching behind the armour, he undid the fastenings along its back, letting the lower portion of the torso fall free in his hands. Wrapping it about his stomach and lower back, his nimble fingers worked the fastenings back into place. Its stiff presence around his midsection was reassuring, supporting his back, squeezing against his sides in a firm embrace.

'War comes upon us, we must bear its dark burden, upon our shoulders.'

Following the lead of the others, Korlandril undid the clasps fixing the upper part of the armour to its stand. He lifted it above his head, solid but not heavy. With careful movements he lowered it onto his shoulders. The plates gripped the surface of the undersuit, extending down his upper arms; the rounded bulge of the power generator slipped easily across his shoulder blades. As before, he returned to a stance of repose and the suit shifted slightly with a life of its own, adjusting itself to his body. When it had stopped moving, he tightened the clasps, fixing the armour in place. He felt top-heavy and adjusted his back to stand straighter.

A moment of fear made Korlandril tremble as the bodysuit extended up towards his face, enclosing his throat and neck, the touch of rippling ridges insistent but gentle. The moment passed as soon as it stopped just below his chin. He took a deep breath to steady himself.

'We stand before Khaine, unyielding in our calling, free of doubt and fear.'

The upper leg armour came next, fitting to Korlandril as snugly as the rest of the suit. He found that if he flexed in a certain way, the plates interlocked delicately, strengthening his stance, offsetting the imbalance of the powerpack. Korlandril's pulse was almost feverish, burning along his arteries, hissing in his ears.

'We do not flee death, we walk in the shade of Khaine, proud and unafraid.'

The lower legs were each protected by a single boot-greave piece, which Korlandril slipped over his feet and knees. He fastened these to the thigh armour, fully encasing his legs. Threads of material grew rigid around his ankles, adding additional support, while the boots shortened themselves to fit his feet. A sensation of solidity, of unmoving permanence, filled Korlandril.

'We strike from the dark, as swift as the scorpion, with a deadly touch.'

The vambrace-gauntlets connected to the upper armour, more clasps linking the two as one. Korlandril flexed his arms, feeling cartilage-like tendrils tightening against his flesh, reinforcing his wrists and elbows. Now fully clad save for his face, Korlandril felt incredible, filled with a heat that did not waver. His armour was his skin; it pulsed along with his thundering heart, drawing life from him and returning its strength.

His next act was to retrieve his waystone from its niche, detaching it from the silver surround of the necklace. It responded to his touch, warming gently, suffusing him with delicate reassurance. He placed the waystone into the aperture of the chestplate. It settled home with a soft click. His armour felt the waystone's presence as much as Korlandril, giving a brief, almost imperceptible quiver and then falling still again.

'That is all for now, there is no need of the mask, we are not at war.'

With the donning of the armour complete, Kenainath gestured for the Striking Scorpions to assemble before him. Korlandril took a step forward, the movement feeling awkward in the armour; its weight was evenly spread across him, but its bulk restricted normal movement. In response, he changed the nature of his stride, his body remembering the motions he had learnt while unencumbered. As strange and stylised as they had felt in his robe, they were natural when armour-clad.

The warriors stood in a single line, a short distance apart, facing the exarch. Kenainath led them through the ritual stances and the Striking Scorpions moved together, each replicating his poses without hesitation or variation. Almost like automatons they mirrored the exarch's thrusts and parries, like marionettes all controlled by the same strings.

Korlandril felt a sense of belonging he had not known for a long time, in perfect synchronisation with his fellow warriors. He was as them, and they were as he; of one mind and one function. Every stance brought a fresh thrill, as he learnt anew their purpose. The armour made him complete, his body now perfected.

For most of the cycle they practised their ritual stances. Some were genuinely new to Korlandril, impossible to attain without the support of the armour. He learnt them without effort, swiftly adapting to each challenge. As the session progressed, the stance changes came more swiftly, the tempo of Kenainath's actions increasing with each round of moves.

The exarch spoke rarely, only to reinforce his previous teachings and adding new insights into the way of the Striking Scorpion.

'With balance we strike, not acrobatic Banshees, flailing and screaming. With strength of motion, strike with sure and deadly grace, power from balance.'

Throughout the exercises the hot temper that had filled Korlandril continued to burn. He began to visualise a foe, formless and shadowy, which he gutted and decapitated, countered and eluded. His imaginary opponent had eyes that burned with a red fire, but was otherwise featureless; an anonymous conglomeration of those who had wronged him, an incarnation formed of his anger and fears. In striking at this apparition, Korlandril drew great strength, feeding on his power to destroy that which had tried to destroy him.

Invigorated, Korlandril was somewhat disappointed when Kenainath signalled for them to stop, returning to the stance of repose, palms touching, legs slightly apart, heads bowed.

Korlandril stood there for a while, expecting some new instruction. Footfalls alerted him to the others moving back to their armour-stands and he did the same. Kenainath had left without word.

Reversing the same series of motions they had used to put on the armour, the Aspect Warriors divested themselves of their battlegear. As he removed each component, Korlandril felt a lightening in his spirit as well as on his body. Though he had felt relaxed throughout the practice, he realised he had been functioning at a far higher state of awareness than normal. Colours seemed a little blander, sounds more muted as he brought himself down from the peak of physical attentiveness and assumed a more relaxed demeanour.

'Welcome to the Shrine of the Deadly Shadow,' said Elissanadrin, extending her palm in greeting. She wore a tight-fitting bodysuit with a pearlescent quality, gleaming with tones of white and ivory. Korlandril laid his hand briefly on hers in reply.

'Let me introduce you to your companions-in-arms,' she said, turning slightly, open hand gesturing towards the others.

'Be known to Arhulesh,' she continued, indicating a warrior a little shorter than Korlandril, his long black hair tied into braids with slender dark red ribbons.

'Greetings Korlandril,' Arhulesh said with a lopsided smile. 'I would have liked to make your acquaintance earlier, but Kenainath is such a stickler for his routines. I must admit, I greatly enjoyed your exhibition, *The Rising of the Heavens*. Did I detect a slight mockery of Khaine in your pieces?'

Korlandril frowned. He could barely remember the sculptures he had created. They were locked away in his memories somewhere, but it was as if he had lost the map and could not find them.

'Oh, Kenainath has drawn you in most conclusively,' Arhulesh said with a raised eyebrow. He turned to the others. 'Careful, we have a real devotee on our hands! I wonder just what, or who, it is that you're hiding from, Korlandril.'

'Hush, Arhu,' cut in Elissanadrin with a dismissive wave of her hand. 'You know that we do not speak of our lives before, unless we wish to.'

Arhulesh directed a nod of apology towards Korlandril, who noted a slight twist to the inclination, a tiny gesture of sarcasm. Elissanadrin laid a hand upon Korlandril's elbow and led him towards the next Striking Scorpion, a serious-faced eldar with gaunt features and stark white hair cropped into a scalplock. He was attending fastidiously to his armour, using a silk-like cloth to wipe away every speck and smear on its surface.

'Speaking of silence, this is Bechareth.'

The name startled Korlandril, for it meant Spirit on the Wind; an appellation given to those whose true identity was not known, usually a stranger. It was also a euphemism for those that had died without the protection of a waystone, their spirits lost to the clutches of She Who Thirsts.

'He doesn't, or can't, speak,' explained Elissanadrin. 'Kenainath brought him to us with that name, and neither has told us anything else. Do not be fooled by his silence, he is a capable warrior.' She paused uncomfortably before continuing. 'I owe him my life.'

Bechareth stood and offered his right hand in greeting: vertical, palm towards Korlandril, a gesture of equality that was rarely used in Alaitoc society except to greet those from other craftworlds. Korlandril raised his left hand in mirror of the gesture, indicating trust, and received a slow blink of gratitude from the warrior. His dark eyes glittered with amusement, and Korlandril felt himself drawn to the mysterious eldar despite his outlandish behaviour.

'Mithrainn,' said Elissanadrin, nodding towards the last of the four. He was of venerable age, probably five hundred passes older or more, with a sharp brow and aquiline nose.

'Call me Min,' he said, eliciting a laugh from Korlandril. The nickname was from the myths of Vaul, after the weak link in the chain that had bound the smith-god to his anvil.

'It is good to meet you… Min,' said Korlandril, touching palms with the elder. 'Forgive my impudence, but I would have thought the Path of the Warrior was more suited to those of less experience.'

'You mean that you think I'm too old for this sneaking about and running around!' Min declared with a grin. He thumped his hand to his chest. 'The heart of a youth still beats within my breast.'

'Powered by the mind of an infant,' added Elissanadrin, rolling her eyes. 'He makes up for Bechareth's silence with his volume. I still think he has some Biel-Tan stock in him, despite his protestations to be pure-blood Alaitocii.'

'You may say that, Lissa, but you have yet to catch me in the swamp.'

Elissanadrin conceded this obscure point with a reluctant nod and a pursing of the lips. She smiled when she saw Korlandril's confusion.

'When you have mastered the arts of the fighting poses, you will join us on our hunts. We go out into the surrounds of the shrine and try to sneak up on each other. The Striking Scorpion is stealth as well as strength.'

Korlandril nodded in understanding.

'And how long do you think it will be before I join you?'

'How long is a star's life?' quipped Arhulesh from behind Korlandril. 'Kenainath has a whim of iron. It could be next cycle, it could be not for another two or three passes.'

'Two or three passes?' Korlandril was taken aback. 'Surely my progress has been swifter than that.'

'Whim of iron, remember, whim of iron,' said Arhulesh, shrugging shallowly.

'Is that before or after I get my war-mask?'

'None can say when you will find your war-mask,' said Min. 'For some it never comes and they leave without truly treading the Path. For others, they wear it from the start.'

Bechareth stepped closer and looked intently into Korlandril's eyes, studying every detail. He held up a thumb and forefinger, a little way apart. His meaning was clear: a short time. The gesture turned to an upraised finger of warning.

'He's right,' said Elissanadrin. 'You shouldn't chase after your war-mask, not until you're ready to take it off.'

'I'm not quite sure I still understand what this war-mask is,' confessed Korlandril. 'I mean, Kenainath wouldn't let us wear our helmets today. I don't understand the connection.'

Arhulesh laughed harshly but his face was serious.

'The war-mask is not a thing, it is a state of mind. You have come close to it, or you would not be here. You will know it when it comes. We cannot tell you what it will be like, for it is unique to each of us.'

'Just know that we have all been through the same experience,' added Min. He laid a hand on Korlandril's shoulder. Korlandril was slightly

uneasy with a gesture of such familiarity, having only just been introduced. He resisted the urge to pull away but Min must have sensed his
reaction. He drew his hand back. 'When it comes, you will share what
we all share and my touch will not be so unwelcome.'

'I did not mean any off– '

'We do not apologise to one another,' cut in Elissanadrin. 'Know that
in this place, with mask on or off, all is forgiven. The past is the past,
the future will be whatever it will be, and we share only the present.
Perhaps it is regret that keeps you from discovering your mask. Leave it
behind – it has no place in your spirit. As a warrior, regret will kill you
as surely as a blade.'

Korlandril pondered this silently. The others turned as one towards
the exarch armour at the head of the hall and Korlandril looked over his
shoulder to see that Kenainath had returned. He had made no sound
that Korlandril had heard and he was at a loss to know how the others
had been aware of his arrival. Perhaps they had not been aware at all;
the thought that the exarch might have heard the conversation disturbed
Korlandril, though he was not sure why.

'It is time for us to depart,' said Elissanadrin.

'Not you,' Min said as Korlandril took a step towards the doorway.

'Enjoy your training, little scorpion,' added Arhulesh, directing a
glance towards the exarch, who stood with arms folded across his chest,
looking sternly at his disciples.

Bechareth passed Korlandril last, giving a short bow in farewell before
leaving with the others. Suppressing a sigh, Korlandril turned towards
Kenainath.

'I am yours to teach,' Korlandril said, dipping his head.

'That is well and good, for there is still much to learn, Striking
Scorpion.'

ANGER

When the eldar first rose from the bosom of the ground, nourished by the tears of Isha, the gods came to them and each offered them a gift. Asuryan, lord of lords, gave the eldar Wisdom, that they would know themselves. Isha gave the eldar Love, that they would know one another. Vaul gave the eldar Artifice, that they would make their dreams a reality. Lileath gave the eldar Joy, that they would know happiness. Kurnous gave the eldar Desire, that they would know prosperity. Morai-heg gave the eldar Foresight, that they would know their place in the world. Khaine gave the eldar Anger, that they would protect what the gods had given them.

The training continued as before; though now in armour and often in the company of the other warriors of the shrine. Kenainath also turned his attention to introducing the disciplines of stealth and ambush, leading Korlandril through the swamps as silently as a breeze. The pair of them travelled to places new to Korlandril – narrow gorges, winding rivulets and shadow-shrouded caves. Despite the bulk of the Striking Scorpion armour, Korlandril moved as soundlessly as if he were naked. So controlled and effortless was Korlandril's motion, so attuned was he to the swaying of the branches and the slightest ripple of water, he was able to blend his movements to those of his surrounds.

For thirty-eight cycles this continued. Korlandril could discern no pattern to the lessons save for some inner timeline that Kenainath maintained for himself. He did not know against which mark he was being judged or to what standard he might aspire, and so could only follow Kenainath's instructions without question. The exarch made no mention of any change in Korlandril's skills, though he knew for himself that they were steadily improving.

In the carefully choreographed ritual of the shrine, Korlandril could now respond so quickly to the exarch's commands it was if he anticipated them. He kept pace with the other Striking Scorpions without thought. His progress, even if unremarked by the others, gave him some satisfaction and he looked forward to the underlying spirit of sharing he felt when he practised alongside the rest of the shrine. Always he felt invigorated when putting on his armour, but now he was left also with a sense of fulfilment when he took it off.

At the rising of the thirty-ninth cycle, Kenainath, clad in his armour but without his helmet, came to the bare dormitory where Korlandril slept. He instructed Korlandril to don his own wargear and led him into a new chamber. Here were arranged the weapons of the Striking Scorpions, hung upon the wall of the circular room. Ten slender chainswords were paired with matching shuriken pistols.

Not quite knowing how, Korlandril walked directly to the arms that he knew belonged to his armour. He ran his fingers along the cladding of the chainsword, able to feel the entwining decorations through the empathic connection to his gauntlet as if he touched it with bare skin.

'Take up your weapon, let it become part of you, feel it in your hand,' said Kenainath.

Korlandril closed his fingers around the guarded hilt of the chainsword and lifted it easily from the curved wall bracket. Like his armour, it was surprisingly light for its size. It fitted snugly into his palm, like an extension of his arm. He twisted his wrist and examined the narrow blades, each sharp enough to slice through flesh and bone with a single stroke. He saw red reflections of his own admiring face in the jewels along its length.

'How do I activate it?' he asked.

'How does your heart beat, your fingers move at your whim, that is the answer.'

Korlandril stalked to the centre of the chamber and took up the stance known as Sweeping Bite, hunched forward slightly. His right fist was raised in front of his left shoulder, but now he could see that the length of the chainsword extended horizontally in front of his face, just below eye level. He rotated, sliding back his right foot, the weapon flashing in an arc, finishing in Hidden Claw.

Growing in confidence, Korlandril moved through the First Ritual of Attack, pacing steadily across the chamber, cutting back and forth with the chainsword. At the fifth stance – Rising Fang – the chainsword purred into life of its own accord.

Shocked, Korlandril stumbled, the weapon almost falling from his grasp. Kenainath made a strange hissing sound and Korlandril turned, expecting to see scorn on the exarch's bare face. The opposite was true. For the first time since Korlandril had met him, Kenainath was quietly laughing.

'As it was with me, first time I took up a blade, now so long ago.' Kenainath's humour dissipated quickly and he gestured for Korlandril to continue.

The chainsword had fallen lifeless in his grasp. Regaining his focus, Korlandril started afresh from the first stance, and almost immediately the chainsword's teeth whirred into motion, making no more sound than the buzzing of a lava-wing. Unperturbed, Korlandril continued, cutting and slashing, each move increasing in speed until the blade was a green and gold blur in the air. He made backhanded cuts and rounded overhead chops, advancing on invisible foes.

As he weaved the blade around him, the shadowy foe he visualised during his routines came into sharper focus. Its eyes still burned red but it took on a more distinct shape, narrow at the hip, broader at the shoulder. In the eye of Korlandril's mind, his foe bobbed and ducked, parried and countered, advanced and retreated.

With an explosion of breath, Korlandril delivered a killing strike, sweeping the blade up beneath the chin of his imaginary adversary, to come to a perfect standstill in Claw of Balance. Drawing a lungful of air, Korlandril stepped back, assuming the stance of repose. He turned towards Kenainath.

The exarch betrayed nothing of his thoughts. There was neither praise nor condemnation in his expression. The pride Korlandril had felt in his performance evaporated quickly under that inscrutable stare.

'You have now begun, the Path continues onwards, you must follow it.'

Korlandril dared a glance towards the shuriken pistol on the wall, and then looked back at the exarch. Kenainath gave one shake of the head and pointed at the chainsword in Korlandril's hand.

'First master the claw, the venomous bite comes next, the sting is the last.'

Korlandril licked his dry lips and nodded. He returned to the centre of the chamber and took up Claw from Shadow. The chainsword responded to his urging before he had so much as twitched a muscle and within moments he was moving again.

For the following cycles Korlandril trained in isolation, until Kenainath was convinced that he could spar with the other Striking Scorpions without undue danger to them or himself. After twenty-three cycles, the exarch informed Korlandril that he was ready to train armed with the other warriors. Kenainath took his warrior-acolyte to a grove not far from the shrine and gestured for Korlandril to seat himself on a moss-covered log

'What of history, the tale of the scorpion, can you tell to me?' Kenain-ath asked. 'What myths have you heard, of Karandras and Arhra, the first of our kind?'

Korlandril raked his fingers through his hair as he remembered what he could.

'Asurmen was the first, the creator of the Path of the Warrior,' he said. 'I guess it was Asurmen that discovered how to don the war-mask. He founded the first shrine and gathered disciples to teach, Arhra amongst them, the Father of Scorpions. Some dark fate befell Arhra, of which I do not know the story, and his greatest pupil Karandras took up the mantle and spread the teachings of the Striking Scorpion.'

'That is true enough, the briefest account of it, but you should know more,' replied Kenainath, crouching opposite his pupil, his eyes intent. 'Arhra fell from grace, touched by the dark of Chaos, and betrayed his kin. He turned on the rest, brought daemons to the First Shrine, hungry for power. The Asurya, the first exarchs of the Path, fought against Arhra. They lost the battle, scattered to the distant stars, and Arhra escaped. He strayed from the Path, consumed by his ambition, and found new pupils. His teachings are wrong, a perversion of the Path, the Fallen Phoenix. It is a great wrong, one that we cannot forgive, the worst betrayal. Karan-dras hunts him, across the stars and webway, for retribution.'

'Arhra still lives?' The tale of the Fallen Phoenix was mixed up with the other myths of the Fall. Not even the eldar had such long lives.

'Who can say for sure, in the warp and the webway, time passes strangely.' Kenainath sighed and his expression was sad, a stark change from his usual indifference or hostility. 'Keep true to the Path, heed Karandras's teachings, remain Korlandril.'

'Have there been others?' Korlandril asked fearfully. 'Warriors that fol-low the Path of the Fallen Phoenix?'

'Not from my pupils, I have guided them all well, taught them prop-erly,' said Kenainath as he straightened quickly. The exarch's familiar stern expression returned. 'Go back to the shrine, tomorrow you fight proper, tonight you must rest'.

Dismissed, Korlandril walked slowly back beneath the dismal bow-ers of the trees to the shrine building wondering why the exarch had chosen that moment to reveal the truth about the founding of the Strik-ing Scorpions. As the lights of the shrine dimmed for the night portion of the cycle, Korlandril lay awake pondering what the following cycle would bring.

He woke early, full of nervous energy. The shrine was still swathed in twilight and he swiftly pulled on a loose robe and left his solitary dor-mitory, feeling confined by its walls. In the gloom outside, the swamp was quiet save for the first chattering of the jade-toads. He took a deep breath, accustomed now to the humidity and heat, though he was far from thinking his present environs were his home.

With that, his thoughts turned to the rest of Alaitoc, as they usually did when he was left with time to think. It was with only a barely intellectual interest that he thought of Thirianna. She was probably upon the Path of the Seer by now. Though it had been a short time, barely a blink in the life of an eldar, that moment when his inner anger had been unleashed by her dismissal seemed distant. Irrelevant. His struggle was not with Thirianna, or Aradryan, or any other eldar. It was with himself.

His body and mind were being perfected for one thing – to slay other living creatures. The thought caused him to shudder. Today he would face one of the other members of the Deadly Shadow, but it would not be a fight to a death. It would be controlled, disciplined, ritualistic. Though he knew nothing of real war, he imagined it to be a desperate, harrowing maelstrom of courage and fear, action and blood. And in that anarchy of battle he would kill. He did not know when, or how, but as surely as he had not been an Artist until he had sculpted his first piece, he would not truly tread the Path of the Warrior until he killed his first foe.

He did not know how he would bring himself to do it. Would it be taken out of his hands? An instinct of defence to protect his life? Would it be cold-blooded, a pre-meditated slaying of another creature defined as an enemy of the Alaitocii by the farseers and autarchs?

Korlandril realised that this was the war-mask Kenainath and the rest talked about. Only on one occasion had he been ready to strike out in anger, truly wishing harm on another individual; that cycle in the swamp, when rage and hate had combined into a moment of pure action. He tried to capture that instance again, but all of his tricks of memory failed him. In that heartbeat his entire being had been focussed on that one effort to hit Kenainath, and nothing else.

For some time he wandered the pathways around the shrine, not straying too far. He knew the twisting trails as well as any other part of Alaitoc, their mysteries unveiled to him through Kenainath. He no longer feared his surroundings. More importantly, he knew that in overcoming his apprehension of this place he had steeled himself against future dread and doubts when confronted by the unknown and unknowable. He was self-aware enough to understand the process being awoken in him by the teachings of Kenainath, weaving layers of the war-mask that would, one day, emerge from within his spirit.

The light was considerably brighter when a resounding chime sounded within the shrine, calling him back.

It was Bechareth. He was armoured save for his helm, and carried his chainsword in an easy grip by his side. There was a tightness to his lips, and fire in his eyes, which spoke of his enthusiasm for the duel about to commence. He appeared relaxed in body, but his eyes were attentive, floating easily but with focus from Kenainath to Korlandril and back again.

As he armoured himself, the mantra of Kenainath flowing through his veins, Korlandril's anxiety slipped away. With each step he became Korlandril less, the Aspect of the Striking Scorpion taking his place. Part of his mind watched the rest with cold detachment, reminding him of the Seven Parrying Sweeps and the Four Rising Attacks. He knew nothing of Bechareth, had only witnessed him performing the practice rituals with the others. Would he be defensive or aggressive? Did he favour a particular style of attack? Korlandril realised that he did not even know how long Bechareth had been treading the Path of the Warrior. He made these observations coolly, without judgement or fear.

He was also unsure of his own strategy. That Bechareth was more experienced seemed certain. Would Korlandril do better to confine himself to fight cautiously until he had more of a measure of his opponent? Or would that hand too much of the initiative to his adversary? Korlandril wondered if he would react well enough to whatever attacks Bechareth made. Part of him considered if the duel would even last more than a few heartbeats.

That thought did bring with it a reaction: a stab of pride. Korlandril had worked hard to learn the fighting stances and the poses of attack and defence. Now was the time to demonstrate that he had learned well. He was determined to give a good account of himself.

At Kenainath's wordless signal, the pair fell in behind the exarch as he led them down a winding ramp to a chamber deep below the pyramid of the shrine's upper storeys. The others followed a little way behind the three of them, walking in single file, clothed only in the undersuits of their armour.

The passageways had a rough, hard-worked surface that seemed odd to Korlandril. The part of him that had been an Artist recognised it for the affectation that it was; nothing on Alaitoc was anything but artificial. Yet the warrior part of Korlandril's mind recognised what the change in surroundings represented. It was tradition, a warrior code that stretched back to the time of the Fall. A shrine dedicated to the teachings of the Striking Scorpion's founder; or rather the teachings of the founder's greatest pupil after his master fell to the darkness.

The ambient light, such as there was in the shrine, was replaced by narrow, flickering tubes. There was pretence here, but one that Korlandril could understand. This was a reconstruction of that first shrine, created by Arhra after learning under the tuition of Asurmen. The Deadly Shadow, as all the other shrines on Alaitoc and the many other craftworlds, was not paying homage to the birthplace of its traditions, but trying to recreate them. Everything was now as it was then. What it was to be a Striking Scorpion had not changed in the thousands of passes that had gone by since that founding.

All of this Korlandril was aware of, with the small critical eye at the back of his mind. The greater part of him, the bulk of his spirit that was now warrior, immersed itself in the atmosphere, heightening his anticipation for the coming duel.

The ceiling was intentionally low, barring the two of them from leaving their feet or swinging their swords too high overhead. The floor was etched with a circle, not much wider than the space the two of them occupied, with the rune of the shrine at its centre. Korlandril knew that the duellists would not be allowed to leave the circle. This was a contest of skill at close confines, of control and precision, the foundation of the Striking Scorpion ethos.

No rules had been explained to Korlandril, but he knew that there would be no actual contact, no risk of drawing blood or damage to the precious armour. He was not even sure this was a contest; he inferred as such from Kenainath's next words.

'This is not a test, a place to prove yourself, to you or to me,' intoned Kenainath, signalling the two warriors into the centre of the oval chamber. The exarch nodded for them to begin and stepped back into the shadows. The other Striking Scorpions watched silently from close to the wall.

The pair shifted instantly, Korlandril assuming Leaf that Cuts, a defensive posture. Bechareth needed no encouragement and stepped forwards and to his left, chainsword humming towards the side of Korlandril's head, the whirring blades stopping short by only the span of a hand.

'Cut!' The word was muffled by the small chamber, coming from the throats of the others at the same time.

Korlandril was taken aback by the speed of Bechareth's attack. The two returned to their positions of repose, staring into each other's eyes. There was intensity in Bechareth's and Korlandril imagined his were the same. This was no war-mask; had it been, the last blow would have sliced off the top of Korlandril's head and Bechareth would not have thought twice about it.

They stood immobile for some time, neither willing to make the first move just yet. Korlandril shifted quickly into Cloud Turning to Storm, feinting high and then spinning low and driving his chainsword toward Bechareth's stomach. His foe deflected the attack, flat of blade on flat of blade, knocking Korlandril sideways by a fraction. Through this miniscule opening, Bechareth stepped forwards again, the tip of his humming blade aimed at Korlandril's throat.

'Cut!' announced the onlookers.

Bechareth stepped back, a flicker of a smile on his lips.

Again and again the same pattern played out: Korlandril countering or attempting an attack, only for Bechareth to manoeuvre into a killing position within a few strokes.

Korlandril shook his head, rapidly losing what confidence he had. It was one matter to execute the strikes and defences he had learnt against thin air, another to perform them against a target that was trying everything to misdirect and unbalance him. His mind, which he had never thought of as particularly slow, seemed unable to register Bechareth's moves quickly enough; any response he might come up with was always too late.

As they paused before their seventh exchange, a sensation of movement, perhaps the slightest sound of a footfall or a breath, caused Korlandril to whirl around, sword cutting the air. He stopped the blade just before it struck Kenainath's outstretched arm. The exarch wore a pleased expression. He moved his gaze from the whirring teeth of the chainsword to Korlandril's stare.

'Do not consider, act without thought or feeling, no hesitation.'

Korlandril understood the lesson, but as he turned to face Bechareth again, he was unsure how to implement the exarch's teaching.

Bechareth flicked up his sword towards Korlandril's thigh, the novice's blade sweeping down and stopping it short. Distracted, he had reacted better than when he had been concentrating. It was not a matter of process, it was a matter of instinct. His body, his inner mind, knew better what to do than his conscious thoughts.

Korlandril focussed on his breathing, relaxing himself, while Bechareth launched a complex assault. At each strike, Korlandril's sword rose to intercept his foe's chainsword with a dull ring. Korlandril could almost see without his eyes, hear without his ears. As never before, he felt enmeshed with his armour, the chainsword an extension of himself and not some foreign object gripped in his fist.

After three more parries, Korlandril took the offensive, sliding a foot forward, lunging towards Bechareth's midriff. Bechareth knocked Korlandril's chainsword downward and flicked his wrist, but Korlandril had already responded, ducking to his left while his blade flashed out towards Bechareth's shoulder. Again the blades met with a brief shudder of contact and then moved on, darting and probing. Korlandril felt like he was standing with the others, simply watching the duel from a distance, amazed at the agility and skill of his body.

'Cut!'

The barked word broke the flow of Korlandril's consciousness. For a moment he felt triumph, for the call had come as he aimed a throat-slashing blow. But Bechareth was smiling, his eyes narrowed. A glance down revealed Bechareth's chainsword barely a finger's width from the inside of Korlandril's thigh – a cut that would have torn through the artery and cut deep into his pelvis.

Kenainath stepped between them, hand raised to halt the duel. He nodded approvingly towards Bechareth, who bowed slightly and withdrew towards the others. The exarch turned on Korlandril, eyebrow raised in question, head tilted ever-so-slightly to one side.

'The lesson is learnt, but you are still a novice, and must practise more.'

'Yes,' replied Korlandril. A moment's reflection and he realised that he was not ashamed of being beaten, he held his head high, his shoulders square. He pondered Kenainath's quizzical expression for a moment, and realised what was expected of him. 'The claw I will master. I am ready to learn the ways of the venomous bite.'

Kenainath nodded in agreement.

Korlandril found the shuriken pistol – the venomous bite of the Striking Scorpion – more straightforward to use than the chainsword. Like his blade, it responded to his thoughts, firing a volley of monomolecular-edged discs that could slice flesh with ease. Though it could be used at some distance, the shuriken pistol in the hands of the Striking Scorpion was mainly a close combat weapon, complementing the cuts and parries of the chainsword. The sweeping movements Korlandril made with his left hand during the rituals became short bursts of fire, to distract or incapacitate the enemy whilst the chainsword delivered the killing blow.

It was impossible to duel with loaded pistols without risking serious harm, and so Korlandril continued to fight with chainsword alone against the others. His skills improved with each encounter, to the point where he would score a cut almost as often as his opponents. Despite this, there was no word of praise from Kenainath, and of the other shrine members only Elissanadrin ever complemented him on his growing skill.

It was with a mixture of trepidation and excitement that, seventy-eight cycles later, Korlandril found himself back in the armouring chamber with Kenainath, about to enter the final stage of his training – the Scorpion's Sting. He suited up as he had done dozens of times before, but on this occasion there was a final line to the mantra intoned by the exarch.

'See not with the eyes, but allow anger to flow, let Khaine's gift guide you.'

Korlandril lifted the helmet above his head and lowered it purposefully, encasing himself fully from toe to scalp. With a hiss of air, the suit sealed itself. He was gripped by a terrifying claustrophobia, trapped inside the helm. It was dark and stifling and he flailed to take it off again, dreading suffocation.

'Be calm warrior, do not let your fears take hold, but extend your will.' Kenainath's voice drifted into Korlandril's consciousness, his tone soothing, patient.

Korlandril forced himself to quell his hyperventilating and took a deep breath, fearing it would be his last.

'See not with the eyes, but allow anger to flow, let Khaine's gift guide you,' Kenainath said again.

The Striking Scorpion performed a mental twist, turning his fear

– defence – into anger – attack. He wanted to master the horror creeping up within him, to slay the sly serpent writhing in his gut that threatened to still his heart.

Almost immediately there was light, blinding in its brightness. Korlandril felt the tendrils of the suit's systems reaching into his mind, probing for connection. He fought the urge to resist and instead surrendered himself to its gentle but insistent exploration. The sensation was deeply unpleasant as the Aspect helmet sifted through his memories and thoughts, seeking purchase. Flickers of past events strobed through Korlandril's consciousness, each too brief to recognise but as a sum stirring up long-dead feelings.

With a shriek of anguish roaring from Korlandril's throat, the memory of Thirianna's rejection engulfed him. That primal scream brought forth a hail of spitting fire from the weapons array built into the helmet – the mandiblasters for which the Striking Scorpions were famed and feared.

Plasmic energy crackled along the discharge of conductive needles fired from the helmet-mounted weapons, spraying across the arming chamber in a burst of fury. The anger looped between Korlandril and the suit, sending him staggering, hands raised to the helmet to drag it off. The suit refused him, pulling him down into its dark embrace.

Blackness swamped Korlandril and he collapsed, clattering to the floor in a twisted heap.

Memory, reality, hope and fear spun with kaleidoscopic chaos within Korlandril's mind. Not even his first Dreaming had been as terrifying. He felt like a mote of dust in a hurricane, a tiny speck of light amidst the furnace of a star. One image burned into his spirit, white-hot in its intensity, inescapable in its magnitude. The rune of the Striking Scorpion seared into his mind.

|Lost|Alone|Pathless|Abandoned|

Laughter – Korlandril dimly recognised it as Aradryan's – turned from humour to taunt. Thirianna's eyes – strangely golden – looked at him with pity and scorn. Kenainath's mocking words, his disdain. Korlandril was child-like, insecure, exposed to the overwhelming sensations of the universe again. There was nowhere to hide. The shadows brought their own perils.

|Darkness|Rage|Hate|Death|

The need to destroy – to eradicate anything and everything – suffused Korlandril. He would tear the throat from laughing Aradryan. He would pluck the scheming eyes from Thirianna. He would slice the head from Kenainath and take it as a trophy. He would heap ruin upon those that had wronged him, slurred his reputation and scorned his advances.

|Light|Hope|Friendship|Love|

Like the waters of a tidal wave flowing down a whirlpool, the doubt and fear and anger swirled away from Korlandril. He heard the joy in

Aradryan's laughter. He saw the affection in Thirianna's eyes. He felt the respect in Kenainath's words.

His hand reached to the spirit stone at his breast, its coolness spreading to each part of him, through his skin, along his nerves, into every organ and bone.

|Calm|Silence|Discipline|Peace|

Korlandril awoke on his cot in the dormitory, unarmoured. He was alone. He could remember nothing save an overwhelming sensation of contentment. The gloom was a comforting embrace, devoid of stimuli to confound and distract him.

Korlandril closed his eyes and slept. He did not dream.

It took six more attempts for Korlandril to finally master the Scorpion's Sting. With each session, he gradually learned to interface with the psychic connections of the armoured suit without suffering the catastrophic feedback of his first encounter. When he finally stood before the others, fully armed and armoured, he was calm and in control.

Bechareth was the first to congratulate him, bowing sincerely and deeply. Elissanadrin came next.

'You have become that which you needed to become,' she said sombrely, her melodic voice tainted slightly by the transmitter of her suit. 'You have achieved the division between your spirit and your war-mask.'

'Which is good news for us,' said Arhulesh, joining the pair.

'How so?' asked Korlandril.

'You will be able to join us outside the shrine,' Arhulesh said. 'The glasses of the Crescent of the Dawning Ages have nothing more to fear from you.'

It was with some shame that Korlandril recalled the incident that had propelled him to the Shrine of the Deadly Shadow.

'Of course,' Arhulesh continued, 'if you feel like smashing anything, make sure you finish your drink first.'

The import of what Arhulesh had first said sank in.

'I will be able to leave the shrine?' said Korlandril. His first reaction was trepidation. What if the others were wrong? What if his anger was not under his control? Korlandril's second thought was of embarrassment. For all that he had discovered about himself as a warrior, he was still ashamed of the journey that had brought him to the shrine's doors. What if he met Thirianna?

'We will be with you,' said Min, laying a comforting hand on Korlandril's arm. 'And if I guess your doubts correctly, you should remember that Thirianna was once a Dire Avenger. In fact, was it not you that judged the warrior more harshly?'

Korlandril had to admit he had confessed as much to the others several times. His views were more conflicted now, but he still felt a certain unease.

'I would like to train for a little more time before I venture out,' he said.

'Nonsense!' declared Min. 'You have learnt too well the art of stealth and secrecy. It is time to step back into the light and enjoy Alaitoc again.'

'Brooding here like Kenainath won't help you,' said Arhulesh. 'What you really need is the company of others.'

'And a carafe or two of summervine!' Elissanadrin added. The suggestion roused in Korlandril a desire to indulge himself a little, to lose himself in talk and wine.

'You are right, this is a time of celebration, not mourning,' Korlandril announced, smiling inside his helm. 'Khaine can keep Kenainath here, but I'm filled with the teachings of Kurnous. Wine and song, and perhaps I might even visit a few old friends.'

The others fell hush and Korlandril felt a presence behind him, a slight chill as if a breeze drifted over his neck. He turned to see Kenainath staring at him.

'I'm sorry, I didn't…'

'No apologies, I would not wish you to stay, who still has freedom. Find happiness now, enjoy your life while you can, you have earned that right.'

Kenainath swung away and then stopped to direct a long stare over his shoulder at Korlandril.

'Do not forget me, and not the Deadly Shadow, who gave you this gift. A pact you have made, with the Bloody-Handed God, he is part of you. Live well and train hard, heed the shrill call to battle, and return to me.'

Korlandril bowed low, humbled by the exarch's words.

'I will return on the morrow, and we will continue. I cannot reject Khaine's gift, and so I look to you to guide me.'

The exarch nodded once and strode away, swallowed by the dark of the shrine.

FEAR

Before the War in Heaven, Eldanesh, sword-brother and hawk-friend, faced the nightmarish horde of the Autochtinii and he was afraid. Countless in number were the foe and the eldar were few. Not for himself did Eldanesh fear, but for the lives of his warriors. As Eldanesh girded himself for the battle to come there was a great tumult of fire in the air. Khaine himself, iron-skinned and fire-blooded, arrived with spear and shield and stood beside the mortal prince. Though Khaine hated Eldanesh and Eldanesh had no love for Khaine, the Bloody-Handed One would protect the eldar from their foes. So it was that Eldanesh's fear was quashed by the presence of the war god and the eldar knew victory over the Autochtinii.

Korlandril smoothed out a graceful curve from the ivory-coloured putty, shaping the thigh of the figurine coming to shape in his hands. The old part of him, the essence of the Artist that had survived into Korlandril the Warrior, knew it to be a crude ornament, but the fingers of the Striking Scorpion still recalled the dexterity and skill of his former Path.

The sculpture was of Isha, as were the four others that he had added to his collection since his first departure from the shrine. It helped him to focus on a moment of purity with Thirianna. Korlandril had also come to terms with the rift that had erupted between him and Aradryan, and recognised that the unveiling had not been the start of that division.

It had been childish not to accept that his friend had changed from the eldar he had known before Aradryan's voyage. With the pragmatic eye of the Warrior rather than the idealistic gaze of the Artist, Korlandril could see that he had changed as much during Aradryan's absence. He looked back at the conceited sculptor he had been and wondered why he had so wished to cling to the past.

The door signal chimed and Korlandril stood up, gesturing for the portal to open. He did not look to see who was visiting him as he crossed into the cleansing chamber to remove the vestiges of the putty from his hand. It was probably Min or Elissanadrin, both had visited him regularly.

'Things change again.' The visitor's voice was not Elissanadrin or Min, though it was oddly familiar. Korlandril turned around to welcome the arrival.

It was Aradryan.

He was dressed in a tight suit of shifting greens and blues, his outline indistinct. He wore a belt and sash with many pouches and pockets and a long knife hung at his hip. The garb of the ranger.

'Things change again,' agreed Korlandril. He remembered his manners and gestured for Aradryan to seat himself. The ranger declined with a slight shake of the head.

'I have come out of courtesy to the friendship we once shared,' said Aradryan. 'I thought it wrong to come back to Alaitoc and not see you.'

'I am glad that you have come,' said Korlandril. 'I owe you an apology for my behaviour the last time we met.'

'It was never the case that we wronged each other intentionally, and neither of us owes the other anything but respect.'

'I trust your travels have been fruitful?'

Aradryan smiled and nodded.

'I cannot describe the sights I have seen, the thrill of adventure that has coursed through my veins. The galaxy has been set out before me and I have experienced such a tiny fraction of the delights and darkness it has to offer.'

'I too have been on a journey,' said Korlandril, cleaning his hands.

'I have heard this,' said Aradryan. Korlandril looked at him and raised his eyebrows in question. Aradryan was hesitant, quiet, when he continued. 'Thirianna. I met with her first. She told me that you are now an Aspect Warrior.'

'A Striking Scorpion of the Deadly Shadow shrine,' said Korlandril. He delicately rinsed his hands and dried them under a warm vent above the sink. 'It does not anger me that you saw Thirianna first. My parting from her is an event of the past, one with which I have wholly come to terms.'

Aradryan's eyes swept the living quarters, taking in the Isha statues arranged around the room. He smiled again and darted a doubtful look at Korlandril.

'Well, perhaps not *wholly*,' the warrior admitted with a short laugh. 'But

I truly bear you no ill-will concerning your part, unwitting as it was, in the circumstances that engulfed me.'

'Have you seen her recently?'

Korlandril shook his head.

'It would serve no purpose. If I happen to cross her path, it will be well, but it is not my place to seek her company at this time. She and I travel to different places, and we make our own journeys.'

'Someone else?' suggested Aradryan.

Korlandril was about to deny such a thing but paused, his thoughts turning unbidden to Elissanadrin. He was shocked and it must have shown on his face.

'Aha!' laughed Aradryan.

'It is not like that,' Korlandril said hurriedly. 'She is a fellow warrior at the shrine, it would be entirely inappropriate for us to engage in any deeper relationship.'

Aradryan's face expressed his disagreement with this notion more than any words, but he said nothing. The two of them stood in silence, comfortable if not pleasant, before Aradryan's expression took on a more serious cast. 'I have also come to give you advance warning that you will be shortly called to your shrine.'

'How might you know this?' asked Korlandril, frowning fiercely. 'Have you spoken to Kenainath?'

'I would not tread foot in an Aspect shrine! And your exarch does not venture forth. No, it is from first-hand knowledge that I am aware of this. I have just returned from Eileniliesh. It is an Exodite world not so far away. Orks have come to Eileniliesh and her people call on Alaitoc for help. I have come back as their messenger. Even now the autarchs and farseers debate the best course of action. There is no doubt in my mind that they will issue the call to war.'

'And I will be ready to answer it,' said Korlandril.

'I have my own preparations to make,' said Aradryan, taking a step towards the door. 'Other rangers are gathering here to share what they know of the enemy. I must join them.'

Korlandril nodded his understanding. Aradryan was at the door before Korlandril spoke again.

'I am glad that you are alive and well, my friend.'

'As am I of you, Korlandril. I do not know if I will see you on Eileniliesh or before we leave. If not, then I wish you good fortune and prosperity until our next meeting.'

'Good fortune and prosperity,' echoed Korlandril.

He watched the ranger depart and the iris door close behind him. He wondered whether to head directly to the shrine or await Kenainath's command. Korlandril decided on the latter course of action; he was in no haste to put on his war-mask.

* * *

Korlandril continued to sculpt into the twilight of the cycle, and still no message from Kenainath arrived. He was putting the finishing touches on the sandals of his miniature goddess when he had cause to pause. Something had changed. He was not sure what had distracted him; a glimmer of sensation at the back of his mind.

He dismissed it and returned to his work, only to be disturbed a few moments later by a more vigorous sense of something untoward happening. It was a feeling at the base of his spine and in his gut. His heart was quickening, growing in tempo along with his breathing. Perturbed, Korlandril sat back in his high-backed chair and concentrated, seeking the source of his discomfort.

It felt like tiny vibrations, running through his spirit rather than his body. Something was awakening his nerve endings, stimulating parts of his mind he did not visit outside of the shrine.

For a fleeting heartbeat he thought he could smell burning and blood, and felt a prickle of heat wash over him. He glanced around the chamber seeking the source but could see nothing. The heat was coming from within him.

Unbidden, the apparition of his imaginary sparring partner flickered through his mind. Like a circuit being completed, the image touched off a chain reaction in Korlandril's mind and body. He flushed with a surge of energy even as he felt a tingling behind his eyes as his nerves sought to connect with something that was not there.

He realised that he was seeking his armour. Even as he thought of the shrine, a ghastly roar echoed in the back of his mind, blotting out all other sensation. Korlandril was almost knocked senseless by the sudden assault of rage and hatred encapsulated in that feral bellow. At once, he knew what was happening, and knew also that he had to go to the Deadly Shadow shrine as swiftly as possible.

War had come to Alaitoc. The Avatar of Kaela Mensha Khaine was awakening.

A small box had been left at Korlandril's door, a simple white cube no larger than the palm of his hand without wrapping or message. Korlandril bent his knee to pick it up and as his fingers neared the package he felt a sensation of warmth. He pulled back slightly, surprised by the feeling. It felt like Thirianna, though there was something else mixed in with the strange hint of presence that lingered around the gift.

He picked it up and opened the lid.

Inside was a rune, shaped from silvery-grey wishstone. He recognised it immediately, the symbol of the Dire Avengers. It was the martial discipline of this warrior Aspect that had merged with the tender thoughts of Thirianna. Holding it in his palm, Korlandril concentrated, teasing the thought-stream with which the rune had been imbued.

He felt momentary sadness and longing; regret at their parting; pride in his actions. Most of all, he felt the sensation of understanding. Korlandril divined the message. Thirianna herself had once heard her call of Khaine and supported him on his current path. Running a finger along the bars of the rune, Korlandril knew she had taken it as a souvenir from her armour, and now she had passed it to him as a token of her friendship, one that he would be able to understand from one warrior to another.

He closed his fingers around the gift and smiled.

It was the first time Korlandril had suited up with the purpose of true battle. Kenainath stood before him with a shallow bowl, a sliver of a blade in his right hand.

'We give of our blood, as Khaine's call roars around us, calling us to war.'

The exarch took the knife and made a cut in the palm of Korlandril's right hand, allowing the lifeblood of the warrior to drip into the bowl and mingle with that of the other Striking Scorpions.

Kenainath then moved around the squad, in turn painting the rune of the Striking Scorpion upon their foreheads. Korlandril was the last and watched with some trepidation as he saw his companions' eyes glaze over, their muscles twitch and their lips curl back from their teeth in snarls.

Then he felt the blood upon his own skin. It felt like the exarch was carving the rune into his flesh with a fiery brand, the pain flaring in Korlandril's mind. The pain turned to anger, welling up from deep within him. The anger drew on the deep-seated frustrations and humiliations Korlandril had put aside, wakening those forgotten emotions.

Quivering, Korlandril did nothing as the war-mask erupted from within him. His blood thundered in his ears and the cut on his palm burned sharply. The air crackled with life and his skin crawled with energy. Like an obscene birth the warrior spirit of Korlandril burst forth through the barriers he had erected, seething and hungry.

The voice of Kenainath cut through Korlandril's senses.

'The peace is broken, harmony falls to discord, only war remains.'

Korlandril began the ritual of arming, following each step without thought. It was as if he walked towards a burning fire and was preparing to pass through the flames. He steadied himself mentally, concentrating on the exarch's mantra.

'Now we clothe ourselves, with bloody Khaine's own raiment, as a warrior.'

Korlandril could not fight back his excitement. This was the moment he had dreaded and longed-for since completing his training. He felt a moment of shame at his own bloodthirst but the regret soon disappeared as he continued to armour himself.

'In Khaine's iron skin, we clad ourselves for battle, while fire burns within.'

Like no other time, the armour felt a part of Korlandril. He was not simply putting on his suit, he was becoming himself. More than putting on plates of armour, he was stripping away the pretensions of civilisation he used to conceal his wrath.

'The spirit of Khaine, from which we draw our resolve, strengthens within us.'

The rune upon his forehead was now icy cold. Its freezing touch spread through him, until it had almost stilled his heart. With its chilling fingers it brushed away his remorse and pity, crushed his compassion and guilt.

'War comes upon us, we must bear its dark burden, upon our shoulders.'

Khaine's iron skin, indeed! Korlandril felt strong, stronger than ever before. He flexed his shoulders and bunched the muscles in his chest, the armour tightening around him, comforting in its hard embrace.

'We stand before Khaine, unyielding in our calling, free of doubt and fear.'

Korlandril's heart was a drumbeat, endless, martial, driving him onwards. He curled his fingers into fists and felt the power in his arms. It felt good, to be so powerful, to be so alive.

'We do not flee death, we walk in the shade of Khaine, proud and unafraid.'

The armour made a creaking noise as it adjusted further. As it knitted together he felt it bonding to him, infusing his spirit with its own. He heard panting, dimly realising that it was he that was breathing so quickly. He closed his eyes and saw the fire-eyed apparition of his anger swirling around him, encasing him as surely as the armoured suit.

'We strike from the dark, as swift as the scorpion, with a deadly touch.'

Korlandril felt his hands empty, and longed for the feeling of sword and pistol in his fingers. He flexed his gauntleted hands in anticipation.

'See not with the eyes, but allow anger to flow, let Khaine's gift guide you.'

As the darkness of the helm enveloped Korlandril, he was frozen in space and time. The universe paused, holding its breath. He stood there in the darkness, savouring it, remembering with scorn the fear he had felt when first he had come to this place. It had made him whole.

Something was placed in his right hand and he gripped it gently. Sharp blades hummed into momentary life and then fell still. With a click, something was affixed to the relay cord on his left arm and his hand curled around a pistol's grip. Thirianna's rune hung from it, a small decoration of his own.

Then his waystone, sliding into place upon his chest, guarding his spirit against damnation. It was his last armour, his true protection against the thing he was becoming, the creature he *wanted* to become.

The darkness was inside him and outside him, the fiery eyes staring directly out of his head. He had known all along the shadowy figure he had been fighting, but only now truly saw it for what it was. It was himself he had fought. He had strained against the urges and desires that lingered within his heart. He had tried so hard to quell the feelings of rage, but he had fought out of ignorance.

The darkness was no more, save that Korlandril had his eyes closed. He opened them and looked out at the world with a fresh view through the ruby-tinted lenses of his helmet.

He took a crouched step forward, easing into his fighting stance. No longer was he a thing of flesh and blood, a mortal being filled with falsehood and crude passions. He was a Warrior. He was part of the Bloody-Handed God, an Aspect of Kaela Mensha Khaine.

Korlandril was no more.

In his place stood a Striking Scorpion of the Deadly Shadow.

The main gallery of the warship was an immense hall, vaulted with rib-like structures that split into tall, narrow doorways leading to the side chambers. Flickers of energy danced along the wraithbone core, merging with hidden psychic circuitry behind walls of shifting, mottled blue and green. The arched ship chambers rang with booted feet, the keen sound of blades cutting air and now and then an explosion or blaze of laser fire as weapons were tested. Warriors from Alaitoc's dozens of Aspect shrines practised their rituals, each in a separate hall that branched from the main arterial passage, the mantras of the exarchs ringing from the high ceilings in a multi-layered symphony of war.

Korlandril stood in line with the other Deadly Shadow warriors, hearing only the voice of Kenainath and the beating of his heart.

The Avatar was aboard. The Bloody-Handed God walked among them. Korlandril could feel its presence lingering on the edge of his senses. It quickened his pulse and filled every motion with greater energy. His mind was fixed upon a single goal – the annihilation of the orks despoiling Eileniliesh.

The thought of battle filled him with expectation. For all that his rituals as a warrior allowed him to separate his anger from his daily life, it was in war that he would find release. The prospect of bloodshed, the visceral conflict of life and death, thrilled Korlandril. It promised an intoxication even greater and fulfilling than the completion of a sculpture or the climax of a Dreaming, though he could remember these previous victories only dimly.

When the exercises were complete, Kenainath dismissed them. Korlandril hesitated, unsure what to do next. Elissanadrin approached him, removing her helmet. Korlandril's eyes were immediately drawn to the rune of dried blood on her forehead. His ruby-tinted gaze moved to her eyes and he saw the dispassionate stare he now recognised as the war-mask.

Hesitantly, self-consciously, Korlandril took off his helmet, fearful that this act would somehow remove his war-mask. Unhelmed, he felt no different. The rune upon his skin bound him to his mental state, an anchor of anger.

He followed the others as they left the chamber and filed along the central nave of the starship, heading towards the stern. Now and then a glimmer of light would pass along the translucent walls, a bright speck amongst pale orange and yellow shimmering. There was no infinity circuit on the ship, though its wraithbone core pulsed gently with psychic energy, playing upon the edge of Korlandril's senses. It was almost overwhelmed with the far sharper, iron-and-blood-tainted presence of the Avatar.

Other squads were likewise assembling, coming together along the arteries of the battleship on foot and skimming platforms: Dark Reapers in their heavy black armour and vane-flanked helms; bone-coloured Howling Banshees, the manes of their helmets flying with psychic energy; and many Dire Avengers, blue-clad, their exarchs wearing bright yellow and white gonfalons on their backpacks. And many others beside, each representing a facet of the War God; each dedicated to a particular fighting style, brought together in a harmony of destruction.

'It will be eight cycles before we reach Eileniliesh,' said Min, stopping in his enthusiastic stride to allow Elissanadrin and Korlandril to catch him.

It seemed such a long time to wait before the bloodletting would begin, but Korlandril knew that such a journey was short compared to most. He was agitated by the inactivity, wondering how he would make the time pass.

'I see the hunger in you,' said Min, baring his teeth in a grin. 'It will come soon enough, do not fret.'

'How many times have you fought?' asked Korlandril.

'This will be my thirteenth expedition,' said Elissanadrin.

'Twenty,' replied Min.

Korlandril looked around at Arhulesh, who had been trailing behind them a little way, with Bechareth a few more paces even further back.

'Two,' said Arhulesh. 'Including this one.'

Korlandril laughed, and then fell silent, taken aback that he could show humour. Arhulesh growled.

'You gave the impression you were more experienced,' said Korlandril. 'I did not realise you were such a babe-at-arms.'

'It is you that is the adolescent, newcomer,' said Arhulesh. 'Feverish to taste that forbidden pleasure, yet as hesitant as an Iybraesillian maiden on coming to full flower. Be assured that nobody expects you to perform perfectly the first time.'

'My first foray into fleshly pleasures met with success and much gratitude from my partner,' said Korlandril. 'I've no fear my battle-virginity will hold me back.'

'For truth, I am sure you practised equally before both,' laughed Arhulesh.

They walked on for a while longer, the chatter of other squads around them.

'I am hungry,' said Korlandril, even as he realised the emptiness gnawing at him. He felt like an engine that had burned most of its fuel.

'We all are,' said Min. 'Tis a strange thing, for a cycle from now your stomach will feel like an endless knot and you won't want a morsel. Eat as much as you can, while you can. Your body burns energy much faster with your war-mask on, it's important to keep up your energy levels.'

Korlandril nodded in understanding.

Their journey took them past vast hangars where the dark shapes of scout ships loomed in shadow. A few were empty, their ranger pilots escorting the warship through the winding half-real maze of the webway. Other halls were also dormant: places where tanks and other war machines would usually be transported. There was to be no such support on this mission – this was a quick strike to destroy the ork threat in its infancy. Only the Aspect Warriors had been called, the farseers judging the situation not so severe that the citizen militia – the Guardians – needed to be mobilised.

Min led them to an eatery where hundreds of Aspect Warriors were sat at long tables, while others moved busily around the circular counters, helping themselves to the food on offer. A force dome glittered overhead, showing a view of the webway. A curving tunnel of energy enveloped the ship with solid walls of rippling colours, streaked through with flashes of star-lit sky. Engineered from the stuff of warp space, the webway burrowed between and through the immaterial and material worlds, part of both but separate from each.

Now and then they passed a branching route, the webway bifurcating through hanging gateways of gold and wraithbone, inscribed with runes channelling and shaping the psychic energy of warp space. There were other features: small tunnels that cut out great loops of the main channels; huge coils of raw wraithbone wrapped around the insubstantial tunnel in places the only evidence of repairs; occasionally the force walls folded and buckled, rippling with light as some malign creature of warp space intersected with the webway and was thrown back by the psychic wards.

There were no other ships to be seen, the route to Eileniliesh had been cleared by the rangers to allow passage for the large warship.

Thinking about the daemons and other creatures loitering close at hand made Korlandril uneasy. The webway was far safer than open warp space, but it unnerved him to imagine the immaterial beasts held at bay by the translucent walls of energy. He pulled his eyes away and looked at the Aspect Warriors gathered in their squads across the circular hall.

'Why does the Deadly Shadow have so few warriors compared to the other shrines?'

'Kenainath will only take on a single pupil at a time,' explained Elissanadrin. 'It is fortunate for you that he had no acolyte at the time of your… dilemma. I would not have been able to bring you to him had it been otherwise.'

Korlandril also noticed that most of the other shrines had their exarchs with them. Kenainath, as far as Korlandril knew, had remained in the Deadly Shadow's allotted shrine-hall. He spied another group of Striking Scorpions, more than twenty of them. Their exarch sat at the head of the table. A long two-edged chainsword hung on a sling across his back.

'The Fall of Deadly Rain,' said Arhulesh. 'That is the exarch, Aranarha. We should pay our respects.'

The exarch looked up at them as they approached; eyes a deep blue, his features smooth like one of Korlandril's sculptures. His hair was cropped barbarically short, save for two long braids that fell across his face.

'The children of Kenainath, a welcome greeting, and a new member with them!' the exarch said with a lopsided grin. He stood up and gave a perfunctory bow towards Korlandril.

'My honour,' said Korlandril, returning the bow. 'I am Korlandril.'

'And now a Deadly Shadow, hiding in your shrine, with Kenainath's dark whispers. Why did you not come to me, my door was open, and I am far less fearsome.'

'I–' began Korlandril, but Elissanadrin cut him off.

'It was I that brought Korlandril to the Deadly Shadow, as was right,' she said forcefully. 'Kenainath teaches us well.'

'I do not dispute that fact, but that is not all, there is more to life than war.'

'He allows us to learn those lessons for ourselves,' countered Min.

Aranarha smiled pleasantly and waved for them to sit themselves down.

'You have come here on your own, without your exarch, so enjoy our company.'

Korlandril glanced at the others for guidance.

'Here is as good a place as any,' said Arhulesh, taking a place between two of the Fall of Deadly Rain warriors. He helped himself to a few morsels from the plate of the warrior to his left. 'We have little else to do.'

'We will join you shortly,' said Elissanadrin, turning towards the nearest food counter. Korlandril trailed slightly behind her, bemused by the exchange.

'I detect some enmity,' he said. 'Do you have some issue with Aranarha?'

Elissanadrin shook her head, taking an oval platter from beneath the heated food station. With dextrous flicks of her wrist, she transferred a pile of steaming multi-coloured grains to the plate. Korlandril took up a bowl and wandered to a stand of low bushes growing from a patch of spongy floor. With quick fingers, he twisted the berries from the living branches and then moved on to a small pool where fragrant blossoms floated on the surface. He plucked a couple of blooms and scattered their petals across his food.

'Aranarha and Kenainath have been rivals for some time, but there is no hostility there,' said Elissanadrin, as Korlandril used a slender knife to fillet slices of meat from the carcass of a shadow-horn. 'Kenainath is old – very old – and he does not approve of Aranarha's methods sometimes. But we are all warriors here, and that is a bond that cannot be broken. For all their differences, they still respect each other.'

'But that does not explain your tone and actions,' said Korlandril, filling his dish with a generous helping of split seeds and twists of angel-resin. He was ravenous and had to stop himself over-filling the platter.

'Kenainath sees his entrapment as an exarch as a curse, but Aranarha takes it as a blessing. The older would rather have no pupils, the younger proselytises his cult, actively recruiting new warriors.'

'Why does Kenainath want to be free of pupils? Is he that disdainful of us?'

Elissanadrin gave Korlandril a sharp look.

'If Kenainath had no pupils, it would mean that there is no need of him – that others were free from the taint of Khaine's Gift. If you think that Kenainath disdains you, then you see something I do not. Perhaps it is merely a reflection of some residual shame you feel.'

'He does not seem to care too much about me,' Korlandril said with a shrug. 'Perhaps I confuse indifference for disdain.'

'Kenainath digs deep, reaching into the very heart of what takes you to him.' Elissanadrin kept her voice quiet as they moved back towards the table with the other Striking Scorpions. 'Aranarha teaches the rituals en masse, taking no personal interest in each warrior. Which of the two do you think cares more?'

Korlandril considered this as he sat down to eat with the rest. Soon his plate was empty and he returned for more. And then a third helping.

'This fire indeed burns brightly, a feast of Kurnous, would not satiate his need,' remarked Aranarha.

Korlandril looked down at the food piled in front of him. He saw no wrong in it. Min had warned him to eat as much as he could while he felt hungry.

'It would be better that I do not go to my first battle weak with hunger,' he said, before setting to his latest course with relish.

'At least our armour is polymorphic,' laughed Arhulesh. 'It won't feel any tighter!'

Korlandril grinned and reached for a goblet of spiced lodefruit juice. He raised it in toast to Arhulesh and downed its contents in a long gulp. Smacking his lips, he thudded the goblet back onto the table.

'If battle tastes so sweet, the greater banquet is yet to come!' he declared.

* * *

The wayseer stood in front of an oval, gold-rimmed portal, one of several such gateways extruded from the wraithbone floor in the webway chambers at the rear of the warship. She was swathed in a voluminous robe of deep purple. Her white hair was parted in the middle and fell in two long locks in front of her shoulders, weighted with rings of a metallic blue. About her extended hand orbited five white runes, twisting gently in the psychic breeze of her magistrations as she aligned the entrance with a temporary webway strand into the material universe. The mirror-like skein of energy within the portal's frame shimmered occasionally, causing the runes to dance with more agitation for a moment before settling into their tranquil circling.

'It is almost time, the portal will be open, we are the vanguard,' said Kenainath. He signalled for the squad to don their helmets.

The red-washed taint on his vision made Korlandril think of a film of blood covering his eyes. He was full of energy; not nervous, just eager. This was the culmination of so much time, so much effort in practice, and just as the webway portal was opening, he felt a new door was opening on his life. He longed to race through and grasp whatever opportunities lay beyond.

Fighting the urge to fidget, forcing himself to stand placidly and wait for the wayseer to complete her ritual, Korlandril idly checked his armour's systems. Rather, he allowed part of his consciousness to merge with the suit a little more deeply than usual. He felt nothing amiss.

Slightly bored, he pulled himself back from the suit's rhythms and gently touched the trigger on his pistol, activating the psychic link. Immediately a view-within-a-view appeared in his left eye, like a keyhole in his vision. Through that small opening he could see the green-veined floor of the portal chamber. Lifting his arm, he played the pistol across the webway portal and settled on the wayseer, the image relayed by the seeing-gem of the pistol's sight. A small rune appeared beside the wayseer – the symbol of Alaitoc – indicating she was friend not foe.

It was a precautionary measure, unlikely to be used, but the designers of the pistol perhaps had lived in more turbulent times, when even the craftworlds had raised their weapons against each other. The viewfinder was useful at range but distracting at close quarters. Korlandril dismissed it with a thought and his vision returned to normal.

The faint padding of boots caused him to turn towards the arched entranceway to the chamber. Seven figures entered, shadowy and indistinct; rangers swathed in cameleoline coats, now the white and pale green colour of the chamber, outlines barely discernable. One pulled back her hood revealing a beautiful face, a tattoo of a red tear beneath her left eye, and winked at Korlandril. Yet for all her charming looks and frivolity, there was something about the ranger that disturbed him. His gaze fell to her waystone and he sensed something otherworldly there. She was not on the Path, her senses and spirit free to soar to whatever heights it could, and to plunge to whatever depths awaited.

Like Aradryan, thought Korlandril. Free, but vulnerable.

'You'll be following us onto Eileniliesh,' she said, turning her attention to Kenainath. The exarch nodded without comment.

The other rangers were unrecognisable. Korlandril wondered if one of them was Aradryan. He surreptitiously angled his pistol towards the rangers and activated the Scorpion's Eye, hoping to see their faces. Flicking through various spectra, both visible and invisible, he discovered the rangers' cloaks dissipated not only ordinary light, but also heat and other signatures as might be detected by an enemy. With a disappointed sigh, he switched it off again and turned back to the portal.

The flat plane was now slowly swirling with colours, mostly blues and greens, with occasional twists of red and black. It was mesmerising, and Korlandril felt himself drawn towards it. Out of curiosity he raised his pistol towards the portal, but Min stepped in front of him, placing a hand on his arm.

'Not wise,' said the warrior with a shake of his head.

Korlandril took the warning at face value and lowered his arm.

'The portal is open,' declared the wayseer. The runes floated in a vertical line above her open palm.

The ranger pulled up her hood, her exquisite features disappearing from view. With a gesture made vague by her long coat, she strode into the miasmic plane of the portal and disappeared. Unslinging rifles almost as tall as themselves, the other rangers followed her.

Kenainath moved his gaze from one Striking Scorpion to the next, as if gauging them. He could see nothing of their expressions, but Korlandril wondered if the exarch had senses beyond those of a normal eldar. With no word of instruction, Kenainath plunged in after the rangers.

Korlandril spared a glance at the rest of the squad, but none of them looked back at him. He wondered if they shared the same sense of achievement as he did, about to embark on his first foray into battle. One-by-one they walked into the webway.

His excitement at a crescendo, Korlandril stepped after them.

The webway passage cut towards the surface of Eileniliesh between the real universe and the otherworld of the warp, a flattened tube cutting through what at first appeared to be roiling water. It was impossible to tell the true colour of the tunnel through his lenses, but he would not have been surprised if it had been a sea green or blue. He half-expected to see the red flashes of a firefish going past, or the silver shimmer of a starfin shoal.

The one thing that was strange was the sense of motion, in that there was not any. Though he stalked forwards at some pace behind the others, nothing changed in his surrounds. It felt like he was walking on the spot. The web-tunnel undulated occasionally, but Korlandril could not tell whether this was due to movement in the warp-passage or simply a shift in the energies that were kept at bay by its immaterial walls.

Peering hard through the invisible force wall, Korlandril could make out the indistinct threads of other webway passages, twisting about this one and each other, coming together and parting like the strands of a thread. Of the squads using these other tunnels, he could see nothing.

'How long is this?' he asked, his voice relayed to the other members of the squad.

'Just a temporary burrowing,' replied Arhulesh. 'We'll be down on the surface in a few moments.'

Korlandril peered past the shoulders of those in front, hoping to see something. In his imagination it would be a shimmering veil through which he would be able to see the trees and grass of Eileniliesh.

Instead, the others flickered out of sight as they passed a certain point, and taking another step, Korlandril found himself walking on soft turf. He was vaguely disappointed.

'Ready your weapons, battle will be soon at hand, Khaine's bloody playfield.'

Korlandril fell into position at the centre of the squad just behind Kenainath and looked around. Above, the sky was filled with clouds, the light of two huge moons dimly pushing through their gloom. They were on a hillside, gently sloping upwards in front of him, and at the summit there stood a narrow, solitary tower. Light burned within its pinnacle, casting long shadows from the scattered rocks and trees. Korlandril scanned the hillside for the rangers but they were already gone, or so well hidden from view that he could no longer see them.

His mouth was dry and he licked his lips, while he flexed his fingers on his weapons to keep himself relaxed, dissipating a tiny fraction of the energy burning inside him. He wondered how close they were to the orks, but refrained from asking. His question was answered as they crested the hill, revealing a swathe of black smoke hanging low over a forest that grew in the valley beyond.

Korlandril heard a growl of anger from one of the others but he was not sure who had made it. It might have even been himself. The sight of the crude billowings of the orks swathing the beautiful trees darkened Korlandril's spirit. Thoughts of glorious battle dissipated and all that remained was a desire to destroy the creatures that assailed this world.

'Follow the river,' came the voice of the lead ranger from the communications crystal just beside Korlandril's right ear.

Kenainath cut to the right and brought them to a narrow, fast-flowing water course, birthed somewhere within the hill and gushing forth along a rocky defile. The exarch and squad crossed easily at the river head, and moved swiftly down the hillside and into the sparse trees at the edge of the forest.

Aside from the gurgling and splashing of the river, Korlandril could hear the rustling of the leaves overhead and the sigh of the wind through the lush grass at his feet. Of his companions, he could hear nothing, moving as silently as shadows. In the distance, as yet barely audible, there sounded a greater disturbance – the noise of rough engines and cruel laughter.

'The orks have occupied Hirith-Hreslain,' reported the ranger.

Another voice came to Korlandril's ear. He did not recognise it, but it spoke with sombre authority.

'The settlement straddles the river,' intoned the speaker. 'The majority of the enemy are on the webward side, closest to our positions. Their leaders are on the opposite bank. Firuthein, position your warriors along the river behind and prepare to disable any transports crossing from the far side. Kenainath, move your squad towards the bridge to deal with any survivors of the Fire Dragons' strike.'

'It shall be, as you command, with Khaine's will,' replied a sonorous voice, presumably the exarch Firuthein.

'The Scorpions wait, we will strike from the shadow, none will survive us.' Kenainath's tone and cadence were instantly familiar.

'That was the autarch,' explained Min when Korlandril asked who he had been listening to. 'He's coordinating the main attack, and we're to stop any enemy reinforcements.'

'An ambush,' said Arhulesh. 'Exactly our type of fighting.'

The river widened and shallowed rapidly as it reached the valley floor. The trees grew close to the banks, but now a wide expanse separated the two sides, the dim light of the night sky a deep orange to Korlandril's eyes. The further the Striking Scorpions advanced, the more they were separated from the rest of the army, which was angling towards the greater concentration of orks on the other river bank. Korlandril glanced over his left shoulder and saw the squad of Firuthein's Fire Dragons striding purposefully along the opposite side of the river.

A sudden movement – or rather the sudden stillness of the rest of the squad – alerted Korlandril to something amiss. He froze in place, poised in the stance of Leaf that Cuts.

A ripple disturbed the placid surface of the water, trailed by a thin stream of bubbles. Something was moving towards the squad, just under the waterline. With a thought, Korlandril brought up the wide-spectrum view of his helmet and gazed beneath the water's reflective surface. The 'something' was large and snake-like, five times as long as an eldar is tall, with three pairs of flippers and a wide-fluked tail. Two large hearts beat beside each other in its chest and Korlandril could see strings of cartilage running the length of its body overlaid with a labyrinth of arteries and strange organs. Korlandril could see the flow of heat from these out to the extremities as the creature swished lazily past, within easy pistol shot.

It gave not a first glance towards the Striking Scorpions swathed from the moonlight by the trees shrouding the bank. Korlandril watched it glide behind him and nodded to Kenainath, signalling that it was safe to continue.

Under the cover of the thickening cloud – the light of the moons now all but gone – the squad made swift progress and were soon within sight of the arcing bridge that connected to the two parts of Hirith-Hreslain. On the far bank – the webward side closest to the eldar army – tall towers rose from amongst the trees. Smoke billowed from narrow windows and soot stained pale walls. On the nearer side the buildings were more widely spaced and a great clearing had been cut into the forest. This had once been pastureland for the grazing beasts of the Exodites. Now it was a ruin, the carcasses of the great reptilian herbivores heaped onto roaring pyres or left in the trampled mud where they had been slaughtered. Crude standards of flat metal icons and ragged banners had been driven into the soil and lashed to the cracked tiled roofs of the outbuildings.

Ramshackle, wheeled vehicles rumbled across the turf, their thick tyres churning up swathes of dirt, cutting gashes into the fertile ground. The air was choked with their fumes. Metal-sided and roofed sheds had been erected over the ruins of farmsteads and barns, where clanging echoed through the night sky and the bright spark of welding torches mingled with the flicker of naked flames and the stark light of artificial lamps. Piles of junk littered the open ground: twisted mechanical workings, badly hewn logs, shredded tyres, the bones of dead food and heaps of steaming dung. Haphazard chimneys jutted from the worksheds spewing oily smoke, leaving a cloud of smog lingering over the filthy campsite.

Through the murk, with the aid of his lens-filters, Korlandril could see the orks, the first he had encountered though he had heard tales from the others of the squad. If anything, their horrific stories did not do justice to the brutal aliens.

There were several dozen of the green-skinned monsters. Most of them were far larger than Korlandril, even hunched and crouching around the fires. Some were enormous, perhaps half again as tall as the Aspect Warriors, and three or four times as broad. They growled and cackled to each other in their brutish tongue, striking out to emphasise their points.

Around and about the encampment scurried a host of smaller creatures, carrying food and weapons, or simply scrabbling about with each other in petty conflicts. Their higher-pitched voices added a dissonant cut through the rumble of the orks' bellows and roars, jarring in Korlandril's ears.

Without thought, Korlandril raised his weapons, disgusted by what he saw.

'It is not yet time, temper your anger and hate, vengeance will come soon,' warned Kenainath.

* * *

The moments crept past as the Striking Scorpions lay in wait. Korlandril watched the orks, wary of discovery, but not a single greenskin warrior or their diminutive servants spared a glance towards the river. He turned his attention back to the towers of the main settlement. Here the destruction of the orks was even more evident.

The bucket-jawed monstrosities had set up their camp in the ruins of the settlement. Walls had been smashed in to widen doorways and windows, and the detritus of the alien invaders was piled everywhere. They had been here for a short while and had made ugly repairs and 'improvements' with sheets of metal riveted into the elegant stone buildings, and planks of untreated wood lashed into place to form balconies and battlements.

Hundreds of the creatures milled about, arguing and fighting, eating and shouting. With each heartbeat Korlandril came to despise them more. They were an affront to everything he had learnt to appreciate and love. They were an oafish, unsubtle, ill-disciplined rabble. They were incarnations of anarchy and violence, having nothing of culture, wit or art. Their brutality was their strength, their ignorance their armour against the darker things of the universe that preyed on more civilised species.

Though every part of Korlandril strained to unleash the wrath of Khaine, to wipe out these barbaric figures that had survived from the earliest legends of the eldar, a small, reasoning part of his brain told him that it would never be so. If the eldar had been unable to remove the blight of the orks from the galaxy when their civilisation had been at the height of its power, before the darkness of the Fall, they had little hope now. They were so few, so scattered, in comparison to the grunting, seething hordes that now held sway over so many worlds that had once belonged to the eldar.

Korlandril found comfort in a singular thought: by the time the next dawn came, there would be fewer orks to despoil the stars. With skill and determination, some would die by his own hand. The prospect renewed his thrill of being in battle, even though not a shot had yet been fired or a blade swung in anger.

He focussed on visualisations of the combat techniques he would employ against the ungainly monsters. He imagined eluding their clumsy blows while his own weapons cut them down with ease. These brutes had slain other eldar – admittedly backward Exodites, but eldar all the same – and he was in a position to exact red payment for that crime.

No more orders came or were needed. The exarchs knew their roles and the warriors knew how to fight. The only announcement of the battle commencing was a thunderous explosion on the webward side of the river. Thin vapour trails marked the passage of missiles from the Dark Reapers as blossoms of incandescent ruin engulfed the orks. The soft whickering of shuriken catapult fire was soon lost in the tumult of the orks' alarms – blaring mechanical horns, resounding metallic drums and deafening bellows.

Korlandril wanted to join the fray and eased himself forwards to stand beside Kenainath. The water lapped gently at the exarch's knees as he stood motionless in the shallows of the river, eyes fixed on the orks on the right-hand bank. Korlandril turned his attention there and saw the greenskins organising quickly. For all their unsophisticated ways, they responded rapidly to the attack; the promise of bloodshed roused them into a unity of destructive purpose.

Buggies with heavy weapons on pivots slewed back and forth, gathering in makeshift squadrons as they headed towards the bridge. Behind them, two clanking, half-track war engines rumbled into life, each as large as the worksheds and of similar crude construction. Huge tyres kicked up clods of dirt, tracks clanked over rusting wheels as the machines lurched towards the bridge.

The burliest orks clambered up steps and ladders onto their open transport beds while others chased behind. Belts of ammunition were slapped into large-bore guns while smaller weapons dotted across the mobile fortresses were pivoted towards the river. Some of the greenskins wildly shot their weapons into the sky in their excitement, all of them hooted and hollered war cries. The armoured carriers belched forth spumes of thick smoke from their many exhausts, the smog washing heavily towards the river on the brisk wind. The mechanical beasts ground forwards implacably, churning through the piles of rotting carcasses and debris.

The first of the war buggies reached the bridge and raced across, two more not far behind. At the webward end of the bridge, concealed in the shattered ruins of a towering gatehouse that arched over the span, Firuthein and his Fire Dragons moved forwards. The exarch stepped up to the jagged remains of a window and levelled his lance-like firepike.

A glaring burst of energy erupted from the weapon and hurtled towards the lead buggy. It caught the light vehicle on the nearside above its front wheel, exploding with the power of a miniature sun. Front axle ripped asunder, the buggy flipped dramatically, screeching along the retaining wall of the arcing bridge, trailing a storm of sparks. Korlandril smiled as he saw the buggy's driver dashed against the wall, flopping like a child's doll, while the gunner was broken and smeared along the white stone of the barrier.

The oncoming vehicles swerved around the smoking remnants, their heavy guns chattering, muzzle flare illuminating the orks' yelling, fanged faces. The bullets tore chunks from the walls of the gatehouse, but Firuthein's warriors stood their ground against the wild, sporadic fire. As the closest buggy came within range, the Fire Dragons unleashed their deadly breath, the air churning with white-hot radiation from their fusion guns.

The gunner of the next buggy exploded in a mist of rapidly evaporating organs and blood, his legs and lower torso spilling from the cradle in which he had been sat. The engine of the buggy burst into flames, swiftly followed by a detonation in the fuel tank, turning the vehicle into a careening fireball that ploughed into the ruined gatehouse before exploding into a cloud of debris and mechanical parts.

The larger transports had picked up speed. The nearest had a great plough-like ram on its front and hurled aside the ruins of the first destroyed buggy. From its back, its cargo of warriors spewed forth a hail of inaccurate fire from their barking guns, streaming bullets in all directions in a frenzy of violence. Heavier arms spat a more staccato beat, thudding their shells purposefully towards the Fire Dragons.

Korlandril watched with horror as one salvo found its mark, tearing great shards of armour from one of the Fire Dragons. The warrior's body – lifeless Korlandril assumed – was flung out of sight into the mangle of the ruined tower.

Korlandril was conflicted for a moment. He was not sure what to think. A distant, whispering doubt told him that this was horrific. He had just seen another eldar brutally slain. Such a thing was perhaps the most traumatic sight he might witness. This quiet voice was drowned out by an altogether more feral roaring, which bayed for Korlandril to avenge the death of the fallen Fire Dragon.

In those few heartbeats of uncertainty, much had happened. At the near end of the bridge the ram-fronted transport had fire licking from under its tracks, gears turned to a molten slurry by Firuthein's firepike. The orks were tumbling over the sides and from the tailgate, gathering around a particularly vast creature with a metal banner pole tied to its back and a necklace of cracked skulls hanging on a chain around its neck. In one hand it carried a short but heavy pistol, in the other a double-headed axe with whirring chainblades.

'The warlord comes out, now it is time to strike swift, and bring down the beast!' cried Kenainath. The exarch was surging forwards through the water even as he gave the shout. Korlandril followed on his heel and the others close behind.

In the darkness and smoke, the Striking Scorpions arrived at the bridge quickly and unseen. The orks had laboured to shove aside the remnants of their transport, urged on by the bellows of their leader and threats from his pistol and axe.

Sudden glimmers of brightness attracted Korlandril's gaze to his right, past the ork warlord and his bodyguard. Like miniature supernovae, sparkling portals were opening up around the orks. Guided by spirit beacons placed by the rangers, the rest of the eldar force was arriving from the webway, surrounding the brutes to ensure none escaped. Squads burst from the ether with their weapons firing; squads of jetbike-riding Shining Spears charged out of the glimmering portals, their laser lances bright with power; caught between the converging squads, the orks died in droves.

Under the bridge Korlandril saw dark shapes, and at first thought they were foes. On closer inspection, he saw more Striking Scorpions: Aranarha's Fall of the Deadly Rain. They moved to cut off the orks' progress at the webward end of the bridge while the Deadly Shadow advanced from the rear.

Beyond Aranarha's squad, battle raged. Bolts of energy and screaming bullets criss-crossed the Exodite towers. The Aspect Warriors attacked with sure and deliberate violence, cutting down all in their path, following in the wake of the Avatar. The shriek of Banshee masks mixed with an unearthly, deafening ululation.

The Avatar of Khaine strode into the orks, the chilling sound coming from the fire-tipped spear in its right hand – the *Suin Daellae*, the Doom that Wails. Twice as tall as the Aspect Warriors surrounding it, the incarnation of the Bloody-Handed One was a nightmarish vision of metal and fire. Its unearthly flesh glowed with a ruddy light from within, its face a moulded visage of pure rage, eyes burning slits of white heat. The Avatar cast its spear through the bodies of a dozen foes before the weapon circled fully and returned to its grasp. Artificial lightning blasts from strange ork weapons crackled across the Avatar's metal hide while bullets pattered and ricocheted all around.

Korlandril had no more time to watch the ongoing orgy of violence – his own desire to shed blood heightened by the sight – for they had reached the winding steps up to the bridge. Kenainath broke into a run, mounting the stairwell swiftly, the rest of the squad following eagerly.

The steps brought them out not far behind the warlord as it advanced towards the main eldar attack, still unaware of the threat emerging from behind. Seven of its brutal subordinates clustered around the alien, shouting encouragement to their smaller minions who were being cut down in swathes by the eldar attack.

Kenainath closed in at a run, his shuriken pistol spitting a hail of razor-sharp discs. Korlandril followed suit, spraying a volley at the closest ork mentor, the salvo leaving a line of shredded flesh across the back of the creature's left shoulder. It turned and glared at Korlandril with beady eyes beneath a heavy, furrowed brow and then opened its fang-filled mouth in a bellow of warning. Its teeth were as long as Korlandril's fingers, spittle flying in heavy gobbets. The creature hefted a large cleaver in both hands, a shimmer of energy playing along its jagged blade. From its eyes to its posture to its roar, everything about the ork signalled murderous intent.

It was a sight Korlandril could never have anticipated and his heart fluttered for a moment, gripped with primitive fear of the gargantuan monster confronting him. As before, Korlandril's response to his fear was a surge of hatred and rage. He pounded forwards, peeling away from Kenainath to close with his chosen foe. The blades of the Striking Scorpion's chainsword blurred into life, fuelled by Korlandril's wrath to such a speed that they screamed as they split the air.

The ork swung its weapon in a long arc towards Korlandril's head. He ducked easily beneath the ponderous attack, his chainsword flashing up towards the underarm of the ork, teeth cutting through muscle and artery. Blood splashed from the wound onto Korlandril's helmeted face as he spun past. Through the Aspect suit he could smell the stench of the ork's life fluid and taste the iron in its blood.

Korlandril's mandiblasters spat laser fire as he sidestepped behind the ork, tearing at the flesh of its back and shoulders. The alien swung heavily around to its right seeking the cause of its pain, blade held overhead. Korlandril did not stand still long enough for the blow to land. He flexed his knees, crouched into Dormant Lightning, and then propelled himself forwards on the tips of his toes, unleashing River of Sorrow. His shuriken pistol fire raked the left side of the ork's face even as Korlandril's chainsword rasped through the thick muscle of its right thigh, gnawing at bone as the Aspect Warrior once again leapt past his unwieldy foe.

The ork collapsed with a grunt, the cleaver falling from its grasp as the alien's muscles spasmed in its death throes. Korlandril performed the coup-de-grace, cleaving his chainsword back-handed into the ork's left temple, shearing through and slicing deep into its brain.

A surge of victory filled Korlandril. The ruined flesh laid out on the stone of the bridge was a greater work of art than any he had ever conceived before. No Dreaming had matched the vitality – the heart-wrenching reality – of combat. Korlandril stood over his fallen foe, admiring the patterns made by the spatters of blood on the pale road-way. He looked at his own armour, smeared with filth, and was jubilant. Korlandril's waystone pulsed in time to the thunderous beating of his heart.

'Korlandril!' Min shouted.

In his ecstasy, Korlandril barely heard his name. He turned to find the rest of the squad.

Something immense loomed in front of him, blotting out the sky with its massive shadow. Korlandril raised his chainsword to Watcher Over Sky, but the defence was pitifully weak against the crushing weight of the warlord's axe. Fang-like chainblades smashed through Korlandril's weapon, sending shards in all directions, and bit deep into the Aspect Warrior's gut.

The force of the blow hurled Korlandril into the air, sending him crashing into the side wall of the bridge.

Horror filled Korlandril as the warlord took a step towards him. The Striking Scorpion was numb with shock and collapsed, his legs suddenly lifeless. He couldn't tear his eyes away from the lumbering ork closing in on him, but could feel his life seeping away through the ragged cut in his belly. His armour tried as best it could to knit the wound, but the damage was too severe.

Kenainath stepped between Korlandril and the ork warlord, the crackling claw of his right fist raised in defiance. The warlord bellowed a wordless challenge and Kenainath responded with offence, smashing the Scorpion's Claw across the chin of the warlord, cracking bone, the fist's powerfield rupturing flesh.

Then the pain hit Korlandril, rippling up his spine, sending a tremor of agony through his brain. He clamped his teeth together to suppress the scream, tears in his eyes.

The rest of the squad wove a deadly dance around their exarch, landing blows upon the warlord, which flailed hopefully at its swifter foes. Blood streamed from dozens of wounds across its chest and upper arms.

The last Korlandril saw was the long blade of Aranarha cleaving into the arm of the warlord, lopping off the limb above the elbow.

Korlandril blinked back into consciousness. He thought he was drowning for a moment, before he recognised the swirling energies of the webway. Hands were around him, carrying him. He eased his head to the left and recognised the armour of Bechareth. He heard voices inside his head but could make no sense of them. They were stern, unflinching. The pain was intense, setting his whole body a-tremble.

He could take no more. He was suffering too much.

He passed out again.

PAIN

During the War in Heaven, Khaine the Bloody-Handed One slew a great many eldar warriors. Mother Isha became fearful that the eldar would be exterminated, so she went to Asuryan the all-seeing and begged for him to intervene. Asuryan also feared that Khaine's rage would destroy not only the eldar, but the gods. He consented to aid Isha, but demanded of her to give up a lock of her immortal hair. This tress of hair Asuryan bound into the hair of Eldanesh so that he and all of his descendants could be healed by Isha's love for them.

Gentle chiming awoke Korlandril. He found himself lying upon a firm, embracing mattress, warm to the touch. A cool breeze passed over his face. He kept his eyes closed, savouring the sensation of tranquility. At the edge of hearing he detected subtle notes, a drifting music that surrounded him, stroked at his spirit.

As he recovered consciousness, conflict disturbed Korlandril's dream-like thoughts. An image pushed at his memories, insistent but formless. He pushed back, trying to keep the memory at bay.

Through his eyelids Korlandril sensed a pulsing red light. His breath came in time to the surges of crimson energy flowing into his brain. It was slow at first but as it quickened in pace, Korlandril's breathing and pulse became swifter. He had no sense of time passing other than the narrowing gap between each breath and each heartbeat.

The red light had become a flickering strobe, alternating between harsh red and soft yellow. Korlandril hyperventilated, gasping rapidly, his chest aching with the exertion though the rest of his body remained motionless. His nostrils flared as he tried to fill his lungs but the flashing lights made him expel each breath before it had barely entered him.

'Awaken,' said a gentle voice. 'Remember.'

The words trickled into his mind and he was powerless to resist their command.

The barrier in his memories ripped asunder and a vast green beast with razor claws burst towards him. Blood drooled from its fangs. Pain flared.

Korlandril screamed with what little breath he had and fell back into darkness.

He floated, his body weightless, tied to the universe by the most slender tether of his consciousness. The voice returned, but this time there were no other sounds, no light save for a dim and distant pale green.

'You are in the care of Isha's healers,' said the voice. Korlandril could not tell if it was male or female, so softly spoken was the tone. 'Nothing can harm you here. You are safe. You heal. You must release the power from the Tress of Isha.'

'It hurts,' Korlandril said, numb, barely recognising his own voice.

'The pain will pass, but you cannot heal your wound until you confront it.'

'The pain is too much,' whispered Korlandril.

'The pain is not of your body but of your spirit. The Tress of Isha will free you from your pain. I am Soareth, and I will help you.'

'I do not wish to die,' Korlandril said sombrely.

'Then you must heal,' replied Soareth. The healer was male, Korlandril decided, and young. Soareth spoke with the language of youth. He did not wish to be healed by a novice.

'What do you know of death?' he demanded, growing angry.

'Nothing,' replied Soareth. 'I am an advocate of life. Listen to me carefully, Korlandril. You still wear your war-mask. You cannot have one hand upon Khaine's sword and the other upon Isha's gift. You must take off the mask.'

'You would leave me defenceless!'

'The only enemy that you must fight is yourself.' Soareth spoke so quietly Korlandril could barely hear him. Or perhaps there was something else that made the healer's voice so distant. 'There is no other battle here, Korlandril. Your wound is grave, but you have the strength to overcome it. I will help you.'

'You are little more than a child, I demand to be attended by someone with more experience,' Korlandril said flatly. He felt himself frown.

'I am trained to help you heal, Korlandril. The power to survive does not reside within me, it is within you. Body and spirit are as one. You must strengthen your spirit to strengthen your body. I will show you how you will do this, and guide you to the Tress of Isha. With its power, you will heal. First you must calm yourself, release yourself from Khaine's grip.'

'I cannot,' snarled Korlandril.

'What is it that you love, Korlandril?'

The warrior dismissed the question. There was no love in battle.

Soareth repeated the question, but this time there was a subtle change in the timbre of his voice. Love. The word began to resonate with Korlandril. There had been something he had once loved, before Khaine had taken him. If only he could remember.

A gentle vibration stirred Korlandril's fingers. It was the slightest tremor but it brought feeling to his fingertips. He felt them brushing through something. Something with fine strands. Brushing through hair.

He stroked Thirianna's head as they watched white-plumed snow finches reeling to and fro across the cliffs in the Dome of Infinite Tides. It was an absent-minded gesture, no intent behind it. Her hand was on his knee as they sat cross-legged on the shale beach and looked up at the towering pale rocks. Though there had been no motive behind that soft caress, the sensation stirred feelings inside Korlandril. Desire rose in him and he stroked her hair again, luxuriating in the closeness between them. He turned his head to look at her, admiring her beautiful face in profile, silhouetted against the low light from the distant wall of the dome. Her gaze was fixed on something far away, seeing something other than birds. Korlandril withdrew his hand, suddenly embarrassed at the gesture. Despite his discomfort, he felt at peace with the feelings now holding sway over him.

Blood sprayed into Korlandril's face, drowning him with a wave of thick red fluid. He sputtered and spat, clawing it from his cheeks, wiping it from his lips and eyes. But the blood kept coming, pouring from his eyes, dribbling from his mouth, seeping from every pore. He coughed, hacking up blood and tissue, despoiling his skin with its sticky gobbets.

Korlandril awoke with a dull ache in every part of his body, and a sharper pain in his abdomen. He suddenly realised where he was and shouted out, a wordless cry of fear echoing sharply around him. Still he could not open his eyes. He wasn't sure why. Perhaps he couldn't bring himself to look upon the source of his pain, the great wound in his stomach that was leeching the life from him.

'Sleep,' said a quiet voice in his ear. He thought he recognised it, but before he could put a name to the voice he was swallowed up by a gentle somnolence.

A rhythmic beating accompanied a slow pulsing of blue light behind Korlandril's eyes. He felt tiny quivers of movement on his skin, like the scampering feet of an insect. It moved simultaneously from the back of his neck down each arm and along his spine, forking at his waist to run down his feet.

'Welcome back, Korlandril.'

Soareth. Korlandril dragged the name from a dark recess in his memories. Something told him not to delve any deeper. He would not like what he saw.

'I am well again?' he asked, surprised by the hoarseness of his words.

'No, not yet,' said Soareth. 'But you have returned to us from the grip of Khaine. You can open your eyes.'

Korlandril prised open one heavy lid, cautious, fearing brightness. The room was softly lit, barely a twilight glow surrounded him. He opened the other eye and glanced around. The shaven-headed Soareth stood at the foot of the bed, a single-piece white robe hanging loosely from bony shoulders. In his hand he held a jewel-studded tablet. His fingers danced over the coloured gems and the room shifted around Korlandril; that is, the colours shifted, creating darker shadows, intensifying the light. The chamber felt smaller.

'Do not be afraid,' said Soareth.

Korlandril tried to sit up so that he could look down at the ruin that he knew his stomach to be. He couldn't move, and said as much.

'I have induced a paralysis for your own safety,' Soareth said. 'The wound has bound but a little. You must help your body complete the healing process. You must draw on the Tress of Isha.'

Korlandril attempted to nod.

'What must I do?' he asked.

'Focus on the ceiling and relax,' said Soareth.

Korlandril looked up, seeing nothing but pearlesque off-white. He was aware of the pain in his abdomen and tried to push it aside so that he could concentrate.

'Do not hide from the pain,' warned Soareth. 'It must be confronted, not dismissed.'

The colours of the ceiling shifted, almost imperceptible at first, a slow merging of pastel colours barely discernable from the white. The colours flowed together and swirled, with no distinct line between them, leaving an impression of a strange meta-colour made up of them all.

'Chant with me,' said Soareth. He started a low intonation, just sounds without meaning, slow and purposeful. Korlandril followed, matching pitch and duration with the healer. His throat hummed with the sound, sending alternating ripples of calm and alertness through his body.

The chanting fluctuated, but Korlandril had the rhythm of it now and matched Soareth exactly. Above the warrior the mottling ceiling was pulsing with life, slow flashes hidden within the maelstrom of colour-energy.

Korlandril shuddered and gave a moan, his synapses flaring from the awakening frequencies pouring into his senses. The tightness in his stomach was sharp, the pain dragging at his thoughts like an anchor. He wanted to fly free of its weight, but the invisible chain held him down.

Eyelids drooping, Korlandril succumbed to the mesmeric influence of the light and sound. He was dimly aware of Soareth moving around him, still chanting, running an angular crystal along nodal parts of Korlandril's body. Psychic energy earthed between Korlandril and the healer, flaring briefly along pain-filled nerves, spasming cells and dilating arteries.

The room went as black as the gulf between stars, swallowing up Korlandril. He could see nothing but inky depths. Raising a hand, he could not even see his waggling fingers. He felt dispossessed of his body and tried to float upwards, buoyed by his own lightness. Something snagged at him, keeping him in place.

A star glittered to his left and he turned to face it. Other pinpricks of light sparkled into life, one at a time, until he was surrounded by a gently revolving constellation of millions of lights. Some were reddish in hue, others bright blue or harsh yellow. He was drawn to a golden star just above him. He reached out and found that he could see the vaguest outline of his hand in the starlight. The stars were close, close enough to touch. His fingers enclosed the warm gold, the light creeping between his fingers, glowing through his flesh.

The star touched his palm and Korlandril was in his chambers, looking up at his mother. Her long silver and black hair hid half her face, but she was smiling. Korlandril played with his animadoll, holding it in his tiny hands, making it wave its flaccid arms with his infant thoughts. The dough-like figure danced jerkily, mirroring Korlandril's own undeveloped movements. Its noseless face creased into a smile.

'This is not where you will find your pain.' Korlandril's mother spoke with Soareth's voice.

He opened his palm and allowed the golden star to drift away. He looked for another, shying away from the baleful ruddy glows behind him, his fingers aiming for a pale blue spark. It bobbed and weaved, trying to elude him, and Korlandril laughed at its antics, still thinking like a child.

Finally his grip ensnared the elusive light.

The lights of the Hall of Inner Harmonies were bright and colourful, dappling the marble-like floor with vitality. Korlandril danced along the line of laughing and singing eldar, linking hands with them as he passed, Aradryan passing down the opposite side of the line. The music was fast and lively, Korlandril's feet skipping quickly across the hard floor, barely touching the ground.

'It is not joy that you seek, Korlandril, it is your pain,' Soareth warned through the mouth of a young, pretty reveller.

Reluctantly, Korlandril spun away from the gala, releasing his hold on the memory-star. He twirled exuberantly a few times more, but his spin brought him closer to the glaring red light that he knew held the memory of pain.

He didn't want to touch it. He could feel its heat, its poison.

'You must,' Soareth told him.

Korlandril's hand trembled as he reached out, arcing his body away from its bloody gleam in fear. His hand closed into a fist, refusing his commands.

'I cannot,' he hissed.

'You will die.' There was urgency in Soareth's tone.

The light of the red star was fading, flickering away into the distance. The constellation around Korlandril dimmed, the darkness and shadows growing stronger, swathing him. He was torn between two fears, his hand refusing to grasp the memory of his injury while his mind shrank back from the engulfing blackness.

The stars, almost gone, began to oscillate slowly and music stirred Korlandril's thoughts. Soareth sang gently, every note calm and measured, setting up a resonance around Korlandril that filled him with their vibrancy. The stars brightened and Korlandril's hope grew, fuelling them further.

The red star was almost invisible, just the slightest smudge in the darkness. In moments it would be gone.

Korlandril lunged forwards, eyes screwed shut, and snatched at the dying star.

With a jolt he felt crushing weight. Opening his eyes, he found himself bound with silver chains. A huge shadow loomed over him as he wrestled and wriggled with his bonds. It was enormous, silhouetted against a sky of dripping blood. Its eyes were red coals and its hands were fanged jaws. The sky growled at Korlandril as he struggled to free himself, voiceless and impotent. He fell limp and rolled to his side, closing his eyes, waiting for the fatal blow.

'Face your fear!' Soareth's voice was a harsh snarl, stinging Korlandril into action.

With an agonised yowl, Korlandril surged up, the silver chains parting, sending shattered links sailing into the air.

On his feet, Korlandril saw something glowing behind the shadow-ork, its golden aura pushing back the curtain of blood that filled his mind. Korlandril dodged to his right, hoping to outwit the shadow-ork, but no matter where he moved, the golden glow was always behind his foe.

'I have no weapons!' Korlandril cried out plaintively. 'My war-mask is gone!'

His words echoed dully. Then silence.

'Soareth? Where are you?'

There was no reply.

'I need you, Soareth!'

Desperate, Korlandril cast about for some weapon but could find nothing, just a featureless plain of grey dust as far as the eye could see. There was no way of escaping; Korlandril was trapped with his would-be slayer.

The shadow-ork did not come at him, it just stood glowering between Korlandril and his prize. Its teeth-fingers gnashed occasionally with a ring of metal that jarred Korlandril's nerves.

Korlandril stumbled suddenly and fell into the dust. It was not dust at all, but ashes, and he spat them from his mouth. He could feel his strength fading.

He was dying.

Korlandril's eyes and limbs felt heavy. It would be easy, to slip down into the ash, to lay down his head and wait for his death. His pain would be gone, his fears and anguish with it. There would be peace.

Then he heard it. It was a thunderous thump, but so very far away. He waited an eternity until he heard it again. It was a double-thud, as of a heartbeat. It seemed so slow. But it was not his heart he heard. It was something else, something far greater than he, something as vast as the galaxy. Yet part of it was within him. Unconsciously, his hand went to his naked chest and there he felt a smooth, oval object. His waystone. Glancing down, he saw it bursting through his skin, ruby-bright, slick with his blood.

Death.

'Not yet!' screamed Korlandril, hurtling to his feet.

He raced towards the shadow-ork, fists raised. Blow after blow he rained down on its incorporeal form, clawing at it with his fingers, smashing it with his knuckles. His strength was sapped quickly; he could feel the last vestiges of his life fluttering away like moths.

With one last effort, Korlandril drove his fist into the shadow-ork's chest, through the heart. It billowed into formless cloud, swept away by a howling wind.

Korlandril saw then the golden coil that had hidden behind the beast. It appeared as a lock of shining hair wound about the twin stems of a red rose entwined with each other, their thorns sharp. Korlandril cared not for the potential pain. He leapt forward and his fingers closed tightly around the rose and its golden tress.

The thorns pierced his flesh but he ignored them, feeling the white heat of the golden thread.

Light exploded. Korlandril unravelled, streaming away in the wind as a million particles, disintegrated into a galaxy of whirling motes of light.

Each mote became Korlandril. He saw himself from within, racing along nerves and synapses; every fibre and cell, every vein and sinew, every corpuscle and protein. The golden light that was Korlandril raced through the systems of his body, purging and destroying the black stain of infection carried into him by the filthy weapon of the warlord. The cleansing fire of his rebirth burned away a budding neoplasm in his gut and cauterised the frayed blood vessels in his abdomen.

Dissipating, losing energy, Korlandril could hold his mind together no longer and slipped away, allowing the Tress of Isha to do its work.

Soareth was waiting for Korlandril when he awoke. The healer sat at the foot of the mattress, gem-slate in hand, watching the warrior carefully.

'You have done well,' said the healer, smiling warmly.

Korlandril groaned. There was still a pain in his abdomen, but it was not as intense as the sharp agony that lingered on the edge of his memories.

'I will live?' he asked hesitantly. Soareth answered with a nod and a broader smile.

'How long must I stay here?'

'Your physical wound is healing quickly,' Soareth said. He stood and moved beside Korlandril to lay a hand on his arm. 'The wounds of your spirit will take longer.'

Korlandril thought about this, confused.

'I feel well,' he said.

'That is because your fears and your woe are trapped inside that part of you which is your war-mask,' said Soareth, sympathy written in his features. 'You must expunge them lest they remain forever, a caustic blight in your psyche that will grow to taint every other part of your spirit.'

'I... I must don my war-mask again to do this?'

Soareth shook his head and gripped Korlandril's arm more tightly for a moment, offering encouragement.

'I can help you explore those parts of your mind now locked within your war-mask. It is not without risk, but I will help you.'

The walls, which had been a steady cream colour, flickered with brief veins of red. Soareth turned towards the door of the small room and Korlandril's eyes followed him.

Dressed in a tight-fitting bodysuit of dark green and orange, Aranarha stood in the doorway.

'Leave!' Soareth said sharply, rising to his feet. The exarch's cold stare passed over the healer and fell upon Korlandril. The room shuddered at the exarch's presence, shimmers of agitation rippling across the ceiling.

'How is our warrior now? I hope he is well, there is much for him to do,' said Aranarha.

'Your kind is not welcome here,' said Soareth, stepping between Korlandril and Aranarha. 'I tell you again, you must leave.'

The exarch shook his head, his twin braids slapping against his shoulders.

'We will deal with pain now, in our own manner, as befits a warrior.'

'No,' said Korlandril. He flinched at Aranarha's scowl but remained strong. 'I will remain here until I am ready. Then I will return to the Deadly Shadow.'

'This is not the place for these words, for these ideas,' hissed Soareth, a hand fluttering across his dark blue spirit stone. 'Do not speak of war in a place of healing.'

'Kenainath failed you before, his way has been wrong, it left you vulnerable. Return with me to my shrine, I will teach you well, make you stronger than before.' The exarch stepped past Soareth, though with care not to touch him, and extended an open hand to Korlandril, as if to help him to his feet.

'No,' said Korlandril, fists clenching by his sides. 'Soareth will help me heal. I trust him.'

'He will destroy your anger, make you weak with fear, and tear away your war-mask. The warrior fights his foes, not parley with them, seeking negotiation. I will show you the true way, the warrior's way, to confront these inner fears.'

Aranarha's tone was implacable and he stooped towards Korlandril, hand still offered.

Korlandril closed his eyes and remained silent. The exarch gave a growl of disapproval and Korlandril waited until his heavy footfalls had receded from the room before opening his eyes. The walls had returned to their placid state.

'I cannot go back, not ever,' he said.

Soareth looked doubtful.

'You think I should return to the shrine?' asked Korlandril, taken aback.

'You have taken only the first steps of your chosen Path,' said Soareth. 'It is unwise to leave early, with issues unresolved, our dreams and desires unfulfilled. Your journey is not yet done. I will help you heal so that you may continue upon it.'

'You heal me to send me back to battle?'

Soareth sighed.

'It is the burden of my Path, far too often, to mend that which will be broken again before too long.'

Korlandril thought about this for a long time before he spoke again.

'It must get depressing. To work in vain so often.'

The healer smiled and shrugged.

'To walk on the Path of the Healer is to give ourselves over to our hopes, to turn our backs on our fear of the future. Hope is an eternal spring from which I drink, and it tastes sweet forever.'

He stood and left the room, the light dimming as he passed out of the door. In the darkness, Korlandril saw vague shapes, moving on the boundary of awareness, looming just out of sight. He shuddered and knew that it would be some time before he was fit to return to the shrine.

RIVALRY

Hawk and Falcon, messengers of the gods both, were close friends. Ever they swept with each other through the skies and danced amongst the clouds. Though filled with regard for each other, they also loved to compete and to set each other dares of skill and bravery. They would race to the moon and back to see who was swiftest. They would goad each other into circling the realm of Bloody-Hand Khaine, daring each other to fly closer and closer to the War God. At dusk one day Falcon and Hawk spied some prey, flying easily upon the mountain winds. Falcon declared that he would be the first to catch it, but Hawk claimed that he was the swifter hunter. The two stooped down upon their prey. Hawk was faster at first, but Falcon beat his wings the harder and dove ahead. Not willing to give up the victory, Hawk surged on, cutting in front of Falcon. Annoyed by his friend's manoeuvre, Falcon batted a wing against Hawk's tail, sending his rival off course. Hawk returned quickly, flying into Falcon to slow down his dive. Their wings became entangled and the two of them fell out of the skies. Their prey flew away, laughing merrily, and the both of them went hungry that night.

The quiet of the shrine was different to the peace of the healing hall. The Deadly Shadow brooded in its silence, the stillness stifling, heavy with melancholy rather than offering solace.

Korlandril walked through the looming trees, choosing to enter by the way he had first arrived rather than the more direct passageways that ran beneath the dome to the shrine building. He had been away for some time and was not sure what welcome, or lack, he would receive from Kenainath and the others. Unsurprisingly, none had visited him in the healing halls. Aranarha's approach had been greatly against tradition, and Soareth had been agitated by it for several cycles after.

So it was with some apprehension that Korlandril walked softly along the winding trails, though not as much as his first coming to the shrine. He began to recover his feel for the place, sensing the presence of the shrine seeping back into his spirit, reawakening emotions that had been dormant. He relaxed as he realised that it had not been the reaction of his fellow warriors he feared but rather he had harboured a lingering doubt that he might not be able to recover his war-mask. The curling mists and strange groans and coughs from the dismal marshes were slowly awakening something inside Korlandril, stirring memories he had avoided whilst in the healing halls.

He came upon the black opening of the shrine's main portal and hesitated, peering into the strange darkness that filled the entranceway. It was the Deadly Shadow incarnate, the gloom of death and war that filled the shrine. Once he stepped into it, he would be back again on the Path of the Warrior.

He took another faltering step forward before a noise to his left distracted him. Min pushed his way through the foliage, exiting the ziggurat by some side door. He started upright, surprised to see Korlandril. Recovering quickly, Min smiled broadly and extended a palm in greeting.

'How have you fared?' asked Korlandril, returning the gesture. Min hesitated before replying.

'It is good to see that you are recovered from your injury,' he said.

'I am eager to recommence my training,' Korlandril replied. He studied Min's face for a moment, noting doubt and worry in the lines upon his forehead and the clench of his jaw. 'You did not answer my question.'

Min's eyes shifted defensively for a heartbeat and then resignation showed in his features.

'I will not be training alongside you, Korlandril,' Min admitted. He looked out through the mangrove, away from the shrine. His gaze remained distant as he continued. 'I am done with the Path of the Warrior.'

Korlandril felt a breath catch in his chest.

'How so? I can think of no other warrior, save Kenainath, more dedicated to the Deadly Shadow.'

'And that is the problem,' Min said heavily. 'My war-mask is fading. No, that is not true. My true face is fading, being replaced by my war-mask. I find myself remembering that which should not be remembered. I enjoy the memories of battle, the surge of excitement I feel when fighting. It is not good.'

Korlandril nodded, unsure what to say. The war-mask of the Aspect

Warrior served a two-fold purpose. The first was to allow the warrior to harness the energy of his anger and hatred and other negative emotions, giving them vent in battle. The second, and more important in some ways, was to act as a dividing barrier between war and peace. When not in his war-mask a warrior knew nothing of the heinous acts of violence he perpetrated whilst in his Aspect. He could slay and maim without guilt; a guilt that would crush the psyche of an eldar if allowed to dwell on it. That Min was haunted by feelings from his war-mask was a grave matter.

'You have made the right choice, Min,' Korlandril said, stepping forward to pat his companion on the arm. 'I will miss you by my side in training, but I am sure we will still see each other outside. What is it that you plan to do next?'

A fervent gleam entered Min's eyes and he grabbed Korlandril's wrists in his hands and stared earnestly into his eyes.

'It is unlikely we will see each other again, Korlandril. I have sailed close to temptation and to see you and the others would not be wise while you remain Aspect Warriors. I have come close to being trapped, of becoming something like Kenainath and Aranarha. I need to leave myself for a while, and think I will take the Path of the Dreaming. Promise me, Korlandril, that you should ever despise your war-mask. Do not allow it to become something you crave, as I nearly did. Realise that it has power over you and you should shun its promises.'

Korlandril laughed and gently prised himself from Min's tight grip.

'I have fought but one battle, I think I have many steps to take along this Path before its lures will tempt me to stay.'

'Do nothing rash! Keep that place of peace, which brings you back from the anger, close to your thoughts at all times. Fear lurks inside your war-mask, no matter what healing you have undergone. Do not let it feed your hatred or stir your anger too far.'

Korlandril waved away Min's concerns.

'I bid you good health and a prosperous journey, Min,' said Korlandril. 'I hope to see you again when my time as a Warrior is done. Until then, our Paths run different courses. If you wish to seek a guide for your Dreamings, I recommend Elronfirthir of Taleheac. Speak to the spirit-seers, they will find him for you.' He turned his back on Min and strode into the shrine, the chill of its shadow sending a thrill through him.

The inner chambers of the shrine were instantly familiar. Korlandril walked through the darkness without hesitation, navigating through the utter blackness to the armouring chamber. The light within was dim, no more than a ruddy glow from the walls, and in the gloom he saw the suits of armour arrayed along each wall.

Korlandril walked to his armour. The gems set into its plates reflected the dawn-like glow of the room, their light brightening at his approach.

He laid his right hand upon the chestplate, over the empty oval where his waystone fitted, and his left hand unconsciously went to the waystone at his breast. Perhaps he imagined the connection or perhaps there was some intangible thread linking him to the suit and back.

'Now you have returned, brought back to us by Isha, whole and well again.'

Korlandril turned his head to see Kenainath crouched upon the dais at the head of the chamber, his elbows rested on bent knees, chin cupped in his hands. The red hue of the room brightened slightly, becoming sharper, causing the shadows to stand out in starker contrast. Korlandril said nothing and returned his gaze to his armour, running the tips of his fingers along the edges of the overlapping parts, dwelling on the fingertips of the gauntlets, caressing gently the mandiblasters on the sides of the helm.

'The armour beckons, seeking its former master, wishing to be whole. Can you feel its will, pushing into your spirit, feeding on your mind?'

'Who made it?' Korlandril asked, stepping away, perturbed by Kenainath's suggestion.

'By me and not me. It was made after the Fall, by First Kenainath.'

The exarch's inflexion and choice of words baffled Korlandril. He switched between tenses, describing himself – Kenainath – as someone both living and dead.

'First Kenainath?'

'I am not the First, though there have not been many, to wear this armour. I am Kenainath, and I am not Kenainath, neither one nor sum.'

'I don't understand.'

'That is for the best, hope that it remains like that, and you stay yourself.'

A dozen further questions came to Korlandril but he stayed his tongue and instead crossed to kneel in front of the exarch in the centre of the chamber.

'I wish to train again.'

Kenainath regarded Korlandril for a long time, a hint of a strange golden glow in his eyes. He looked deep into the warrior's eyes, seeking something of what passed in Korlandril's thoughts, perhaps seeing things even Korlandril did not see.

'Begin tomorrow, this coming night you must rest, training will be hard,' Kenainath said as he stood. He turned towards the shrouded door at the end of the shrine and then stopped and looked back at Korlandril. His lips pursed in appraisal and an eyebrow rose in inquiry. With a nod, the exarch seemed satisfied. 'You are welcome back, Korlandril the Warrior, to Deadly Shadow.'

The exarch faded into the gloom, leaving Korlandril alone with his conjecture and apprehension. For all the worries and anticipation that fired Korlandril's mind, his body was tired. Sleep seemed a very good idea.

* * *

Korlandril ached. Every part of him was stretched thin, every muscle and tendon quivered and twanged. He realised how honed his body had been before the fight with the orks and how much of a toll his inaction in the Shrine of the Healers had taken. Though his injury had healed it would be some time before he regained the physical perfection he had attained in the shrine.

It was odd to train without Min. It nagged at Korlandril, like looking at a familiar smile with a tooth missing. It was an imperfection in his world, a departure from what he had known as he had become a warrior. In an effort to ignore the distraction, Korlandril turned his thoughts inward during training. His near-death had shown that he was not so accomplished in the deadly arts as he had thought. He strived to find what had been missing from his fighting technique, analysing himself as he made the cuts and thrusts and moved from stance to stance.

As his strength and suppleness returned, so too did Korlandril's precision and style. He was confident that his measured strokes were exact replicas of those demonstrated by Kenainath. It was not his technique that had failed him, it was something else.

It was hard to learn from an experience he could not remember. Objectively he was aware of what had happened to him – the fight with the ork and then the crushing blow from the warlord – but he had no sense of what he had been feeling, what he had been thinking. Those recollections were tied up in his battle persona, hidden behind his war-mask. Though he did not allow them to disrupt his practices and duels, questions surfaced in Korlandril's thoughts when he was outside the shrine; when eating with the others or sculpting in his rooms.

What mistake had he made? Had he made any error, or had it simply been ill fortune that had seen him injured? Had he hesitated or been afraid? Had he been cautious or over-confident?

It nagged at Korlandril that he could not find the answers. His only course of action was to focus everything upon his fighting technique and his decision-making in the duels. The latter was difficult. He fought without conscious effort, allowing reaction and instinct to guide his weapons.

Perhaps that was the problem, he realised. Did his instincts make him predictable? Did he need to intervene occasionally to change his style, to move against instinct? Was it the ritual itself that had been his undoing?

Sixty-three passes had come and gone since his return to the shrine, during which Korlandril's body had been restored to its peak of speed and strength. His actions were second nature, his weapons once more an extension of his will. He was due to face Bechareth again in a training duel. Korlandril decided that he would try to maintain more of a conscious awareness of his actions during the faux-combat.

The two of them faced off in the chamber beneath the shrine, Kenainath hidden in the shadow, Elissanadrin and Arhulesh calling the winning strikes. Korlandril began as usual, reacting and acting without thought to the attacks and defences of Bechareth. The contest was even, with perhaps Bechareth having slightly the upper hand.

As he ducked and wove, slashed and stabbed, Korlandril allowed himself to engage more closely with his body. He saw it as a globe of light in his mind's eye, his warrior instincts envisioned as a miniature sun, ebbing and flowing with energy, his body moving around and within it. His conscious thought, his reasoning, Korlandril saw as another orb, its surface still and calm. As he fought, Korlandril tried to bring the two spheres together, so that conscious and unconscious might overlap.

He faltered, allowing Bechareth a strike to the abdomen that would have torn open his old wound. Korlandril hesitated, a flicker of memory touching on his thoughts. He retreated into ritual, taking up Hidden Claw, pushing aside the tatters of recollection.

Korlandril began again, forming the globe of tranquil consciousness, but rather than imposing it upon the fire of his intuition, he tried to meld the two, to make them as one. He parried and counter-attacked, recognising the move his body had chosen, and the calm sphere slid a fraction closer into place. He lunged forcefully, his unthinking will recognising an opening.

Slowly, atom by atom, Korlandril merged the two parts of his consciousness. His mental exercise was far from finished when Kenainath called for the pair of them to cease their duel. Returning to repose, Korlandril fixed the last image in his mind, a partial eclipse of his warrior instinct by the rational mind, hoping to recreate it the next time he duelled.

Bechareth bowed his head in appreciation and gratitude, a knowing look in his eye. Korlandril mirrored the respect, his gaze not leaving that of his opponent.

'You are taking steps, moving swiftly on the Path, to fulfil your will,' said Kenainath, signalling for the others to leave. 'Your spirit responds. I sense it developing, becoming as one. We are all conflicted, many parts vying to win, yet none may triumph. You must seek balance, in all things not just battle, to be whole again.'

Korlandril nodded and remained silent.

'Practise your focus, see yourself from the inside, and master your will. The Path is wisdom, to control that which taunts us, to find true freedom.'

'And when I am done, will I be free of my anger?'

'We are never free, that is to have no feelings, we hope for control. Our spirits soar high, on a fierce wind of feeling, that ever threatens. Learn to still that wind, to glide on it where you wish, and not become lost.'

'I never thought I would miss Min's bad puns,' said Korlandril.

His gaze drifted to the empty space on the bench opposite, drawn to the social vacuum created by his former companion's absence.

Arhulesh seemed similarly perturbed, sitting next to the void, fidgeting with the scraps of food on his plate and staring absently over the balcony of the Crescent of the Dawning Ages. Korlandril looked over his shoulder. Within a bubble of blue and green captured in an invisible field, shoals of yellow cloudstars bobbed up and down, their slender tendril appendages wafting on gaseous currents. Their motions usually brought a mesmeric peace to those that watched them, but Korlandril was agitated.

'It is a shame that Min had to leave, I feel the squad is incomplete,' he said to break the uneasy quiet.

'It is a good thing that Min has left for another Path,' said Elissanadrin. She looked at Korlandril. 'It is the proper way. We move on, we grow, we change. You have never been comfortable with change, have you?'

Korlandril did not reply, though he knew she spoke the truth.

'It is dread of the future that makes us cling to the past,' said Arhulesh. 'Perhaps Korlandril is scared that he will become an overbearing dullard!'

'And what is it that you fear?' demanded Korlandril, his tone fuelled by sudden annoyance. 'Being taken seriously?'

The hurt in Arhulesh's expression sent a stab of guilt into Korlandril, who reached out a hand in apology. Arhulesh waved it away, his smile returning.

'Harsh, but perhaps true,' he said. His smile faded a little. 'If I cannot take myself seriously, how can I expect anybody else to do so?'

'You are a warrior, it is a sombre responsibility,' said Elissanadrin. 'Surely you can take some respect from that.'

Arhulesh shrugged.

'In my war-mask, that is certain. The rest of the time… I would laugh at myself if it was not so depressing.'

'Surely you became an Aspect Warrior to develop some gravitas,' said Korlandril.

Arhulesh laughed but it was a bitter sound, devoid of humour.

'I joined for a wager,' he said. He lowered his gaze sorrowfully while the others frowned and shook their heads in disbelief. 'It is true. I went to Kenainath for a bet. I thought he would reject me.'

'An exarch cannot send away those that come to them,' said Elissanadrin.

'I wish I had known that now. He kept me there, like he kept both of you, until he'd delved inside my spirit and placed the seed he would nurture.'

'Why did you not leave?' asked Korlandril. 'I mean, after your first battle?'

'I may have stumbled onto the Path of the Warrior by mistake, but I am not so self-centred that I would glibly depart from it. Maybe it was the lesson I needed to learn. Still need to learn.'

Korlandril glanced to his left, across a row of empty tables and benches, to where Bechareth sat looking over the park and lakes beneath the cloudstar bubble.

'And you know nothing of his story?' Korlandril asked.

'Nothing,' said Arhulesh. 'I know more about Kenainath than Bechareth, and that is little enough.'

'I think he was one of the earliest exarchs on Alaitoc,' said Korlandril. 'He told me he was not the first but said that the Deadly Shadow has not had many.'

'That chimes with what I have heard, in rumour and whispers from others that once fought with him,' said Elissanadrin.

'Of all the shrines to go to for your wager, why in all the galaxy did you choose Kenainath's?' asked Korlandril.

'I cannot reason it,' replied Arhulesh, giving another shallow shrug. His brow furrowed. 'He is a hard taskmaster. I have spoken to warriors from other shrines – they train half as much as we do.'

'I would rather be over-trained than under-trained,' said Elissanadrin. 'In battle, at least.'

'Yes, in battle, perhaps, but we wear our war-masks for a fraction of our lives, it seems such a waste.'

'He is serious-minded, I like that,' said Korlandril. 'Take Aranarha, for instance. He seems too eager. I do not think I could trust him.'

'He was once a Deadly Shadow,' Arhulesh confided quietly. 'I have spoken with Aranarha several times, and I think he resents the ancient exarch a little. He is trapped on the Path, dedicated to Khaine's bloody service, but locked away in there is some kernel of anger at Kenainath for allowing him to become trapped.'

'I think there is more the hand of destiny at work here than any ill-doing on the part of Kenainath,' said Elissanadrin. 'It is inevitable that some will become enamoured of battle after much time, as surely as a farseer turns to crystal with the passing of an age. If nobody became exarchs, who would train the generations to come?'

Korlandril pondered this for a time, trying to imagine a universe without the touch of Khaine. The others continued to talk but he did not hear their words. He pictured Alaitoc free of bloodshed, free of the iron beast at its heart, the pulsing blood-wrath fragment of Khaine that dwelt inside every eldar just as it lay dormant in its chamber at the centre of the craftworld.

He then pictured Alaitoc overrun, by orks perhaps, or maybe humans, or some other upstart race. Without Khaine, without war, the eldar would be defenceless. Little enough remained as echoing vestiges of their great civilisation. Without anger and hate, they would be wiped from the stars.

'It is a dream without hope,' he said eventually. 'Peace is merely an illusion, the momentary absence of conflict. We live in an age of bloody war, interspersed with pauses while Khaine catches his breath. I think I understand Kenainath a little better now. It is right to wish that the universe was otherwise, but it is foolish to think that it ever will be.'

'You see?' chuckled Arhulesh. 'You are a warrior now, and fear a future where you will no longer have a place.'

'Things change,' said Elissanadrin. 'You should learn from your healer – there should always be room in your spirit for hope.'

'All things change, and yet nothing alters,' said Korlandril, awash with philosophic thought. 'We know that everything is a great cycle. Star becomes stardust to become another star. War becomes peace to become another war. Life becomes death…'

'…becomes life?' said Arhulesh. 'I hope you're not referring to my spirit meandering around the infinity circuit when this handsome yet fragile body finally succumbs. That isn't life, is it?'

Korlandril had no answer. He was not quite sure what his point had been, and reviewing his words brought back nothing of the momentary insight he thought had occurred.

'As warriors, our deaths may bring life – for other warriors and for those on Alaitoc that we protect,' said Elissanadrin.

'I do not think that was the conclusion I had in mind,' said Korlandril. He stretched and stood up. 'With that being said, I think it suffices for now.'

As he walked across the Crescent of the Dawning Ages, Korlandril felt eyes upon him and glanced back to see Bechareth staring intently in his direction. The Striking Scorpion made no attempt to hide his interest and raised his goblet in wordless toast. Korlandril gave a half-hearted wave in return and hurried out, unsettled by the attention of the silent warrior.

The cycle of life continued. Korlandril practised and duelled, and when not in the shrine he made an effort to visit his old haunts around Alaitoc – taking the air carriage across the swirling seas of the Dome of Infinite Suns, climbing the cliff paths of the Eternal Spire, swimming in the gravity-free Well of Tomorrow's Sorrows.

He sculpted too, moving on from his Isha fetish to portraits of his shrine-companions that he gifted to each of them, save for Kenainath, whose essence refused to be captured by the psychic clay in any fashion satisfactory to Korlandril. He toyed with the idea of Dreaming for a while, but was hesitant to find a partner to join him, knowing well the dark places such memejourneys might take him. He even met with Soareth a few times, though not within the healing halls. They walked along the sandy shores girdling the circular Sea of Restoration and spoke of things other than Korlandril's injury and Soareth's healings.

Korlandril enjoyed the normality of it all. He knew that at some time, near or far, he would be called again to bring out his war-mask. He did not know what awaited him when that happened. He believed himself content, though he would sometimes wake from sleep with the lingering edge of a dream in mind, a momentary after-image of a shadowy red-eyed figure left in his thoughts.

As the dawn of a new cycle flickered into artificial life, he returned to the Deadly Shadow to find his companions in much agitation. They were gathered in the central chamber, where Kenainath paced aggressively back and forth across his dais. Red-tinged darkness swathed everything, flowing along the chamber in unsettling waves.

'What is occurring?' Korlandril asked quietly as he took his place beside his armour.

'A grave dishonour, done to me and to you all, that must be addressed,' growled Kenainath. 'An insult to us, an affront to our true code, a doubt to be purged.'

Korlandril turned to Elissanadrin for explanation.

'Arhulesh has left the Deadly Shadow and joined the Fall of Deadly Rain,' she replied in a terse whisper, her eyes narrowed. 'He has chosen Aranarha's teachings over those of Kenainath.'

Korlandril redirected his attention to the exarch, who stopped his prowling and crouched at the front of his stage, his eyes roving from one follower to the next. They settled on Korlandril.

'You will represent, champion of this great shrine, against Arhulesh. To end this dispute, affirm the Deadly Shadow, the shrine of first truth.'

'I have no dispute with Arhulesh,' replied Korlandril. 'It seems to me that your division is with Aranarha as much as anybody. If a duel is to be fought, it should be between the exarchs of the shrines.'

'Not my skill in doubt, a question of battle-lore, it mocks my teachings. Pupil faces pupil, this shrine's technique against theirs, to show the true Path.'

'It would be unwise to choose me to represent the Deadly Shadow in an honour-duel,' said Korlandril. He remained calm in demeanour, but inside his heart fluttered at the prospect of representing the honour of the shrine. It was a burden he felt unable to carry. 'Bechareth is the finest warrior amongst us, bar you. He should be your champion.'

Kenainath shook his head.

'It is you I choose, my most recent of students, my faith is certain. It is Korlandril, the newest of our number, who I believe in. No greater lesson, no better demonstration, than your victory.' Kenainath made a slashing gesture with his hand to show the matter had been settled and he would brook no further argument. The exarch's agitation was replaced with satisfaction at this pronouncement. 'Six cycles from now, in a place neither ours nor theirs, you face Arhulesh. Prepare yourself well, fight with bravery and skill, compete with honour.'

Korlandril stood dumbstruck as the exarch stalked from the chamber. He started as Bechareth laid a hand on his shoulder. The warrior winked and nodded his approval. Elissanadrin was less convinced, if her expression was to be judged. She cocked her head to one side, examining Korlandril.

'It would destroy the last remnants of Kenainath's reputation if you fail,' she said sternly. 'It is not only the honour of the Deadly Shadow that rests on your shoulders – it is the shrine's entire future. If you defeat Arhulesh he must renounce his change of heart and return. If you lose to him, he will remain with Fall of Deadly Rain.'

'I see,' said Korlandril, speaking out of instinct. He rubbed his chin with a slender finger. 'Actually, I don't. The loss of Arhulesh is no great thing.'

'Number us,' said Elissanadrin. Korlandril did so: Himself, Bechareth and Elissanadrin, as well as Kenainath. That made four…

'Oh, I *see*,' said Korlandril. 'Unless Kenainath brings back Arhulesh or replaces him quickly, there are too few of us to operate as a squad.'

'Kenainath will be forced by tradition to send us away and the shrine will be disbanded.'

'What would happen to Kenainath? What do exarchs without warriors do?'

Elissanadrin shrugged and shook her head mournfully.

'I do not know, but it cannot be good. For Kenainath, surely it would be the end of him. He has dwindled in reputation for an age. Perhaps this will be the blow that finally finishes him.'

Korlandril glanced towards the portal that led to the exarch's private rooms. He disliked Kenainath, had done so since they had first met. But he did have respect for him, and for what he had taught Korlandril. Something else passed across his thoughts. Arhulesh had not only abandoned the exarch, he had walked away from all of them, and the memories of those who had been Deadly Shadow in time past. The thought that the Deadly Shadow would be no more irked Korlandril, and to be sacrificed by the whim of Arhulesh was meaningless. Dormant for some time, the serpent of Korlandril's anger flicked out its tongue, tasting his annoyance. It uncoiled slowly, basking in its return to favour. Korlandril did not fight the creature, but instead allowed it to wind itself into his heart and around his limbs. Its embrace brought resolve, brought strength.

'It will not come to pass,' Korlandril said, fixing Elissanadrin with a stare. 'I will make sure of that.'

The warriors of the Deadly Shadow followed their exarch along the narrow tunnel, walking at a measured pace. Kenainath held a sceptre, the head of which was fashioned in a glowing representation of the shrine's rune. It was the only illumination, bathing the close walls with its red glare.

They had departed the Shrine of the Deadly Shadow beneath the armoury through a mist-filled portal none of them had seen before.

Korlandril tried to work out the direction they were taking but could come to no clearer conclusion than that they were heading rimward. The passageway was walled with small glassy tiles, of varying shades so dark that they seemed to be black with the barest hint of purple and blue, green and red. There was no pattern to the colours that Korlandril could discern, though on the periphery of vision he was reminded of the mangroves of the Deadly Shadow shrine, their shadows and dismal colours hinted at but not revealed.

The squad's armoured footfalls were stifled by an earthy layer under-foot as they snaked along the straight corridor. The air was chill in comparison to the humidity of the shrine's dome, so that faint breath steamed the air as they advanced.

'Do not allow Arhulesh to take the initiative,' whispered Elissanadrin from behind, repeating the advice she had constantly given Korlandril for the past five cycles. 'The Fall of Dark Rain style relies less on the guile of the Dark Shadow and more on aggression.'

'Yes, I understand,' said Korlandril, keeping his gaze on the back of Kenainath.

'But be careful, Arhulesh is still Kenainath-trained, and he has faced you many times.'

'No more or less than I have faced him,' said Korlandril with a smirk. His joke settled his nerves a little though Korlandril sensed irritation from Elissanadrin and glanced over his shoulder to see that it had brought forth a scowl.

'He will have not changed much in the short time he has been with Aranarha, but perhaps just enough to make things difficult for you.'

'It may be to my advantage, a conflict in his thoughts, in his technique,' said Korlandril, trying to look for something positive in Elissanadrin's warnings. He returned his gaze to the front. He felt Elissanadrin's hand on his shoulder.

'You will be the better warrior,' she said firmly. Korlandril took strength from her conviction, detecting no deception in her tone.

Light flickered ahead, filling Korlandril with the urge to hasten his pace, nervous energy propelling him forwards. He resisted, keeping step behind the exarch. He focussed on the deliberate strides, turning them from a source of frustration to a purposeful meter, regulating his pulse and breathing in time to the solemn steps.

The tunnel led them into a broad octagonal chamber, the walls clad in the same tiles as the corridor. The circle at its centre was built from a low lip inscribed with narrow runes. From three other directions at right angles to each other, more portals led into the duelling chamber. At the same time as Kenainath stepped across the threshold, Aranarha entered from the left, also bearing the glowing sigil of his shrine.

The two exarchs signalled for their followers to take their places along the wall flanking their entrance, and then stepped up to each other, face-to-face within the circle. The Fall of Dark Rain outnumbered the Deadly Shadow by many members.

'Challenge has been set, so that honour is settled, and the truth be known,' intoned Kenainath. There was no anger in his tone, only the solemnity of the occasion.

'The challenge is taken up, to settle honour, to put to rest our dispute,' replied Aranarha with equal gravitas.

They turned to their respective champions. Both bowed and waved their representatives into the duelling area, withdrawing to stand side-by-side a few paces away. Korlandril strode into the circle, chainsword held lightly in his grasp, his eyes intent on Arhulesh as he approached. His opponent's face was set in a serious expression but Arhulesh could not stop the briefest flickers of a smirk from his lips. Korlandril welcomed Arhulesh's amusement; he judged it to be a sign of overconfidence.

The two of them nodded their heads in greeting, eyes fixed on each other, the light from the two shrine-totems casting long shadows across the floor. Slowly, the pair drew up their heads and moved unhurriedly into their fighting stances: Korlandril in Waiting Storm, Arhulesh in a subtly modified version of Rising Claw.

In the back of Korlandril's mind floated the twin spheres of instinct and reason, hovering through and around each other. With his warrior intuition, he sensed that Arhulesh's weight was more balanced to the left, while his reasoning eye calculated that a dropping slash would create the greatest problems from this position.

Without a word, Korlandril flowed into action, stepping forward and twisting into Moon's Falling Wrath, his chainsword flashing towards Arhulesh's chest. His opponent reacted in time, pushing the chainsword aside at the last moment before a strike would be called, but his balance had been shifted to his back foot, to the right.

Korlandril feigned a reverse cut towards Arhulesh's front leg, sending him backwards, and then pivoted on one foot, ducking beneath his foe's blade to bring his own towards the knee of Arhulesh's back leg.

'Cut!' came the call from the surrounding warriors. Korlandril detected a note of triumph in the voices behind him, from the Deadly Shadow. His warrior-spirit throbbed with pride while his reasoning mind told Korlandril that the strike was just reward for a well-worked strategy.

The two exarchs nodded their agreement with the decision, their heads bowing briefly towards Korlandril. The two combatants straightened and returned to repose.

With a flash of foresight, Korlandril guessed that Arhulesh was expecting him to strike first again. Korlandril dropped his left shoulder by the tiniest movement, and as Arhulesh's chainsword swung across his chest in response, Korlandril surged to his right, his feet dancing quickly across the tiled floor. Spinning, Arhulesh barely blocked the cut towards his lower back, and then launched an ill-judged thrust towards

Korlandril's throat. The Deadly Shadow warrior delayed his reaction by the tiniest of margins, leaning out of the blow's path at the last moment so that Arhulesh was over-committed. A simple sweep brought Korlandril's blade to within a finger's breadth of Arhulesh's neck.

'Cut!' The call from the Deadly Shadow was excited, that of the Fall of Dark Rain muted. Again the nods of the exarchs conferred the strike to Korlandril.

The third strike went to Arhulesh, who launched a blistering attack from the start, overwhelming Korlandril with the surprise of its feral ferocity. The next onslaught favoured Korlandril, who had expected a repeat, so that he led Arhulesh on a merry dance, defending and parrying but offering no counter-attack until his foe was thoroughly off-balance and unable to ward away the strike.

Korlandril had no idea how the duel was ended. Was there a set limit, a score he needed to achieve? Or was it simply a matter of one exarch giving way to the inevitable?

Distracted by this consideration, Korlandril left himself open to a cut to his left thigh. Inwardly cursing his lack of focus, Korlandril raised his chainsword in salute to gain himself a little time to settle.

From then on, the duel was as one-sided as it had begun. Arhulesh's blows were well-timed, some of them downright devious, but Korlandril had the measure of his opponent. As he fell further behind in the strikes, Arhulesh became more and more aggressive, striving after the victory.

Korlandril tried to be patient, but the ever more desperate attacks of Arhulesh were like a goad to him. The fiery sun of his warrior instinct grew in strength, while the pale moon of his reason shrank. It was enough, Korlandril realised. Arhulesh was fighting on instinct alone now, reducing the duel to a matter of reactions and animal guile.

'Cut!' The call echoed around the chamber once again. Korlandril was eight strikes to Arhulesh's three. Kenainath raised a hand to halt the proceedings.

'The matter is done, the Deadly Shadow prevails: the honour is ours.'

Aranarha's eyes went to Korlandril first and then to Arhulesh. The exarch of the Fall of Dark Rain opened his mouth to speak but Arhulesh cut across him with a strained rasp.

'No! I can do this!' Arhulesh squared off against Korlandril, his expression turning sly. 'If an ork can best him, so too can I...'

Korlandril's eyes narrowed as something surged inside him. Arhulesh launched an attack, aiming a cut towards Korlandril's gut, hoping to capitalise on the distraction caused. Korlandril's weapon swatted aside the predictable blow and he drove forwards, raining down strikes on the chainsword of Arhulesh. The red of his helmet filled Korlandril's vision and there was a strange whirring noise in his ears as he relentlessly pressed forwards, hammering his blade from the left and right, from above and below.

Arhulesh's eyes widened with terror as he desperately fended off each brutal attack.

Hands grabbed Korlandril's shoulders and he was dragged out of the circle whilst others pulled Arhulesh to safety. As Korlandril's back hit the tiles, he was jolted into sensation again. With mounting horror, he remembered that he was not wearing his helm; the red mist had been in his mind. The whirring sound had been the noise of his chainsword, activated by his anger.

He had been heartbeats away from donning his war-mask in a duel.

TRAP

With Khaine by his side, Eldanesh vanquished the foes of the eldar. None could stand before the might of the Bloody-Handed One and his disciple. One evening as the crows feasted on Eldanesh's slain foes, Khaine congratulated Eldanesh on his victories and promised him many more. The War God granted Eldanesh a vision of the future, releasing a drop of his fiery blood onto Eldanesh's forehead. Eldanesh saw what would come to pass under the patronage of Khaine. Enemies unnumbered fell beneath Eldanesh's blade and the might of the eldar grew to its zenith. All creatures were cowed before the strength of Eldanesh and all eldar paid homage to Eldanesh for his rulership. When the vision had passed, Khaine told Eldanesh that the War God would put aside his animosity for the Children of Isha if Eldanesh would simply swear fealty to the Bloody-Handed One. Eldanesh cared not for the bloody future of Khaine's dreams and refused to give his oath to the War God. Enraged, Khaine struck down Eldanesh and the War in Heaven began.

Though Korlandril had lost his control at the end of the duel, it was agreed that he had gained the victory. Korlandril was the first to welcome Arhulesh back, greeting him in the armouring chamber.

'Your place is with the Deadly Shadow,' said Korlandril. 'We are whole with you numbered amongst us.'

Arhulesh studied Korlandril, seeking some hint of reproach or gloating. Korlandril offered neither.

'I am sorry I insulted you,' said Arhulesh. 'It was a sly ploy, one not worthy of the Striking Scorpions.'

'It was ill-judged, but I am glad that I did not make you pay too high a price for the error. I apologise for my reaction, it did not befit the conduct of a warrior facing one of his own.'

Arhulesh extended his hand with fingers outstretched and Korlandril touched fingertips with him, sealing the agreement.

'Kenainath has me training on my own again for the time being,' confessed Korlandril. 'Also I am forbidden from leaving the shrine for the next twenty cycles. I think he trusts me, but he wishes to make a statement. I would not be surprised if he has something planned for you.'

'I'd deserve it,' Arhulesh said heavily. 'Running off to Aranarha to spite Kenainath? I am truly my worst enemy sometimes. Such a fool.'

Korlandril said nothing. Arhulesh's brow creased in a frown of disappointment.

'Was I supposed to argue?' Korlandril asked, keeping the smile from his face.

'I shall become a philosopher next and found a new Path,' said Arhulesh. He lifted a finger to his chin in a pose of mock thoughtfulness. 'On this Path one shall be required to do the exact opposite of what one thinks to be right. I shall call it the Path of the Idiot.'

Korlandril laughed and clapped a hand to Arhulesh's shoulder.

'I shall become your first disciple. While I have dabbled in idiocy several times, truly I should learn its intricacies under a great master. Short of running off to join the Harlequins, I can't think of anything I could do to best your latest exploits.'

'Best not to mock the Harlequins,' Arhulesh said, becoming serious. 'Cegorach still stalks the webway, after all. No point attracting attention to yourself.'

There was something in Arhulesh's tone that betrayed a deeper meaning to his words, though Korlandril could not think what it might be. There was a story here, one that Arhulesh was unwilling to tell.

'You should see the others before Kenainath catches you,' Korlandril said with forced levity. 'And before he sees you with me and extends my penance for another twenty cycles!'

'Good health and prosperity, Korlandril. If we are both fortunate, I will see you in twenty cycles' time.'

Korlandril watched Arhulesh depart. When he was sure he was alone, he took up Rising Claw, continuing his ritual from where he had been interrupted. Out of the corner of his eye, Korlandril saw twin glimmers of red from the darkness of the doorway to the inner shrine and Kenainath's quarters. In a moment, they were gone.

Korlandril endured his solitary punishment without complaint. When released by Kenainath, his first instinct was to meet the other warriors.

He counselled himself against the urge and decided that he needed to seek less warlike company. It came to mind that he should see someone he had not visited in quite some time.

Thirianna's surprise was a reward in itself. After a brief foray into the infinity circuit – the spirits within were not keen to be disturbed by active Aspect Warriors – Korlandril found her in the Garden of Heavenly Delights, poring over a scroll beneath the white-blossomed bower of a snowpetal. Thirianna was dressed in the deep folds of a blue robe, hung with rune charms and bracelets glittering with their own energy. Her hair was swept back in a long plait, coloured a deep auburn and decorated with ruby-red gems. She stood quickly, laying aside her text, and embraced Korlandril. Taken aback, he hesitated before wrapping his arms around her.

'I heard that you had been injured,' Thirianna said, stepping back to regard Korlandril critically, assuring herself that he was well.

'I am healed,' he replied with a smile. 'Physically, at least.'

Korlandril gestured to the bench and the two of them sat side-by-side. Thirianna opened her mouth to say something but then closed it. A flash of concern marred her features.

'What is wrong?' Korlandril asked.

'I was going visit you, as there is something you should know. I would rather we spoke about other matters first, but you have caught me unawares. There is no pleasant way to say this. I have read your runes. They are confused, but many of your futures do not bode well.'

'There is nothing to fear. I have suffered some tribulations of late, but they will not defeat me.'

'It is that which worries me,' Thirianna said. She reached out and laid her palm briefly on his cheek, but he flinched at the touch. 'I sense confrontation in you. You see every encounter as a battle to be won. The Path of the Warrior is taking its toll upon you.'

'It was one slip of concentration, nothing more,' said Korlandril, standing up. He stepped away from Thirianna, seeing accusation in her expression. 'I stumbled but the journey goes on.'

'I have no idea what you are talking about. Has something else happened?'

Korlandril felt a stab of shame at the memory of his mistake during the duel. He did not consider it the business of Thirianna; it was a matter for the Deadly Shadow to resolve.

'It is nothing important, not of concern to the likes of you.'

'The likes of me?' Thirianna was upset more than angry. 'No concern of a friend?'

Korlandril relented, eyes downcast.

'I almost struck a genuine blow during a ritual settlement.'

'Oh, Korlandril...'

Her pitying tone cut sharper than the rebuke he had endured from Kenainath and Aranarha.

'What?' he said. 'You speak to me like a child. It happened. I will learn from it.'

'Will you? Do not forget that I have been a Dire Avenger. Though that time lives in the mists of my past, it is not so old that I forget it entirely. Until recently I trod the Path of the Warlock. As a warrior-seer, I revisited many of my battle-memories, drawing on them for resolve and strength. I recall the lure of the Warrior's Way: the surety of purpose it brings and the comfort of righteousness.'

'There is no fault to be found with having the strength of one's convictions.'

'It is a drug, that sense of power and superiority. The war-mask allows you to control your rage and guilt in battle, it is not meant to extinguish all feeling outside of war. Even now I sense that you are angry with me.'

'What if I am? You sit there and talk of things you do not understand. It does not matter whether you have trodden the Path of the Warrior, you and I are not the same. That much you made clear to me before I joined the Deadly Shadow. Perhaps *you* felt tempted by the power. I have a stronger will.'

Thirianna's laugh was harsh, cutting to Korlandril's pride.

'Nothing has changed with you. You have learnt nothing! I offer comfort and you take criticism. Perhaps you are right. Perhaps it is not the Path of the Warrior that makes you this arrogant. You have always been so self-involved.'

'Self-involved?' Korlandril's incredulity heightened the pitch of his voice. He took a breath and moderated his tone. 'You it was that fluttered in the light of my attention, promising much but ultimately willing to give nothing. If I am selfish it is because you have taken from me that which I would have happily given myself to.'

'I was wrong, you are not selfish. You are self-deluding! Rationalisation and justification is all that you can offer in your defence. Take a long look at yourself, Korlandril, and then tell me that this is my fault.'

Korlandril stalked back and forth for a moment, analysing Thirianna's words, turning them over to divine their true meaning. He looked at her outraged face and realised the truth.

'You are jealous! Once I was infatuated with you, and now you cannot bear the thought that I might live my life outside of your shadow. Elissanadrin, perhaps? You believe that I have developed feelings for another, and suddenly you do not feel you are unique in my affections.'

'I had no idea that you have moved your ambitions to another. I am glad. I would rather you sought the company of someone else, as you are no longer welcome in mine.'

'This was a mistake. You are not worth the grief you bring, nor the time you consume.'

Thirianna began to sob, burying her face in her hands. It was pathetic; an obvious attempt at sympathy and attention. Korlandril wanted no more of Thirianna's manipulation. Without farewell, he ducked beneath the branches of the snowpetal and walked away.

Following his argument with Thirianna, Korlandril sought to banish the episode from his thoughts with a sculpture. He returned to his quarters to do so but could not settle. He paced about the living space, surrounded by his representations of Isha, each beautiful face a reminder of Thirianna. Every time he sat at his bench with white putty in hand, he could not bring forth a vision to fashion. His mind was full of barbs and edges. Far from creating a thing of beauty that would calm him, his attempts at sculpture brought to mind those things that vexed him the most.

Restless, Korlandril returned to the Shrine of the Deadly Shadow. He found Elissanadrin shadow-sparring in the armour chamber.

'Perhaps you would appreciate something to aim at?' he said, moving to put on his armour.

Elissanadrin smiled and nodded in reply. She spoke quietly as Korlandril armoured himself.

'There is a familiar agitation about you. Thirianna, I would say.'

Korlandril said nothing, his mind focused on the mantra of arming. Pulling on his breastplate, he spared Elissanadrin a brief flicker of a nod.

'It is unfortunate that we grow apart from those we love, but take comfort that as you change, as your life goes on, there will come others with which to share yourself.' said Elissanadrin.

Korlandril activated the suit and he flexed his arms as it tightened around him.

'Is that an offer of congress?' he asked.

'You are very blunt today,' she replied. 'I would not put myself up as substitute for Thirianna. I am not her, so you must take me as I am.'

'I would not want you to be Thirianna,' Korlandril said coldly. He balled his hands into fists and loosened his wrists. 'And you are not. I would very much like to court you and, if all goes well, we could share an intimacy.'

Elissanadrin laughed gently.

'You are so traditional at times, Korlandril. Perhaps we should "share an intimacy" and then see if we wish to court? I regard physical compatibility highly.'

Neither spoke as they walked to the arming hall and took up their chainswords. They followed the passageway down into the heart of the shrine in silence.

'I already feel compatible with your physique,' said Korlandril. He raised his chainsword to his brow. 'Perhaps the intimacy of the blade will convince you.'

Elissanadrin returned the salute and took her place in the duelling ring. She tossed her hair over her shoulder and smiled coyly.

'I do not doubt your energy or your endurance, but I fear you may be out of practice with your technique.'

'Let me prove to you that I still remember well the tricks and skills hard-learnt in the past.'

Korlandril entered the circle and stood face-to-face with Elissanadrin, so close he could taste her breath and smell her skin. His heart raced, from the prospect of the duel and the pleasures beyond.

The sound of scraping on stone caused both to spin toward the doorway of the duelling chamber. Kenainath stood there, armoured save for his helm. His dark eyes regarded them both, unblinking, his mouth a thin line.

'No time for duelling, we are summoned to battle. The autarch awaits.'

Shocked from their flirting, Korlandril and Elissanadrin exchanged a glance and followed the exarch hurriedly as he disappeared from the doorway.

'Battle with whom?' asked Elissanadrin. Kenainath gave no reply.

The others were waiting in the main chamber, unarmoured. Kenainath said nothing as the squad fell in behind their exarch. He took them through a narrow doorway and down a long ramp that led into a circular chamber. Lights glowed quickly into life, revealing four sleek transports, coloured the same green as the squad's armour. They hovered slightly above the metallic floor, curved swept-back wings and the high arch of a dorsal stabiliser casting shadows over the squad.

Arhulesh hurried to the closest, touching a rune on its side to open the shallow-domed canopy. He leapt nimbly aboard and moved to the front of the craft. Korlandril waited for the others to seat themselves in the back before taking a place next to Bechareth, thinking it best not to be too close to Elissanadrin considering the playful flirtation they had just been engaged in. Arhulesh closed the canopy and the skimmer breathed into life, a faint hum the only signal that it was now active.

Under Arhulesh's guidance, the craft swung towards an opening at the far side of the chamber, beyond which a row of yellow lights lit the way along a winding tunnel. Arhulesh steered the craft effortless along the concourse, gathering speed until the lights flashing past were a single blurred line.

'Where are we going?' asked Korlandril. Elissanadrin turned from the front and hung an arm over the back of her seat.

'The Chambers of the Autarchs,' she said. 'It is where the shrines usually gather to receive news from the farseers before we don our war-masks.'

Korlandril took this information in silence. He had never heard of the Chamber of the Autarchs and he wondered whereabouts on Alaitoc it was located. The skimmer flew along tunnels and conduits he had never seen before and he assumed that these were in substrata of channels used solely in times of war.

Three other transports of similar design swung into view ahead, coloured in deep blues and black.

'Dark Reapers,' said Elissanadrin. She leaned forwards to study the markings as the skimmers converged. 'Shrines of Dark Moon Waning, Cold Death and Enduring Veil.'

This last one Korlandril knew – the shrine to which Maerthuin and Arthuis belonged.

Craft from other shrines hove into view behind them, joining the line of skimmers converging quickly on the Chamber of the Autarchs. The concourse ended in a wide space, its dome a black hemisphere through which nothing could be seen. The floor stepped down into an amphitheatre. Three figures stood upon a circular dais at the heart of the hall, two clad in heavy robes, the third in blue and gold armour, a crested helm beneath his arm and a long scarlet cloak on his back.

The gathering Aspect Warriors dismounted from their transports on the upper level of the hall as squads took up their places around the autarch and farseers. Korlandril looked at the white stone of the broad steps and saw runes in gold etched into its surface, each indicating the place of a different shrine, arranged by Aspect. Several hundred warriors were already in place and as many again were following their exarchs into position.

'Arhathain,' said Arhulesh, pointing to the autarch. 'He wore the masks of the Dark Reaper, Howling Banshee and Dire Avenger before he became autarch.'

'His name seems familiar,' said Korlandril. Kenainath stopped and Korlandril looked down to see the rune of the Deadly Shadow beneath his feet.

'Commander of Alaitoc during the Battle of Whispers, and co-commander with Urulthanesh at the Thousand and One Storms.' said Elissanadrin.

Korlandril recognised the names of the two battles, both long campaigns that had taken a heavy toll of Alaitoc's warriors.

'I do not know the farseers,' said Arhulesh. Both were male and of stately poise. One was younger than Korlandril, which surprised him. The other was venerable and even at this distance it was possible to see the strange glint of his skin, the first hint of his body turning to crystal, undergoing the transformation wrought upon him by his psychic abilities.

'Time is short, so brevity is required,' announced Arhathain, his voice filling the air, projected by a sonic field to every part of the hall. 'Farseer Kelamith,' the autarch indicated the elderly farseer, 'and his acolyte have foreseen a terrible tragedy for Alaitoc. A silver river turns to black and its boiling waters flow towards Alaitoc. The Dancing Death is seen on the shores of a white sea, her hair braided with the skulls of our children. She Who Thirsts casts her greedy eye upon the stars and in times to come her infernal gaze will fall upon our lives.

'It is vital that we move to prevent this event coming to pass. The Dark Gods have extended their reach once more, into the hearts and minds of the easily-corrupted humans. Though they do not yet know it, they are starting upon a path that will not only damn their own world but will bring forth a host of the Dark Gods' creations. Such is their ignorance that in only three of their short generations they will unleash a cataclysm that will savage planets and bring ruin to the doors of Alaitoc itself. We cannot allow this to happen.'

'The curiosity of the humans shall be their downfall if we do not intervene,' continued Kelamith. His voice was cracked and quiet, weighed down by an eternity of peering into possible futures, all of which eventually led to death and the destruction of Alaitoc. Korlandril wondered what manner of mind could stare into the face of such doom time and again, to avert each disaster as it became known. 'We cannot warn them of dangers yet to come to pass, for in doing so we risk creating the very desire we seek to end. A swift move now, bloody but necessary, will eliminate the threat to Alaitoc and also keep safe the future generations of humans.

'Those we need to eliminate are few, and if we strike hard and with haste they will receive no reinforcement. Overwhelming force will bring capitulation quickly. Those we wish to destroy have in their possession, unwittingly, an artefact that must be retrieved and destroyed safely. You will know it when you are close at hand. On no condition must you approach the artefact itself, and endeavour at all times to keep it from your thoughts lest it ensnares your spirits also. It concerns that which we do not speak of, and so you understand this is no idle caution.'

Korlandril shuddered with the thought of She Who Thirsts. His spirit stone pulsed cold once in sympathy and other Aspect Warriors exchanged glances and gave each other nods of assurance and comfort.

'We will attain orbit secretly and create temporary webway portals in order to strike at the heart of the target's fortifications,' said Arhathain. 'Their army will respond, and we must be prepared to withdraw under attack. Speed is of the essence, lest our ships in orbit be discovered and forced to break their webway connections. The rangers will gather what information they can about this human planet and the place where they store this vile prize. Detailed battle-sagas will be relayed to each exarch en route to the human world.'

The autarch raised a fist and turned slowly, acknowledging the assembled warriors.

'Alaitoc once again must turn to Khaine's bloody messengers. You will not fail us.'

'It is time to go, to don armour and war-masks, to quicken the blood,' said Kenainath, signalling the squad back to the transport.

Though he had no training as a farseer, Korlandril knew the principles at work: every action had a consequence and it was the duty of the farseers to guide the weapons of the Aspect Warriors to bring about the destiny most favourable to Alaitoc. He felt some small pity for the savage humans that would have to die in this attack, for it seemed that they were unknowing of the harm they would cause. Yet it was a necessary tragedy, the shedding of human blood so that eldar lives were made safe.

He wondered for a moment if killing a human would be harder than killing an ork. The ork was a creature of pure malevolence, of no benefit or advantage. Humans, though crude and unmannerly, were useful pawns and possessed of an innate spirit to be valued. That they were weak and easily corrupted – in body and in mind – was lamentable, but as a species they were more desirable as neighbours than many others in the galaxy. As he took his seat in the transport for the return to the shrine, Korlandril wondered what he would feel when he killed his first human. The thought gave him doubts concerning his chosen Path. Killing orks was simple extermination; killing humans one might consider a form of murder, albeit of a minor kind. Then he realised the ridiculousness of the question.

He would be wearing his war-mask; he would feel no guilt and remember even less.

Korlandril followed Kenainath from the webway portal with chainsword and shuriken pistol ready. They found themselves inside a wide compound surrounded by wood-and-earth walls several times Korlandril's height. The glimmer of other webway portals crackled in the night air, the shadowy figures of the Aspect Warriors emerging from the gloom. The air was bitterly cold, gentle snow falling from the dark clouds above; a carpet of frost on the cracked slabs that paved the courtyard; frozen rivulets on the brick walls around the open space.

Snaps of laser fire crackled down from the surrounding wall, targeting a squad of Dire Avengers advancing up an inner ramp. They responded with deadly bursts of fire from their shuriken catapults, cutting down several humans wearing thick grey coats and floppy fur-lined hats with flaps that hung over their ears.

The Striking Scorpions, supported by other Aspect Warriors, were to lead the assault against the human stronghold. While other troops secured the outer defences, the Deadly Shadow and others would strike at the central buildings, searching each until they had located the accursed artefact that was their goal. Though a great number of Alaitoc's warriors were to stage the attack, there was to be no long engagement with the enemy; it was a human world and would be home to many times the eldar's numbers. It was imperative that Alaitoc's warhost did not get drawn into an extended battle, which would risk the extraction of the artefact.

Kenainath led the squad away from the walls, towards a complex of four buildings at the heart of the compound. Three were single storey, built of rough grey brick. The fourth was five storeys high, hexagonal in shape, windowless and made of a rock-like substance strengthened with a criss-cross of metallic girders. It towered over the compound, the hub around which everything else was built.

Battle felt different this time. Colder, not just in temperature but also in temperament. There was none of the burning anger Korlandril had felt before, no hatred brought on by the orks or the sweeping bloodthirst of the Avatar to distract him. He watched with detachment as Howling Banshees, bone-coloured and wailing, sprinted towards the nearest compound building, their gleaming power swords slicing effortlessly through the humans spilling from its large gateway.

The Deadly Shadow veered left, alongside the Dire Avengers from the Star of Justice shrine and Fire Dragons from the Rage of Khaine, heading towards the next closest warehouse. Heavy doors rolled together to close off the entrance, sporadic las-fire springing from the narrowing gap but finding no mark amongst the eldar.

With a loud clang, the doors shut. The Dire Avengers directed their weapons against the harsh lamps along the edge of the roof, bringing more darkness. Kenainath motioned the squad to take cover beside the wall of the building as the Fire Dragons closed on the doors with thermal charges in hand.

There was little fire coming from the walls now. A glance around the perimeter showed the Dire Avengers had scoured three-quarters of the wall of its defenders. Black-clad squads of Dark Reapers took up firing positions, their missile launchers directed outside the compound.

With blasts of white fire, the Fire Dragons' thermal charges turned the warehouse doors into a river of cooling slag. The Aspect Warriors ducked through the holes created, the red glare of their weapons sending long shadows back into the compound.

'Strike without mercy, rejoice in Khaine's bloody toll, leave nothing alive!' cried Kenainath, waving the squad forwards with his glowing power claw. Arhulesh was first into the breach, followed by the exarch. Korlandril followed Bechareth through the tangled metal, Elissanadrin at his back.

The inside of the warehouse was empty save for a few metal crates piled neatly to Korlandril's left. A thin wall portioned a separate area to the right. Helmeted heads bobbed up and down at the narrow windows and two small doorways.

The Fire Dragons unleashed their fusion guns' fury, blasts of energy tearing through the flimsy wall. Under the cover of this fire, the Deadly Shadow charged, the occasional las-bolt zinging past them or striking up small clouds of vapour from the floor.

At the closest door, three humans levelled their weapons at Arhulesh and Kenainath. Without thought or order from his exarch, Korlandril raised his shuriken pistol and spewed a hail of lethal discs into the doorway, his fire converging with that of the others. Two of the humans fell back, their chests and faces lacerated; the third fired his weapon, catching Kenainath a glancing blow across the right shoulder. Unbalanced, the exarch took a shortened step to right himself, allowing Bechareth to surge ahead. He and Arhulesh reached the door, chainswords simultaneously decapitating and eviscerating the human remaining there.

Steered by instinct, Korlandril cut to the right of the doorway and hurdled through the shattered remains of a window. The humans within had turned towards Arhulesh and Bechareth, leaving their backs exposed. Korlandril's whirring blade opened the first along the spine from neck to waist, showering the Aspect Warrior with blood and fragments of vertebrae, creating a harmony of wet spatters and bony pattering. He hamstrung a second human, drawing the chainsword swiftly across the back of both knees.

Korlandril turned his gaze on another human and activated his mandiblasters. A flurry of shards spat from the pods on either side of his helm and arcs of blue energy lanced out, earthing through his prey's left eye to send azure coruscations across the blackening skin of the man's face. He collapsed with smoke trailing from his open mouth and ruined eye socket. Almost as an afterthought, the Aspect Warrior turned and drove the point of his weapon into the throat of a fourth human.

Korlandril finished with a flourish, flicking blood from his blade into the eyes of another enemy, blinding him momentarily. In the heartbeat the human flailed at his face, Korlandril slid sideways and brought his sword up and under his target's left arm, chopping through the side of his ribcage and cutting into heart and lungs. The chainsword stuck for a moment, juddering angrily in Korlandril's grasp before he wrenched it free.

Korlandril heard panicked shouts to his right and turned to see three more humans trying to clamber out of the window behind him. One fell to a burst of pistol fire from Korlandril, the other two exploded into ruddy clouds of super-heated matter as the Fire Dragons opened fire from the main floor of the warehouse.

Korlandril paused, eyes and ears searching for prey. There was a groan and he remembered the human he had hamstrung. He turned back to the crippled soldier; he was crawling towards the doorway leaving a smeared trail of blood. Korlandril watched him for a moment, the Artist part of him intrigued by the swirls of red painted on the floor by the human's desperate scrambling. The Aspect Warrior saw himself dimly reflected in the life fluid of his enemies, a distorted portrait in blood.

The moment passed and Korlandril stepped after his wounded foe, only to be beaten to the kill by Bechareth. The Striking Scorpion let his pistol drop to hang from its feed-lanyard and grabbed the human's hair, yanking him up to his ravaged knees. A swift cut separated head from neck, the body flopping into the blood pooling at Bechareth's feet.

Still holding the severed head, Bechareth looked up and saw Korlandril. They could see nothing of each other's expressions, but each realised Bechareth had taken a kill that was rightfully Korlandril's. Bechareth gave a florid bow of apology – face averted, legs crossed – and presented the head to Korlandril.

'There are more than enough foes to spread around,' said Korlandril. 'I do not begrudge you this one.'

Bechareth straightened, nonchalantly tossing the head out of the doorway. He nodded in appreciation.

'The building is clear, Khaine's wrath still waxes strongly, onwards to more death,' announced Kenainath, waving them forward with his claw.

A quick search revealed two back doors to the warehouse, both leading out into a small walled courtyard at one side of the compound's central tower. A metal door set into the side of the tower proved little obstacle; Kenainath's power claw tore through it with two strikes.

Inside was a mess of rooms and corridors. Humans scurried to cover as the Star of Justice squad arrived, salvoes from their shuriken catapults ripping along the olive-coloured walls, cutting down a score of greatcoated humans caught in the open. The Striking Scorpions followed behind, despatching any foe that had survived the deadly hail from the Dire Avengers. Room-by-room, the two squads worked methodically across the bottom storey in a circle, leaving nothing alive. Behind them, other squads raced into the tower and up the stairwells.

Detonations sent showers of dust from the pipe-lined ceiling above, indicating stiffer resistance in the upper floors. Korlandril switched to his thermal vision to watch the motes of debris settling on the cooling bodies of his slain foes, the dust draping over them like shrouds.

They found an enclosed spiral stairwell and Kenainath took the lead, the Striking Scorpions surging past the Dire Avengers to take advantage of the close confines. They were only a few strides up the steps when four small objects clattered from the wall above and bounced down the stairs.

Kenainath reacted first, throwing himself forward to get out of the grenades' blasts, while the rest of the squad hastily retreated down the stairwell, using the central pillar as cover. Shrapnel and splinters of wall showered down the stairs, but the Striking Scorpions were left unharmed. The ring of las-bolts echoed from the walls and the squad leapt forwards to rejoin their exarch.

They found Kenainath with the remains of a dead human in the grip of his claw, the soldier's left arm sheared clean off. A headless corpse lay crumpled on the stairs at Kenainath's feet. A few las-impacts had left craters in the exarch's armour, wisps of vapour drifted lazily around him.

Another las-volley shrieked down the stairs, sending the squad back a few paces. Korlandril joined Kenainath and the pair rounded the curve of the stairwell swiftly, shuriken pistols at the ready. A group of humans clustered on a landing above – Korlandril counted eight as he glanced around the turn before pulling back out of harm's way.

'My wrath will go left, direct your fire to the right, and we will slay them,' ordered the exarch.

'As Khaine wills it,' replied Korlandril. He brought back the visual memory of the humans' locations, fixing them in his mind as clearly as if he was standing in front of them. It was a moment's thought to calculate the best sweep of fire to catch them in one burst.

'I am ready,' he told Kenainath.

The two of them sprang around the turn of the stairs, a blur of deadly discs hissing from their pistols. Korlandril's burst struck two kneeling humans across their throats, killing them instantly. He continued to fire as he moved to his left, raising his aim to send a torrent of shots into the stomachs of those stood further back from the steps. They went down with ugly grunts, sprays of blood showing up as bright yellow in Korlandril's thermal gaze.

Korlandril and Kenainath were stepping over the bodies, chainsword poised, before the last of the humans hit the ground.

The landing had two doorways, one to each side. With the tread of the others sounding close on the steps behind, Kenainath flicked his head to the left and signalled Korlandril to stay near at hand.

The open archway led to a series of small cell-like chambers sparsely furnished, with bare walls. Korlandril guessed them to be the quarters of menials; how like the humans to degrade their own kind in an attempt to prove superiority. The true demonstration of civilisation recognised all as individuals, equal and important. An eldar who chose to serve others did so as a means of developing their humility and sense of duty – something that as yet held no appeal for Korlandril.

He brushed aside the philosophic notion as a distraction and quickly scanned the doorways ahead, searching for any heat signature. He registered nothing. The subservient humans had most likely fled at the first sign of attack, perhaps hoping the guns of their masters would keep them safe. Their faith was misplaced. Any who had come into contact with the Chaos artefact were at risk of corruption, none could be left alive.

A more thorough search confirmed that this storey, complete with kitchens and storerooms, was devoid of foes. Sounds of fighting from above announced more squads advancing ahead of the Deadly Shadow and Star of Justice.

'We shall go higher, ascend to the very heights, catch our foes at bay,' announced Kenainath. Uriethial, exarch of the Star of Justice, was quick to agree. The two squads headed back to the stairwell and bypassed the next two storeys, where there was evidence of much heavier fighting. Human corpses littered the landing, but amongst them were broken eldar weapons, pieces of armour and the bright splashes of eldar blood.

Korlandril wondered absently whether he knew any of the fallen. Now was not the time to mourn.

Several more squads joined the attack on the upper level, converging from the third and fourth storeys. As Korlandril ascended the steps, he felt a growing sense of unease. Something tugged at the edge of his spirit and his waystone began to tingle upon his chest.

'Kill them cold and fast, take no joy in the slaying, She Who Thirsts looks on!' warned Kenainath as they reached the last turn of the stairs.

The upper storey was a single open chamber, lavishly panelled and furnished. Humans sniped from behind overturned couches and upended bookcases, tomes of simple human script lying ripped and scattered across the dark lacquered floor. Flares of blue energy criss-crossed the room, as Dire Avengers and Howling Banshees boiled up several stairways leading into the chamber.

One particular knot of humans hunkered down behind a large desk set on its side, scraps of paper, crude writing implements and scrawled ledgers piled on the floor where they had fallen. From here, something seeped across the room, touching upon Korlandril's psyche. The thrum of las-fire resounded in his ears and the tight closeness of his armour was a lover's embrace. The scent of the varnish and blood, the whickering of shuriken fire and cries of pain, all combined into a symphony for Korlandril's senses.

Spurred by the thrill, he fired his pistol at a human cowering behind the torn remains of an armchair. The flash of discs buried in his forehead, some slicing through his eyes into his brain. The corpse slowly tumbled to the floor, its gun clattering loudly on the wood.

At the far end of the hall, sheltered amongst a press of drably coated guards, lurked three male humans clad in thick robes of purple and red, edged with fur and gold. The trio were elderly, by human standards, their creased faces twisted in grimaces of shock and terror. The ostentation of their garb marked them as personages of power in the hierarchy of the humans, if not the eyes of the eldar.

Soon this last group were all that remained.

One of them – his thick hood fallen back to his shoulders to reveal a hairless head mottled with blemishes – stood up and shouted in his unintelligible tongue, brandishing a box no larger than his hand, encrusted with pale blue and pink gems. His wide-eyed expression may have been of fear or anger, it was impossible to tell. His contorted face was a grotesque caricature of expression, a gross parody of emotion.

Korlandril's eyes were drawn back to the box, a faint whisper in the back of his mind. The human fell to his knees and his bodyguards threw down their weapons, holding up hands in capitulation. His two magisterial companions fell forwards and debased themselves, looking up imploringly at the warriors surrounding them.

It was the box that called to Korlandril and he stepped forwards, ignoring the human soldiers. The gems upon its surface glittered so brightly, entrancing him. He heard the murmurs of other Aspect Warriors around him.

It would be a sweet prize indeed. Korlandril pictured the bloody ruin he would make of the decrepit creature that kept the beautiful box from him. Korlandril would tear out the human's innards and use them as garlands. His bones would make fine pieces of sculpture, suitably painted and rearranged.

Touch nothing. Free your minds of desire and temptation.

Korlandril recognised the thoughts of Farseer Kelamith. They cut through the strange fog that had clouded his spirit since entering the room.

The air crackled behind the surrendering humans. Where a moment earlier had been empty air, seven heavily-armoured warriors appeared. They were clad in red and black, their backs and shoulders encased in broad, beetle-like carapaces decorated with the designs of white spider webs. In their hands they wielded bulky weapons, deathspinners, glowing blue from within, their muzzles surrounded by spinning claw-like appendages.

As one the Warp Spiders opened fire on the last humans. The muzzles of their weapons flashed with bright blue as gravitic impellers spun into a blur. The air filled with a swirling cloud, indistinct but nebulous. The writhing monofilament wire mesh unleashed by the deathspinners engulfed the humans, slicing effortlessly through skin, flesh and bone. The grey cloud turned red with gore as the humans disintegrated into thousands of miniscule pieces, each small part further sliced and dissected by the streaming wire cloud until only a faint red mist remained.

The sight brought a tear to Korlandril's eye. Such destruction, wrought so quickly and so beautifully. For a moment he entirely forgot the presence of the box, until it clattered to the floor, the remnants of the human's fingers dripping from the enticing gems.

There was a presence and Korlandril stepped aside, sensing new arrivals at the doorway behind him. The Aspect Warriors parted to allow Kelamith and Arhathain to enter. Three dozen runes gently orbited the farseer, intersecting and parting with each other's paths as he strode forward. Arhathain wore his blue armour, in his right hand a spear almost twice as tall as the autarch, its leaf-shaped head inscribed with thousands of the tiniest runes, each burning with its own energy.

With them came a coterie of grim-faced seers, all clad in plain white, heads shorn of all hair. Between them floated an ovoid container, dark red in colour and patterned with silver runes. Korlandril recognised wraithbone – a psychoplastic woven into existence by the bonesingers, the living core of Alaitoc and every other eldar creation. Korlandril's waystone fluttered warmly as the casket slowly glided past him.

From amongst the wreckage to Korlandril's right, a human surged forwards, one arm hanging limply by his side, a long wound in his thigh spraying blood as he sprinted across the room towards the artefact.

Arhathain reacted quickest, his spear singing across the hall to catch the human in the chest, hurling him bodily through the air. A blink later, several shuriken volleys and laser blasts passed through the air where the man had been. Arhathain beckoned to the spear and it twisted, ripped itself free of the dead human and flew back to his grasp. Unperturbed, the autarch approached the box and lowered to one knee beside it, studying the artefact closely.

Whispering protective mantras, the white seers closed around him, their robes obscuring all sight, their sibilant incantations growing in volume. When they parted a moment later, silence descended. The box was gone but the wraithbone casket gleamed with a darker light, an aura of oily energy seeping from it. Korlandril took another step back, unwilling to get too close to the accursed contents now that he was freed from its lure.

The white seers departed with their tainted cargo.

'Humans gather in force to destroy us outside the walls,' Arhathain announced, standing up. 'The garrison are all slain. Return to the webway and we will be away. Take our dead, we cannot leave them in this forsaken place.'

With the others, Korlandril descended to the level below. Here they found several dead eldar, armour pierced by bayonets or cracked by las-blast and bullet. Korlandril stooped and picked up the remains of a Howling Banshee. His faceplate was shattered, revealing an empty eye socket and bloody cheek. Korlandril lifted him gently in his arms and carried him back to the webway portal.

The solemn notes of pipes and a slow and steady drumbeat heralded the arrival of the funeral cortege. Three long lines wound slowly into the Dome of Everlasting Stillness; two lines of eldar flanking the bodies of the dead borne upon hovering biers. The bodies were covered with white shrouds, each embroidered with their names. On the left of each bier the Watcher bore the spirit stone of the deceased: the dead eldar's waystone now imbued with their essence, ready for transference to the infinity circuit. On the right of each departed walked the Mourner in a heavy white veil sobbing and occasionally giving vent to plaintive wails – an eldar who trod upon the Path of Grief. Other eldar of Alaitoc gathered in their thousands to watch the procession, tears in their eyes, memories of the fallen stark and bright in their minds.

They lamented the deaths of those they knew, but could not give full voice to their sorrow lest it consume them. That was for the Mourners, who had devoted themselves to the outpouring of the emotion death brought about, freeing others to remember the fallen with calm regret without being destroyed by guilt.

Korlandril watched sombrely as covered body after covered body slid past, the growls and choking cries of the Mourners falling deafly on his ears. He remembered the sorrow of past occasions, but felt little of it now. It seemed a matter of numbers, though each of those numbers represented a life no more. Twenty-four had died during the attack.

There would be other burials in the cycles to come, but none to match the communal grieving taking place. Twenty more were in the Halls of Healing, some of them fighting with little hope against wounds even the Tress of Isha could not heal. This was for all of Alaitoc to feel its woe. Smaller ceremonies for friends and families would take place after, when the spirit stones of the deceased became one with the infinity circuit.

A shroud marked with the rune of Arthuis passed. Korlandril closed his eyes, memories flooding back.

It was the eve of the Festival of Illuminations. Korlandril danced with Thirianna, while Arthuis and Maerthuin poured large measures from a black crystal decanter.

'What is that you have brought?' Thirianna asked gaily. 'Is it a special treat?'

She had been drinking summervine since mid-cycle and was a little unsteady on her feet. Korlandril relished the opportunity to hold her close as he supported her, though not so close that it would be inappropriate.

'It is a secret family recipe,' said Arthuis. He proffered two half-full glasses towards Korlandril and Thirianna. The dancers broke apart and seated themselves at a low table beside the gently bubbling stream that wound through the Valley of Midnight Memories. The dome lights were still bright, shining above like a hundred suns, but soon all would become as black as the deepest shadows between stars, save for the ghost-light of waystones and the glittering ornaments worn in hair and around necks. It was the Time of Shadow, the cycle before the Festival of Illuminations; the night before day, hidden and dark delights before revealing light. It was the night that all could indulge their passions without regret, to expunge themselves of the memories the next cycle.

Korlandril tasted the thick liquid, which was as black as the bottle it came from. There was a hint of effervescence about it and a subtly bitter edge that sweetened into a pleasant aftertaste.

He raised the glass to Arthuis and Maerthuin.

'I congratulate your family on keeping such a delectable tipple a secret for so long!'

'It's just duskwater and nightgrape, mixed with firespice, cloudfruit and dustsugar,' laughed Arthuis. 'Be careful, it tastes innocent, but it hides a sting like Anacondin's spear at its heart!'

'Nightgrape?' said Thirianna, placing her glass on the table untouched. Her eyes flashed with anger. 'That is not respectful. To take the crop from the Gardens of Immortal Solace and use them for intoxication! What would you do if your grave flowers were so used?'

Arthuis grinned, took up the glass and downed its contents in one gulp.

'If it was from my plot, I'd expect you to choke on it!'

The memory disturbed Korlandril. He should not have recalled it – the Festival of Illuminations should have swept away all recollection. What other doors in his mind had he opened when he had drawn on the Tress of Isha?

Korlandril closed his eyes and pictured Arthuis as a statue, immortalised in black gemstone, full of strong corners, but with a hollow within containing a vial of his secret midnight cocktail. It would be a fitting tribute to one who embraced his darkness so openly, and yet strove so hard to bring light to the lives of others.

His death was unfortunate. Sacrificed, like so many others, so that future generations would know peace.

Korlandril opened his eyes and scanned the gathered crowds. Many were Aspect Warriors but the majority were not. None were exarchs, for tradition dictated that the priests of Khaine were not welcome at these ceremonies. Peddlers of destruction were not allowed to mourn their handiwork. To the rest of Alaitoc the exarchs were already dead, and none would mourn their passing, though their deeds would be honoured and cherished. The crowd looked on in demure silence as the glorious dead passed through the Gate of Farewells, a white arc crowned with the golden rune of Alaitoc.

The quiet disturbed Korlandril. These eldar had given their lives, not for quiet contemplation and respectful peace, but for life, for the joys to be experienced by those around them and those yet to come. Their deaths were sad but the accomplishments of their lives were not rendered obsolete by such ending. Even their spirits would live on within the infinity circuit. This was a transition from the corporeal to the incorporeal, not the ultimate termination of life, and for the first time Korlandril saw the funeral rites with different eyes.

'Farewell, Arthuis!' Korlandril called out, raising a hand in salute to the departing body of his friend as it disappeared into the glow of the gate. 'You lived as you wished, and died most nobly! I will visit you soon!'

Korlandril felt the heat of agitation around him and the stares of others fixed upon him. He turned to the eldar next to him, a young male eldar perhaps only on his first Path. The youth was frowning in reproach.

'Is what I say not true?' Korlandril demanded. 'Will you one day be ready to give your life like my friend? Would you want those you have been cleaved from to whinge and whimper, or would you want them to roar out their tributes to you?'

'This is not the place...' said an austere eldar to Korlandril's left. She laid a hand on his arm and pulled him closer to whisper in his ear. 'You discredit yourself, and the spirit of your friend.'

Korlandril pulled his arm from her grip and pushed her away. He had meant the contact to be gentle, but she fell, landing heavily. Korlandril stooped to offer her a hand but others pushed him aside with pursed lips and glares of reproach.

Righted once more, the matriarchal eldar straightened the folds of her robe and faced Korlandril.

'You are not welcome,' she said sternly, and turned her back on him, deliberately and slowly. Others did the same, leaving Korlandril in a spreading circle of isolation.

'What need have I for the fawning attentions of others?' he snarled. 'Once you all craved to be known by me, and I indulged you. You are less than Arthuis. He I called friend and did not judge, and in return he did not judge me and called me friend. Who else here could say the same?'

With a last growl, Korlandril stalked through the flower-studded meadow towards the waiting air-rider.

Part Three

Exarch

LEGACY

During the War in Heaven, Khaine unleashed untold evils upon the eldar. Ulthanesh at first refused to fight, claiming the quarrel of Khaine was with the House of Eldanesh, not all eldar. Khaine's wrath was not so confined and there were those in the House of Eldanesh who remembered the bitter parting with Ulthanesh. Those tainted by Khaine fell upon Ulthanesh's followers and there was war between the Houses. Khaine was pleased, but Ulthanesh finally relented from his pacifism and took up his spear, not to confront the House of Eldanesh, but to bring war to the Bloody-Handed One. Seeing their common foe was the War God, the House of Eldanesh made their peace with Ulthanesh and the two fought side-by-side as the warriors had done of old. But there were those of both Houses so enamoured of war that Khaine worked them against each other, and they would slay any foe, regardless of loyalty. They became creatures of the Bloody-Handed God and turned against their own kind.

The longer Korlandril spent at the shrine, the less he thought of death. He was surrounded by it now, its messenger and its target. He dimly recalled flickers from the fighting with the humans: brief vignettes of destruction and slaying lasting no longer than a heartbeat. The recollections brought no sensation with them, like a play with no words, or a silent opera. They were simply things that had happened.

One particular cycle after training, Korlandril mentioned this in passing to Arhulesh. His fellow Striking Scorpion stopped in his stride and directed a penetrating look at Korlandril.

'You are remembering scenes of bloodshed?'

'Just images,' replied Korlandril. 'Do you not?'

'No! Nor would I wish to. I can feel those memories inside me, down in the shadows of my spirit, and that is enough to make me sicken with guilt and woe.'

'I do not understand. We all know that we have drawn blood and slain. It is irrefutable fact. We are Aspect Warriors – it is what we have trained to do. I am no longer an Artist but I can still visit the sculptures I created.'

'There is a difference between intellectual acknowledgement and emotional connection. Your sculptures were the product of your actions, not the memory of them. Tell me, Korlandril, what did it *feel* like to sculpt your first masterpiece?'

'It was…' Korlandril foundered. He was not sure of the answer. 'There was a sense of achievement, for certain. And release. Yes, definitely a moment of creative release when it was completed. Much like the surge of energy I felt in my first battle.'

'This is dangerous!' cried Arhulesh, backing away from Korlandril.

'Your fright is unwarranted,' said Korlandril, extending a hand to placate his companion. 'What has so shocked you?'

'You compare acts of creation and destruction. That is not healthy. If you continue in this way, you will remember the joy you felt, and that would signal something very grave indeed.'

'Why do you separate death from life, destruction from creation, in such an arbitrary way?'

'Because creation can be undone, but destruction cannot! You may come to hate a statue that you crafted, and can smash it to a thousand pieces, but the memory of it will remain. It is not so with death. You can never bring back those who have been slain – you cannot grant them the gift of Isha. As the act cannot be undone, the memory must not remain.'

'Korlandril still wears his mask, since the last battle, and he cannot remove it.'

Korlandril and Arhulesh spun to see Aranarha walking out of Kenainath's chambers. The Deadly Shadow exarch was close behind.

'It would be too soon, more swiftly than I have seen, I am not so sure,' said Kenainath.

'He has confessed it himself, sees what our eyes see, voiced that which we hear within,' replied Aranarha.

'No, that is not true!' snapped Korlandril. 'I performed the rituals. I removed my war-mask.'

'Then you have nothing to fear, walk from this dark place, go into the light outside,' said Aranarha, his tone challenging.

'I shall!' declared Korlandril. He turned to Arhulesh, who still eyed him warily. 'Come, my *friend*, let us go to the Meadows of Fulfilment and you can tell me more of Elissanadrin.'

He hooked an arm under Arhulesh's and dragged him towards the door. As they walked down the passageway, the admonishing voice of Kenainath drifted after them, his words intended for his fellow exarch.

'That was a mistake, confrontation fills his mind. He will seek a foe.'

'Ignore them,' Korlandril said with a forced laugh. 'They are jealous of our freedom.'

Arhulesh said nothing.

Arhulesh extricated himself from Korlandril's invitation shortly after the two had left the shrine, citing a former appointment. Korlandril considered his options.

He felt no desire to sculpt, there were already three half-finished works in his chambers and none of them appealed. He was not hungry or thirsty. His attempt to inveigle Arhulesh into an outing had been borne more out of boredom than a desire for company.

He decided that Elissanadrin would be able to drag him from the ennui that had slowly grown within him since the last battle. She was a Striking Scorpion and would understand the tedium Korlandril felt.

He found an infinity circuit terminal not far from the shrine portal, hoping to locate Elissanadrin. Placing his hand upon the crystal interface, Korlandril attempted to align with the pulsing spirits within. The connection was fleeting, the energy of the infinity circuit reluctant to conform to his requests. Korlandril was no spiritseer and had no means to commune with the infinity circuit to divine its agitation. He removed his fingers from the crystal, concentrated his thoughts more clearly on Elissanadrin, and tried again.

As before, Korlandril experienced the briefest glimmers of Alaitoc, envisaging the craftworld as a whole, but was not able to detect any presence of Elissanadrin. Perturbed, he stepped away from the interface. The passageway was devoid of other eldar who might assist him, so Korlandril headed towards the Dome of Midnight Forests, the entrance to which was a short walk away.

The bright light of the path gave way to the more diffuse twilight of the dome as Korlandril passed through the wide arch into the trees. This part of the parkland was sparsely traversed due to its proximity to several Aspect shrines. Korlandril headed towards the lakes at the centre, knowing them to be a popular haunt of many Artists and Poets. Perhaps he would see Abrahasil. He had not met his mentor since first going to the Deadly Shadow.

As Korlandril walked through the trees, his thoughts broke in many directions. Memories of encounters beneath the shady foliage flickered through his mind, but he did not linger on any in particular. The shades of the leaves intrigued him, moving into purplish autumnal hue. The softness of the grass underfoot was welcoming. He ran his hands across the craggy bark of a lianderin, his fingers detecting every whorl and knot.

All these thoughts occupied him, but they could not drive out his foremost experiences. A patch of light might reveal him and he kept to the shadows. He changed direction at irregular intervals so as not to approach his target from a direct line. He constantly scanned root holes and branches for signs of danger, though the Dome of Midnight Forests was devoid of any threat larger than a dawnfalcon.

Korlandril's paranoia grew as he heard fleeting voices from ahead. He had covered a considerable distance, unaware of the passage of time. The twilight was darkening through the heavy canopy, signalling the beginning of the dome's night cycle. He had entered not long after the Time of Cleansing at mid-cycle.

The glitter of water could be seen between the trees. There was movement and a figure appeared on a path ahead.

Korlandril was behind the concealing bulk of a tree before he realised it, clinging to the shadow like a spider on its web. From his hiding spot, Korlandril eyed the arrival. She was a little shorter than him, with black and gold hair swept high from her pale forehead. Her soft white tunic had a long tail that danced in the subtle dome breeze, twisting on itself and curving invitingly in her wake. She was laughing, a crystal reader in hand, eyes focussed on its pale display.

'Forgive my intrusion,' said Korlandril, stepping on to the path.

The maiden shrieked and the reader fell from her grasp. She caught it before it hit the wood bark of the path, swiftly straightening as Korlandril approached, a hand held out in apology.

'I did not mean to startle you,' he said.

'Why would you sneak up on me like that?' she demanded. Now that she had been given a moment to study Korlandril, she took a fearful step back. Her voice was subdued. 'What do you want from me?'

Korlandril could not fathom the cause of her disquiet. He had surprised her, but that did not warrant such a guarded reaction.

'I have a question. Have you experienced any problems with the infinity circuit of late?'

'I have not,' she said stiffly. Her tone was clipped, her language formal and cold. Though they were strangers, there was no reason for such bad manners.

'It was a simple enough request,' said Korlandril. 'I do not understand your hostility.'

'Nor I yours,' she said, turning away. 'Leave me alone.'

Korlandril stood dumbfounded as she strode quickly back towards the lakes. He took a moment to review what had happened.

Korlandril was behind the concealing bulk of a tree before he realised it, clinging to the shadow like a spider on its web. From his hiding spot, Korlandril eyed the arrival. She was a little shorter than him, with black and gold hair swept high from her pale forehead. Her soft white tunic had a long tail that danced in the subtle dome breeze, twisting on itself and curving invitingly in her wake. She was laughing, a crystal reader in hand, eyes focussed on its pale display.

'Forgive my intrusion,' said Korlandril, stepping forwards into Claw with Rising Sun, right arm crooked ready to defend, left arm raised for a strike.

The maiden shrieked and the reader fell from her grasp. She caught it before it hit the wood bark of the path, swiftly straightening as Korlandril approached, moving forwards in a crabwise fashion, right arm extended in Lunging Serpent.

'I did not mean to startle you,' he said, shifting to the posture of repose.

Korlandril looked at her retreating back, wondering how it was he had slipped into the ritual postures without effort, and why he had not been aware of it. The two versions of the same event vied in his mind – the one the experience as it had happened, the second his more conscious reflection upon it.

The stranger's fearful and angry reaction proved that his recollection of events was true; it had been his experience of them that was amiss. He had stalked her like prey. Troubled, Korlandril turned away from the lakes and headed back into the woods as the light dimmed and the Midnight Forest earned its name.

Korlandril could not think. There were too many distractions: rustling leaves, skittering insects, hooting birds, yelping creatures.

He tried to centre his thoughts but every movement triggered his instincts and he was instantly aware, eyes fixed on a snuffling thorn-eater or ears pitched to detect the next beat of a wing overhead. Even the gentle swaying of the trees and the dappling of Mirianathir's light demanded his attention, each shifting shadow requiring his scrutiny before he could settle again.

For most of the night cycle he sat frustrated in the grove, far from the paths used by lovers and philosophers, trying to attain a measure of equilibrium.

Frustrated, as the dome's field depolarised to let through more of the dying star's rays, Korlandril quit his attempts at meditation and headed for the Deadly Shadow.

Korlandril found the shrine empty, or those parts to which he had access. He suspected Kenainath was present somewhere – where else would the exarch be? – but the chamber of armour and hall of weapons were deserted. In silence, the mantra running through his head, Korlandril equipped himself for training.

He went through his opening routines with ease, stringing together a series of attacks and defences to loosen his muscles, tightened by his unsettling experience in the forest. As he went through these motions, he began to frame the shadow-foe in his mind, readying himself for more extreme exertions.

He found that zone of control and instinct he desired, his chainsword flickering in and out at his whim, weaving a deadly dance of blade alongside imaginary shurikens and bursts from his mandiblasters.

Korlandril stopped, halfway between Rising Claw and Serpent from Shadow.

His shadow-prey had a face. Several in fact. The faces of the humans he had killed. He saw them morphing into each other, eyes dead, mouths agape.

With a laugh, Korlandril slashed at the apparition's throat, taking the head clean off. Its ghost whispered away into cloudy shreds and disappeared. Korlandril continued his training without it. He needed no imaginary foe to fight; he had drawn real blood and taken real lives.

He practised for most of the cycle and was quite weary by the time he hung up his chainsword and took off his armour. Despite his fatigue, his mind was still aflame, not the least satiated by his exertion. Hunger and thirst gnawed at him, but it was not just for food and drink that he craved. He wanted something to occupy himself. He needed some entertainment.

He found the others at the Crescent of the Dawning Ages and sat with them, a full platter on the table before him.

'I am of a mind to hear a recital, or perhaps see a theatrical performance,' he told the others between mouthfuls of food. 'Something stirring, with drama, and perhaps a little bit of sensuousness.'

'There is a rendition of *Aeistian's Tryst* in the Dome of Callous Winters,' Elissanadrin told him, helping herself to the carafe of summervine Arhulesh had brought to the table.

'Too rhetorical,' Korlandril replied.

'There's a *Weaving of the Filigrees* in the Hall of Unending Labours,' suggested Arhulesh. His eyes flickered between Korlandril and Elissanadrin in a suggestive manner. 'Perhaps the two of you could attend.'

Korlandril considered this for a moment, but dismissed the idea. He did not want to be distracted during his first congress with Elissanadrin. The more he thought about it, the less appealing the notion of physical intimacy with his companion became.

He shook his head.

'We could race skyrunners along the Emerald Straits, I've always wanted to try that,' suggested Elissanadrin.

Korlandril sighed.

'It's not as dangerous or thrilling as it looks, not if you've any experience with a skyrunner at all.'

'I'm not going to waste my time with this,' said Arhulesh, standing up.

'It's clear that you have no appetite for any suggestion I might make. Enjoy the summervine.'

'Wait!' Korlandril cried out. 'I am sure we can think of something. I just want to find something to kill time.'

All within earshot turned towards Korlandril. Across the Crescent of Dawning Ages a shocked silence descended.

'What are you all staring at?' rasped Korlandril, rising angrily to his feet. 'Have none of you ever suffered from a momentary boredom that cannot be satisfied?'

There was a tight grip at his elbow and Korlandril felt himself dragged back to the bench.

'You cannot say something like that!' hissed Elissanadrin. Her expression was a mixture of exasperation and shock.

'Was it my tone? Did I raise my voice too much?'

Elissanadrin's look turned to incredulity and her mouth opened twice without words. Korlandril considered his words innocent enough, but his experience in the Dome of Midnight Forests gave him a moment of doubt. He reviewed the past few moments.

'We could race skyrunners along the Emerald Straits, I've always wanted to try that,' suggested Elissanadrin.

Korlandril sighed, his lips turning to a scornful sneer.

'It's not as dangerous or thrilling as it looks, not if you've any experience with a skyrunner at all.'

'I'm not going to waste my time with this,' said Arhulesh, standing up. 'It's clear that you have no appetite for any suggestion I might make. Enjoy the summervine.'

'Wait!' Korlandril cried out. 'I am sure we can think of something. I just want to find something to kill.'

Korlandril rose back out of the memory with shock.

'Kill time!' he barked. 'I want to find something to kill time!'

Elissanadrin appeared unconvinced. Korlandril was about to argue his point, that it was an innocent slip of the tongue, but he stopped himself.

Korlandril's whirring blade opened the first along the spine from neck to waist, showering the Aspect Warrior with blood and fragments of vertebrae, creating a harmony of wet spatters and bony pattering.

The moment had been sweet indeed. All he had remembered before had been the faces, but now the artistry with which he had wielded his weapons came back to Korlandril. And the sensation… The hint of it sent a thrill through him, rousing his blood, making every detail of his surroundings stand out in sharp detail. Elissanadrin's breath on his cheek and the scent of gladesuns in her hair. The heat from her body. Even her blood, pulsing though her arteries and veins, flushing just beneath the skin.

What a rich, red paint it would make.

'I do not like the way you are staring at me,' she said, pulling back from Korlandril.

With a shudder, Korlandril forced himself to focus. He stood up, gave a stiff bow of apology, and fled.

The Shrine of the Deadly Shadow would not welcome back Korlandril. He had tried the entrances of which he was aware and none of them would open at his approach. Even the infinity circuit refused to acknowledge his presence. Unsure what this presaged or what course of action to take, Korlandril resorted to returning to the main gateway and banging upon the iris-door with his fist.

'Is this your doing, Kenainath?' he demanded, his voice echoing coldly around the accessway.

His demand was met with silence and he stood fuming and impotent for some time. As he was about to turn away, the door peeled open to reveal Kenainath in full armour, complete with helm.

'You are not welcome. I am exarch of this place, your shrine is elsewhere.'

Kenainath's voice was flat, emotionless. Korlandril took a step forwards but halted when the exarch raised his claw.

'This is where I belong! You cannot cast me out.'

'You have lost your way, you must find another shrine, it is tradition. The Path ends for you. Khaine has taken your spirit, you are an exarch.'

'Nonsense!' Korlandril's laugh was harsh. 'One does not become an exarch after two battles. This is ridiculous.'

'Your journey was short, but now it is completed, you must accept it. There are other shrines, empty and without leaders, one will call to you. As it was with me, as it was with all of us, those trapped on the Path. We will meet again, not master and his pupil, but as two equals.'

'Tha–'

The door whispered shut, cutting off Korlandril's retort. He slumped against the wall, head in hands. It made no sense to him. He had barely taken two steps upon the Path of the Warrior. There could be no way he was trapped. Something had gone wrong, but he was no exarch.

Taking a deep breath, Korlandril straightened, fists clenched. He would not accept this without a fight.

He took several steps away from the door and then halted. Self-realisation blossomed within him. The more he fought this fate, the tighter its grip had become. What was it he was fighting against? Himself? Thirianna? Aradryan? It was senseless, this craving for confrontation. The listlessness that had filled Korlandril since returning from the battle against the humans nagged at him. Would it last forever? Would he ever be rid of the drifting, formless feeling that consumed him?

Kenainath was right. Korlandril craved that dance between life and death, more than anything he had craved in his life – adulation, recognition, self-awakening, all were trivial in comparison to the rush of blood from war and the exquisite delight of a foe slain and a victory achieved.

There was one place left that might provide him with the answers he needed. Moving away from the Deadly Shadow, Korlandril located a bay of skyrunners. Taking one, he turned on the automatic guidance and entered the Chamber of Autarchs as his destination. Thoughts a-whirl, he gunned the engines into life and sped away.

The massive audience hall was empty save for Korlandril. He paced around the broad steps, looking at the long circles of runes around the central platform, each an Aspect shrine. Some were worn thin by generations of feet, others as bright as the day they had been inscribed. As he circled slowly, he recognised the pattern. The oldest shrines were at the centre, many of them Dire Avengers, Striking Scorpions, Howling Banshees, Swooping Hawks and Dark Reapers. There were duplicates, their runes careful variations of their parent shrines, each moving further from the dais. New runes appeared, of Aspects unknown before – Crystal Dragons, Warp Spiders, Shining Spears. Outwards and onwards the history of Alaitoc's warrior past spiralled.

On the innermost step, Korlandril stopped. He stood on a Striking Scorpion rune. Examining it closely, he read its name in the simple curls and curving cross-strokes. Hidden Death. It was unfamiliar, though he was sure he did not know the name of every Aspect shrine on Alaitoc.

In hiding he had come to the Aspect Warriors, and in death he was trapped. It seemed to make a form of sense. Was this what Kenainath had meant?

Korlandril quickly returned to the skyrunner and entered the Shrine of Hidden Death as his destination. Lifting into the air, the skyrunner turned a half-circle and then darted towards the rimward exit from the chamber. This led into the labyrinth of tunnels Korlandril had seen when coming from the Deadly Shadow. Left, right, and then ascending through a vertical fork, the skyrunner climbed towards the dockside area of Alaitoc, gaining speed. The wind pulled at Korlandril's hair and face and tugged hard at his flapping robes as the skyrunner banked sharply to the right around a curve, spiralling downwards once more, flashing past other junctions.

Even with the considerable speed of the skyrunner, Korlandril was able to memorise the route, ingraining every twist and change of direction into his mind. The further he flew, the greater his hopes surged. It was not the thrill of speed that filled him, but the sense of belonging he yearned for. Along the tunnels and concourses the skyrunner took him closer and closer to his destiny. It sang in his ears with the thump of his heartbeat, coursing through every fibre.

This was the call mentioned by Kenainath.

It was the Time of Contemplation before the skyrunner began to slow, perhaps halfway around the rim of Alaitoc from the Deadly Shadow, nearly as far away as it was possible to get. Was this coincidence?

Korlandril was quick to dismiss the idea. There was no coincidence at play. The infinity circuit, the great mind of Alaitoc, had guided him here, by some means or other. Korlandril did not fool himself that he understood everything that was happening, but was content to be buffeted along on its tide for the moment. He had wandered from the Path and become lost; it mattered not who guided him now. Only a single hope remained – to find the peace of battle he so sorely missed.

The skyrunner came to a halt outside an inconspicuous archway, sealed with a solid gate of deep emerald colour. Dismounting, Korlandril dismissed the skyrunner and it sped off around a bend in the corridor. Hesitantly, fearful that this place would reject him also, Korlandril approached the gates.

With a sigh, they swung inwards and a wash of warm air billowed out to engulf Korlandril in an airy embrace. He closed his eyes, savouring the smell of strong spice and the light touch of the breeze on his flesh, the brightness through his eyelids as of a sun close at hand. Opening them, he blinked twice to settle his eyesight and looked upon his new home.

Low dunes of red sand stretched across the dome, their boundaries obscured by distance. Here there grew scrubby patches of candlewood, their violet blossoms small but pungent. A burning orb hung low to his left, like an impossibly close sun, and even as Korlandril watched it sank further and further from view, until all that remained was a dusky glow, though the rest of Alaitoc was perhaps not much past mid-cycle.

Korlandril threw off his boots and robe and undid the ties from his hair, letting all fall free. Bare-footed and naked, he crossed the threshold and walked into the sandy swathes, feeling the particles beneath his soles, sliding between his toes.

Unnoticed, the gates swished shut behind him.

Korlandril wandered this new worldscape for some time, getting a feel for his position and for its atmosphere. It was like no other dome he had seen. The artificial sun disappeared, leaving only a red haze. Far in the distance he could see the glimmer of a forcefield and the glow of Mirianathir. He headed towards it.

Approaching the centre of the desert, his footprints gently swept away by the breeze, Korlandril felt a tremor. Stopping, he located the source of the disturbance, some way off to his left. As he headed in that direction the tremors became stronger, sending waves of sand cascading down the dunesides.

Cresting a particularly high dune, Korlandril came upon a deep crater-like bowl, edged with a thin, high wall. The sands within the wall danced and bounced in agitation. With a rushing of sand, something erupted from the bowl, the red grains pouring from the stepped shelves of its structure. It was a ziggurat, a little smaller than the Shrine of the Deadly Shadow, made of yellow rock. The force of its arrival almost threw Korlandril from his feet as the sands slipped from underneath him.

A white light glowed from the slit-like windows and doorways of the lowest level. With a joyous shout, Korlandril ran down the slope towards the shrine. He paused at the low doorway – barely high enough to enter without stooping – and took a deep breath. The act did nothing to quell the excitement he felt. This place was like a Dreaming made real. Korlandril touched the rough surface of the doorway to assure himself that it was no phantasm. The light spilling from the shrine felt thick in his hands and heavy on his skin, but the stones were real enough.

As he stepped into the doorway, almost blinded, the light vanished, plunging all into darkness. Korlandril's heart quavered for a moment and he stopped, taken aback by the sudden change. As his eyes adjusted, he became aware of a red glow, coming from around a corner ahead. Walking quickly, he followed the patch of dim light, turning left from the main passage into a side chamber. The glow was stronger, coming from an archway opposite, through which seven steep steps led down into the shrine. Coming to a U-shaped landing, Korlandril was confronted by two more archways. The light came from the left, now strong enough for him to see the walls to either side.

Along more corridors and through more arches Korlandril followed the strengthening glow, until it brought him to a low-ceilinged room much like the Deadly Shadow duelling chamber. There was no circle upon the floor but a stand holding an elaborate suit of armour. It was from the red gems encrusting the dark green plates that the light was coming. There was movement in the light; the gems were spirit stones. Seven in all, each containing the essence of a dead eldar.

Korlandril stood before the suit, admiring the curve of its plates, the solidity of its presence. He reached a hand out and touched the breastplate. His waystone flared in response, its glow merging with the spirit stones of the armour. A glimmer of a memory fluttered across Korlandril's consciousness and he snatched his hand back.

The memory was gone. Perhaps he had imagined it.

Walking around the armour, Korlandril studied it closely. It was heavier than normal Aspect armour, the plates reinforced with additional spines and ribbing overlaid in gold. The craftsmanship was exquisite, every curve and line a harmony of functionality and style. Korlandril ran a finger along the back of a gauntlet, shivering with anticipation.

A spark of recollection jolted him away again.

'This is mine,' he whispered, his voice swallowed by the chamber.

Yours...

The voice was not a voice, but a thought. Was it Korlandril's own thoughts, or something else?

'I shall be the Hidden Death.'

Hidden Death...

179

The thought-echo lasted for a moment and disappeared, leaving no trace in his memory.

Korlandril stared at the armour for a long while, wondering who had created it, who had worn it, which enemies had fallen to its wearers.

Answers…

The time for hesitation and contemplation was over. For good or ill, Korlandril had come to this place – been led to it? – and it was here that things would change. For one who feared change so much it was the final answer. He would change no more. He would become the Hidden Death and remain so until he was slain. He could surrender willingly, leave the doubts behind, the struggle to adapt would be no more, the war within would be called truce.

All he had to do was accept what had become of him and put on the armour.

'War, death, blood, all that remains. I am Exarch Korlandril.'

Exarch Morlaniath.

The name meant nothing to Korlandril, save for the most distant shimmer of a recollection, though he could not place it. It was someone else's memory of a myth Korlandril had once heard, or the name one keeps for oneself and never shares with another.

The time had come.

As he took the armour from the stand, he whispered the mantra that would have him take up his war-mask forever more. Unbidden, the words changed between brain and tongue, but he spoke them surely, as if this was the way he had always meant to say them.

'The peace has been broken, balance falls to discord, only battle remains.'

A shadow-voice joined his as he drew on the first parts of the armour.

'Now we array ourselves, with bloody Khaine's raiment, as a true warrior.'

Now we array ourselves, with bloody Khaine's raiment, as a true warrior.

Images flashed through his mind: memories not of his life. His mind burned with pain, his thoughts stretching to accommodate a whole new lifetime's worth of experiences. Faces of friends he had never met, of parents who had not created him, of foes he had never slain. So many dead faces, thousands of them, in a torrent of anguish and death, and throughout all a jubilant laughter rang in his ears.

And finally a moment of blackness, of agony and ending.

As an automaton, Korlandril continued with the armour, the next line of the mantra barely a breath from his lips, another voice taking it up in his mind.

'In Khaine's own iron skin, we clad ourselves for war, while fire burns hot within.'

In Khaine's Own Iron Skin, We Clad Ourselves For War, While Fire Burns Hot Within.

Another storm of memories, more pain, more death. Korlandril tried to fix upon something he knew to be his own life.

He ran his fingers through Auriellie's sapphire hair, kissing her neck, her sharp cheeks illuminated by firelight.

No! That was not his memory. He had never done that. He had never known Auriellie. He tried again, but the mantra continued to spill from him and he was swept away on another tide of false recollection.

'The iron blood of Khaine, from which we draw our strength, grows greater within us.'

THE IRON BLOOD OF KHAINE, FROM WHICH WE DRAW OUR STRENGTH, GROWS GREATER WITHIN US.

'Battle comes upon us. We bear its dark burden, upon our broad shoulders.'

BATTLE COMES UPON US; WE BEAR ITS DARK BURDEN, UPON OUR BROAD SHOULDERS.

Smaller and smaller, vanishing to a single point. Korlandril's individuality was engulfed by the tide of personalities from the spirit stones. He drowned in darkness, flailing to retain some sense of self against the torrent heaping upon his frail mind.

'Come to stand before Khaine, unyielding in our fate, free from all doubt and fear.'

COME TO STAND BEFORE KHAINE, UNYIELDING IN OUR FATE, FREE FROM ALL DOUBT AND FEAR.

The dead numbered in their tens of thousands. Countless lives extinguished at the hands of those who had worn this armour. Creatures of all races, some warriors, many not. Victims of Khaine's bloody murders.

Korlandril wailed with the last vestiges of his grief, giving his last compassion for those that had been killed, saving none for those to come.

'We do not flee from death. We stride in Khaine's shadow, proudly and with no fear.'

WE DO NOT FLEE FROM DEATH; WE STRIDE IN KHAINE'S SHADOW, PROUDLY AND WITH NO FEAR.

WE STRIKE FROM THE DARKNESS, AS THE SWIFT SCORPION, WITH A MOST DEADLY TOUCH.

SEE NOT WITH EYES ALONE, BUT ALLOW RAGE TO FLOW, LET KHAINE'S GIFT COMFORT YOU.

Korlandril was all but gone, a swirl of motes in a far greater consciousness.

Morlaniath returned. The exarch opened eyes closed for an age and turned to the great double-handed biting blade upon the wall behind. Taking it up, Morlaniath remembered the weapon's name: *Teeth of Dissonance*. Like two lovers of old meeting, Morlaniath and the immense chainsword became as one, the exarch stroking a hand along the length of the casing. Morlaniath's fingertips danced across the point of every blade. Taking up a ready stance, Morlaniath willed the weapon to life, stirring her from a long sleep. Her purring was as smooth as when she had first been baptised in blood.

Together they would bring death again.

REBIRTH

When the War in Heaven was at its height, the followers of Khaine numbered many. They were dire foes to the Children of Eldanesh and Ulthanesh, for they had given in wholly to their bloodlust. Yet, one-by-one the Champions of Khaine fell. Khaine would not relinquish his servants so easily, and kept their spirits, armouring and arming them to continue the war. Though they were as bloody-handed as their master, these warriors also were defeated and fell. Still Khaine would not release them. Despite Khaine's threats and tortures the Smith-God, Vaul, would forge no more armour and arms for the Bloody-Handed God to rebuild his armies. Khaine would not release his grip on those that had sworn themselves to his cause, and he crushed them together in his iron fist, so that several would fight as one, sharing such weapons as Khaine could spare. Filled with the wrath of Khaine, the spirit-warriors slew many of Eldanesh and Ulthanesh's children. Yet such was their anger these spirits fell to fighting amongst themselves. Each spirit-part vied for control of the whole and they splintered. Khaine's spirit army fell to ruin as the spirits finally fled his grip.

It was a place of bones and skulls, where blood rained from thunderous skies and the clash of blades and screams of the dying sounded across an unending plain.

He floundered through the bones, slipping and falling with every other step. He cast about for some sense of place or direction, seeing nothing but death. He called out but the wind whipped away his voice as soon as it left his lips. He was lost. Alone. What was his name? Who was he?

He examined the skulls, small and large: eldar, human, threeshan, ork, demiurg, tyranid and many others. Tiny witchlights glowed in their eyes. He picked up a misshapen head, its snout pronounced, the eyes set wide, a ridge of bony nodules across its brow. He stared deep into the eyes, connecting within the remnants of spirit within.

The sky burned with black flames while dazzling yellow beams criss-crossed the ruins of an alien settlement. The hrekh poured out of their stilt-legged towers, running on bow-legs, guns chattering in their long arms. He sprang easily aside, muddy water splashing up around his legs as he ran through the sluggish river. Vyper jetbikes screamed past, their gunners directing torrents of scatter laser fire into the wood and stone towers, gunning down the hrekh by the dozen. He leapt up to a walkway above the shallow lake, pulling himself over the rail in one easy motion. The Hidden Death followed, their mandiblasters crackling, shuriken pistols spitting. Pursued by the gleaming jetbikes of the Shining Spears, a hrekh clan leader hurried around the corner, looking over its shoulder. He pounced, driving the *Teeth of Dissonance* between the creature's swaying paps to erupt from its back. He ripped the biting blade free and kicked the corpse into the water.

The skull dropped from his fingers and the memory disappeared.

How many thousands of deaths were collected here? How would he find one that he recognised?

He picked up another skull, of a human, but in the first flash of recollection he knew it did not belong to him. He threw it to the ground and stamped on it, but the skull only bounced away from beneath his naked foot.

Somewhere there was a memory that was his. He needed to keep looking.

Dim red light reflected from the mock-stone walls of the chamber. He looked down and saw sandy footprints on the floor. His footprints. That was confusing. For three generations he had waited in the chamber, waited to be found by the one who answered his call.

Who was he?

We Are Morlaniath.

The thoughts were his, but not his alone. Others stared out of his eyes with him, flexed his fingers around the grip of the long chainsword in his hand, felt the whistle of air into his lungs.

Who was I?

We Were Morlaniath, And Idsresail, And Lecchamemnon, And Ethruin, And Elidhnerial, And Neruidh, And Ultheranish, And Korlandril.

Korlandril.

The name focussed his attention. It was not his only name, but it was his most recent. This body, these limbs and brain and nerves and bone, they had been called Korlandril. With this knowledge, he delved into his memories, seeking the truth of what had happened.

He waited. For a timeless span, there was only spirit. Ultheranish's body had been slain. They had carried the suit here – Kenainath, Aranarha, Liruieth and the other Striking Scorpion exarchs. The sands piled on the doors and the light disappeared. It mattered not. One would come, sooner or later. What was time? A meaningless measure of mortals.

The shrine trembled. Miniscule movement. He awoke. He could feel the anger. The shrine resonated with it. The Avatar had roused. Still none had come. He fell dormant again.

The Avatar was unleashed again, stirring his spirits to awareness. None came. He did not sleep. There was a whisper echoing through the shrine. So far away, so quiet. He listened and learned. One would be coming. He had heard the thoughts of the New One. He shared the New One's anger and rage, felt the pain of his wound. Soon, he realised. Soon he would be coming.

He waited.

The sands shifted. The New One was coming. His thoughts rang like cymbals around the chamber.

Come To Me. I Am Peace. I Am Resolution. I Am The Ending.

The silver chain between them shortened and he pulled harder. The shrine responded, throwing off the detritus of generations. Soon. So soon.

The New One entered. He recognised himself. He touched his armour and the two parts of him became one for a moment.

You are we, and we are you.

'This is mine,' he said, and heard, and replied.

Yours…

The New One spoke and he listened.

'I shall be the Hidden Death.'

Hidden Death…

There was a moment of doubt, of contemplation. He knew what he was seeking. He had always been seeking the same. He was what he was seeking.

Answers…

The New One took up the armour and Morlaniath began the chant. Glorious return was nigh.

He understood now where he had come from. He was not-Korlandril. He was not-Morlaniath. He was both, and others beside. He was all and they were him.

He explored his memories. They were all his, but some he had not seen before. Time passed in a blur of old relationships, battles lost and won, friendships long and short, enemies slain and escaped, love and hate, births, romances, disappointments, old hopes and new dreams, and a half-dozen painful deaths. He flitted from one to the next without effort, seeking nothing in particular.

He came across one that caused him to stop. A face he knew. He recognised all of the faces, but this was one of the old memories, unknown before to this body. He put a name to the face.

Bechareth.

It did not fit with the other memories. The Bechareth of this body was a Striking Scorpion. The Bechareth of the memory was something else. He searched further back, seeking the genesis of the memory, the start of the story.

He was Ultheranish, the vessel before this current one. They were in the webway, aboard a ship. Through high-arched windows, he watched the glowing rivulets of psychic energy swirling past.

Alarms sounded. Something else was in the webway. He was one of the Hidden Death, just another warrior ready to defend the starship. Not-Neruidh was exarch. He flitted between the two memestrands, watching himself as exarch and seeing himself through the exarch's eyes. The Hidden Death followed the exarch into the outer corridors, waiting for the attack. Another vessel came alongside, a bladed, sinister reflection of their own warship: the kin of Commorragh. With cutters and forcefields they breached the hull, a swarm of raiders armed with splinter rifles and crackling blades. The Aspect Warriors fought back, the Hidden Death at the fore.

He met sword-to-sword with one of the Lost Kindred, a cruel-eyed wych almost naked save for a few slender straps and curving shoulder armour. His foe was swifter than he, her twin daggers darting and weaving around his chainsword. His armour bore the brunt of her strikes, sparks of energy flying from her blades as they struck. He brought up his pistol to her face and she ducked, to be met by the rising point of his chainsword. Her face split in twain and she fell to the ground, her beautiful features now a gory mess.

Others followed the wyches. They wore armour also, not unlike his, though coloured in black and white. He recognised them immediately. Incubi. A perversion of Khaine's Aspects, debased and immoral. Mercenaries without principle or code.

In a rage he hurled himself at the closest, his chainsword plunging towards the helmeted head. The incubi swayed back, his powered glaive rising to deflect the attack. Spinning, the incubi delivered a kick to his midriff, sending him staggering. His chainsword flashed up to ward away a strike towards his chest, sending the glaive's gleaming head screaming past his right shoulder.

The pair parted and circled, feinting and jabbing with their weapons. The incubi's eye lenses gleamed with a yellow, ghostly light. Sickened with rage, he launched another flurry of attacks, mandiblasters spitting, chainsword weaving left and right. The incubi ducked and swerved aside from each blow, the tip of his glaive carving figures-of-eight in front of him.

A chance salvo from the Striking Scorpion's pistol caught the incubi in the thigh. He followed up with a blistering series of strikes towards the head and throat, each caught at the last moment on the haft of the incubi's weapon. A sudden change of direction and a twist to the left sent the chainsword's teeth into the incubi's lower back, slivers of torn armour spraying to the floor.

A backwards sweep caught the enemy a glancing blow to the side of the head, shearing away part of his armour, splintering the eye lens on the left side of his face to reveal a glimpse of the creature within.

The incubi looked up at him with a horrified eye, hand thrown up defensively in front of him. It was the face not-Korlandril knew as Bechareth.

The Striking Scorpion had no time for the death-blow; more warriors swept from the pirate vessel, engulfing the Hidden Death in a swirling melee.

The memories of Ultheranish and not-Ultheranish shed no more light on what had happened. He delved into the past of not-Neruidh.

'He must be accepted, pupils are not turned away. It is not a choice.' Kenainath stood in the Chamber of Autarchs with not-Neruidh, Aranarha, Liruieth, Kadonil and Elronihir. Beside the Deadly Shadow exarch stood the former incubi, Bechareth, eyes downcast, demure and silent. He wore a plain white robe from the Halls of Healing, several spirit-aligning gems hung about his person to aid his recovery.

'He is the enemy, one of the dark kin. He cannot be one of us!' Kadonil was vehement.

'This is no debate, I have made my final choice, I will not change it.'

'What you say, it is true, he is yours,' said Liruieth, her voice quiet but firm. 'Watch him close, tell no one, work him hard.'

'He will be silent, none but us shall ever know, a Scorpion's secret,' Kenainath assured them.

Kadonil whirled away in disgust. Aranarha stalked off without a word. The remaining exarchs nodded in compliance, and departed.

Though he had always known it, the memory was a shock. Bechareth, who he had befriended, who he had trusted in battle, was not of Alaitoc. He was not even of the craftworlds.

He felt betrayed. Kenainath had kept this secret from them all, swearing Bechareth to silence to protect his own reputation.

Rash.

It Was Decided. The Vote Was A Majority. You Cannot Revisit That Decision.

I Was Always Dubious, But You Would Not Listen To Me.

You Are Dubious About Everything.

Quiet! thought not-Korlandril.

The voices fell silent as Morlaniath strained his senses. Someone was approaching the shrine.

'Hello?' a quavering voice called out.

Greet Him.

Let Him Wait.

Who is it?

Your First Pupil.

One To Be Taught.

So soon?

Always It Is So. A New Exarch Needs Followers. The Shrine Calls To Them. Stirs Their Blood. Most Are Deaf To My Call.

There Will Be More In The Times To Come.

How do I teach him?

We Have Taught Many Already.

Remember.

The First Of Many. Hidden Death Will Rise Again.

With trembling hands Morlaniath took off his helmet. Slowly and precisely, he unfastened the clasps of his armour and took it off piece-by-piece, reverentially placing each part back on its stand.

The other voices subsided, but their presence remained. His head still contained names of those he had never met, faces he had never seen with these eyes, foes slain in bloody combat by hands other than his.

Clad in the undersuit, Morlaniath turned to his left, knowing that the steps through the archway there led directly to the main chamber of the shrine. He could feel the presence of his first acolyte; nervous, frustrated and angry. Just as he had been.

He ascended the stairway swiftly and silently, entered the main chamber behind the aspirant. The newcomer was young – younger than he had been when he had approached Kenainath. He could feel his anxiety, pouring out in waves.

'We are the Hidden Death. You hearken to our call, who is troubled in mind.' Morlaniath barely recognised his own voice and was unsure if he had spoken the words. There was a ritual cadence to them, phrases so oft-spoke in times past that they spoke themselves.

'I dreamt of a river of blood, and I bathed in it,' said the young eldar, his voice querulous, his eyes fixed on Morlaniath as he stepped slowly across the chamber floor.

'Dreams of death and bloodshed, Khaine's hot touch on your mind, a hot thirst for battle. These have brought you to me, Exarch Morlaniath, the keeper of this shrine. I will lead you to truth, take you on that dark path, into your mind's shadows.'

'I am afraid, exarch.' The youth's subservience was both refreshing and yet familiar. As an Aspect Warrior, Morlaniath had quickly grown used to suspicion and dismay from others not on the Warrior Path. Now he was exarch, feared but revered.

He took the other's arm in his grip and pulled him to his feet. He fixed the warrior-to-be with a long stare, gauging his mood. He wondered if he had appeared as pitiful to Kenainath. So full of ignorance, so afraid of himself.

'The Path will be bloody. You walk alongside Khaine, and may not make the end.'

The eldar nodded dumbly, fingers fidgeting at the loose robe he wore.

'The urge is strong in you, to shed blood and bring death. You must strive for control. We will bring your war-mask, unleash your death-spirit, so that it cannot hide. You will control its wrath, it will hold you no more, you will gain your freedom.'

'Why has this happened to me?'

Such a familiar question! He remembered it from his own lips and from dozens like him. All faced the same shadows in their spirits, all had to deal with Khaine's double-edged gift. Why did each one of them believe themselves different? Did they truly think they were free of Khaine's touch, or that there would be a time when Khaine's hold on the eldar would be broken for good?

'You are not so special, to feel these darkest moods, and wish to act on them. You are but a mortal, with a mortal's nature, for the good and the ill. Learn to embrace this gift, love Khaine's dark legacy, and you will master it.'

'I… I am so weak…' the eldar sobbed.

'You are at your weakest, so we will make you strong, strong enough to prevail.'

Morlaniath headed towards the archway leading to the shrine's central corridor, beckoning his aspirant to follow.

'Weak in body and mind, full of doubt and sorrow, but we will remove them. A farewell to your guilt, no remorse or lament, a warrior in truth.'

He led the youth out into the heat of the desert, the warmth on his skin like a homecoming. Here he had first learnt the ways of the Striking Scorpion from Nelemin, who had been taught by Karandras the Phoenix Lord. For life-after-life he had come to this place, first to learn, and then to teach, reinventing himself with each episode, an unending link to the founding of the Striking Scorpions.

'I am Milathradil.'

Morlaniath regarded the youth without expression.

'You are Milathradil, of the Hidden Death Shrine, a Striking Scorpion.'

The night-cycle of the desert dome was dry and frigid. Morlaniath stood at the gate of the shrine and looked out over the sands, feeling at home. The dome's fields dampened the dying star, leaving only the faintest glimmer of scarlet to light the dunes, ever-shifting in the artificial winds.

Constant but changing, like Morlaniath. Every cycle-start, at the Time of Wakening, he looked over his domain. For an age this had been his place. It was still his place, through this new body.

The shrine alerted him to the presence of Kenainath and Aranarha. He felt them crossing the threshold from the sub-strata tunnels. He turned and made his way to his chambers, walking along feet-worn corridors and down ancient steps without thought.

The two exarchs waited for him in his private arming room, clad in loose robes, their spirit stones lighting the gloom.

'A welcome return, from the void of somnolence, with new life inside,' said Kenainath, giving a polite bow.

Morlaniath smiled.

'It is good to return, you trained this body well. I am fully restored.'

'Yet the spirit was weaker, it is trapped with us, doomed to tread this path with us,' said Aranarha.

'Another always comes, be it soon or later, the nature of Khaine's gift.'

Morlaniath felt his newest disciple stirring in the chambers above. Out across Alaitoc, others were responding to his presence, troubled by their thoughts, fearing their own anger. They did not yet know it, but they would come to him soon.

'Do you feel his anguish, sense his dark destiny, the burning in his blood?'

The others nodded.

'He will make a fine pupil, so full of anger, his resentment is his key,' said Aranarha. 'He will train ferociously, you must watch him close, temper him with much patience.'

Morlaniath nodded in agreement. The three exarchs exchanged gestures of parting and then Morlaniath was alone.

He felt nervous inquiry resonating through the shrine. Milathradil was awake and seeking him. It would not be well for him to wander the shrine without a guide. Invigorated by his fresh life, Morlaniath headed up the stairs to find his new pupil.

The students were willing and growing in number. Over the last sixty cycles, Milathradil had been joined by Euraithin, Lokhirith and Nurianda and the four of them were attentive to Morlaniath's instruction as he taught them the rituals of combat. Much of the teaching was in the style of the Hidden Death, but in places the stances and strikes were subtly evolved, incorporating Deadly Shadow techniques from not-Korlandril's experiences.

The Hidden Death desert was the opposite of the dank swamps of the Deadly Shadow, but Morlaniath's previous lives had been spent in this arid dome and he adapted to the environment without hesitation. He learned afresh what he already knew, the instinct of the residual spirits dwelling within him guiding him effortlessly across the dunes, leading him to the training areas and the tests to put before his acolytes. He knew the haunts of the sandserpents that burrowed beneath the dunes; the piping calls of the windhoppers; the trails of the scurrying worm-hunters and the coiling casts left by their prey.

Without his armour, he walked across the drifts, comforted by his sense of place and the residual presence of his other selves. They were always there, though speechless, guiding him indirectly, steering him this way or that.

The former exarchs were stronger when Morlaniath wore his armour. Nagging doubts and unconscious knowledge were given voice by their spirit stones. Their counsel was sometimes at odds with Morlaniath's own inclinations, and even with each other, though all professed a common goal.

At night Morlaniath did not sleep, but instead retreated to his private chamber and donned his armour, to rest his body and commune with his other selves. It was one such night-cycle that Morlaniath pulled on his armoured suit, his thoughts on the progress of his nascent squad.

You Are Too Lenient With Your Pupils. They Are Not Focussed. They Chatter Aimlessly When You Do Not Attend Them.

Nonsense! It Is To Attain Balance That We Strive, Not To Create More Exarchs. Their Division of War And Peace Is Proceeding Well.

An exhausted mind makes mistakes. I show them the rewards of control, the freedom they will earn for themselves when they have separated their warrior spirits, when they have grown their war-masks.

I Sense Kenainath's Hand In This. He Has Too Much Influence Over You.

I Too Learned At The Deadly Shadow. Kenainath's Teachings Grant Perspective And Offer Challenge.

I will teach as I see fit.

Foolish, To Dismiss Our Experience So Quickly.

I share your experience, it is mine also. The Hidden Death is being reborn, but it will take some time. I will show patience, as Aranarha suggested.

Another Upstart!

You Are Jealous Of Him. He Is Popular With His Warriors. Your Aloofness Was Always Your Weakness.

Some Will Die. It Does Not Benefit Master or Pupil To Grow Too Attached To Individuals. Warriors Come And Warriors Go. The Hidden Death Is Eternal.

And it shall remain so under my leadership. I am now the Hidden Death.

We Shall See.

For all his patience, Morlaniath was eager for his squad to complete the first stages of their training. Heedful that rushing matters could risk everything, he waited until all four of his students were ready to take the next step. He introduced them to their armour, allowing each to pick their suit. He felt a perverse delight when Milathradil picked the suit once worn by not-Ultheranish when he had been a simple Striking Scorpion. It stirred something in his memories, a nugget of information he had not examined before, when he had chosen his first suit of armour, which now concurred with an older fragment of knowledge.

His first instinct was to stand beside Elissanadrin, seeking the familiar, but he dismissed the urge. It was change and renewal that he needed, not the comfortable. Out of the corner of his eye, Korlandril thought he saw a momentary glitter in the eyes of one suit. He turned towards it. There was nothing to distinguish it from the others, but something about it tugged at Korlandril.

'This one,' he said, striding towards the armour. He stood beside it and turned to face the exarch.

'That is a wise choice, a noble suit you have picked, which has served us well,' said Kenainath. 'You are now ready, in body if not in mind, to don your armour.'

'Which has served us well?'

Kenainath was referring to himself, the exarch, not the shrine as an entity. He had once worn the armour that Korlandril had picked. The thought gave Morlaniath pause, to wonder if perhaps he had been destined to become himself at the moment he had first stepped into the Deadly Shadow.

He led the others in their armouring, teaching them the Hidden Death mantra, which had been passed to him by his fore-spirits when he had donned his exarch armour.

It was intriguing to watch the reactions of his pupils, and to see himself again as that novice wearing armour for the first time, more than half a dozen times over. He felt again the surge of power, of strength, that had flowed through him, the first glimmerings of his war-mask shining through.

Milathradil was the most eager. Morlaniath could feel his war-mask just beneath the surface. It resonated with the exarch, feeding him and drawing on him at the same time. Morlaniath would have to watch Milathradil closely; his passion could be his undoing.

Nurianda and Euraithin were more hesitant, sharing excitement and fear in equal measure, as it should be. Lokhirith was afraid. He was fearful of his own power, afraid to embrace his war-mask, holding back on the tide of emotions that needed to be given freedom before they could be controlled. Morlaniath decided he would pair Lokhirith with Milathradil for a while; they were in an odd balance together and would bring each other closer to internal harmony.

When the warriors were full-clad, Morlaniath began the rituals again. He moved without thought, called out the names of the poses. With that part of his mind not occupied by the training, he wondered which of his followers had shadow-foes and which did not. They moved with poise and precision, but it was not their technique that Morlaniath examined as he called out Rising Sting from Darkness. He was connected; connected to the shrine and through it to the Striking Scorpions, those in front of him now and all of those that had come before.

He read the micro-expressions in their faces and sensed their emotions. Euraithin was too focussed on his body, tightly controlling every motion. He needed to allow his instinct to prevail so that his attention to his environment was not lacking. Nurianda, she was a study of balance, at once a whirling maelstrom and a tranquil lake. Milathradil was distracted, too intent upon the creation of his shadow-foe. Morlaniath could read the fierce visualisation in his gestures, in the determination of his thoughts and the slightly curtailed, clipped nature of his technique. Lokhirith was still uncertain, second-guessing his body, his eyes straying to Morlaniath or his companions, seeing too much of the real world to lose himself entirely in the battle.

Progress had been made, but there was still a long way to go.

Morlaniath communed, resting his body in his armour while his spirits digested the events of the cycle. There came a sudden interruption to their deliberations.

One Is Coming.

Morlaniath sensed a presence at the borders of his domain, at the main portal to his desert dome. It was not an aspirant, though he felt a great deal of tension from his visitor. It was not an exarch: he would recognise his kin instantly. There was something familiar in the presence; a similarity to someone locked away within his memories, but dissimilar enough that he could not locate it. The person approached and then went away, and then approached again. There was hesitancy, a mixture of fear and doubt.

He opened his eyes, feeling change afoot.

Still armoured, Morlaniath took a skyrunner from the shrine's depths and sped across the desert leaving a plume of sand in his wake. He flew directly to the main portal, the nagging sense of recognition tantalising in its closeness but still eluding him. Dismounting, he opened the wide gateway with a thought command.

A farseer turned quickly, taken aback by his arrival. She was dressed in a long robe of pure black, embroidered sigils of silver and white decorating the hem and cuffs of her gown. She fidgeted with a pouch at her waist, while her eyes widened with a mixture of surprise and disgust.

He recognised those eyes. It was Thirianna.

Oh, It's Her. Troublemaker, That One.

'It that you, Korlandril?' she asked.

'I am not Korlandril, though he is part of me, I am Morlaniath.'

You Should Say 'We'. It Is Very Rude To Ignore The Rest Of Us.

We Are One. 'I' Is Correct.

Ignore Them Both. This Argument Never Ends.

Thirianna took a step away, shoulders hunching.

What Does She Want?

She Doesn't Belong Here. Send Her Away!

Look How Scared She Is Of Us.

'Why do you disturb us, coming here unbidden, breaking the gold stillness?'

She took a few steps further back, shaking her head.

'This was a mistake. I should not have come. You cannot help me.'

Good Riddance.

She Has Already Roused Us. We Have Nothing To Lose By Letting Her Speak.

We Have Wasted Enough Time. Let Her Go.

She might return and disturb us again.

'Now that you have come here, seeking guidance and truth, speak your mind with freedom. If I can assist you, if you have hard questions, perhaps I can answer.'

Thirianna approached and stared past Morlaniath, taking in the wide vista of the desert. Her gaze turned to the exarch.

'Is there somewhere else we can speak?'

Always the Same. Farseers Want To Know Everything. Do Not Let Her In. She Is Not Welcome.

The Shrine Is Soaked In The Memories Of Blood. She Cannot Go There.

'The shrine would not be fit, farseers enter with risk, and I am loathe to leave.'

'Can we perhaps walk awhile? I do not feel comfortable discussing matters on your doorstep.'

Morlaniath turned away, assuming she would follow. The sands shifted under his booted feet but he walked with purpose and balance, heading towards a shallow oasis gently fed by irrigation webs beneath the sands. Clusters of red-leaved bushes hid the water's edge, bright white stars of blossom poking from the foliage.

The water was still. Sometimes he came here to contemplate without his companions. This was the first time he had come here in the full presence of the others. Memory came without asking, swamping him for a moment with recollections of this place as each spirit clasped to some distant event, seeking to relive them. He pushed them away and gestured for Thirianna to seat herself beside the still pool.

'This is… pleasant.' She looked at her surrounds and sat down, gathering her robes to one side, her black hair tossed over her shoulder, head tilted away from Morlaniath.

'It is the birth in death, the hope in hopelessness, life amongst the barren.' She did not look at him when he spoke. She gazed thoughtfully into the waters. Insects skimmed the surface, sustained by its tension.

'I have foreseen troubling times for Alaitoc, perhaps something worse.'

A Farseer Foresees Trouble? That Is The Nature Of Things.

Listen To What She Has To Say.

This Is A Waste Of Our Time. We Should Wake The Warriors And Begin Their Training In The Dark Stalking.

'You are now a farseer. Such things will be your life, why do you come to me?'

'I am told that I am in error. The farseers, the council of Alaitoc, do not think my scrying will come to pass. They say I am inexperienced, seeing dangers that do not exist.'

They Are Right.

Pompous And Conceited, All Of Them. She Thinks She Sees Something They Cannot. They Cannot Conceive Of Being Blind To Anything.

Not all of them.

Yes, All Of Them.

'Likely they are correct, your powers are still weak, this path is new to you. I do not see my role; I am the exarch here, not one of the council.'

'You don't believe me?'

'You offer me no proof, and there is none to give, belief alone is dust.'

Thirianna stood and walked to the pool's edge. She dipped her booted toe into the waters, sending a ripple across the surface. The ripple disturbed Morlaniath. This was a place of calm and Thirianna had brought disquiet. He said nothing and watched as she allowed the droplets to fall from her boot, moving her foot so that they dribbled a swirl in the sand.

'I followed the fate of Aradryan.' Morlaniath spent a moment recalling the name. One who had been friend to Korlandril, unknown to not-Korlandril. He had started Korlandril on his path to this place. Thirianna continued without pause. 'Our three destinies are interwoven. More than we have seen already. Yours is not ended, but will soon. His is distant and confused. Mine… Mine is to be here, to tell you these things to set in motion future events.'

Fanciful And Untrue. All Destinies Are Interwoven.

'What is it you have seen, what visions bring such woe, what do they mean for us?'

'Aradryan dwells in darkness, but there is also light for him. But his darkness is not confined to him. It spreads into our lives, and it engulfs Alaitoc. I do not know the details: my rune-casting is very crude at the moment. I feel he has done something gravely wrong and endangered all of us.'

'Your warnings are too vague, they contain no substance, we have no course of action.'

Thirianna snorted, a sound of bitter resentment and dark humour.

'That is what the council says. "How can we prepare against something so amorphous?" they asked. I told them that more experienced seers should follow the thread of Aradryan. They refused, claiming it was an irrelevance. Aradryan is gone from Alaitoc, they told me, and he is no longer their concern.'

Who Are We To Argue?

This Is Not Our Concern. We Are Warriors, Not Philosophers.

Morlaniath listened to this, perplexed. The council were correct. They could no more act on such a vision as they could an unfounded rumour. Other memories came to mind, rebuilding his picture of Thirianna. She was always seeking attention, always looking to be the centre of things. It was no surprise that she had not yet removed this flaw from her character, and now sought to garner an audience by claiming some personal insight into Alaitoc's doom.

'Continue your studies, delve further into this, to seek your own answers.'

'I fear there is no time. This is imminent. I lack the strength and the training to see far ahead.'

If She Is So Weak, How Have Others Not Seen This Disaster?

That Is A Good Point. Her Story Is Incomplete. Send Her Away!

'Others have not seen it, your fresh cataclysm, who are stronger than you. I must concur with them, who have trodden the Path, who see further than you.'

'It is such a small thing, whatever it is that Aradryan does.' She stooped and took a pinch of sand, rubbing her fingers to spill it to the ground until she held a single grain. She flicked it into the waters of the pool. 'Such a tiny ripple, we can barely see it, but a ripple nonetheless. The anarchy of history tells us that momentous events can start from the most humble, the most mundane of beginnings.'

'I have no aid for you, no council influence, and I agree with them. Go back to your studies, forget this distraction, I will not assist you.'

She looked at him for the first time, eyes misted, lips trembling.

'I feared the worst, and you have proven me true. Korlandril is not dead, but he has gone.'

'Which you once predicted, that both of us would change, for better or for worse. I am Morlaniath, you are Thirianna, Korlandril is no more. Seek contentment from this, do not chase the shadows, only darkness awaits.'

'Do you not remember what we once shared?'

'I remember it well, we shared nothing at all, I have nothing for you.'

Thirianna straightened and wiped a gloved finger across her cheek, a tear soaking into the soft fabric.

'You are right. I will leave and think of you no more.'

She bunched up her robe and strode up the encircling dune, heading towards the main portal. Morlaniath followed a short way behind and stopped on the dune's crest to watch her retreating back. She reached the gateway and Morlaniath willed it open. Then she was gone and with a thought he closed the gate behind her.

* * *

The *Teeth of Dissonance* thrummed in Morlaniath's hands, carving the air with beautiful sweeps. All in the shrine was quiet save for the sound of the blade and the tread of the exarch's booted feet on the stone. His followers were all asleep, exhausted by the day's training. Only their dreams broke the stillness, edged with blood, tinged with death. Morlaniath smiled.

He finished his practice and returned the blade to its rightful place. Taking up the stance of repose, he thought about Thirianna's visit.

Were we too dismissive?

You Gave Her Full Chance To Speak Her Case. We Are Unconvinced.

We Have Other Concerns. It Is Not Our Place To Debate With Farseers. Let The Autarchs Do That.

She came to us as a friend.

We Are Exarch. We Have No Friends. She Came To Us In Desperation When All Others Had Turned Her Away. It Is Shameful.

Then I ask not for her sake, but for Alaitoc. If what she says is true, it bodes ill for us.

What She Says Is Fantasy. Do Not Give It Further Consideration.

If There Is To Be War, We Will Fight. We Train Our Warriors For Battle. There Is No More That We Can Do. That Is What It Is To Be Exarch.

There It Is Again: 'I'. This Individuality Is Unbecoming.

I am still myself, Morlaniath and not-Korlandril both. I will make my own decision.

To Be Exarch Is To Know Sacrifice. Not For Us The Twilight Of The Infinity Circuit. Darkness Is Our Domain. If It Comes To Pass That This Body Dies, We Will Endure. That Is The Reward For Our Sacrifice.

Do Not Meddle In The Affairs Of Others. It Is Not Welcome And It Is Not Our Duty.

We Do Not Understand Her Motives. If What She Says Proves True, We Will Be Informed. If It Is Untrue Our Interference Risks Bringing Disharmony.

I am unsettled by this. If my fate and Aradryan's is still entwined in ways not yet revealed, it would be wise to heed her warning.

Farseers Always Speak Of Fate. It Is Their Reason For Everything. Sometimes Things Happen Without Purpose. All Warriors Know This. We Train, Perfecting Our Art, But It Is In The Nature Of War That The Random And The Uncontrollable Appear.

It was Thirianna and Aradryan that set me on this course, to our rebirth, to the return of the Hidden Death. I conceive that it is possible my future and theirs are not wholly separate.

Then What Will Happen, Will Happen. Let The Farseers Chase The Possibilities, We Will Deal With The Consequences.

Now it is you that is willing to surrender to fate.

This Debate Is Inappropriate. She Is A Distraction. Ignore Her.

I Concur. Concentrate On The Training Of Your Warriors.

Morlaniath stripped off his armour, unable to shake the disquiet, annoyed by the conflict of thoughts raised by Thirianna. While the direct thoughts of Morlaniath faded into memory, their effect lingered on, confusing him. The question of faith·vexed him the most. He had seen her conviction, but had ignored it. Whatever the reality, *she* certainly believed something terrible was going to happen.

It irked him that he was powerless, or so it seemed. He was entirely in the hands of the farseers, and they had chosen to ignore her.

He focussed on this train of thought. His distaste was not with the actions of Thirianna but with the inaction of the council. Part of him was too willing to simply accept their judgement. It was against his nature to submit, to blindly concur, now more than ever. The vestiges of not-Korlandril struggled against Morlaniath, urging him to do something.

Still in a state of conflict, Morlaniath gathered his squad at the start of the next cycle and led them in the combat rituals. It diverted his attention away from the dilemma posed by Thirianna.

Nurianda was proving to be the most capable of his students. Her technique was impeccable and she had found her war-mask without trauma. She had mastered the chainsword and the pistol without drama, and was at one with her suit. The others still struggled. They seemed reticent to lose themselves fully, still clinging to fragments of their past lives, gripping tight to the last vestiges of their former selves. While they resisted their own temptations they would never be able to progress.

Morlaniath tried to remember what it was like when he had been Korlandril. It was unpleasant, full of conflict and fear. The memories of the other Morlaniaths intruded upon his recollections, blurring the line between what had been his life and theirs. He had welcomed becoming the Hidden Death, yet the vestiges of his former life clung to his mind; or perhaps he clung to them. It occurred to him that perhaps he had been right to dismiss Thirianna. She was a tie to the past that no longer held any relevance for him.

He dismissed the squad and was about to leave when he noticed Nurianda lingering next to her armour.

'There is something amiss, you are free to leave here, yet here you still remain,' he said, approaching the Striking Scorpion.

'I find it difficult,' she admitted, eyes downcast. 'I tried to speak to my father, but he does not understand.'

'He cannot understand. Each of us has a Path, which only we can walk. I am merely a guide, the journey is all yours, you must walk it alone.'

'What if... What if the journey does not have an end?'

'It ends eventually, at one place or other, though I do not know which. Do not dwell on the end, but move along the Path, striving for your own goal. Know what you leave behind, the suffering and fear, seeking a place of peace. The love for your father, his affection for you, should act as your anchor. While you drift it remains, as it was at the start, so too at the ending.'

Nurianda smiled, wistful and thoughtful.

'Thank you. I will be patient with him.'

Morlaniath waved her to leave and stood for a while longer, gazing at the empty suits of armour. Each had belonged to many warriors. He could remember all of them – the ones that had lived, the ones that had died; the ones that had moved on, and those who had become him. He was all of them and none of them. What was he? Nothing more than dismembered spirits sharing a corporeal prison, unable to welcome the peace of the Infinity Circuit, unable to die because She Who Thirsts would claim him. He was nothing if he was not his experiences, his memories. He was the walking dead, stuck in the limbo of this body.

He could sense himself losing touch. This fresh body, it had stirred old feelings and old thoughts: memories of freedom and love; moments of pleasure and pain; moments of mortal senses and mortal thoughts. Its touch remained for the moment, but Morlaniath knew from several experiences that it would not last. Not-Korlandril invigorated him for the time being, but soon that spark would gutter and he would be Morlaniath wholly, the immortal servant of Khaine.

Let go of the past? That was foolish. Though many were the ways he had become Morlaniath, each was unique to him, each was a journey he had made. The Path had ended for him, but that did not eliminate the route he taken to reach this point. That route had meaning, and the people who had walked beside him for a while also had meaning. He had no future, save an eternity of violence and death, but they did.

He did not like unfinished business. The past was not irrelevant, but he had to leave it behind. Morlaniath made a decision and headed for the skyrunners.

'Perhaps you seek war, for that is your nature,' said Arhathain.

'I cannot make a war, if that is my desire, it is the council's choice,' replied Morlaniath.

He knew the autarch well; had fought beside him on many a battlefield. Like all autarchs he was strong-willed, determined enough to tread the Path of the Warrior several times without being ensnared by Khaine's curse. He remembered Arhathain as a young Dire Avenger, and a Howling Banshee in more recent memory. As an exarch he was far older than Arhathain, but not-Korlandril had been less than half his age. A dichotomy of feelings warred within Morlaniath, causing him to feel ancient and infant at the same time, unsure of his place and his time.

He had called Arhathain to the Chamber of Autarchs and spoken of Thirianna's predictions. Arhathain defended the council's decision, as was to be expected. Morlaniath tried to find the words that conveyed his thoughts, but it was difficult; he wanted to seize the autarch and force him to agree. Keeping his temper in check, he listened to what Arhathain had to say.

'Every day our seers uncover a thousand dooms to Alaitoc. We cannot act on every vision. We cannot go to war on every doubt. Thirianna herself cannot provide us with clarity. We might just as well act on a superstitious trickle of foreboding down the back of the neck.'

'She lacks the proper skill, the means to give you proof, hold that not against her. Give her the help she needs, to prove her right or wrong, she will keep her silence. This doubt will hold her back, it will consume her thoughts, until you release her. You have walked many paths, seen a great many things, lived a great many lives. That life you owe to me, I remember it now, so many cycles past. I was your guardian, the protection you sought, a true companion. I remember the debt, the oath you swore to me, it is now time to pay.'

Arhathain frowned and turned away, pacing to the far side of the rostrum at the centre of the hall.

'The one I made that promise to died ten passes and more ago,' he said softly, looking up at the circular opening at the top of the dome. A distant swathe of stars was strewn across the blackness of space. 'I did not swear that oath to you. It is not Elidhnerial that asks me to repay that debt, it is Korlandril.'

'I am Morlaniath, Elidhnerial too, and also Korlandril. The debt is owed to me, to all the parts of me, united in spirit. Who save me remembers, can repeat the words used, heard them spoken by you?'

'If I do not do this?'

'Your honour is forfeit, and others shall know it, I will make sure of that.'

The autarch turned and directed an intent stare at Morlaniath.

'You will not call on me again in this way?'

'Your debt will be repaid, to Elidhnerial, and we shall speak no more.'

Arhathain nodded reluctantly and stalked up the shallow steps of the chamber.

Morlaniath smiled at his departing back; the part that was not-Korlandril was pleased. He did not know what would become of his intervention, what the future would hold for him or Thirianna. Yet he was content. As a last act before he wholly became Morlaniath, it was worthwhile. Soon she would be unimportant, just another one of the memories, no greater and no less than the thousands of others he had met and loved and hated and been indifferent to. This was his parting gift. Even now the memory was becoming lost in the haze.

By the time he returned to the shrine, he would no longer care.

TRANSFORMATION

When the Great Enemy was born, the Bloody-Handed God brought war against She Who Thirsts but was quickly vanquished by the newborn horror. The Prince of Pleasure and the Lord of Skulls fought over possession of Khaine's spirit, for the Bloody-Handed God was a child of both but belonged to neither. Great was the struggle in the remnants of heaven, but neither She Who Thirsts nor the Master of Battle prevailed. When both the rivals were exhausted, they drew up their boundaries and in the calm eye of their wrath Khaine fell into the world of mortals. Here the Bloody-Handed One shattered into many fragments, unable to exist as a whole in the material realm. His power spent, his body divided, Khaine's wrath was finally diminished. Though suppressed, his rage lingers on in these fragments, drawn to war and strife, awaiting the time when blood awakens him and his vengeful essence gains form once more.

The shrine throbbed once, a frisson of rage that peaked in less than a heartbeat and was gone; a spasm of energy that distracted Morlaniath for a moment, causing him to almost miss his next instruction. He put the tremor to the back of his mind and completed the training period with his pupils, dismissing them abruptly when they were done.

He was uncertain of the cause for the momentary flux of psychic energy that had disturbed him, though he had strong suspicions. He took a skyrunner from the shrine and flew through the bowels of Alaitoc, following an instinct.

The tunnels he navigated were lit by the solitary beam of his skyrunner, a circle of light in the blackness. In the darkness around him, strands of wraithbone glittered occasionally with psychic force as the spirits of the infinity circuit pulsed to and fro. This was the life of Alaitoc – the heart and arteries, skeleton and nervous system, thoughts and feelings of the craftworld. The disturbance that Morlaniath had felt did not come again as he rode, though he sensed a residual after-shock of its occurrence, a tension that filled the air.

At the hub of Alaitoc, where the many psychic veins and nerveways of the craftworld converged, Morlaniath exited the service passage and brought his skyrunner to a halt inside a darkened chamber. The infinity circuit glowed with a ruddy light, the red of a womb. A gate was open before him, its two huge doors opened wide to reveal a wraithbone-wrapped chamber. At the centre of that room was a great throne of iron. Upon that throne sat a statuesque figure, twice Morlaniath's height, its skin fused metal, its eyes black, empty sockets. The immense figure brooded, sucking the light from the throne room, iron fingers in fists, face contorted in a silent roar.

He felt the approach of someone behind him and turned.

'You felt it also, a heartbeat of Khaine, the Avatar stirs?' asked Iriethien, Dire Avenger, exarch of the Light That Burns.

'I felt something stirring, the Avatar still sleeps, the time has not yet come,' Morlaniath said.

'War is approaching, Khaine knows of these things, he senses battle,' said Iriethien. He gazed at the immobile giant, seeking any sign of life.

'We will know soon enough, there will be no doubting, when the war god calls us.'

The presence of Iriethien had confirmed Morlaniath's suspicions. As he returned to his skyrunner, a single thought troubled him: his warriors were not yet ready for battle.

The tremulous sensation from the Avatar of Khaine did not repeat itself, but Morlaniath knew that it had not been an aberration. Once it began to waken, the Avatar did not fall into slumber again without blood being shed. The other exarchs felt it also, and sent warning to the council of Alaitoc that events were unfolding that would take the craftworld to war.

Filled with a new urgency, Morlaniath pressed on as quickly as he could with the training of the Hidden Death Striking Scorpions. All of them had now progressed to mastering the helmet and mandiblasters but progress seemed slow to the exarch. He had to be certain that they were ready for battle and was still unconvinced. If their training was insufficient it might mean disaster, not only for themselves but for the other warriors that would be relying upon them.

Morlaniath did not fret, did not waste time worrying about this state of affairs. The matter was a simple one: when war came they would either be ready or they would not. If they were not suitably prepared, they would not fight.

The voices were no more. The nights brought silence and solitude, a time for contemplation. Morlaniath found peace in the memories of battle, reliving the glories of his past, sometimes even dwelling upon the moments of his deaths, learning from them, seeking ever to improve himself.

He found his memedreams lingering more frequently on his bloody encounters with humans. Was it because his last battle had been against the followers of the Corpse-Emperor? Was there some deeper force at play that led him to relive these wars?

His pondering was interrupted, seven night-cycles after he had felt the tremor of the Avatar. Through the strands of the infinity circuit he was aware of a new arrival coming to Alaitoc, a presence that resonated through all of his lives, all of his spirits. There was a counter-echo in the midst of his consciousness, a responding tremble of awareness from the other shrines, and again the great pulse of Khaine's heartbeat thudded briefly across the infinity circuit.

The docking bay glimmered with light from the webway portal, swirling purple and blue dappling the curved walls and the armour of seventeen exarchs. They waited in silence, each called from his or her shrine; Swooping Hawk, Dark Reaper and Striking Scorpion. Morlaniath felt the same as the others, a primal instinct to gather, to greet their arrival.

They had been brought to the Star-Wreathed Stair, the docks where warships came and went, keeping their taint of blood from ships of peaceful purpose. This was the place where the Aspect Warriors boarded their vessels. It was where their remains were brought back. From here Alaitoc had launched its warriors into the Night for an age, sending them to slay or be slain. This was a place of destiny, from whence the fate of Alaitoc had been steered: expeditionary forces to uncover rising threats; fleets bent on vengeance for eldar deaths; armies that had destroyed worlds; missions to kill the ignorant and the innocent; warriors sent to slaughter inferior races, whose only crime had been their existence.

Death stained the twining branches of wraithbone around the dock, the infinity circuit singing a mournful dirge at the back of Morlaniath's mind. It nourished him and he drew a deep breath of satisfaction.

The bow-wave of psychic energy from the webway grew stronger, the arrival of a ship imminent. It carried with it a sensation of belonging, of acceptance and stability. These thoughts were touched with blood, images of destruction played out in bursts of mental activity. It was similar to the sensation he felt from other exarchs, though greater in its intensity, increasing in its power the closer the ship came.

As when Thirianna had come to the shrine, Morlaniath knew who it was that came to Alaitoc, but could not recognise him. The whole had changed but parts remained familiar, much in the same way as an exarch's spirit slowly evolved into a new personality with each warrior that took up the armour.

Ageless immortality was the backdrop to each of the sensations, older even than Morlaniath, a spirit so deep that it swallowed everything that touched it.

The webway portal pulsed, readying for the ship's exit. A surge of psychic energy swept through the assembled exarchs, bringing flashes of insight, visions of distant worlds and ancient places.

The ship broke through the portal at incredible speed: one moment the bay was empty, the next the sleek black hull filled the void. Its surface rippled with faint colour, waves of dark purple and blue shimmering from shark-like nose to slender tail fins. It lowered silently to hover just above the deck, merging with its own shadow.

A circular portal opened, creating a disc of faint white light. Morlaniath strained forward, pulse racing.

Three figures appeared at the portal as the tongue of a ramp extruded itself to the floor. They wore armour, their suits versions of the exarch armour of those that waited but far heavier and more elaborate, and even more ancient: Swooping Hawk, Dark Reaper, Striking Scorpion. Their weapons were ornate artefacts of the time before the Fall when eldar power had been at its height; beautiful instruments of destruction salvaged from the ruins of an entire civilisation.

The first wore wings that shimmered in a thousand colours, a curved blade in one hand, a multi-barrelled las-blaster in the other, helm adorned with a single feathered crest, his armour a mottle of summer blue and winter grey. The next had armour of black, sculpted with golden bones, his helm a red-eyed skull, the image of Death itself, a scythed shuriken cannon in his grip. Last came the Scorpion, and upon him Morlaniath fixed his gaze, the flow of connection between them strengthening as the new arrival approached. His yellow and green armour was banded with obsidian ribbing, his helm curved back in a series of plates like a scorpion's tail, crackling mandiblasters pods to either side. One hand was an elegant claw wreathed with energy, the other gripped the hilt of a biting blade, its teeth so sharp that rainbows of cut light danced around them.

They were the first exarchs, those who had walked the Path of the Warrior in the wake of the Fall and studied under the guidance of Asurmen. Morlaniath knew them immediately, remembered them from previous encounters while legends of their deeds surfaced in his mind.

Three founders of the Aspect shrines: The Cry of the Wind, Baharroth; The Harvester of Souls, Maugan Ra; The Shadow Hunter, Karandras.

Three Phoenix Lords, almost without precedent, had come to Alaitoc for a single purpose: war.

* * *

The arrival of the Phoenix Lords was both a reaction and a catalyst. They had sensed a new doom approaching Alaitoc and had been drawn to the coming conflict. Their presence reacted with the somnolent essence of Khaine's Avatar, speeding its wakening. Morlaniath's memories were clouded with blood, his training sessions with his warriors interrupted by waves of bloodthirsty sensation. The other exarchs felt it too, and the Aspect shrines and infinity circuit gently thrummed with the nascent rage of Kaela Mensha Khaine.

Faced with these events, the council of Alaitoc summoned its greatest seers to divine which potential cataclysm was most likely to engulf the craftworld. They studied the runes of Thirianna, ready to listen to her half-formed tale of approaching death. Eyes more ancient than hers scanned the skeins of possibility, following the threads of Aradryan's life and the interwoven fates of Alaitoc.

All agreed: a great darkness was descending upon the craftworld. The rune of the humans blackened when touched and the farseers felt the irrational hatred of mankind directed at Alaitoc.

The autarchs called the exarchs to assembly in their circular hall, Alaitoc's deadliest warriors all gathered in one place. The air seethed with their fierce pride and lust for battle. Morlaniath was drenched in their growing anger and strengthening hatred, soaking it into his spirit, elevating his own anticipation to a peak.

Arhathain, accompanied by Alaitoc's three other autarchs, addressed the restless throng of shrine leaders.

'It is the humans,' he said solemnly. 'The followers of the Emperor will come to Alaitoc intent on conflict. Why they choose to do so is unclear, but some slight against them has stirred their wrath. As a single pebble may start a landside, so the act of one has led the humans to Alaitoc. Though the farseers have travelled the strands of destiny, there is but one consequence that cannot be averted: Alaitoc will be attacked.

'It is not our place to speculate on the shortsighted decisions of humans. It is our task to prepare for war and deal with the consequences. Rangers have returned to Alaitoc, bearing grave news. Imperial ships forge their way through the Sea of Dreams, heading in our direction. There is insufficient time to elude them: they are too close and Alaitoc is not yet at full energy peak. Our starships will intercept them, deter them from coming, but humans are ill-counselled and stubborn. It is likely they will attempt to breach Alaitoc and bring battle to our homes. Though they think that they come with surprise as their weapon, we have not been taken unawares.'

The autarch had calmly relayed this information, but now his voice rose, stoked by feeling.

'We will not allow this absurd action to go unpunished! The temerity of the humans staggers belief, even if their ignorance is well-recorded. It is not just Alaitoc that we must fight to protect, but all of our people. If the humans think that they can attack craftworlds with impunity, it will signal the end of our species. They must learn the folly of their action, through the bloodiest lesson we can give them. They are cowards, and superstitious. We will write new legends for them – myths of how the eldar slaughtered them for their stupidity. Stories written in their entrails and blood.'

Arhathain walked slowly around the circumference of the podium, bright blue eyes passing over the circles of exarchs. His lips formed a snarl.

'We abhor you! We who are free are fearful of you, the living reminders of the consequences of weakness and indulgence. Rightfully you are shunned, for your spirits are cursed by Khaine. You are warmongers and murderers. Those of us who have passed along the Path of the Warrior stand absolved of the atrocities we have committed and have found peace. You are trapped, relishing your bloody deeds, glorying in your hatred and rage.

'But we who are free also need you. Without the exarchs, we would all be lost. You carry the burdens of our guilt. You stand between our fragile spirits and the degradations of war.'

His voice became a harsh whisper as he continued to circle, tense, shoulders hunched, fists tight.

'This is your time! The humans seek to violate our beautiful homes. They *dare* to bring war against us! You are our bloody messengers. You are Kaela Mensha Khaine's anointed slayers, our vengeance incarnate, our anger given form. You are merciless, and rightly so. Our survival allows no compassion. Our continuing existence depends upon the unthinking doing the unthinkable.

'Feel now the pulse of Khaine throbbing through your veins. We who are free, we feel it also. But it is but a cold trickle in our veins compared to the white heat of its ferocity in your hearts. The Avatar awakens. Feel his call. Take to him that which he needs.'

The autarchs and exarchs turned as one to the main gate at the height of the stepped auditorium. A lone figure stood there, silhouetted against an orange light beyond. It was the Shining Spear exarch, Lideirra of the Midnight Lightning shrine. She wore her silver and gold armour and carried an immense spear, its head as long as her arm and as broad as her face – the Suin Daellae, the Doom that Wails, the weapon of the Avatar.

'Behold the Young King!' announced Arhathain. 'Your gift to Khaine in return for the awakening of his Avatar.'

With a fierce shout, the exarchs raised their right fists in salute to the Young King. Chosen from amongst their number, the Young King served as their spiritual leader for five hundred cycles and then passed on his or her crown to another. For most, their rule passed without sacrifice; for a few their reign would end in blood, their spirit offered up to Khaine to breathe life into the metal husk of Khaine's Avatar.

Lideirra stood calmly in the archway, accepting of her fate. It was not only a great honour to be chosen as Young King – named after Eldanesh's epithet as a child, though the chosen exarch could be male or female – it was also a promise of release. To be consumed by the rage of Khaine's fiery spirit was a release from immortality, one that few exarchs would ever know.

The six exarchs of the innermost ring, the oldest of their Aspects, headed up the steps to the Young King: Morlaniath, Striking Scorpion; Iriethien, Dire Avenger; Lathorinin, Howling Banshee; Faerthruin, Fire Dragon; Maurenin, Dark Reaper; Rhiallaen, Swooping Hawk.

They formed an honour guard around the Young King, three on the left and three on the right, and walked slowly from the hall. Another triumphant shout echoed behind them as they passed from the sight of the exarchs.

The walls of the passageway were covered with holographic images of the oldest myths of the eldar, the tales that had inspired the Aspects. Scenes of destruction from legend enveloped the entourage as they paced slowly towards the shrine of the war god. The doors closed silently behind, leaving them bathed in the soft glow of the projections. This was the Bloodied Way. It wound gently downwards, bringing the procession to the antechamber of the Avatar's throne room. The great bronze doors were closed, a thick trickle of ruddy light creeping from beneath it.

Morlaniath could feel the presence of the Avatar; its heat on his body, its spirit in his mind. The ground reverberated beneath the exarch's feet with a sonorous beating. His heart matched the rhythm.

From hidden doorways, masked and robed seers entered: the warlocks. Former Aspect Warriors, the seers too felt the pull of Khaine. They brought with them a long cloak of red and a golden pin fashioned in the shape of a dagger. The two bearers stood before Lideirra as the exarchs slowly removed her armour. They handed each piece to one of the remaining warlocks.

When Lideirra was naked, Iriethien took the dagger-pin in his left hand. Another warlock garbed in white robes came up next to him, an ornate golden goblet in his hands: the Cup of Criel. The myths of the eldar held that when Eldanesh had been slain by Khaine, his followers had caught his blood in seven cups, to keep it from the war god. Khaine fought hard to reclaim the life and spirit of his victim, but Eldanesh's people had held the war god's armies at bay, preserving Eldanesh's spirit forever.

Standing behind the Young King, Iriethien used the point of the pin to cut the rune of the Dire Avenger into the flesh of Lideirra, beneath her left shoulderblade. The dagger-pin cut through skin and flesh effortlessly. Blood ran in rivulets across the Young King's pale flesh, dripping from her buttock to be caught by the cupbearer.

When he was done, Iriethien passed the knife to Morlaniath, who drew out the sigil of the Striking Scorpions on the other side of Lideirra's back. He passed the knife to Lathorinin, who carved the rune of the Howling Banshee beneath Lideirra's left breast. Next came Faerthruin, making the mark of the Fire Dragon on the Young King's right side. Maurenin and Rhiallaen cut Lideirra's arms, inscribing the runes of the Dark Reaper and Swooping Hawk respectively.

All the while Lideirra stood in silence, trembling slightly but not once flinching from the blade worked upon her flesh. Her eyes were bright with anticipation, fixed upon the bronze doors in front of her. Her white skin was criss-crossed with trails of blood.

One of the warlock attendees brought forth Lideirra's waystone, clasped into a fixing upon a pale silver chain. This was hung around her neck. The stone bearer then took up the dagger-pin and delicately cut the rune of the Avatar into Lideirra's forehead. Crimson trickled into her eyes but she stared unblinking, red tears streaking her cheeks.

The mantle of the Avatar was hung from her shoulders, fixed with the bloodied dagger-pin. Its great length was wrapped about her body twice, and still it trailed on the floor behind her. Darker shadows spread across the red cloth as her blood soaked into the tightly-woven fibres.

Next she was presented with the Suin Daellae, taking the immense spear in her right hand. Into her left was placed the Cup of Criel, now brimming with her blood.

The warlocks formed a circle around the Young King and her honour guard. One of them raised her voice, giving vent to a piercing wail which flowed into the opening words from the *Hymn of Blood*. Another took up the refrain, adding a discordant tone beneath the first, and then another and another until the warlocks filled the antechamber with the sound of harsh singing.

Morlaniath turned his attention upon the throne room doors. The light from beneath was growing bright, flickering, reflected from the entwined wraithbone of the antechamber. The heat from the bronze portal increased steadily, until the air shimmered and Morlaniath blinked sweat from his eyes inside his helmet. Crackles and splintering noises sounded dully from within the throne room. Hisses of steam and the snap of flames grew louder.

The exarchs joined their voices to the chants and shrieks of the warlocks, adding another discordant harmony to the hymn.

Morlaniath felt the stirring of the Avatar at the base of his spine, its presence tingling up to his neck and then flowing along into his fingertips, into his gut and down to his toes. Energy suffused every part of him, setting his nerves alight.

He sang on, roaring the praises of Khaine, his voice cutting across the ululations and wails of his companions.

In the midst of the ritual, Lideirra stood immobile, skin stained with blood, a thickening crimson pool around her bare feet. Cup and spear were unmoving in her hands, and save for the subtlest rise and fall of her chest she was no more than a statue.

Another reverberating heartbeat throbbed through Morlaniath. Then another, and another. The bass pulsing fitted with the tempo of the strident hymn, both quickening with each other.

With a rush of heat, the bronze doors opened, bathing the antechamber with dazzling light. Morlaniath could barely make out the form of the Avatar in the brightness, a hulking ember sat on its throne, a shadow amongst the light.

The Young King paced into the throne room, spear and cup held before her. She was swallowed by the light and then briefly appeared before being engulfed again by the shadow of the Avatar.

With a dull thud, the doors slowly closed, ending the hymn, the quiet that followed eerie, full of febrile tension. Still the sounds of metal melting and fire burning came muffled through the doors. A rumble as of distant thunder gently shook the bronze barrier.

The warlocks departed wordlessly as the exarchs formed a circle, standing hand-in-hand with each other, Iriethien to Morlaniath's left, Lathorinin to his right. The ring thus formed, the exarchs' spirits flowed into one another, mingling and swirling together. Their voices were raised in a single chant, a soft, bass humming that set the chamber to vibrating. Morlaniath drifted away, losing himself in the maelstrom of spirits created by the conjoined exarchs.

Morlaniath's next moment of awareness came as he stepped back from the circle. Aranarha had taken his place at the vigil. Morlaniath returned to the Chamber of Autarchs where the other exarchs waited.

He rested, waiting for his time to come again. Around his dormant form, exarchs came and left, but he did not notice them. He dreamt, wandering in his memories of battle, delighting in the recollections of previous times spent fighting alongside the Avatar. The dreams became more vibrant, more distinct and he knew the Avatar's awakening was coming closer.

The exarchs began to drift away from the chamber, singly at first, and then in small groups, returning to their shrines. Morlaniath lingered a while longer, revelling in the life that flowed into him.

His contemplations halted abruptly. He sensed Kenainath behind him. Opening his eyes, he turned to his fellow exarch.

'There is something amiss, I feel a disturbance, your spirit is troubled.'

'Your thoughts are correct, I have need to speak with you, come now to my shrine.'

Morlaniath felt for the presence of the Avatar, knowing that he would have to return soon to the Hidden Death and ready them for the Avatar's awakening. He knew that there was yet still time. He nodded his acquiescence and accompanied Kenainath from the hall.

Morlaniath followed the other exarch into the armouring chamber of the Deadly Shadow. Silence reigned, the squad not yet called to war by their leader, though surely they felt the coming of the Avatar.

'Where are your warriors? The time is approaching, they must soon be ready,' said Morlaniath.

Kenainath took off his helmet and placed it upon the top of its stand. His face was emaciated, his eyes sunken and dull, his dry skin clinging to the sharp bones of his cheeks.

'I cannot lead them, I will not see this battle, my time here is short.' Kenainath's voice was barely a whisper. 'This body is old, the time of its end draws close, and will pass away. No other comes here. The Deadly Shadow will sleep, waiting for rebirth.'

'It is a cruel ending, on the eve of battle, one more glorious war,' replied Morlaniath.

Kenainath gripped Morlaniath's shoulders and fixed him with a penetrating stare.

'There is not much time; I have something to ask you, a boon to request. Your squad is untested, your warriors not ready, you cannot lead them.'

Morlaniath opened his mouth to argue but Kenainath ignored him and continued on.

'You need warriors, take on the Deadly Shadow, lead them in battle. They need an exarch, let them be the Hidden Death, with you their exarch.'

A reflex shimmered through Morlaniath's consciousness: the Avatar's awakening was approaching. Time was short. He looked at Kenainath, seeing him through a hundred different memories. It was a harsh fate that took his life from him, at the brink of Alaitoc's greatest need. Yet this body had fought longer than any other exarch. Perhaps he deserved peace for a little while; perhaps this was a battle others needed to fight for him.

'It shall be an honour, to lead your warriors, to make them Hidden Death.'

A thin sliver of a smile twisted Kenainath's cracked lips.

'The honour is mine, to stand in such company, to be found worthy.' Kenainath looked sharply past Morlaniath's shoulder, as if someone had entered the room. 'My pupils approach, I will send them on to you, at the Hidden Death. The Avatar comes, make them don their masks swiftly, take me from their minds.'

Morlaniath nodded in understanding. There should be no time for the Deadly Shadow to dwell on the passing of their exarch, and there would be time enough for them to mourn after the coming battle. He clasped Kenainath's hands for a moment, their spirits mingling for a moment before he broke the contact.

'Enjoy your coming rest, it will not be forever, and we will fight again.'

Morlaniath turned away and headed to the skyrunners below, sensing others approaching the shrine.

As he straddled the skyrunner, he felt a surge of power coursing through him. He would have to be swift: the Avatar was almost awake.

Morlaniath sped for the throne room of the Avatar, dragged on by the call of the war god incarnate. He had readied his own shrine, joined shortly after his arrival by the warriors who had been the Deadly Shadow. Though Elissanadrin, Arhulesh and the others had been full of questions, Morlaniath had allowed them no time to ponder the turn of events. He had left them ready to bring forth their war-masks; waiting in silent expectation for the Avatar's coming, along with the dozens of other Aspect Warrior shrines across the craftworld. At the moment of his awakening they would don their helms and be suffused with his bloody power, ready to bring death to the humans.

He took his place in the circle of founders, heart racing, breaths coming in short gasps. The doors of the throne room shuddered violently, smoke and flames licking beneath them. The humming incantation of the circle was drowned out by a metallic pounding and the roar of flames.

A piercing scream cut through the chant, and silence fell. Morlaniath shuddered in the grips of ecstasy, the rage and hatred of the Avatar coursing through his body. Through the infinity circuit, the war-call of Khaine echoed through the Alaitocii, bringing everything to a stop. For a single instant every eldar on the craftworld, alive and dead, were joined as one, their psychic energy bringing forth the incarnation of their rage, their living idol of violence.

In a quivering rapture, Morlaniath watched the bronze doors crash open.

The Avatar's eyes burned with dark fire, glowing coals of hatred. Its iron skin was blistered, cracked and pitted, molten rivulets dribbling over the plates. Between them, fiery hide burned bright, tongues of flame licking along metal muscle, flickering within immortal joints.

In its right hand it wielded the Suin Daellae, the arcane weapon glittering with power, the runes upon its haft and head writhing with flaming sparks. Upon its shoulders it wore the ruddy cloak, its cloth and dagger-pin still stained with blood. Of Lideirra there was no sign, save for a gory slick of blood encasing the Avatar's arms from burning fingertips to sharp elbow. The blood hissed as it dripped to the floor.

All of this Morlaniath saw in a moment before the Avatar swamped his mind. The exarch relived every death he had inflicted, his joy reaching a crescendo. It was almost too much, a blurring kaleidoscope of pain and bloodletting, every flitting image heightening Morlaniath's pleasure until he could restrain it no more.

He arched his back and let loose a roar of rage, venting every atom of his hatred, his call joined across the craftworld by thousands of throats.

WAR

In the time following the Fall, Asurmen rallied the shattered remnants of Eldanesh and Ulthanesh's children. Upon the craftworlds they fled, the ravages of She Who Thirsts following them swiftly. Asurmen knew that the children of Eldanesh and Ulthanesh could not flee forever, for the obscene god that had been born out of their lustful desires and perverse nightmares was still a part of them. Asurmen led a handful of his followers to a barren world free of distraction and temptation. Here Asurmen founded the Shrine of Asur. Dedicating his life to the preservation of the domain of Asuryan, king of the gods and arbiter of heaven, Asurmen taught his followers that they must give up their love of the gods, for indulgence had led to decadence and wickedness. The destructive impulses of Khaine had to be tempered with wisdom, and so Asurmen taught his followers how to forget the joy of slaying and the thrill of battle. At the Temple Shrine of Asur, his pupils each developed their own fighting technique, channelling only a part of the Bloody-Handed God's rage. They were the Asurya, the first exarchs. When the treachery of Arhra destroyed the Temple Shrine of Asur, the Asurya escaped to the craftworlds to found new shrines to pass on their disciplines of war. The Asurya created the Path of the Warrior and would be known in ages to come as the Phoenix Lords, each reborn out of death until Fuegan of the Burning Lance calls them to the Rhana Dandra, the final battle, ending of the children of Eldanesh and Ulthanesh.

All was still in the Dome of Crystal Seers. Trees of multicoloured wraith-bone jutted from the exposed infinity circuit, their glass-like leaves casting rainbows across the white sand-covered ground. Beneath their contorted limbs stood the immortal seers, flesh turned to ice-like crystal, their robes hung upon glassy bodies, their spirits long departed.

The dome throbbed with the energy of the infinity circuit as Alaitoc readied to defend itself. Morlaniath and the Hidden Death had been stationed to guard the dome alongside four other squads: Shining Spears on their silver jetbikes; Howling Banshees with their flowing manes and screaming masks; Dire Avengers in their blue and white; Warp Spiders with their glowing deathspinners.

Behind them hovered three Wave Serpents, elegant troop transports coloured in the blue of Alaitoc with purple thorn patterns wreathing across their sleek hulls. Energy vanes crackled with power along their bows, distorting their shapes with a shimmering protective field. Each had a turret sporting shuriken cannons or pairs of brightlances that swivelled watchfully.

Morlaniath spared no time for these sights. His attention was fixed far above, through the transparent force dome. Here the first battle for Alaitoc was being waged in the cold vacuum of space.

Bright flares of light from crude plasma engines betrayed the positions of the Imperial ships. Ghost-like, the warships of the eldar flitted past, only the shimmer and glint of their solar sails giving them away, their hulls as dark as the void.

Trails of fire criss-crossed the starry sky, as missiles and torpedoes streaked across the firmament. The blinding flash of laser weapons flitted through the darkness, while blossoms of brief flame erupted in the void. Squadrons of graceful destroyers tacked effortlessly to bring their weapons to bear while battleships slid gently through the maelstrom, their batteries unleashing salvoes of destruction, open bays spewing wave after wave of darting fighter craft and wide-winged bombers.

An Imperial frigate hove into view, so close that Morlaniath could see its white hull and golden eagle-headed prow. It was a slab-sided, brutal vessel, encrusted with cornices and buttresses, its prow a giant golden ram shaped like an eagle's beak. Flashes rippled from bow to stern as it opened fire with deck after deck of guns, the flashes cut through by the searing beams of laser turrets arranged along a crenulated dorsal deck. Alaitoc responded, a storm of lightning and laser leaping from the craftworld's defence turrets and anti-ship guns. The human ship was engulfed by a torrent of fire and its hull quickly broke, sending plumes of burning air into the vacuum. Wracked by the eldar weapons, the frigate's plasma reactors detonated in a blossom of white.

It was as if the stars themselves fought, and Morlaniath stood entranced by the spectacle of destruction.

The eldar ships glimmered with holofields, appearing as shimmering ghosts to open fire before disappearing against the star-filled backdrop. Human void shields sputtered with blue and purple flares as they unleashed bursts of energy to shunt the attacks of the eldar into warp space.

For all the skill of the eldar crews and the agility of their ships, the humans drew inexorably closer, their coming heralded by fresh waves of torpedoes and the glare of attack craft. Burning hulks drifted in their wake, both human and eldar, debris gently spiralling away from shattered wrecks. The humans seemed bent on their course, coming straight for Alaitoc like armoured comets, punching through the craftworld's fleet, heedless of the damage inflicted upon them. Morlaniath had to admire the humans' single-mindedness, misguided as it was. Blind faith in their decrepit Emperor gave them a zeal that overrode all logic and sensibility.

A massive shape loomed through the dome, dozens of armoured doors opening along its side to reveal bristling gun batteries. Defensive fire converged on the cruiser and its shields rippled, dissipating the blasts with actinic flares. Its bow erupted with blossoms of orange and moments later the streak of torpedoes hurtled towards Alaitoc, breaking into hundreds of smaller missiles as they crashed into the craftworld.

Morlaniath felt the tremor of their impact, not through his flesh but in his mind, the infinity circuit reverberating with a spasm of pain. More salvoes from the cruiser's gun decks slammed into Alaitoc, crashing against the energy shields that protected the domes. This time the ground did shudder, so close were the impacts of plasma and rocket. The barrage continued for some time and then fell silent, the flare of laser and shell replaced by the small pinpricks of assault craft engines.

The humans were sending their boarding parties.

'The Tower of Ascending Dreams is under attack.' Arhathain's voice cut through Morlaniath's trance. 'Stand ready to respond on my command.'

The exarch signalled to his warriors to mount up in the Wave Serpent. As they ran up the ramp at its back, he saw the Warp Spiders wink out of existence, while the Shining Spears gunned the engines of their jetbikes and sped out of sight between the wraithbone trees.

Morlaniath crouched in the back of the Wave Serpent as the ramp closed, sealing them inside. Above him motors whined quietly as the turret lowered into the hull, the pilot readying the transport for departure.

The Striking Scorpions waited for the autarch's orders, every heartbeat slowly tickling past. Arhulesh fidgeted with anticipation, flexing his fingers around the grip of his chainsword. Elissanadrin crouched next to Morlaniath, forearms gently resting on her knees, head bowed in concentration. Bechareth remained as silent as ever, his gaze fixed on Morlaniath. The exarch stared back, wondering what passed through the former incubi's mind. Did he confuse Morlaniath with Korlandril, thinking perhaps that they shared some kind of bond? Did he ponder his fate now that Kenainath's protection was no more? Morlaniath had questions of his own; questions that only time would answer. Was Bechareth truly reformed? He had fought as Hidden Shadow many times, but would he be willing to lay down his life for Alaitoc, an adopted home? Could he be trusted to fight if it seemed that Alaitoc was waning?

'The humans have broken into the lower levels of the Tower of Ascending Dreams,' announced Arhathain. 'Move forward to contain them. Do not over-commit. More human ships are closing along the starward rim. Be ready to fall back and redeploy. Guardian forces moving in support.'

The thrum of the Wave Serpent's engines filled the cabin as it lifted higher and turned on the spot. There was little sensation of movement save the slight pull of inertia as the transport accelerated, but on internal screens Morlaniath saw the crystal seers skimming past as the pilot steered the Wave Serpent towards the main artery to the docking area being attacked.

They passed through the low portal at high speed, veering onto a thoroughfare lit by bright bands of green and blue. The lights flashed past the screen, increasing to a rapid strobe as the Wave Serpent picked up speed. Other vehicles joined them at intersections; several Wave Serpents fell in behind them while two Falcon anti-grav tanks sped past, their helmeted pilots and gunners glimpsed briefly through armoured canopies.

Suddenly deceleration pushed at Morlaniath as the Wave Serpent cornered sharply. He swayed with the momentum, readjusting himself on his haunches to keep his balance. The Wave Serpent picked up speed again as it accelerated along the ramp leading towards the dock towers.

They burst onto the broad plaza of the rim, the whining of the engines lost in the cavernous space of the empty docks: all of the ships had let slip from their moorings as soon as the Imperial fleet had broken out of warp space.

The Wave Serpent slewed to a halt and the ramp lowered even as the transport settled down into a low hover. Morlaniath raced down the ramp, the squad close behind. The outer part of the dock was deserted. Only the occasional flash of a laser or torpedo trail beyond the shimmering force curtain betrayed the battle that was raging.

A spiralling rampway led up to the lower levels of the Tower of Ascending Dreams. The building formed a tapering curve into a soaring pinnacle that jutted out from the craftworld's rim. Slender windows pierced the walls, sometimes lit by a flash of energy from within.

Their armoured boots thudding softly on the rampway, the Striking Scorpions entered the lower level – several storeys of arched rings surrounding the central core of the tower – with the sounds of other squads just behind. Morlaniath looked over his shoulder to see Erethaillin's Maidens of Fate catching quickly, the lightly-armoured, swifter Howling

Banshees passing the Striking Scorpions as they turned a loop of the ramp onto the second level.

Morlaniath could hear gunfire; the chatter of barbaric solid-shot weapons, the zip of laser fire and the air-splitting shriek of shuriken ammunition. He pulled free the *Teeth of Dissonance* from where the blade had been hanging across his back, wielding it in both hands as the spiralling passageway took them up another level.

The Hidden Death ran onto a wide concourse that curved gently along the rim of the craftworld. A sea of stars spread out beyond the blue-tinged force wall, burning debris floating across the starscape.

The whirr of wings caught the exarch's attention and he glanced up to see a squad of Swooping Hawks flying above him, the wings of their flightpacks a multi-coloured blur in the dim yellow glow of the chamber. He saw Phoenix Lord Baharroth gliding amongst his followers, his las-blaster sending shafts of brilliant energy into the upper levels of the docking tower.

Ahead, through an archway that arced far above him, Morlaniath could see blue-clad eldar with yellow helmets gathered in a defensive semi-circle: Guardian squads protecting the landing beyond the arch, shuriken catapults spitting salvoes into a foe that the exarch could not yet see. Amongst the Guardians glided heavy weapons platforms, their crews close at hand with psychically-linked controls. Brightlances spat blasts of laser, starcannons unleashed torrents of blue plasma and missile launchers filled the air with screaming trails. The Swooping Hawks dove through the arch, their weapons criss-crossing the chamber beyond with white ripples of fire.

Morlaniath reached the archway and looked up at Alaitoc's attackers.

They had taken cover on a sweeping gallery above and opposite the archway, hiding behind rows of slender columns that rose to the ceiling far above. The stunted, thick-limbed enemy were clad in rumpled suits, grey and black camouflage, skull and eagle insignias stitched onto arms and chests, their flat faces hidden behind silver-visored helmets. In fat, gauntleted hands they carried crude laser weapons that fired bolts of red. Pinned back by the eldar counter-attack, the humans clumsily bobbed into view, loosing off scattered shots before hiding again.

The Swooping Hawks swept majestically up, slaloming between the pillars, grenade dispensers on their thighs showering the humans below with blasts of plasma and shrapnel. The Maidens of Fate – Erethaillin's Howling Banshee squad – were already at the left-hand end of the ramp-way that led to the human-occupied gallery, the exarch at the forefront of their charge, a gleaming, curved sword in each hand. Forced back by the heavy weapons of the Guardians, the grenades of the Swooping Hawks and the approach of the Howling Banshees, the humans directed no fire towards Morlaniath and his squad as they raced across the tiled floor between the arch and the right-hand access ramp.

Morlaniath could see human officers amongst the throng of their men, swathed in long dress coats with golden epaulettes, wearing silver-peaked caps with winged skull badges. None of the humans noticed the Hidden Death quickly but quietly stalking up the ramp, keeping to the long shadows cast by the pillars above.

Morlaniath broke from the ramp at a full run, the others directly behind him. Their shuriken pistols spat a blurring volley into the nearest humans, shredding grey fatigues, cracking mirrored visors. Their sergeant turned in dismay, a moment before the *Teeth of Dissonance* separated his head from his shoulders in one sweep.

The Hidden Death did not pause to finish off the wounded, following closely as Morlaniath charged into the group of humans huddled behind the next column. The exarch's mandiblasters exploded across the face of a black-coated officer, the human's face twisting into an agonised, wordless scream as energy flared across his swarthy skin. Morlaniath swept his biting blade across the officer's left arm, severing the limb at the shoulder.

A flash and a roar at close range heralded a shotgun blast, a moment before a storm of pellets crashed into Morlaniath's left side, staggering him for a moment. He turned quickly and saw the panicked human trying to load more shells into the gun's slider, his movements slow and fumbling in Morlaniath's eyes. With a laugh, Morlaniath gutted the impudent creature, spilling his intestines over the white-and-gold tiles of the gallery. Around him, the Hidden Death chopped and hacked, coating the floor with blood and limbs.

The Striking Scorpions and Howling Banshees converged from opposite ends of the gallery, cutting down all in their path. The humans got in each other's way, the few shots they fired woefully inaccurate. Six more of their number fell to the blade *Teeth of Dissonance* and Morlaniath growled in tune to his weapon, relishing every death.

Las-blasts and the thudding of feet heralded the arrival of more humans coming down the broad stairway that swept down to the gallery from the docking spire above. The Swooping Hawks greeted the reinforcements with las-fire, shrouding the steps with a fusillade of deadly light. Guardians poured along the gallery from either end, adding their own fire to the defence.

The snap of the humans' lasguns was drowned out by the piercing shriek of the Howling Banshees as they charged again, their masks projecting a psychosonic wave before them. Some of the humans fell to their knees, ears and eyes bleeding, others dropped weapons from numbed fingers or simply collapsed with spasmodic fits. Even those that were not incapacitated stood in quivering shock, unable to defend themselves as Erethaillin and her warriors closed for the kill, power swords cutting through flak jackets, flesh and bone without resistance.

Morlaniath was about to lead his squad forward in support of the

Howling Banshees when Arhathain's voice cut through his thoughts.

'Enemy numbers are strengthening. They have breached our defences in several positions and are establishing a landing zone. Stage a withdrawal from the Tower of Ascending Dreams to avoid being isolated. Bring the enemy into the Concourse of the Suffering Heart. Additional forces will join you at the Plaza of Alaithir.'

In response to this new plan, the entirety of the tower plunged into darkness, the dim light of the walls extinguished by Alaitoc. Through the augmented vision of his helmet, Morlaniath watched the Imperial soldiers toppling down the stairway, tripping over each other, flailing in the blackness for balance. The bright flash of the Swooping Hawks' lasers and the flare of missile detonations highlighted faces contorted in terror at this sudden change of environment.

The eldar withdrew from their foes behind the fire of the Swooping Hawks and Guardian weapons platforms. With their attackers thrown into disarray, the Alaitocii withdrew from the Tower of Ascending Dreams into the concourse outside, squads taking it in turns to stand rearguard while the rest retreated. Outside once more, the Striking Scorpions boarded their Wave Serpent and turned to speed along the rim, heading for the Plaza of Alaithir, a broad junction between the Concourse of the Suffering Heart and the Mourning Way. Behind them, the Imperial troops staggered out into the lighted concourse to be cut down by Falcon tanks and soaring Vyper jetbikes.

At the Plaza of Alaithir, forces were converging from three directions, falling back from all across the starward side of the craftworld. Silhouetted against the orange glow of the dying star, Falcons hovered at each intersection, weapons trained above the incoming squads of Aspect Warriors and Guardians. Wave Serpents converged on the immense fountain at the centre of the plaza, from which reared an enormous statue of the autarch after whom the plaza was named. The marble warrior stood with sword and fusion pistol at the ready, glaring balefully down the Mourning Way towards the Spire of Tranquillity.

The Hidden Death disembarked to join the line defending the concourse along which they had just travelled. The Vypers and Falcons slid back into view occasionally, firing their weapons at foes hidden behind the curve of the craftworld's rim. Eventually the humans came into view again, resolutely advancing in a column hundreds-strong. Gawky walkers strode on double-jointed legs beside the squads of infantry, their multi-barrelled lasers spewing a torrent of fire at the eldar vehicles. Human heavy weapons teams ran forward, dragging wheeled lascannons and bulky autocannons behind them. They set up firing positions alongside the advancing companies, adding the fury of their fire to the walkers' as cover for the advancing soldiers.

As shells cut dark streaks through the air, a Vyper was clipped by a salvo, losing a control vane. It careened out of control into the jade-coloured interior wall. Another volley ripped into the armour of a Falcon, which listed sideways before grinding into the ground with a crumpling of armoured plates. More shots punched through the wreckage, cracking sensor gems and showering pieces of shattered canopy across the tiled floor. Its anti-grav engines destroyed by a laser blast, another tank flipped awkwardly upwards, pulse laser still firing burning bolts of light. The turret of a third Falcon erupted in flames from a hit and the tank spun crazily about its axis until it crashed into the energy field on the spaceward side of the plaza, ripples of lightning spreading across the force shield.

Faced with the continuing onslaught, the Falcons' and Vypers' pilots increased the speed of their retreat, eventually turning completely and boosting away from the Imperium's soldiers on plumes of light. The throb of their engines vibrated through Morlaniath as they soared over-head into the relative safety of the plaza.

To the advancing humans it must have seemed as if they had their foes at bay, trapped in the open space of the plaza. The grass-covered hills and marble-like roadways provided little cover for the sheltering troops. The eldar waited in silence while the angry orders and triumphant shouts of the Imperial officers echoed along the concourse.

A shimmering force wall blazed into existence barely a dozen paces in front of Morlaniath and the other squads at the concourse edge of the plaza. Everything beyond was tinted by the blue of the field, as if the army marched along the bed of a shimmering sea. Las-bolts and bullets sparked from the force shield, which quivered with each impact but held firm. Morlaniath smiled. The shield wall was not to protect the eldar from attack. It had another, far more deadly purpose, as the humans were about to discover.

The fine tendrils of the infinity circuit within the inner wall of the concourse flickered and then darkened. Deprived of energy, the outer force wall collapsed with a flare of light. Exposed to the ravening vacuum of space, the humans were swept from their feet by the explosive outrush-ing of air, hundreds of them hurled out of the craftworld in moments. Their screams were lost in the void as their skin froze and blood vessels tore open while weapons and helmets spun around them. Even the walkers could not fight against the explosive depressurisation, their awk-ward metal legs flailing as the sudden hurricane hurled them out into the stars along with their dying comrades.

The massacre lasted only a few moments and silence descended. Glit-tering particles of frozen blood lingered in the air, before falling like rain in the artificial gravity of the craftworld. With a grim fascination Morla-niath watched the red pattering, interspersed with plummeting corpses that thudded upon the tiled concourse in mangled heaps. Though the depressurisation had been done out of necessity and lacked the true artistry of a well-placed shot or cut, there was a simple beauty to be found in its effective results.

'Human forces have pushed into the sub-levels beneath the docking dome,' Arhathain informed the warriors of the craftworld. 'More assault craft are inbound. They must be driven back.'

Morlaniath gestured for his warriors to follow him back to the Wave Serpent.

'No overconfidence, this is but the first strike, the humans will fight hard,' he told them as they strode up the boarding ramp. 'We will be pitiless, make them pay heavily, every step shall be pain. Look to one another, strike with single purpose, fight as the Hidden Death.'

The ramp closed behind them and within moments the Wave Serpent was moving again, angling towards the Mourning Way.

'How do we fare in other battles?' asked Elissanadrin.

'That is not our concern. We fight the foes we face, to their destruction. Focus on this sole task. Allow no distraction, until our foes are slain. Listen for the autarchs, they will guide our swift hand, to land the deadly blow.'

'Their looks of terror when the darkness came, that is something I will treasure,' said Arhulesh with a sharp laugh. 'Did you see their surprise? Such stupidity, to think that Alaitoc would tolerate their filthy presence.'

'It is a shame that those who knew such fear are now dead,' said Elissanadrin. 'Terror is a disease – it spreads through an enemy as swift as a plague.'

'Let us hope that they communicated some of their dread before they perished.' Arhulesh turned to look at Bechareth. 'How can you keep your delight to yourself? Does it not eat at you, to hold in that delightful moment of death, when an enemy's spirit is extinguished?'

Bechareth's helmeted head cocked to one side. His gaze moved between Arhulesh and Morlaniath. The Striking Scorpion shrugged and shook his head. He raised a finger to the grille of his helmet and pulled free his chainsword. The bloodstained blades of its teeth gleamed in the light of the compartment.

'Though his voice is silent, Bechareth speaks to us, his blade's words come loudly,' explained Morlaniath, eliciting a laugh and a nod from Arhulesh.

'It certainly does,' said the Striking Scorpion. 'I slew thirteen of them, but could not match your tally. Eighteen, was it not?'

Bechareth nodded.

'We shall see who has the greater score when the humans have been driven from Alaitoc. I think I may even beat you this time.'

'The count will be many, the humans come in force, plenty for each of us,' the exarch assured his squad.

As their minds turned to the prospect of much death to come, the squad fell silent. Morlaniath allowed himself to briefly recall his latest slayings, while part of him kept an eye on the crystal screen displaying the Wave Serpent's position. Along with many others, the Hidden Death had dropped several layers beneath the main inhabited zone of Alaitoc; the Wave Serpent raced along an arterial supply route usually used to transport wares from the Exodite colonies and other craftworlds to the various parts of Alaitoc.

These depths were totally enclosed, divided from the emptiness of space by solid walls and floors, not force shields that could be switched off. Listening to the irregular comments from the autarchs, Morlaniath learnt that the humans had been over-confident in their speedy assault, but now they advanced with more caution. This did not make them any less dangerous. They would gather their strength and attack relentlessly, knowing that they had the advantage of numbers. They could not be allowed to gain a worthwhile foothold on Alaitoc. If they did, it could well herald a slow doom for the craftworld.

As Morlaniath considered this, he felt a ripple through the wraithbone skeleton of the Wave Serpent as it connected to the infinity circuit with a flutter of psychic energy. He felt another mind touch upon his thoughts and instantly recognised Thirianna, remembering the sense of her from their encounter at the shrine. Through the psychic connection Morlaniath felt the fleeting presence of other eldar: exarchs and Guardian squad leaders, vehicle pilots and support weapon gunners. All were joined together for a moment.

The enemy make progress along the Well of Disparate Fates. Walk the red path with them, drive them back to their landing craft. There followed a flutter of brief images: Imperial soldiers setting up crude barricades; the small one-man walkers stalking through unlit corridors, searchlights playing across curving walls; an officer with a pistol in hand bellowing at his troops.

She was gone, leaving only an aftertouch in Morlaniath's mind. The exarch opened up the communications channel with the Wave Serpent's pilot, Laureneth.

'Put us down close to them, we will advance on foot, cover us with your fire,' he told the driver.

'I understand, exarch,' the pilot replied, his voice flat. The telemetry display close to Morlaniath changed to show a schematic of the conduits and tunnels beneath the docks. A rune flashed at an intersection a short distance from the place they had seen in Thirianna's message. 'Will that be suitable, exarch?'

'That will be suitable. A bloody trail follows, as we walk in Khaine's shade.'

The deadly struggle between the Alaitocii and the invading humans filled the sub-strata levels of the docks. The Imperial forces were desperate to gain a foothold into which they could move their heavier materiel. Despite the Alaitoc fleet taking a serious toll of the transports attempting to reinforce the landing zone, with perhaps only one in every three of the human's craft making fall at the craftworld's rim, the enemy continued relentlessly. A growing field of burning craft, debris and corpses coalesced around the dock facilities in ponderous orbits, kept close by Alaitoc's artificial gravity field.

The eldar held their ground in a large nave-like intersection between three transit routes from the docks to the central arterial concourses. The humans advanced along two vaulted tunnels, scampering from pointed arch to pointed arch, sometimes using the mounds of their own dead as cover. They offered little in the way of fire – by the time they had closed the range, their numbers were so low they were swiftly eliminated by the Guardians. On levels above and below, to the left and right, similar firefights wracked the craftworld.

'They fight like maniacs, not counting any cost, the price paid by fanatics,' Morlaniath commented to his squad as he watched the grey-clad soldiers charging headlong into a volley of missiles fired by several squads of Dark Reapers. With the Hidden Death, other squads of Striking Scorpions, Howling Banshees and Warp Spiders were positioned a little way behind the fighting, ready to move forward to stave off any breakthrough or counter-attack if an opportunity presented itself. Occasionally the Wave Serpent behind the squad unleashed a torrent of plasma from its starcannons, the flickering shots disappearing into the gloom of the passageway.

'Numbers are no tactic, to be hurled like bullets, a limitless supply,' the exarch continued. 'They render death pointless, each life a statistic, that no one is counting. They use the hammer, to smash at formless fog, to destroy only air.'

Though Alaitoc could not empty the air from this section, the craftworld did not permit the humans easy advance. The light dimmed and changed, from bright mid-cycle glare to late-cycle twilight, interspersed with brief periods of blinding whiteness and utter darkness.

Infinity circuit energy coursed through the walls; Morlaniath could feel the spirit energy within rippling on the edge of consciousness. Amidst the turmoil, ghostly apparitions, brief psychic phantasms, appeared amongst the enemy ranks, no doubt guided by the seers: raving, fire-wreathed monstrosities; weeping human mothers cradling the bloodied swaddling of children; fluttering flocks of giant wasps; shimmering lights that contained the screaming faces of the humans. Locked inside the walls of the craftworld the enemy had no gauge of time passing and could not know whether they fought for a heartbeat or a lifetime; the eldar were free from such doubts, subconsciously attuned to the internal rhythms of Alaitoc.

The terrifying assault on the senses of the humans had only a limited effect. Occasionally a soldier would break and run screaming from the fight, but more often the bellows of the humans' leaders cut through the clamour, urging the soldiers forwards. Morlaniath watched a robe-clad human with a bald head raising a book in his right hand, frothing and shouting, his homilies keeping the soldiers at their positions despite the horrendous casualties. Grim-faced officers with peaked caps and skull-shaped badges instilled discipline with more brutal means, turning their pistols on their own warriors when they showed signs of cowardice.

'Their faith is a façade, layered onto cowards, driven by fear more than hate,' Morlaniath observed. 'Superficial hatred, falsely righteous anger, is no motive for war. Our hate and rage is pure, Khaine's lasting gift to us, a true strength of spirit. Do not pity these fools, they can learn nothing new. Any mercy is wasted. They die without meaning, no one counting the toll, no one heeding their deaths. Their lives are meaningless, no lasting potential, short spans easily spent. No true aspirations, just fear and resentment, minds filled with hollow thoughts.'

Crude as the humans' techniques were, they were slowly gaining ground by sheer weight of numbers and raw belligerence. The autarchs had acknowledged as much when Arhathain next communicated to the exarchs and Guardian squad leaders.

'A new wave of forces is closing on the humans' landing area. These reinforcements cannot be allowed to bolster the attack. Push the humans back to their ships and eradicate them.'

A flash of awareness from the infinity circuit brought Morlaniath's attention to a circular opening in the curving wall behind him. The covering melted away, revealing a narrow but navigable conduit that ran alongside the main passage.

Erethaillin and her Howling Banshees were already at the tunnel mouth, ducking their maned helms into the service duct. Morlaniath and the Hidden Death followed as swiftly as their heavier armour allowed, the iris-door coalescing across the gap behind them, plunging the passage into gloom. The glow of psychic energy trailed along crystal-line fibres in the wall and by this witchlight the two squads advanced quickly. There was no need to guess the relative positions of the enemy in the parallel corridor; Alaitoc would lead them to where they were needed.

Bent over, the Howling Banshees sped along the conduit on light feet, their bone-white armour cast with a blue gleam from their power swords. Morlaniath watched them getting further and further ahead until the glow of their weapons and eyes was no more than a quickly receding haze in the distance.

The tunnel curved gently upwards, taking it away from the main route by which the humans were attacking. Morlaniath surmised that they were being taken direct to the landing zone, but wary of the limits of estimation, sent a message to Arhathain.

'Into the foes' dark heart, a fatal blow unseen, is that our new purpose?' he asked. It was but a few heartbeats before Arhathain responded.

'The enemy will be caught twixt doom and death, with no escape. The new arrivals are imminent – do not allow them to join the ongoing attack.'

The glow ahead grew bright again, and soon the Striking Scorpions saw the azure-dancing blades of the Howling Banshees squad, crouched around another iris door having been told to wait for the following squad.

'Strength in our unity, together we fight, in victory renowned,' said Erethaillin.

'With the Maidens of Fate, the Hidden Death will fight, doom and dark together!' laughed Morlaniath.

They waited in silence, eyes fixed to the closed portal. The sound of booted feet reverberated through the conduit from the passageway on the other side of the door, an occasional guttural human command added to the noise.

The iris door widened and the Aspect Warriors streamed through, pistols blazing.

They were at the skin of Alaitoc itself, a large domed hallway filled with humans. Blunt-nosed landing craft squatted on the curving starquays, the air shimmering with cooling engines. Dozens of humans marched down the ramps from these assault boats, utterly unprepared for the sudden attack.

As a human fell with a volley of shurikens in the back of his neck, Morlaniath saw Aranarha and his squad attacking from close to the rim wall. Warp Spiders materialised in the midst of the foe, their death-spinners ripping through whole squads. From above, Swooping Hawks dropped down through the arching arms of loading cranes, plasma grenades blossoming beneath them, their las-blasters sending streams of white death through the milling humans.

Morlaniath spared no more thought for the other squads as he chopped the head from an Imperial soldier with a twist of his wrists. One of the peak-capped officers bellowed incoherently at him, raising a fist sheathed in a crackling mechanical gauntlet. Morlaniath sliced the human's arm at the elbow, the powered glove clanging to the floor. Las-bolts sprayed from the officer's pistol, catching the exarch on the right side of his chest, leaving smoking holes in his armour. Annoyed, he flexed his arm and sent the *Teeth of Dissonance* through the officer's other elbow, leaving him literally disarmed. The officer collapsed to one side, still shouting, kicking out with his legs in hopeless defiance. Morlaniath ended him with a surge from his mandiblasters, the laser bolt punching through the human's gilded breastplate. The whole affair had taken less than three heartbeats.

A human crouched over a buzzing piece of equipment looked up in horror as Morlaniath loomed over him – on the end of a coiling wire he held a cup-shaped receptacle to one ear. The *Teeth of Dissonance* cleaved through the human's upraised arm and came to rest halfway through his skull, showering the fizzing electrical box with blood. Morlaniath let go of his sword with one hand and stooped to pick up the receptacle and hold it close to his helmet's auditory pick-up. Between bursts of static, meaningless human gibberish rang tinnily in the exarch's ear.

Being overrun at sector six – by the Emperor's holy shrivelled gonads, we need more ammunition – did you see what they did to the captain? Is that him over there? Where did the rest of him go? – Remain at stations, reinforcements incoming – The door won't open, Command. It swallowed Sergeant Lister – Say again, corporal, report position – Reinforcements imminent, the Asta–

Morlaniath dropped the comm-device and looked across the wide hangar. A few pockets of humans held out, defending their shuttles to the last soldier. His squad was too far away to intervene, there would be none left by the time the Hidden Death reached the landing craft. He watched with a twinge of envy as Aranarha boarded one of the assault boats with his warriors.

'Enemy reinforcements have reached the docks,' announced Arhathain. 'All units fall back to the Dome of Midnight Forests. Do not engage the enemy, fall back at once.'

Morlaniath was confused. The hangar and docking platforms were in eldar hands. Heavy weapons were moving up the access ramps. Any enemy foolish enough to make a landing in the teeth of the eldar squads would be cut down as soon as they set foot on the craftworld. He turned towards the glimmering one-way field that protected the dock opening. There was no sign of approaching craft outside, just a swathe of stars.

Of the attacking ships, there was nothing to be seen save for a handful of flaring plasma drives against the darkness. Morlaniath could not see how so few reinforcements had so unsettled the autarchs.

The docks shook with a thunderous impact as a torpedo-like craft smashed through the outer wall to Morlaniath's left, the nose cone of the boarding vessel surrounded in a red haze of energy. Two more slammed into Alaitoc to either side of the first, sending cracked shards of wall flying across the docks. Light within recesses around the torpedoes' noses flared and Morlaniath dropped to his belly in an instant, warned by instinct. A barrage of rockets filled the dockside, a mass of fire and smoke trails and deafening blasts that cut through the eldar. Secondary detonations tore apart the human landing craft, creating a fresh storm of shrapnel.

Morlaniath jumped back to his feet and checked on his squad. Arhulesh held his arm where a long gash had ripped through his armour, and there were minor cracks and scratches in the suits of the others, but no serious injuries. The same could not be said for other eldar forces. The limp forms of Guardians lay sprawled across walkways, sparks fizzing from the remnants of their heavy weapons. Erethaillin's squad had been close to the wall and bloodstained armour littered the hangar floor, the tattered strands of the Howling Banshees' helmet manes floating around their corpses.

In every direction Morlaniath looked, he saw dead and dying eldar.

His gaze was drawn back to the three glowing projectiles jutting through the wall surrounded by a lingering haze of smoke. Though scorched, they were painted in white and red. In unison, the noses broke into four petal-like segments, opening up to reveal a harsh white interior. The bottom petal touched down like a ramp and in the dizzy aftermath of the rockets blasts, the dock rang with heavy feet.

A dozen fiery trails snarled from of the opening portals, followed by the sharp crack of detonations, the bloodied remains of eldar warriors flung across the hangar floor. With morbid curiosity Morlaniath focussed on one, seeing a miniature rocket at least the size of his thumb propelled out of the white light. It hit a Guardian in the leg and punched through the thin armour into flesh. A moment later it detonated with a blossom of bone and blood, ripping the limb apart from the inside.

Morlaniath knew this weapon.

He had faced it once before: the time when not-Lecchamemnon had been slain. The memory of his death was unpleasant and the exarch looked at the boarding torpedoes with a disconcerted feeling as more of them burst through other parts of the dock wall. Hugely armoured figures ran down the ramps, their guns spitting fury.

Imperial Space Marines!

DEATH

In the moment between Khaine's sword blow and Eldanesh's death, Asuryan the Phoenix Lord came down from heaven. Eldanesh asked why it was that the eldar had to die. Asuryan laughed at the question. He told Eldanesh that he could not die. The father of the eldar would live on in the spirit and memory of his children, reborn anew in every generation. While his children prospered, Eldanesh would be immortal. As death's grip tightened on Eldanesh and the stars dimmed, Asuryan gave him one last message. The gods had no descendants, only they could truly die.

The retreat from the docks was swift. Faced with the devastating onslaught of the Emperor's most fearsome creations, the eldar melted away into the inner corridors and halls of Alaitoc. The craftworld secured their retreat, delaying the pursuing Space Marines with closed doors and energy fields. Driven by the energy of the infinity circuit, Alaitoc remapped entire parts of its layout to stall the enemy advance, sealing corridors and collapsing walkways to strand the enemy and separate them from each other. When all was done, the infinity circuit shrank back from the docks, rendering the crystal network dead, leaving no means for the foe to exploit or infiltrate its energies.

As the squad boarded their Wave Serpent in silence, Morlaniath sensed the numbed shock of his warriors, the realisation that there existed foes in the galaxy that were the match of them.

'It is not the right place, to face our foes head on, standing with blade-to-blade,' he said as the Wave Serpent lifted off and turned sharply, heading for the Dome of Midnight Forests. 'We are part of the whole, a sole Aspect of Khaine, not complete of itself. With others we will fight, much greater together, victorious in time. Space Marines are dire foes, deadly in their own right, but so few in number. They are strong of body, they know not dread or doubt, yet still they can be killed. No swift victory comes, this is a war of will. Alaitoc must prevail.'

'The enemy have secured many landing points behind the spearhead of their finest warriors,' Arhathain cut through Morlaniath's encouragement. 'Their numbers will swell and they will bring vehicles and heavier weapons. We cannot be dragged into their crude way of war, meeting them headlong. They will lumber after us with great crushing blows. We must be the blade that cuts a thousand times. We have killed many of the humans and we must kill many more before we know victory. There will be no swift road back to peace. The true war for Alaitoc begins now.'

The exarch sensed lingering doubt in the minds of his followers.

'The autarch speaks the truth: we fight for survival, to avoid extinction. Harbour no weaknesses, dispel the seed of doubt, harden yourselves for war. Know there is no retreat, we fight to guard our home, to keep our future safe.'

'Space Marines, tanks, countless soldiers, how can we fight against such things?' asked Arhulesh.

'With blade and with pistol, we fight what we can kill, trust others for the rest. We are not without arms. We have our own weapons, to meet these kinds of threats. Defeat is not our fate, not by the hands of men, not in this place and time. Let hate be your courage, let anger be your shield, let Khaine watch over us.'

Their disquiet receded as the Wave Serpent sped on. In silence, they each fell into a meditative state, drawing on their resolve to quench the fear that had risen. Morlaniath had no need to bolster his convictions with abstract contemplation. He had a very real reason to despise the Space Marines of the Emperor.

The fields around the town burned, pockmarked with craters. The bodies of gigantic miradons lay in burning heaps, their scales glistening in the flamelight. More blasts rained down from the skies, crushing the buildings of Semain Alair. Charred corpses were flung high into the air by the plasma impacts, while the screams of the burning Exodites mingled with the agonised bellows of their herds.

The exarch watched the devastation from a stand of burning trees on a hill overlooking the farming settlement, the canopy overhead a crackling inferno. In irrigation ditches and hollows, others lay in wait.

He turned to Farseer Alaitharin.

'We have arrived too late, the slaughter has begun. Now we must count the dead.'

The seer's ruby-like eye lenses fixed him with a stare. She reached into the pouch at her waist and drew forth a handful of wraithbone runes. They lifted from her open palm and arranged themselves into a circling pattern, slowly revolving around the farseer.

'It was not our fate to protect them,' she said slowly. 'We cannot stop the humans from taking this world.'

'I do not understand, what is our purpose here, if not to drive them back?'

'One is coming who will become a greater military leader. In a generation from now, he will lead his forces against the fleet of Alaitoc in the Kholirian system and destroy many of our ships. I have followed his strand. He is most vulnerable here, during this conquest. Extinguish his light now and it will never burn our people.'

'Who is this great leader, a threat to the future, no human lives so long?'

'He is no human,' replied Alaitharin. The runes ceased their orbit and floated back to her hand. She looked up into the evening sky. 'He comes upon a shooting star.'

Morlaniath and the other Hidden Death warriors followed her gaze. Pinpricks of light appeared in the sky, swiftly growing larger. As they neared, Morlaniath could see black liveried craft falling through the atmosphere, the glimmers of light the glare of their heat shields. The exarch counted them, fourteen in all.

Dart-like shapes appeared over the hills in front of Morlaniath, closing fast: Nightwing fighters. Lasers lanced from their prows, striking the falling drop pods. The armour of many shrugged aside the attack, but three exploded into clouds of fire and debris, exploding into parts that burned away into nothing. The Nightwings twisted and fired again, destroying two more.

Bulkier shapes appeared in the twilight, rockets flaring from their wings – the gunships of the enemy. They were high-sided, clumsy craft, laden with weapons. The Nightwings were forced away from the falling pods by the weight of fire as they turned to meet this new threat.

With blazes of plasma, the drop pods slowed their descent and slammed into the soft earth of the farms. Heat shimmer disturbed the air but Morlaniath could make out white cross-shaped markings on their sides. Explosive bolts crackled and ramps crashed to the burnt ground, disgorging squads of bulky, armour-clad warriors.

'This one,' said Alaitharin, pointing to a squad sergeant forging up the slope towards the burning settlement, his squad in close formation behind him. A rune – the symbol of fate sealed – appeared in Morlaniath's vision, dancing over the head of the Space Marine. Even when he disappeared into a dell, the rune betrayed his whereabouts. 'It is destined that you slay him. Go now, bring his doom swiftly.'

Morlaniath headed towards the burning buildings with his squad in tow while other eldar forces formed a ring around the disembarking Space Marines. The rune of fate was a constant presence, dragging him on. Gunfire erupted across the devastated field but he did not spare a glance backwards, intent only on the prey he stalked.

The outskirts of the settlement were as ruined as the centre, the high towers and long halls crushed to piles of rubble. Morlaniath skirted around a complex of half-fallen walls that had once been a storehouse. Twisted harnesses and saddles jutted from the shattered masonry. Here and there an arm or leg could be seen, dust sticking to the drying blood.

He found it hard to understand the farseer's attitude. Surely this warrior could have been killed before the attack was launched? It was one matter to expend the lives of lesser species to further the cause of Alaitoc; it was another to sacrifice eldar, even if they were only Exodites. There may have been greater risk in an orbital attack, but it was the duty of the Aspect Warriors to face such dangers. The farmers lying dead in the ruins of their homes had made no such commitment.

Yet, it was the farseers that could foretell the perils facing the craftworld, and if this was the best course of action he was in no place to resist their judgement. He was glad he did not have to deal with the vagaries of divination. He had a clarity of purpose it was hard to argue against: kill the enemy. The fulfilment of that simple goal brought him contentment, often joy.

His prey had taken up a position in the ruins of a meeting hall, on the debris-strewn floor of the second storey. The squad's fire screamed out over the ravaged fields, covering their comrades as they took up defensive positions against the eldar attack. Their attention was focused outward, unsuspecting of the Hidden Death that came at them from behind.

Morlaniath trod gently across a ramp of broken stone, careful not to move the smallest grain of debris. Crouched at the sill of a shattered window, he set eyes on his prey once more. The sergeant stood with one foot up on the lip of a wall, directing the fire of his squad. The white edging of his shoulder pads and the cross symbol they enclosed could be seen in the shadow of the ruin. Bursts of muzzle flare illuminated his craggy face as he stared intently out across the fields.

With a nod to his squad, Morlaniath slipped through the remnants of the window and across the rubble-strewn street, gliding between patches of burning material and smoking corpses.

They were halfway across the open space when the prey suddenly glanced down at his left wrist: Morlaniath could see a red light winking quickly on a device attached to his arm. To Morlaniath it seemed as if the sergeant turned slowly in his direction, raising his pistol to fire, mouth opening to bellow a fresh order even as his other hand raised the Space Marine's helmet towards his head.

The Striking Scorpions needed no command. They leapt forward at full speed, entering the bottom storey of the building occupied by the Space Marines. Riethillin and Lordranir sprinted up the stairway while Morlaniath led Irithiris, Elthruin and Darendir up the slope of a collapsed floor, into the heart of the enemy squad.

Harsh light blazed as the Space Marines unleashed the fury of their bolters. Darendir was in their line of fire and was torn apart, fragments of armour and body tumbling down the floor-slope. Morlaniath tossed a handful of small grenades, each exploding into a white-hot cloud of plasma that sent the Space Marines reeling back. He charged through the dissipating mist, the *Teeth of Dissonance* carving into the chest of the closest enemy. Blades screeched as they hacked through the gold-embossed eagle on the warrior's plastron. The Space Marine twisted away, almost wrenching the weapon from Morlaniath's grasp. The exarch ducked beneath a fist almost as large as his head and kicked his foot against the Space Marine's stomach to wrench his biting blade free. He lithely twisted aside as the Space Marine tried to bring an armoured elbow down on the exarch's shoulder, the *Teeth of Dissonance* cutting into the flexible armour behind the warrior's left knee.

The Space Marine toppled as the lower half of his leg spun away, his weapon blazing as his finger instinctively tightened on the trigger, the flare of the bolts disappearing into the darkening sky. Morlaniath drove the point of his blade into the faceplate of the Space Marine's helmet, the whirring teeth cutting through the grille-mouth until blood sprayed heavily and the Space Marine fell still.

Something slammed into the exarch's back and he felt ribs fracturing. Morlaniath snarled in pain and his mandiblasters spewed an arc of energy as he twisted with the force of the blow to confront his new attacker. The Space Marine ponderously swung overarm with a long combat knife, the blow falling wide as Morlaniath slipped aside. The exarch rained down three blows on the arm of the Space Marine, the last severing his wrist so that hand and knife fell to the blood-spattered floor.

The rune of fate danced across the exarch's vision and he plunged past the wounded Space Marine to attack the sergeant. His prey raised a chainsword in defence, the *Teeth of Dissonance* deflected away in a storm of sparks. Morlaniath adjusted his attack, feinting towards the sergeant's gut before bringing his blade down hard against the side of his head. The teeth skittered across the rounded helm, shards of armour splintering, but the blow did not bite home and the *Teeth of Dissonance* rebounded off the Space Marine's helm and shoulder pad.

The Space Marine clubbed down with the butt of his pistol, catching the exarch on the left shoulder. The eldar's arm went numb and his fingers lost their grip on the *Teeth of Dissonance*. Something sent grinding pain along his spine when he stooped to recover the fallen weapon. A booted foot crashed into his chest, lifting Morlaniath fully off his feet, pain flooding through every part of him. He felt his heart rupturing from the blow, his lungs filling with blood.

This cannot be, he thought distractedly. He coughed and blood filled his helm. Even his eyes hurt as he watched the sergeant turning away with a snarl of contempt. Morlaniath held on for a few moments longer to see Ethruin pounce.

As Ethruin, he saw his exarch fall. Ethruin surged forward, triggering his mandiblasters to scorch the eyes of the sergeant, blinding him. His blade found the Space Marine's throat, ripping open the flexible protective collar, biting into windpipe and arteries with a solid thrust. Blood frothed from the wound as the sergeant fell back, crashing through a window to the ground below.

With their target dead, the eldar withdrew into the night, the Hidden Death taking the armoured body of their fallen exarch with them.

Morlaniath snapped back to the present with a fierce growl. Such were the convoluted strands of fate that the farseers had to follow, with lives and spirits overlapping one another across the skein of time. There were no such machinations to contend with in this battle. The goal was simple. Slay the humans and drive them from Alaitoc.

Nothing else mattered.

The Dome of Midnight Forests was dark, lit only by the glow of Mirianathir. Beneath the ruddy shadows of the lianderin, the Alaitocii gathered. Grav-tanks prowled along the pathways while scores of Wave Serpents shuttled back and forth delivering squads to their positions. The eldar had forsaken any defence of the dockward corridors, knowing that the Emperor's Space Marines excelled at such close quarters fighting. Swooping Hawks and Warp Spiders harried them, hitting and retreating, drawing the human forces on towards the forest dome. Here the eldar would make their next stand, able to rake fire across the wide clearings from the cover of the scattered woods. Every valley would become a killing field, every brook and meadow a graveyard for the invaders.

The Hidden Death were joined by Fiorennan and Litharain from the Fall of Deadly Rain shrine – the only survivors from the squad. Five of them had been scythed down by rockets during the initial Space Marine assault, caught as they cleared the Imperial landing craft. The exarch and three more of his warriors had died trying to fall back, cut down as the Space Marines drove into the eldar. Aranarha's armour had not been recovered and the loss hung heavy in his warriors' minds.

'What if they desecrate his suit?' asked Fiorennan. 'What if they break apart his spirit stones? He could be lost to us forever!'

'It is unwise to dwell, there are many such fates, but not all come to pass,' Morlaniath assured them. 'The enemy come fast, with no thought of the dead, he will be overlooked.'

'Out of spite and ignorance, they could cause harm they do not under-stand,' argued Fiorennan.

'Aranarha is lost, for the moment at least, we cannot change his fate!' snapped Morlaniath. Talk of the eternal death displeased the exarch. If Alaitoc was to fall, then all of his kind would finally die, the infinity circuit would be raped of its power and She Who Thirsts would feast heavily. He shuddered. No mortal creature scared him, not even the Emperor's Space Marine abominations, but everlasting torture con-sumed by the Great Enemy was a doom best not contemplated.

'Do not countenance death, dispel thoughts of defeat, think only of winning. Morai-heg was fickle, but it is in our hands, to shape our own future. Responsibility, to create our own fate, lies within our own grasp. To kill and not to die, to slay and not to fall, this is the end we seek.'

In silence, the Striking Scorpions stalked between the towering trees to their allotted position. As they flitted through the shadows, an enor-mous Cobra anti-grav tank slid past along a broad road, a nimbus of blue energy playing around the muzzle of its distortion cannon. The leaves trembled and grass flattened at its passing, though it made no more sound than the hum of a honeywing. The Hidden Death followed close behind until the Cobra turned off the road into a bowl-shaped clearing ringed with ancient lianderin.

This too was the Hidden Death's appointed place. Morlaniath quickly scanned his surrounds to get a sense of the geography. The clearing was like an amphitheatre on three sides, shallow-sloped and rimmed with trees. It opened out into a broad valley that led towards the docking bays, along which the enemy would have to advance.

Something amongst the trees caught Morlaniath's eye: a large statue entwined with the branches of a lianderin looking down the length of the valley. The statue would provide valuable cover if needed, while the trees gave ample shelter to circle behind a foe that entered the dell.

More figures converged on their location – two Vyper jetbikes appeared from the trees on the far side just ahead of several squads of Guardians clad in blue and yellow. They were followed by figures almost twice as tall, which strode silently through the undergrowth, eyeless, domed heads turning left and right as they picked their way forwards: unliving wraithguard. Within the armoured shell of each was encased a spirit stone containing the essence of an eldar drawn from the infinity circuit. Morlaniath's thoughts grew heavier upon seeing the artificial bodies of the wraithguard: even the dead had been roused to defend the craft-world. The exarch could feel the undead spirits touching on his senses, bringing with them the dry emptiness of the infinity circuit, leaving a trace of bitterness in the exarch's mind. Psychic energy coursed through their construct bodies and writhed within the wraithcannons they held.

Behind them came a coterie of seers – three warlocks carrying glitter-ing spears and a farseer armed with a rune-carved Witchblade.

Our fates share the same path again for a while.

Morlaniath looked over towards the farseer and recognised Thirianna. She raised her Witchblade in salute.

'Is this coincidence, or a machination, brought about by your hand?' the exarch asked.

I am not senior enough to influence the judgement of the autarchs. Some have fates closely entwined; others have strands that never touch. We are the former. Do you not remember where you are?

Morlaniath looked around, reliving moments from his many lives, seeking a memory related to this place. His eyes fell upon the tall statue, of an eldar warrior kneeling before the goddess Isha, catching her tears in a goblet.

'I present *The Gifts of Loving Isha*,' he announced with a smile.

There were a few gasps of enjoyment and a spontaneous ripple of applause from all present. Korlandril turned to look at his creation and allowed himself to admire his work fully since its completion.

It was a recent memory, yet no closer and no further than any other. His was an existence spread across all of Alaitoc and a hundred other worlds.

'I remember clearly, when disharmony reigned, when my spirit was split. This was my new birthplace, the path leading from here, which brought me full circle. It is no more than that, a place in a past life, of no special accord.'

Many new paths sprang from this place. Some for good, others that led to darker places. Your work began those paths, even if you did not intend it. We are all linked in the great web of destiny, the merest trembling on a silken thread sending tremors through the lives of countless others. Just a few cycles ago a child sat and stared at your creation and dreamed of Isha. He will be a poet and a warrior, a technician and a gardener. But it is as a sculptor that he will achieve great fame, and in turn will inspire others to create more works of beauty down the generations.

'I need no legacy. I am an undying, eternal warrior.'

No creature is eternal: not gods, not eldar, not humans or orks. Look above you and see a star dying. Even the universe is not immortal, though her life passes so slowly.

'What will become of me, have you divined my fate, looked upon my future?'

We all have many fates, but only one comes to pass. It is not for me to meddle in the destiny of individuals, nor to look into our own futures. Trust that you shall die as you lived, and that it is not the True Death that awaits you, not for an age at least. Your passing will bring peace.

'I suffer many deaths, I remember each well, never is it peaceful.'

An explosion rocked the dome, a plume of smoke billowing from the rimward edge above the trees as human explosives tore through the outer wall. Flocks of birds erupted into the dark sky with screeches and twittering, and circled above the trees in agitation. The crack of Space Marine bolters and the zip of lasers echoed in the distance.

'The enemy are upon us!' Arhathain's voice was quiet but firm in Morlaniath's ear. 'The next battle begins. Do not sell your lives cheaply, nor forget the artistry with which we fight. The day has not yet come when the light of Alaitoc will be dimmed.'

The Hidden Death waited, concealed beneath the trees. Their swords and pistols were of no use in the battle being waged, and so the Hidden Death waited for the enemy to come into the trees where the Striking Scorpions would excel. Or, Morlaniath hoped, he would get the command to move along the valley to deal a deadly blow to a force already torn apart by the rest of Alaitoc's army.

Arhulesh fidgeted with his bandaged arm, Elissanadrin whispered quietly to herself. Bechareth crouched beside the bole of a tree, staring intently down the valley towards the enemy. Waves of anger poured from Fiorennan and Litharain, touching the minds of the others. Morlaniath fed on the rage their exarch's death had unleashed, drawing it in as one might take a draught of refreshing air.

Nothing could be seen of the humans save for the flash of explosions. Their gunfire became a constant rumbling, mixed with the clanking of combustion engines and grind of tracks. Filthy smog stained the air above their advance, smoke from dozens of exhausts carpeting the treetops.

The padding of feet caused Morlaniath to turn. A squadron of war walkers advanced quickly into the clearing, the bipedal machines making no more noise than an eldar on foot. The cloven feet of the machines left shallow indents in the earth as they stalked forwards on their slender, back-jointed legs. The closest pilot, his open cockpit enclosed in a shimmering energy field, looked towards Morlaniath and raised a hand in greeting. The exarch nodded in return and watched the machines break into loping runs, turning rimwards to head into the trees lining the valley, weapon mounts swivelling to keep balance.

A ripple of explosions tore across the left slopes of the valley, still some distance away. Morlaniath traced the trajectory of more shells as they plunged down into the shallow-sided gorge, judging the artillery pieces that launched them to be at the far end of the valley: far too distant to be viable targets for his squad. With growing impatience he saw columns of human vehicles crushing trees beneath their bulk, forging up both slopes in an effort to gain higher ground. Squat tanks with large turrets lumbered at the heads of the columns, their large bore guns spewing fire and smoke every time they fired. Falcons and Vypers slid effortlessly between the trees, ignoring the lead tanks to fire at the clanking transports sheltering behind them. Detonations racked the columns and the tanks slewed to a stop, their turrets swinging ponderously to track their elusive targets while infantry spilled from their burning carriers.

The flicker of Warp Spider jump generators sparkled in the distance as they closed in on the debussed infantry. From beyond the valley walls, doomweavers – gigantic versions of the Aspect Warriors' deathspinners – sent immense clouds of monofilament wire into the air above the valley. The Warp Spiders disengaged and the Vypers broke free as the deadly wire descended, so thin it sliced branch and bone alike.

Behind the lines of halted tanks more vehicles appeared, painted in the red and white of the Space Marines. They charged fearlessly up the valley past the halted advance, ignoring the brightlance bursts and pulse laser blasts screaming around them. With them came attack bikes, three-wheeled contraptions with heavy weapon-armed sidecars. Bursts of plasma and laser criss-crossed between the two forces. More Space Marine tanks crashed forwards like mobile bunkers, the flash of lascannons erupting from armoured sponsons. The eldar withdrew again, leaving the shattered wrecks from both sides burning on the hillsides.

Behind the shield of the Space Marines' vehicles, human tanks advanced again, hundreds of soldiers following behind. From left and right explosions and other sounds of war echoed across the dome. The Emperor's warriors pressed forwards on a broad front, starshells hanging in the air to illuminate their path, the roar of great guns booming out above the splintering crash of falling trees and the crackle of flames.

Beside Morlaniath, the Cobra lifted effortlessly from the flattened grass, arcs of energy coruscating along its distortion cannon, throwing dancing shadows across the clearing. The lead Space Marine tanks were almost three-quarters of the way along the valley. Lascannon blasts stabbed from them into the darkness, setting fire to trees, gouging furrows in the ground as the enemy sought the elusive eldar.

With a thrum that set the ground shaking, the Cobra opened fire. The air itself screamed as the distortion cannon tore at its fabric, a rent appearing in the air above the closest Space Marine vehicle. The gap widened into a whirling hole framed with purple and green lightning, its depths a swirl of colours and reeling stars. Even at this distance, Morlaniath felt a slight nausea tremble through his body and a burning in his spirit stones. The warp rift tugged at his spirit, immaterial fingers prying into parts of his mind locked away behind barriers learnt as a child. Tempting whispers and distant laughter echoed in the exarch's thoughts.

The Space Marine tank was dragged to a stop by the implosive energies of the warp hole, its tracks grinding vainly through the soil, smoke belching from its exhausts as the driver gunned the engine in an effort to maintain traction. With a drawn-out creak, the vehicle lifted from the ground, tipping backwards, stretching and contorting as the breach into warp space opened wider. Rivets sprang free and disappeared into the ravening hole, followed quickly by the tangled remains of the gun sponsons. An armoured figure was drawn out of the top hatch and spun crazily into the maw of the warp a moment before the tank slammed upwards and was sucked into the spiralling vortex. With a crack like thunder the vortex closed, sending out a shockwave that sent a nearby Space Marine transport slamming into a tree with a shower of wood splinters and leaves.

The clearing fell still again as the Cobra's cannon recharged. Undaunted, the humans continued their advance, almost reckless in their haste to close. The whine of descending shells caught Morlaniath's ear and he looked up to see several black shapes falling from the flickering skies. Their trajectory was taking them somewhere off to his right and he followed their fall until they disappeared into the trees a moment before a series of ground-shaking detonations. Flames and smoke leapt into the air. Amidst the flash and turmoil, the exarch saw eldar bodies being tossed like leaves on the wind.

Lascannon blasts flashed across the clearing, shrieking off the Cobra's curved hull. The super-heavy tank lifted again as more power surged along the length of its main gun. Again came the scream of tortured reality and the concussive blast of the warp vortex forming. More than a dozen armoured figures and a pair of troop transports were sucked into the energy maelstrom, their forms thinning and twisting before they disappeared from sight while raw psychic energy forked to the ground from the breach's undulating rim.

Morlaniath strode to the statue and pulled himself up onto Isha's knee to gain a better vantage point, looking past the bulk of the Cobra. He felt that it would soon be time to act; he chafed at being a witness to the battle so far and longed to let the *Teeth of Dissonance* cut a bloody path through Alaitoc's foes.

Wrecks and bodies littered the valley floor, but the Space Marines had gained the higher ground to either side and from their vantage point their tanks poured chattering fire into the tree line. Within this cordon, batteries of self-propelled guns lumbered into position, bringing them into range of the dome's heart. A least twenty tanks grumbled towards Morlaniath's position, painted in the same grey as the soldiers' fatigues. Four brightly-coloured Space Marine transports charged ahead of the advance and would be at the edge of the clearing shortly.

Morlaniath flexed his fingers in anticipation and was about to lower himself to the ground when something crashed through branches behind him, their snapping audible above the din of war. He turned to see a trunk bending and then cracking violently under some unseen pressure. The ground trembled slightly from a massive tread, and a patch of earth sank, squashed by a tremendous yet invisible weight. Craning his neck, the exarch looked up and saw a shimmering presence, a vague outline of contortion against the dark red of the dome's sky.

Holofields shimmered and Morlaniath found himself staring up along the giant, slender leg of a Phantom Titan, half again as tall as the lianderin trees. The Titan was like a giant rendition of Korlandril's sculpture of Eldanesh, its slender limbs and narrow waist a perfection of proportion and design. For all its beauty, it was the perfection of destruction embodied by the Titan that impressed Morlaniath more. Instead of arms, the immense walker had two elegant guns, each longer than a grav-tank. From the Phantom's right shoulder hung the ribbed barrel of a tremor cannon; from the left a lance-like pulsar.

A flurry of missiles streaked from shoulder-mounted pods either side of the swept dome of the Titan's head, engulfing the enemy tanks in a curtain of plasma blossoms. The air shimmered around the vane-like holofield wings splayed from the back of the Phantom, blurring its shape unto a dazzle of fractured images as the Titan took another step forwards. A broad, clawed foot swung gracefully over the clearing to find purchase beside the Cobra, the massive machine's tread delicate for its size, dextrously avoiding the eldar warriors in and around the dell.

Bending one knee slightly, the Titan swung its tremor cannon into position, aimed along the left-hand valley slope. Even within his suit, Morlaniath felt a compression of air around him a moment before the weapon fired. A bass growl reverberated in the exarch's gut, swiftly rising in pitch to a shriek that tightened his throat and set his ears ringing, until it scaled higher, out of the range of even an eldar's hearing. He traced the path of the sonic pulse by the dancing of air molecules: overlapping sine waves of near-invisible energy that ended in the midst of the advancing humans. Where the line touched, the ground erupted, a huge gout of earth and rock rupturing into a widening crack that zigzagged along the hillside. Tanks shook themselves apart as the beam crossed over them; Space Marines were flattened inside their armour; unarmoured soldiers were torn limb from limb by the disharmonious sonic energy coursing through their bodies.

The whine returned and descended to a low rumble as the weapon powered down. There was no respite from the Phantom; more clusters of missiles streamed from its shoulder pods while its pulsar unleashed a glittering salvo of laser energy that tore along the front squadron of tanks, punching through armour, exploding engines and melting the crews inside. The Cobra fired again and the valley descended into an anarchy of swirling vortexes, wailing sonic explosions and the steady strobe of the pulsar. Shells screamed in return, flashing past the wavering image of the Titan to crash into the trees beyond the clearing.

Morlaniath climbed down from the statue, his excitement at the prospect of combat dissipated by the arrival of the Phantom. What use were mandiblasters and biting blade when compared to the awesome energies being unleashed upon the enemy? He rejoined the rest of the Hidden Death, who stood under the shadows of the trees watching the carnage in the valley.

'Do you think any will reach us here?' asked Elissanadrin.

'Not while we have our tall friend watching over us,' said Arhulesh, looking up at the Phantom Titan. 'Oh…'

Morlaniath looked to see the Titan turning away, its outline refracting into a shimmering cloud as the holofield cloaked its movements. In a few strides it was gone, lost past the canopy of the trees. With a whisper, the Cobra followed, sliding between the thick boles of the lianderin. Clearly their weapons were needed more elsewhere. Morlaniath brightened at the prospect that the battle was not yet over.

The exarch directed his gaze back to the valley. He could see red-armoured figures moving between the smoking wrecks and grey-clad soldiers taking up positions in the rents and craters torn into the ground by the Titan's weapons. Though the heaviest enemy vehicles had been destroyed, more of the gangling Imperial walkers advanced through the shattered stumps of the lianderin. Light anti-grav skimmers in the colours of the Space Marines streaked through the air, moving out to the flanks of the advancing force.

'They are needed elsewhere, but enemies remain, our blades will taste more blood,' said Morlaniath. He wondered whether to await the enemy attack, or to head out into the valley to take the fight to the foe. He felt the touch of Thirianna's mind in response to these thoughts.

Arhathain is mustering forces for a counter-attack along this axis. We wait for the reinforcements and then we will advance.

'Make ready your wargear, more warriors arrive, we shall be fighting soon,' the exarch told his squad.

They waited patiently, keeping an eye on the invaders as they approached along the valley, more circumspect than in their initial charge. Morlaniath saw squads of Imperial soldiers digging defensive positions into the hillsides: heaping up the earth to make barricades for trenches and mortar pits; creating semicircular redoubts for their anti-tank weapons; erecting spindly communications masts for their commanders to talk with each other. It was clear that they had abandoned their foolish hope of sweeping away the Alaitocii with a single attack and were now preparing to hold the ground they had taken.

'Their strategy is false, a folly of battle, to think that ground matters,' the exarch remarked to his squad. As he spoke, he pointed out the growing system of works. 'Their minds think in straight lines, seeking grand engagement, counting only in numbers. Our way of war is swift, the fast and fluid strike, not tied to a sole place. They hope we will attack, throw ourselves on their guns, to drive them out of here. We will be more patient, we have the advantage, Alaitoc is our home. Their presence is fleeting, it cannot be sustained, without food and water. They defend an island, cut off from their supplies, and we will rule the sea.'

'Perhaps their attacks are meeting with more success elsewhere?' said

Litharain. 'They make solid their position knowing that advances are being made on other fronts.'

Morlaniath directed a beckoning thought to Thirianna. The farseer acknowledged the question and crossed the clearing to speak directly with the exarch.

'We have abandoned the Dome of Lasting Vigilance, and the humans control more than a quarter of the access ways to Alaitoc's central region.' Her voice was quiet, her tone non-committal. 'We still hold the domes around the infinity circuit core. It is Arhathain's wish that we drive these humans from this dome so that we can mount an attack on the flank of their other forces, severing them from their landing zone in the docks.'

'The enemy prepare, waiting is a peril, how soon do we attack?' said Morlaniath.

Thirianna said nothing for a while, her head cocked to one side as she communed with her fellow seers.

'The counter-attack is almost ready,' she said eventually. 'The humans' rough defences will be no obstacle. They think only of left and right, forwards and backwards. They still forget that we do not have to crawl along the groun–'

The farseer stopped and turned her gaze beyond Morlaniath. The exarch knew what had interrupted Thirianna, for he felt it too: a sensation in the blood, a quickening of the heart.

The Avatar was approaching.

Its presence joined the minds of the hundreds of eldar converging through the trees around Morlaniath, linking them together in one bloody purpose. The exarch saw Guardians and Aspect Warriors advancing through the woods around him, heading for the valley. Far above, Swooping Hawks circled in the thermals of the burning tanks while Vampire bombers with wings like curved daggers cruised back and forth awaiting the order to strike.

Amidst the increasingly strong background throb of the Avatar, Morlaniath felt something else touching upon his spirit, something cold, yet keen and familiar: a direct call to him unlike the burning beacon of the Avatar's presence. He scoured the trees looking for the source. In the shadow of a split lianderin trunk, he saw a pair of yellow eyes flash. From the darkness appeared Karandras, oldest of the Striking Scorpion exarchs.

The Phoenix Lord stalked forwards, his helmet turning slowly as he looked at each of the Hidden Death in turn. He stopped a short distance away, gaze directed towards Bechareth. Morlaniath felt a quiver of worry. Did Karandras sense something of Bechareth's past? Did the Phoenix Lord realise he had once been counted amongst the most hated foes of the Striking Scorpions? The Shadow Hunter stared for a long time, the only movement the dancing reflection of flames in the lenses of his heavy helm and the slow flexing of his power claw. Anxiety flowed from

Bechareth, his shoulders hunched, fist clenched tight around the hilt of his chainsword

'You will join me,' said Karandras, turning to Morlaniath. His voice was as of many speaking in unison, deep and full of power. Every syllable resounded through Morlaniath's mind like they were his own thoughts given life by another. The exarch breathed out slowly, struggling to remain calm. 'Serve as my guard.'

'It will be our honour, Hidden Death stands ready, for the Shadow Hunter,' replied Morlaniath, briefly bending to one knee in deference. As his psyche touched upon the Phoenix Lord's, Morlaniath felt a huge depth opening out beneath him, a bottomless well of life and death. Morlaniath was old, almost as old as Alaitoc, yet the creature that stood before him was even more ancient.

'Your shrine has done well, it is a pride to the Aspect of the Striking Scorpion,' the Phoenix Lord said, gesturing with a nod for the Hidden Death to follow him into the trees.

'The teachings are not mine, the wisdom is from you, I am the messenger,' said Morlaniath.

'Yet the message can become confused, distorted by the passing of ages, from lips to ear to mind, and on to fresh lips. The ideals of the Striking Scorpion remain strong on Alaitoc. It is not so in all places. It is to your credit.'

The Phoenix Lord led them away from the others, the presence of the Avatar receding as Karandras forged on through the trees towards the enemy. A blur of shadow followed Karandras, an aura of darkness that surrounded the squad even when they crossed paths and clearings. Its tendrils lingered behind, caressing the trunks of the trees, lightly striking the Aspect Warriors that followed. One diaphanous trail passed across Morlaniath's arm, chill to the touch. It came from the darkness between stars, the shadow of the deepest void. The tendril dissipated into the air and the sensation passed.

The crack of breaking twigs and the crunch of footfalls rang through the trees. To the left, three of the Imperial walkers advanced quickly through the woods. They lacked the grace of the eldar war walkers, strutting forward on their servo-powered limbs, swaying awkwardly from side-to-side. They were about twice Morlaniath's height, the leaves brushing the top of the pilots' open cockpits. Each was armed with a multiple-barrelled weapon that swung back and forth as the driver scanned the trees for enemies. Smoke drizzled endlessly from twin exhaust stacks mounted on an engine behind the cabin, leaving a sooty stain on the foliage of the lianderin.

More trampling alerted the squad's attention to another squadron passing to their right. Immobile, they waited for the reconnaissance sweep to pass by and then moved on again, heading close and closer to the human line.

* * *

Karandras brought the squad to a halt beneath the eaves of the woods, within gunshot range of the leading human squads. They squatted in the shadows and watched as several squads of soldiers fanned out into the woods, though none turned their eyes upon the Phoenix Lord and his companions.

The slope of the valley was a scene of crude industry, the humans digging-in like parasites on Alaitoc's flesh. Many of the soldiers were engaged with shovels and picks whilst their officers stood around, shouting orders or berating their men. A few sentries stood guard, but it was not these that drew Morlaniath's attention.

In front of the progressing defences were thirty Space Marines, each squad stood beside a slab-sided transport. They held their weapons ready, their helmeted heads turning with metronomic precision as they patrolled the hillside, watching the woods for any threat. At the near end of their line stood another walker, different in design from those that had passed earlier. It was almost as tall, but far broader, almost square in shape, painted in the red and white livery of the Space Marines. It was mostly thickly-armoured hull on squat legs flanked by two massive shoulders; from the right a short arm extended tipped with a claw wreathed in crackling energy; from the left protruded a short-barrelled weapon fed by several fuel tanks that reminded Morlaniath – in a very crude and human way – of the fusion guns used by the Fire Dragon Aspect.

'Which ones are we after?' whispered Arhulesh.

Karandras kept his gaze ahead as he replied, raising a finger of his claw to point at the Space Marines.

'The hardest prey makes for the worthiest prize,' said the Phoenix Lord.

'What will be our approach, the ground gives no cover, our enemies alert,' said Morlaniath.

'There will be a... distraction,' replied the Phoenix Lord in a mellifluous tone. Morlaniath detected a hint of humour.

They waited in silence. Above, the Swooping Hawks continued to circle slowly out of range of the enemy. Morlaniath detected the faintest of compression at the back of his skull, the passing touch of an immaterial presence. He knew that it was a leftover trail, a collateral effect of a Warp Spider's jump generator being activated not too far away. Not for the first time in his long existence, Morlaniath wondered what manner of eldar would become a Warp Spider, willing to expose themselves to the perils of warp space. There was a violent darkness in the core of every exarch and Aspect Warrior, but the Warp Spiders balanced on a precipice of self-destruction. They were not only risk-takers, they had a bleak outlook on life, rarely mixing with warriors from other shrines.

'Be ready,' warned Karandras, driving away Morlaniath's pondering. He had some inkling of what was to be expected and looked up into the sky. In the flickering, dim light of the humans' starshells, winged shapes swooped down from the heights of the dome. The shriek of the wind from their wingtips grew in volume as the Vampires dived, six of them in a V-formation.

A cluster of spheres arced down into the human soldiers as the Vampires swooped overhead. No mundane detonations rocked the valley: each sonic bomb exploded above the defence lines to send out rippling shockwaves. The sonic pulses pulverised bodies and barricades – expanding, ethereal globes of devastation swept across the hillside to create a screaming storm of debris. Morlaniath saw soldiers lifted into the air, their fatigues ripped from lacerated bodies. Those at the outer edge of the sonic eruptions fell to the ground with blood streaming from ears, eyes and mouths, crimson seeping from the pores in their skin, bursting from ruptured blood vessels.

The Space Marines turned as the Swooping Hawks descended in the wake of the bombing run, their bolters rising towards the flying Aspect Warriors. Karandras was already out of cover and dashing along the crest of the hill towards the enemy. Morlaniath pounced after him, the rest of the Hidden Death close on his heels.

A Space Marine gunner sitting in a hatch atop one of the transports spotted the Striking Scorpions and heaved around his pintle-mounted weapon. Bright flares streamed towards the squad as the Space Marine opened fire, his twin-barrelled gun spraying explosive bolts. Two rounds streaked past Morlaniath and he heard a scream of pain. Glancing back, he saw Elissanadrin writhing on the ground, right arm missing below the shoulder, a gaping hole in the side of her chest. In a moment, the exarch took in the frothing blood, splinters of bone and spurting arteries in the wounds. More bolts whined past. There was no time to spare for the fallen warrior. The exarch surged after Karandras, the *Teeth of Dissonance's* blades spinning up to full speed, powered by Morlaniath's growing rage.

Karandras cut to the right and plunged into the closest Space Marine squad as more bolter shells whickered past. With two steps, Morlaniath leapt up the sloping front of the transport, biting blade level. Without breaking stride, he bounded past the gunner, the whirring teeth of his blade sweeping through the Space Marine's neck as the exarch dashed past, thick blood spattering on the white hull of the vehicle. Swift retribution for Elissanadrin's death sent a thrill through the exarch as he ran across the engine grille and jumped down to rejoin his squad.

Four Space Marines lay at the feet of Karandras, their armour carved apart by his sword and crushed by his power claw. The Phoenix Lord's mandiblasters unleashed a torrent of blasts that hurled another foe from his feet, his armour shattering from the pulses of green energy.

The Hidden Death joined their Phoenix Lord in the melee, pistols singing, chainswords screeching. A bolter shell flashed across Morlaniath's vision, the flare of its propellant almost blinding him, his helmet lenses polarising to avoid permanent damage to his eyes. He instinctively ducked and spun, lashing out with the *Teeth of Dissonance*, the blade crashing against an armoured leg. A fuzzy red shape stumbled back to his right. Morlaniath drove forwards, angling the point of his biting blade high, catching the Space Marine across his heavy shoulder pad. The exarch fought back a brief flash of not-Lecchamemnon's death with a feral snarl.

'Destroy the invaders, set free your enmity, let the red river flow!'

Morlaniath launched himself at his foe, mandiblasters crackling into the Space Marine's eye lenses. With a growl, the exarch smashed the roaring teeth of his blade across the Space Marine's gut, slicing through pipes and cables in a spray of electrical sparks. The Space Marine swung his bolter like a club, Morlaniath catching the weapon on the armoured guard of his sword. The strength of the blow forced the exarch back three steps, but in a moment he regained his balance and sprang again, ducking beneath the Space Marine's outstretched arm, the *Teeth of Dissonance* tearing a furrow through the ribbed armour protecting the warrior's exposed armpit. Blood spewed from a severed artery, bathing Morlaniath's legs as he spun behind the Space Marine.

With a shout, the exarch hammered the biting blade into the vents of the Space Marine's power plant backpack. Fractured energy cells discharged their contents in an arc of bluish light, mirrored by a flurry of laser fire from the exarch's mandiblasters. Coolant hissed in a cloud from the Space Marine's ravaged armour, frosting across Morlaniath's left arm. The thin layer of ice crystals flaked to the floor as he brought back his sword for a final blow. The Space Marine turned lopsidedly towards the attack, to be met full in the face by the teeth of Morlaniath's weapon, which sheared through the helm, removing the top of the Space Marine's skull. As the Space Marine collapsed, Morlaniath delivered another burst from his mandiblasters into the exposed brain matter, reducing it to steaming grey slurry.

A shadow loomed over the exarch and he saw the blocky shape of the Space Marine walker towering above him. The metal beast had its massive hand upraised, energy crackling between long claws. The exarch lifted up the *Teeth of Dissonance* to parry the attack, but knew he did not have the strength to fend off such a blow.

Something hit the exarch hard in the side, pushing him out of the way of the claw's lighting-wreathed descent. Morlaniath rolled to the side, Bechareth between him and the walker, a moment before the claws slashed down, cleaving away the side of the Aspect Warrior's helm before parting the left arm from his body.

Karandras leapt across Bechareth as he fell, his powered claw raking trails of ceramic splinters from the walker's armour. Morlaniath was filled with the urge to drag Bechareth to safety, instilled in him by a thought from the Phoenix Lord. He could do nothing but act in tune with the compulsion. He held the *Teeth of Dissonance* in his left hand and grabbed Bechareth by his remaining wrist, hauling him from under the walker's clawed feet. The walker's fist caught Karandras in the stomach, glittering fingers punching out of the Phoenix Lord's back.

Morlaniath looked down at Bechareth's face, almost a mirror image of the first time they had met, the Striking Scorpion's eyes staring from a mask of bright blood. Morlaniath saw the hatred and anger of an Aspect Warrior in that gaze, but sensed something behind the war-mask.

The exarch understood why Karandras had sacrificed himself to save Bechareth.

'You must survive this war, move on along the Path, find the peace that you crave,' Morlaniath whispered. 'Fight the darkness in you. Prove that the Path is right, that Khaine does not own us!'

Bechareth's hand flapped against Morlaniath's arm, seeking to grasp him. He fell back with a shuddering gasp, eyes fixed on the exarch.

'I will,' said Bechareth, lips twisted with pain.

Morlaniath nodded and turned back to the walker, which was lumbering after the rest of the Hidden Death as they retreated down the hill. The exarch took two steps after the mechanical beast, eyeing the vulnerable pipes and exhausts jutting from its back.

He stopped, gaze drawn to the body of Karandras lying just ahead. The Phoenix Lord's armour was rent open from stomach to throat, but there was no blood splashed, no organs ripped apart. In the gouge, a galaxy swirled; motes of light circled around a central brightness, each a spirit of Karandras.

Morlaniath was entranced. He could feel the faint beating of a heart at the base of his skull. It grew in strength as he approached the rent form of Karandras, drawn closer by an irresistible instinct, filled with the same external purpose as he had been when he had dragged Bechareth to safety. He was not in control of his body and watch in detachment as Morlaniath knelt beside the fallen Phoenix Lord, dragged deeper and deeper into the circling lights. The call of Khaine waxed strong, roaring in the Morlaniath's ears to the drum of the heartbeat.

He reached out a hand to touch the glittering stars.

With a wrench, Morlaniath felt himself drawn from his weak physical vessel, every part of him: Morlaniath, the First, the Hidden Death; Idsresail, the Dreamer; Lecchamemnon, the Doomed; Ethruin, the Dark Joker; Elidhnerial, the Weeping One; Neruidh, The Forgiver; Ultheranish, the Child of Ulthwé; Korlandril, the Artist.

Not-Korlandril was but an atom in the star of Morlaniath, and Morlaniath nothing but a star in the whole galaxy that was Karandras. Countless essences, endless voices drifted slowly together. Spirits from across the galaxy, of warriors born on every craftworld in every age, and the spirit-parts that made them, and the memories of those other spirits that had touched them, stretching out, far out into the infinity of the universe, all connected, all brought together in this one body.

Morlaniath fragmented, became his parts, each seeping away into the glitter of the Phoenix Lord's essence. The silence of space greeted them. Not for them the life-in-death of the infinity circuit. Not for them the ravages of She Who Thirsts. Here they would end, truly and forever. Only Karandras lived on. Briefly, Korlandril lived again, and then was gone.

Peace.

He hid behind the tumbled arch of the old temple, shivering in his nakedness. Hunger gnawed at his gut. His limbs trembled with weakness, his breath wheezing in his throat. And the pain inside, the throbbing in his heart and head, the needles of agony that coursed through his mind, stretching him in all directions, more unbearable than any physical pain.

A foot scraped on dusty stone and he shrank bank further into the shadows, eyes desperately seeking an escape. There was none, he was trapped. Through the tears, he saw a figure silhouetted against the light from outside the shrine.

'Do not be afraid,' the stranger said, his voice quiet but strong.

He remained as still as death, holding his breath. The stranger crossed the bone-littered floor of the temple with easy strides, his green gown flowing behind him. The stranger's eyes were unlike any he had seen before. They were empty of hatred, empty of lust, empty of jealousy and malevolence.

He flinched as the stranger reached out a hand. He pushed himself back until his spine was against the cold wall. There was nowhere else to hide. The stranger smiled, but there was none of the leering desire he usually associated with such an expression.

'What is your name?' the stranger asked. His voice was low, calm, not screaming, not shouting.

'Karandras,' he whispered back, his voice barely a breath.

'Karandras? That is a good name, a strong name.'

'What do you want with me?'

'I want to help you.'

'Where are you going to take me? The others wanted to take me into the dark web, but I ran. I was scared.'

'You were right to be scared. The others are not to be trusted.'

'Trusted?'

'I will teach you about trust. It is a good thing. Come with me and I will teach you many things.'

'What will I learn?'

'You will learn not to be afraid. You will learn about happiness, and peace, and balance. Do you want to learn these things?'

'I do not know... What are they?'

'They are what will make us strong again.'

'Will you teach me how to hide?'

'There are no places left to hide.'

'Will you keep me safe?'

'Nowhere is safe.'

Karandras considered this for a moment.

'Will you protect me?'

'Better than that, I will teach you how to protect yourself. I will teach you how to fight.'

Karandras reached out and hesitantly grasped the proffered hand. The stranger's grip was firm but gentle. He allowed himself to be lifted to his feet, his head no higher than the stranger's chest.

They turned towards the door together and walked across the light, Karandras's hand in the stranger's.

'Where are we going?' the boy asked.

'To a place where my friends are waiting. To a place where you can learn how to fight, to battle the enemies of the body and the spirit.'

They reached the cracked steps of the doorway, the harsh light causing Karandras to blink heavily, tears in his eyes.

'Who are you?' he asked.

'I am Arhra. I am your new father.'

Whiteness faded away to the colours of life and death. Karandras pulled himself to his feet, his armour fusing the wound that had allowed his energy to escape. The Phoenix Lord looked down at the empty suit of the exarch that had given him this new life. He felt nothing of the eldar that he had been. There were no memories, save his own. There was no spirit, save the one he had been born with.

He was Karandras, and Karandras alone.

He looked around, assessing the raging battle. The Alaitocii were fighting hard and driving the humans from the dome, but the fate of their craftworld was far from decided. Karandras stooped to pick up his chainsword, reassured by the feel of it in his fist. The Striking Scorpions who had joined him were retreating back to the woods, carrying two of their wounded number between them. The Phoenix Lord turned his back on them and headed after the Imperial Dreadnought that had killed him. The Phoenix Lord felt the thrill of retribution singing through his body.

Another war, another death. Such was to be his fate, until the final battle, the Rhana Dandra, when all things would end.

PATH OF THE SEER

'Life is to us as the maze of Linnian was to Ulthanesh, its mysterious corridors leading to wondrous vistas and nightmarish encounters in equal measure. Each of us must walk the maze alone, treading in the footsteps of those that came before but also forging new routes through the labyrinth of existence.

In times past we were drawn to the darkest secrets and ran wild about the maze, seeking to experience all that it had to offer. As individuals and as a civilisation we lost our way and in doing so created the means for our doom, our unfettered exploration leading to the darkness of the Fall.

In the emptiness that followed, a new way was revealed to us: the Path. Through the wisdom of the Path we spend our lives exploring the meaning of existence, moving from one part of the maze to another with discipline and guidance so that we never become lost again. On the Path we experience the full potential of love and hate, joy and woe, lust and purity, filling our lives with experience and fulfilment but never succumbing to the shadows that lurk within our thoughts.

But like all journeys, the Path is different for each of us. Some wander for a long while in one place; some spread their travels wide and visit many places for a short time while others remain for a long time to explore every nook and turn; some of us lose our way and leave the Path for a time or forever; and some of us find dead ends and become trapped.'

– Kysaduras the Anchorite,
foreword to Introspections upon Perfection

PROLOGUE

A blue sun reflected from the still waters of the lake, its yellow companion peeking just above the red-leaved trees that surrounded the edge of the water. Red-and-black birds skimmed above the lake with wings buzzing, their long beaks snapping at insects, their chattering calls the only sound to break the quiet.

A white stone building bordered the water, its long colonnaded veranda stretching over the lake on thick piles. Beyond the portico, it reared up amongst the trees, square in shape, turreted towers at each corner. Thin smoke seeped lazily from vents in the wall, the breeze carrying it away across the forests. Narrow windows shuttered with red-painted wood broke the upper storeys, small balconies jutting from the wall beneath each one.

Armed figures stood guard at the high doorways and patrolled walkways running along the red-tiled roofs. The men were dressed in loose black trousers tucked into knee-high boots, with bulky red jackets buttoned and braided with gold. Their heads were covered by black hoods, with tinted goggles to protect their eyes from the strange light of the local star. They walked their rounds and chatted with each other, thinking nothing was amiss.

Behind the line of trees that bordered the grounds of the manor, the air shimmered with colour. A swirl of energy broke reality and from the breach emerged a thin line of warriors. Clad in blue and gold armour, the Dire Avengers of Alaitoc stepped foot upon the humans' world, their shuriken catapults held at the ready.

They moved quietly between the trees as more Aspect Warriors appeared: the black-armoured Dark Reapers, the bone-coloured Howling Banshees. At the centre of the ten-strong squad from the Shrine of One Hundred Bloody Tears, Thirianna looked impassively at the imposing but severe structure of the mansion, assessing the lines of fire from its rooftops and windows.

There were fewer defenders than had been expected, but the farseers and autarchs had taken no chances with the size of the force that had been despatched. Several dozen Aspect Warriors converged across the grounds, more than enough to cope with the stiffest defence yet small enough to attack and withdraw without alerting the wider defences of the world. It was imperative, so said the farseers, that this seemingly idyllic place was wiped from the skein of fate, lest some disaster spawned here befall the craftworld in the future.

Thirianna felt the touch of Farseer Kelamith upon her mind, as did the others around her.

The heavy blade pauses while the shadows deepen.

She knew exactly what was meant; the main force was to halt out of view while the rangers and Striking Scorpions infiltrated the humans' defences. She settled to her haunches in the shade of a tree and waited, mind fixed on the task ahead.

There was a flash of light through the sky and a massive explosion rocked the front of the manor house, shards of stone and cracked tiles thrown high into the air by the impact. A moment later, another blast seared down through the clouds and detonated, destroying one of the turrets in a cloud of dust, spilling mangled bodies to the close-cut lawn beside the mansion.

To Thirianna's right, the Dark Reapers had opened fire with their missile launchers. A rippling burst sent a volley of projectiles towards the roof of the house while the Dire Avengers and Howling Banshees dashed across flower-filled beds, vaulted over stone benches and skipped across bubbling fountains trailing splashes of water.

Nimreith, Thirianna's exarch, led the squad towards a long porch alongside the waterfront. Thirianna could see the heavily armoured forms of Kenainath's Striking Scorpions emerging from the lake, pistols and chainswords ready.

The Deadly Shadow launched their attack as Thirianna's squad reached the end of the portico, the Striking Scorpions' pistols spitting hails of molecule-thin discs, their chainswords purring. Caught by surprise, the soldiers stood no chance and were cut down in moments, dismembered, disembowelled or beheaded by the blades of the Striking Scorpions.

The warriors of the One Hundred Bloody Tears leapt over the balcony rail and joined the Deadly Shadow. Together they headed towards the back doors.

The Striking Scorpions and Dire Avengers scattered for cover as fire erupted from one of the windows, bullets and splinters from a wooden planter punching through the armour of one of Kenainath's warriors.

Thirianna returned fire without thought, her weapon sending a hail of shurikens through the window, slashing across the chest of the human within while volleys from the others tore apart his throat and face.

Without hesitation, Nimreith leapt across the breach and the One Hundred Bloody Tears followed her through. Thirianna was the fourth through the window and broke to the right as they had trained, her eyes scanning the shadowy interior for foes. She spied a door opening beneath an arching staircase and brought up her shuriken catapult. Another fusillade of monomolecular discs filled the air as a human guard clumsily burst into the hallway, his padded armour ripped and bloody in a heartbeat.

'To the ascent, we walk in blood, Dire Avengers,' said Nimreith, heading towards the stairs.

Thirianna fell into her place in the line, stepping effortlessly up the stairway as she trained her shuriken catapult on the landing above. There was movement and she opened fire instantly. The body of a human tumbled properly into view, throat slashed open.

Reaching the landing, the squad was directed to the right by Nimreith, towards a set of wooden double doors. Thirianna felt the wild presence of the Howling Banshees approaching from behind and then diminishing as they turned left along the landing. A dull aura of fear had settled on the manse, the dread of the human occupants polluting her thoughts.

She kept her eyes and weapon fixed on the doorway at the end of the landing, while subconsciously registering the explosions of more Dark Reaper missiles and the shouts of dying humans from below.

Luadrenin and Minareith opened the double doors while the rest of the squad stood ready. The chamber within was empty, the rough furnishings of wood suggesting some kind of recreational area. There was a wood-burning fireplace and a low table surrounded by couches. The carpet underfoot was threadbare from the passage of many feet. A painting of a human with heavy jowls hung above the fire.

Thirianna took it all in at a glance, her focus drawn towards another door on the opposite side of the room. The squad moved quickly, securing the door and a window that led to the balcony.

Thirianna was first into the next room.

It was some kind of eating area. A long table flanked by high-backed seats stretched the length of the room, set with plates and candlesticks as if ready for a meal. Thirianna heard a whimpering noise and leapt onto the table. She ran along its length, picking her way between the dishes and candlesticks without effort.

At the far end of the room was another seating area, with overstuffed chairs and a round table. In the corner cowered a female human. With her were three children: one male, two female. Their faces were red and wet, their eyes glistening.

The taint of Chaos permeates this place, said Kelamith. *All must be purged.*

The humans made whimpering, animal noises as Thirianna brought up her shuriken catapult.

The ambient light in Thirianna's bedchamber was dimmed. She lay on the soft floor and looked at the shadows on the ceiling, watching the slowly-changing patches of dim light and dark shifting. Her slight body, narrow waisted and slender shouldered, was immobile. Her thin face was half hidden by the long sweep of white hair that lay across it, obscuring the tattoo of Alaitoc's rune on her right cheek. Thirianna's deep blue eyes roved from side to side as her gaze hunted the darker shadows, which constantly slipped to the edges of vision, refusing to give up their secrets.

She smelled something strange: blood. A moment later she felt a pain in her hands. Lifting them up, she saw that she had dug her nails into her palms. She watched a droplet of her life fluid slide down to her wrist and drip onto her bare stomach.

Something was wrong.

A presence squirmed in the recess of her mind. The smell and the sight of the blood stirred it. The touch of Khaine, the anger of the Bloody-Handed God awakened. Thirianna closed her eyes, seeking peace in the darkness. Her vision was filled with the blood red of her war-mask.

With a gasp she opened her eyes again. She whispered the mantras she had been taught, seeking to put aside that part of her that was Thirianna the Dire Avenger. Her brow itched, feeling upon it the rune of her shrine that had been painted there in blood.

She lifted her finger to her forehead but felt nothing. There was no blood there. She had removed the rune and chanted the verses and still a remnant, a dagger shard, remained in her mind.

Trying to relax, Thirianna took a deep breath and laid her hands on her chest. She felt the beat of her heart through her fingertips, swift and strong. The nagging sliver of Khaine would not go.

She wondered if perhaps she should go to the shrine, to seek the guidance of Nimreith. She dismissed the idea. Thirianna felt that if something was amiss, she would be able to deal with it.

Closing her eyes again, she probed at the wound in her psyche, feeling around the raw edges, hesitant to look deeper. Veiled with mental curtains, the memories within were part of her war-mask, detached from the rest of her thoughts. She felt them throbbing behind the locked synapses of her brain, insistent for attention.

What could be so important that it demanded to be seen?

Slowly, Thirianna folded back the curtains of her thought for a glimpse, the tiniest flicker of acceptance.

She screamed, mind awash with a vision of crying children and the dying shrieks of their mother.

Part One

Poet

FRIENDSHIP

Tower of Torments – Vaul's Gaol. This is a rune of opposition, appearing in conjunction and used alongside the runes of two individuals. It represents the prison of Vaul, in which the Smith God was bound to his anvil by Khaine the Bloody-Handed One. When used deliberately, the Tower of Torments can guide one along the skein to a breaking of bonds, as Vaul broke free from his chains; when appearing unheralded upon the skein the Tower of Torments signifies abrupt departure, though whether the breaking is for good or ill requires further divination.

The stylus nib hovered over the shard of crystal set in its stand before Thirianna. She sat on a brightly embroidered rug in front of the writing stand, her legs crossed, free hand held to the small of her back. She focussed her thoughts, composing herself to commit her sentiment for eternity. Three runes intertwined in her mind, forming the concept, embellished with a unique flourish Thirianna had been devising for several cycles.

Picturing the edges and curves of the rune overlaying the facets and contours of the crystal, Thirianna started to move her hand. Light flowed between stylus and shard. Molecules rearranged, forming a design of shifting colours in the heart of the crystal. Her hand moved back and forth, left and right, shaping the poem-design in glimmering rainbow.

When she was finished, she returned the stylus to its holder on the writing tray. She regarded her work with critical eyes but was pleased with the result. Warm reds flowed into cold blues and jade green, separating the three runes yet linking them with the oranges and purples between. Thirianna plucked the crystal from the claw-like holder and turned it around in her fingertips. The colours shifted and the runes interleaved in different ways, each perspective creating a subtle new verse of shape and hue.

The poem-form came full circle in her hand, flowing without hindrance back to the beginning.

Thirianna smiled at the accomplishment. She read the poem again, satisfaction replaced with longing. Standing, she left the small composing area of her habitat and went into the main living chamber. Crossing the rug-scattered space Thirianna stopped before a blister-like protrusion on the wall. It peeled open at a wave of her hand, revealing rows of shelves, each holding a dozen poem-crystals. Thirianna placed her latest composition in its place on the lowest row.

She took a while to review them all, picking up each, reading and re-reading them, feeling the story of her life, of her love, unfolding once more. From the first few crude slashes to the elegant lines of her latest works, the poems told a story not only of her feelings but of her growing proficiency.

The poet delved deeper, examining the meaning as well as the form. The crudeness of the first poems mirrored their raw content, the pain and suffering she had felt. As she had moved away from that hard time, pushed her war-mask deeper and deeper into the past, the movements had come more fluently, the language more assured as her thoughts and emotions had settled. She smiled again at the recurring themes, her playful delves into possible futures of happiness.

Thirianna snapped out of her contemplation, suddenly aware that she was running late. She stepped into her robing area and swiftly chose an outfit suitable for the coming occasion. She pulled on a white ankle-length dress pleated below the knee, delicately embroidered with thread just the slightest shade greyer than the cloth, like the shadows of a cloud; sleeveless to reveal pale arms painted with waving patterns of henna. She wrapped a diaphanous scarf of red and white about her shoulders and summoned up a mirrorplate to appear in the wall of the chamber. Something wasn't quite right.

She opened a drawer and pulled out the pigment-comb. Its teeth were a haze of blue, which shifted to glittering silver. Thirianna's lustrous black hair changed to white as she ran the pigment-comb through her long locks. With deft movements, she picked out two stripes of blue to frame her face. She completed the transformation with a swift touch of an iris-petal to her eyes, turning them from bright green to dark blue.

Satisfied if not entirely happy with these hasty preparations, Thirianna left her apartment and headed to the docks. She had hoped to enjoy a leisurely journey to the Tower of Eternal Welcomes, but instead hailed a star-runner. The small tri-winged craft spun up to the docking lock of the dome in which Thirianna lived, gravitic vanes trembling in the fluctuating field of Alaitoc's artificial gravity as she boarded. The exterior portal cycled open, allowing the craft into the airlock, which gleamed with golden light. The ambient hue turned a deeper orange in warning as the outer gate detached. The star-runner was propelled out into the vacuum with a puff of air and freezing water droplets.

Thirianna relaxed and looked down at Alaitoc below as the star-runner skimmed towards the starward rim. That star, Mirianathir, bathed the craftworld with its ruddy glow. To Thirianna's right the glimmering webway portal rippled against a field of stars.

With a fluctuation of golden light, the webway portal dilated for a moment and where there had been vacuum drifted *Lacontiran*, a bird-like trading schooner just returned from her long voyage to the stars of the Endless Valley. Trimming her solar sails, she turned easily along the starside rim of the craftworld and followed a course that led her to the Tower of Eternal Welcomes.

Thirianna sighed with relief. Aradryan was aboard *Lacontiran*, and would not arrive before the star-runner made it to the Tower of Eternal Welcomes. She activated the filterglass and the stars were replaced with an opaque sheen so that it seemed as if Thirianna sat inside a pearl.

She hummed quietly, testing out timing and cadence for her next poem, trying to capture her mood of excitement and expectation.

Wending her way easily through the assembled eldar thronging the walkways of the Tower of Eternal Welcomes, Thirianna sensed the ebb and flow of emotion around her. It was not just from the snatches of conversation or the poise and expressions of the other eldar that she drew this information; as a poet she had taught herself to attune her feelings to the emotions of others, sensing their mood on an instinctual level.

She passed couples in love, groups of friends, siblings both loving and jealous, friends and rivals. She felt the heady swirl of these overlapping, colliding feelings washing over her from the crowd, enjoying every moment of expectation, every thrill of excitement; even the worry and dread felt by some was a sensation to be savoured. Without sadness happiness could not appreciated; without darkness light had no meaning.

In the midst of this kaleidoscope of craftworld life, Thirianna spied Korlandril. His slender frame was draped in an open-fronted robe of shining silk-like gold, his neck and wrists adorned with hundreds of molecule-thin chains in every colour of the spectrum so that it seemed his hands and face were wound with miniature rainbows. His long black hair was bound into a complicated braid that hung across his left shoulder, kept in place with holo-bands that constantly changed from sapphires to diamonds to emeralds and every other beautiful stone known to the eldar.

Thirianna saw something of the work of the ancient artist Arestheina in her companion's attire, though displayed somewhat too brashly for her liking. All the same, she felt a buzz of familiarity as she laid her hand upon Korlandril's in greeting, feeling the warmth of his affection.

They swapped intricate pleasantries while *Lacontiran* glided effortlessly towards the docking pier. Thirianna complimented Korlandril on his outfit and he replied in kind, a little too enthusiastically for Thirianna's comfort. She could see the longing in the sculptor's eyes, took considerable pleasure from it being directed towards her, but there was something else lingering beneath the surface. There was a hunger hidden away, and it gave Thirianna pause, frightening her with its intensity.

She dismissed it as part of Korlandril's assumed artistic temperament. Though the Poet and the Artist were close Paths, they were not trodden for the same reason. The Artist sought inspiration, to be utterly open to all influence from outside in order to render the universe into his work. The Poet was about reflecting the universe, using it as a mirror to examine oneself and one's feelings. The first was extrovert, the second introvert, and though they complemented each other well, Thirianna and Korlandril's chosen paths meant they viewed Alaitoc and its eldar with very different eyes.

Thirianna turned towards the approaching starship, alive with the excitement of Aradryan's return. Korlandril was good company, a very loyal friend, but she had missed Aradryan greatly. His humour, his laugh, had been taken away when he had chosen to tread the Path of the Steersman, and she longed to see his face again and listen to his soft voice. She trembled at the prospect and felt Korlandril stir with unease beside her. She glanced at him out of the corner of her eye and saw a frown briefly crease his brow as he looked at her, before he too turned his gaze towards *Lacontiran* sliding smoothly against the dockside.

A dozen gateways along the hull of *Lacontiran* opened, releasing a wave of iridescent light and a honey-scented breeze along the curving length of the dock. From the high archways passengers and crew disembarked in winding lines. Thirianna stretched to her full height, poised effortlessly on the tips of her boots, to look over the heads of the eldar in front, one hand slightly to one side to maintain her balance.

'There he is, our wanderer returned to us like Anthemion with the Golden Harp,' said Korlandril, pointing to a walkway to their left, letting his fingers rest upon Thirianna's bare arm for the slightest of moments to attract her attention.

Thirianna's gaze followed her friend's pointing finger. At first she did not recognise Aradryan amongst the dozens of eldar streaming down to the dockside. Only by his sharp cheeks and thin lips did Thirianna finally pick him from the crowd. His hair was cut short on the left side, almost to the scalp, and hung in unkempt waves to the right, neither bound nor styled. It struck Thirianna as roguish and she smiled. He had dark make-up upon his eyelids, giving him a skull-like, sunken glare, and he was dressed in deep blues and black, wrapped in long ribbons of twilight. His bright yellow waystone was worn as a brooch, mostly hidden by the folds of his robe. Aradryan's forbidding eyes fell upon Korlandril and then Thirianna, their sinister edge disappearing with a glint of happiness. Aradryan waved a hand in greeting and made his way effortlessly through the crowd to stand in front of the pair.

'A felicitous return!' declared Korlandril, opening his arms in welcome, palms angled towards Aradryan's face. 'And a happy reunion.'

Thirianna dispensed with words altogether, brushing the back of her hand across Aradryan's cheek for a moment, savouring the touch of his flesh, assuring herself he was real. She laid her slender fingers upon his shoulder, an exceptionally familiar gesture of welcome usually reserved for close family. Thirianna did not know why she had been so intimate, but enjoyed the touch of Aradryan's fingers on her shoulder as the steersman returned the gesture. Thirianna felt a hint of coldness from Korlandril and realised that she was being rude to monopolise their friend's attention.

The moment passed and Aradryan stepped away from Thirianna, laying his hands onto those of Korlandril, a wry smile on his lips.

'Well met, and many thanks for the welcome,' said Aradryan.

Thirianna noticed Korlandril holding Aradryan's hands for a moment longer than might seem necessary, and saw her friends scrutinising each other carefully but subtly. With the same slight smile, Aradryan withdrew his grasp and clasped his hands behind his back, raising his eyebrows inquisitively.

'Tell me, dearest and most happily met of my friends, what have I missed?'

The three reunited friends spent some time catching up with each other's news, each noticing the differences in the other since Aradryan's departure. The steersman wanted to feel Alaitoc again beneath his feet and so they walked along the Avenue of Dreams, through a silver passageway that passed beneath a thousand crystal archways into the heart of Alaitoc. The dim light of Mirianathir was caught in the vaulted roof, captured and radiated by the intricately faceted crystal to shine down upon the pedestrians below, glowing with delicate oranges and pinks.

Korlandril was being garrulous, speaking at length about his works and his accomplishments. He could not help it; the mind of the artist had no place for circumspection or self-awareness, only sensation and expression. Thirianna exchanged the occasional patient glance with Aradryan as they walked, while Korlandril extolled the virtues of his sculptures.

Now and then Aradryan would intervene, sometimes when Korlandril was in mid-flow, to ask Thirianna about the changes in her life. Korlandril would take these interruptions with forced grace and was always eager to steer the conversation back to himself, as though he competed with Thirianna for Aradryan's attention.

'I sense that you no longer walk in the shadow of Khaine,' said Aradryan, nodding in approval as he looked at Thirianna.

'It is true that the Path of the Warrior has ended for me,' she replied, her eyes never straying from Aradryan. In a hidden part of her mind a memory stirred. Though she could not recall what was locked away there, she sensed the pain within and forcefully quelled the urge to examine it. 'The aspect of the Dire Avenger has sated my anger, enough for a hundred lifetimes. I write poetry, influenced by the Uriathillin school of verse. I find it has complexities that stimulate both the intellectual and the emotional in equal measure.'

'I would like to know Thirianna the Poet, and perhaps your verse will introduce me,' said Aradryan. 'I would very much like to see a performance, as you see fit.'

'As would I,' said Korlandril. 'Thirianna refuses to share her work with me, though many times I have suggested that we collaborate on a piece that combines her words with my sculpture.'

'My verse is for myself, and no other. It is not for performance, nor for eyes that are not mine,' Thirianna said quietly. Korlandril's attention-seeking was beginning to test her patience and she cast a glance of annoyance at the sculptor. 'While some create their art to express themselves to the world, my poems are inner secrets, for me to understand their meaning, to divine my own fears and wishes.'

Admonished, Korlandril fell silent for a moment. Thirianna felt a stab of guilt immediately and the brief silence that followed gnawed at her conscience. Korlandril recovered quickly enough and asked Aradryan whether he intended to stay. The steersman jested with him, showing some of his old wit, while Thirianna merely enjoyed seeing the two of them together again.

'Your return is most timely, Aradryan,' Korlandril said after another silent interlude. 'My latest piece is nearing completion. In a few cycles' time I am hosting an unveiling. It would be a pleasure and an honour if both of you could attend.'

'I would have come even if you had not invited me!' laughed Thirianna. For all of his patience-sapping self-aggrandising, Korlandril was exceptionally gifted and his sculptures allowed her to better see the spirit hidden behind the gregarious facade of the artist. 'I hear your name mentioned quite often, and with much praise attached, and there are high expectations for this new work. It would not be seemly at all to miss such an event if one is to be considered as a person possessing any degree of taste.'

Aradryan did not reply for a moment and Thirianna cast a concerned look at her friend. He seemed almost expressionless, as if a blank mask had been placed upon his face.

'Yes, I too would be delighted to attend,' Aradryan said eventually, animation returning. 'I am afraid that my tastes may have been left behind compared to yours, but I look forward to seeing what Korlandril the Sculptor has created in my absence.'

Thirianna spent the next few cycles alone as Aradryan reacquainted himself with his family and other friends, and Korlandril continued the labours on his latest sculpture. She began the composition of a new poem, inspired by the return of Aradryan. His reappearance had stirred up old emotions; some pleasant, others not so.

She passed much of the time in the Dome of Wandering Memories, where archives of Alaitoc's greatest writers and poets were kept. She sought out her favourites – Liareshin, Manderithian, Noiren Alath and others – and spent whole cycles losing herself in their verses. She sought the runes that would blend the two facets of her feelings, not merging to grey but speaking in clear tones of black and white, light and dark.

In her research, Thirianna spoke with some of the other poets that she met there, never revealing her intent but seeking recommendations that would further her understanding. She enjoyed this phase of composition immensely, excited by possibility, unfettered by the reality of committing her words to eternity.

The evening before Korlandril's great unveiling she received a message across the infinity circuit from Aradryan, inviting her to join him at the dawn of the next cycle. She agreed and left arrangements for them to meet on the Bridge of Glimmering Sighs, one of her favourite haunts when away from the Dome of Wandering Memories.

She slept fitfully that night, alternately excited and oppressed by the thought of spending some time alone with Aradryan. He had lost much of his gaiety since becoming a steersman, not only in look but demeanour. She wondered what experiences had wrought such changes, and wondered also if she really wanted to learn of them.

It was the nature of the Path that friends and family changed, becoming new people, relationships waxing and waning as individuals made their own way through their long lives. Yet Aradryan, and Korlandril more so in his absence, had left a lasting impression upon her that she could not shake. He seemed more like a brother than a friend – Thirianna had no real siblings to compare – and it was hard for her to reconcile her warmth for him with the stranger who had returned upon *Lacontiran*.

Aradryan was already waiting for her when she arrived at the Bridge of Glimmering Sighs. The silver arc crossed over a ribbon of white-foamed water that cascaded through the Dome of Silence Lost, its span curving as it rose to the crest high above the river. Green-and-blue snapwings and red-crested meregulls trilled and squawked as they dived beneath the bridge and swept along the fern-filled banks.

She smiled as she approached Aradryan, who stood alone at the edge of the bridge looking down into the rushing waters. There was no rail, and he stood with the toes of his high boots poking over the edge, his balance poised at the delicate edge between stability and falling. With an impish grin, he looked over his shoulder as Thirianna called his name, and waved her to join him. The expression flooded her with happiness, reminding her of the Aradryan that she had waved goodbye to long ago.

'A very pleasant location,' he said, stepping back from the edge of the bridge to face Thirianna. 'I do not recall coming here before.'

'We never came here,' Thirianna replied. 'It is a well-kept secret amongst the poets of Alaitoc, and I trust that you will keep it so.'

'Of course,' said Aradryan. He looked out over the edge again. 'It reminds me a little of the gulfs of space, an endless depth to fall into.'

'I would prefer that you did not fall,' she said, reaching out a hand to Aradryan's arm to gently tug him back as he looked to take another step. 'You have only just come back, and we have much to talk about.'

'We do?' he said, delighted by the thought. 'Perhaps you have a verse or two you would like to share with me, now that Korlandril does not intrude upon us.'

'As you were told before, I do not perform my poems.' Thirianna took her hand away from Aradryan's arm and cast her gaze into the distance, seeing the haze of the dome's edge beyond a maze of winding rivers and gushing streams that cut through golden lawns.

'I thought perhaps they were written for a very select audience,' said Aradryan. 'It must be such a gift, to compose one's disparate thoughts; to embrace them and order them in such a way.'

'They have an audience of one,' said Thirianna, still not meeting Aradryan's gaze. 'That one is me, no other.'

'You know that we used to share everything,' said Aradryan. 'You can still trust me.'

'It is myself that I do not trust. I cannot allow any fear that my compositions might be seen by another to restrict my feelings and words. I would be mortified if my innermost thoughts were put on display to all-comers.'

'Is that what I am?' said Aradryan. He took Thirianna by the arm and turned her towards him. 'One of many?'

'It is no slight against you, nor against Korlandril or any other,' explained Thirianna. 'I choose to share what I share. The rest is mine alone, for no other to know. Please appreciate that.'

'Such an attitude does not sit well aboard a starship,' said Aradryan. 'One is part of the many, and in confinement with others most of the time. It takes several to pilot such a vessel, and we must each trust the others implicitly. I have learned that friendship is not the only thing that must be shared. Co-operation, the overlapping of lives in ways beneficial to all, is the key to understanding our place in the universe.'

'A grandiose conclusion,' laughed Thirianna. 'Perhaps there is something of the poet in you!'

Aradryan did not seem to share her amusement. He let go of her arm and glanced away. When he looked at her again, the expressionless mask had returned to his face, sincere but otherwise featureless.

'Korlandril will not be entertaining us until the dusk of the cycle begins,' he said. 'If you will not grace me with your poems, perhaps you could suggest other entertainments that will divert us until the unveiling.'

Thirianna did not like the change, the abrupt closing off of emotion. She supposed that she had deserved it, but could not bring herself to apologise for any unintended offence she might have caused Aradryan. It was his error to press her on her poetry and he would have to learn that she was not willing to talk about it.

With an effort, Thirianna brightened her mood and laid a palm upon the back of Aradryan's hand.

'The Weathering of the Nine takes place later today,' she said. 'I have not been for many passes.'

'Nostalgia?' said Aradryan, a smile breaking through his demeanour, eyebrow lifting in surprise.

'A return,' Thirianna replied. 'A return to a place we both know well.'

Aradryan considered the invitation for a moment, the conflict showing in his shifting expressions. The internal argument ended with a look of happy resignation and he nodded.

'Yes, let us go back a while and revisit our youth,' Aradryan said. 'A return to happier times.'

'It is a truth that as we progress, our grief increases and our joys diminish,' said Thirianna.

The two of them started down the slope of the bridge towards the coreward bank.

'It does not have to be so,' said Aradryan. 'The universe may have grief in plenty to heap upon us, but it is in our power to make our own joy.'

Thirianna was about to argue that the greatest grief came from one's own making, but stopped herself. Such thoughts led to a place she was not willing to visit. Not yet. Not ever again, perhaps.

They walked on a little further and she considered what Aradryan had said and her reaction to it. Had she become morose, she wondered? Aradryan's return was a cause for celebration, a positive event. It was up to her to make the most of it.

'Yes, you are right,' said Thirianna, cheered by his words. 'Let us recapture the past and create some new happiness.'

'She is so serene,' Thirianna said. 'Such calm and beauty.'

Korlandril's creation was remarkable, stirring dormant thoughts within Thirianna's mind. *The Gifts of Loving Isha* it was called. She was struck by the simplicity of the sculpture, which hid a very complex web of themes.

The statue was bathed in a golden glow and tinged with sunset reds and purples from the dying star above. It depicted an impressionistic Isha in abstract, her body and limbs flowing from the trunk of a lianderin tree, her wave-like tresses entwined within yellow leaves in its upreaching branches. Her faced was bowed, hidden in the shadow cast by tree and hair. From the darkness a slow trickle of silver liquid spilled from her eyes into a golden cup held aloft by an ancient eldar warrior kneeling at her feet: Eldanesh. Light glittered from the chalice on his alabaster face, his armour a stylised arrangement of organic geometry, his face blank except for a slender nose and the merest depression of eye sockets. From beneath him, a black-petalled rose coiled up Isha's legs and connected the two together in its thorny embrace.

It was a monument to love, and the grief that it brought; a motif with which Thirianna was all too familiar of late.

Aradryan did not seem to share her opinion, flicking his fingers slightly in a sign of disagreement.

'It is self-referential,' Aradryan explained, his gaze moving from the statue to Thirianna. 'It is a work of remarkable skill and delicacy, certainly. Yet I find it somewhat… staid. It adds nothing to my experience of the myth, merely represents physically something that is felt. It is a metaphor in its most direct form. Beautiful, but merely reflecting back upon its maker rather than a wider truth.'

Though the criticism was evenly spoken, Thirianna sensed tension in her companion, as though his critique was directed at something more elemental than a sculpture. Intimidated by what Aradryan might have made of her verses had she shared them, Thirianna sought to defend Korlandril's work.

'But is not that the point of art, to create representations for those thoughts, memories and emotions that cannot be conveyed directly?'

'Perhaps I am being unfair,' said Aradryan. 'Out in the stars, I have seen such wondrous creations of nature that the artifices of mortals seem petty, even those that explore such momentous themes such as this.'

Thirianna felt a surge of anger close at hand and turned in time to see Korlandril, his face twisted with a sneer.

'Staid?' snapped Korlandril, stepping forwards. 'Self-referential?'

Her stomach lurched with sudden shared guilt at Aradryan's words, which the sculptor must have overheard. Aradryan seemed unperturbed, his posture calm, expression radiating sincerity.

'My words were not intended to cause offence, Korlandril,' he said, offering a placating palm. 'They are but my opinion, and an ill-educated one at that. Perhaps you find my sentimentality gauche.'

Korlandril hesitated, blinking and glancing away in a moment of awkwardness. The pause lasted only the briefest heartbeat before Korlandril's scowl returned.

'You are right to think your opinion ill-informed,' said the artist. 'While you gazed naively at glittering stars and swirling nebulae, I studied the works of Aethyril and Ildrintharir, learnt the disciplines of ghost stone weaving and inorganic symbiosis. If you have not the wit to extract the meaning from that which I have presented to you, perhaps you should consider your words more carefully.'

Thirianna stepped away from the pair as Aradryan folded his arms.

'And if you have not the skill to convey your meaning from your work, perhaps you need to continue studying,' Aradryan snarled back. 'It is not from the past masters that you should learn your art, but from the heavens and your heart. Your technique is flawless, but your message is parochial. How many statues of Isha might I see if I travelled across the craftworld? A dozen? More? How many more statues of Isha exist on other craftworlds? You have taken nothing from the Path save the ability to indulge yourself in this spectacle. You have learnt nothing of yourself, of the darkness and the light that battles within you. There is intellect alone in your work, and nothing of yourself. It might be that you should expand your terms of reference.'

Horrified, Thirianna wanted to intervene, but found herself helpless. She looked from Korlandril to Aradryan and back again, torn between her two friends. She detected animosity deeper than was being revealed, and wondered at its cause.

'What do you mean by that?' said Korlandril.

'Get away from this place, from Alaitoc,' Aradryan said patiently, his anger dissipated by his outburst. Now he was the picture of sincerity, his hand half-reaching towards Korlandril. 'Why stifle your art by seeking inspiration only from the halls and domes you have seen since childhood? Rather than trying to look upon old sights with fresh eyes, why not turn your old eyes upon fresh sights?'

Korlandril parted his lips for a moment, but then shut his mouth firmly. He directed a fierce glare at Aradryan, before stalking away through the blue grass, scattering guests in his flight.

As if realising for the first time that Thirianna had been witness to the confrontation, Aradryan turned towards her, hands raised in apology.

'I am sorry, I d–'

'It is not I that deserves your apology,' she said curtly, her feelings hurt more by Aradryan's treatment of Korlandril than his disregard for her. 'Perhaps such behaviour is tolerated on a starship, but you are back on Alaitoc. You are right, you have become gauche.'

With that parting remark, she left Aradryan, ignoring his call after her. She fought to retain her composure as she made her way through the dispersing audience, smiling at those who met her gaze though inside she felt like screaming.

She had been content with her life. Aradryan's return had thrown that into turmoil and she worried what that would bring. She had sought serenity and calm through her poetry, but it seemed that matters beyond her control were about to make her life far more turbulent.

After little sleep, Thirianna woke before the next cycle had begun. She lay in the twilight of her apartment and thought about what she should do. It was unlikely that Korlandril and Aradryan would reconcile of their own accord. The prospect of choosing one of her friends over the other or, worse still, losing both of them, stirred her to action. Neither would be happy for her to interfere, but Thirianna was sure that if she was subtle she could bridge the sudden divide that had come between them.

It was not something she could attempt alone. She knew well the peril of unintended consequences when trying to steer the course of others' lives. Yet it was not an insurmountable obstacle. There were older, wiser minds that could be brought to bear on the problem.

As the darkness lightened into the glow of a new cycle, Thirianna ate a swift breakfast, cleansed herself and dressed in simple attire. She left the tower in which she lived and, along with a handful of other early wakers, crossed Alaitoc on a grav shuttle. The few eldar with whom she shared the carriage sat quietly, keeping to themselves. Thirianna was glad for their recognition of her desire for solitude and spent the time considering the changing nature of her relationships with Aradryan and Korlandril.

So wrapped up did she become in these thoughts that she almost did not notice her arrival at the Dome of Golden Sanctuary. There were no other eldar alighting from the shuttle as she stepped down to the curving platform, but she could feel the presence of many others close at hand: the infinity circuit.

Close to the heart of Alaitoc, the Dome of Golden Sanctuary was a maze of chambers and corridors, its walls gleaming with the energy of the craftworld's psychic energy conduits. Flickers of colour flashed past along the crystal matrix, each bringing a brief buzz of life to the empty rooms and tunnels.

It was in this place that the farseers conducted much of their esoteric work. All of the eldar aboard Alaitoc knew of it, though few ventured here. It was the first time Thirianna had visited, and she wondered if it was true that the layout of the dome's winding streets and soaring towers did indeed change over time, reflecting the will and whim of the infinity circuit and the farseers that used its power.

She came upon a broad space that at first glance appeared like any of a thousand other parklands that could be found across Alaitoc's many domes. In many ways it was quite mundane; the grass was green, as were the leaves on the trees, and the water that glittered in a pool at its centre was clear and filled with fish. There were certainly more exotic plants and habitats elsewhere on the craftworld; where gravity was inverted and waterfalls poured upwards; where species of birds extinct off-world continued to fly the skies; where pools of liquid silver reflected clouds of coloured gases.

Yet first impressions were deceptive. Walking along the narrow path of white stones, Thirianna could sense more than could be seen with the naked eye. Here the power of the infinity circuit was being used to weave a landscape across more than the usual number of dimensions, and the results could be felt rather than touched or heard. She passed across a bridge and was filled with a gentle melancholy; stopping beneath the wide boughs of a tree Thirianna felt a moment of adoration for the beauty and complexity of life.

Distracted, she wandered the park for a while, enjoying the changes of mood and emotion that the different areas brought. Thirianna found a bench that looked out at a tumble of rocks and boulders at the bottom of a grassy slope. There was a blue-robed eldar sitting on the bench, a number of rune pendants hanging on golden chains across his chest, his wrists laden with gem-clad bracelets and intricately crafted charms. His hands were sheathed in soft velvet-like gloves of pure black.

'You are late,' said the eldar, turning purple eyes to Thirianna. His expression was one of pleasant surprise rather than admonition, which further confused her.

'I did not know I was expected,' she replied. The eldar gestured for her to sit next to him and she did so.

'I am Alaiteir,' said the eldar. 'I have been waiting for you a little while.'

'You are a farseer,' Thirianna said, laughing at herself for foolishly asking if she had been expected.

'You are right,' said Alaiteir. 'Your coming here has been known to me for several cycles.'

'And do you know what I wish to ask?' Thirianna said, her smile fading.

'No,' admitted Alaiteir. 'Physical things, the interactions of beings, can be foreseen with practice, but their purposes and desires are far harder to discern. The will of an individual is a fleeting, capricious thing that is hard to locate.'

Thirianna accepted this explanation with a shallow nod. She looked at Alaiteir for a moment, wondering if she was doing the right thing.

'All that you say shall be kept in confidence,' Alaiteir assured her. 'You may ask without regret or shame. It is the burden of the farseer that we see and hear many things, but only few can we even discuss.'

Taking a deep breath, Thirianna steadied her thoughts and launched into her tale. She explained to Alaiteir how she had come to know Korlandril and Aradryan, and her changing feelings for both of them. She talked about her own life, the Paths she had walked that had brought her to this place. She finished with the story of Aradryan's return and the disruption it had caused. All the while Alaiteir said nothing, but listened patiently with the occasional nod of understanding or a brief smile to Thirianna to persuade her to continue.

When she was done, Thirianna asked the question that had been on her mind since Aradryan had stepped off *Lacontiran*.

'What is going to happen to my friends?'

Alaiteir laughed, earning himself a shallow scowl of annoyance from Thirianna. The farseer held up a hand in apology and he seemed genuinely contrite.

'A question that is so simple to ask, yet so difficult to answer,' he said. He moved closer to Thirianna and laid a hand on her leg: a bold intrusion of her space but well meant and a gesture of assurance. 'What you ask cannot be answered. Not by me and not in the way you have asked it. Could I see what will happen to them tomorrow? Possibly. The cycle after? Very likely. A pass from now? To the ends of their lives?'

Thirianna sighed, realising the enormity of what she had hoped and the futility of hoping for it. She moved to stand up but a gentle pressure from Alaiteir stopped her.

'Did Anatheineir give up so easily on the quest for the Silver Star?' said the farseer. 'I cannot see these things for you, but there is another way. It is this that truly brought you here.'

'You have seen something?' Thirianna asked, her excitement growing. 'Something about Korlandril or Aradryan?'

'No,' said the farseer, deflating Thirianna's mood. 'I know nothing more of these individuals than that which you have just told me.'

'Why can you not simply tell me what you have seen?' said Thirianna, annoyance replacing her anticipation. 'Why not give a straightforward answer?'

'You have not yet asked the right question.' Alaiteir held up a hand to quell Thirianna's next outburst. 'I do not speak riddles out of choice, but necessity. We each ask ourselves and others a myriad of questions in every cycle. Some are trivial, and some are not. Which are the trivial ones and which are important? We do not know until we hear the answers. I cannot give you a truthful answer to a question that has been unasked but I can tell that you have not yet divined your inner purpose in coming here.'

'Inner purpose?' Thirianna was sure she knew exactly what she wanted to know and said as much. 'I just want to know if things will be better between Korlandril and Aradryan.'

'And now we start to get to the heart of the matter,' said Alaiteir. He stood up, took Thirianna's hand and gently pulled her to her feet. The two of them looked down the slope towards the broken rocks. 'By what measure can "better" be defined? Better for Korlandril? Better for Aradryan?'

Thirianna knew the answer immediately but hesitated in saying it, suddenly ashamed of the realisation. She glanced at Alaiteir, who was studying the rocks below.

'Better for me?' Thirianna said quietly. Alaiteir nodded but did not look at her. Thirianna thought some more, working out what she meant by the statement. It was strange that her conclusion came as no shock to her. The farseer had been right, she had known all along what she really wanted to know. 'How will this division between Aradryan and Korlandril affect me?'

'That is good,' said Alaiteir. He looked at Thirianna, his expression stern. 'It is perhaps the first and last question we ask of any person or situation. Our selfishness is inherent and nothing that should bring you shame. Turmoil and change is upon you and you fear for what the future may hold. That is entirely natural.'

'And my wish is for Aradryan and Korlandril to mend this wound between them for my benefit,' said Thirianna. 'Surely it is to their benefit as well?'

'Who can say?' said the farseer, his necklaces swaying as he gave a shallow shrug.

'I thought perhaps a farseer could say,' said Thirianna, smiling again.

'You seek answers, but I cannot give them to you,' said Alaiteir. 'All I can do is steer you to the right questions. The answers you will have to find for yourself. The time is upon you to make a choice, Thirianna. It is this choice that I saw; this choice that persuaded me to come to you in this place at this time.'

'I must choose between Korlandril and Aradryan?' said Thirianna, dismayed by the prospect. 'How could I do such a thing?'

'Or perhaps choose neither,' said Alaiteir. 'Perhaps you must choose yourself over both of your friends. If you truly wish to know what the future holds, there is only one decision you have to make.'

Thirianna looked at Alaiteir for some time, trying to discern any extra meaning from his expression, seeking further guidance, but none was to be found. The farseer obviously intended that she must come to this decision entirely without direction from him.

It was only after much thought that the answer came to Thirianna.

'You think that I should move to the Path of the Seer?' she asked quietly.

'What I think is irrelevant,' replied Alaiteir. 'All I can tell you is that every cycle we each stand upon a branch in the threads of fate, every decision we make shaping the future we will live in. Some cycles the choices we face change little of what will happen. This cycle, this moment, is not such a day. What you decide to do next, free of coercion or persuasion, guided by your own mind and heart, will set you on a new trail, whether you stay a poet or become a seer.'

'I cannot take such a decision now,' said Thirianna.

'I would not expect you to do so,' said the farseer. 'If I am to be honest, I must tell you that you have already made the decision. Now you must spend some time finding out what road you have chosen.'

Thirianna nodded and took a few steps along the path. She stopped and turned back to Alaiteir.

'Thank you,' she said. 'What should I do if I choose to follow you on the Path of the Seer?'

'If that is revealed to be your choice, I will know it and come to you.'

INTROSPECTION

Rod of Light – The Staff of Asuryan. This rune is one of conjunction, lacking any power or significance on its own, but of the highest potency when cast or seen alongside another. Its appearance colours the reading of any other rune, and characterises wisdom from within. When the Rod of Light comes unbidden to a seer, it signals great change, representing the flame of the Lord of the Heavens that consumes the old and brings rebirth.

On returning to her quarters, Thirianna was greeted by a thrum of recognition from the infinity circuit interface in her main chamber. Placing a palm onto the smooth slate, she allowed her consciousness to touch upon the energies of Alaitoc. Thirianna's thoughts touched with an after-echo of Aradryan's presence; he had come to her apartment seeking her.

She detached herself from the infinity circuit while she considered what she should do. Part of her wished for solitude, so that she could think upon the choice presented to her by Alaiteir; the other part of her wanted to lose herself in mundane matters so that she could forget the dilemma for a while and return to it refreshed.

Thirianna decided on the latter course and meshed with the infinity circuit again, seeking the signature of Aradryan. She found him on the Boulevard of Split Moons, not far from the tower where she lived. Through the infinity circuit, she touched upon his thoughts, gently gaining his attention. In a moment they had exchanged feelings of greeting and conciliation and came to an understanding; Aradryan would wait for her amongst the storefronts and arcades and she would join him shortly.

Breaking the link, Thirianna changed her clothes, swapping her robe for a tight bodysuit of glittering purple and silver. She wrapped a light scarf about her neck and shoulders and a wide belt studded with sapphire-like gems about her waist. She pulled several torcs up her arm and finished with a long pair of white gloves and matching boots. She quickly coloured her hair and eyes green to finish the striking look and hung a small waistbag from her belt. Feeling ready to meet Aradryan, she set off for the Boulevard of Split Moons.

She found Aradryan waiting beside a jewellery stall, picking through an assortment of plain gold earrings. He wore a wide-shouldered jacket of dark blue, flared at the hips, fastened by a line of tiny buckles from waist to neck and wrist to elbow. A heavy kilt of subtly blended greens and blacks covered his upper legs, above narrow boots studded with golden buttons. It was a style that had not been seen on Alaitoc for some time, and the sight of her friend caused a moment of nostalgia in Thirianna.

Aradryan looked up at her approach, smiling broadly, and held up a pair of earrings shaped vaguely like two leaping fish.

'Not really to my taste,' said Thirianna as they touched hands in greeting.

'Not for you, for me,' said Aradryan, nonplussed.

'I know,' said Thirianna, laughing softly. She took one of the earrings and held it up to the side of Aradryan's face. The curve of the jewellery matched well with his features and she nodded. 'Yes, they would look very good.'

'Then it is decided,' said Aradryan, recovering his composure. The steersman signalled his desire to take the jewellery to the stallholder, who nodded his head in appreciation of a choice well made and waved for the pair to continue on their way.

The two of them spoke little as they moved between the stalls and stores, examined gems and scarves, robes and headdresses. Thirianna was grateful for the opportunity to divert her attention away from herself and Aradryan. She enjoyed feeling the textures of cloth and seeing the rainbows of light in the gems, losing herself in every detail. When Aradryan spoke, he raised trivial matters, commenting on the wares on display and those offering them. After a while, Thirianna realised that much of what he said was negative, and though never offensively phrased his words came across as a quiet but constant denigration of Alaitoc.

Eventually Aradryan's subtle complaints started intruding on Thirianna's appreciation of the objects on display and she turned to him, letting her irritation show.

'What is it about life here that chafes so badly that you must constantly gripe and find fault?' she snapped, taking Aradryan by the arm and guiding him to a small alleyway between two stores where they would not be overheard.

'I am sorry if I have broadened my view beyond the petty baubles on display here,' Aradryan replied. He was about to say something else but stopped himself and his expression changed to one of contrition. 'No, I am genuinely sorry. You say that life here chafes, and I can think of no better word to describe it. It rubs against my spirit, binding my thoughts like a cord around my limbs. Alaitoc is safe, and controlled, and suffocating. It offers comfort and dependability. I no longer desire these things.'

'So why did you return at all?' Thirianna asked, feeling guilty for judging her friend so harshly. 'There must have been a reason to come back.'

Aradryan gave Thirianna a look that she did not recognise; it seemed to be desire mixed with pleading, and a hint of desperation. The look passed quickly and Aradryan glanced away, pretending to flick away an imagined piece of thread from the shoulder of his jacket. When he looked at her again, he showed the studied, expressionless mask that he had worn almost constantly since his return.

'My memories of Alaitoc were fonder than the reality,' said Aradryan. 'Or perhaps the reality has changed to one of which I am less fond.'

'You speak of Korlandril,' said Thirianna. The mention of the artist's name caused a brief flicker of emotion to cross Aradryan's face; annoyance that turned to shame.

'And you,' said Aradryan. He sighed and leaned back against the wall of the alley, crossing his arms over his chest. 'I do not know my place here any longer.'

'It will take time, but you will adjust again, and learn anew to find the delight in each moment that passes, and meaning in the things you now find trivial,' Thirianna assured him. 'Alaitoc is your home, Aradryan.'

'Is it?' he replied. 'I have little bond to the family left here, and my friends are not those I left behind. Why should I choose to stay here when all of the galaxy is open to me?'

'Though it would sadden me to see you leave again, I cannot argue against your desires,' said Thirianna, feeling helpless against the force of Aradryan's disaffection.

'Is there some reason I should stay?' he asked. He directed a look at Thirianna similar to the one he had given her earlier; longing and hopeful. She could not hide her shock when she realised what he wanted to hear from her.

'I have only my friendship to offer,' Thirianna said. Aradryan's disappointment was instant, showing as a furrowed brow and parted lips for a moment before the emotionless mask descended again.

'Friendship was once enough, but not now,' said Aradryan, his tone even and quiet. He directed a quick bow of the head to Thirianna, in deference to her feelings, eyes closed out of respect. When he opened them, there was a glimmer of sorrow. 'It seems that even friendship is not possible with Korlandril. He has grown arrogant, I think, and he has no time for others. Thank you for your candour, Thirianna. I hope I have not caused you undue embarrassment or woe.'

Before Thirianna could reply, Aradryan had stepped out of the alley, quickly striding through the thickening crowd of eldar milling along the Boulevard of Split Moons. Thirianna considered whether to go after him and decided against it. She was certain that she could not offer what Aradryan desired and no other argument would convince him to stay.

It is probably for the best, she told herself. As much as it pained her to think of Aradryan leaving again, his return, and the feelings he had hinted at, had made her life a lot more complicated in a very short space of time. Thirianna was confident that whatever ennui or wanderlust plagued Aradryan, he would overcome it.

The question she had been ignoring returned to her, prompted by the thought that perhaps she could free herself from the uncertainty that surrounded her life. This brief episode had highlighted to her how little control of her situation she had, and that made her feel uneasy. To know something of what would come, to glimpse the possible consequences of these endlessly difficult decisions, was a huge temptation.

The door chime woke her in the early part of the following cycle. She sensed Alaiteir. Quickly slipping on a loose robe of white and silver, she thought open the door and welcomed her unexpected visitor.

'I apologise for the inconvenience, but I bear news that you will wish to hear,' said the farseer. 'I would not normally intervene in such a small matter, but considering the delicate balance of choice on which your life is currently poised I think it wise that you should know that your friend, Aradryan, has set himself aboard the crew of a new ship.'

'And why does this news bring you to my door at such an inopportune time?' said Thirianna. She could not remember the dream that had been interrupted but a hollowness lingered inside her, a vague after-memory that disturbed her.

'The starship is *Irdiris*,' said Alaiteir. 'It is due to slip its moorings before the dawn cycle begins.'

'So soon?' said Thirianna. 'Why such a swift departure?'

'Why not?' said the farseer. 'Your friend is in pain and seeks swift resolution to it. He is acting rashly, but we cannot blame him for that.'

'If he does not wish to share the courtesy of saying goodbye to me, then perhaps he is not the friend I thought he was,' said Thirianna, sitting cross-legged on the rug at the centre of the main chamber. She indicated an invitation to Alaiteir to seat himself on one of the low couches but he declined with a raised hand.

'The *Irdiris* is no normal vessel,' said the farseer. 'She is a void-runner bound for distant stars beyond the reach of the webway. It will be many passes until your friend returns, if he comes back at all.'

'A ranger ship?' said Thirianna, one hand moving to her mouth in shock. 'You think that he chooses to make himself outcast, leaving the Path behind him?'

Alaiteir simply nodded, his eyes never moving from Thirianna.

'I have to convince him to stay!' She jumped to her feet and made for the dressing room next door. She hastily dressed herself in the same outfit she had worn earlier in the cycle and hurried from the apartment. She stopped on the landing outside and waited for Alaiteir to join her. Realising that she did not know where the *Irdiris* was docked, she returned to her quarters and moved towards the infinity circuit terminal.

'The Bay of Departing Sorrows,' said Alaiteir from the doorway, just as Thirianna's hand was about to make contact with the smooth plate. He waved a hand towards the docking balcony behind him. 'You can take my cloudskiff if you wish to travel swiftly.'

'I do not understand why you have such an interest in this,' said Thirianna, hurrying past the farseer. The two-sailed anti-grav vessel hovered alongside the sky quay, its engines gently humming. 'You have my sincere thanks for passing on this news.'

'Wait!' Alaiteir called out as Thirianna nimbly leapt over the side of the cloudskiff. She turned, one hand on the tiller controls. 'Do you really want Aradryan to stay?'

Thirianna hesitated, and in turn that hesitation gave her a moment's pause for thought. Were her reasons selfish? She decided that it was in the interests of both herself and Aradryan that he stay, regardless of the difficulties that might cause.

'I cannot bear to think of him out there in the darkness, adrift from the Path and alone,' she said, thumbing the grav motors into life via the rune on the tiller handle.

She steered the cloudskiff away from the quayside and down towards the floor of the dome, the hum of its engines becoming a soft purring as she picked up speed. She brought the craft level with one of the many transit routes that stretched from dome to dome, and guided the cloudskiff towards the arched opening.

Glancing back she saw Alaiteir standing with arms crossed at the railing outside her apartment. As she passed into the shadow of the passageway she wondered if she was not being manipulated by the old seer. How could she tell if the decisions she was making were truly her own and not a meaningless dance to some design that favoured Alaiteir?

She dismissed her doubts, realising that such speculation could lead nowhere. She reassured herself that the life of one poet was far below the machinations of the farseers of Alaitoc and forced herself to believe that Alaiteir was acting out of genuine regard for her, if not outright kindness.

She guided the cloudskiff from dome to dome, cutting across the disc of Alaitoc by the shortest route, passing over the central divide towards the darkward rim. Coming close to the edge of the craftworld, she saw the

Bay of Departing Sorrows in the distance: a crescent of quays and docks attached to the darkside rim at a steep tangent. There were three ships moored there, but the *Irdiris* was easily recognised by its small size and single solar sail. It was little more than an armed yacht, built for speed, efficiency and range, crewed by only a handful of eldar. At the moment its hull was coloured a deep green mottled with black stripes, its sail glowing gold in the light of dying Mirianathir.

Steering the cloudskiff lower, she passed alongside the white hull of a short-range barque, dipping beneath its twin loading ramps along which a procession of egg-like package crates were floating into its hold. Coming around the prow of the barque, Thirianna saw two figures walking up the gantry beside the *Irdiris*. She recognised the tall, gaunt figure of Aradryan and slowed down, bringing the cloudskiff gently alongside the larger vessel. Stepping down to the quay, she saw Aradryan turning in her direction.

'Aradryan!' Her voice disappeared into the depths of the dimly lit hangar.

He stopped, hands on hips. Thirianna broke into a run and reached him as Aradryan's companion, a female eldar in a tight bodysuit of yellow and blue, shook her head and continued up towards the void-runner.

'This is madness,' Thirianna said as she reached her friend. She reached out a hand to his arm but he stepped away, avoiding the contact. Aradryan was dressed in the same severe outfit he had worn on his arrival and his expression was stern.

'It is freedom,' he replied, glancing over his shoulder towards the open iris-like door of the starship. He looked back at Thirianna and his expression softened. 'I did not wish to be parted like this. It is too painful to say goodbye.'

'It does not have to be this way,' said Thirianna. 'Do not leave.'

'You wish me to stay?' said Aradryan, one eyebrow raised. 'Would there be a purpose in remaining on Alaitoc?'

Thirianna had wrestled with the idea on the journey from her apartment, but had resolved no solid argument she could offer. It simply felt wrong that Aradryan should go in this manner, abandoning the structure and protection of the Path for a life as an outcast.

'There must be more to this than your desire to be with me,' she said. 'How can you hate Alaitoc, who has raised and nurtured you and given you so much?'

'I do not hate her,' said Aradryan. 'I am merely bored of her. Perhaps in time my thirst for new vistas and experiences will be sated and I will return. Would you come with me?'

Arguments sprang to Thirianna's mind, but they seemed trite against the yearning she felt in Aradryan's spirit. She stepped back, bowing her head.

'Be safe,' she said. 'See the stars and come back to us.'

'I will, Thirianna,' Aradryan replied. He strode close to her and laid a hand on each of her shoulders. 'Take care of Korlandril for me. I sense that he needs a good friend at the moment, if only to save him from himself.'

'And who is going to save you from yourself?' Thirianna asked, tears moistening her cheeks. She could not look at Aradryan and kept her gaze on the marble-like floor of the docking pier.

'Nobody,' Aradryan said.

Thirianna still did not look up as she felt Aradryan remove his hands and back away. She heard his faint footsteps on the gantry followed by the delicate whisper of the closing doorway.

Lights sprang into life along the length of the *Irdiris*, bathing the dock in a warm glow of oranges and reds. Thirianna turned away, not wanting to see the starship leave. With barely a sound, the breeze of its passing ruffling her hair, the void-runner lifted from the platform and tilted starwards. The forcefield enclosing the dock shimmered into silvery life as the *Irdiris* passed through it.

Thirianna looked up at the last moment, catching a glimpse of the vessel's swallow tail before it disappeared through the energy barrier and was obscured from sight. She waited for the forcefield to settle, returning to its transparent state. By then, the *Irdiris* was accelerating swiftly towards the webway gate aft of Alaitoc. It became a shimmer against the stars as its holofield activated, and then it was gone from view.

Thirianna found Alaiteir sitting on the same bench as before. The aging farseer sat with his hands neatly clasped in his lap, watching yellow-feathered sawbeaks duelling over the tumble of rocks at the bottom of the hill.

'There is a final warning I must give you,' Alaiteir said as Thirianna sat beside him. She arranged her robe carefully and looked down the slope. 'Though you may step onto the Path of the Seer like any other part of the Path, and step off again when you feel the time is appropriate, it has the strongest lures of any we might tread.'

'I resisted the call of Khaine,' said Thirianna. 'That is perhaps the most treacherous trap of all.'

'It is not,' said Alaiteir. Thirianna detected a subtle note of annoyance in his tone and realised she had spoken out of place. She dipped her head in apology.

'The call of Khaine is strong but it is a harsh, unsubtle snare,' the farseer continued, mollified by Thirianna's contrition. 'The lure of the Seer is far more potent, for it promises unbounded power. Those of us who tread the Path of the Seer to the fullest extent know the doom to which we walk.'

He held up a hand, silencing another comment from Thirianna before she could make it.

'I do not mean the visions of our own deaths,' Alaiteir continued. He chuckled. 'When you have seen the hundredth possible way you might die a gruesome death, the fear tends to have lost its edge.'

The farseer paused and Thirianna sensed that he was inviting her to speak.

'As a warrior I learnt to accept that all things die,' she said. 'I have faced real death many times; what is the phantasm of a possible future compared to that?'

'Yet none of us wish to truly die,' said Alaiteir. Without turning, he gestured towards the spirit stone fixed in an ornate brooch upon Thirianna's left breast. 'Our spirits pass on to the infinity matrix when our physical forms are spent.'

'This much I already know, as would any child of Alaitoc,' said Thirianna. 'I do not understand how that is so different for a seer.'

'For a seer one's spirit retains a greater sense of consciousness after death, but it is not of that which I speak,' said Alaiteir. He tugged at the fingers of his glove, removing it to reveal a hand that glittered like a diamond. The skin was transparent, slightly edged like a shaped gem, and within shining flashes of colour hinted at veins and capillaries and muscle. He held it up to the light of the dome, each fingertip sparkling like a star. He wiggled his fingers and laughed quietly. 'To tread the Path to its furthest end, to become a farseer, is to resign oneself to a different fate. We do not join with the infinity circuit; we become it!'

Thirianna had heard of such a thing, indeed had walked in the Dome of Crystal Seers, but it was a different matter to see the effect first-hand whilst it was progressing. She stared at the jewel-like flesh of Alaiteir's hand, marvelling at the rainbows of light that danced from the surface.

'Does it hurt?' she asked.

'Not at all,' replied Alaiteir. 'It is quite pleasant in a way. It is not the changing of the flesh that I warn against, but the hardening of the spirit. When a farseer becomes part of the infinity circuit his mind is wholly intact. Not for us the half-limbo of the physically dead, dimly aware of the fate that has befallen us. Consciousness is retained, an eternity ahead to spend without form stretched across the reaches of the skein.'

'The skein?'

'If you choose to become a seer you will learn more,' the farseer said, pulling on his glove.

'If I choose?' said Thirianna. 'I have already chosen. You know this or you would not have been waiting for me.'

'You will reconsider your choice and the two eventualities of that decision still exist,' said Alaiteir. He stood up and extended a hand to Thirianna, graciously helping her to her feet, a sign of equality. 'If you choose the Path of the Seer, go to Farseer Kelamith and he will be your guide.'

'Not you?' Thirianna was saddened, having already become a little attached to the farseer's strange but charming ways.

'No, Kelamith's thread and yours will entwine if you choose as such. He has more of a gift with novices than I.'

'Even with your warning, I feel certain of my choice.' Thirianna asked. 'Why will I reconsider?'

'I do not know,' admitted the farseer. He glanced at Thirianna and smiled slyly. 'And if I did, do you think I would tell you?'

FATE

The Raven – Messenger of Morai-heg. One of the most powerful runes, the Raven can be used only by the most experienced seers, for it can be a wayward guide to the unwary. The eyes of Morai-heg see all, and the Raven leads the follower to a single point of fate, from which there is no escape. Such nodes of destiny are rare, for the future is eternally mutable, but where they exist, the Raven will find them.

Thirianna was at Korlandril's statue, sitting at one end of a curving bench, gazing at the dim glow beyond the dome. She wondered what it would be that might cause her to change her mind. As far as she knew herself, her mind was set on taking the Path of the Seer. The possibilities it offered were genuinely endless; the ability to gaze into the furthest reaches of the future and control her own fate.

She felt another approaching and turned to see Korlandril crossing the grass. He was a little late, but she did not mind; their appointment had not been precise. She smiled as he sat next to her, pleased that one of her friends seemed to be in good spirits.

The moment passed, as did her smile, when she turned her thoughts to the news she needed to pass on.

'Aradryan has left Alaitoc,' Thirianna said quietly.

Korlandril's face was a flurry of emotion. Assuming the mantle of artist he had rendered himself incapable of self-critical thought and restraint. Every feeling etched into his features; shock and then disappointment.

There was another look, just at the end, and Thirianna detected a small measure of satisfaction. She was not wholly surprised at this. After all, Korlandril and Aradryan had parted on bad terms.

'I do not understand,' said the sculptor. 'I know that we had a disagreement, but I thought that he planned to remain on Alaitoc for some time yet.'

'He did not depart on your account,' said Thirianna, though doubtless the disagreement between the two had contributed. She realised that discussing Aradryan's declaration of feelings for her would not be prudent.

'Why would he not come to see me before he left?' Korlandril asked. 'It is obvious that some distance had grown between us, but I did not think his opinion of me had sunk so low.'

'It was not you,' Thirianna said, knowing she could have persuaded Aradryan to stay but had chosen not to.

'What happened?' asked Korlandril, a slight tone of accusation in his voice. 'When did Aradryan leave?'

'He took aboard *Irdiris* last cycle, after we spent some time together.'

Korlandril did not seem to recognise the name. That was no surprise; Thirianna had not heard of the starship a cycle ago.

'*Irdiris* is a far-runner, destined for the Exodites on Elan-Shemaresh and then to the Wintervoid of Meios,' she explained.

'Aradryan wishes to become a… *ranger*?' Incredulity and distaste vied with each other across Korlandril's face. He stroked his bottom lip with a slender finger, calming himself. 'I had no idea he was so dissatisfied with Alaitoc.'

'Neither did I, and perhaps that is why he left so soon,' confessed Thirianna. 'I believe I spoke hastily and with insensitivity and drove him to a swifter departure than he might otherwise have considered.'

'I am sure that you are no–' began Korlandril but Thirianna cut him off with an agitated twitch of her finger.

'I do not wish to speak of it,' she said. Her guilt gnawed at her and bringing out the sorry details into the open would do neither Thirianna nor Korlandril any good.

They sat in silence for a while longer, while littlewings darted amongst the branches of the trees above them, trilling to one another. Deep within the woods a breezemaker stirred into life and the leaves began to rustle gently: a calming backdrop.

'There was something else about which I wish to speak to you,' said Korlandril, rousing Thirianna from thoughts of Aradryan. 'I have a proposal to make.'

There was something about Korlandril's look that excited Thirianna. The passion she could see in his eyes stirred the feelings she had kept secret between herself and her poems. She indicated with an inclination of her head that they should stand.

'We should discuss this in my chambers, with something to drink, perhaps?' she said.

'That would be most agreeable,' said Korlandril as the two of them made their way towards the dome entrance.

They were about to step onto the sliding walkway up to the towers where Thirianna lived when a large group appeared from the gloom ahead of them. Sensing something dark, Thirianna strayed closer to Korlandril, who put a protective hand upon her shoulder though she felt him tense and could sense his discomfort.

The group were Aspect Warriors and an aura of death hung about them as palpable as a stench. They were clad in plates of overlapping armour of purple and black, their heavy tread thunderous in the still twilight. Thirianna could feel their menace growing stronger as they approached, waystones glowing like eyes of blood. They had taken off their war-helms and carried them hooked upon their belts, leaving their hands free to carry slender missile launchers.

Dark Reapers: possessed of the war god in his aspect of Destroyer.

Something in the depths of Thirianna's thoughts stirred; a memory hidden away, an aftertouch of Khaine on her spirit. It both excited and appalled her, disgust warring with the thrill it brought.

Though their helmets were removed, the warriors still bore the rune of the Dark Reaper painted in blood upon their faces. Thirianna and Korlandril shrank closer to the edge of the passageway as the Aspect Warriors passed, seeking the faces of their friends. Thirianna took several deep breaths in an attempt to calm down, but she felt a quiver running through her as the Aspect Warriors approached. Korlandril's hand on her shoulder felt heavy and reassuring.

Thirianna pointed, directing Korlandril's attention to Maerthuin. Arthuis walked a little way behind. The brothers stopped and turned their eyes upon Thirianna and Korlandril. Their gazes were empty, devoid of anything but the remotest recognition. Thirianna could smell the blood of the runes on their faces and suppressed an urge to reach out towards it.

'You are well?' asked Thirianna, her voice quiet and respectful.

Arthuis nodded slowly.

'Victory was ours,' intoned Maerthuin.

'We will meet you at the Crescent of the Dawning Ages,' said Arthuis.

'At the start of the next cycle,' added Maerthuin.

Korlandril and Thirianna both nodded their agreement and the two warriors moved on. Thirianna relaxed and Korlandril gave a sigh of relief.

'It is inconceivable to me that one should indulge in such horror,' said Korlandril as the two of them stepped upon the moving walkway.

Thirianna said nothing. Horror was not the sensation she had felt, though she was sure it was there, hidden away behind the careful meme-blocks erected by her war-mask.

They made a spiralling ascent, languidly turning upon itself as the sliding ramp rose around the Tower of Dormant Witnesses. Thirianna considered Korlandril's words and as they reached the top of the ramp realised the error in them.

'It is not an indulgence,' said Thirianna.

'What is not an indulgence?' replied Korlandril, who had been looking at the stars beyond the dome.

'The Path of the Warrior is not an indulgence,' she repeated. 'One cannot simply leave anger in the darkness, to fester and grow unseen. Sooner or later it might find vent.'

'What is there to be so angry about?' laughed Korlandril. 'Perhaps if we were Biel-Tan, with all their talk of reclaiming the old empire, then we might have a use for all of this sword-waving and gunfire. It is an uncivilised way to behave.'

'You ignore the passions that rule you,' snapped Thirianna.

'I meant no offence,' he said, obviously embarrassed.

'The intention is not important,' said Thirianna, still annoyed by Korlandril's flippancy. 'Perhaps you would care to ridicule the other Paths on which I have trodden?'

'I did not mean…' Korlandril trailed off. 'I am sorry.'

'The Path of Dreaming, the Path of Awakening, the Path of the Artist,' said Thirianna, shaking her head slightly. 'Always self-indulgent, always about your needs, no sense of duty or dedication to others.'

Korlandril shrugged, a fulsome gesture employing the full use of both arms.

'I simply do not understand this desire some of us feel to sate a bloodlust I do not feel,' he said.

'And that is what is dangerous about you,' said Thirianna. 'Where do you put that rage you feel when someone angers you? What do you do with the hatred that burns inside when you think upon all that we have lost? You have not learnt to control these feelings, merely ignore them. Becoming one with Khaine, assuming one of his Aspects is not about confronting an enemy, it is about confronting ourselves. We should all do it at some time in our lives.'

Korlandril shook his head.

'Only those that desire war, make it,' he said.

'Findrueir's *Prophecies of Interrogation*,' said Thirianna, knowing the quotation. It was a trite statement that she had once believed as well. 'Yes, I've read it too, do not look so surprised. However, I read it after treading the Path of the Warrior. An aesthete who wrote about matters she had never experienced. Hypocrisy at its worst.'

'And also one of Iyanden's foremost philosophers.' Amusement danced on Korlandril's lips.

'A radical windbag with no true cause and a gyrinx fetish,' countered Thirianna.

Korlandril laughed. His levity bordered on disrespect and Thirianna allowed her displeasure to show.

'Forgive me,' Korlandril said. 'I hope that is not an example of your poetry!'

Thirianna vacillated between annoyance and humour before breaking into a smile.

'Listen to us! Gallery philosophers, the pair! What do we know?'

'Little enough,' agreed Korlandril with a nod. 'And I suppose that can be a dangerous thing.'

The two of them reached Thirianna's chambers. She noticed Korlandril examining the interior in some detail and they made some small talk while she prepared drinks. They discussed Aradryan's leaving again, though Korlandril turned the conversation around to himself, and it was clear he was more concerned about Aradryan's low opinion of his sculpture than the fate of his friend, which irritated Thirianna.

'Your friendship has been important to me,' said Thirianna, wishing to change the subject.

'I have a new piece of sculpture in mind, something very different from my previous works,' Korlandril announced.

'That is good to hear,' said Thirianna. It was obvious it was this that Korlandril wanted to talk about. She was a little bit disappointed. 'I think that if you can find something to occupy your mind, you will dwell less on the situation with Aradryan.'

'Yes, that is very true! I'm going to delve into portraiture. A sculptural testament to devotion, in fact.'

'Sounds intriguing,' said Thirianna. 'Perhaps something a little more grounded in reality would be good for your development.'

'Let us not get too carried away,' said Korlandril with a smile. 'I think there may be some abstract elements incorporated into the design. After all, how does one truly replicate love and companionship in features alone?'

'I am surprised.' Korlandril's talk of love intrigued her. She watched him closely, trying to discern his mood, but he did not seem to notice her scrutiny. Thirianna thought of her poems, and the love they expressed. 'I understand if you do not wish to tell me, but what inspires such a piece of work?'

The artist looked perplexed, and Thirianna realised there was more to what he had said than she had seen. Before she could apologise for not responding to his gentle overtures, Korlandril spoke again.

'You are my inspiration,' he said quietly, eyes fixed on Thirianna. 'It is you that I wish to fashion as a likeness of dedication and ardour.'

Thirianna was shocked by Korlandril's openness, and a little dismayed that it perhaps had come too late. Her infatuation with him, hidden away within her verses, had always been her secret, and in writing her poems she had lessened its power over her.

'I... You...' She looked away, not sure what to say. For a moment she wondered if Korlandril knew what she had written about him. Suddenly she was scared by the whole issue and affected an air of distance. 'I do not think that is warranted.'

'Warranted?' Korlandril leaned towards her, his face intent on Thirianna. 'It is an expression of my feelings – there is nothing that needs warranting other than to visualise my desires and dreams. You are my desire and a dream.'

Thirianna did not reply. She stood and took a couple of paces away before turning to face Korlandril, her face serious.

'This is not a good idea, my friend,' she said gently. She wondered why he had said nothing before, when perhaps she would have been in a position to reciprocate. She realised that this was the dilemma that would make her reconsider becoming a seer. There was no doubt in her mind, and it was best to disappoint Korlandril as gently as possible. 'I do appreciate the sentiment, and perhaps some time ago I would not only be flattered but I would be delighted.'

'But not now?' he asked, hesitant, scared of the answer.

She shook her head.

'Aradryan's arrival and departure have made me realise something that has been amiss with my life for several passes now,' she said. Korlandril reached out a hand in a half-hearted gesture, beckoning her to come closer. Thirianna sat next to him and took his hand in hers. 'I am changing again. The Path of the Poet is spent for me. I have grieved and I have rejoiced through my verse, and I feel expunged of the burdens I felt. I feel another calling is growing inside me.'

Korlandril snatched his hand away.

'You are going to join Aradryan!' he snapped. 'I knew the two of you were keeping something from me.'

'Don't be ridiculous,' Thirianna rasped in return, trying to hide her guilt that Aradryan had offered to stay for her. 'It is because I told him what I am telling you that he left.'

'So, he did make advances on you!' Korlandril stood and angrily wiped a hand across his brow and pointed accusingly at Thirianna. 'It is true! Deny it if you dare!'

She slapped away his hand.

'What right do you have to make any claim on me?' she snapped. 'If you must know, I have never entertained any thoughts of being with Aradryan, even before he left, and certainly not since his return. I am simply not ready for a life-companion. In fact, that is why I cannot be your inspiration.'

Korlandril's trembling lip was a cliché of sadness and it melted through Thirianna's anger. She took a step closer, hands open in friendship.

'It is to save you from a future heartache that I decline your attentions now,' she continued. 'I have spoken to Farseer Alaiteir and he agrees that I am ready to begin the Path of the Seer.'

'A seer?' scoffed Korlandril. 'You completely fail to divine my romantic intents and yet think you might become a seer?'

'I divined your intent and ignored it,' lied Thirianna, laying a hand on his arm. 'I did not wish to encourage you; to admit your feelings for me would be to bring them to the light and that was something I wished to avoid, for the sake of both of us.'

Korlandril waved away her arguments, pulling his arm from her grasp.

'If you have not the same feelings for me, then simply say so. Do not spare my pride for your comfort. Do not hide behind this excuse of changing Paths.'

'It is true, it is not an excuse! You love Thirianna the poet. We are alike enough at the moment, our Paths different yet moving in the same general direction. When I become a seer, I while not be Thirianna the poet. You will not love that person.'

'Why deny me the right to find out?' Korlandril's fists were balled at his side and anger flashed in his eyes, scaring Thirianna. 'Who are you to judge what will or will not be? You are not even on the Path and now you think you can claim the powers of the seer?'

'If it is true that you feel the same when I have become a seer, and I feel the same too, then whatever will happen will come to pass.'

Korlandril caught an angry reply before he said it. His expression changed to one of hope.

'If you feel the same?' he said. 'You admit that you have feelings for me.'

'Thirianna the Poet has feelings for you, she always has,' Thirianna admitted.

'Then why do we not embrace this shared feeling?' Korlandril asked, stepping forwards and taking Thirianna's hands in his. Now it was her turn to pull away. She could not bring herself to look at him when she spoke.

'If I indulge this passion with you, it would hold me back, perhaps trap me here as the poet, forever writing my verses of love in secret.'

'Then we stay together, poet and artist! What is so wrong with that?'

'It is not healthy!' Having seen what obsession had done to Aradryan, Thirianna was in no mind to suffer it herself. 'You know that it is unwise to become trapped in ourselves. Our lives must be in constant motion, moving from one Path to the next, developing our senses of self and the universe. To over-indulge leads to the darkness that came before. It attracts the attention of… Her. She Who Thirsts.'

Thirianna waited while Korlandril flexed his fingers. She could hear the quick beating of his heart and feel his pain rising to the surface. Yet for all that she felt for him, he would have to be the second friend in a cycle that she would turn away.

'What we feel is not *wrong*!' said the artist. 'Since the founding of the craftworlds our people have loved and survived. Why should we be any different?'

'You use the same arguments as Aradryan,' Thirianna admitted softly, turning on Korlandril. 'He asked me to forget the Path and join him. Even if I had loved him I could not do that. I *cannot* do that with you. Though I have deep feelings for you, I would no more risk my eternal spirit for you than I would step out into the void of space and hope to breathe.'

Seeing the agonised expression on Korlandril's face was too much for Thirianna. To part with Aradryan had been a heartache; to spurn Korlandril for whom she had once felt so deeply was too much. Tears welled up in Thirianna's eyes.

'Please leave,' she said.

Korlandril's anguish was all-consuming and it frightened Thirianna. His eyes narrowed to slits and he bared his teeth as he stalked back and forth across the room.

'I cannot help you,' Thirianna said, staring with misery at the anguish being played out in Korlandril's actions. 'I know you are in pain, but it will pass.'

'Pain?' spat Korlandril. 'What do you know of my pain?'

Korlandril half-raised his hand, fist clenched. Stepping back, fearing he would strike her, Thirianna raised a hand to her mouth in horror.

Korlandril fled, crying and trembling. Thirianna took a step after him, full of concern. She stopped herself, fearful more of what he might do to her than himself. She had seen something in his eyes that she had only before witnessed in the sanctuary of the Aspect shrines: hate and anger.

This did not bode well for either of her friends and more than ever she wanted to know what would happen.

Walking amongst the forest of seers past, Thirianna allowed her mind to open to their thoughts. She passed between them, near the heart of the Dome of Crystal Seers, intrigued by their diamond-like bodies, still clothed in the robes they had worn when they had finally passed into the otherworld of the infinity circuit.

Their thoughts were like a background noise in her mind. It pulsed around her, under her, over her, threading along the microscopic veins of psychic crystal that enmeshed the dome. She could feel their sentience around her, each coming to the fore as she walked past his or her immobile form.

She caught glimpses of life in the infinity circuit; a world of colour and sound and light. She saw also beyond the veil, peering at snippets of the realm of the purely psychic. Since she was a child she had been taught to raise barriers against that world, to protect herself and others against the creatures that lingered within.

It was a hard habit to break and she could not open anything more than a chink in her psychic defences to let in the vibrant minds of the crystal seers. Just as she glimpsed something interesting, instinct would snap her away, moving her thoughts elsewhere, throwing up defences against the psychic intrusion.

'It will be the fate of Kelamith to end here,' said a voice behind her. 'Perhaps it will be the fate of Thirianna. That is not yet known.'

Thirianna turned to see a farseer standing beside one of the statue-like eldar, one hand on its shoulder. He was clad in a robe of thick black velvet, embroidered with runes and sigils in golden and silver thread. About his neck and wrists were many charms.

He was a little shorter than Thirianna, and broad of shoulder for an eldar. His eyes were mismatched; one a vibrant purple, the other a luminous yellow. They glittered with psychic energy.

The farseer had his other hand outstretched and above it a single rune gently spun in the air, turning end over end. Thirianna recognised it immediately. It was her name, her rune.

'Are you Kelamith?' she asked. 'You were expecting me?'

'Kelamith will expect you, yes,' replied the seer. His voice carried more gravitas than any other Thirianna had heard. His intonation, his choice of words, seemed archaic yet spoke of the future. It was difficult to understand what he was saying. 'He will know that you would come. He will be here.'

'When will he be here?' she asked. 'If you are not Kelamith, who are you?'

'He will be here now,' said the seer. His hand closed around the rune and his eyes dimmed. They focussed on Thirianna. 'Apologies, child. I am Kelamith. I will guide you on the Path of the Seer.'

VISION

The Seeking Shaft – Arrow of Kurnous. A guiding rune, the Seeking Shaft will always find its mark, no matter where or when it is released. In the most complex journeys across the skein, cause-and-effect cannot be easily attributed to a single personality. In these circumstances, a wise seer will turn to the Seeking Shaft to identify a particular individual not yet known to the seer.

A sense of relief filled Thirianna as she watched the crystal-verses of her poems melt away in the reblender. As she fed each into the warm interior of the device, their words lifted away from her, seeping deeper into her memory, becoming a thing of the past rather than the present.

She had saved this task until last, unsure what the destruction of her work would do to her. She was glad: a final closing of the chapter of Thirianna the Poet, as Thirianna the Seer would concern herself only with the future.

As the last of the crystals dissolved in the orange glow of the reblender, Thirianna felt the last ties to her previous life slipping away. For many poets what she had done bordered on vandalism, but in her mind Thirianna knew that nothing good could ever come from her poems being known by another, least of all Korlandril.

She had not heard from him since their argument; she had missed the appointment with their friends while she had been in the Dome of Crystal Seers. She had spent the last cycle tidying up her apartment for whoever next chose to live there, and her few belongings were gathered in a shoulderbag waiting for her by the door. There was little she wanted to take with her on the next part of her life, and even less that she wanted to keep to remind her of the past.

Content that she was ready, Thirianna stood up, slung the bag over her shoulder and left the rooms. From now on she would dwell in the Chambers of the Seers.

Arriving in the heart of Alaitoc, close to the gardens where she had met Alaiteir, Thirianna secured herself new quarters. Having received no guidance or instruction from Kelamith on how to proceed, Thirianna located a suite of unoccupied rooms – the trace on the infinity circuit showed that the seer who had lived there had moved on to walk the Path of Service, which Thirianna considered a good omen.

It took hardly any time at all to unpack the few books and crystals she had brought with her. She inspected the view from the apartment's balcony and found that it overlooked the rock-strewn slope where she had spoken to Alaiteir. Never one to trust coincidence when farseers and the infinity circuit were involved, Thirianna smiled to herself.

'Thirianna will be late.'

Kelamith had arrived without announcement by the infinity circuit. Surprised, Thirianna blushed as the farseer stepped onto the balcony. He had the same strange, distant look in his eyes as when they had first met.

'I did not remember receiving an invitation,' she confessed.

'Kelamith will not send the invitation as he sees that Thirianna will be late, so instead he will come here for Thirianna himself.'

'Do you always speak like that?' Thirianna asked, annoyed at the farseer's presumption.

Kelamith slowly closed his eyes. When he opened them again the witchlight had disappeared. He bowed his head slightly in apology.

'A risk attached to the work I undertake,' he explained. 'I delve deeper along the skein than my companions. I examine with the narrow eye that which attracts the attention of their broad gazes.'

'Where will I be late?' Thirianna said.

'I do not remember,' said Kelamith. 'The thread has gone. My presence here has assured that.'

'You do not remember?' Thirianna said. 'Only a moment ago you spoke about it.'

'And a moment ago it ceased to be a possibility and thus never existed,' said Kelamith. 'One cannot remember a thing that has not existed. Really, child, you need to grasp these fundamental realities quickly if we are to make any sort of progress.'

Taken aback, Thirianna had no answer to that. She thought it better to keep to a specific topic.

'Where are we going?' she asked.

'Into the mind of Alaitoc,' Kelamith announced with a broad smile. 'I hope you are ready.'

The chamber was one of many, egg-shaped and arranged alongside the others like a maze of bubbles in a foam, joined by narrow archways. The walls were glowing with the conduits of the infinity circuit, thousands of crystalline capillaries interwoven with each other and the fabric of the rooms.

As they had walked through an arterial tunnel into the depths of Alaitoc, Thirianna had glimpsed other eldar in the adjoining chambers, some alone and others in groups. Each was surrounded by a small constellation of runes, turning in the air, bobbing up and down, spiralling and climbing, curving and dipping in their eccentric orbits. Kelamith paid them no attention and offered no explanation as to what they were looking for.

Kelamith stood in the centre of the room and held out his hands, palms down, thumbs splayed and touching. Thirianna felt a surge of psychic energy and a node of the infinity circuit extruded from the interlaced conduits on the floor, pulsing with green and blue light.

'Our minds are a fragile thing, child,' said Kelamith. 'From the moment we are born to the moment we pass on, our thoughts are open for all of the universe to see. There are creatures that desire them, powers that hunger after them, and for that reason even as you learnt to speak and walk, to master your joy and woe, you were taught how to suppress the energies of your mind.'

The farseer took a step back and waved to Thirianna to stand beside the node. She did as he instructed, wanting to reach out and touch the glimmering crystal stalagmite but afraid to do so.

'We all possess the ability to unleash the power of our minds in amazing ways, child,' said Kelamith. 'Whether it is in the shaping of a thought or the mastery of the deadly Aspect arts, our mind is our most powerful tool. We suppress that power to ward away the dangers such ability will bring, but as a seer you must embrace it.'

'What do you wish me to do?' asked Thirianna, full of trepidation.

'You must let go of your thoughts,' said the farseer. 'You must allow them to be free and boundless. You must give up a lifetime of worry and cast away all of the protection, unlearning that which you had to learn.'

'Does that not attract the attention of the Great Enemy?' The slightest thought of She Who Thirsts sent a shudder through Thirianna, of fear and loathing.

'In time you will use the runes as your shield, focussing the psychic energy you will channel,' explained Kelamith. 'The defences will always be there, yours to call upon should you need them. Do not be cautious though, for such interruptions may set back your development and retard your ultimate power. At first you will conduct this unlearning within the safety of the infinity circuit. And do not be afraid, for I am also here with you, child.'

Kelamith gestured for Thirianna to place her hands on the infinity circuit node. It was cool to the touch, though veined with warmth on her palms.

'Speak after me, and let your thoughts flow with the words,' said Kelamith. Thirianna closed her eyes, concentrating on the feel of the node in her hands and the voice of Kelamith, which came slowly, rhythmically on the edge of hearing.

'In the skein there is nothing. There are no names and there are no beings. This is where the mind originates. There is the mind but nothing is physical. Forms obtain the mind and thoughts are created. This is called Passing. In the not-yet-formed the skein divides and splits but there is no time passing. This is called Being. There is an energy that gives life to all things, allowing form to obtain mind and create thought. Forms that create thought share in this energy. This is called Life. Let slip Life, and become Being. Let slip Being and become Passing. Let slip Passing and become Mind. Become Mind and be one with the skein.'

Thirianna chanted the words, matching the pitch and cadence of the farseer. She dimly recognised them from her childhood, though they seemed in a different order. As she spoke each syllable, she felt herself relaxing, in body and thought.

She could no longer feel the node between her fingers. She continued chanting, repeating the words, feeling them entering her subconscious, triggering reactions in her thoughts that she could not feel but sensed in other ways.

Her body dissolved away, as the crystals had melted in the reblender. Her limbs, her torso, her fingers, her face, all had gone, leaving Thirianna as a floating core of thought.

'Open your eyes, child.'

Thirianna did so, though she had no eyes to open.

She found herself in a realm of light and movement. She could see the flicker of other eldar around her, like candles in twilight. A tracery of white, the infinity circuit, linked every other light together, stretching on without horizon into the impossible distance.

Energy flowed along the maze, back and forth, surging and ebbing, binding everything together with its movement, linking the eldar with one another.

And beyond.

Beyond was something even more spectacular, defying rationalisation. Beyond were the constantly shattering panes of existence; the overlapping planes of destiny; the interwoven threads of fate. The present surrounded Thirianna, but just out of reach was the future, and in the darkness behind was the past. Every life, every thought, every movement, every motive, every emotion, weaving together in a dazzling tapestry of cause and effect. It branched out, splitting and dividing like cells, spawning entire new universes and possibilities with every passing moment.

This was the skein, and it was beautiful.

And too much. Too much to see, to comprehend, to understand.

Thirianna passed out.

It took three cycles until Thirianna had recovered sufficiently from her first experience of the skein to contact Kelamith. The farseer had been notably absent as Thirianna had rested in her new rooms, and had offered no explanation of what had happened to her. Thirianna considered the possibility that Kelamith had known what would happen, and had foreseen that she would regain her mental harmony in time, and chosen not to intervene.

Just that briefest glimpse of the skein had opened Thirianna's mind to the wondrous possibilities that lay before her. Rather than being fearful of approaching the infinity circuit again she was excited by the prospect. Yet it had taken three days of meditation and contemplation before she had been able to think of the skein without being dizzied by its power.

Midway through the fourth cycle after the episode, she received an invitation from Kelamith to join him in the gardens next to her chambers. He made it clear that the two of them would be venturing into the infinity circuit again, which set Thirianna's mind racing in all directions.

As she made her way down towards the parkland, her first thought was one of concern. What if she were incapable of interacting with the skein? What if she lacked the psychic power to deal with its infinite possibilities? She dismissed the idea as she reached the edge of the gardens. Kelamith had hinted that her mind's defences would be more of a hindrance than a help at this early stage; if he had any further worries over her suitability he would have voiced them or refused to become her mentor altogether. His lack of concern for her wellbeing led Thirianna to believe that what she had encountered, and her reaction, was commonplace.

Following the path up to the top of the rock hill, she wondered how many attempts it would take before she could interact with the infinity circuit. She was impatient, more than at any time in her life. She had a lifetime to perfect any art or skill she turned her mind to, but her desire to see what the future held for her propelled her forwards more swiftly than on any previous Path. It was possible, she concluded, that in her haste to comprehend the skein she was unwittingly stalling her development.

Kelamith stood beneath the branches of a tree near to the bench atop the hill. His eyes were free of witchlight and his expression was one of almost paternal pride, which confused Thirianna.

'Greetings, child,' said the farseer. Thirianna nodded her head in return and sat on the bench. 'I trust you feel restored and recuperated? You have not been unduly perturbed by your recent experience?'

'I am rested,' said Thirianna. She smiled at the farseer as he walked over to her and stopped in front of the bench. 'And I am eager to try again. I hope that with your guidance I will not fail this time.'

'Fail?' Confusion knotted Kelamith's brow. 'There was no failure. Not on your part, at least. I failed to divine the extent of your instinct and natural ability, and did not take suitable precautions for your safe-keeping.'

'I do not understand.'

The farseer sat beside Thirianna, closer than would normally be acceptable between recent acquaintances. Thirianna tried to ignore the intrusion into her personal space.

'You went further into the infinity circuit than I considered possible,' explained Kelamith. 'For most of us, our first steps upon the Path are tentative and short-lived. We see no more than a fraction of the infinity circuit, and nothing of the great realm of which it is part. You, on your first attempt, looked upon the skein itself. The skein is a thing of wonder, but it cannot be seen without training and preparation.'

Thirianna tried not to look smug at the thought that she had done so well, but evidently failed. Kelamith's frown of confusion turned to one of annoyance.

'You have natural power but no control, child,' he said. 'Once the shackles have been loosed from our thoughts it is easy to look at the skein. The skill comes in understanding it; in seeing only a part and choosing a singular thread to follow. Any fool can look at the mass of the future, but a seer must separate the detail from the noise, the important from the unimportant.'

Kelamith stood up and waved for Thirianna to follow him.

'We will return to the infinity circuit and we will try again,' said the farseer. 'This time I want you to only peek at what can be seen.'

'And how do I do that?' Thirianna asked as they started down the hill.

'As a child we blinded you, and now that you have opened your eyes again the light burns them,' said Kelamith. 'I will teach you the means to open them only slightly and protect yourself from the harsh glare of the unbounded skein.'

As before, they made their way into the heart of Alaitoc, walking through the interlinked Chambers of the Seers until they came to the same room as before. The infinity circuit node rose from the floor at Kelamith's command and he indicated for Thirianna to approach it.

'Do you still remember the words?' he asked.

'I do,' replied Thirianna. The verses were etched into her thoughts as deeply as her poems had once been. Oddly, she realised, she could barely remember her compositions when once they had come to mind at the slightest thought. The destruction of the crystals had been mirrored by her memory.

'Concentrate on the sense of form,' said Kelamith. 'Retain a foundation within your form rather than letting your spirit free. Chain your mind with the reality of your being and the restrictions of form.'

Thirianna did not quite understand what the farseer meant, but she was eager to link with the infinity circuit again. This time when she placed her hand on the node, she tried to picture the way she had interacted with the infinity circuit countless times before, skimming across its surface without delving into it.

'That will not do,' said Kelamith, sensing her intent. 'You cannot simply look upon the infinity circuit, you must still become part of it, while keeping yourself detached.'

'That is a contradiction, surely?' said Thirianna.

'Remember: Mind, Being and Form,' said the farseer. 'Three intertwined parts of you, each separate and the same. If such concepts prove difficult, there is nothing I can do to help you.'

Nodding her submission to this logic, Thirianna took a breath and allowed herself to slip into the infinity circuit.

At first she did as she had planned, touching only lightly upon the huge matrix of psychic energy that ran through every part of Alaitoc. She allowed her thoughts to dance towards the distant rim, where ship manifests and passenger lists inhabited the frameworks of the docks; to the Pinnacle of Mornings, where a group of poets were reciting the *Epic of Eldanesh*; to the Dome of Crystal Seers; to the Arc of the Turning Suns.

She felt a presence beside her: Kelamith, not physically, but within the structure of the infinity circuit.

'Thirianna will delve a little deeper,' he said.

She felt warmth from his presence, like the glow of safety that wrapped her as a child when her mother had held her. It was sanctuary and it bolstered Thirianna's confidence. She started to recite the words taught to her by Kelamith and felt her consciousness slipping further into the infinity circuit.

'Thirianna will stay where she is, deep enough to see,' said the farseer.

The sensation was different this time. Thirianna understood what Kelamith meant about being part of the infinity circuit while remaining separate. Her form had become the infinity circuit but her being remained as it was and her mind lingered between the two.

Her world had become a glittering web of power, but rather than try to see it all, she concentrated on what was close at hand. She was inside the Arc of the Turning Suns. She could feel the flutter of the engineers touching upon the infinity circuit as they tended to the star-sails gathering energy from the dying sun. With another part of her mind she could witness them at their stations, making gentle adjustments to the massive solar collectors to maximise their efficiency.

She became aware of Kelamith beside her, watching without comment. He appeared as a golden spark in the infinity circuit, his psychic energy diffusing along dozens of conduits but concentrated close at hand.

Something else flickered into her consciousness. At first they were too fast to comprehend; flashing pinpricks that had raced past by the time her mind had become aware of them. Thirianna narrowed her focus, picking a handful of crystalline threads to interact with. The speed of everything seemed to slow as her thoughts coalesced, making the workings of the infinity circuit plainer to see.

The constant thrum of psychic energy became a slower pulse, moving outwards along the conduits of the infinity circuit in rhythm to Alaitoc's ponderous heartbeat. It rippled from the core to the rim, near-instantaneous in reality, but to her mind's eye becoming subtle, entrancing waves.

More of the bright sparks she had seen passed close by and Thirianna caught them with her thoughts, her scrutiny slowing their progress.

There were several dozen of them, clustered in groups each a handful strong. They appeared as tiny creatures, each group occupying the area of a fingernail. Yet there was immense power contained in their miniscule forms. Looking even more closely, she saw tiny clawed legs splaying across the threads of energy and she realised she looked upon the warp spiders from which the Aspect Warriors of the same name drew inspiration.

Each warp spider raced along the infinity circuit's threads, dozens of legs moving faster than thought. They rode upon the pulses of energy, then dashed back to the core before the next, heaved out on the tide of psychic power before returning to the hub.

They became aware of Thirianna and investigated. They circled around the mote of consciousness that was her mind, scurrying to and fro while they inspected her. Created to guard the infinity circuit from malign presences, the warp spiders quickly realised that Thirianna was no foe and relaxed their guard.

Rather than move on, they circled playfully around her, excited by this new presence. She could feel the tiny pinpricks of energy passing through her as the warp spiders danced across the infinity circuit, joyfully clambering around and through her thoughts.

The warp spiders were like a psychic tickle running through her mind, each a particle of purity and happiness that left a warm trail where it touched her, criss-crossing her memories and thoughts with tiny footsteps.

The experience was cleansing, the warp spiders feeding on tiny shreds of negative energy that leaked from Thirianna's deepest fears and worst emotions; fears and emotions kept locked away in the recesses of her mind but never wholly secured.

'It will be enough for the moment.' Kelamith washed through Thirianna, scattering the warp spiders. 'Thirianna will have her first true taste of the infinity circuit, but she must quell her curiosity and retain control.'

Kelamith's mind linked with Thirianna's and pulled her across the infinity circuit back to the Chambers of the Seers. For a strange moment

Thirianna found herself looking at her own form. She realised that no matter how graceful and poised her body seemed, to the realm of the purely psychic it was crude as any other physical structure, with the same imperfections and compromises as any living being.

It was a humbling moment, right before she was reunited with the shell of her body.

Thirianna felt a wave of claustrophobia as she was restricted to her normal, physical senses again. The weight of her form was a burden to her thoughts, which struggled across chemical synapses and along physical nerves.

The sensation of loss passed and Thirianna opened her eyes, looking at her hands upon the infinity circuit node. Kelamith stood to her right, eyes blazing with psychic energy. He turned that otherworldly stare upon Thirianna.

'Thirianna will do well, but she must be told that this is only the beginning,' said Kelamith. 'She will return here in the next cycle and we will continue.'

'Yes, she will,' Thirianna said, her mind still tingling with after-effects from the warp spiders.

For cycle after cycle Thirianna returned to the Chambers of the Seers and explored the infinity circuit with Kelamith. Often he would guide her, leading Thirianna to strange places she had never seen before: places made of crystal cliffs and plains of sapphire, ruby seas and star-lit voids. Sometimes Thirianna was left to wander. Though never wholly alone – Kelamith's presence could always be felt in the distance – Thirianna started to learn how to navigate the infinity circuit more speedily.

Freeing herself from the constraints of form, she noticed junctions and pathways that were separate from the physical crystalline matrix, existing only in the psychic realm. At first these transitions jolted her consciousness, bringing the strangest sensation of disassociation, almost bereavement. In time the translocation of her spirit became less jarring, her consciousness slipping between the nodes of the infinity circuit with less effort.

Thirianna spent more time with the warp spiders, following them back to their roosts in the core and letting her mind free to be washed across the infinity circuit on the tides of psychic energy. Kelamith encouraged her, in his own odd fashion, and from the warp spiders she learnt more of the secret routes of the infinity circuit and the space in-between. Thirianna would chase the creatures, following them around the complex maze, never quite catching them. The warp spiders were more than happy with her company, staying just ahead of her flowing mind, teasing her with their presence.

When she was not delving into the secrets of the infinity circuit, Thirianna spent her time studying the runes of the seers. Kelamith furnished her with a learning crystal that contained thousands of the sigils, embedded with commentary from Alaitoc's greatest farseers.

At first, like the skein they represented, the volume of the runes was overwhelming: a near-incomprehensible labyrinth of meaning that overlaid and meshed in mysterious ways. Through the learning crystal, Thirianna was able to focus on one rune at a time, absorbing its meanings and uses, before following the branches and threads that led to other runes. Cycle by cycle her understanding expanded exponentially, her knowledge of the seers' codes and language spreading even as her comprehension of the infinity circuit broadened.

Thirianna admired the pattern and asymmetry of both; the organic flux of circuit and rune in conjunction with each other. Even as she was chasing warp spiders through the psychic maze of Alaitoc, Thirianna was associating the runes from the crystal with the experiences she underwent.

Yet not every cycle was a playful or joyous experience. The infinity circuit delved into every part of Alaitoc, from the restoration chambers to the weapons batteries. Through her deepening knowledge of the circuit's ways, Thirianna learnt to read the telltale signs of danger that appeared when she encroached upon areas she was not yet ready to look upon. Some of these she ventured into later with the aid of Kelamith; others remained a mystery to her.

Some of these regions were the places haunted by the spirits of the disquieted dead. While the energy of most eldar was subsumed into the greater consciousness of the infinity circuit, there were some that refused to relinquish their grip on the physical world. Many were warriors, killed in battle, trapped with their rage and their bloodlust. Some were great leaders, notable orators and philosophers, acclaimed artists; their personalities so strong that they existed after death to suffer eternity in the limbo of near-life.

Not all of the spirits that survived were dangerous. Many were simply mournful, filled with self-loathing and depressed at their fate. Some had strange mood swings, moving across the infinity circuit between joy and despair.

Kelamith advised Thirianna to be wary of such spirits, but not to shun them entirely. They were wise and many had noble intent, but their division from the world of the living gave them a twisted view of affairs. Thirianna had not yet developed the skill or focus to converse with these wandering ghosts, but communicated merely in sense and emotion, feeling happiness or woe, longing or regret when she came upon them.

Of particular distaste to Thirianna was the increasing habit of the warp spiders to seek refuge near the Aspect shrines during their games of psychic hide-and-seek. Thirianna could sense the brooding presence of the Aspect Warriors, their warlike minds corralled within the infinity circuit away from the thoughts of others. Like a shadow cast across the psychic maze, the temples of Khaine's followers touched on the infinity circuit with rage and hatred, tainting its energy.

The psychic landscapes of the infinity circuit were twisted as well. Gone were the rainbow bridges and waterfalls of silver, replaced by dank grottos, forbidding caverns of black ice and harsh red deserts. Fire glimmered across the infinity circuit, corrupted by iron and war, ash and blood.

It was not just a general abhorrence and fear that kept Thirianna from exploring these dark reaches further. The memory of her time as a Dire Avenger grew in strength when she came closer to the power of the Aspect shrines. It nagged harder and harder to be free from the bounds that kept it within Thirianna's unconscious, forcing her to withdraw, feeling polluted by its presence.

Part Two

Warlock

CONTROL

The Brother's Gaze – Eye of Ulthanesh. It is often tempting to follow a thread across the skein in a single direction, linking event to event, catalyst to outcome, to arrive at a final fate. While this allows one to see the progression of the future, it is to surrender the initiative to fate. The Brother's Gaze is a rune of contradiction, approaching a juncture from the opposite angle, providing the path from outcome to catalyst so that the course of destiny might be better steered.

Several dozen cycles had come and gone since Thirianna's first foray into the infinity circuit when Kelamith came to her early after the artificial dawn. She awoke, sensing his presence in her chambers, and found the farseer standing on the balcony of the apartment. Thirianna was instantly aware of something different; not about Kelamith but Alaitoc itself. The atmosphere was pregnant with energy, the infinity circuit buzzing with a growing presence, stronger here near the Chambers of the Seers than she had felt it before.

No, not stronger, just different. It had been stronger in the Shrine of One Hundred Bloody Tears.

The Avatar of Khaine was waking. The incarnation of the Bloody-Handed God was coming to life, stirring on its iron throne.

'War comes,' she said, pulling on her robe.

Kelamith turned towards her, eyes alight with psychic power. He said nothing for a moment and the light faded.

'Yes, child, war is coming,' he confirmed. 'You have the opportunity to

311

witness something you have only experienced from afar.'

'No,' said Thirianna. 'I do not wish to see the Avatar awakening. I am a warrior no longer, and I will not suffer Khaine's touch upon me again.'

'You must,' said Kelamith. 'It is not the fate of the seers of our age to look upon joyous ends. War and death, blood and misery are the veils we must lift to see what the future holds for Alaitoc. We must confront our own destruction every cycle, in order that it can be avoided. If you cannot resist the lure of Khaine, if you cannot tread in his fiery trail, you are of little use as a seer.'

Shuddering at the thought, Thirianna finished dressing. She felt Kelamith's eyes on her, curious and invasive, but pushed away the self-consciousness his attention brought forth. She looked at the farseer but he said nothing, features set in a look of polite determination.

'There is no other way?' asked Thirianna. Kelamith shook his head, eliciting a sigh from her. 'Very well. I will come with you into the infinity circuit.'

'Our journey does not end in the infinity circuit, child,' Kelamith said, raising a finger in a gesture of correction. 'The nerves of Alaitoc are a cipher of the skein, an artificial construct that is only a representation of the realm into which you will eventually delve.'

'I understand,' said Thirianna. 'I remember seeing the skein itself.'

'And the coming battle will provide us with a great opportunity to return there,' said Kelamith.

'Battle?'

'Surely, child,' replied the farseer. 'In battle the skein is a stark, living thing. It will be an excellent introduction for you. Where else do fate and chance come into such vivid contrast? A battle narrows the score of the skein, revealing the myriad twisting ways of destiny in a confined space and time. You are fortunate.'

'Fortunate?' Thirianna laughed with bitterness. 'I have tasted battle, and though I do not remember it, a sense of fortune is not my recollection.'

'Your protests are tiresome, child,' said Kelamith. He shrugged dismissively. 'We both know that you will accompany me. I know this because I have seen it. You know this because in your heart you desire to become a seer and this is what you must do.'

'You think I should just accept what you decide?' snapped Thirianna. 'I am a slave to your instruction because you have seen the results?'

'Never succumb to fatalism, child,' said Kelamith, growing concerned. He approached Thirianna and laid a hand on her shoulder. 'There are rarely no choices. As a seer you will find that there are too many decisions to make, not too few. In time you will have a power that lesser creatures dream of possessing; you will be able to shape the future consciously and not be a powerless leaf on the river of time.'

The farseer's words conjured up vistas of possibilities in Thirianna. She was momentarily suspicious that Kelamith seemed to know the right thing to say when it mattered, but her doubt faded as she envisaged the power he described. It was the desire to have that power and control that had brought her to the Path of the Seer and it would be foolish to be fearful now of the obstacles she would have to overcome.

With great trepidation, Thirianna walked along the corridor that led to the Shrine of One Hundred Bloody Tears. It had not changed since she had quit the Path of the Warrior; had not changed in ten lifetimes of the eldar since it had been founded. The portal to the shrine was a pointed arch at the end of the corridor, of blue metal embossed with runes in gold, like etching on crossed sword blades. One hundred tear-shaped rubies decorated the edge of the metaphorical swords, symbolic droplets of blood, their tiny facets each reflecting ruddy images of Thirianna as she approached the shrine.

The gate opened as she stepped up to it, revealing a landscape of wooded hills. Over the trees soared the pinnacle of the temple tower, its summit lit with silver light, its walls a smooth ochre. The only light came from the tower, bathing the woodlands in an odd twilight that seemed to hang on the edges of narrow leaves and clung to the deep ridges in the bark.

Taking a step across the threshold, Thirianna felt a surge of different feelings. She remembered her fear when she had first come here, mind awash with rage at her father. Other recollections danced in her thoughts as she followed the strip of golden slabs that led to the tower: learning the mantras of the Dire Avengers; taking up her armour for the first time; the hiss of the shurikens the first time she fired her weapon.

Deeper memories, of acts committed while she wore her war-mask, edged into consciousness but were held back by the mental barriers she had put in place. Her war-mask writhed inside her subconscious, brought into life by the growing presence of Khaine's Avatar, awakened by her coming to the shrine.

Eventually she came to the base of the tower.

The doorway was open, golden light spilling from within. Thirianna walked into the light, feeling its warm touch envelop her like the arms of a lover, caressing the memories that were hidden away behind the locked doors of her mind.

Thirianna swiftly ascended a spiralling set of stairs to the armouring chamber in the upper reaches. She could hear the soft chants of the Aspect Warriors as they prepared themselves for battle, but blocked out the urge to speak them herself.

Coming to the main hall, Thirianna found eight Dire Avengers half-dressed in their armour. The rune of the shrine was already upon their foreheads, written in the blood of each warrior, and between the two lines of Dire Avengers walked Nimreith, her voice leading the chant. Thirianna recognised the glazed looked in the eyes of her former squad members, and another memory, a longing for acceptance and harmony, wriggled in her mind.

Nimreith paused in her ceremony, eyes falling upon Thirianna. The exarch said nothing, but waved a hand towards an archway to Thirianna's right. It had always been closed when she had been a Dire Avenger, but now the portal lay open, the room beyond dark.

Nimreith had taken up the chant again, turning her back on Thirianna. Realising that she would receive no further instruction, Thirianna stepped through the open doorway and into the room beyond.

There was no light save that which glowed from several objects hanging upon the far wall. A deliberate rumble and a hiss of air caused Thirianna to turn around. The door had closed behind her, leaving her alone in the antechamber.

Crossing the small room, Thirianna examined the glowing objects. There were three triangular breastplates, wrought from silver wraithbone, formed into rune-shapes and inscribed with tiny sigils from which the light was glowing. The psychic energy emanating from the rune armour was palpable, connecting with Thirianna as she held out her hand towards the closest piece. Above each set of armour was a helmet, studded with gems, the eyepieces seeming to glint with their own power as they reflected distorted images of Thirianna.

Between the armour and helmets were several swords. An aura of menace surrounded each one, leaking thoughts of death into Thirianna's mind. Her war-mask quivered in response, rising from the depths of her unconscious like a hunter scenting prey, eclipsing her other thoughts.

Thirianna moved to the armour on the far left, drawn to its organic form. She lightly drew her fingers along its lines, feeling the small indentations of the runes and a surge of psychic energy.

She realised she was chanting, whispering the mantra that would bring forth her war-mask. Part of her wanted to stop, knowing that pain and suffering was waiting for her beyond that bloody veil. Another part of her, a stronger part, wanted to embrace the oblivion of the death-dealer, to shred away conscience and remorse and become Khaine's Bloody Hand.

She lifted the armour from its hooks and turned it around so that she could slip it over her shoulders. Bands and belts writhed like tentacles, wrapping around Thirianna's body, drawing the armour tight to her chest. It felt reassuring to be in the armour's embrace and its protective energies flowed through and around Thirianna, surrounding her with a dim gleam of power. The armour melded around her waystone, drawing it from its brooch to move it over Thirianna's heart. The waystone was bright with power, throbbing in time to her racing pulse, hot to the touch.

The matching helmet came next, resplendent in the blue and gold of the shrine. Still chanting, Thirianna brought the helm over her head, taking a deep breath as the darkness consumed her. Flashes of memory were surfacing now; glimpses of battle and death. Looking through the eyepieces was like seeing with fresh eyes.

Lastly she took up the accompanying sword. As Thirianna's fingers curled around its hilt, the blade glimmered, every rune glowing blood red for a moment. It felt like taking the hand of a child, uplifting and comforting yet bringing a sense of responsibility. The Witchblade's murmuring desires for blood trickled into Thirianna's consciousness, pushing back the last of the barriers holding her war-mask in check.

She felt complete.

She stood in the centre of the room and held the Witchblade in front of her at the salute. From this pose she began a series of slow movements, the memory of her ritual fighting stances coming back to her. The sensation was strange. She had practised countless times with a shuriken catapult, but now every gesture and manoeuvre seemed to match perfectly with a blow or defence with the sword. Something was subtly different. With a mixture of surprise and happiness, Thirianna realised that it was the Witchblade that moved her, teaching her its unique style of fighting, directing her limbs and body in the way of war imbued within the weapon.

Faster and faster she practised, her muscles, her instinct, remembering everything. She whirled and chopped, spun and sliced, sidestepped and parried. An age ago the Witchblade had been given its purpose and now it had another vessel through which it could act.

She allowed her mind to drift from its anchors as she had learnt with the infinity circuit. Mind detached from Being, Being detached from Form, leaving her as a single moving entity of pure thought. The sword was no less a part of her than an arm or a foot or even her heart. Its edge shone bright as Thirianna allowed herself to be drawn into the blade, her own essence powering its lethal energies.

Thirianna and Witchblade became one.

'It is a simple enough task,' said Kelamith, betraying no sign of impatience.

The same could not be said for Thirianna. She glared at the Witchblade lying on a purple rug spread out across the floor of her room, where it had been for the best part of the last cycle.

'Lift the sword, child,' said Kelamith.

Gritting her teeth, Thirianna held out her hand towards the hilt of the Witchblade and tried to imagine it in her grasp. She pictured it floating gently upwards, blade downwards, and gliding across the room to her waiting hand.

The sword did not so much as twitch and sat on the rug with what Thirianna thought was a defiant expression, if such a thing could be said of a sword.

315

'It won't move,' she snapped, letting out an explosive breath and letting her hand drop to her side.

'Perhaps it is not the sword that needs to move, child,' said Kelamith.

'If I am allowed to move, then I would simply cross the room and pick it up!' said Thirianna, exasperated by Kelamith's tone and cryptic suggestions. She was sure the farseer spoke in improbable riddles simply to prove himself superior.

'I did not say to move your form,' Kelamith replied. 'You are a seer now, a mystic with limbs not made of flesh. The sword is not of your form but it is now part of your being, linked to you by the power of mind. You are bound together, sharing your travels along the skein.'

'I cannot do it,' said Thirianna. 'It will not come.'

'The paralysis is in your thoughts, just as paralysis in your arm would stop you from lifting your hand. Do that now. Lift your hand.'

With a sigh of reluctance, Thirianna did as she was asked, holding her right hand up to Kelamith.

'Was there any difficulty?' asked the farseer.

'Of course not,' said Thirianna. 'My hand is attached to me by my arm. I do not feel this link you speak of.'

'You ignore it,' said Kelamith. 'You allow your warrior-self to intrude upon the mind. The warrior is a creature of Form and Being and no thought. The warrior cannot lift the sword, only the seer can.'

Thirianna turned back towards the Witchblade, sneering at its reluctance to be commanded. She was not going to lose a battle of wills with an inanimate object.

She extended her mind, focussing her thoughts again on the lifting of the blade. She visualised as Kelamith had instructed, imagining the Witchblade to be as light as a feather, gently wafting across the room at her beck and call.

Nothing happened.

'How much longer are you going to force me to do this?' Thirianna snarled, folding her arms petulantly. 'I promise I will not drop my Witchblade.'

'Perhaps you would rather I tied it to your wrist?' Kelamith replied, with no hint of mockery. 'It is not the blade that you require; it is the act that you need to perform.'

He delved a hand into one of the pouches at his belt and brought out three runes. With a flick of his fingers he cast them into the air. As they fell the runes slowed and veered, coming together in a group to spin around the farseer's pointing finger. Two of them continued to circle slowly and the third sped up, passing around twice for each rotation of the others. One of the others then began to move up and down, describing an undulating wave in its orbit.

'The mastery of our minds is an exercise in control, child,' said Kelamith. He moved his hand to his nose and the runes changed their route, circling around his head. As Kelamith lifted his hand away a rune took its place, gently turning end over end in front of his nose like a propeller. Thirianna laughed, the ridiculousness of the scene puncturing her annoyance.

In the next moment, the runes flashed across the room, darting past Thirianna's face. She ducked out of instinct and it was Kelamith who now laughed.

'Grab one,' said the farseer as the runes started to weave around Thirianna's body.

She swept her hand towards the closest, but it darted between her fingers as they closed, pinging gently from her forehead. She tried again, lunging after the next, but it swerved away from her hand and took up a fresh orbit around her leg. Thirianna kicked at the rune out of irritation and instinct, but missed once more, almost unbalancing herself.

'Mind is quicker than Form,' said Kelamith. 'In the time it takes your thought to move to your arm, to your fingers, to your knee and toes, I can have five thoughts.'

The runes spun faster and faster, circling around Thirianna's head. In quick succession they bobbed against her nose, her lips, her ear, like a group of especially irritating flies. Thirianna glared at Kelamith and saw a brief smile of amusement.

'Pick up the sword,' he said, bouncing a rune from the back of Thirianna's hand.

She reached out towards the Witchblade. She did not will it into her grasp, did not visualise its movements. She simply desired it in her hand so that she could swat away the annoying runes.

With a screech, the Witchblade flew from the rug and slapped into Thirianna's open fingers. She closed her hand quickly and turned on her heel, looking to knock the runes out of the air.

The runes were already back with Kelamith, dancing to and fro from outstretched fingertip to fingertip.

'When you move your arm, you do not think about it, you simply do it,' said the farseer. 'When you are hungry you feel it. When you fall asleep, it happens without consent. Form must conform, but Mind is free, bound together by Being. Try it again.'

Heartened, Thirianna returned the Witchblade to its place on the rug. She walked back to her position and flung out her hand.

The sword did not move and Thirianna's exasperated sigh filled the chamber.

The time to depart was fast approaching. For six cycles Thirianna returned to the Shrine of One Hundred Bloody Tears. For six cycles she and her Witchblade became accustomed to one another, learning a little bit more about the other with each encounter. For six cycles she practised the exercises taught to her by Kelamith, seeking to refine her psychic control so that it came as easily as breathing and walking.

In contrast to her worries before going to the One Hundred Bloody Tears shrine, Thirianna found no difficulty in letting her war-mask slip away when she had concluded each session. It was as if she had moved that part of her into the Witchblade, allowing it to take possession of the anger and the hate, soaking up the merciless desire for death that came from the war-mask.

The next time she put on her rune armour and took up her sword, Thirianna would not be removing it again for some time. She and Kelamith would be amongst the Aspect Warriors of the strike force being assembled. She would be returning to battle.

The rune projected from the crystal consisted of three glowing loops, bisected by two crossbars. The image turned slowly in front of Thirianna as a female voice spoke quietly.

'The Sign of Daitha was first configured by Nemreinthera of Iyanden and its use spread quickly to other craftworlds, coming to Alaitoc during the Fourth Pass of the Wintering in the Age of Hallowed Dusk. It was first adopted by Kordanrial Alaineth, who introd–'

The recording paused as it detected the door chime. Thirianna realised she had been so intent upon her studies that she had not noticed the approach of a visitor. She cast her mind into the infinity circuit – feeling a moment of pride that she could do so now without physical contact with a node or interface – and suddenly recoiled in surprise at the identity of her guest.

She thought open the door and plucked the crystal from the floor, stowing it in a pouch at her belt.

'Aradryan!' she said, turning towards her visitor. 'This is unexpected.'

He was dressed in a tight-fitting suit of greens and blues that were constantly shifting, masking his form. It was a holo-suit, frequently used by rangers, though there was no sign of the heavier cloak or coat that such eldar usually wore. Thirianna noticed a long knife was sheathed at his hip, and he wore a belt laden with packs and pouches.

'Hello, Thirianna,' said Aradryan, stepping into the apartment. He smiled and offered a palm in greeting. Thirianna laid her hand on his for a heartbeat, still nonplussed at her friend's arrival. 'Sorry I could not warn you of my return.'

'I did not expect to see you again for much longer,' said Thirianna. She sat down and waved to a cushion for Aradryan to sit but he declined with a quick, single shake of the head.

'I cannot stay long,' he told her. 'It seems my attempt to get far away from Alaitoc was destined to be thwarted. The *Irdiris* intercepted a transmission from Eileniliesh. It's an Exodite world that has been attacked by orks. We thought it wise to return to Alaitoc with the news.'

'Preparations are already under way for an expedition,' said Thirianna.

'Farseer Latheirin witnessed the impending attack several cycles ago.'

'Such is the way of farseers,' Aradryan said with a shrug. He laughed. 'Of course, you are becoming a seer now. Perhaps I should choose my words more carefully?'

'I do not take any offence,' replied Thirianna. 'They are an enigmatic group, that is sure. I have been around them for some time and I do not yet understand their ways.'

She studied Aradryan and sensed restlessness. It was something more than the wanderlust that had taken him away from Alaitoc; an unsettling energy emanated from her friend.

'How have you fared?' she asked.

Aradryan shrugged again.

'There is not much yet to say,' he said. He gestured at his outfit. 'As you see, I have decided to join the rangers, but in truth I had not set foot off *Irdiris* before we had to return. On Eileniliesh we will fight the orks.'

'That would be unwise,' said Thirianna. 'You have never trodden the Path of the Warrior. You have no war-mask.'

'It is of no concern,' said Aradryan with a dismissive wave of the hand. 'My longrifle will keep me safe. It seems I have a natural talent for marksmanship.'

'It is not the physical danger that concerns me,' said Thirianna. She stood up and approached Aradryan. 'War corrupts us. The lure of Khaine can become irresistible.'

'There are many delights in the galaxy. Bloodshed is not one that appeals to me,' said Aradryan. His brow creased deeply. 'I never realised how blinkered you could be. You see the Path as the start and the end of existence. It is not.'

'It is,' said Thirianna. 'What you are doing, allowing your mind to run free, endangers not just you but those around you. You must show restraint. Korlandril, he has been touched by Khaine. His anger became too much.'

'He is an Aspect Warrior now?' said Aradryan, amused by the news. His smile was lopsided and there was something else, something fey in his eyes. 'I did not realise my critique of his work was so harsh.'

Aradryan's short laugh cut at Thirianna's spirit. There was a harshness there that had not existed before. Her friend had always possessed something of a delight in irony and sarcasm but his happiness at Korlandril's predicament was entirely misplaced.

'Why have you come here?' said Thirianna. 'What do you want from me?'

'Nothing,' said Aradryan. 'You made it very clear I should expect nothing from you. I came as a courtesy, nothing more. If I am not welcome, I shall leave.'

Thirianna was not sure how to respond. Having Aradryan here, in her apartment, was unsettling. She could feel the wildness hovering beneath the surface of his spirit. He appeared normal and polite, but every now and then that unfettered spirit showed itself. He was prey to every passing whim and fancy, every vague emotion and thought that came to him, and was unpredictable and dangerous because of it.

'Yes, I think you should leave,' said Thirianna. Aradryan's lip curled a fraction but he nodded his acquiescence. For a moment the look of hurt and betrayal he had worn before he left returned. Thirianna relented slightly. 'Please take care of yourself, Aradryan. I am pleased that you came to see me.'

The ranger seemed caught in two minds, taking a step towards the door but keeping his eyes fixed on Thirianna, perhaps hoping for her to change her mind. She hardened her spirit to his departure, knowing that he was a distraction she could not afford, especially this close to leaving for Eileniliesh.

'Goodbye,' he said, one hand on the edge of the open door. 'I do not expect us to meet again. Ever.'

It was difficult but Thirianna refused to respond to the overly dramatic statement. It was nothing more than a blatant attempt at emotional blackmail and she was determined not to succumb.

'Goodbye,' she replied. 'Travel well and find contentment.'

With a sigh, Aradryan turned away and moved out of view. The door swished across the opening, leaving Thirianna alone with her thoughts. She stayed there a moment and then dashed towards the door, which opened before her. She shouted Aradryan's name as she ran out onto the landing. He was just at the turn towards the stairwell and stopped to look over his shoulder.

'Please see Korlandril,' Thirianna called out to him. He nodded and raised a hand in acknowledgement, and then disappeared down the stairs.

As the cycle entered the night period and the lights of her apartment dimmed, Thirianna sat in the main room with a small object in her lap. It was a simple thing: a small white box. Inside was a rune, shaped from silvery-grey wishstone. It was the mark of the Dire Avenger, a small souvenir she had kept from her time as an Aspect Warrior. She was not sure why she had taken it. It had once hung from the grip of her shuriken catapult and in a moment of foolishness or sentimentality she had brought it with her when she had quit the Path of the Warrior.

She did not know what to do with it, but the rune nagged at her. Returning to the shrine had awakened dormant passions and desires, and though they were faint now, the rune was responding in some way. She could not throw it away; that would be disrespectful to herself and the Shrine of One Hundred Bloody Tears. She could not keep it, its presence was becoming a distraction. She would feel embarrassed to return it.

Another option occurred to her.

Though she had concentrated of late on her own development, she had heard that Korlandril had been overpowered by his rage and succumbed to the lure of Khaine. In a move that Thirianna thought of with delicious irony, Korlandril had become an Aspect Warrior, a Striking Scorpion of the Deadly Shadow. The name of the shrine struck a chord in her thoughts when she had heard it, resonating with that memory she kept placated in a way she did not understand.

She was a seer now, and Korlandril a warrior.

Thirianna remembered their argument about the Path of Khaine before Korlandril's turn to anger. Knowing that, just as with Aradryan's abandonment of the Path, she was in part responsible for Korlandril's lapse into rage, Thirianna thought that she could show her former friend some measure of understanding and atonement. It was a message from one warrior to another, one that she was sure he would appreciate in the difficult time he was surely experiencing.

Thirianna waited in front of the door to Korlandril's apartment. She knew he was not inside; she felt none of his presence and with her heightening psychic awareness needed no foray into the infinity circuit to discern his whereabouts.

She wondered if it would be better to wait for him, to place the gift in his hands and explain its meaning.

Thirianna decided against this course of action. It would be of no benefit to Korlandril or her to meet again under these circumstances. To whatever end, both of them had changed, moved on to new Paths, and they were still discovering their new selves.

She placed the box in front of the door where it could not be missed. Leaving her hand lingering on it for a moment, she allowed a little of herself to seep into the rune within: sadness and longing, regret at their parting, pride in his actions and, most of all, forgiveness and understanding.

BATTLE

The Suin Daellae – Spear of Khaine. As with all runes associated with the Bloody-Handed God, the Suin Daellae reacts only to bloodshed. Its purpose is the location of pivotal moments of war and is used to detect the violent death of a significant individual. It must be employed with care and strictly controlled; the Spear of Khaine has an inherent desire to show the seer myriad versions of his or her own bloody demise.

'Keep your mind closed,' warned Kelamith. 'You are not yet ready to see the webway with your thoughts.'

Thirianna and her mentor sat on the padded bench of a light skiff, awaiting the arrival of the seers that would join them. The vehicle was a slender deltoid, its wings flaring sharply at the stern, the lights of the launch bay blocked by the golden, curving sail above, leaving the two seers in shadow. Seated in a small cockpit behind the passenger compartment, the driver adjusted the trim of the vehicle, the sound of the engines increasing briefly to a soft purr.

The farseer was garbed in his full regalia: flowing dark robes beneath the golden chestpiece of his armour, rune-furnished clasps and jewellery hanging from neck and wrists. His face was hidden behind the mask of an ornate helm with a high crest decorated with oval gems. A long Witchblade was scabbarded across his back, and in his hand he carried a staff taller than Thirianna, topped with a sculpted detail of Vaul's anvil surrounded by lightning bolts.

Thirianna also wore her rune armour and helmet, her long Witchblade hanging at her left hip, a shuriken pistol holstered on the right.

Another farseer and three warlocks hurried up the extended ramp into the main body of the skiff, murmuring apologies for their late arrival. They sat on the opposite bench as the crystalline canopy extended from the hull and encased the group, distorting the glow of the hangar lamps into a rainbow. With a momentary surge that pushed Thirianna into her seat, the skiff lifted off and turned towards the shimmering field that acted as the door to the flight deck.

Thirianna was apprehensive as the skiff detached itself from the dock of the starship. Through the canopy Thirianna looked out at the webway with only her eyes. She had travelled it many times as a Dire Avenger, but her thoughts had always been engaged on the upcoming battle. Now her war-mask was less intrusive, her anger held in check for the moment. The Witchblade twitched in its sheath, sensing her thoughts.

The starship receded into the distance as the webrunner accelerated through the psychic tunnels of the eldar webway. Burrowing through the space between the real universe and the immaterial realm of the warp, the webway appeared as a shimmering tunnel of energy. The psychic field enclosing the corridor moved constantly, like a branch swaying in a breeze, undulating gently across the shifting warp tides. It appeared red through the lenses of Thirianna's helm, but in truth was of no real colour; the mind interpreted the swirling energies of the warp held at bay as a kaleidoscope of ever-changing rainbows and patterns.

Thirianna could feel the weight of psychic pressure surrounding her and was not in the least tempted to disobey Kelamith's instruction. She had no desire to let her mind free so close to the lair of daemons and other warp entities.

A pulsing gateway opened ahead, ringed with shimmering gold. Thirianna felt the wash of reality pouring into the webway like the draught from an opened door. It prickled her senses, bringing images of life and vitality after the cloying numbness of the webway's protective barriers.

The webrunner's driver steered towards the opening. There were other craft too – grav-tanks with sleek hulls and transports carrying Aspect Warriors. Around the main webway tunnel other passageways were forming – temporary creations that delved through space directly to the surface of Eileniliesh. Thirianna could see rangers moving on foot through these ad-hoc tunnellings, followed by squads of Striking Scorpions.

She wondered if one of them was Korlandril.

'Breaching the gate,' the driver told them.

The portal loomed around the webrunner, large enough for several vehicles to pass through at a time. It hung across the webway like a gate to the heavens, twin pillars of white and gold topped by a sharply curving arch. The runes on its surface shimmered with the light of the webway, small flickers of psychic energy dappling its pale surface. From this perspective, it seemed as if the webway simply carried on past the archway, but even without opening herself to the skein, Thirianna could feel the strange interface of warp and reality contained within the faint haze that spanned the gateway.

A Wave Serpent transport swept past, its curved hull a mottled blue and white, marked with the symbols of Alaitoc. Glancing back, Thirianna saw a swarm of jetbikes closing fast, their riders wearing silver, blue and white, laser lances in their hands: Shining Spear Aspect Warriors.

As the skiff approached the opening, Thirianna sensed the titanic energies contained by the web gate's crystalline circuitry. Passing through the plane, she felt as if a strong wind blew through her mind, sweeping away the background noise of the webway, leaving only the calm and quiet of the natural world. Peace and clarity filled her thoughts.

One moment Thirianna was in the webway, the next she was on Eileniliesh, looking back at the towering gateway of the web portal set against a star-filled clear sky. It was situated in a forest-ringed dell, two curving stone-like upthrusts marked with runes, a crackling sheen of energy flaring between them. The Shining Spears burst from the portal, banking their jetbikes to skim towards a roadway leading towards the settlement of Hirith-Hreslain. At the direction of Kelamith, the skiff pilot brought the craft to a gentle stop, hovering just above the ground.

Immediately, Thirianna ventured a portion of her mind into the skein and felt a familiar-yet-different sensation. Eileniliesh, like all Exodite planets, possessed a world spirit that ran through large parts of its crust. It seemed to Thirianna to be a locked, barren place in comparison to the throng of the infinity circuit, barred to her entry. For the briefest moment she was aware of the entire world, her mind spanning continents, flowing along gushing rivers, soaring between mountain peaks and delving into deep caverns.

The sensation passed and Thirianna was brought back to herself by Kelamith's light touch on her arm.

The canopy slid back and Thirianna took a breath of air through the filters of her helm. She smelt the freshness of the night air, leaves mulching beneath their branches bringing an undercurrent of autumnal decay. She could hear the buzzing of insects and a moth the size of her hand fluttered past in the light of Eileniliesh's moons. Over the tips of the trees Thirianna could see a tall tower, its summit a blazing beacon of bluish light that threw harsh shadows through the forest canopy.

Kelamith and the other farseer, Donoriennin, dismounted from the webrunner as a similar craft pulled alongside. A heavily armoured figure wielding a long spear and sporting an impressive crest of white hair on his helm alighted from the vehicle and met the two farseers on the soft turf.

'Arhathain,' said one of the other warlocks, an eldar almost twice Thirianna's age, called Keldarion.

'The autarch,' replied Thirianna, recognising the name. Arhathain was one of Alaitoc's foremost military leaders, destined to be remembered for generations for his victories. Thirianna was filled with admiration and a little fear by the fabled warrior. Like all autarchs he had trodden the Path of the Warrior several times in different Aspects, and that spoke of a frightening bloodlust unfamiliar to Thirianna; yet he had emerged from each occasion without succumbing to the entrapment suffered by the exarchs, and that spoke of immense willpower, discipline and personality.

Autarch and farseers held a short discussion, during which it seemed that Kelamith did most of the talking. Arhathain nodded frequently, listening to the advice of his counsellors. He made a few quick replies and returned to his transport. Kelamith and Donoriennin took their seats in the webrunner and the driver turned the craft after the departing autarch's vehicle.

'The settlement straddles a river,' said Donoriennin. 'The orks still revel in their destruction and their stain has yet to spread. The Exodites have done well to destroy the crude landing craft and keep the aliens from expanding their conquest, though they lack the strength to drive the invaders from the lair they have built. We will contain the orks in Hirith-Hreslain and then destroy the foul horde. Our ship will deal with the ramshackle ork transport in orbit, ensuring there is no possibility of reinforcement or escape. The main attack will come from this side of the river, into Hirith. Fire Dragons and Striking Scorpions have been despatched to intercept ork reinforcements coming across the river from their camp in Hreslain, the other part of the town.'

'Thirianna will accompany me in the main attack,' said Kelamith. Even through the lenses of his helm Thirianna could see the psychic light in the farseer's eyes. 'Donoriennin and Keldarion will be with the vanguard, Lurithein and Simmanain will lend their support to the flanking force moving along the river bank to relieve the squads lying in ambush at the bridge.'

There could be no argument. Kelamith and the other farseers had spent much of the journey to Eileniliesh delving into the various future paths the battle might take, reviewing each for the best outcome for Alaitoc. Though no fate was ever assured, their foresight did not just provide an advantage for the eldar, it guaranteed it; they had seen the victory for Alaitoc and divined the means by which to bring about that outcome. If the eldar stuck to the plan as drawn up by Arhathain from the prophecies of Kelamith and the others, they could not fail. The only uncertainty remaining was the courage and discipline of the individual warriors taking part.

The skiff was zipping between the broad trunks of the trees, cutting away from the roadway towards a glittering curve of river ahead. Jetbikes swooped and swerved between the boles, flashes of brightness in the darkness, while the larger vehicles made their way along the road.

Turning to follow the river, the eldar army stopped a short while later when they came into sight of the first buildings. The woods did not end abruptly but diminished in density as Hirith-Hreslain took over, nature and settlement blending seamlessly into each other.

The bulk of the town formed a crescent, arcing away from a curving span that crossed the slow river, leaving a wide space at its centre. The air was thick with smoke from ork fires and the stench of their encampment hung in Thirianna's nostrils despite her helmet's filtration systems. She snorted with disgust as the army moved out slowly, breaking into two distinct parts: transports carrying Howling Banshees crept along the river bank accompanied by Shining Spears. Kelamith and Thirianna dismounted along with the main force, the skiff moving away quickly to take the other seers to their appointed positions. Dire Avengers loped through the trees, shuriken catapults at the ready. Dark Reapers made their way into the nearby buildings, their dark forms reappearing at windows and balconies in the high towers. A pair of Falcon grav-tanks glided across the grass, heading towards an archway that led to the main thoroughfare.

Ahead of the main force, vague flitters of movement in the shadows showed the progress of the rangers, Aradryan most likely amongst them. They carried with them psychic beacon-markers that would enable the squads still in the webway to create openings in the heart of the town and launch the first wave of attacks against the orks.

Coming closer to Hirith-Hreslain, Thirianna could see the evidence of the ork occupation. Several towers had broken roofs and the walls were pocked with shell holes. Soot from burning marked many buildings, windows had been smashed and doorways broken in.

Worryingly, Thirianna could see no bodies and she shuddered to think of what had become of the Exodites slain in the ork attack.

The raucous talk of the orks echoed along the white-paved streets, along with the crackle of fires and the snap of random gunshots. Engines could be heard from across the river, faint but discordant against the sighing of the wind and the calls of night birds in the forest surrounding the settlement.

'Join me,' said Kelamith, coming to a halt in an arched alleyway at the edge of the town.

It was a moment before Thirianna realised the farseer wished her to conjoin their minds. Thirianna whispered the mantras, letting her psychic defences slip away so that her spirit and Kelamith's could enter the skein together. She felt the farseer's thoughts overlapping hers, soft but insistent. Relaxing, Thirianna allowed herself to drift into a psychic trance, trusting the warriors around her to protect them in this vulnerable state. Her last sight was of a dozen runes dancing above Kelamith's outstretched palm, and then she was inside the skein.

* * *

At first everything seemed to be anarchy.

Threads of fate wound about each other in impossible knots, tying together and splitting, writhing like a disturbed nest of serpents. Dozens of images flashed through Thirianna's thoughts: images of death and destruction, of dying orks and slain eldar. It was impossible to make any sense of the confusion, to discern meaning from the mass of seemingly random information. Her mind recoiled as it had done during her first foray into the infinity circuit, but now she knew how to respond.

Thirianna ignored the huge tides of fate washing over her and picked out a single thread, as she might locate a node or conduit of the infinity circuit. She concentrated all of her thoughts on that short stretch of time, pushing away everything else. Like leaves falling from the tree, the other fates being revealed to her fell away, allowing the thread on which she was focussed to expand and gain detail.

Before she could work out what she was looking at, Thirianna felt Kelamith's touch on her thoughts. Runes appeared across the skein, glowing with power, moving in strange patterns, interacting with the ever-shifting warp and weft of time.

'Follow me,' said Kelamith.

He seemed like a bolt of gold on the threads of fate. Latching on to Kelamith's psychic signature, Thirianna allowed herself to be dragged along in the wake of his divination, seeing flashes of the battle unfold. The runes acted as navigation beacons, and Kelamith steered towards one and then another, before veering wildly from the path for a short time to investigate a newly unfolding passage of events.

As they travelled, Thirianna was bombarded with sights and sensations. The crackle and bark of guns, the hiss of shurikens cutting the night air, the roars of the orks and the war shouts of the eldar. Warriors fought and died over and over, buildings crumbled and rebuilt, vehicles exploded and were miraculously restored as possible futures laid themselves upon Thirianna's mind.

The filth of the orks was everywhere, a cloying, overwhelming brutality that blotted out rational thought and compassion. Their bestial urges ran through every future, a mass of green-skinned violence and anger. Its power obliterated armies and engulfed planetary populations, fuelled by war and domination. It was in every ork and every ork was in the mass, a surging force of nature, elemental in its randomness, cataclysmic in its devastation. It could be beaten back, sometimes even tamed, but never destroyed.

And then came fire and blood.

'The Avatar!' said Thirianna.

It was like a vortex of fate, dragging in hundreds of other threads to itself, the rune of Khaine lingering above it. The Avatar's presence was like flames on a woven cloth, burning along the weave, destroying everything nearby. Blood soaked the skein, drowning lives by the score, washing over Thirianna with a wave of hatred and base rage.

The sensation almost overwhelmed her as her war-mask surged from the depths of her psyche, threatening to obscure her witch-sight. She struggled to keep her bloodlust at bay, to concentrate on the unfolding patterns of destiny, and after some struggle she repressed the urge to kill, the desire for war and death.

In doing so, she looked upon the skein with greater clarity. Suppressing the bright glare of the Avatar, she could see the winding and unwinding of lives in the knots and coils that had formed around it; enemies slain and followers tainted.

Thirianna had come to a standstill, halted by the encroachment of the Avatar; Kelamith blazed across the skein, seeming to be everywhere at once. Through his mere observations the skein was changing, becoming simpler, as redundant fates were cast away, never coming to pass. To see and reject a future was to consign it to non-existence, paving the way for new threads to emerge, new fresh possibilities to weaken or grow in strength.

All of a sudden, the farseer was back with Thirianna, surrounding her in an aura of gold.

'Tell me what you see,' said Kelamith.

Thirianna concentrated again, not seeing the skein itself but delving into its contents. She noticed a rune she recognised from her teachings – the Cave of the Mon-keigh. She allowed her thoughts to be guided by it, plunging into one possible future. She saw a massive ork, blade in hand, cutting apart Striking Scorpions, only to fall to the blades and shimmering fists of their exarchs; the alien's death howl echoed in her thoughts.

As she was about to depart, Thirianna caught a sense of something else, flavoured with recognition. Retracing her steps, the scene seeming to rewind through her thoughts, Thirianna paid more attention to the ork warlord's victims.

She froze, gripped by sudden anguish.

Korlandril was one of those that would fall to the ork's attack. Panicked, Thirianna pulled back, seeking the life-cord of Korlandril. It continued for a little while and then frayed, becoming dozens of ragged threads before disappearing into a haze of uncertainty.

'Does he die?' she asked.

'I cannot see any more than you,' said Kelamith.

'I should warn him,' said Thirianna. 'He could die.'

'There are some that die tonight and he may be one of them,' said Kelamith. 'You cannot prevent them all, and it may not even be desirable to save them.'

'He is my friend,' said Thirianna. 'I cannot just ignore this.'

'You focus on the wrong detail, child,' replied Kelamith. 'It is not the injury of your friend that is important. The ork warlord will die if we follow that path, and in its death others will be saved.'

'How…' Thirianna gave up trying to argue.

A miniature battle raged inside her thoughts. Her instinct was to save her friend, but Kelamith's logic fought back and the two sides reached an impasse. Was Korlandril's life worth two other eldar? Ten? Twenty?

'I understand,' she said, guilt threatening to consume her.

'There is no time for self-pity, child,' said Kelamith. 'The battle begins and Arhathain must make a few changes to the plan.'

Blotting the image of wounded Korlandril from her memory, Thirianna allowed herself to be drawn back into her body. She opened her eyes and saw in the small time display of her helmet that everything she had seen had taken less than two heartbeats to pass in the physical world.

Even as she was making sense of this, feeling disjointed and split between the real and the psychic, another presence intruded on her thoughts. It was like the bow wave of a boat, pushing everything before it, sending ripples far out through the skein.

Blood and fire.

Thirianna turned, as did many of the eldar moving into the town. A patch of air was alive with psychic energy, like fire crawling along an ember. The scent of blood, of charring flesh and melting iron filled the air, and again Thirianna was forced to fight back against her rising war-mask.

In the skein it had only been the Avatar's potential that she had fought against. Here she struggled against its actuality, with her mind still open like a portal left unlocked.

Waves of anger and hatred poured into her. Her Witchblade threw itself out of its sheath into her hand, crackling with psychic energy, its edge keening for blood. As the air split and a coruscating ring of fire appeared, Thirianna gritted her teeth and fought back the urge to slay and maim.

Feeling her will buckling as the Avatar approached, Thirianna became desperate. She ripped her mind free from the skein altogether, letting the barriers of her mind slam back into place, shutting her off from the deluge of rage. She fought to stay conscious, blood pounding through her veins, vision swimming.

The Avatar stepped from its portal, trailing smoke and sparks.

More than twice the height of Thirianna, the incarnation of the war god was a towering creature of metal and flame. The air around the Avatar recoiled from its heat, causing smoke and steam to writhe wildly. Psychic energy emanated from the creature, bringing a distant screaming and wailing to the edge of hearing. Its body was of ancient iron, a form of shifting plates barely holding in check the fiery being within.

A cloak of red cloth and flame trailed from its shoulders, held in place by a pin shaped like a long dagger. In its right hand, the Avatar held aloft a spear of immense proportion, its triangular head engraved with runes that burned with white flame. The weapon shrieked its bloodthirst – the Wailing Doom. The Avatar's left hand formed an enormous iron fist, blood dripping and steaming from its spiked knuckles.

Eyes of fire turned on Thirianna, who backed away from the apparition. The Avatar's gaze pierced her spirit for a moment, burning through her mental defences, bringing forth flashes of dying aliens and slain beasts – memories long repressed. The Avatar turned its head away and Thirianna let out a gasp of relief.

Leaving smoking footprints in its wake, the Avatar strode into the town, the eldar following close behind.

The eldar attack struck like lightning.

Guided by the web-beacons and signalled by Kelamith, the warriors that had remained in the webway opened temporary portals around the centre of Hirith-Hreslain. Tiny stars expanded into glowing gateways through which Dire Avengers, Howling Banshees and Fire Dragons stormed.

Power swords gleamed in the darkness of the night; the whisper of shurikens echoed from the white walls of the half-ruined town; the blaze of thermal guns and detonating plasma grenades lit up the plazas and streets. The orks, many of them still slumbering, died in their dozens to the sudden assault.

Roars and shouts, drums and horns sounded the alarm as the main force of the eldar closed in, sweeping around the ork camps to pin them against the river while the strike force tore into their centre.

The Avatar raced forwards, Wailing Doom in hand, charging directly for the greatest concentration of orks. More Aspect Warriors followed close behind, their exarchs leading their squads along rubble-choked streets and through the shells of destroyed buildings.

Kelamith and Thirianna followed a little distance behind. Every now and then the farseer paused to consult his runes; Thirianna joined with him during these moments to see the battle unfolding upon the skein.

As Kelamith had told her, the battle was a microcosm of the whole skein. Every bullet and shuriken, every sword blow and axe swing created uncertainty and possibility, the future branching out so quickly that it was impossible to follow every thread. Shadowing Kelamith, Thirianna observed how the farseer used his runes to seek out the pivotal moments, following the course of the Avatar, the ork warlord, the autarch, individual exarchs. Through these means, sense could be made of the senseless. The white noise of destruction gave way to specific detail and vivid scenes.

Thirianna moved back from Kelamith as his mind ventured towards the fighting on the bridge, fearing to look again at the fate of Korlandril. Instead she turned her attention to one of the other seers: Simmanain. He had progressed far further along the Path of the Seer than Thirianna, though his presence was a candle flame compared to the bonfires of the farseers. She watched Simmanain dancing along the narrow threads, moving from fate to fate, focussed on a handful of individuals.

As those threads were severed, she realised with a shock that she was witnessing the deaths of those Simmanain was fighting. It was frightening and yet invigorating to see cruel fate in action, brought about by the warlock's Witchblade.

'Come, child, our presence is needed,' said Kelamith a moment before he withdrew from the skein.

Thirianna detached her mind and followed the farseer as he broke into a run, stepping nimbly over fallen blocks of masonry that littered the street ahead. Kelamith brought them to a small square just a short distance from the main plaza. Fire and smoke erupted from a building on the opposite side, followed by the crash of large cannons. Shells screamed along a street towards the main eldar attack, detonating out of sight; Thirianna felt the sense of life lost as pinpricks of tragedy on her consciousness.

A squad of Dire Avengers appeared from the rubble to Thirianna's right, summoned by Kelamith. She recognised the rune on the back banner of their exarch: the Shrine of the Golden Storm. Together the Aspect Warriors and seers converged on the ork artillery.

'Ready your weapon,' warned Kelamith.

Thirianna felt the touch of his mind on hers, coaxing her into the skein for an instant. She glimpsed a wall of fanged, green faces and saw herself with Witchblade raised, fending off the swing of a heavy maul.

Reacting without thought, Thirianna swung her Witchblade up to the guard position as the eldar leapt through a broken wall into the artillery position. Deflected, an ork club swung harmlessly past her shoulder. The Witchblade moved in her hands, taking off the beast's arm below the elbow as it pulled back for another swing.

Reality and possibility flashed together, creating a near-instantaneous flow of images in Thirianna's mind. With her eyes she saw more than a dozen orks pouring from an adjoining room; with her thoughts she saw the ork next to her blazing a hail of bullets into her chest.

She leapt to the right as the ork opened fire, its shots spewing wide of their mark. Taking her Witchblade double-handed, Thirianna thrust the point into the ork's chest. The psychic sword thirsted for energy and she poured her power into it, plunging the blade through breastbone and heart and spine.

The growls and grunts of the orks filled the room along with the blare of pistols. Muzzle flashes illuminated leering, savage faces. In Thirianna's mind she saw an ork jumping down from the shattered floor above, its axe carving into the shoulder of a Dire Avenger.

With four swift steps she crossed behind Kelamith and shouted a warning, pointing her Witchblade towards the hole in the ceiling. The Dire Avengers parted as an ork almost twice their size plunged into their midst. Shuriken catapults sang, shredding the greenskin from several directions.

A shockwave of psychic power burst from Thirianna and she stumbled forwards as something crashed into her back. Her rune armour crackled with energy as she spun around to face her attacker. She had been too occupied by warning the others to foresee the blast of the ork's pistol into her back. Kelamith's sword parted its head from its neck with one sweep, blood spattering across the farseer's gem-encrusted helm. Kelamith said nothing as he turned away, directing the tip of his staff towards more orks lumbering through a doorway to his left.

Psychic lightning crackled.

The closest ork exploded into a mist of vaporising blood and bone dust. The one behind it was engulfed in flames as its padded jacket caught fire, fat bubbling away, muscle charring. A third juddered uncontrollably, finger tightening on the trigger of its gun, sending a hail of rounds into the back of another green-skinned brute.

As the glow of the attack faded, the Dire Avengers opened fire, sending a storm of shurikens into the survivors, slicing flesh and bone.

Behind their exarch, the Aspect Warriors dashed into the next room, shuriken catapults at the ready, Kelamith and Thirianna just two steps behind. They opened fire again, cutting down the small slave creatures manning three large-bore cannons.

'Disable them,' said Kelamith, nodding towards the artillery pieces.

Thirianna moved forwards, sword gripped in two hands. Copying the exarch, she brought the blade down into the breech of the crude gun, sending up a shower of sparks and droplets of molten metal as she poured psychic energy into the weapon. The Witchblade sheared through the breech and lock, cracks running along the poor-quality metal of the barrel with loud crackles and shrieks.

Glancing out of the ragged hole in the wall through which the pieces had been firing, Thirianna could see the main plaza. The Avatar was surrounded by a swarm of greenskins, the war god's incarnation carving left and right with the Doom that Wails. The flare of Dark Reaper missiles fizzed across the dark sky, exploding inside the buildings where a large number of orks had taken refuge.

'We must join the battle,' said Kelamith.

Seers and Aspect Warriors sprinted along the road towards the rest of the Alaitocii. Feeling the presence of other eldar, Thirianna glanced up and saw the dim figures of rangers, their longrifles rested on the broken rails of balconies and the sills of shattered windows. Unseen in the distance, orks died to their silent fire.

Reaching the main space at the heart of Hirith-Hreslain, the picture of the unfolding battle was clear. The orks occupied the few buildings left standing near to the river, a horde of leering faces and muzzle flares at the windows. The wreckage of several vehicles burned on the bridge, and in the light of the flames a squad of Fire Dragons and two groups of Striking Scorpions battled against the ork reinforcements. Thirianna wondered if Korlandril had fallen yet, but could not bring herself to seek the answer in the skein, fearing to see his thread cut short like those of the orks.

Two Falcon grav-tanks pounded the tallest of the remaining towers with pulse laser and shuriken cannon fire while other eldar forces moved from building to building, avoiding the killing field of the open plaza. A wildly corkscrewing rocket erupted from one of the ork lairs, fizzing across the square with a trail of sparks to hit the curved prow of a Falcon grav-tank, ricocheting from the angled armour before exploding. The thud of heavier weapons drowned out the whispering of shurikens and zip of lasers.

A sizeable mob of orks appeared from the river banks, clad in heavier armour than the others. More rockets and heavy calibre shells flared from their weapons as Thirianna and Kelamith took shelter behind the ravaged remains of a pool and fountain. The warriors from the Shrine of the Golden Storm broke to the right, crossing the cracked flags of the plaza as gunfire erupted around them.

Thirianna saw two Dire Avengers fall to the fusillade before they reached the shelter of a wall. She glanced at Kelamith, wondering why he had not warned them, but the farseer was intent on the newly arrived orks pushing forwards from the river.

From a sidestreet emerged the Shining Spears, their laser lances crackling with energy. In two lines, the jetbike riders curved around a toppled statue of Kurnous the Hunter and arrowed into the heart of the ork reinforcements. Laser blasts exploded with white light, smashing open armour and disintegrating flesh. Axes and claws gleaming with power fields were swung back at the swift Aspect Warriors, unseating one and smashing the jetbike of another. The Shining Spears swept past out of range and turned sharply, the shuriken catapults of their jetbikes spewing a hail into the orks that had survived the first charge. As the green-skinned brutes returned fire another jetbike exploded, sending the rider crashing into the burnt remnants of a tree. The Shining Spears lowered their weapons and dashed in again, sweeping away the last of the barbaric aliens in a bright ripple of laser lance detonations.

Fuelled by battle-lust, or perhaps possessing just enough foresight to realise they were trapped, the orks poured out of the buildings they had occupied in a haphazard counter-attack. Gunfire roared from the ruined buildings and flashed across the plaza. The orks charged in groups towards the eldar, their bellows and roars turning to shouts and howls of pain as las-fire and shurikens greeted them.

The Avatar strode towards the fray, spear keening madly. The war god's incarnation hurled its rune-etched blade into the approaching orks, the burning tip of the Wailing Doom ripping through half a dozen aliens in a bloody arc before returning to the Avatar's hand. Howling Banshees sprinted into the fray, their masks emitting piercing shrieks that coursed along the nervous systems of the orks, stopping them mid-stride. Swords gleaming with blue power fields sliced effortlessly through armour and flesh, flashing and sweeping in sinuous arcs.

Following Kelamith as he advanced on the orks, bolts of energy leaping from his fingertips, Thirianna skimmed across the surface of the skein, glimpsing the possible movements of her foes. A half-track vehicle that had eluded the ambush on the bridge appeared in her vision, its turret spewing flames. She glanced towards the alley from which it would emerge and saw that a squad of Fire Dragons were already waiting, alerted to the attack by Kelamith or one of the other farseers.

No sooner did Thirianna glance in that direction than the crude ork vehicle burst out of the darkness, fire licking from the muzzle of its small turret. The Fire Dragons opened fire as one, their thermal guns melting through the fuel tank being towed behind the orkish contraption. The explosion filled the narrow street with flame and debris, coating the walls and roadway with patches of burning oil.

The orks were now desperately trying to break through the encircling eldar line, hurling themselves forwards despite their heavy casualties. At a mental nudge from Kelamith, Thirianna headed right, glimpsing a possible breakthrough amongst the many futures unfolding. Dire Avengers poured hails of shurikens into the orks.

Yet the aliens pressed on, heedless of the growing number of deaths. Detonations erupted amongst the attacking aliens, scores cut down by the missiles of the Dark Reapers now in position in the upper storeys of the surrounding buildings. Still it was not enough to halt the reckless ork assault and the Dire Avengers took the brunt of the charge, firing their weapons until the last possible moment.

Their exarch leapt to the fore, a glimmering shield of energy on one arm deflecting the first flurry of blows, power sword slashing at limbs and throats. Kelamith and Thirianna arrived a few heartbeats later, their psychic weapons shimmering with energy. Thirianna slashed the tip of her Witchblade across the neck of the closest ork, cutting through its spine. She side-stepped the clumsy lunge of an ork with a growling chainsword and chopped away its leg as it stumbled past, swiftly following with a thrust into its back, her sword erupting from its chest as it fell.

Thirianna's rune armour flared as bullets hammered into her from the left. She winced at the shock of their impact, unhurt but startled by the unexpected storm of fire. There was simply too much happening to pre-empt every enemy action. Kelamith came to her assistance, casting a serpent-shaped rune into the air above the orks. A whirling apparition appeared out of the night sky, a burning snake that enveloped a handful of orks in flaming coils.

Recovering quickly, Thirianna rejoined the fight, her Witchblade moving with speed and precision, slicing and thrusting, despatching three orks in quick succession. Guided by her precognition, the warlock evaded their counter-blows, swerving away from danger, picking the right moment to strike at every instant.

Darkness fell upon the skein, blinding Thirianna's othersight. A torrent of brutish rage pummelled her thoughts, crushing her mind. A wave of cataclysmic energy engulfed her, accompanied by a psychic roaring that swamped all other sensation.

Mid-stride, Thirianna was hurled from her feet by an explosive blast. The detonation echoed in her mind as much as it had hurt her body, a wall of pure psychic power unlike anything she had experienced.

While patches of light danced across her vision, Thirianna righted herself and saw an energy-wreathed ork beyond the scattered bodies of the Dire Avengers. Green crackles of power crawled across its near-naked form and sparked from wildly wide eyes. It held a copper staff in one hand, trailing copper wires that jumped and fluttered with more psychic energy.

Thirianna delved into the skein, trying to find out why she had not detected the ork psyker earlier. She was swamped again by a deluge of orkish brutality, like a mental war shout that drowned out everything else. Like a volcano erupting, the psychic ork was a detonation of power, shredding the skein with its presence, blotting out everything else.

The ork shaman had a bodyguard of half a dozen warriors who laid down a curtain of fire from their automatic weapons, sending poorly-aimed volleys into the disorientated Dire Avengers. Kelamith threw out a blanket of darkness, shrouding the Dire Avengers from view as they leapt into the cover of a nearby ruin.

Ripples of green energy pulsed from the shamanistic ork, cracking the paving tiles underfoot. The waves hit the eldar, tossing them from their feet, a deep welt opening up in the ground beneath them.

Thirianna leapt nimbly over the widening crack, running into the darkness projected by Kelamith. The gleam of her Witchblade was extinguished and she could see nothing for a moment. Keeping in a straight line, she sprinted on, sword ready for the attack. Bursting from the psychic cloud, Thirianna found herself just a few strides from the closest of the shaman's minders. A moment later and her Witchblade had taken off its head, fiery sparks pouring from her sword.

As Thirianna ducked beneath the crackling power claw of the next ork, five figures appeared from the shadows behind the orks. Clad in heavy, segmented armour, their chainswords purring quietly, the Striking Scorpions fell upon the unsuspecting orks. Their exarch wielded a long, two-handed chainsword with which he cleaved down the spine of the shaman, splitting the alien's body to the waist.

The psyker's bodyguard were hacked down in moments, but there was little time to hesitate. The orks had been funnelled towards a single street by the rampaging Avatar and the missiles of the Dark Reapers. There were only a few dozen left, but their desperation made the orks dangerous.

Above the bark of guns and the whine of shurikens, ear-splitting screeches split the night air. Monstrous winged shapes dropped down from the clouds, silhouetted against the setting moons. Blasts of multicoloured lasers stabbed into the orks as the Exodite dragon riders plunged into the attack.

Thirianna felt a surge of awe when a chorus of ground-shaking bellows reverberated through the town as more of the Exodites' war-beasts entered the battle. Gigantic forces of nature harnessed by the Exodites, the immense reptiles thundered across the plaza towards the orks. With laser lances and fusion pikes, the Exodites closed, determined to exact revenge for the destruction of the town and the deaths of their kin. To them Arhathain had granted the final act of destruction, an opportunity to settle a bloody score with the green-skinned invaders.

Some of the Exodites were mounted on bipedal, predatory lizards with dagger fangs and slashing claws. Armed with pistols and blades, the Exodite knights slashed into the retreating orks, striking and withdrawing continuously. Other eldar crewed heavier weapons in howdahs upon the backs of gigantic reptiles. Pulses of white fire and burning lasers strobed through the orks, cutting down a score in one salvo. The dragons soared above, their riders raining down more las-fire and showers of plasma grenades.

Against the fury of the Exodites, the orks did not survive for long. They were cut down in short order, the wounded crushed beneath the feet of the advancing behemoths.

'The battle is won,' announced Kelamith.

Thirianna looked around the square and saw the hundreds of dead orks and several dozen wounded and slain eldar. She knew she should be sickened by the sight, that the memory would be enough to drive any eldar mad, but her war-mask shielded her from these dark thoughts, leaving them only as an abstract, intellectual consideration.

The warlock felt composed, recognising the scene from many like it witnessed on the skein. Thirianna was relieved; some of the glimpsed vision had showed far more eldar dead. She detached her thoughts from the skein, left with lingering images of the Alaitocii and Exodites scouring the ruins for hidden ork survivors.

The battle was indeed won, but the killing was not yet over.

LOST

The White Guardians – The Warp Spiders. The skein is not a benign realm, to be wandered without heeding its dangers; perils of a very fatal kind await the unwary. Not only this, the skein is open to manipulation, and there is no power more mutable than that of the Great Powers of the warp. In dealing with matters associated with such entities, the employment of the White Guardians is essential to keep the seer safe from both physical harm and psychical misdirection, as their namesakes guard the infinity circuit for similar dangers.

A cloud had settled upon Thirianna's spirit. Following the battle with the orks, she had returned labouring beneath a feeling of guilt and shame; guilt of foreseeing Korlandril's injury and shame for allowing it to happen. She cried for a cycle and half, swallowed by frustration and the burden of what she had seen. The limitation of her power was very evident. Without Kelamith to guide her, Thirianna could not find out what lay in wait for her friend, and she did not know whether he would live or die.

Something more tenebrous also nagged at her subconscious. It was not the misery of death or the bloodlust of battle; these things she had experienced before and her war-mask protected her from them. She could dimly recall being overwhelmed by the shamanic power of the orks, swept away by its elemental force. Like a rock caught in an avalanche, she had been tumbled across the skein, unable to find purchase, while Kelamith had remained unaffected.

She had seen nothing of the farseer in the five cycles since they had arrived back on Alaitoc, and knew better than to seek out Kelamith. If he was not to be encountered it was of his choosing.

Left to her thoughts and worries, Thirianna felt a stirring of jealousy for the farseer. His powers were prodigious, in reality as well as upon the skein. There were few places he would not venture – places he had forbidden his apprentice to enter – and Thirianna was sure that there were secrets out on the skein that she could uncover. Glimpsing the short, obvious intent of an attacking ork was one matter; discerning the interweaving web of motion and action of a group was something beyond her. Thirianna needed to know how to look further and deeper into destiny, and chafed at having to wait for Kelamith to lead her back into the infinity circuit.

At dawn-light on the sixth cycle since coming back to the craftworld, Thirianna decided to take matters into her own hands. She rose early from her bed, ate a light breakfast and headed to the Chambers of the Seers by herself. She easily found the node employed by Kelamith and started her preparations to immerse herself into the infinity circuit.

Before completing the mantra, Thirianna paused, her hand hovering above the warm, inviting curve of the node. Kelamith had explained nothing of the mores and taboos about the skein and Thirianna felt a pang of guilt, wondering if she was about to commit a transgression of seer tradition. Was it disrespectful to proceed without the authority of Kelamith? Would she be bringing disorder to the work of the other seers by her solo intrusion?

Thirianna dismissed her concerns; Kelamith had made no edict or ban on her using the infinity circuit by herself, and even for one whose communication was as esoteric as Kelamith she concluded that he would have made any such prohibition plain.

She placed her hand onto the node and started the mantra anew, peeling off the layers of physical form, ego and consciousness, allowing her unfettered mind to slip into the realm of dreams and futures.

To acclimatise herself, Thirianna headed first to some of her familiar haunts, allowing herself to be borne along by the pulsing energies of the infinity circuit. She loitered around the Eye of Aetheniar, dancing on the starlight that poured into the observatory, becoming one with the waves and particles that fell upon the banks of sensors and lenses.

Her mood lightened and she moved her presence across Alaitoc, spanning a distance in an instant that would take the best part of a cycle to travel by conventional means. She swam through the crystalline threads beneath the Dome of Haunting Whispers, catching snatches of poetry and lectures from the early cycle orators performing before crowds only they imagined. Thirianna bored quickly though, having spent too often in this place in her body, and skimmed along the craftworld's conduits towards the docking spires.

Even now she could still feel the after-presence of Aradryan, a light echo of his parting etched on the fabric of the infinity circuit. She delved into the transmissions and archives, seeking any news of where her friend's ship had gone after the battle with the orks. There was nothing, an emptiness left by the desire of the rangers to travel unheralded.

Saddened by this, Thirianna was about to head to the Dome of Crystal Seers when she felt a ripple through the infinity circuit. It was the gate astern of Alaitoc dilating, sending a shivering pulse of energy through the craftworld as a ship emerged from the near-warp of the webway.

Thirianna bobbed on the ripple for a moment, enjoying the sensation of distant stars seen and far-flung planets visited that was borne to Alaitoc in the starship's wake. As the webway closed again, Thirianna noticed something she had not seen before. Kelamith had warned her not to stray too close to the portal, for reasons he had not disclosed, but Thirianna now felt herself drawn in that direction. Curiosity, helped along by no small measure of petty defiance, urged her to have a closer look.

She was taken aback by what she discovered, though when she had thought about it for a moment she realised it should not have been a surprise.

The infinity circuit did not stop at the webway portal, but continued along insubstantial threads woven into the energy of the webway itself. Freed from crystal conduit and psychic lattice, the infinity circuit became a hazy fluctuation of energy that dispersed into the fabric of the webway tunnels.

It made sense, Thirianna decided. Though in many ways the webway was a physical thing, a tunnel that delved between the warp and the material universe, it was just as much a psychic construct. It was fixed in places, but for the most part was a shifting, ephemeral thing, its gates linking the distant, moving craftworlds together.

She had not considered such a thing before, or the implication of it. The webway was more than just a means of travel, it was the interstellar link between the surviving craftworlds, powered by and powering them in equal measure.

Edging closer, a little fearful of the power sustaining the webway, Thirianna saw that there were smaller portals, extending from other parts of the craftworld. In theory she had known about such things; to be part of them was a different experience entirely. Many of the older Aspect temples had small webway doors; there were likewise others that led to the Chamber of the Autarchs; the private residences of Alaitoc's oldest families had openings erected in the times before the Fall. Many were little more than vestigial passages, cut off and defunct, their purpose now forgotten or unnecessary. Some were still active but locked, barred by psychic shields and rune-forged barriers. She veered away from these, knowing that they had been closed for good reason. Like the Mirror of Nandriellein, they were tainted forever, doomed to betray any that used them.

Thirianna hesitantly moved into that part of the infinity circuit that was not physically encompassed within Alaitoc. The transition was seamless, from the partly physical to the purely psychic. As she neared the webway portal, the vagueness of the threads ahead resolved into more distinct pathways. Emboldened by this discovery, Thirianna ventured further.

There was a brief moment of dispersion as she moved into the fabric of the webway itself. She stopped, suddenly aware of how far she was from her body. The thought of her physical self interfered with her clarity of thought and for an instant she struggled to retain her collective presence, fighting against a pull that threatened to drag her back to her mortal shell.

Repeating the last verse of the mantra she had learnt, she stabilised her presence, reassuring herself that in the world of the skein, distance was as meaningless as time. Should she get lost or in trouble, Thirianna was confident that she could detach herself from the infinity circuit and would be brought back to her body without effort.

For a while she lingered close to the webway portal. There was a coldness here that seeped through her spirit. She realised that she was alone, though the presence of other seers flickered past occasionally as they made their own forays across the interstellar distances between craftworlds.

She felt a tremor of life as the portal opened and a ship passed into the webway, bringing its own miniature version of the infinity circuit. Spirit stones at the heart of the starship sent out psychic tendrils, their feathery touch on the webway moving through Thirianna as the ship accelerated away from Alaitoc towards its unknown destination. The crystalline matrix within the ship drew energy and information from the structure of the webway, becoming part of its psychic construction whilst its physical form remained distinct.

Thirianna suppressed an urge to take hold of one of the psychic tendrils and slide aboard the departing vessel. That would be too much of a risk, and she was content to wander by herself, glorying in the ever-widening branches of the infinity circuit as it traversed the galaxy.

There was no sense of time in this place, but Thirianna knew that she had been inside the infinity circuit for quite a while. In comparison to her earlier travels, this journey was by far the longest. Undeterred, she allowed herself to drift away from Alaitoc, following the after-echoes of the ship that had left, buffeted gently by its psychic wake.

The webway split not far from the Alaitoc portal, becoming several large shafts and many more smaller ones. With a metaphorical last glance back at the portal, Thirianna chose one at random and swooped along it, breaking free from her worries as she broke free from the psychic well of her home.

Here it was truly lifeless.

The coldness of the void between stars permeated the webway's walls, dissipating its energies. As Thirianna moved on, she encountered patches of resistance, areas of thinness in the fabric of the webway where the physical universe was trying to encroach upon the framed space created between realities.

There were signs of damage, or perhaps poor maintenance. She did not see them, she had no eyes to speak of, but became aware of the frailty of the infinity circuit along certain stretches.

Everything had been silent and blissful after the relative metropolis of the dead that was Alaitoc's circuitry. Now came a distant whispering.

Fear gripped Thirianna as she realised how far she had come and how foolish she had been to venture here without protection or escort. She felt alone and tiny, a mote of existence suspended between life and death by a fragile thread of ancient engineering.

As the whispering grew louder, coming closer, Thirianna moved away from it, frightened by its presence. It was not just the material world that could break into the webway; the warp also exerted its own pressures on the structure, and where it was breached, the denizens of that immaterial realm could enter.

Thirianna stopped her retreat, aware that she could not discern whether she was moving back towards Alaitoc or further from it.

She had ventured far enough and it was time to return, Thirianna decided. The seer let her grip on the psychic matrix loosen, expecting to be drawn back to her body.

Nothing happened.

She tried again, thinking of her body, of the physical Alaitoc, of the singularity of Mind and Being and Form. Still she was bound within the twining energies of the webway and the haunting whispers were now almost upon her, chilling her spirit with their presence.

Thinking that perhaps she could broaden the vista of her interaction and find the way back, Thirianna allowed her presence to dissolve, spreading along the skein in every direction. She thought she saw a glimmer of heat, of life, of energy that could be Alaitoc. Yet at the same time, her spirit touched upon something utterly alien and utterly repellent.

Disembodied, Thirianna could not scream. Her flare of despair and dread caused a ripple across the skein as she drew herself back to a single point of consciousness. The wave of fear seemed to echo forever, betraying her presence to every sentience in the vicinity. Thirianna was aware of being discovered, of being exposed to any passing predatory thing. She tried to make herself invisible, to blend with the fabric of the webway, but her fear caused convolutions to pulse across the infinity circuit, spasming its structure as sobs might wrack her physical form or a twitching fly might alert a waiting spider.

Like a noose tightening around her, the things that hunted Thirianna closed in. If she stayed where she was, she would be trapped and helpless. Mustering all of her courage, Thirianna summoned up as much willpower as she could find. She became a sparkling mote of energy in the webway and in a moment she had fled, flashing across the infinity circuit, turning left and right, heading up and down, turning around and about, heedless of the direction as long as it was away from the things that had stalked her.

Stopping, Thirianna knew that she was truly lost now. There was not the faintest glimmer of Alaitoc's warm presence.

There was something else though, bending the skein with its weight, distorting the webway. Thirianna could not sense it directly; whatever it was had a masking field around it, shielding it from detection. It was only by its effect on the nearby strands of the webway that it could be located, like a glass lens that can only be seen because of the light passing through it.

Thirianna had a suspicion that she knew what it was: a reality pocket. A piece of the material universe had been wrapped up in the fabric of the webway, hidden from both the mortal and immortal realms. There were many reasons for such pockets to exist, and most of these webway sanctuaries pre-dated the Fall. Given her recent experiences, Thirianna was reluctant to investigate further, but necessity outweighed caution; she had to find some means of getting back to Alaitoc and the bubble world might contain someone that could help.

Thirianna moved towards the reality pocket, probing gently at its borders. It did strange things to her sense of self, like a convex or concave mirror bending her image; she felt herself simultaneously stretched thin and yet terribly heavy.

Pushing past the discomfort, Thirianna slid into the pocket world. A moment later she saw that she had made a terrible mistake.

A spire of dark material speared up from a rocky foundation, extruded from the inner surface of the webway duct. At first Thirianna had no comprehension of scale; she was a fragment of consciousness with no form to judge her surroundings. As she observed the black tower, she realised that it was enormous, and that the flecks of darkness spiralling around its summit were in fact eldar with winged flight packs.

Everything moved with such slowness here, compared to the thought-quick interactions of the unfettered infinity circuit. Dragging herself around the edge of the reality pocket, catching a glimpse of a miniature dark blue star above the tower, Thirianna saw three long walkways extending from one side of the tower. The pair of starships docked at two of them revealed their function as quays, but the ships were like nothing Thirianna had seen coming or going from Alaitoc.

They were undoubtedly warships: weapons blisters extended the length of their hulls. Their lateen-like solar sails were raked heavily back, two large and one small, and the prow of each vessel had a ram-like extension that glittered with an energy field.

The webway encompassed the world of the tower but did not penetrate it. The threads of the infinity circuit surrounded the bubble but made no inroads towards the tower itself. Thirianna could see small figures of eldar walking along gantries and the docks, but she had no means of approaching closer.

When she realised what the eldar on the dockside were doing, she decided that it was for the best that she could not come any closer.

The eldar, garbed in highly stylised, barbaric clothing, bearing whips and scourges, were leading a seething mass of aliens from their ship to a yawning gate in the side of the tower. As the portal opened, the sound of shrieks and moans filled the air. Thirianna felt wave after wave of torment roiling around the reality bubble; agony unending poured like a flood from the gate of the tower.

Turning her attention to the newest arrivals, Thirianna recognised humans, several dozen of them, amongst the miserable throng. The other creatures, some hairy, some scaled, some squat and misshapen, others upright with two arms and legs like eldar, were not known to her. They were all bound in energy cuffs, glowing bands of red around their ankles and necks. She could not see any more detail, and for that she was grateful.

Thirianna felt herself being ripped apart as a portal appeared in the fabric of the pocket, tearing from the webway into the compressed region of reality. Another ship appeared through the gate, an armed sloop smaller than the two other vessels. Its black and red hull glistened like the scales of a fish as it banked towards the highest of the docks.

The pirate lair could not provide the information Thirianna required and to be here was dangerous in the extreme. She extricated herself from the reality pocket with another mind-churning sensation, leaving the raiders to their despicable lives.

Now that her panic had subsided, Thirianna was able to take better stock of her situation. She was lost in the webway, some distance from Alaitoc. The best way to locate the craftworld would be aboard a ship, and her best chance of finding a ship would be to locate one of the larger arterial routes. She could sense that the webway around her was a tangled mess of smaller passages and tunnels, caused in no small part by the distortion of the pirates' sanctuary. She would be lost in here forever if she tried to get past the lair, so she turned back, her nervousness returning as she considered the fact that she was moving back towards the place where whispering creatures had come for her.

A moment or an eternity passed, it was impossible to tell which. Thirianna was sure that she was heading in the right direction. The webway seemed to be widening, but Thirianna could not shake the nagging feeling that the further she moved, the greater the distance was growing between her and Alaitoc.

Her mood flitted through various phases: frustration, fear, hope, anxiety, and back to frustration. The infinity circuit responded to her presence, her state of mind, echoing back her inner thoughts, reflecting her sudden moments of excitement and dread.

After some time Thirianna realised again that she was not alone. This time she tried her hardest to master her fear, balling it up deep inside her, not allowing it to disturb the skein of the webway. Things, formless things of dead eyes and dagger fangs and eternal hunger, flitted past her.

Their touch was freezing, but Thirianna did not respond. She was a patch of energy in the webway, an aberration not prey, nothing of interest to the mindless hunters.

The predators circled slowly, nudging at the fabric of the webway from without, trying to push their way in. Thirianna moved slowly away, so slowly it was almost imperceptible in comparison to the lightning-fast speeds she had travelled before.

Now and then she stopped, sensing the hunters coming closer again, their interest piqued by this fuzzy patch of warmth and life. Thirianna tried not to panic, tried hard to dim her thoughts, to suppress memories of home and friends, giving nothing for the predators to seize upon. She was a mote of existence, a part of the universe, and nothing more.

Heat suffused the infinity circuit. It grew gradually, like dawn breaking. From its warmth the hunters turned tail and fled.

Relief flooded through Thirianna. She was sure the warmth was something good. As it crept across the skein, it filled her with hope. It was like the caress of a lover, gentle and relaxing, coaxing her into sleep. It was the embrace of a mother, swaddled in soft cloth, gently rocking into somnolence.

Violet surf lapped at the pale blue sand, the warm water touching Thirianna's toes. Above, a bright orb of silver illuminated the scene, casting soft shadows across the rippled beach. A figure approached from Thirianna's right still some distance away. She smiled, recognising the gait of Aradryan. He was dressed in a loose-fitting robe of white and grey, and held a hand to his brow to shield his eyes, which glittered in the silvery light.

Thirianna stood up, reaching out a hand in welcome. As her friend came closer she realised she had made a mistake. It was not Aradryan that approached, but Korlandril. The sculptor's face was masked by his hair, tousled across his features by the gentle breeze. He was smiling, eyes alight with amusement.

'This is a nice place,' said Korlandril, stopping beside Thirianna. He looked out across the glittering water. 'It was nice of you to invite me.'

'I thought we should spend a little time together,' said Thirianna, though in truth she could not recall any agreement to meet her friend. 'We have to talk.'

'We can spend more than a little time,' Korlandril said, smiling lopsidedly. He reached out a hand and stroked Thirianna's arm. His touch set her nerves alight, sending a shiver of pleasure through her body. 'We can stay here as long as we want.'

'I'm not sure,' said Thirianna. She wanted to pull away her arm, but Korlandril gently gripped her wrist and tugged her closer. His dark eyes bored into hers, full of passion.

'I made something for you,' he said, producing a fine golden bracelet from his robe. He held it out for Thirianna to slip her hand into.

She hesitated.

'When did you start making jewellery?' she asked. 'I thought portraiture was your speciality.'

'Let us see what it looks like on your arm,' said Korlandril, ignoring the question. He pulled her hand closer. 'Just put it on and we can see.'

'You have never given me a gift before,' said Thirianna, disturbed by Korlandril's insistent manner.

'You have never declared your love for me before,' replied her friend. He moved the bracelet towards Thirianna's fingers but she snatched away her hand.

'This is not right,' she said. Thirianna looked around, not recognising where she was. There were few parts of Alaitoc she had not visited, in person or in spirit, and her surroundings felt unfamiliar. The thought spurred a memory.

'You stopped being a sculptor,' said Thirianna, taking a step back from Korlandril. 'You became a warrior.'

'I could not bear to be away from you,' said Korlandril, pacing forwards to stay beside her. 'Your love has conquered my hate. Why not just accept my gift for what it is? Put it on and we will sit here and talk. We have as much time as we want, nobody will disturb us.'

'No,' said Thirianna, shaking her head. She tried desperately to recall how she had come back to Alaitoc. She could not. The last thing she remembered...

'This is not real,' Thirianna said, backing away from Korlandril. 'I was stuck in the webway. I still am, aren't I? What are you?'

'I am your friend,' said Korlandril. 'You know who I am. Put on the bracelet and together we will go home. I know the way.'

'You are not Korlandril.' Thirianna felt panic rising in her breast. She did not know what the apparition was, but it was certainly not her friend.

Korlandril looked genuinely hurt, his brow furrowing with disappointment. Clouds gathered quickly overhead, obscuring the silver sun, swathing the beach in gloom. The figure of Korlandril pursed his lips and gently shook his head.

'Why did you have to spoil this beautiful time together?' he asked. 'I thought you wanted to be with me? Is that not what you desire?'

'You are not Korlandril,' Thirianna said again. She glanced over her shoulder and saw that the beach stretched away to the horizon in every direction. The thing pretending to be Korlandril grabbed her wrist again and held up the bracelet.

'Put it on,' he insisted. Thirianna splayed her fingers as Korlandril tried to force the band over her hand. He snarled and twisted her arm, forcing her to her knees. 'Put it on or I will get angry!'

The clouds had become very dark now and the sea was heaving, flecked with foam, the waves crashing noisily against jutting crystal shards that had thrust up from the sandy shore.

'Leave me alone!' shrieked Thirianna, squirming in the grasp of the imposter.

'We will be together for eternity, just as you desire,' said Korlandril. 'It is what you want above all other things.'

'It is not,' said Thirianna, falling still. 'I do not love you.'

'Everybody loves me,' said the apparition. 'Do not lie. Do not resist your own heart's desire.'

Thirianna kicked out at the creature's leg, ripping free her hand as it stumbled. The sand had become beads of black glass, shifting underfoot as Thirianna tried to get to her feet. The waves were black too, and the sky a menacing purple and red.

'You cannot leave me,' Korlandril shouted after her as Thirianna turned and ran.

She had taken only a few paces before she stopped, the apparition appearing in front of her.

'It is better that you choose to spend eternity with me,' it said. 'I can make your existence an unending pleasure. Love me as I love you and you will never know fear or anger or sadness again. Accept our love for what it is, binding and forever.'

The thing took a step closer, hand held out, but stopped and glanced up at the sky. Thirianna looked to the clouds as well and saw that they were parting. It looked like snow was falling, though the clouds were shredding above, turning to thin wisps of grey. The white shower fluttered closer and closer.

'No!' snarled Korlandril. 'Leave us in peace!'

As the flickering downfall of white came closer, Thirianna could see beyond that the world was melting away. The sky had becoming the whirling miasma of the webway, the sea likewise dissipating into tatters of colour.

There was not just one of the creatures, there were dozens. They were all possessed of half-male, half-female bodies, with a single breast each, and huge, glittering, entrancing eyes. Thirianna was surrounded by them, as the daemons stalked forwards on bird-like legs and taloned feet. They had long claws for hands, which snickered and snapped in a staccato rhythm as they closed in. The closest held a golden manacle and chain, and lunged for Thirianna, but she dodged aside to evade its clacking grasp.

Thirianna recognised them immediately and was terrified. They were lesser daemons, servants of She Who Thirsts, embodiments of the Great Enemy.

She tried to flee but was surrounded.

The daemonettes paused and looked around, themselves frightened in turn.

Trailing crystalline threads, the warp spiders descended upon the webway, tens of thousands of the tiny creatures. In a pale wave they swept over the daemons, miniscule mandibles biting deep, covering the creatures from clawed feet to crested scalps. The daemons fought back, slashing with their claws, raking great furrows in the mass of the white Guardians.

More figures appeared from the gloom, shining white silhouettes bearing swords and spears. As blazes of pure light they struck into the daemons, shattering them, leaving blossoms of fading sparks as they cut and slashed at the immaterial creatures.

Thirianna felt the light folding around her, forming a cocoon of energy, gentle yet strong. The light infused her, seeping through her spirit, transforming her into pure energy. She felt the touch of another presence upon her thoughts, wordless yet reassuring.

She allowed the light to lift her and in moments she was away, flashing across the webway, leaving the battling apparitions far behind.

With a gasp, Thirianna opened her eyes. She swayed for a moment and then collapsed, her hand falling from the infinity circuit node.

She did not lose consciousness, but felt weak and dizzy, her vision swimming. It was not her body that ailed but her mind. Images from her experience flashed through her thoughts, disorientating her further. She struggled to compose herself and between the visions half-glimpsed a ring of other eldar around her, five in all.

She recognised Kelamith, his face contorted in a fierce scowl of concentration. His fingers twitched at his sides, while several runes spun around him, whirling about on eccentric orbits.

In a few moments the nausea passed and Thirianna was able to sit back against the curve of the wall, catching her breath. She shuddered at the recollection of what happened and her waystone burned bright upon her breast, glowing blue, hot to the touch.

She had been so foolish, so naive. What had she been thinking, to dare the webway alone, inexperienced and helpless? She started to sob, realising how close she had come to being trapped by She Who Thirsts. She had risked not just death, but an eternity of torment devoured by the creation of the eldar's own hedonistic past.

Still shuddering, she flinched as a hand touched her shoulder.

Looking up, she saw Kelamith. She expected a rebuke, but his face was kindly, his lips curved in the slightest of smiles. Taking his hand, Thirianna allowed herself to be helped to her feet.

'I am sorry,' she said, burying her face in the cloth of his robe, more tears flowing.

'It is I that am sorry, child,' said Kelamith, holding a hand to the back of her head. 'I should have been more watchful.'

Thirianna pulled back and looked at the farseer.

'I put all of us in danger,' she said. 'What if those… things had taken me, turned me to their cause?'

'They did not,' said Kelamith, patting her hand. 'That is a credit to you. You are stronger than you think. Not every person can resist their wiles. Yet I apologise again, for I had seen that you would venture forth on your own. I did so, when I first started, and I thought it would be good for you to find your own way. I did not see how much peril awaited you, and I should have done.'

'You knew I would get lost?' said Thirianna. 'You allowed me to wander free, knowing what it might have led to?'

'Heed this warning,' said Kelamith, now with a stern expression. 'Of the many possible outcomes, only this one put you at risk. I judged it worthwhile to let you have your own time, thinking the chances of disaster were remote. Yet no matter how unlikely an outcome might be in regards to all of the others, while it remains possible it must be considered. Had I known for sure that this would happen, I would have intervened. As it is, I did not think you powerful enough to travel so far and become so embroiled in the eternal matrix.'

'The eternal matrix?' said Thirianna. She had not heard the phrase before.

'It is the realm that binds together the infinity circuits of all the craftworlds, part of the webway and part of something else,' explained Kelamith. 'It is as close to the unbound skein as any artifice of ours can be, made of the raw stuff of the ether. A novice such as yourself cannot usually travel far upon it.'

'And what will you do now?' said Thirianna, casting her gaze at the marble-like floor. 'I suppose I have proven myself very short-sighted. I will understand if you do not wish to be my teacher any more.'

'I think that more than ever I wish to be your teacher, child,' said Kelamith. 'You show great potential, not just of psychic power, but of curiosity, resolve and self-belief. These are vital attributes if you are to reach the full extent of a seer's abilities. I would be more worried if you had not explored on your own.'

Thirianna looked around and saw the other seers nodding in agreement.

'Return to your chambers. You have had an ordeal that would test the greatest of us,' said Kelamith. 'Think on what has happened to you, and with the next cycle come to me again and we will continue with your training.'

REUNION

The Twin Birds – Hawk and Falcon. All runes work in conjunction with each other, but there are several pairing and sibling runes that can only facilitate a true reading together. The most prominent of these are the Twin Birds, formed as one and divided only upon the skein. In many cases the two fates of different individuals may be deeply entwined, seeming as one; in such circumstance the Hawk and Falcon are able to discern points of digression, each following its own path to highlight possible divides and moments of reunion.

After her dramatic first foray into the eternal matrix, Thirianna was content to roam the more orderly confines of Alaitoc's infinity circuit. Areas previously seen as staid and safe were now sanctuaries of stability for the seer, refuges she attended constantly to maintain her sense of self and a degree of mental balance.

She progressed well under the tutelage of Kelamith, using the infinity circuit to open up the vistas of the wider skein with greater control and focus. Her wanderings became more concentrated, though she lacked the true ability of free navigation and frequently required the guiding spirit of Kelamith to show her the way.

For some considerable time this continued and Thirianna honed her powers every cycle, growing again in confidence, the dark memories of her near-capture by the daemons receding.

After her latest session in the infinity circuit, Thirianna was not dismissed by Kelamith. Instead the farseer invited her to walk with him in the gardens outside her residence.

They talked about the lessons learnt and Thirianna's hopes for the coming cycles, but it was obvious that something else was on the farseer's mind. The pair of them stopped at the height of an arcing white bridge over a shallow ravine, the shadows of the dome's towers long across the hills and scattered woodlands.

'You have come a long way to mastering your psychic sense,' said the farseer, hands clasped behind his back. Thirianna leant on the rail and glanced down at the thin rivulet of water passing under the bridge.

'I feel as if I have only stepped into the shallows,' said Thirianna. 'The sea of knowledge extends far further than we have travelled already.'

'That is true, and it is why we must now venture further from the shore,' said Kelamith. 'Until now, you have acted as your own anchor. As you experienced in your time upon the eternal matrix, there are limits to our power while confined by our bodily conduit. To see further, to wade further into the sea of knowledge, we must lay before us beacons to follow. In this way we can follow their direction far out into the future, but be assured of the direction home.'

The farseer brought forth a rune from his belt, no larger than the tip of his thumb. It was made of dark blue wraithbone, gleaming slightly with its own power. The rune spun lazily at the end of Kelamith's extended finger.

'The runes are our beacons, our stepping stones into the distance,' he continued. 'Until now you have used your mind and body to channel the power of the skein, and there are limits to what we can withstand. The runes provide new avenues of exploration. If you think of the barriers between reality and the future as a wall, the runes open new gates for us to pass through. Each has its own specific purpose, opening up new vistas beyond that wall and guiding our minds to their destinations. They also act as a valve, ensuring that the power we tap into does not overcome us, shielding our thoughts from She Who Thirsts.'

Thirianna shivered at the mention of the eldar's darkest foe and almost lost the meaning of the farseer's words. She pushed aside the rising memories of the webway to concentrate on what Kelamith had said.

'Each rune increases our power,' said Thirianna.

'In a way,' replied Kelamith. 'In themselves they contain no power, but they enable us to channel more psychic energy. It is a balance. To control a number of runes requires considerable mental dexterity and focus. At first, we begin with a single rune.'

'You think it is time for me to learn runecraft?' said Thirianna, excited by the prospect.

'Certainly it is, child,' said Kelamith. 'Each rune is a unique thing, bonded to its seer, an extension of their Form. When you come to me next cycle, I will take you to have your first rune fashioned.'

'Which shall it be?' Thirianna asked. There were several hundred that she knew of now, each with its own benefits and challenges, abilities and traps.

'We all begin with the same,' said Kelamith. 'The rune of Self. Our personal rune. It is our incarnation upon the skein and no runecraft is possible without it.'

They arranged to meet in the following cycle and Kelamith departed, leaving Thirianna to think on this next stage of her development. The possibilities intrigued her and the idea of taking this important step gave her a sense of achievement she had not felt since becoming a seer. The image of the rune of the seer and the rune of herself were as one in her mind, inseparable, one the symbol of the other. It was a sign of her progress that she was about to embody that image she held in her mind, and she returned to her chambers full of anticipation.

'Is this a trick?' Thirianna demanded, as Kelamith waved for her to enter the bonesinger's workshop.

'There is no trickery,' the farseer assured her.

'Yet you must know who practices his craft here,' said Thirianna.

'I do know,' said Kelamith, expression impassive. 'Yrlandriar is one of the foremost bonesingers of Alaitoc. He has fashioned many seer runes.'

'He is my father!' said Thirianna, knowing that Kelamith had to be aware of the fact.

'So you no longer profess to be the child of Wishseer Aurentian? A strange time to make such a confession,' said Kelamith, his eyes showing intrigue.

'Aurentian was more my father than Yrlandriar, after the death of my mother,' replied Thiriama. 'Yrlandriar is no father to me.'

'Yes, he is,' said Kelamith, unperturbed. 'You are very fortunate.'

'Fortunate?' Thirianna almost spat out the word. 'Yrlandriar is a selfish, cantankerous tyrant. I will have nothing to do with him.'

The farseer's patient expression did not change. He turned at the high archway and clasped his hands together. A glow of psychic energy lit up Kelamith's eyes and his voice took on the otherworldly cant Thirianna now associated with the farseer's forays onto the skein.

'Yrlandriar will fashion the rune of Thirianna,' he intoned slowly. 'With it, she will continue on the Path of the Seer, learning her own fate and that of many others.'

'There are other bonesingers,' said Thirianna, unconvinced by this fatalistic declaration. 'I will have one of them fashion my rune.'

'That is not what will happen,' said Kelamith, his voice returning to normal, eyes dimming. 'Your objections are juvenile, not worthy of a seer of Alaitoc.'

Thirianna stood firm, unwilling to indulge in the farseer's manipulation. 'You think that I make this choice out of whim or spite?' asked

Kelamith, a touch of anger now showing in his furrowed brow. 'Listen to me, child. As a seer you will see many fates that you cannot change. If you cannot accept them, you will be driven mad, tormented by possibilities that never existed. If your father does not fashion your rune, your time with me is finished.'

'Perhaps another farseer will continue my instruction,' said Thirianna, crossing her arms defiantly. 'Surely there is at least one other that sees my potential.'

'That is pride,' snapped Kelamith, causing Thirianna to flinch. It was the first time the farseer had raised his voice to her, and she felt a momentary pang of guilt. 'No other will take you, I will ensure that.'

'You are not being fair!' said Thirianna. 'It has been many cycles since my father and I spoke last, and I do not wish him to be a part of my life.'

'If that is the case, you have a difficult choice to make,' said Kelamith, calm again. 'You can continue to shun your father and find another Path, or you can become a seer and reconcile yourself to his existence.'

Thirianna wrinkled her lips in distaste, prompting Kelamith to turn away and start back down the passageway towards the grav-disc that had brought them to the Dome of Artificers.

'Wait!' Thirianna called after him. She clenched her fists in annoyance, but kept her frustration from her voice. 'I will speak with Yrlandriar, but only to ask for a rune.'

Kelamith stopped and turned back, waving a hand towards the doorway.

'That is all you have to do, child,' he said.

Thirianna took a deep breath and headed through the archway, steeling herself for the impending confrontation.

The chamber beyond was large and semicircular, opening out onto an even wider expanse that ran across a large part of the width of Alaitoc. The room was bare, in surprising contrast to Thirianna's expectations. A few pedestals displayed small works of art; an open cabinet held various works-in-progress; a central table was home to an assortment of cups, dishes and plates holding the remnants of several meals.

All of this Thirianna took in at a glance; her attention was snatched away by the scene beyond. In the massive nave-like chamber there hung what appeared to be the spine and ribcage of some vast primordial animal. As Thirianna approached the open side of the room she recognised what she was seeing – the central structure of a starship.

Gleaming lights shone from the ivory-coloured wraithbone, illuminating every part of the ship-to-be. It was the first time she had seen such a vessel under construction and it took her breath away. All thoughts of Thirianna's many disputes with her father were forgotten, swept away by the majesty of the creation before her. It was a large vessel, though by no means the largest, stretching for half of the hangar's length. The scale was only brought home to her when she saw the tiny figures on the gantries surrounding it.

Though she was not well versed in such things, it looked to Thirianna that the bulk of the work had been completed. The dorsal structure and splay of curving spars towards the prow put her in mind of a shark, front-heavy but delicately poised. The rib-like spurs shortened towards the stern before they abruptly widened into a three-finned tail. Looking up, she could see the massive round apertures where the solar sails would be fitted and in the unlit gloom above she caught the glitter of the panels ready to be lowered into place.

As much as Thirianna saw the starship, she could feel it as well. The wraithbone pulsed slowly with psychic power, barely registering against the background of the infinity circuit, but with its own distinct timbre. The skeletal structure nestled on a cradle of crystalline towers, connecting it to Alaitoc, feeding it the power of the craftworld.

Thirianna studied the details, recognising some of the fluted work along the sides of the fuselage as settings for gun batteries. It was a warship, and the knowledge brought a hint of menace to the entire affair. She imagined the laser turrets and plasma accelerators that would be fitted, turning this graceful piece of art into a machine capable of dealing unimaginable destruction. The steady throb of psychic power now seemed edged with waiting potential, a beast slumbering, waiting for the command to unleash its fury.

The eldar working on the slender gantries and scaffolding were dressed in light tunics and tight-fitting bodysuits. They were implanting crystal nodes and gem-like energy studs into the wraithbone, coaxing the psychoplastic to accept the jewels with whispered words and intricate gestures.

'This is… unexpected.'

Thirianna turned at the sound of her father's voice. He walked from under the crystal cradle to her right, his open-fronted robe reaching to the floor, an intricate set of musical pipes under one arm. His expression was stern, eyebrows meeting in a frown beneath a high forehead. Yrlandriar's black and purple hair was bound up in an intricate knot fixed with several jewel-headed pins and his hands were encased in metallic gloves, delicately segmented and chased with golden rune designs.

'Kelamith sent you,' he said, walking past Thirianna into his workshop.

'I did not desire this meeting, but I have been left no choice,' said Thirianna. 'Kelamith is stubborn.'

'A trait with which you are all too familiar,' said Yrlandriar. He gestured and a stool rose up from the blue fabric of the floor, next to the table. As the bonesinger sat down, placing his pipes in front of him, Thirianna noticed he did not offer her a seat.

'I see you have lost none of your hypocrisy,' she said. 'If you could but spare a few moments of your precious time I am sure you could compose a whole treatise on the merits of intractability.'

Yrlandriar eyed her coolly, legs and arms crossed.

'Your foolishness begets response,' he said. 'That you chose to ignore my advice is further proof of your selfishness.'

'Advice?' Thirianna made no attempt to hide her scorn. 'You wanted to control me, and nothing less. Just as you wanted to control my mother.'

'You have none of your mother's qualities,' the bonesinger said, a sneer creasing his face. 'It is only good fortune that you did not share her doom. And now you wish to play at being a seer? How long before you grow bored of that?'

'It was your manner that fanned the fire of Khaine within me and drove me to the shrines of the Aspect Warriors,' Thirianna snarled back. 'Perhaps it was the same for my mother.'

'How little you understand,' said Yrlandriar, looking away. 'It was a desire to protect you, her child, that called to Mythrairnin.'

'And you blame me for that,' said Thirianna. 'I was only a child when she died, but you held me responsible. You could never accept that she chose me over you.'

'Perhaps it was your behaviour, your spoilt demands and incessant complaints that drove her into the embrace of Khaine.' Thirianna could see her father was quivering with emotion, though whether grief or anger she could not tell. He looked at her again, eyes slitted. 'And despite what happened to her, you had to follow in her steps. I lost a life-companion to Khaine's wars, and my daughter abandoned me for his bloody embrace too.'

Thirianna sighed and took a step towards the door.

'Did you not have something to ask of me?' Yrlandriar asked.

'No,' Thirianna replied. 'You have not changed at all. You belittle everything I have achieved and I see that you seek only to use this arrangement to further spite me. I do not care what Kelamith says, I will find another bonesinger to fashion a rune for me.'

'So I was right,' her father said. 'You speak of spite, and then discard your future simply because of your feelings for me. You have no dedication. When Kelamith first proposed this to me, I had hoped you had matured. I see that you have not. If you cannot ask a straightforward favour of me, what hope have you of walking the twisting paths of fate? You are far too capricious, Thirianna. You always have been. You are too young to be a seer, and I will not help you.'

Thirianna deadened her thoughts to her father's continuing insults as she headed for the door. She stopped at the threshold, unable to leave without retort.

'You are lonely and bitter, and seek to blame others for your own short-comings,' Thirianna said quietly. 'Perhaps I should pity you, but I cannot.'

Before he could say anything further, Thirianna left, hot tears welling up in her eyes.

Kelamith was waiting for her, sat on the padded couch at the centre of the grav-disc. Thirianna sat opposite, and buried her face in her hands. Saying nothing, the farseer commanded the disc to rise up, tilting gently as it took them back to the Chambers of the Seers.

Three more cycles passed before Kelamith contacted Thirianna, requesting that she join him in their usual chamber. She had spent the intervening period in brooding isolation, frustrated by her father's attitude, the old wounds of their parting reopened by the encounter.

Kelamith said nothing of his intent for her, and Thirianna feared to ask. The farseer had been adamant that Yrlandriar would be the one to make her rune, and it was with little hope that Kelamith had changed his mind that Thirianna travelled to the Chambers of the Seers. She fully expected to learn that his tutelage would cease, and Thirianna prepared herself for disappointment.

'To see the future is a powerful ability,' said Kelamith, after the two had exchanged their formal greetings. 'Yet it is a transient thing compared to the ability to learn from the past. It is in the understanding of past, present and future that true knowledge lies. The past informing the present, the future judged on events that have passed. Without seeing the past and the present, the future lacks context and becomes a meaningless barrage of possibilities.'

'One does not need to extend great psychic power to learn the mistakes of the past,' said Thirianna, unsure what Kelamith was trying to tell her. It did not seem relevant to her current predicament.

'It is not required, but it can certainly aid us,' replied the farseer. 'We each have our memories, preserved for eternity. We can consult records, to witness the decisions and conclusions of our predecessors. These are valuable sources of knowledge, but the infinity circuit provides us with another.'

Kelamith gestured for Thirianna to merge with the infinity circuit node. She did so, lowering her consciousness into the psychic web of the craftworld. The transition was smooth, without effort, no longer requiring the mantras she had learnt from Kelamith. In many ways, becoming one with the infinity circuit felt to Thirianna as if she returned to her natural state, that being clothed in mortal flesh was a temporary inconvenience that would one day be discarded.

Kelamith's thoughts overlapped with Thirianna's, mingling yet remaining distinct.

'Until now you have only looked forwards upon the skein,' he told Thirianna. 'You know that time is not a fixed point, but a seamlessly unrolling stream of cause and effect. Upon the skein, we can not only seek that which will happen, but also that which has already happened.'

Thirianna felt a tug at her spirit and she complied with it, shifting from the artificial state of the infinity circuit to the realm of pure thought that was the skein. The last time she had travelled here, during the battle with the orks, she had kept her gaze low, glimpsing only the futures immediate to her. This time she allowed her gaze to roam more widely, drinking in the complexity and beauty of the unfolding universe, seeing the haphazard mesh of fate being revealed.

'You do not yet have your rune,' said Kelamith. Thirianna noted a hint of admonishment in his thoughts. 'I will have to guide you back, to memories you have misplaced and events that you have never witnessed.'

To Thirianna it seemed as if the skein inverted itself. The unravelling threads were spiralling together, becoming one, a myriad probabilities becoming defined causes. The images she glimpsed resolved themselves in reverse as time flowed backwards. She struggled to keep up, so swiftly did Kelamith lead the way, but she half-saw herself again and again, in various situations that she knew well: becoming lost in the webway; meeting Kelamith for the first time; her argument with Korlandril; sitting composing poetry in her room; eating a meal with Aradryan and Korlandril in the shade of a golden-leafed tree.

Back they went, further and further, Thirianna's life flashing past, until they stopped during her youngest childhood. Thirianna was amazed, watching her infant self sitting in her mother's lap, trying to grab at her long braid of hair. Sadness filled Thirianna at the sight, even as the warmth of the scene filled her with a sense of love.

'I remember this time,' said Thirianna, trying to think clearly amongst the tumble of emotions that threatened to consume her. 'Mother is singing to me the *Lay of Eldanesh*. She had a wonderful voice.'

'And as a child that was what you remembered, your mother's voice, imprinted forever in your thoughts,' said Kelamith. 'However, our memories alone do not define a moment.'

He brought the pair of them out of the vision, sliding sideways to an intertwining thread, like stepping from one gravrail platform to another. The scene returned, subtly different.

Thirianna felt shock as she realised she was experiencing the scene through the memories of her mother. She had her baby daughter on her lap, and was idly singing to her while she waited for Yrlandriar to return. He had been called away from Alaitoc, to effect repairs to a starship that had been attacked by humans. She was worried, afraid he might never return, afraid of what would become of her daughter to be raised without her father.

Yrlandriar entered and her mother's relief flooded through Thirianna. She saw his warm smile as he slung his bag from his shoulder to the floor. Infant Thirianna had fallen asleep and she never stirred as Yrlandriar knelt and placed a kiss upon her head.

Thirianna broke from the scene, pulling herself back to the abstract whorl of threads, seeing the three lives entwined in that moment, one of them her own. She was both appalled and fascinated by what she witnessed. Kelamith was right; the power of the skein went far beyond simply showing images of the future. It provided her with the means to witness herself from the perspective of others, to learn what they had intended, what they had thought and felt beyond her knowledge.

'Now do you see why it is Yrlandriar that must cast your rune?' said Kelamith.

'No,' replied Thirianna. 'You seek to prove that he loves me, by showing me a scene from before my mother died. He changed at that moment and his love turned to disgust. I do not doubt that he loved me as a child, but I fail to see how any of this is relevant to my current path.'

'You have not paid attention to what I have told you, child,' said Kelamith, showing his irritation. 'To understand the universe we must understand ourselves. Your past influences your future, and just as you must come to terms and accept the possible futures, you must also reconcile yourself with the truth of the past. That is the purpose of the Path of the Seer, to seek self-awareness.'

'I know all too well the effect my father's behaviour has had on me,' said Thirianna. 'I suffer no delusions on that account.'

'Examine the threads of your life, and note those which are most closely bound to yours,' said the farseer.

Thirianna did so and though other lives touched upon hers, coming and going, there were two constants: her mother and father. It was to be expected and Thirianna did not see how this changed things. She followed the interlocked threads and then halted, suddenly terrified. One of the threads stopped abruptly.

Her mother's death.

'I have no desire to see this,' said Thirianna.

'Your desire is irrelevant, child,' said Kelamith. 'Examine closely the future course.'

The seer did as she was told, seeing the unravelling of the threads representing her life and her father's becoming distant from each other, spiralling away towards their own dooms. Witnessed in this way, the divide became even starker than the memory of that growing distance.

'More than any other, this moment has shaped your fate, though through no act of your own,' said Kelamith. 'If you are to learn from it, you must experience it.'

'No!' said Thirianna, but her protest went unheeded. Thirianna felt Kelamith's spirit merge with hers, dragging her down into the moment of the event, becoming a singularity with the thread of her mother's fate.

Twin suns of blue fire blazed overhead, shining down upon a dismal plain. Hills covered with brown grass and stunted trees stretched to the horizon, broken by shallow pools of dank water. The landscape was broken by bizarre ruins, jutting up from the soil in rows that radiated out from an immense pyramid at their heart. Most were little more than hummocks of overgrown stone, any markings long faded. Here and there needle-like monoliths speared from the grass at haphazard angles, their sides etched with odd geometric designs that flickered with fitful bursts of energy.

The pyramid glowed, bathing in the light of the two suns, reflecting them with a baleful sheen, its smooth surface marked out with large designs similar to those on the needles. Black lightning crackled about its golden peak and leapt to the tips of angular monoliths arranged about its base.

The army of Alaitoc approached swiftly, embarked upon Wave Serpent transports and Falcon grav-tanks. Their shimmering shadows flitted across the dull heathland as they closed in from three directions. The engines of jetbikes flared as they sped ahead to scout out the ruins.

Mythrairnin disembarked from the Wave Serpent with the other warriors from the Shrine of the Cleansing Dawn, her shuriken catapult at the ready as she leapt over the remnants of a low wall to take cover. With a whine of engines, the Wave Serpent moved away to take up a supporting position, its twin bright lances swivelling left and right as the gunner sought targets for the weapons.

In a constricting ring, the eldar moved in on their objective.

Ahead, the pyramid blazed with a pulse of power, a beam of disturbing pale green light erupting from its summit to pierce the greyish-yellow sky. An immense portal ground open, revealing a shimmering gate crisscrossed by forks of sickly green energy.

Warnings were passed on from the jetbike riders, but all who approached the pyramid could see the cause of their concern. Rank after rank of warriors marched from the portal, their bodies fashioned in the likeness of golden skeletons. Each carried a rifle set with a long crystal that crackled with the same unnatural energy as the gateway.

The heavy weapons of the grav-tanks opened fire, lances of laser energy converging on the emerging phalanx of artificial warriors. Gold-coloured bodies were shattered, robotic limbs sent whirling through the air.

The command came through to advance and Mythrairnin followed her exarch, Gallineir, as he vaulted over a toppled monolith, heading directly for the foe. Around the squad, other Aspect Warriors advanced, flashes of colour amongst the dismal surrounds.

The emerging necrontyr paid no heed to their casualties. Indeed, those warriors that had fallen still possessed a spark of life. Some crawled onwards, others paused to reassemble their broken bodies, the strange metal of their construction flowing and churning as legs and arms and heads were reattached.

Other infernal creations emerged from hidden gateways around the pyramid. Across the ruins, floating machines with skeletal torsos and heavy cannons emerged from the depths. Gleaming warriors with sleek bodies and halberds edged with glowing energy fields stalked through the remains of the necrontyr city. Clouds of beetle-like constructs each as large as an eldar helmet boiled up from the depths, the swarms hissing and spitting arcane energy.

Dark Reapers added their missiles to the fusillade of the vehicles, the trails of their shots cutting through the flickering mesh of laser fire. Squadrons of jetbikes jinked and swerved in unison as they duelled with the metal scarabs, their shuriken catapults unleashing volleys with each pass. The scarabs engulfed the machines and riders, overloading engines with their energy fields, detonating in blossoms of green fire to destroy the eldar.

A squad of Howling Banshees just ahead of Mythrairnin readied their weapons and leapt from cover to charge towards the closest necrontyr warriors. Like puppets controlled by a single hand, the necrons turned as one and levelled their weapons. Blinding green energy flared, rippling through the Aspect Warriors. Mythrairnin felt fear tugging at her as she saw a Howling Banshee struck by one of the beams. The energy pulsed through the unfortunate Aspect Warrior, stripping away her armour, then her flesh, then her bones, disintegrating her into nothing in a matter of moments.

With an angry shout, Mythrairnin aimed her shuriken catapult and fired at the necron warriors. Her hail of fire caught one of the artificial soldiers in the chest, slashing through metal in an explosion of sparks. The necron stumbled and fell on its face.

Mythrairnin turned her attention to another and fired again, but no sooner had she let loose another burst than the first warrior was pushing itself to its feet again, surrounded by a nimbus of unnatural light. Its glassy eyes flared menacingly as its ruined torso rearranged, the discs of the shurikens spat from its reforming metal flesh to fall to the ground.

Mythrairnin fired again, and again, and again, as did the rest of her squad. Under the barrage of fire, the necrontyr were knocked down time and again. With each volley, those foes who recovered grew fewer. Yet the necrontyr did not pause in their relentless advance.

Metallic creatures shrouded with cloaks and tatters of decaying flesh joined the attack, their wickedly long claws slicing through the Striking Scorpions fighting to Mythrairnin's left. The death of each eldar was greeted by an unsettling screech of triumph.

The eldar fell back, pulling away from the main necron advance under the cover of their tank fire. In rippling lines they retreated before the necrontyr and then attacked again, the army of Alaitoc constantly shifting, never allowing itself to be trapped in the ruins.

Mythrairnin did not know how many times she had fired or how many of the constructs she had destroyed. The battle became a delicate dance of attack and withdrawal, its tempo dictated by the ebb and flow of the necron assaults.

The ruins themselves became weapons. What had first seemed to be decorative, geometric structures revealed themselves to be weapon turrets. The pylons spat forth coruscating blazes of disintegrating energy, killing two or three eldar with every blast.

It was clear to Mythrairnin that they had come too late. The slumber of the necrontyr on this world had ended and their awakening could not be halted. Still the commands were to maintain the attack. She did not question her purpose, filled with the knowledge that the farseers had predicted this tomb world would at some time in the distant future despatch a harvesting fleet that might well fall upon Alaitoc's ships.

The risk to the craftworld would have been enough to stiffen Mythrairnin's resolve, but through the fog of battle-lust she could feel something else pushing her on. Dim memories of her daughter flickered through her mind as she fired incessantly into the necrons. If there was a chance, no matter how remote, that these evil creations might harm her child, she would give her life to prevent it.

One of the suns was setting and in the dimming light, the pyramid changed. Another section of gleaming metal slid away to reveal an immense hangar-like space. From the darkness emerged a terrifying apparition, glowing with green energy. It looked like a cross between a building and a warrior, a huge construct with a dozen heads and batteries of weapons set about a complex, ever-shifting geometric core.

The necrontyr war machine loomed over the battlefield, sheathed in a baleful glow that warded away the blasts of bright lances and scatter lasers. An orb at its centre spun faster and faster, crackling with energy that crawled along arcane circuitry to the blisters of the weapons turrets.

With a blinding flash, green lightning arced down upon the eldar army, shredding tanks and Aspect Warriors in a barrage of pyrotechnic destruction. Whole squads were vaporised in a heartbeat. Falcons exploded or were sheared into small pieces or crashed into the ruins of the city.

The order came to retreat.

Within moments, the Wave Serpent that was to carry the Dire Avengers slid into view just to one side of the squad, sheltering behind a crumbled archway. Mythrairnin and the four other survivors headed towards the transport, pausing only to unleash one more volley at the necron warriors closing in on them.

They were almost at the Wave Serpent when the shadow of the necron war engine fell across them. A moment later, the ancient stones around them detonated as lightning engulfed the Wave Serpent. The transport exploded, sending a shard of hull scything through the Dire Avengers.

Mythrairnin was flung back by the blossom of fire and hurled into the remains of a wall. She stumbled as she tried to stand and realised dully that her right leg had been cut off by the blast of debris.

She saw the necrons advancing and suppressed a cry of fear and pain. Khaine was with her, and with Khaine's strength she would not die without some retort. She fixed on the image of her daughter's face and activated her shuriken catapult, sending volley after volley into the necron warriors stalking closer.

A bolt of green energy hit her, and for the briefest of moments her entire body filled with pain, every molecule torn apart.

Thirianna clawed and struggled to rip herself from the grip of the skein, but Kelamith would not permit her to leave. Trapped, Thirianna caught herself in a loop, experiencing the last moments of her mother's life, desperate to cling on to any connection to her, yet torn apart by the nature of her doom.

Kelamith intervened, prising Thirianna's spirit away from the thread of her mother, withdrawing from the intimate contact so that she could establish some semblance of rational thought and balance.

'Why?' demanded Thirianna, recoiling with horror from the memory of what her mother had experienced.

'It is not the pain of your mother that you must understand,' the farseer replied, his voice distant and dispassionate.

Before Thirianna could raise any objection, she felt herself drawn down into the material of the skein again, this time flowing along a faint after-thread left by her mother's death, to where it intersected with the line of her father's life.

The glowstone let out only the feeblest amount of light, barely touching the blackness of the room. Yrlandriar sat cross-legged in the middle of the chamber, hands on his knees, staring at the darkness.

How could he tell Thirianna what had happened? How could he explain to her why her mother would not be returning?

These questions nagged at him, more than the grief that was even now crushing his heart and running veins of chilling venom through his gut. In a moment of self-reflection, Yrlandriar realised that it was not the thought of answering these questions for his daughter that so vexed him; he could not answer them for himself.

He knew it was a fallacy to expect meaning from the random chance of fate, and still he struggled to find some sense in the death of his beloved Mythrairnin. He could find none. He could find no solace in a meaningful death because he could not comprehend how it was that she had first taken to the Path of the Warrior. The causality of her ending led back to that decision, and it was this that defied logic more than anything else that crowded Yrlandriar's thoughts.

She had known death was a possibility and yet against all reason, Mythrairnin had abandoned her child to his care to follow in the footsteps of the Bloody-Handed God. It was a decision that seemed perverse to the artisan, to seek destruction instead of the joys of her own creation.

He had not wept. It seemed a pointless exercise in vanity, a physiological response that would do nothing to fill the gulf that yawned wide in the core of his being. He was empty and cold, all sense of love and warmth ripped from him for no reason at all.

The child would need him.

It was too painful to contemplate. Yrlandriar was surprised by his own reaction, yet every thought of Thirianna mutated into memories of her mother. They were so alike in many ways the slightest thought of his daughter sent spasms of grief through Yrlandriar.

There was nothing he would be able to do to ease the hurt, and Thirianna's grief would compound his own. Yrlandriar's misery would reflect in his daughter and her woe would stir his own. She would be better free from such a taint, able to live her life untouched by the gnawing sadness that would now be his burden.

Thirianna was still absorbing this, trying to reconcile her own memories of the time with the thoughts of her father, when Kelamith moved them again. This time it was to a juncture of her life and Yrlandriar's, and from the first moment she recognised it: the time before she had left to become a Dire Avenger.

'You cannot tell me what to do!' screeched Thirianna, snatching up her bag of belongings. 'You just don't understand.'

'No, I do not,' said Yrlandriar, his heart sinking as Thirianna took another step towards the door. He had failed, and now Thirianna would suffer the same fate as Mythrairnin. He tried to calm himself, but the mere thought of his daughter becoming an Aspect Warrior filled him with foreboding.

'Can you not see how selfish this is?' he said, spitting the accusation at his daughter. Her anger deepened and Yrlandriar realised he was not conveying what he meant properly. She simply would not listen to what he was saying. 'Why do you have to do this to me?'

'This is not about you, father,' said Thirianna. 'Why does everything have to be about you? And you accuse me of being selfish!'

'You are making a mistake,' he said. He had let Mythrairnin leave for the shrines without argument and was not going to do the same with Thirianna. 'You are being hasty and immature.'

'I am not being immature,' said Thirianna, her tone cold. 'As a child you would always tell me what to do. I will not accept that any more. You cannot control me; I am not your possession. You should support me, and understand that I have to do this. I have little left to remember mother, but perhaps I can know her a bit better if I follow upon the Path she trod.'

'That path leads to death and despair,' said Yrlandriar. The slightest hint of the thought that Thirianna would die as well sent a chill through every part of him. It would be too much to bear and he could not allow it, for the sake of both of them. 'I forbid this. As your father, I cannot allow you to do this.'

'Forbid?' Thirianna's voice rose to a piercing pitch. 'Forbid? I am not some lump of wraithbone to be moulded and shaped and teased by your command. That is your problem, father. You think that you can be the master of everything you touch. Well, you will not be my master. Turn your fingers to another purpose and leave me to live my life as I choose.'

Yrlandriar could think of nothing else to say that he had not said already, over and over. He had known that he and Thirianna were becoming estranged, and had expected her to leave even sooner. Yet to learn that she was to tread in the footsteps of Khaine was too much for him to accept.

Thirianna stopped at the door and gave him a final backwards glance. Was that hesitation he saw? Did she wait for some last argument from him to dissuade her from this madness?

It did not matter. Clearly he had failed. He had failed Thirianna and he had failed the legacy of Mythrairnin. Both of them were lost to him and perhaps they were the better for it.

'Just leave,' he said, turning away, finding no consolation in his decision.

After returning to her body, Thirianna excused herself from Kelamith and left the Chambers of the Seers. She did not return to her own rooms, but instead took the gravrail across Alaitoc, back to the Tower of Ascendant Flames where she had been raised.

The tower was close to the hub of Alaitoc, the highest on the craftworld, a massive edifice of walkways and bridges and balconies and windows. She sat on a bench hidden away in the depths of the park surrounding the tower, beside a pool filled with blue-scaled skyfins and purple dawn-sails. In the bushes nearby, a green-furred leathervole rustled through the fallen leaves, its ridged proboscis nuzzling through the mulch.

Thirianna allowed herself to relax, concentrating on the small details of the scene. Yet for all that she tried to separate herself from what Kelamith had shown her, the experience continued to tickle away in the depths of her mind. She had deliberately closed off the memories from the skein, unwilling to relive them until she had settled herself. It had been a cruel tactic of Kelamith, one that was now blatantly manipulative, and part of her railed against the farseer's transparent bullying.

Though she refused to recall in detail what she had witnessed, she could not avoid the imprint they had left upon her consciousness. Thoughts of her father were still overwhelmingly associated with frustration, but the edge was not so keen, her anger not quite so sharp.

Thirianna could not quite believe the cold-hearted behaviour of Kelamith in subjecting her to such distress, but she realised that whatever his intentions she was left to deal with the consequences.

Carefully, like someone opening a door a crack to peer into the room beyond, Thirianna peeled back the layer of ignorance shielding her recent memories. She veered away from those of her mother, instantly feeling a stab of pain as soon as she approached them. It was her father that concerned Kelamith, and now her, and so it was to that train of experience that she now paid attention.

Reviewing what she knew of Yrlandriar, she was no closer to forgiving him for his selfish ways. It had been wrong of him to shut Thirianna out from his feelings after the death of her mother, no matter how he justified it to himself.

Yet despite that, Thirianna had now seen herself through his eyes, and that was something she could not simply ignore. While his behaviour had been poor and his reasoning unsound, Yrlandriar's decision to withdraw into himself had not been helped by Thirianna's increasingly demanding nature. The more she had pushed for his attention, the further he had withdrawn from it, fleeing his daughter as if she were the spectre of her dead mother.

As hard as it was to accept, Thirianna came to the conclusion that she had acted selfishly as well. She had made no attempt to bridge the dark gulf between them and had simply expected her father to cross the divide and come to her.

Thirianna was upset and scared by how little empathy existed between her and Yrlandriar. How could father and daughter grow apart so swiftly? In retrospect, it occurred to her that it was what they had both desired, even if only subconsciously. Without Mythrairnin to bind them together, each of them considered themselves and the other best left to be on their own.

If Kelamith had expected some great change of Thirianna's outlook, some revelatory thawing of her feelings towards her father, he was going to be disappointed. The farseer's callous stunt in the infinity circuit did not deserve such a reward and Thirianna was appalled that Kelamith had thought it plausible. Despite everything, she still considered her father a stranger, and she owed him nothing.

Rousing herself from her reverie, Thirianna looked up at the Tower of Ascendant Flames, silhouetted against the dim glow of the dying star. She had been born up amongst the cloud-wreathed heights of the tower, but her life had not started until she had left. She could not defend her father in any way. He had not tried to do his best; he had made little attempt to give her the love and affection she needed.

With that thought came a realisation. It was not her father's love she desired, not his apologies nor his forgiveness. All she required of him was a rune, fashioned from wraithbone.

He was a stranger and she was attaching too many other emotions to the relationship. It did not matter whether they were father and daughter, whether they agreed on her choices in life. He was a bonesinger and she was a seer. She required a rune, and he would make it for her.

* * *

The following cycle, Thirianna returned to her father's workshop. Yrlandriar was working on the starship frame, but she waited patiently for him to return, examining the pieces on display. Many were unfinished, their purpose, whether functional or artistic, not clear. Others were little more than three-dimensional sketches, rough shapes and angles that held some semblance of the form they would become but nothing more. There seemed to be quite a few of these which she had not seen before, which led Thirianna to wonder if perhaps Yrlandriar was trying in his own way to come to terms with their fresh meeting and not yet succeeding to find the means.

Her father announced himself as he returned, and Thirianna put back the object she had been looking at with a pang of guilt. Remembering how mortified she would have felt had someone been examining her poems, she suddenly wondered if she was intruding into Yrlandriar's privacy.

The bonesinger did not seem surprised at her presence.

'So you have come back, Thirianna,' he said, sitting beside the table again.

'I wish you to fashion a rune for me, father,' she replied, using her most formal tone.

'And why would I do that for you?' said Yrlandriar. 'What you ask for is not some bauble. What assurances will I have that my efforts will not be wasted? That half a pass from now you will not have tired of being a seer and moved on to your next flight of fancy?'

Thirianna refused to rise to the taunt, and held her temper in check.

'None of us know for how long we might tread a Path, and it is not for you to judge anyone but yourself,' said Thirianna. 'I am committed to learning the secrets of the seer. Such is my commitment, I am willing to offer you an apology so that we might understand one another better.'

Yrlandriar raised an eyebrow in surprise.

'An apology?' He seemed genuinely pleased. 'What is it that you regret so much that it is worth apologising to me?'

'I am sorry that we do not like each other better, and do not know each other better,' Thirianna said. She bit back the criticisms that surfaced in her thoughts and paused, taking a breath before she continued. 'I am sorry that I did not realise that as much as I needed your comfort and attention following the death of my mother, you equally deserved the time and solitude to deal with your own loss.'

Yrlandriar swallowed hard, his expression softening. He glanced away, towards the looming bulk of the starship, and his next words were softly spoken.

'I am sorry also, Thirianna,' said the bonesinger. 'Sorry that I cannot mend the past as I might repair a broken spar or heal a splintered node.'

'I need your help now, father,' said Thirianna, the words coming with difficulty. 'Will you fashion a rune for me, so that I might learn to be a seer?'

Still looking away, Yrlandriar touched a finger to the side of the table. A shallow drawer slid out, and from this the bonesinger brought out a small object, as slender as one of his fingers. Finally he turned his gaze to Thirianna and his face was stern.

'It is not yet finished, but I was going to bring it to you when it was complete,' he said. 'Your coming here stirred up many painful memories for me, but I cannot blame you for that. More than anything else I have created, this has caused me much hardship. It is your rune, wrought in wraithbone, conjured forth by my hand and my will. Perhaps you will care for it better than I cared for you.'

'Thank you,' said Thirianna, bowing her head. 'It means much to me that you have done this.'

'Though it was not my intention, I raised a daughter who was strong of will and knows what she desires,' said Yrlandriar, placing the unfinished rune on the table top. 'I wish I could take some pride from that, but it leaves me hollow.'

'Pride is fleeting,' said Thirianna. She felt uncomfortable with the silence that followed and Yrlandriar was faring no better, fidgeting with the fittings of his gloves. 'I hope you will deliver it in person when it is finished.'

'I hope it guides you to a fulfilling future,' said Yrlandriar.

'It is folly to chase after fulfilment,' said Thirianna. 'If you taught me anything, it is to accept what fate brings us, good or ill. To deny that is to forever postpone contentment.'

Yrlandriar nodded thoughtfully, his gaze straying back to the starship.

'I will not keep you from your other work,' said Thirianna.

Her father said nothing in reply, so she turned and left, resolving to find Kelamith as soon as possible.

POWER

The Siren Mirror – Eldanesh's Shield. As the ward of the Sire of the Eldar turned back the blows of his foes, so the Siren Mirror acts to reconstitute the energies of an enemy. One of several runes whose use is specific to battle, Eldanesh's Shield works by channelling the power of the skein harnessed by the enemy, so that it might be wielded in the favour of the seer.

The rune of Thirianna floated a little more than an arm's reach in front of her, utterly still. She drew the image of the rune into her thoughts as Kelamith had shown her, creating a bond between the mental and the physical. The rune glowed slightly with the psychic power and Thirianna could feel more energy flowing into her mind.

She sat in the middle of the main chamber of her apartments, performing the exercises passed on by the farseer. At first she attained control of the rune, mastering it to her purpose. When balance was met, she took the power of the rune into herself.

Now that she had completed the first two stages, she could choose how to wield the psychic energy that was now hers to possess. Thirianna chose an external focus, using the rune to extend her influence on the physical world. She concentrated her thoughts, narrowing them to a single point at the centre of the rune.

The rune acted as an amplifier, adding power from the skein to Thirianna's innate psychic energy. With this, the seer reached out across the room, picking up several objects from the tables and shelves: a brush, a necklace, her discarded bag and a small bust of Asuryan. Thirianna's eyes flickered from one to the other as she moved them around the chamber, delicately placing each one in a new position.

She repeated the exercise, moving the objects back to their original places, but this time with her eyes closed, using only the psychic aura of the rune to guide her thoughts. With gentle psychic pushes, she nudged each object back into place.

Opening her eyes, Thirianna noted with some satisfaction that she had restored the room perfectly. She turned her attention to a wide dish set on the floor in front of her, a small square of cloth laid inside the metallic bowl. Thirianna set her mind to the task of examining the cloth scrap at the smallest level, passing into its weave, down to the individual molecules of the material. She set the atoms dancing, agitating them with the power of her thought, exciting the air molecules around the cloth.

After a few moments, the scrap burst into flames, burning with a pale blue colour. It quickly turned to ash, settling into the bottom of the dish, gently stirred by the breeze drifting in through the open window.

They were small things she did, but it was not safe to practise the greater powers that were being unveiled to her, at least not in the confines of her apartment. There were rooms in the Chambers of the Seers, rune-shielded and psychically warded, where she had unleashed some of the more extreme abilities she was now learning to control.

The rune had another purpose and it was to this that Thirianna now turned her attention.

With the image of her symbol still fixed foremost in her thoughts, Thirianna made the transition to the skein. No longer did she need the infinity circuit to make the journey; her thoughts were able to flow between the realms of the real and unreal with the smallest effort.

It was a liberating experience for Thirianna to know how far she had progressed. As Kelamith had told her, the runecraft increased her powers exponentially. As she floated in the aether of the skein, Thirianna marvelled at how much she could do with just a single rune, and was eager to increase her powers further. The most experienced farseers, like Kelamith, could control a dozen or more runes at a time. Thirianna could only speculate at the possibilities that would open up to her, though such a thing was still a distant dream.

Being one and the same with the rune, Thirianna was able to instantly find her own life thread in the insane tangle of the skein. She fixed herself upon the current moment, her rune appearing as a marker in her thoughts.

Kelamith had warned her not to roam too far ahead of the present, not until she was strong enough to cope with the multiplicity of fates that would unfold. After her wayward adventure in the webway, Thirianna heeded her tutor's warning and restricted herself to peeking just a few cycles ahead.

She was amazed by the number of overlapping threads, the volume of lives upon which every life touched, whether directly or indirectly. Decisions she made echoed up through the possible futures, creating branch after branch of potential fates. In turn, her life thread twisted and turned, shaped by events and the actions of others, sometimes becoming hazy during periods of great uncertainty, other times becoming taut and thick when she was in full control of her destiny.

One thread in particular bonded itself to hers very shortly, the next cycle in fact. She investigated, and found that it belonged to Korlandril. Everything became uncertain as she looked closer, the act of her observation obscuring the potentialities that were being revealed.

Leaving her rune as a beacon to bring her back, Thirianna moved away from her own life and followed Korlandril's. It was steeped in darkness and bloodshed, tainted by Khaine's touch as Korlandril followed the Path of the Warrior.

Something strange happened next and Thirianna could not quite work out what it foreshadowed. One of Korlandril's possible futures merged with that of another. The two existences did not just entwine or knot together, they became a single thread. Looking more closely, pushing back visions of bloodshed and battle that tried to encroach on her thoughts, Thirianna examined the composite thread and saw that it was not just Korlandril's life that was meshed within its fibres. There were others, coming from across the skein at different times, each becoming a small part of the whole.

The merged life of Korlandril and the others stretched on without turning or breaking, slashing through the future like a bloodied blade. With some shock, Thirianna realised what the skein was showing her. Korlandril's spirit was being subsumed into a greater presence, that of an exarch of the Bloody-Handed God.

Korlandril risked becoming trapped on the Path of the Warrior.

Thirianna located her rune and returned to it, before she effortlessly slipped out of the skein and back into her body.

She wondered what to do. She had not nearly enough skill or experience to delve further into Korlandril's possible paths and what she had seen was only one of several possible outcomes. As when she had foreseen his injury during the battle against the orks, there was no means by which she could accurately predict what would happen in the long term should Korlandril take one course over another.

The perils of causality, a lecture oft-repeated by Kelamith, came to Thirianna. It was a simple premise: by acting upon an observation one might bring about the foreseen, undesired event. Sometimes a seer's actions would influence the passage of fate, so that the observer became the cause. It was just one of many pitfalls waiting for the unwary voyager into the future, one that every seer had to confront if they were to fulfil their potential. The very essence of the seer was to guide Alaitoc and its people past the dangers and conflicts of the future; yet it was a delicate balancing act judging when to intervene and when to allow fate to take its own course.

In short, as Thirianna had once summarised it to Kelamith, the lesson was not to interfere unless you were sure of the outcome.

Thirianna was far from sure of the outcome if she chose to act on what she had seen. Could she prevent Korlandril's entrapment, or would she somehow, or had she already, precipitated it? Not only that, if she was to find herself in the position that she could avert Korlandril's journey to becoming an exarch, was it right that she should do so? Until she was more accomplished, she could not venture far enough across the skein to see the possible implications of Korlandril's futures.

Like so many of the questions posed by Kelamith, it was an impossible conundrum, one that was far beyond Thirianna's rudimentary scrying skills and ethical reasoning.

There was only one conclusion she could come to, though it pained her to admit, just as it had pained her to allow Korlandril to be injured. She was in no position to judge what was right and wrong and would simply have to allow what was to come to pass to do so. Though it might turn out to be a personal tragedy for Korlandril, and for Thirianna, Korlandril's possible entrapment could have implications far beyond their lives, and to change it might be to endanger the lives of others.

Thirianna waited beneath a snowpetal in the Garden of Heavenly Delights, reading a treatise on the Rune of the Golden Sail passed to her by Kelamith. She had seen herself meeting Korlandril here and despite her decision not to interfere with the course of events as she had foreseen, Thirianna had decided to allow the meeting to take place.

She felt Korlandril approaching, his warrior spirit cutting across the skein like a bubble drifting across a pool of blood. She turned and feigned surprise as he reached the shade of the tree.

Korlandril was dressed in a pleated robe of dark green, the same colour as the Striking Scorpion armour he wore in battle. He walked with quiet assurance, his eyes scanning the parklands constantly, seemingly poised for action. Thirianna could sense the spirit of Khaine hiding under the surface, a coiled serpent waiting for the opportunity to strike.

Pushing back a rising distaste, Thirianna remembered that they were friends and she embraced Korlandril, trying not to shudder at the warrior's cold touch. Taken aback, he hesitated before wrapping his arms around her.

'I heard that you had been injured,' Thirianna said, stepping back to regard Korlandril, assuring herself that he had recovered. It was better that she did not reveal her foreknowledge of his grim injury.

'I am healed,' he replied with a smile. 'Physically, at least.'

Korlandril gestured to the bench and the two of them sat side-by-side.

Thirianna was about to ask him how he was feeling, but stopped herself. It was a foolish question, and one that would invite her to say something she might regret.

'What is wrong?' Korlandril asked.

Despite her earlier confidence, seeing her friend's concern weakened Thirianna's resolve. She could not simply let him become trapped as a warrior. She decided that even if she did not act directly, a timely reminder of the perils associated with being an Aspect Warrior would not go amiss.

'I was going to visit you, as there is something you should know.' It was a lie, but Thirianna believed it would be better for Korlandril not to know that she had intended to allow him to travel to his doom without her intervention. 'I would rather we spoke about other matters first, but you have caught me unawares. There is no pleasant way to say this. I have read your runes. They are confused, but many of your futures do not bode well.'

Korlandril spoke with assurance, dismissing her concerns with a frown. 'There is nothing to fear. I have suffered some tribulations of late, but they will not defeat me.'

'It is that which worries me,' Thirianna said. She reached out and laid her palm briefly on his cheek, but he flinched at the touch. 'I sense confrontation in you. You see every encounter as a battle to be won. The Path of the Warrior is taking its toll upon you.'

'It was one slip of concentration, nothing more,' said Korlandril, standing up. He stepped away from Thirianna. 'I stumbled but the journey goes on.'

'I have no idea what you are talking about,' said Thirianna. Korlandril's confidence had become defensiveness, his remarks an overreaction. 'Has something else happened?'

'It is nothing important, not of concern to the likes of you.'

'The likes of me?' Thirianna was upset more than angry. How swiftly Korlandril had forgotten the past they shared. 'No concern of a friend?'

Korlandril looked guilty, eyes downcast, unable to meet her gaze.

'I almost struck a genuine blow during a ritual settlement.'

Thirianna knew what a dishonour that would be. It also confirmed her suspicions. If Korlandril could not maintain control of his murderous impulses in the shrine, it was a sign of the growing grip Khaine had on his spirit.

'Oh, Korlandril…' she said.

'What?' he said. Anger flashed across his face, his brow knotted, teeth briefly bared. 'You speak to me like a child. It happened. I will learn from it.'

'Will you?' There was no contrition in Korlandril, as if he sought confrontation. Thirianna remembered Korlandril's comment of 'the likes of you' from earlier and wanted to assure him that she understood better than he realised. 'Do not forget that I have been a Dire Avenger. Though that time lives in the mists of my past, it is not so old that I forget it entirely. Until recently I trod the Path of the Warlock. As a warrior-seer, I revisited many of my battle-memories, drawing on them for resolve and strength. I recall the lure of the Warrior's Way; the surety of purpose it brings and the comfort of righteousness.'

'There is no fault to be found with having the strength of one's convictions.' Korlandril's fists were balled and his shoulders hunched with aggression. It frightened Thirianna to see him this way, and the surety of what she had seen made her more determined to help him back from the brink of a lifetime of hatred and bloodshed.

'It is a drug, that sense of power and superiority,' she warned. 'The war-mask allows you to control your rage and guilt in battle, it is not meant to extinguish all feeling outside of war. Even now I sense that you are angry with me.'

'What if I am? You sit there and talk of things you do not understand. It does not matter whether you have trodden the Path of the Warrior, you and I are not the same. That much you made clear to me before I joined the Deadly Shadow. Perhaps *you* felt tempted by the power. I have a stronger will.'

Thirianna could not stop herself from laughing at the ridiculousness of the accusation. She had successfully passed from warrior to poet; he was the one that was becoming trapped.

'Nothing has changed with you,' Thirianna replied, angry as much with herself as her friend, for allowing herself to get involved. 'You have learnt nothing! I offer comfort and you take criticism. Perhaps you are right. Perhaps it is not the Path of the Warrior that makes you this arrogant; you have always been so self-involved.'

'Self-involved?' Korlandril's voice rose with disbelief. He stepped back and visibly took a breath, trying to calm himself. When he spoke next, his voice was scornful. 'You it was that fluttered in the light of my attention, promising much but ultimately willing to give nothing. If I am selfish it is because you have taken from me that which I would have happily given myself to.'

'I was wrong, you are not selfish,' said Thirianna.

She wondered how the two of them had ever been friends. Her patience was wearing thin with Korlandril's sense of self-importance. Had he always been this pompous?

'You are self-deluding! Rationalisation and justification are all that you can offer in your defence. Take a long look at yourself, Korlandril, and then tell me that this is my fault.'

Korlandril stalked back and forth for a moment, like a caged animal seeking escape. For a heartbeat, Thirianna feared the Aspect Warrior would become violent. It was clear that his war-mask was thinning, the rage of his battle-spirit mingling with his personality away from the shrine and war.

'You are jealous!' Korlandril rasped. 'Once I was infatuated with you, and now you cannot bear the thought that I might live my life outside of your shadow. Elissanadrin, perhaps? You believe that I have developed feelings for another, and suddenly you do not feel you are unique in my affections.'

'I had no idea that you had moved your ambitions to another,' replied Thirianna. She had no idea who Elissanadrin was, but if she was fool enough to consort with Korlandril, Thirianna felt sorry for her. 'I am glad. I would rather you sought the company of someone else, as you are no longer welcome in mine.'

'This was a mistake,' he said. 'You are not worth the grief you bring, nor the time you consume.'

A grim realisation dawned on Thirianna. Her fear of involving herself with Korlandril had been correct. Their confrontation was just another blow upon the slender barricade that kept Korlandril's anger in check. She began to sob, burying her face in her hands, knowing that she had probably moved him closer to entrapment, against her every intention.

She recovered a little and looked up, finding that Korlandril had departed without any farewell or parting word. It was with bleak thoughts that Thirianna left the park. Her unsubtle interference, despite knowing that it might prove ill, had possibly doomed her friend. Far from helping Korlandril, her clumsy attempts at a warning might well have brought about the very fate she had wanted to avoid.

Thirianna wondered, for the first time since she had escaped the webway, whether she was suited to the life of the seer. She had wanted answers, to know the consequences of her actions and their effect on others. In reality, the more she learnt, the further she delved into the secrets of the skein, the less certain she was of anything.

The flames that licked along the edges of the Witchblade were a pleasing violet hue. Thirianna's rune glowed with the same colour as it slowly orbited the hilt of the weapon, its aura dimming and brightening in tune with the ebb and flow of the psychic flames. The purple haze gleamed from Thirianna's rune armour and was reflected from the golden sigils inscribed into the walls of the hexagonal chamber.

Thirianna wore no helm – and had not drawn up her war-mask – and her eyes glittered with psychic power as she concentrated on the Witchblade. When first she had taken it up, it had been an extension of her body. Now it was becoming an extension of her mind. With a thought, she reduced the flames to a dull gleam; with another they burst into full life.

Thirianna stepped and chopped, leaving a violet trail of light where the blade passed. She cut and thrust, side-stepped, parried and thrust again, the tip of the sword leaving a glowing imprint in the air. She had not noticed it before, but the burning trail of the Witchblade left rune-impressions on the air, writing death and destruction in its wake.

Spinning to a new posture, Thirianna levelled the Witchblade at chest height and unleashed the power of the psychic fire. The violet flames roared across the room, splashing against the rune-covered walls. Thirianna's rune spun madly, turning over lengthwise as she poured more psychic energy into the blast, adjusting the aim of the Witchblade with small wrist movements.

Imagining an unexpected attack, she brought the weapon up to the guard position, as her mind wreathed the flames into a disc of fire to ward away the blow. She whirled, her robe flapping at her legs, bringing the Witchblade to the attack in a new direction, setting loose three pulses of flame that exploded against the psychic shield of the wall in purple blossoms.

A chime sounded, alerting her to an approaching visitor. As she drew back her power, the swiftest delve into the infinity circuit revealed the arrival to be Kelamith. It was unexpected. She had not seen the farseer for more than a dozen cycles and it seemed that he had been content to allow her to practise with blade and rune without supervision.

Stowing the weapon in its sheath, Thirianna powered down the protective runes and opened the archway to allow Kelamith to enter. The farseer was dressed in his full regalia, his crystal-lensed helmet tucked under one arm.

'Battle approaches,' he said. 'Come with me to the council of seers. The autarchs will be needing our guidance.'

Thirianna nodded, and with a twitch of her finger sent her rune into a pouch at her belt. She opened her sword hand and the Witchblade reluctantly floated back to its place on the wall. She followed the farseer through the Chambers of the Seers, heading towards the central hall where the council gathered. She had seen it before, a high-ceilinged dome of dark blue, pierced with diamond-like gems that glittered as the starry sky. Benches lined the walls, and to one of these Kelamith led Thirianna. He directed her to sit as other seers filed into the chamber, the farseers gathering on the central dais while the warlocks and lesser seers took their places on the marble benches.

It was quite a crowd, all thirteen of Alaitoc's farseers present and nearly four times that number of other psykers. Thirianna exchanged thoughts of greeting with those around her and received the same in reply, some formal, others genuinely warm and welcoming. All was done without lips moving, telepathic contacts that took moments to convey what would take a lengthy conversation to say. A few remarked that this was Thirianna's first council and she responded with nervousness and excitement.

The autarchs then entered, emerging from the gravrail station beside the hall, coming from the Aspect shrines where they held their own gatherings.

The autarchs, three of them, were dressed in ornate armour. Thirianna could sense the antiquity of their wargear, generations of death steeped in the plates and mesh. Arhathain wore dark blue armour chased with gold detail, a white cloak hanging from his shoulders, a long spear in his right hand; Neurthuil's armour was also blue, though of a clear sky and decorated with silver, the metallic wings of her flightpack folded close, a three-barrelled lasblaster hanging from its strap over her shoulder; Akolthiar's armour was red and orange, his face hidden behind the grille of a Banshee mask, a long-muzzled fusion pistol at his waist, a red-bladed axe in hand.

All three had trodden the Path of the Warrior many times and all three had proven strong enough to resist the lure of Khaine. Though Thirianna had no desire to become a warrior again, she was filled with admiration and respect for the three commanders, inspired by their discipline and purpose.

It was Arhathain, chief amongst the autarchs, who spoke first.

'We have received warning from this council that a threat emerges.' His voice was quiet and assured, deep and full of authority. 'The word has been passed to the exarchs and the Aspect shrines ready for battle. We seek guidance from the council.'

'The council is ready to guide,' Alaiteir replied formally, the farseer gesturing to one of his companions.

'The skein ripples with conflict,' said Laimmain, her fingers moving as three runes emerged from her belt and took up station in front of her. 'Worse, the taint of the Great Enemy falls upon the thread of Alaitoc.'

An aura of consternation filled the hall and Thirianna's heart beat faster while recent memories threatened to surface. She pushed back the rebellious recollections and focussed on the farseers.

'An artefact has been unearthed, brought out of hiding by the reckless inquisitiveness of the humans,' continued Kelamith. 'It is a small thing but possessed of a great power to corrupt.'

'For the moment it is dormant,' said Laimmain, picking up the explanation again. 'Yet the humans' curiosity and greed will cause them to delve into its properties and their spirits will be ensnared, their dreams given form by this subtle and deadly creation.'

'This wicked artefact will work its malice, eating at their minds, perverting their ambitions,' said Alaiteir. 'They will become enamoured of this thing, slaves to the will of She Who Thirsts.'

'Their depravity will be hidden at first, yet they are rulers of a world, important agents of the Emperor, and their corruption will go unnoticed but reach far,' said Kelamith. 'In just a short time, a passing of three of their generations, they will secretly revere the Great Enemy. In madness and desire, they will call upon She Who Thirsts to deliver them power so that they might escape the rule of the Emperor and thus seal their pact with darkness.'

'Such a thing would be ill enough,' said Anuraina. She summoned an image into being with a wave of her hand. It showed an arc of the galaxy, a swirl of stars that Thirianna recognised as being only a few light years from Alaitoc. 'In their ignorance, the humans will fail, but their inexpert ritual shall weaken the boundaries between the realm of the mortal and the immortal.'

The projected image swirled and changed. Thirianna recognised it as a vision from the skein, similar to the ever-fluctuating, slightly amorphous view from her own journeys into the possibility of futures. The vision centred on a particular star and then closed with the fifth planet in orbit. The sky around the orb seethed with daemonic energy, as the warp breached into the material universe, bringing the power of Chaos into the physical realm.

'The contagion from this daemonic invasion will spread to neighbouring star systems,' said Kelamith, as the image continued to evolve, presenting a view of debasement and destruction across seven worlds. 'These forces will be harnessed by those who wish us harm. Guided by the Great Enemy, the forces of Chaos will strike at Alaitoc.'

The next vision was even more horrifying. It showed the vessels of the craftworld overrun by daemons of She Who Thirsts, breaking open the crystal vaults of the ships' infinity circuits, supping at the eldar spirits held within. Gasps and disgusted whispers rippled through the auditorium. Thirianna looked away, sickened by what she saw.

'All of this can be averted with a strike now,' said Alaiteir. The vision presented by Anuraina dissipated and was replaced by a shadowed view of a human citadel. 'The object that will cause so much strife is being brought here. It is poorly defended, a journey of no more than a few days from Alaitoc.'

'And what is the objective?' asked Arhathain. 'The item must be recovered or destroyed, that much is clear. What of its corrupting effect?'

'All in the citadel may have been touched by its presence,' said Kelamith. 'Even if we recover the artefact, who can say what its lingering taint might damage in the future?'

'All in the citadel must be slain,' said Alaiteir.

'Are you sure that is necessary?' asked Akolthiar.

'You seem concerned to protect the humans,' said Kelamith. 'We speak of only a few hundred lives, nothing more.'

'It is not the expenditure of the humans that I question,' replied the autarch. 'The more to be slain, the greater the risk to eldar lives. Not only will it require more warriors to risk themselves in battle, such a strike may provoke a response from the humans.'

'We have delved into this,' said Kelamith. 'There is no consequence to Alaitoc if we strike swiftly and surely. The humans will remain unaware of our part in the attack, and those that suspect will be left no proof of our involvement. Alaitoc will not be blamed.'

'If that is so, then I agree,' said Akolthiar.

'We have consent,' said Arhathain. 'We will begin preparations for a battleship to convey the warhost to this world. Opposition will be minimal. The Aspect temples will be sufficient to deal with the matter.'

'We shall continue to scry the battle-fate of your warriors,' said Laimmain. 'Several of us will accompany you to the world to ensure that nothing goes amiss.'

'And the artefact?' said Arhathain.

'We have already despatched a message to the white seers,' said Kelamith. 'They will meet us at the human world and stand ready to take possession of the artefact. The Great Enemy's wiles are many. Be sure that your warriors are fully prepared.'

'The Aspect Warriors will not be turned by this object,' said Arhathain. He looked at the assembled seers. 'Be sure that none of your number are beguiled by its presence either.'

The farseers looked displeased at the suggestion, but bowed their heads in deference to the autarchs, formally passing on the burden of the battle to the military leaders.

When the autarchs had departed, a discussion ensued between the seers. It was decided that Kelamith and Laimmain would accompany the force, along with Thirianna, Aladricas and Naomennin.

'To practise one's skills in the peace and safety of the craftworld is one matter,' Kelamith said to Thirianna as they walked back to her apartment. 'It is another to employ them in the anarchy of war and unleash them upon living creatures. This will be a valuable if somewhat difficult experience for you.'

Thirianna said nothing, something in her memories stirring inside, haunting her. Kelamith detected her reticence.

'This is not some scheme of mine to have you confront your unkind past,' said the farseer. 'We will need your skills if we are to avert this threat to our people. Whatever issues you may have with the slaying of potential innocents, set them aside now. To see the peril and not act would not only doom Alaitoc, it would be an insult to those who have long striven to harness this power for our protection.'

'I understand,' said Thirianna, though she felt uneasy about the coming battle.

'We do not leave for another two cycles,' said Kelamith. 'Use that time to confront whatever doubts are nagging. In battle, you will not be given the luxury of hesitation or laxity.'

'I will be prepared,' Thirianna assured him, though she was loath to reveal to herself the malign memory she had taken great pains to lock away in the deepest parts of her mind. 'When you call, I will be ready.'

Thirianna waited in the dark antechamber in the Shrine of One Hundred Bloody Tears, sensing the exarch in the room behind her calling the Dire Avengers to battle. She knew that she would have to reach into her memory and bring out the experience she had shut away. It was concealed firmly behind her war-mask, and Kelamith had hinted that the coming battle might bring it forth without Thirianna's volition. Better now, she had decided, to confront this potential nightmare in the sanctuary of the shrine, than risk it taking her unawares at a critical moment.

She began the mantra that brought forth her war-mask. She paused as it was settling into place, keeping a hold of her normal self to avoid being consumed with bloodlust. The Witchblade in her hands thrummed with life, woken by her dark thoughts.

Placing the blade to one side, disassociating herself from its war-hunger, Thirianna sat cross-legged in the middle of the chamber and closed her eyes. She pushed through the red film of the war-mask and opened herself to the memories that lay beyond.

Dozens of recollections flooded through her, each a vista of death, a vignette of bloodshed. She shuddered, caught between the horror of the atrocities she committed and the ecstatic feeling that had flowed through her when she had perpetrated them.

Yet there was nothing there that caused her greater concern than before. She had seen these things when she had prepared for the battle with the orks. There was another memory, so vile to her she had cast it down into the abyss of her thoughts, where even her warrior-self would not have to contemplate it.

She baulked for a moment, afraid to venture further. Her skin felt slick with the blood of those she had slain, her ears rang with their wounded cries and death rattles, her heart pounded with the sensation of their fleeing life.

Thirianna withdrew a little way, allowing the warrior-memories to recede, leaving her in peace again. She slowed her heart and breathing, instilling calm. If she were to unleash this dark memory she would have to do it swiftly, diving past the other recollections into its lair.

Hardening her heart as much as she could, filled with trepidation, Thirianna thrust herself into the past, sweeping past the battles into the dark maelstrom of her innermost secret thoughts.

It was some kind of eating area. A long table flanked by high-backed seats stretched the length of the room, set with plates and candlesticks as if ready for a meal. Thirianna heard a whimpering noise and leapt onto the table. She ran along its length, picking her way between the dishes and candlesticks without thought.

At the far end of the room was another seating area, with overstuffed chairs and a round table. In the corner cowered a female human. With her were three children, one male, two female. Their faces were red and wet, their eyes glistening.

The taint of Chaos permeates this place, said Kelamith. *All must be purged.*

The humans made whimpering, animal noises as Thirianna brought up her shuriken catapult.

The eldest female, the mother, shrieked something, covering the children with herself. Thirianna ignored her wails and opened fire, shredding the woman's body.

The children screamed, their tear-streaked faces spattered with the blood of their mother. The largest of them, the boy, leapt to his feet and charged Thirianna. She reacted without thought, stepping aside from his clumsily swinging fists. She swung the shuriken catapult, bringing it down on the back of the boy's neck, easily snapping the young human's spine. He flopped to the lacquered floor without a further sound.

The two girls squirmed, trying to free themselves from the dead weight of their mother, eyes wide with horror as their brother's corpse twitched in front of them.

Thirianna looked at the youngest. She was barely old enough to walk, yet the look in her eyes seemed weighed with a lifetime of sorrow. The Aspect Warrior fired again, ripping out the child's throat with a short salvo. The last struggled to her feet and turned to run. It was futile and she went down in a mess of blood and ragged dress, her blonde locks covering her face as she tumbled onto a rug.

Thirianna looked at the sprawling bodies, the swirl of their blood and the splay of their dead limbs. They had been so fragile, so easy to slay.

She laughed.

Falling to one side, Thirianna let out a wild howl of despair. Her own laughter echoed around the chamber, haunting and deliberate, full of contempt for life. The seer clasped her head in her hands, filled with guilt and shame, her body convulsing as she remembered every fleck of blood on the faces of the dead children. She saw the edges of the mother's ribs, bloody and scratched from the shurikens, poking out from beneath her laced bodice. She could smell the blood, hear the crying.

Every part of her wanted to flee. Thirianna resisted the urge to hurl the memory back into the blackness, a tiny part of her strong enough to face the full fury of her own violence. Over and over she watched the family dying, yet it never dimmed, and the memory of her exultation at the act wrenched at her spirit each time.

Panting, Thirianna forced herself to her feet. She had to accept this; she had to acknowledge that part of her capable of committing such an act. They were only humans, she told herself, but her justification felt hollow. They were not innocent, she reasoned, they were tainted by Chaos, but she knew that it was a delusion.

I am a murderer, she thought.

Another part of her mind railed against the accusation. Her war-mask flowed, bringing out her warrior spirit. She had been a Dire Avenger, incarnation of a purifying flame. She had slain hundreds, guilt or innocence were irrelevant.

It was not the act itself that so appalled Thirianna, it was the joy it had brought.

It sickened her, that laugh, the utter disregard for life that she had shown. It rang again in her ears, chilling, devoid of compassion. The slaughter may have been justified or not, it may have been a necessary precaution or cold-blooded murder. What Thirianna could not deny was the satisfaction it had brought. It had not been an act of instinct in the heat of battle, a life-or-death decision to slay or be slain. It had been cold-hearted, reasoned, and was all the more enjoyable for it.

The heinous act had thrilled her so much because she had known full well what it was she was doing. It was the simple matter of doing the unthinkable, without blame or shame, which had been exhilarating. It was a true moment of Khaine's bloody work, unhampered by logic or morality.

Another thought burst through Thirianna's internal recriminations. Even in her moment of high-handed triumph, she had known she was bewitched with the bloodshed. After the battle she had quit the Shrine of One Hundred Bloody Tears, turning her back on the Bloody-Handed God, forever expunged of her desire for war.

The act, callous as it was, had freed her from Khaine's grip.

Focussing on this, Thirianna recovered some of her equilibrium. As the visceral nature of the memory subsided, she was able to hold on to that simple fact: at her darkest moment she had triumphed. She had stood upon the brink of accepting Khaine's embrace, of becoming enamoured of death and blood-letting, but it had not trapped her.

It was the nature of the Path that a life be composed of many such moments, where one trod the line between safety and utter obsession. Thirianna had passed the test, and she had moved on. It was only from shirking her duty to those she had slain, by trying to forget them, that she had poisoned herself.

The memory was quickly losing its power to unbalance her. The more she examined it, the more Thirianna consoled herself to the grievous act. Confronting what she had done, she could feel the guilt and shame she had not felt at the time. In accepting the punishment, the raw feeling that sang along her nerves, she could atone for her bloody ways.

Reaching out a hand, Thirianna called to her Witchblade. It leapt to her grasp, singing its own deadly song. She Who Thirsts threatened again, through the humans once more. Thirianna would have to kill again, not only to save her own life, but to save the lives of future Alaitocii. Human lives would be saved too, though they would never comprehend the benefit for themselves. The thought did not make what she had to do easy, but it made it a fraction more palatable.

Thirianna heard the dull chanting of the Dire Avengers in the adjoining chamber. Their ritual was coming to its climax, as each would be daubing the rune of the shrine on their foreheads and taking up their war-masks.

She crossed the room and lifted her helm from its hook. She too was ready.

The eldar battleplan was a thing of complex beauty. Like so many human worlds, the eyes of the defenders were ever turned outwards, seeking threats that would approach openly. Not only had they allowed the machinations of Chaos to enter unhindered into their lives, the humans were incapable of defending themselves against any foe more advanced. Their orbital stations and crude surveying satellites scanned the void for disturbances in the warp, expecting enemy ships to enter their system in the outermost reaches, far from the gravitational pull of their sun.

The eldar suffered from no such restriction. The webway passed close by to the human world and though it was not without some effort, it was a straightforward task to extend a temporary tunnel into the system. The battleship *Fainoriain* and two destroyers had exited the webway inside the ring of detection devices, and hidden by holofields and other screening devices, the eldar had devised their method of attack.

The Chaos artefact had been taken to the citadel seen in the visions of the farseers. Swiftly monitoring the humans' unencrypted communications revealed that this fortress was a retreat for members of a mercantile cadre that effectively ruled the world under the auspices of the Emperor's agencies. It was protected by physical walls and gun turrets, but had no defence against the eldar.

In layout the fortress was an octagon, protected by walls of hewn stone, within which a courtyard of dull grey slabs contained several buildings. At each angle of the walls was located a defence battery, multi-barrelled cannons pointing to the skies beside small guardhouses. The main citadel was located not quite at the centre, a slightly smaller tower in its shadow. Several one-storey buildings surrounded these two structures, storehouses with wide doors and no windows. Flags hung limply from poles along the walls, and spotlights glared out into the night beyond.

Such defiance was in vain against the eldar.

The first wave of Aspect Warriors emerged from the webway within these defences and swiftly secured the walls and outer courtyard, cutting down all resistance with shuriken catapults and missile launchers. As the anti-air batteries were overrun, Swooping Hawks descended from the night skies to bolster the attack, dropping onto the worn battlements with plasma detonations and strobing lasblasters.

Thirianna noted in passing that Korlandril was amongst those fighting, the Striking Scorpions of the Deadly Shadow tasked with taking one of the warehouse-like outer buildings. He seemed to have recovered from his injury and his thread across the skein was strong.

Glad that her former friend would not suffer a repeat of the trauma of his last battle, Thirianna followed Kelamith down an alley between two of the warehouses. While Dire Avengers, Dark Reapers, Howling Banshees and Fire Dragons made the initial assault, the seers and a bodyguard of more warriors had left the webway in the vicinity of the command tower close to the northern wall.

Two squads of Warp Spiders heralded the second phase of the attack. Using their warp jump generators, the Aspect Warriors teleported directly into the main guard room within the tower, silently slaying the occupants in a matter of moments.

Thirianna and Kelamith led the squad of Dire Avengers from Thirianna's old shrine, the One Hundred Bloody Tears, accompanied by Arhathain. Poised between reality and the skein, Thirianna quickly led the others to a large portal of iron. She had foreseen the door opening as the occupants of the tower emerged to respond to the attack on the wall.

Sure enough, a few moments later, the sound of grinding gears and swinging levers could be heard. The gates opened inwards to reveal several dozen human soldiers wearing drab grey fatigues. Their uniforms were more like labourers' clothes, heavy overalls stitched with many pockets worn over white shirts. Their helmets were of grey-painted metal, steeply sloped with narrow cheekguards, and their squad leaders wore gorgets of silver and vambraces of the same.

The humans raised their lasguns slowly, eyes widening with shock and fear. The Dire Avengers opened fire, gunning down many, while Thirianna, Kelamith and Arhathain charged into the doorway.

Thirianna cut the legs from the first soldier as a blue las-blast deflected from her rune armour. She ducked under the butt of a rifle and chopped off the hands holding the weapon. A step to the left brought her behind the screaming man and a swift cut to the neck ended his suffering. Forewarned by the skein, Thirianna brought up her Witchblade to deflect another las-bolt, before unleashing a fury of flames through a doorway to her right, incinerating another handful of humans.

Thirianna briefly felt the spirit of Kelamith as he flashed through the minds of the defenders, searching for information, stealing their dying thoughts. It felt a little like ransacking their graves, prising open their last hopes and fears for glimmers of useful intelligence.

'We seek the darkness below,' said the farseer. Thirianna glimpsed a vision of a room filled with crude communications devices. 'Their voice must be silenced.'

Arhathain led the next attack, the shuriken weapon mounted in his gauntlet spewing a hail of discs as he leapt down a flight of stairs towards the underground levels. The glow from his spear mingled with the light from Thirianna's blade and Kelamith's staff, bathing the stairway in a multicoloured swirl.

The Dire Avengers followed after their autarch, the two psykers bringing up the rear. More soldiers emerged from a row of rooms holding narrow bunks; unarmed, they were swiftly despatched.

At the end of the corridor, the room to the communications centre started to swing shut. Thirianna felt a huge build-up of pressure in the back of her mind, as Kelamith extended his will. The door was thrown open by the power of his thought, hurling back the two men who had been closing it.

Dial-filled consoles exploded as the Dire Avengers opened fire. Thirianna went through the door beside Arhathain, blocking a bayonet aimed at her gut. She slashed the tip of her Witchblade through the human's throat, sending him reeling into another soldier. Jumping high over both men, Thirianna drove her blade into the back of another, before spinning on her heel to deliver the killing blow to the man who had been tripped.

Arhathain's spear blazed as he swept it through the bank of speakers and levers, sending molten metal splashing up the dark stone walls. An ear-splitting whine erupted from a damaged grille, a moment before Kelamith's staff silenced it, the farseer driving the ornate head into the bowels of the spark-spitting machine.

'It is done,' said Kelamith. The whine of shuriken catapults filled the passageway outside as the Dire Avengers responded to a fresh attack.

'The cordon is formed,' reported Arhathain. 'All squads are in position to move on the central building.'

'Wait!' snapped Kelamith.

A heartbeat later, Thirianna also felt something changing. The skein was shifting, mutating and bending as new futures unfolded. A malign presence was spilling out across the threads of fate, bending them to its purpose.

'She Who Thirsts,' muttered the farseer.

Thirianna recognised the taint, awash with memories of being hunted in the webway. Now there was no attempt to beguile, no subtle twisting of desire. The daemons of the Great Enemy swamped the skein with their presence, responding to the threat to their artefact.

'We do not have time to wage two battles,' said Arhathain, also sensing something of the gathering daemonic threat. 'We have a limited time before we are detected and the humans respond in force.'

'Continue for the main tower,' said Kelamith. Thirianna felt him binding for a moment with the mind of Laimmain as the two farseers devised a plan to defend against the daemons. 'We shall protect your spirits as you protect our bodies. Thirianna, come with me.'

The two of them headed up through the communications tower, as Arhathain and the Dire Avengers left to join the main attack. Thirianna flowed between reality and unreality, the material and immaterial overlapping in her thoughts. As she negotiated a turn in the stairs, she felt the first pull of the artefact.

Tenebrous tendrils plucked at Thirianna's mental defences, seeking a means to penetrate her mind. Her rune glowed white-hot, fending off the attack, redirecting the psychic power pushing at the barriers erected around her mind.

Though she suffered no physical damage, the psychic attack left her dizzied. She could smell a sweet perfume, alluring, intoxicating. Her skin tingled within her armour, while a melodic harmony disorientated her, tempting her deeper into the skein.

She resisted the alluring deception, hardened to it by previous experience. Enraged, the daemons hurled themselves at the minds of the eldar, clawing and screeching, trying to overcome with brute force that which they had failed to circumvent by seduction.

Thirianna lashed back with her mind, sending a pulse of fire across the skein. Kelamith did likewise, and she felt the flames from the other seers scorching along the threads of the future, purging the daemonic presence.

Reaching the uppermost storey of the communications building, Kelamith withdrew from the skein for a moment, leaving Thirianna to fend for herself. Keeping only the smallest fraction of her essence in her body, she ventured further across the skein, following the path blazed by Laimmain, picking off stray motes of Chaos energy left in the wake of the farseer's offensive.

Immaterial hands plucked at Thirianna's thoughts, trying to prise open her passions, seeking weakness in her resolve. She felt the heartache of her discord with Korlandril and Aradryan and quickly responded with thoughts of her partial reconciliation with her father.

The daemons recited the words of her poems, calling them out in trite snippets, twisting the meanings of the verses, making them sound pathetic and hollow. Thirianna refused to be goaded into a response. Instead, she followed the psychic echoes of the voices, tracking down the daemons and bringing the fire of purity to bear upon them. White flames licked across the skein, silencing the evil chatter.

There came a lull in the onslaught, the daemons retreating from the wrath of the eldar seers. Thirianna returned her consciousness to her body, noting that the entire psychic battle had taken less than a dozen heartbeats.

'Our foe is not yet defeated,' warned Kelamith, gesturing towards the door. 'We must join the attack on the central tower.'

The seers left the communications building and headed towards the central compound. Fires could be seen burning at several of the windows in the upper levels. There were eldar dead at the main gate, Howling Banshees riddled with bullets. Thirianna stepped over the corpses without a second glance, her war-mask inuring her to the horror of the scene.

As she followed Kelamith up a winding staircase, she was aware again of powerful energy flowing across the skein. The daemons came again, focussing their malice upon the psykers, drawn to their bright spirits.

Drawing power through her rune, Thirianna divided her attention between the real and unreal. With the daemons flooding the skein with their corrupting energy, it was impossible to draw on the power of her foresight, so it was with some caution that she stepped off a landing into one of the chambers of the citadel. She scanned the room quickly, while on the skein the daemons manifested themselves, appearing in a variety of hideous forms. The daemonettes she had encountered before could be seen, claw-hands slashing, jewelled eyes bewitching. With them came six-limbed monstrosities with lashing tongues. Thirianna focussed her powers, meeting the daemonic incarnations with an apparition of her own, flaming sword in hand.

Blade met claw in the ethereal world, as Thirianna leapt behind the toppled remains of a bookcase, las-bolts searing along the stained wood. She pulled out her shuriken pistol and fired back, felling one of the soldiers taking cover in a doorway opposite.

A claw snapped at Thirianna's face, deflected at the last moment by the hilt of her Witchblade. She darted under another slashing claw and brought the sword up into the creature's chest, turning it to ash.

Kelamith entered the room, a ball of light erupting from the tip of his staff, hurling the humans back from the doorway. On the skein, a handful of daemons disintegrated into bodiless screams at the touch of his mind.

'Others are coming, stall their advance,' said the farseer, waving a hand towards another, smaller doorway at the far end of the ruined library.

Thirianna dashed down the long carpet, sword in hand, arriving at the door a moment before a human stumbled through, a pistol in one hand, chainsword in the other. Thirianna blocked the chainsword with her Witchblade and fired her pistol into the man's gut, sending him backwards through the door.

In the skein, the daemons were acting strangely. They circled the bright sparks of the eldar psykers, constantly moving, feinting but not attacking. Thirianna could sense other energies at work, the power of the warp leaking through to the material world, the unreal becoming real through the machinations of the daemons.

Beyond the door was a small set of stairs leading down, no doubt used by servants so that they would not disturb their masters as they moved about the citadel. There were sounds of a struggle coming from below and Thirianna hurried down the steps.

The daemons were pouring their power through the nascent breach into the material universe, seeking anything to anchor upon. The dull, lifeless minds of the humans were hard to detect, but utterly unprotected. Urged on by a thought from Laimmain, the seers tried to intervene, placing themselves between the daemons and the humans, hurling bolts of fire to drive back the creatures of the Great Enemy.

The room below was some kind of storage area, the walls lined with shelves, barrels and crates stacked neatly to one side. A human female crouched behind one of the boxes, her head in her hands, mouth open in a silent scream. Thirianna stepped forwards, Witchblade raised.

The woman's flesh pulsed, rippling with unearthly power as something slid into the body, pushing its way into the material world through her weak mind. Spines erupted from her back and shoulders and her hair fell out in clumps, leaving a distorted scalp coloured a dark pink. Fangs erupted bloodily from her gums and her fingernails turned to white claws.

With a screech, the daemon-thing leapt at Thirianna, slashing at the eye lenses of her helm. Sparks erupted from the seer's rune armour, throwing the daemonic creature back, the woman-daemonette smashing into the shelves to send shards of pottery crashing to the hard floor. Thirianna did not hesitate, lunging at the possessed human with Witchblade outstretched. The sword passed into the daemon's gut, violet fire springing from the wound.

A psychic backlash ripped along the Witchblade, taking Thirianna by surprise. She stumbled back, losing her grip on the weapon as she tumbled over piled sacks. The daemon-thing was not destroyed. A forked tongue rasped in and out of its fanged mouth as it stalked forwards, its dagger-like claws outstretched.

Thirianna formed a fist, enveloping her hand with psychic power. She sprang to her feet and punched the creature in the chest, driving her hand forwards with every ounce of physical and mental strength. The blow tore the daemon in half, a ring of purple fire exploding outwards, hurling body parts into the cluttered stores.

Here and there, the daemons were making other breakthroughs from the skein. Try as they might, the eldar could not shield every human mind. Thirianna could feel the artefact weighing heavily on the psychic plane, bending everything around it, forming an immaterial gravity well that drew everything towards it. Its presence was erratic though, coming in ebbs and flows, its power constrained by the will of the seers. It flared, sending out a corona of energy, shadowy tentacles seeking a mind to latch on to, to bring it to full awakening.

Thirianna heard the creak of a door behind her opening. Her Witchblade flew into her hand as she spun around, ready to strike.

The blade stopped a hair's-breadth from the boy's throat.

Thirianna trembled, looking into the wide, brown eyes of the youth. He was dressed in drab grey clothes, his jerkin buttoned tight, short trousers flapping around his knees. She noticed he was barefoot.

The boy said something to her in the garbled tongue of the humans, his face a mask of fear. He started backing away towards the door, eyes roving around the room, taking in the gore splashed everywhere.

'Slay him!'

Kelamith's command was a shout in the heart of Thirianna's mind. She almost acted on impulse, but stayed her hand again, refusing to strike the killing blow.

She could not do it. The council had decided that all had to die, but Thirianna could not bring herself to slay the boy out of hand. She was not the cold-blooded slayer of Khaine any more. Her Witchblade twitched, eager for blood, but she held it back. Even with her war-mask in place, she could not spill the blood of the boy. He was no threat.

In the moment of her hesitation, Thirianna's guard in the skein wavered. A daemonic entity slipped past her straying thoughts, sliding into the youth. She watched in horror as his skin paled and his eyes darkened.

Flickering between the skein and reality, Thirianna could see the daemon within the boy's form, yet still she could not deliver the deadly blow. On the skein, she seized hold of the daemon and tried to drag it from the youth's body.

The child snatched up a broken piece of wood and smashed it across Thirianna's chest. Her rune armour absorbed the blow, flashing with light.

She struggled with the daemon, its psychic claws and teeth slashing and biting at her mind as it fought to keep the boy; she delved her thoughts into the raw stuff of the daemon, sickened by its touch but determined not to let go.

She warded away the swinging plank with her Witchblade, guiding the blow harmlessly past her shoulder. The boy snarled and spat curses at her in his own tongue before jabbing the broken end towards her face. Thirianna ducked aside, slapping the plank from the possessed boy's grasp with the flat of her Witchblade.

Now the daemon changed, melding itself around Thirianna, trying to draw her into the remnants of the boy's mind. His memories flashed across her consciousness: so few and all of them of a lifetime of drudgery and servitude.

'The boy is dead. There is nothing left to save.'

Kelamith's voice was calm, the words like cooling water on a fevered brow, calming Thirianna's ire. She realised her fear was giving strength to the daemon. The harder she struggled to free the boy from its grip, the stronger it became.

Distracted, Thirianna reacted slowly to the youth's next attack. He snatched up a clay jug and hurled it into the side of her helm. The material held and she was unharmed, but the impact made her ears ring.

The Witchblade called to her, resonating with Thirianna's war-mask. She was a killer, and the boy's life or death would not change that. The stain of blood was on her spirit forever. What was one more short existence in the torrent of blood she had unleashed in her life?

The daemon swelled with power, fuelling itself from Thirianna's doubt.

The boy's body rippled and bulged, hunching over as a tail tipped with a barbed sting erupted from the base of his spine. The sting jabbed towards Thirianna, almost catching her unawares. She ducked beneath the attack and stepped back out of range.

The boy smiled at her, the expression one of sublime innocence.

The daemon had gone too far and it flinched as it realised its mistake.

Thirianna levelled her Witchblade at the boy. Purple flames sprang from the sword, engulfing the possessed child from head to foot. On the skein, Thirianna ripped free from the daemon, tearing it apart from within, shredding it with her naked rage.

The thing screamed, such a piercing, plaintive wail that Thirianna almost broke off her attack. She steeled herself and poured out more of her rage, turning the creature's physical body to a smouldering cinder even as she scattered its power, banishing it across the breadth of the skein.

As the charred remains collapsed into ash, Thirianna fell to her knees, moaning with despair. Her blade grew dark and her rune clinked to the ground as she retreated inside a hard shell thrown up around her thoughts.

Kelamith came to her quickly, on the skein and in person. He peeled away the protective layers encircling her mind while he helped her to her feet.

'Come and see that which has caused us so much grief,' he said.

Thirianna locked away the encounter with the daemon alongside her previous child-slaying, bringing her war-mask into full focus, shutting off the rampaging guilt that wracked her whole mind.

She was calm again.

The threat of the daemons had been dissipated but still Thirianna could feel the brooding presence of the artefact. It became a more diffused energy, spreading across the skein, looking for escape. The minds of the eldar were like a field of stars, and in turn each flickered with pale blue and delicate green shades as the Great Enemy sought to tempt them.

'Touch nothing,' warned Kelamith, his words echoing across the skein to the minds of the other eldar. 'Free your minds of desire and temptation.'

As the two seers headed up another staircase, Thirianna caught sporadic sounds of fighting. On the skein she could see the last few humans holding out in the room at the pinnacle of the tower.

The artefact made a last grab for attention, pouring its filthy power into the humans. Thirianna felt a moment of triumph from the object and saw a vision of a human leaping towards the box that held its power in check.

Something else flickered across the skein. They were there for a moment and then gone: Warp Spider Aspect Warriors, forewarned by

Kelamith. The thread of the human's life ended abruptly.

A new aura of light filtered across the immaterial realm as Kelamith and Thirianna were joined by Arhathain on the top landing. Kelamith gestured for Thirianna to wait as the farseer and autarch entered the chamber together.

Thirianna turned at a sudden presence behind her. A group of grim-faced seers made their way up the stairs, all clad in plain white, heads shorn of all hair. Between them floated an ovoid container, dark red in colour and patterned with silver runes. Thirianna stepped out of their way, disturbed that they had no presence on the skein. As they passed, her spirit stone glowed white for a moment, touched by their energy.

When the white seers had entered, Thirianna moved to the door, just in time to see that not all of the humans were dead. The artefact gave a last pulse of power, imbuing life into the near-lifeless with a flailing tendril of energy. A human soldier surged from the wreckage of the room's furniture, one arm hanging limply by his side, a long wound in his thigh spraying blood as he sprinted across the room towards the artefact.

Arhathain reacted quickest, his spear singing across the hall to catch the human in the chest, hurling him bodily through the air. A blink later, several shuriken volleys and laser blasts passed through the air where the man had been. Arhathain beckoned to the spear and it twisted, ripped itself free of the dead human and flew back to his grasp. Unperturbed, the autarch approached the box and lowered to one knee beside it, studying the artefact closely.

Whispering protective mantras, the white seers closed around him, their robes obscuring all sight, their sibilant incantations growing in volume. The skein bent around them also, becoming a protective bubble that reflected back the thoughts of Thirianna as she tried to peer inside.

When they parted a moment later, silence descended. The box was gone but the wraithbone casket gleamed with a darker light, an aura of oily energy seeping from it. The casket weighed heavily on the skein, even the warding powers of the white seers unable to stop it from affecting the paths of fate around it. There was much blood and death surrounding the artefact, but Thirianna knew not to pry too closely, and averted her thoughts.

The white seers departed with their tainted cargo.

'Humans gather in force to destroy us outside the walls,' Arhathain announced, standing up. 'The garrison are all slain. Return to the webway and we will be away. Take our dead – we cannot leave them in this forsaken place.'

'Who are they?' Thirianna asked, as she and Kelamith followed the white seers back to the transport pod that had brought them through the webway.

'A bridge, between the craftworlds and the Black Library,' replied the farseer. 'They are steeped in the knowledge of Chaos, and are immune to its charms and wiles.'

'They do not look like Harlequins to me,' said Thirianna, remembering the garish troupe of warrior-performers she had seen once as a child.

'Though the Harlequins know the location of the Black Library, they are not its only Guardians,' explained Kelamith. 'They are far too capricious to be entrusted with such a thing, no matter how devoted they profess to be about the destruction of the Great Enemy. Wiser, sounder minds than those of the Laughing God's followers will study this thing and learn its secrets before it is destroyed.'

Thirianna thought how sheltered her life had been on Alaitoc. She had thought she had known everything about her people, both those of the craftworld and those beyond, but she was learning quickly that the remnants of the great civilisation they had once been were far more diverse and secretive than even she had known.

'That is true,' said Kelamith, detecting her thoughts. 'There are many things of eldar and alien origin that we have forgotten.'

'That is not a comforting thought,' said Thirianna.

'It was not intended as such,' replied Kelamith. 'Though you faltered today, you will grow the stronger for it. Though you can perfect the arts you have already learnt, honing your runecraft and powers, you face another choice, child. It is not an easy decision, and while many decisions may influence the course of your fate, this one will without question decide your doom.'

Part Three

Farseer

SKEIN

The Hooded Shadow – Cloak of Morai-heg. The balance of fate can be both robust and delicate. Some dooms cannot be avoided, while others hang by a slender thread for their duration. Of the latter, there are some fates so highly attuned to influence that the simplest observation, the knowledge of their possibility, can render them inert. In order to look upon such visions, the seer must go forth in the guise of Morai-heg herself, protected from repercussion by the Hooded Shadow, lest their awareness of what they witness brings it to pass or quenches its potential.

Thirianna held her rune just above her fingertip as she contemplated her future. It was to this point that she had been moving since leaving the Path of the Poet, an instance in her life that would have a profound effect on her existence, both of what came next and what she had already experienced.

She sat on the low couch below a window overlooking the parklands. The dome had moved to the dusk-like period of the cycle, an artificial twilight of deep reds and purples casting long shadows from the trees and rocks. The croaking of nocturnal amphibians could be heard in the distance, while moonsparrows and rasp owls disturbed the peace with their roosting cries and haunting calls. Swarms of tiny bats, each no larger than a fingernail, fluttered from their nests in the boles of the kaidonim trees, appearing as a drifting haze that floated just above the grassy hills.

All of the calm of the scene was lost on Thirianna as she studied the slowly revolving sigil of wraithbone. She admired the craft her father had put into its making. At first glance it appeared quite plain, a simple shape of two bars and three curves, encompassing the syllables of her name. On closer inspection, the surface was rippled with whorls and lines, almost invisible to the naked eye, like the print of a fingertip. Stranger still, the wraithbone was not static. The pattern shifted slowly; so slowly it could not be seen, but it definitely changed from one cycle to the next in subtle ways.

The design could be taken as a map, perhaps, charting the possible futures being played out by Thirianna's life. It might be a record of her past life, constantly updating as she moved across the skein of fate. For all Thirianna knew, it might well be a simple conceit of her father, an embellishment of purely decorative value.

Whatever the mutable pattern was, it could not offer Thirianna any guidance on the matter at hand. There was no pressure to decide her course; she continued to practise her scrying and her psychic abilities, and in a sense that was a choice in itself, a choice of non-commitment. Yet Thirianna knew her continued studies were not a resolution, but simply a means to allow her time to think.

It was tempting to use the rune to delve the future path, to see the consequences of one act or another on Thirianna's life to come. It was for that very reason she had chosen the Path of the Seer, after all.

Kelamith had warned against such a thing. Reading one's own rune was commonplace amongst seers. Thirianna had done it several times, but always the ending had been blurred, lacking true meaning or context. When she had fought in battle against the humans, it had been her rune guiding her step and her blows, but only from one moment to the next.

In this matter the rune could not help.

Thirianna had to decide whether the Path of the Seer would be just one stage of her life, as had the Path of the Poet and the Path of the Warrior and the other paths she had trodden before; the alternative was to dedicate herself to the ever-deeper study of the skein and to ultimately become one with the infinity circuit. There was no alternative. If she wished to be a farseer then she would be treading upon a road that led to two fates: accidental or violent death, or the near-life of the Dome of Crystal Seers. To truly understand the skein, to glean its most vital and hidden secrets, was to share in its power, to become part of it, eventually leaving behind Form and Being and becoming Mind alone.

The rune could not help because the situation presented Thirianna with a paradox. If she were to hold back and stay a simple warlock, she could not see far enough ahead to understand the future implications. If she wanted to know where her fate would take her if she became a farseer, the extension of her powers would continue to grow exponentially, taking her to places in the skein she could not yet comprehend, and thus would not understand yet.

Against Kelamith's advice and the logic of the problem, Thirianna had tried to locate her future self on the skein, as the farseer must have known she would. It had been a frustrating experience, full of circles and loops that became ever more complex and self-referential the further ahead she scryed. The divergences in her life became so maddeningly complicated and obscure that she had abandoned her forays into her future in order to preserve her sanity. She had stood on the brink of becoming wrapped up in her own convoluted destiny, never to escape, and at the last moment had heeded Kelamith's warning.

As many important decisions come to be, it was a straightforward question of whether she desired a varied life, or an existence dedicated to a single goal. Without any foresight, reduced to second-guessing fate, Thirianna could apply logic and feeling, but nothing more, and it was these two qualities that she had come to distrust and had led her to becoming a seer.

She looked again at the rune, wondering if there was some kind of message or secret intention of the spiralling design worked into its surface. There was only one person who could answer that question, and Thirianna found herself wondering what other advice Yrlandriar might give her.

She had not seen her father since he had presented her with the rune, passing by her apartment on a brief visit. The two of them had exchanged formal pleasantries but both had grown quickly uncomfortable with the notion of discussing deeper matters.

Part of Thirianna was loath to seek help from Yrlandriar. She had done well enough without his opinion before and it was likely to disagree with her own desire. Yet the avoidance of confrontation was morally cowardly; Thirianna's instinct was to continue on the Path and it was appropriate that she sought out challenges to that intuition to test her resolve. Yrlandriar was likely to provide such a thing, even if his opinion only served to bolster her dedication out of opposition to her father's wishes.

She reached into the infinity circuit, seeking the signature of Yrlandriar. He was working on the starship again and their consciousnesses touched only briefly long enough to agree a meeting later in the cycle.

Thirianna took off her seer robes and placed her rune inside a cloth-lined drawer in the wall beside her bedding. She pulled on a skin-tight suit of ochre, threaded with veins of gold, and a pair of high boots of dark blue. She styled her hair, strapped on a broad white belt, and drew on a long coat that matched the colour of her boots. She activated the mirrorplate and examined the results. She looked nothing like a seer, as had been her intent. If she was to make this decision clearly, she had to divest herself of the accoutrements of the seer, to discover if she was comfortable merely being Thirianna.

It was liberating at first, as she walked out of the apartments and joined the growing group of eldar at the gravrail platform at the edge of the park. Other than passing acknowledgement, no one else paid her any heed. Garbed as a seer she had been treated with more dignity and respect, but also a little suspicion.

The bullet-like carriage of the gravrail arrived and Thirianna boarded, joining a crowd of eldar heading rimwards for the night shows and darkened domes of dockwards Alaitoc. The carriage swiftly accelerated, turning the scattered lights of the towers and park to a blur, before the gravrail passed into a tunnel between domes and all became a soft white light.

Thirianna felt strangely alone. She was tempted to delve into the infinity circuit, but decided against it. Instead she sat watching the other occupants of the carriage as they travelled in pairs and threes and small groups, chattering happily or taking part in deep discussions with their peers.

At a glance it was impossible to say which path each of them was currently treading. There were a few subtle signs in clothing, jewellery, hairstyle and manner, but Thirianna felt half-blinded by having to resort to such techniques. As a seer she could glimpse the thread of everyone in the carriage and know instantly who they were, and what they did.

She tried to turn it into a game, to see if her old skills of observation had withered under the glare of her growing psychic ability. It was something to pass the time on the long journey.

Some of the others left and more came on board as the carriage moved from dome to dome, bringing in revellers from the Arcade of Distant Gravitas, dropping off severely dressed aesthetes in the Dome of the Kites. With each new influx, Thirianna studied them afresh, watching the changing relationships and unfolding destinies being played out in the flesh as she denied herself the vision of them on the skein.

Would they stay friends, she wondered? Who would grow closer and who would be drawn apart by the nature of the paths they followed? Would they be happy or sad? Which of them would lead lives of fulfilment or frustration?

It was an intriguing experience, to speculate on such matters. It reinforced the opinion of Kelamith, that rarely could the lives of individuals be turned to one fate or another. Only the great swathe of destiny could be altered, the life of Alaitoc steered on the correct path. It was a trap to think that every ill could be avoided and every boon enjoyed for each person. The gain of one was often the loss of many, and the gain of many made at the expense of a few.

As the carriage neared its destination at the docks, Thirianna was left with only a handful of others. The cultured landscapes outside were swathed with darkness except for the scattered glow of lanterns on the rivers of the Dome of Eternal Winters and the gleam from the windows of spire-like habitats.

She was in no hurry and when the gravrail arrived in the dock area, she found a small vendor offering a variety of hot confectionery. Thirianna was amused to see that they were cooked over an actual open flame, giving them a rustic flavour she had not tasted before. Nibbling on the soft lumps of sweetness, she wandered to her father's workshop.

As she entered, she immediately heard voices raised in song.

She hurried to the hangar where the starship was being crafted, having never seen a chorus of bonesingers working together. She located them arranged around the prow of the ship, accompanied by several dozen lesser artisans lining the gantries and walkways surrounding the ship's skeleton.

The huge space was filled with rising and falling harmonies, resonating from the ribbed walls, rebounding from the vaulted ceiling. The sounds of pipes merged with the voices of the eldar, adding an undercurrent of a different rhythm and pitch. Every harmonic was precise, guided by the bonesingers to a particularly frequency, moulded to the pitch and tone desired.

The air was alive with psychic energy. The starship skeleton resonated with the power and the walls hummed with it. It was too tempting not to witness this extraordinary feat from the skein, so Thirianna slipped part of her mind sideways into the infinity circuit to observe the act of creation both physically and psychically.

The infinity circuit thrummed with the energy being channelled. The structure of wraithbone blended with the psychic circuitry of the craftworld, attached at several key nodes. Drawing on this power, the bonesingers were weaving a pattern of resonant psychic energies, overlapping matrices of power that when combined formed solid matter: fabled wraithbone.

Two curving spurs were being added to the front of the ship. Thirianna's guess was that the area would later house some form of sensory array, such was its position. With her eyes and ears, she had some vague idea of the wraithbone forming out of the air, growing from the existing skeleton, its creation setting up vibrations that cut across the psychic choir.

With her mind, she could appreciate the true beauty of the act. The nascent wraithbone existed as a potentiality within the skein, taking on infinite forms. As the bonesingers led the other artificers, the skein pulsed and flowed with their desires, their imagining of the ship's design acting as the guide of fate. Conforming to this shaped destiny, the wraithbone solidified from its amorphous state into a physical material, fulfilling the self-destiny of its existence.

Fuelled by the infinity circuit, the wraithbone was a distillation of the skein, an amalgam of hope and despair, opportunity and disappointment, love and hate, life and death. The songs of the artisans encompassed joy and woe, the realisation of dreams and the dashing of ambitions.

The wraithbone was glowing with its own chill light, its future shape appearing as a fluttering image on the edge of vision, molecule by molecule emerging from its potential to fulfil its destiny.

Thirianna's waystone, attuned to the psychic voice of Alaitoc, throbbed with the beat of the song of creation. It sang through her body and mind, filling her with vigour and hope. Her mind was ablaze with possibilities as she glimpsed the voyages of the starship-to-be, the trials and tribulations and triumphs of its crews splaying out from the wraithbone core at its heart, a thousand and more new fates unveiled in the act of its creation.

Slowly the chorus quietened. One by one the artisans finished their songs, until only the pipes and voices of the bonesingers were left, echoing faintly through the great hall. Each sang and played in isolation now, honing the last parts of the structure, discordance rising from the harmony. Sadness gripped Thirianna. Potential was becoming reality. Infinite possibilities were resigning themselves to a singular fate.

The last notes hung in the air for a time, shimmering along the whole skeletal structure. And then they were gone, leaving a perfect moment of silence.

Thirianna realised she was crying.

It was as if she had lived and breathed with the ship. In the last moments of the song she had been taken to distant stars and far-flung worlds. And at the very end, she had seen the destruction of this mighty vessel, its conflagration in battle. Even in its birth had been sown the seeds of its death, the fate of all things, from eldar to starship, flower to star.

As she recovered, it was hard for Thirianna to match the beauty of what she had experienced with her knowledge of Yrlandriar who had orchestrated it. The starship was as much part of him as it was anything else, something more than just the fruit of his labours. His imprint was within every part of it, meshed with the presence of the others who had joined in its making, a physical extension of his own thread of destiny.

For a moment Thirianna felt jealousy. It was such creations, such children born of wraithbone, which had occupied her father when he should have attended to the needs of his actual child.

She tried to suppress the feeling as she saw her father approaching, not wishing to engage with him in a negative frame of mind. She tried to mask the envy she felt, but could not help but wonder if the satisfaction of being involved in such a creation had outweighed Yrlandriar's feelings on becoming a father.

'I fear I am under-dressed,' said Yrlandriar as he stopped in front of Thirianna, his eyes quickly taking in her extravagant outfit. He wore his rune-embroidered robes and carried his pipes under one arm, hair tied back by a bland but neat band of silver.

'I felt like a change,' said Thirianna, taken off-guard by the comment.

She followed Yrlandriar into the workshop, and sat down as a low seat emerged from the wall at a gesture from the bonesinger. He placed his pipes on the table and sat next to her, somewhat stiff and formal.

'I have a question,' said Thirianna, unsure how to phrase it.

'A question for me?' replied Yrlandriar, blinking with surprise. He regained his composure quickly. 'Ask your question.'

'The designs on the surface of the rune you wrought for me, do they have a meaning? Was it a pattern of your creation?'

Yrlandriar relaxed, comfortable with the nature of her inquiry. He stood up, opened a cabinet in the wall and took out a small crystal bottle and two goblets. He passed a cup to Thirianna and filled it with amber liquid from the decanter, before serving himself and placing the bottle back in its place. Thirianna noticed his actions were crisp and premeditated, a mark of physical as well as mental discipline.

'The design that you see is not an invention of mine,' said the bonesinger, shaking his head. 'The wraithbone is psychoreactive, as you know. It is responding to you, forming itself from your thoughts and feelings, binding itself to your spirit. What you see is a reflection of yourself, as realised by the wraithbone.'

'And will it ever stop changing?' Thirianna asked. She took a sip of the drink. It was honeywater, sweet and aromatic.

'Only if you stop changing,' replied Yrlandriar. He sat down and looked at Thirianna but said nothing more. His finger tapped on the rim of his goblet, though whether from contemplation or impatience Thirianna could not tell.

'I sense that you have more than one question to ask of me,' he said eventually. 'Your first could have been easily answered via a more distant communication, yet you come to visit me.'

'I stand upon the crux of a choice,' said Thirianna, choosing her words carefully. She did not wish to betray her own feelings on the matter lest it influence her father's opinion. 'My runecraft has progressed well. I must choose whether I will devote myself to further study of its lore, or remain a warlock for the time being.'

'You are too young to become a farseer,' Yrlandriar replied promptly. He took a mouthful of honeywater and Thirianna realised that he was not going to offer any further explanation.

'Age is not an issue,' she said.

'Of course it is,' said Yrlandriar. 'You have more than half of your life ahead. It would be obscene to walk a single Path for all of that time.'

Thirianna was about to argue her case but stopped herself. What her father had said was true and it was not something she had properly comprehended. However, it irked her that he seemed so dismissive of the idea.

'If it is what I wish to be, what my destiny should be, that is of no concern,' she said.

'It should be a concern,' said Yrlandriar. 'There are a great many things you might yet accomplish even if you do not attach yourself to this single path.'

'You are a bonesinger and shall remain so until you die,' Thirianna pointed out.

'That is different,' said Yrlandriar.

'How is that so different?' asked Thirianna. 'What accomplishments of yours outshine the creations you now render? Is not your final path also your finest?'

Yrlandriar looked to speak, but then took another drink. He glanced around the workshop, the slight hint of a frown creasing his brow.

'Yes, that is true,' he said when he returned his gaze to his daughter. 'You will have a great deal of experience by the time you are my age. For many passes I have been a bonesinger and yet I still cannot reach the heights achieved by some of my predecessors.'

Thirianna was not sure if that was an endorsement or just a passing comment. Yrlandriar's expression was doubtful, but his words seemed to lend weight to Thirianna's choice by instinct.

'I did not learn to create starships from the air in a single cycle,' Yrlandriar continued, his expression lightening. 'Perhaps you are right. With many passes of study and experience you might become one of the greatest farseers of Alaitoc. That would be the reward for the sacrifice you would make.'

'Sacrifice?' Thirianna was not sure what she would be giving up. It seemed to her that now she had tasted the potential of seerdom, it would be hard to live without it.

'To experience a life not bound to the skein,' said Yrlandriar. 'Would you ever fall in love, in the knowledge of all the potential disasters that might befall the relationship? Would you have a child, risking seeing its death a thousand times over every time you travel the skein? The life of a bonesinger can be lonely, I assure you. There is little in the physical world that can match the harmony of spirit that comes from the act of pure creation. Yet it is nothing to the loneliness of the farseer. At a whim you can choose to see the death of everyone you have ever cared about and yet you must often choose to let it happen, for fear it will bring doom to others to interfere.'

Remembering her last encounter with Korlandril, Thirianna had known a little of that dilemma. She had hoped that by increasing her experience and power she would bring more surety to her decisions, but recent exploits trying to divine her own future had betrayed that belief as a myth. The further one could venture, the wider the uncertainties involved.

'I see that perhaps I have opened your eyes to something you had not considered before,' said Yrlandriar. He turned slightly towards her, goblet clasped in his lap. 'You alone will make this decision and you alone will bear the consequences of it. You ask what I think you should do? I can tell you that I would never exchange my time with your mother or the raising of you for a few extra passes studying the way of the artificer. There is a level I will never be able to attain, but it is a small price to pay in compensation for the legacy I have left in other ways.'

'I see,' said Thirianna. Her father's honest words had sown doubt in her mind. She was back to the conundrum of the rune. How could she decide when she could not know what she would be giving up? She might not be a farseer and yet spend her life alone, leaving it without a legacy, her existence nothing more than something that happened and then was gone.

'Nothing is certain,' said Yrlandriar, reading something of Thirianna's dilemma in her pensive expression. 'You choose between two unknowns, and in this you are not less and no greater than any of us.'

'And if I choose to become a farseer, against your wishes?' Thirianna was not sure why she wanted to bait her father in this way, but it was a habit hard to break.

'My wishes are irrelevant,' said Yrlandriar, much to Thirianna's surprise. He smiled slightly at her reaction. 'We both know you will ignore them, and I cannot force my views upon you, that much is clear. So it is that I choose not to have any. Whatever you choose, I will try to remember that I am your father and I will give you whatever support I can. That is the best I can offer you.'

Thirianna could not quite believe what her father had said, and she ran his words through her mind again, trying to detect some hint of sarcasm. There was none.

'To be counted amongst the greatest of Alaitoc is not something to be dismissed lightly,' said Thirianna. She had read treatises and works from philosophers, poets and seers who had all left their lasting mark on the craftworld. To have her name listed amongst their like was tempting indeed.

'You think that fame is reward enough to forgo the life you might enjoy?' asked Yrlandriar. 'Is that a good reason to give up on everything else that might be?'

'It is *a* reason,' said Thirianna, laughing at herself. 'Only history will judge if it is good enough.'

'You are committed to this,' said Yrlandriar. 'I see it in your eyes. You see a future unfolding before you, shaped to your desire. It is not with joy that I realise this, but it is plain that you have cast your stone into the pool and now it remains to see how far the ripples will stretch.'

'I have,' said Thirianna. 'Too few of us pass our lives with true meaning and I will not be counted amongst those who came and went and were forgotten. I cannot change the past that exists between us, but I am happy that we have reached an understanding.'

'Enjoy it while it lasts,' said Yrlandriar, his expression stern. 'In time, the past and the present will be of no importance to you. I will be just another thread in the great tapestry of your destiny.'

The flux that had beset Thirianna's thread on the skein settled with her decision. She spent some time exploring the possible fates, though she heeded Kelamith's advice not to stray too far into the future at this early stage.

Her life took on a regular pattern of study, exploration and tuition. Progress was steady but slow, the unwinding possibilities of the skein gradually revealing their secrets as Kelamith guided Thirianna along the pathways of fate.

Twenty cycles after making her decision, Thirianna was met mid-cycle by Kelamith, who took her to their favoured place in the parklands, overlooking the tumbled rocks on the hillside.

Kelamith had a box with him, no larger than his hand, fashioned from the wood of a liannin tree. A simple pattern was carved in the lid, showing a knotted design representative of the skein, winding about the rune of Morai-heg, the goddess of fate.

Thirianna took the proffered box uncertainly, surprised by the gift from her mentor.

'It does not come from me,' he said with a delicate shake of the head. 'Open it and things will become clearer.'

Intrigued, Thirianna lifted off the lid of the box and placed it beside her. Within, nestled in the velvet lining, sat two more runes. One was the Scorpion, the other was the Wanderer. Confused, Thirianna looked to Kelamith for an explanation.

'They come from Yrlandriar,' he said.

'Yes, I understand that,' replied Thirianna. 'I appreciate the gesture and the effort. What I do not understand is why he chose these two runes. Did he speak with you about the choice?'

'No,' said Kelamith. He leaned a little closer and spoke softly. 'Your father had paid greater attention to your affairs than perhaps you realise. Remember why it was that you first came to Alaiteir.'

'I was distraught, worried about my…' Realisation dawned. 'The Scorpion represents Korlandril. The Wanderer is Aradryan.'

With a nod, Kelamith stood up.

'It is a fine gift, and I am happy to deliver it on Yrlandriar's behalf,' said the farseer. 'What have you learned about the Scorpion and the Wanderer?'

'The Scorpion is a rune of concealment,' said Thirianna, remembering the first descriptions from the texts she had read. 'It is used to find those fates that would otherwise be hidden to the observer. The Wanderer, well, that one is easy. It allows the seer to travel to distant threads, unconnected to others.'

'A very useful combination, and one that is within your power to wield wisely,' said Kelamith. 'I shall leave you to investigate your gift in your own time. Call on me if you need further guidance.'

Kelamith left her sitting at the top of the hillside. With a thought, Thirianna lifted the two runes from the box. Her own rune joined them from her belt and the three wove orbits around each other, interchanging positions as Thirianna concentrated on them, the circles and ellipses they described in the air pleasing to her eye.

The park was not the place to begin this new exploration of the skein. Thirianna allowed the runes to settle in the box. Kelamith was already out of sight, so she made her way to the Chambers of the Seers on her own, excited by the new possibilities presenting themselves.

As she arrived, she remembered to send a message across the infinity circuit, expressing her sincere thanks to her father for the gift. It was, she told him, the best thing he had ever done for her.

Thirianna was baffled by her next forays onto the skein. She had thought that with the power of three runes to draw upon, the maddening anarchy of diverging futures would be made clearer. If anything, the skein had become even more complex to navigate.

She asked Kelamith about this, having become lost several times trying to locate occasions when her thread and that of Korlandril and Aradryan would overlap again. It was an exercise in curiosity more than anything else; thoughts of her friends came infrequently and it was with dispassionate interest that she viewed their unfolding lives.

'It is the nature of the skein that the greater we become, the more of it we see,' explained Kelamith.

The two of them shared a simple lunch in Kelamith's rooms at the heart of the Chambers of the Seers. His apartment consisted of two areas: one for sleep and one for study. Little space was given over to anything except the basic essentials for eating, drinking and sleeping. The rest of the apartment was filled with copies of treatises, complex fate charts notated by Kelamith himself, rune boxes and storage crystals.

The apartment was quite cluttered, unlike the cold, streamlined mind that Thirianna detected when she was on the skein with her mentor.

'But that does not make sense,' said Thirianna. 'The greatest seers can make distant, accurate prophecies. How is that possible if the skein becomes ever more complicated?'

'You are using the power of the runes to expand your horizon,' said Kelamith. He picked at the scraps of food left in the dish set between them. 'You must learn to use their particular qualities to focus your vision on what you wish to see. The true art of the seer is to combine the power of many runes to hone in on a specific instance. Do not use them to look at the whole of the skein, but employ their channelled power to add layers of meaning to a narrow point of reference.'

'I think I understand,' said Thirianna. 'How should I proceed? What instance should I examine?'

'It does not matter,' said Kelamith. 'There is no means to know the import and probability of a divergence or convergence until one examines it.'

Thirianna was not satisfied by this answer, and Kelamith picked up on this.

'Do not be too hasty to know everything,' he said. 'Start with something simple, something small. Pick something that you know well.'

'I have tried that,' said Thirianna. 'I looked for Korlandril's thread, but I could not locate it. It is as if he has disappeared from the skein, and even the Scorpion cannot find it.'

'You are looking in the wrong place, then,' said Kelamith. 'If you are looking for an unknown, you must first begin with a known. I have shown you how to wind back the skein and look to the past. Use this to locate Korlandril's thread and then follow it forwards. Really, you should know this. It is a fundamental procedure.'

'You are right,' said Thirianna, pricked by the farseer's disappointment. 'I am sorry. I have been over-reaching myself, forgetting the process you taught to me. I will apply myself with more attention to detail.'

'It is not wrong to strive to see everything,' Kelamith said. 'It is the lure that brings us all to the skein. Do not fall into the trap of seeing everything whilst observing nothing. Small gates will often be the start of long roads.'

Thirianna was not quite sure what this last enigmatic statement meant, but she was eager to visit the skein again, fortified by Kelamith's advice. She asked leave of her mentor and returned to the Chambers of the Seers.

Remembering to apply herself to the basics, Thirianna forced herself to go through the entire ritual, even using one of the infinity circuit nodes to slip into the skein. She spoke the mantras in full, visualising and focussing on every syllable, concentrating on the meanings behind the words.

The skein appeared as it had done previously, a baffling labyrinth of emerging potentials. Thirianna ignored the temptation to go exploring and instead used her rune to latch onto her own thread. She wound it back, tugging the past to the present, until she found her last encounter with Korlandril.

Now that she had located his thread, Thirianna allowed time to wind forwards again. As she had done so before, she came across a tightly wound interlacing of threads, into which Korlandril's disappeared but did not emerge.

It was now that Thirianna channelled some of her energy through the Scorpion, allowing herself to pass into the tight knot of destinies, making her presence fine enough to pass through the grain of the tangle.

With some sadness, she realised what had come to pass. As she had feared, Korlandril had become too enamoured of his war-mask and was now trapped on the Path of Khaine. He was now an exarch, one spirit amongst many, his essence bound within a suit of ancient armour, rapidly losing its individuality as it was subsumed into the greater consciousness of the being known as Morlaniath.

So much for Korlandril, she thought. She felt a stab of momentary guilt at the thought that perhaps she had precipitated his fall into Khaine's clutches, but it quickly passed. Regret was misplaced on the skein. Here more than anywhere else it was plain to see the missed opportunities and squandered moments that passed by every living thing with each breath. The past, with its simple straight lines, fixed in place, could not be changed.

Thirianna corrected herself, remembering one of the early lessons taught to her by Kelamith. It *was* possible to change the past, through the power of the warp. Time in the realm of Chaos did not flow forwards and backwards. It churned and looped, and a seer with enough skill could, with great effort and a large amount of risk, move sideways from one flow to the next, and thus if gifted with a little luck, move his or her consciousness back in time.

There was grave danger to the seer; channelling so much power in the heart of Chaos itself was an invitation for daemonic attack even with the protection of the runes. This was not the greatest peril though. The past was meant to be set and it was impossible to foretell the consequences of any change made. Only the greatest catastrophes could be averted in this way, yet such action led to futures that were impervious to prophecy.

As Kelamith had concluded, it was far better to change the present than influence the past.

Thirianna switched her attention to Aradryan, having seen nothing of her friend since the battle at Hirith-Hreslain. She withdrew her focus from the Scorpion and channelled her power through the Wanderer, flinging her gaze wide to locate Aradryan's tangle of threads.

It took some time to find him. For a period he had been lost altogether and it was impossible to discern the reason. Thirianna noted this for a future conversation with Kelamith and concentrated on the slender threads she could find. Each was a tenuous causal link, made vague by Aradryan's unfettered desires. He was being ruled by emotion and whim, straying far from the Path, and thus cause and consequence changed quickly as his moods and feelings swung widely from one extreme to another.

Aradryan's growing capriciousness was clear to see as a series of threads that rapidly spiralled into a festering mess of contradictory lines of fate. Thirianna picked the closest, glimpsing her friend fighting aboard a starship of human design. She could not precisely locate the event in time and space, but it was not that distant; he was close to Alaitoc and the battle she saw would take place soon.

From this nodal point, Thirianna busied herself exploring the possible outcomes. In some futures, Aradryan died during the battle, shot or cut down by huge warriors garbed in the armour of Space Marines from the so-called Imperium of Mankind. Thirianna was amused by the conceit of the humans to claim the galaxy as their dominion, especially since such a claim was made in the name of a piece of rotting flesh sustained only by sacrificing their own kind. An Alaitocii philosopher, Nurithinel the Outspoken, had once claimed that the humans' worship of their corpse-Emperor was no worse than the interment of eldar spirits within the infinity circuit and had been hounded from the craftworld for the distasteful comparison.

Putting aside this diversion, Thirianna continued her exploration. In other futures, Aradryan survived, returning to his ship in triumph. In either case, he had risen to a position of some prominence in quite a short space of time, but backtracking along his life-thread did not reveal how this had come to pass. It must have been something that happened during the period in which his fateline disappeared from the skein.

Following the threads forwards again, Thirianna cast her vision further ahead. Here there was a dizzying multiplicity of outcomes: Aradryan dying in a variety of unpleasant manners; Aradryan travelling the webway to the Dark City of Commorragh; Aradryan returning to Alaitoc with wanderlust spent; Aradryan being taken in by the Harlequins; Aradryan captured by humans and experimented on by their crude scientists.

Thirianna stopped, suddenly noticing a small detail that had flashed past in one of the first visions. She tried to find it again, but already the lines of fate were blurring together and splitting afresh as her friend's actions spawned new fates for him.

Thirianna withdrew from the skein, concerned with what she had seen. Detaching herself from the infinity circuit, she closed her eyes and concentrated, bringing back the image that had flickered past.

She saw Aradryan, garbed outlandishly, a pistol in one hand and a gleaming power sword in the other. He was fighting a human clothed in a garish uniform, with golden epaulettes and a peaked cap. It was not this that worried Thirianna; she had seen Aradryan fighting many different foes from orks to hrud to humans to other eldar. What had nagged her as it flashed past was where Aradryan was fighting.

She examined the vision again, bringing it to a stop at a certain point where she could draw back and see more clearly what was going on. She shuddered at what she saw.

Aradryan fought alongside other eldar, armoured in the colours of Alaitoc. Around him were many bodies, of human and eldar, and approaching was a squad of Imperial Space Marines liveried in red and white. What appeared to be the smouldering remains of a Phantom Titan, one of Alaitoc's greatest weapons, formed the backdrop.

Past this vignette, Thirianna saw something that horrified her as it confirmed her first suspicion. It was the glint of muzzle flare on crystal, and in that speck of light she could see what the las-blast was reflecting from. It was a crystal seer. In fact, she recognised him immediately, having spent some time in the Dome of Crystal Seers learning about her predecessors from Kelamith. The robe-clad statuesque seer was Anthirloi, who stood at one end of the Sighing Bridge.

At some time in the future, there was the possibility that humans would invade Alaitoc.

Thirianna opened her eyes, hands trembling, her heart thundering in her chest at the thought. It was not chance that had drawn Aradryan to that moment, it was entwined with his destiny, an emergent possibility brought about by his actions. Thirianna had not seen how or why Aradryan was tied up with the humans, or how it was that they had come to Alaitoc, but her instinct had been right to notice it.

She calmed herself, remembering that she had seen only potential, not certainty. Many had been the warnings made by Kelamith and the other seers not to take everything she witnessed as coming to pass. The vague nature of the vision, the uncertainty with which she had come across it and the fact that she had not been able to locate it again all pointed to an extremely rare happenstance. The chance course of events required to bring it about were astronomically slim, verging on the impossible.

Overcoming her first reaction, Thirianna returned to her chambers to think a little more on what she had seen. She revisited the vision several times in her memory, convincing herself that Alaitoc was the scene of the fighting. It was unmistakeable.

Yet if the violence she had seen would come about, the whole craftworld was embroiled in the battle. Such an event would be a massive weight upon the skein, entwining the fates of every eldar on the craftworld and every human they fought against. Other seers must have surely seen the possibility of such a cataclysmic event before.

Thirianna poured herself some sunbloom nectar and sat by the window. It was arrogance of the highest order to think she had unwittingly stumbled upon such a momentous occasion when the most experienced farseers of Alaitoc had no inkling of its existence. It was more than arrogance, it was vain fantasy.

She laughed at herself for being so concerned. In this she had really proven herself a novice. Kelamith had seen the doom of Alaitoc many times, and Thirianna was sure she would see it again too in the future. It was folly to react to such an unlikely possibility.

To occupy herself with other thoughts, Thirianna studied for the next few cycles, avoiding the skein except to strengthen her links to her new runes. Yet try as she did to forget what she had seen, it continued to haunt her. She dreamt about that moment, that silent scene of death and destruction, her mind giving voice to the fierce war cries, hearing the crackle of the flames and the snap of the humans' weapons. She smelt the blood and felt the fear, and woke in a terrible state of panic.

Frustrated with this turn, Thirianna sought out Kelamith. They met in the Chambers of the Seers and Thirianna explained what she had seen and how it had affected her.

'It is natural,' Kelamith assured her. 'No matter how rational and logical we may try to be about such things, we cannot fight against the visceral nature of such a vision. To be unaffected would be strange. The contemplation of our own death is serious enough. To witness the potential downfall of Alaitoc is of a much higher magnitude.'

'And it grows less with time?' asked Thirianna. 'It will diminish?'

'The sensation becomes less extreme and of shorter duration with each experience,' Kelamith told her. He looked away. 'It never wholly disappears.'

'Such a remote possibility is not worthy of consideration, is it?' asked Thirianna.

'It is not,' replied her mentor. 'To dwell on such possibilities is to invite a creeping doubt, one that will gnaw away at your ability to travel the skein with freedom. If you let such a thing hook its barbs into your thoughts, it will constantly drag at you, leading you back to the improbable and the destructive.'

'Yet what I saw could happen,' said Thirianna, remembering the vividness of her dreams. 'Is not the most distant possibility worthy of investigation? This was not some minor battle I saw – it was a war for survival. If there is even the remotest chance that such a thing will come to pass, should we not bring it to the council's attention?'

'As a theoretical possibility, it is not without merits for discussion,' said Kelamith. He stood up and smoothed a crease in his robe. 'As a spur for further action, it is inconsequential. You are welcome to raise the matter at the next gathering of the council in four cycles' time.'

Thirianna thanked Kelamith for his time and consideration. When he left, she realised she had much to do if she was to present what she had seen to the farseers and autarchs. Even if the catastrophe she had seen was of almost no import, it would be a good opportunity for her to present her first real vision to the council members.

The farseers and autarchs came together in the Hall of Communing, an open, column-lined dome at the edge of Alaitoc. Only a force wall shielded the inhabitants from the depths of space, so that the council was surrounded by a field of stars with only the ground beneath.

Thirianna waited patiently while other matters were attended to. The council discussed several visions reported by the senior farseers and the autarchs requested guidance on military endeavours and excursions they were planning. Thirianna listened with interest to everything said, noting the lyrical, narrative form adopted by the farseers when they explained their visions. There was a style to the language that conveyed the sense of what they had seen, taking those who had not witnessed the visions as close as possible to the experience.

Thirianna hastily reconsidered her own submission for the council's deliberations, couching her report in more fanciful terms while the members discussed messages that had arrived from Ulthwé warning of a renewed attack against the Imperium of the humans, launched by renegades dwelling in the warp storm that had engulfed the heart of the ancient eldar empire. It was decided that a small force would be despatched to aid Ulthwé should the need arise, but the farseers saw no need to investigate more fully; Ulthwé was home to Eldrad Ulthran, agreed by all to be the most powerful farseer alive, and there was little Alaitoc could add to his greatest divinations.

The council proceeded for most of the cycle, until the open invitation was accorded to the members to bring up minor matters for discussion. Thirianna caught Kelamith's eye, who introduced her to the council as his pupil and then motioned for her to begin her address.

'I have seen the death of Alaitoc,' Thirianna began, wanting to capture the attention of everybody present. 'In flame and smoke, by plasma and missile, our world is ravaged by the unending hatred of the humans.'

She paused and looked around. Some of the seers watched her with polite, vacant expressions. A few were holding conversations with those around them. Many seemed bored or amused by what she said. It was not the reaction she had hoped for and she considered her next words carefully.

'The Space Marines will come, the fell warriors of the Emperor, and they will bring with them the doom of many,' she continued. 'I have seen Alaitoc's domes torn asunder, our halls ravaged by war, our people slain in their thousands.'

Her claim was not technically true – she had been unable to locate the thread again despite many attempts in the last few cycles – but the spirit of what had been locked into her memory was the important point.

'A time will come when we must stand strong against this threat, for all that we hold dear, our very existence, will hang in the balance,' Thirianna told them, eyeing the assembled council members. She tried not to look to Kelamith for assurance, but glanced in his direction nonetheless. Her mentor looked no more interested than any of the others. She forged on, skipping the rest of the introduction, hoping that it was her delivery that fell on deaf ears and not her message. 'Cataclysm will come, brought upon us by the actions of one of our own. I have seen this fate, spawned by the recklessness of one that I know. In hi–'

'When?' asked Arhathain, cutting through Thirianna's tale. 'Please be more specific.'

'I…' Thirianna's nerve broke as she looked at the autarch, who sat with one eyebrow raised in questioning, lips pursed with irritation. 'I am not sure, autarch. The thread is indistinct, the timing uncertain.'

'Very well,' said the autarch. His expression softened, yet his look of benign pity stung Thirianna more than his annoyance. 'Such is the nature of the skein. Perhaps you could tell us what this acquaintance of yours will do to precipitate this unheralded attack on Alaitoc?'

Thirianna looked down at her feet, feeling guilty for wasting everybody's time with her nonsense.

'I am not sure, autarch. He is an outcast, his future wild and free, difficult to follow.'

'That is to be expected also,' said the autarch, not unkindly. 'You are Thirianna, yes? I know that this must be quite frightening for you, so please do not feel you are being judged. Your inexperience should not be held against you. Is there another here who can better explain what form this threat will take, or the nature of the event that must be averted to prevent it?'

The assembled eldar looked at each other and Thirianna desperately wanted one of them to indicate that he or she had also seen something of what Thirianna had encountered. None did so, and a quiet murmuring spread through the council, adding to her embarrassment.

'Thank you, Thirianna,' said Arhathain. 'If you do discover any more information on this matter, be sure to bring it to the attention of Kelamith.'

Thirianna's shame could not delve any deeper into her heart. Instead it turned to anger, her frustration with herself becoming frustration at the council.

'Please let me finish,' said Thirianna. 'This is important. I saw Alaitoc under attack. I was not mistaken. If what I saw comes to pass, we shall all be slain and the craftworld destroyed.'

Thirianna heard quiet laughter and looked around the council, furious with the disrespect they were showing her.

'At least we should investigate further,' said Thirianna. 'The remotest possibility that Alaitoc might be attacked is surely something we should take seriously?'

'An attack that none of us has foreseen except you?' This came from Anatharan Alaitin, the eldest of the farseers. 'While we spend our time chasing this dream of yours, who can say what other issues we might miss? I am sorry, Thirianna, but you will have to present us with a better case than you have. Spend some more time on it and if there is more to be learnt you will learn it.'

'I need your help to do so,' said Thirianna. She held out an imploring hand to those around her. 'I have not long trodden this Path. I have but three runes to control. There are those here that can steer a dozen times that number. Will one of you follow me and help me locate this disastrous fate?'

She looked now at Kelamith, but Thirianna's mentor gently shook his head. None of the others offered her any comfort. Thirianna turned her attention back to Arhathain, hoping that he might indulge her, even if only out of pity.

'A life lost, a starship destroyed, an Exodite world attacked, a threat to another craftworld, all of these things I could dismiss,' she said. 'Yet I saw none of those things. However faint the possibility, no matter how tenuous the thread I found, it is there. And if it is there, it may come to pass. This is our home of which I speak: Alaitoc. Judge this wrongly and we all suffer.'

'The council has heard your petition, yet we have found no cause on which to act,' said Arhathain. His narrowing eyes betrayed his irritation at Thirianna's continued insistence.

'My apologies for wasting the council's time,' said Thirianna, sitting down. Inside she raged at her casual dismissal by the great of Alaitoc. Had one of them seen what she had seen, she had no doubt that further action would be called. Their doubt was personal, and all the more hurtful for that. It was Thirianna they did not trust and it did not matter what she said, they could not submit to the idea that she had glimpsed something that they had all missed.

For several cycles after the council, Thirianna avoided the Chambers of the Seers, ashamed at the reaction she would receive. She stayed in her rooms, brooding on the indignity of what had happened. The more she considered the events of the council, the greater her conviction became that something had to be done about the vision.

Spurred on by the desire to redeem herself, Thirianna tried to rise to the challenge posed to her by Arhathain. If she could locate something on the skein that vindicated what she had seen, it would give her a reason to broach the subject again with Kelamith and the others.

Knowing what she did might be dangerous, Thirianna delved into the skein again, determined to find some other evidence of the possible fate she had witnessed. Ignoring the warnings made against spending too much time away from her physical self, Thirianna spent most of each cycle skimming across the skein, using the Wanderer to guide her to random shreds of future, hoping that she might come across the previous thread she had found.

It was hopeless. It had been a rare chance that had brought the vision to her in the first instance, and it would require hundreds of cycles of searching at random to find it again. At the end of the second cycle of hunting, Thirianna tried a different approach. She reasoned that if what she saw would come to pass, at some point in the future it would affect her. If she followed enough of the threads of her own destiny, one of them would lead her to the catastrophe she had seen.

For a whole cycle Thirianna searched, pausing only briefly to eat and drink, but still she could not find the elusive thread she sought. She blazed across the paths of her future selves looking for the slightest glimmer of recognition. Yet the further ahead she looked, the more unlikely it became that she would find what she was looking for. The event she had witnessed would happen sometime in the current pass, that much she was certain. She restricted her search, ignoring the more distant echoes of times to come, hoping to come across some evidence of the turmoil that would surely engulf her should the humans attack Alaitoc.

She found nothing.

Thirianna verged on abandoning the search. It seemed most likely that whatever Aradryan might have done had passed by and that a different course had been set. The glimmer of possibility had not come to fruition and Alaitoc was safe.

This conclusion did not sit well with Thirianna as she once again resumed her quest. As she looked for a link between herself and the momentous event, using the Scorpion to delve deeper into her near-future to divide and tease out all of the half-chances and near-misses, she stumbled upon an unexpected scene.

The threads she followed barely touched on hers, yet there was a causal link somehow. The essence of Morlaniath, the exarch Korlandril had become, was also involved, entwined momentarily with the fate of Arhathain. Following the course of these events, Thirianna saw Arhathain bringing the council together again, instructing the senior seers to direct some of their effort into investigating Thirianna's claim.

Thirianna left the skein, amazed at what she saw. Somehow it was possible that she could convince Arhathain to take her seriously; that was all she wanted. She knew it was likely a fool's errand to seek out the fate of Aradryan and expect a revelation, but it rankled that the council had given her no credence at all.

Thirianna slept for a short while, her dreams still mired in the death of Alaitoc, and rose again as soon as she had regained a little of her strength. The long journeys into the future had taken their toll on her mind and body, even after only a few cycles, but she gathered what stamina she could and set out again, following the trail left to her by the Scorpion. After a while, she located the moment of Morlaniath and Arhathain coming together.

She focussed all of her thoughts on that event, prying open the skein to witness what might come to pass.

The exchange took place in the Chamber of Autarchs, empty save for Morlaniath and Arhathain. At first Thirianna could not hear what passed between them, but as she focussed her mind, blocking out the peripheral information, concentrating on the two speakers alone, she caught scatters of their conversation.

'Perhaps you seek war, for that is your nature,' says Arhathain.

'I cannot make a war, if that is my desire, it is the council's choice,' replies Morlaniath.

'Every day our seers uncover a thousand dooms to Alaitoc,' says Arhathain. Thirianna senses disinterest in him. He has heard the arguments before. 'We cannot act on every vision. We cannot go to war on every doubt. Thirianna herself cannot provide us with clarity. We might just as well act on a superstitious trickle of foreboding down the back of the neck.'

'She lacks the proper skill, the means to give you proof, hold that not against her,' counters the exarch. Thirianna wondered why it is that he takes up her cause. 'Give her the help she needs, to prove her right or wrong, she will keep her silence. This doubt will hold her back, it will consume her thoughts, until you release her. You have walked many Paths, seen a great many things, lived a great many lives. That life you owe to me, I remember it now, so many cycles past. I was your guardian, the protection you sought, a true companion. I remember the debt, the oath you swore to me, it is now time to pay.'

A distant time flickers across the thread, distracting Thirianna for a moment. She sees a young Arhathain, fighting as a Swooping Hawk on the world of Nerashamensin. A human twisted by the worship of the Chaos gods emerges from the shadow of a broken doorway, a crude gun in her hands. She aims at Arhathain. The Chaos-worshipper falls, a chainsword cutting her head from her body as the Striking Scorpion Elidhnerial strikes from the dark interior of the building.

Several lifetimes pass. Elidhnerial becomes an exarch, joining Morlaniath. Morlaniath is awakened by the anger of Korlandril and the two become as one.

Thirianna marvels at the convoluted nature of history and destiny. The original Morlaniath, Elidhnerial, Arhathain, Korlandril and Thirianna bound together by distant ties that none of them is aware of.

Arhathain frowns and turns away, pacing to the far side of the rostrum at the centre of the hall.

'The one I made that promise to died ten passes and more ago,' he says softly, looking up at the circular opening at the top of the dome. A distant swathe of stars is strewn across the blackness of space. 'I did not swear that oath to you. It is not Elidhnerial that asks me to repay that debt, it is Korlandril.'

'I am Morlaniath, Elidhnerial too, and also Korlandril. The debt is owed to me, to all the parts of me, united in spirit. Who save me remembers, can repeat the words used, heard them spoken by you?'

Thirianna remembers the words too. She can repeat them. She saw the debt of thanks sworn by Arhathain. The debt Elidhnerial-Korlandril-Morlaniath now wishes repaid.

'If I do not do this?' asks the autarch.

'Your honour is forfeit, and others shall know it, I will make sure of that.'

The autarch turns and directs an intense stare at Morlaniath. Thirianna senses his loathing for the exarch.

'You will not call on me again in this way?' says Arhathain.

'Your debt will be repaid, to Elidhnerial, and we shall speak no more.'

Arhathain nods reluctantly and stalks up the shallow steps of the chamber.

Thirianna broke from the vision with her head pounding, her breath coming in shallow gasps. It was the first time she had witnessed the future in such specific detail and her mind throbbed with the energy she had used to render it.

Arhathain's change of heart now made sense, but it left Thirianna with another question: why had the exarch Morlaniath intervened on her behalf?

Thirianna did not have the strength at that moment to delve back into the skein to discover the truth. She would have to apply some reasoning to the matter herself. She lay on her bedding and closed her eyes, pushing away the numbness that was welling up inside her thoughts, trying to focus on the problem.

The only connection she shared with Morlaniath was Korlandril, who had become part of the exarch's fractured personality. It was possible that some remnant of the relationship between Thirianna and Korlandril was inside the lingering spirit of her former friend. She wondered if she could appeal to that transient fragment of the exarch, to entreat him to act on her behalf.

Yet that provided another problem. If she was to reveal how she knew the exarch had influence over Arhathain, it would invite suspicion from Morlaniath. Though it was accepted that the seers had to scan the fates of every individual, Thirianna had intruded upon a very private matter, one that would cause the exarch to take offence.

She would have to approach the matter in a different way, without giving away the fact she knew about Morlaniath and Arhathain's history. If she could somehow sow the seed of the idea in the mind of the exarch, there was a chance he would act as she had seen, and thus Arhathain's command to the council to help her would be realised.

Thirianna smiled. The disastrous last meeting with Korlandril had shattered her confidence in her ability to intervene in the way a seer should. This latest encounter renewed her confidence. This was exactly why she had become a seer, to act and not react. By her hand she could set in motion a course of events that would be to her benefit.

The thought of such a thing thrilled Thirianna. For her whole life she had been prey to the whims of fate, unseeing of the future, unable to do anything but respond to protect herself. Now she would prove that she had moved beyond that.

She would truly be a farseer.

* * *

On the long journey to the Aspect shrines, Thirianna's determination started to falter. Caught up with ideas of how she would prove her worth to Kelamith and redeem herself in the eyes of the council, she had commissioned a skyrunner to take her across Alaitoc. Her enthusiasm had ebbed as she considered how she was going to confront the exarch Morlaniath.

Her nervousness increased as she approached the forbidding portal that concealed the Shrine of the Hidden Death. She had allowed herself to forget a cardinal rule of farseeing: not all futures come to pass. It was only a possibility that Morlaniath would heed her, and then only a possibility that he would intervene for her, and on top of that there was no assurance that the help of other seers would aid her in detecting even a glimmer of what she had seen before.

In the heat of the moment she had failed to consider the alternatives. Enthused with sudden optimism, she had not investigated the other outcomes of the encounter. Morlaniath might refuse to see her. She might be humiliated, turned away by the exarch. Worse still, Arhathain might learn of her manipulation and her reputation would be forever tainted by the act.

This thought expanded, as Thirianna realised that her movements on the skein had been open to see. The use of the Scorpion made it less likely she would be discovered, but if Kelamith or any of the other farseers investigated thoroughly they would easily follow the trail she had left. Even success might damage her standing.

The gate to the shrine was inconspicuous in itself, a small emerald-coloured doorway within a narrow archway. Thirianna stopped in front of the gateway, unsure how to attract the attention of Morlaniath. When she went to the Shrine of One Hundred Bloody Tears, she was admitted without effort; the gate before her was solidly closed.

There was still time to pull back from the thread she was about to spin. She could turn around and return to the skyrunner, allowing events to follow their natural course. She had not committed herself to any act that would change anything.

The door sighed open behind her. Thirianna turned quickly, surprised by this. A tall figure clad in ornate armour stood in the open gateway, face hidden behind the expressionless mask of his helm. Thirianna felt the rune of the Scorpion in a pouch at her belt jostle in recognition, tugging at her thoughts.

Foolishly, she had expected to see Korlandril. Instead she was confronted by a Striking Scorpion exarch, full of brooding menace. Death surrounded the warrior like a cloak, its touch cold to Thirianna's psychic sense. She retreated from the presence, suddenly afraid.

'Is that you, Korlandril?' she asked.

'I am not Korlandril, though he is part of me, I am Morlaniath.'

It was as Thirianna had feared. Korlandril had been absorbed by the meta-spirit of the exarch. Morlaniath did not seem to recognise her. Beyond the exarch stretched low dunes of red sand, the haze of heat obscuring the distant dome wall. Here and there scrubby patches of candlewood broke the undulating wilderness, the scent of their small but pungent blossoms wafting from the open gate. A blood-red orb hung low on the artificial horizon, bathing the scene in a dim, ruddy light.

'Why do you disturb us, coming here unbidden, breaking the gold stillness?' asked Morlaniath.

There was anger in his voice and Thirianna backed away, every doubt she had crowding into her thoughts. She shook her head, wishing she had not come here.

'This was a mistake,' she told the exarch. 'I should not have come. You cannot help me.'

Morlaniath stayed silent for a moment. Thirianna could detect turmoil in his spirit, but was too frightened to examine it any closer. She kept her mind firmly detached from the skein, not wishing to experience the horror of the exarch in anything but his physical form.

The exarch's disturbed spirit settled again. 'Now that you have come here, seeking guidance and truth, speak your mind with freedom,' said Morlaniath. 'If I can assist you, if you have hard questions, perhaps I can answer.'

Thirianna approached and stared past Morlaniath, taking in the wide vista of the desert. Her gaze turned to the exarch.

'Is there somewhere else we can speak?' she said

'The shrine would not be fit, farseers enter with risk, and I am loath to leave,' the exarch declared.

Thirianna agreed. She had no desire to set foot in the Striking Scorpion shrine. It was a hard enough task to attend the Shrine of One Hundred Bloody Tears; to enter an unfamiliar Aspect shrine would test her nerves to their limit.

'Can we perhaps walk awhile?' she suggested. 'I do not feel comfortable discussing matters on your doorstep.'

Morlaniath turned away without a further word. After a moment the door did not close and Thirianna assumed she was to follow the exarch. She stepped into the dome, booted feet sinking into the soft sand. Morlaniath strode ahead, poised and graceful, while Thirianna struggled to keep up with his long strides. Squinting against the artificial sunset, she saw that they headed towards a shallow oasis gently fed by irrigation webs beneath the sands. Clusters of red-leaved bushes hid the water's edge, bright white stars of blossom poking from the foliage.

It was a place of surprising peace, an oasis in more than just the physical sense. Morlaniath crouched at the water's edge for a moment. At the back of her thoughts Thirianna could feel the skein undulating as the exarch's many memories of this place came together.

'This is... pleasant,' said Thirianna. She looked for somewhere to sit and on finding no seat or rock, lowered herself onto the warm sands.

Morlaniath looked at her, eyes concealed behind the red lenses of his helm. It was an unsettling sensation and Thirianna gathered her robe about herself and tossed her hair over one shoulder as a distraction from that dead gaze.

'It is the birth in death, the hope in hopelessness, life amongst the barren,' said Morlaniath.

Thirianna gathered her thoughts. She counted the present situation a success, uncomfortable as it was. The harder part was perhaps to come. She had to put across her thoughts in such a way that the exarch would wish to help her. She did not look at him when she spoke. She gazed thoughtfully into the waters. Insects skimmed the surface, sustained by its tension.

'I have foreseen troubling times for Alaitoc, perhaps something worse,' she said.

'You are now a farseer. Such things will be your life, why do you come to me?' said Morlaniath. His voice was flat, giving away nothing of his mood.

'I am told that I am in error,' explained Thirianna. 'The farseers, the council of Alaitoc, do not think my scrying will come to pass. They say I am inexperienced, seeing dangers that do not exist.'

'Likely they are correct, your powers are still weak, this path is new to you,' said Morlaniath. Though the exarch's words were disheartening, Thirianna drew some strength from the indication that Morlaniath knew who she was. It was possible some part of Korlandril still existed inside. 'I do not see my role. I am the exarch here, not one of the council.'

'You don't believe me?' said Thirianna.

'You offer me no proof, and there is none to give, belief alone is dust,' replied Morlaniath.

This was proving even harder than Thirianna had envisaged. She needed a strategy, an approach that might appeal to the vestiges of Korlandril harboured inside the group-mind of the exarch. To give herself time to think, Thirianna stood and walked to the pool's edge. She dipped her booted toe into the waters, sending a ripple across the surface. It was a subconscious act, but it created a reaction in the exarch. His thoughts were disturbed, just as the water was disturbed. Thirianna thought of the skein; of the ripples caused by action that spread across space and time.

Korlandril was in there somewhere; perhaps she could bring him to the fore with something familiar to both of them.

'I followed the fate of Aradryan,' she said. She could not judge his thoughts, his face hidden from view, but she could sense another bubble of activity within Morlaniath's spirit as he searched his memories. She pressed on, hoping that Korlandril still recognised the name. 'Our three destinies are interwoven. More than we have seen already. Yours is not ended, but will soon – his is distant and confused. Mine... mine is to be here, to tell you these things to set in motion future events.'

This last was not entirely true, but Thirianna considered herself an agent of destiny now.

'What is it you have seen, what visions bring such woe, what do they mean for us?'

A single personality was asserting itself; Thirianna could sense it in the skein, one thread growing thicker than the others. Her eyes confirmed as much; one of the spirit stones in the exarch's armour glowed brighter while the others dimmed. It had to be Korlandril, becoming more focussed, drawn out by familiarity. That he had asked the question bolstered Thirianna's confidence again. The exarch wanted to know what she had seen.

'Aradryan dwells in darkness, but there is also light for him,' she said, affecting the tone of language used in the council. If it was right for the autarchs it might work on the exarch. 'But his darkness is not confined to him. It spreads into our lives, and it engulfs Alaitoc. I do not know the details – my rune-casting is very crude at the moment. I feel he has done something gravely wrong and endangered all of us.'

'Your warnings are too vague, they contain no substance, we have no course of action,' replied Morlaniath. He turned his head away, his attention straying back towards the shrine hidden somewhere in the dunes.

Thirianna gave voice to her disappointment, finding no more support here than in the council.

'That is what the council says. "How can we prepare against something so amorphous?" they asked. I told them that more experienced seers should follow the thread of Aradryan. They refused, claiming it was an irrelevance. Aradryan is gone from Alaitoc, they told me, and he is no longer their concern.'

The exarch did not reply to this immediately. Thirianna felt a tremor of contact buzzing through her mind. She risked a glance into the skein and saw Korlandril's thread touching upon hers. Korlandril's, not Morlaniath's. He was remembering her. Hopefully the memories were good ones. His next words dashed that hope.

'Continue your studies, delve further into this, to seek your own answers,' said the exarch.

'I fear there is no time,' said Thirianna. She had to force Morlaniath to confront the issue now. 'This is imminent. I lack the strength and the training to see far ahead.'

'Others have not seen it, your fresh cataclysm, who are stronger than you,' remarked the exarch. Korlandril's spirit was weakening again, moving away from Thirianna. 'I must concur with them, who have trodden the Path, who see further than you.'

'It is such a small thing, whatever it is that Aradryan does,' Thirianna said quickly, making a last effort to establish a connection with the afterthought of Korlandril. She reminded herself that she had seen Morlaniath convince Arhathain to help her. It was possible, if she could find the right approach. She stooped and took a pinch of sand, rubbing her fingers to spill it to the ground until she held a single grain. She flicked it into the waters of the pool. 'Such a tiny ripple, we can barely see it, but a ripple nonetheless. The anarchy of history tells us that momentous events can start from the most humble, the most mundane of beginnings.'

'I have no aid for you, no council influence, and I agree with them,' said Morlaniath. 'Go back to your studies, forget this distraction, I will not assist you.'

The words were harsh, the essence of Korlandril fading away. Disappointment welled up from within Thirianna. She had failed to accomplish even this simple task.

'I feared the worst, and you have proven me true,' she said, trying hard to hold back the tears that threatened to spill down her cheeks. 'Korlandril is not dead, but he has gone.'

'Which you once predicted, that both of us would change, for better or for worse,' said Morlaniath. Thirianna wondered if the exarch was throwing that sentiment back at her out of spite or merely making an observation. 'I am Morlaniath, you are Thirianna, Korlandril is no more. Seek contentment from this, do not chase the shadows, only darkness awaits.'

'Do you not remember what we once shared?' she said, out of desperation.

'I remember it well, we shared nothing at all, I have nothing for you.'

Thirianna straightened and wiped a gloved finger across her cheek, a tear soaking into the soft fabric.

'You are right,' she said. 'I will leave and think of you no more.'

She bunched up her robe and strode up the encircling dune, heading towards the main portal. She felt the presence of Morlaniath behind her for some of the way, shadowing her progress, and then he stopped, leaving her to depart.

She felt a trickle of psychic energy and the portal ahead opened. In that instant, the exarch's mind was open, and out of desperate instinct, Thirianna made contact for a moment, propelling her sadness and shame into the mind of the exarch.

The link broke and she passed out of the dome, at a loss as to what she would do next.

It was late in the following cycle when Thirianna received a summons from Kelamith to attend him in the Chambers of the Seers. It was most definitely a summons and not an invitation, and Thirianna's thoughts were quivering with trepidation as she made her way to see her mentor.

She found him alone, standing in front of the Orb of Elmarianin, a great sphere of ruby-red crystal almost as tall as the farseer, which glimmered with psychic energy, motes of power moving slowly through its depths. The farseer's face was reflected ruddily in hundreds of its facets, each appearing slightly different.

Kelamith turned at her approach, expression stern.

'It is a curious thing,' said Kelamith, gesturing to the orb. 'Created by Elmarianin before I was born, this device allows the seer council to combine their powers of divination. Its use takes a toll on the infinity circuit and those who employ it.'

'Yes, I have read about the Orb of Elmarianin,' said Thirianna. She was confused, unable to see the point being made by the other farseer.

'Speaking of curious things, I have just returned from a gathering of the senior seers,' continued Kelamith, eyes fixed on Thirianna. 'We we're called together by Autarch Arhathain. He has reconsidered your contribution to the council and feels it merits more attention.'

Thirianna felt a surge of satisfaction, though she tried hard to conceal it. Then worry took its place.

'I am honoured,' she said. She kept her expression neutral, wary of betraying any sense of guilt. 'Did the autarch explain his change of mind? Did my arguments perhaps persuade him to judge again what I have seen?'

'He was reluctant to expand on that point,' said Kelamith, still staring intently at Thirianna. She sensed curiosity rather than suspicion and relaxed a little. 'It is almost without precedent, for the council to return to such a decision. Arhathain was most eloquent in his persuasion, insistent even. We have acquiesced to the autarch's wishes, and will search for this doom you witnessed.'

'I am pleased,' said Thirianna, knowing that it would be strange for her to pretend indifference at such a turn of events. 'I also hope that I am mistaken, and that more experienced minds brought to the matter will allay any fears the autarch may have.'

'Indeed,' said Kelamith.

He turned back to the orb, laying a gloved hand upon its surface. When he spoke his tone seemed casual, but his words struck a chill through Thirianna.

'It is a grave offence to mislead the council,' said Kelamith. 'The skein is not a plaything. It is a powerful force, one that we must always approach with due gravitas and dignity. To use its power for selfish means, to pursue self-aggrandisement, is to invite anarchy.'

Thirianna said nothing, though her heart beat faster. She calmed herself quickly, rationalising that if Kelamith and the others believed she had acted wrongly in some way, they would not have agreed to Arhathain's request for further investigation. Kelamith was baiting her, she decided, trying to get her to reveal her secret.

'Do you know the punishment for such a transgression?' said the senior farseer. Thirianna could see him watching her in the reflections of the orb. She shook her head. 'It is a cruel thing, one that we each despise, yet it is one of our oldest laws. One who misuses the skein in a grievous manner is banished from the council of seers.'

'That seems justified,' replied Thirianna, unsure what was so heinous about such a punishment.

'The offender is barred from all rune-casting, and to ensure compliance the perpetrator is taken to the Halls of Isha,' continued Kelamith. His voice was quiet, filled with sadness. 'He or she is subjected to a procedure that removes the parts of the brain that bolster our psychic strength. The criminal is cut off from the skein, unable to interact with the infinity circuit.'

That sounded a lot worse to Thirianna, though she still did not understand why Kelamith seemed to loathe it so much. His following words brought home the full extent of the injunction, as he turned and looked at Thirianna directly.

'It is a far harsher punishment than death,' he said. 'It is the ultimate banishment, Thirianna. Forget for the moment the power to traverse the skein and witness the future. Think on those things that you take for granted, small acts you perform every day. Your chambers respond to your thoughts, warming and cooling, lightening and darkening as you desire. You would only be able to communicate through the spoken word, unable to access the infinity circuit.'

He took a step closer, eyes boring into Thirianna.

'Even more than that, you do not see what you would lose by such a punishment. We each touch upon one another in subtle ways. We read each other not just physically but with our thoughts. We have bonds between us stronger than family and friendship. Every Alaitocii is bound together through the infinity circuit, and every craftworld tied to a single fate through the eternal matrix. To be cast from that is to be something other than eldar. Loneliness and despair, cut off from that most instinctive of contact, will haunt the criminal. They will watch and hear life around them, but they will not feel it.'

It was truly a greater punishment than Thirianna had appreciated. To lose one's sight, one's hearing, one's sense of touch or smell would be unfortunate enough. To have part of one's spirit taken away, to be rendered mundane, to lose a huge part of the essence of being eldar, would be crippling.

'That is severe indeed,' she said, keeping her tone even. 'With such an injunction as a threat, I cannot imagine anyone wishing to transgress such a law. I cannot imagine it has ever been put into practice.'

'Then your studies are incomplete,' said Kelamith. He waved a hand to the orb. 'Elmarianin suffered such a fate. His genius in creating this device was marred by his motives for doing so. He did not like the idea of the council holding power over him and so he sought to place himself above the other seers. He was the most powerful seer Alaitoc has known, and could wield the orb by himself. He used its power to interfere in the lives of the council, placing them in his debt, creating weakness and division.'

'How was he stopped?' Thirianna asked. She was horrified by the tale and wondered why she had not heard it before.

'One of the seers, Aranduirius, was brave, and spoke to the others of Elmarianin's manipulation of her,' said Kelamith. 'Each put aside their pride and confessed Elmarianin's control, spurred by Aranduirius's example. Together, as a council, they confronted him and subjected him to the law.'

Kelamith came closer, seeming to grow in height as he approached, until he was standing less than an arm's length away; his presence invaded the space around Thirianna but she could not step back. The witchlight gleamed in the farseer's eyes and when he spoke, it was with the distant tone Thirianna recognised as his voice of prophecy.

'Thirianna is taken to the Halls of Isha, where she undergoes the Ritual of Cleaving,' intoned the farseer. This was not idle threat; this was a vision, one of Thirianna's possible futures. She backed away, frightened by the pale blue orbs that stared at her. Kelamith followed, taking a step closer, keeping within touching distance. 'She is shamed, cast out of the council. Her mind is broken, her ambition crushed. In atonement she seeks the Path of Service. Still she does not find peace. Her empathy has been taken, her telepathy stolen. She wanders Alaitoc, a ghost-like creature subjected to scorn and pity in equal measure. Alone, cast out, terrified by the long half-existence that stretches before her, Thirianna takes the star-walk, casting herself into the void from the Bridge of Tranquillity.'

The horrifying gleam of Kelamith's eyes seemed to envelop Thirianna as he projected the vision. She drifted for a moment in the freezing vacuum, as empty as the void that consumed her.

Thirianna shrieked and fell back, landing heavily. When she looked up, Kelamith was standing over her, the witchlight gone, one hand extended to help her up.

'That future will not come to pass,' said the farseer, pulling Thirianna to her feet. He shook his head with disappointment. 'You think I am so vile as to heap such a punishment upon a misguided act?'

'I don't know,' said Thirianna. She trembled, the memory of her freezing death still grasping her heart with its cold touch.

'What you did was vain, and foolish, but no more than some of the other things you have done since coming to me,' said Kelamith. He laid a hand on Thirianna's shoulder and squeezed gently. 'I must believe that you acted out of genuine concern for Alaitoc, and your persistence does you credit. So too the manner of your manipulation. Now you have witnessed properly the power the skein grants to us, and I trust that you will not abuse it again.'

'Does the council know of this?' Thirianna asked, wondering if Kelamith's forgiveness might prove irrelevant.

'They do not,' said the farseer. 'They are quick to put down Arhathain's change of heart to a whim of interest. You must recover yourself. Other members of the council will be arriving soon.'

'They are coming here?' Thirianna glanced at the glowing orb.

'It will be the quickest way to put this matter to rest. If there is some echo of Alaitoc's doom to be found, we will find it.'

The skein was alight with the prying minds of the eldar. They stood in a circle around the Orb of Elmarianin, each surrounded by a small constellation of orbiting runes. The air glowed with the ruddy power of the orb and the witchlight of the seers, casting marbled reflections of red and blue across the chamber. The facets of the massive gem reflected the assembled seers, picturing them from every perspective, alone and together. The bright points of light shifted in its depths, converging and splitting, forming arcs of light that mirrored the patterns being woven by the seers' runes.

The gleam of the orb grew stronger as each psyker moved his or her mind into its crystalline form, refracting their spirits through the prism of its construction, their foresight multiplying and diverging.

Thirianna channelled herself through her rune, letting consciousness slip into the orb, feeling its cold edges breaking apart her thoughts, disassembling her mind. Ignoring the strange sensation, she did her best to guide her fellow seers to the location of the event she had seen.

She cast the Wanderer, attaching it to her own rune, so that it would bring her to the thread of Aradryan. She felt the minds of the council nearby, watching her, judging her. She tried to put aside their scrutiny. It did not matter if they faulted her technique as clumsy or her divination as naive; all that mattered was finding the glimmer of Alaitoc's death.

Aradryan's life unfolded rapidly as Thirianna surged across the skein, following the winding trail of his fate. She felt a little guilty, exposing her friend's being to the observation of so many, but she knew no other course to take.

Some of the seers were already branching off, intrigued by spiralling possibilities hinted at by the outcast's actions. Having agreed to Arhathain's wishes, they put their full effort into resolving the problem. Thirianna would have felt pleased by this dedication had not a few of them remarked beforehand that they were keen to get this nonsense dealt with quickly so that they could return to their normal studies.

Aradryan's immediate future settled quickly, the disparate strands melting away as possibilities were ended. His fate was narrowing to a point, a single strand from which he could not escape.

The farseers crowded close, eager to see this pivotal moment.

A pulse shook the skein. To the eye of Thirianna's mind, it took on a blood-red hue and a deep rumble echoed across its length and breadth. Crimson blood flowed along every strand, dripping from life to life, while fire sprang into being, burning vast swathes of the skein.

A single rune blazed above all others. Like a beacon of white fire, the symbol of Khaine the Bloody-Handed obliterated the skein, devouring all life.

The war god's heartbeat reverberated again, and was answered by another thunderous tremor. In the heart of the craftworld, nestled in the wraithbone core of Alaitoc, the Avatar of Kaela Mensha Khaine started to awake.

War. Terrible, all-destroying war.

In the light of the baleful rune, the seers scurried and panicked, racing across the skein, searching desperately for the catalyst of such devastation. They fragmented into splinters of thought through the power of the orb, hunting along several strands at once, covering swathes of history.

As the light of Khaine faded, as the flames died and the blood dried, the skein was rewritten, revealing its secrets.

The thread of Aradryan coiled about Alaitoc like a serpent constricting around its prey. His fate, his life, surrounded the craftworld, squeezing it from existence.

The seers delved through the knot, confronted by images of burning towers and falling spires. Human tanks rumbled along the Boulevard of Languid Praise, while Imperial Space Marines blasted at the doors to the Dome of Eternal Peace.

Death, fire, war. All of Alaitoc was crushed beneath it, the craftworld's future disintegrating under the weight of attack.

This was no distant possibility. The threads of fate were growing rigid, hardening into certainty, coalescing into a single unavoidable destiny.

The seers conversed quickly amongst themselves, recovering from the shock of the sudden change in fortunes. They needed to know what had happened, what Aradryan had done to create such a doom and why they had not been able to witness it earlier.

Thirianna already knew, or guessed she knew. She had seen it before and the memory of it had lodged like a shard in her mind.

She called to the other seers as she raced back through the outcast's life. As she expected, the possibility had become reality. She peeled open the skein to reveal Aradryan's piratical attack on a flotilla of Imperial ships.

The humans sought revenge for their fallen.

It was an extreme response. The attack on the Imperial convoy did not seem to merit such an overwhelming attack. Yet the consequences were clear to see, the path from the cause to the effect as straight as possible, one linked directly to the other.

Several of the seers departed, Kelamith amongst them, to bring this dire news to the autarchs, so the council of war could be gathered and plans set in motion. Those that remained, Thirianna included, began to search for a solution that would avert the disaster.

They examined the future potential of Aradryan, but no alternatives were revealed. The seers turned their attention to the humans, picking up the straggling strands of their lives. Military commanders, a planetary governor, the Chapter Master of the Sons of Orar Space Marines; all were examined and all could not be diverted from their course. Something had been set in motion, larger than any individual. There could be no timely assassination to curb the growing threat. No pre-emptive strike would stall the Imperial behemoth gathering its might.

Thoughts then turned to moving Alaitoc, though the craftworld was only part of the way through its star-fuelled regeneration and to leave now would be a major hindrance to her future health. The seers explored the possibilities regardless, but found that escape from the attack was impossible. Whether they remained or moved, the humans somehow were able to find Alaitoc and launch their attack.

They were too late. They would have to stand their ground and fight.

One-by-one the remaining seers departed, leaving Thirianna alone amongst the frayed threads of Alaitoc's future. Her heart was heavy with grief, no thought of vindication entering her mind.

Kelamith intruded upon her woe.

There is still hope. The attack cannot be forestalled, but the war is not lost. The future beyond is filled with immense uncertainty. We will fight the humans and we will be victorious. Dark days will beset us, but we will endure and we will recover. This is not the first time Alaitoc has faced immediate peril and through our endeavours it will not be the last.

The farseer was gone again and Thirianna was alone.

She moved her consciousness to the present, to a moment experienced with Aradryan. He was asleep in his cabin aboard his ship, intoxicated with a cocktail of exotic spirits and narcotics. Thirianna felt weak, her force dissipated by the effect of the Orb of Elmarianin. She gathered up what was left of her psychic strength and concentrated it into a single thought: a warning.

She touched upon Aradryan's drug-fevered mind, connecting him for an instant to the coil of his life strangling Alaitoc. The craftworld was in grave danger and would need every Alaitocii, outcast or not, to help defend her. Aradryan had to return, to restore the balance he had self-ishly disrupted.

Thirianna lurched out of the skein, utterly drained. Pain thrummed through her synapses and her body ached, tested to the limit by the amplifying effect of the orb. She decided to return to her chambers. Other, loftier minds could concern themselves with what would happen. When she had recovered she would play her part in the events to come.

War was fast approaching and she would need all of her strength.

WAR

The Bloody Hand – Khaine. There is one rune that a seer loathes to employ, for it is a terrible rune; all too often it is the doom of the seer. Yet there is no other rune that can replicate its power, for in war and bloodshed are many fates decided. In matters of battle, the rune of Khaine must guide the eye of the seer, to bring about the demise of the enemy and ensure the Bloody Hand does not fall upon the friend. A terrible rune, used to trace the fate of Alaitoc's Avatar. It is a treacherous rune, possessed of its own fierce pride, and will try to steer the seer only to fates that end in tragedy.

The Avatar was awakening.

Thirianna could feel its bloody call in her bones. The touch of the Avatar stretched to every part of Alaitoc, its wakening dreams of bloodshed permeating the infinity circuit, rousing the ire of all on the craftworld.

As a former Aspect Warrior, Thirianna was more susceptible to the sensation than those who had never walked the Path of the Warrior. Her war-mask, held in dormancy, quivered inside her mind, seeking to rise up in response to Khaine's call to arms. It was ever-present, gnawing at her thoughts when the council of war was convened between the autarchs and the seers. She could sense its effect in the warlocks and felt its power swirling from the military leaders.

The task was straightforward. The seers would divine the nature of the human attack, trying to foresee the direction and nature of the assault. With this information the autarchs would devise a suitable battle plan. In turn, the seers could travel the skein to explore the possibilities opened up by the courses of action chosen.

Straightforward, but far from simple. So many strands of fate had to be examined it was impossible to foresee every eventuality. Promising threads petered out into inconsequence, while mundane events proved to have profound implications. The life or death of a particular individual could hold the balance between victory and defeat; whether that was an autarch or a guardian, a Space Marine captain or a lowly human soldier. Whether a squad held its ground for a moment longer, or fell back a moment sooner, created new vistas to contemplate.

The greater part of the burden of prophecy fell on the shoulders of the most experienced farseers. They could utilise their runes of Khaine to travel the bloodiest pathways, weighing up life and death with incredible accuracy.

For the warlocks, and lesser seers such as Thirianna, their task was to provide an overview of the unfolding events. They lingered on the periphery of the skein while the most powerful minds delved deep, watching the great play of events as the senior seers used their many runes to twist and bind, separate and cut the threads of destiny.

Thirianna had been presented with the rune of Alaitoc by Kelamith. It was a powerful symbol, binding her fate to that of the craftworld. As the seer who had first witnessed the potential doom, it was her responsibility to stay focussed on that moment.

Over and over she saw the craftworld destroyed or overrun.

If the fleet engaged the attackers early, the enemy smashed past and landed without interference; if the starships protecting the craftworld held off their attacks the enemy were too numerous to hold back while they bombarded Alaitoc from space.

If the eldar held the landing points, they were drawn into bloody, attritional fighting. Victory came at too high a price, the population of Alaitoc so diminished that it never recovered. If the humans were allowed to gain too much of a foothold, large portions of Alaitoc were destroyed, never to be rebuilt.

It was an agonising experience for Thirianna, who sat at the heart of the destruction like the silver scales of Morai-heg, weighing one outcome over another.

The autarchs asked constant questions, demanding details of the forces the humans would bring to bear, the types of weapons they carried, the tactics they would employ. No detail was considered insignificant. The war host of Alaitoc was deadly but finely tuned. Each squad of Aspect Warriors, each tank and transport, each Titan and starship had a role to fill in the great tapestry that was being woven. If part of the thread was too weak, the whole picture came apart.

Arhathain, veteran commander and hero to Alaitoc, suggested a swift counter-attack, taking the battle to the humans before they had approached Alaitoc. The seers complied, investigating the outcomes of such a strike.

Too few warriors, came the response. The Imperial fleet being sent against Alaitoc would absorb any damage inflicted and the surviving Aspect Warriors would not have the strength to hold against the humans left behind.

Seeing that invasion was inevitable, the autarchs considered their alternatives. Did they fight for every piece of the craftworld or sacrifice areas for strategic gain? Here the prophecies were more encouraging. As sufficient as the Imperial ships were to break through the orbital defence, the skein showed that they could not hold onto large amounts of territory. An occupation of Alaitoc would be impossible, the threat of a long, drawn-out war remote.

This pleased the autarchs, and they pried further into the potential strategies they might employ. The war host was a fluid, moving thing, able to strike and withdraw, constantly attacking whilst using speed and misdirection as its defence. If it was possible to avoid fighting the humans head-on, the eldar would gradually sap the strength of the invaders.

Thirianna was overwhelmed by the vision that followed. Large swathes of Alaitoc lay in ruins. Domes were shattered and the passageways choked with the dead. The delicate ecological balance of Alaitoc was destroyed, deserts encroaching on forest domes, swamps swallowing terraces and vineyards, wildernesses engulfing parks and gardens. The infinity circuit faltered, sporadic and weak.

Yet the Alaitocii survived; enough to renew and rebuild. Their homes were devastated, many loved ones lost, but the people of Alaitoc endured. In time the craftworld would recover, and though most of a generation would be lost, Alaitoc would rise from the ashes of invasion like the phoenix of Asuryan, its power diminished but not gone.

The exhausting work continued, honing the strategy over the coming cycles. The seers came and went as their stamina dictated, adding their power to the effort when they could, resting and recovering when they were spent. Thirianna was sent back to her apartments several times by Kelamith, to sleep amongst dreams of flank attacks and diversions, air assaults and orbital battles.

Slowly the plan came together, like the orchestration of a great composer. The autarchs pored over the visions of the seers, homing in on areas of vagueness, mustering the resources of the craftworld to meet the threats that emerged with each prophesied scenario.

The resultant consensus was in part a military strategy and in part an ethos to be adhered to. War brought too much flux to the skein for every outcome to be known, and despite every effort of Thirianna and the rest of the seer council, there was no surety of any particular event coming to pass. The plan consisted of layer after layer of contingency, of response to gains and losses as fluid as the war host itself. Every margin of victory or defeat was analysed, and plans constructed to deal with the consequences.

After so much effort, the best the autarchs hoped for was a chance for victory. They could be no more prepared than they were, yet chance, or perhaps fate, would still play a major part in the battles to come. Victory was not guaranteed, indeed was far from certain, and depended upon a great many things coming to pass as the eldar desired.

In that time, Thirianna learned a lot about humans and their way of war. Through the visions granted by the skein, she saw the paradox in their nature. In one regard they were blunt and predictable. They lacked any kind of subtlety, preferring their brute strength over sophistication. They could be trusted to tackle any obstacle the eldar placed before them head-on, and in this was found their greatest weakness. They could be lured and directed, forced into battles that favoured the eldar. Their xenophobia, their creed of self-punishment and sacrifice could prove their undoing, bringing them into battles that they could not hope to win yet ones they would fight out of blind devotion and hope.

Yet for all their barbaric ways, the humans were also fickle. In each of them nestled the seed for great heroism and great cowardice. Compared to the lives of the eldar, the humans lived for a brief moment, and their threads were little more than remnants scattered across the skein, the vast majority passing their lives without meaning or impact on the wider universe.

A few of them were different, but were not necessarily marked out by status or rank. A lone sergeant might rally a line rather than flee; a medic might brave a storm of fire to rescue an officer who goes on to lead a new attack; a gunner mans his weapon when others have retreated to hold back an Alaitocii counter-attack.

Not only did moments of positive qualities make the picture unclear. Unexpected cowardice, ill discipline, poor communications on the part of the humans could unsettle the plans laid by the eldar. Just as the Alaitoc war host had to be precise and focussed in its movements and attacks, the responses of the enemy had to concur with the desires of the eldar.

It was with hope rather than confidence that Thirianna left the final meeting of the council. She had played her part in preparing Alaitoc for war; now was the time for her to ready herself so that she might influence the battle by her own hand.

Throughout the scrying and the planning, the pull of Khaine had strengthened. The Avatar's coming was fast approaching and Thirianna could feel the white heat of its awakening burning through the infinity circuit.

The exarchs were assembling, ready to present the Young King to the Avatar of Khaine. The infinity circuit trembled with the impending events, flashing images of war through the mind of Thirianna. She saw not just the battles to come, but conflicts past, across the galaxy. In her dreams she was a hundred different warriors striding across a hundred different battlefields. She brought death to the foes of Alaitoc as the war god incarnate led the battle host of the craftworld.

As the ceremony reached its climax, the skein fell still, pregnant with potent possibility. Thirianna felt the moment of sacrifice as the Young King was offered up. The rune of the Young King disappeared from the skein and the rune of Khaine took its place, dimly glowing, casting its presence across every future.

The Avatar's spirit roused itself from dormancy with a psychic roar that caused all on the craftworld to pause, shaken by a wave of anger and a momentary thirst for blood.

Thirianna had been asleep, dreaming of skies alight with green fire and dark towers toppled by the might of Alaitoc. She sat bolt upright in her bedding, heart pounding, breath coming in shallow gasps. Her war-mask surged up from the interior of her mind, blanketing all other thoughts. The seer relived her own battles, each passing in an instant, a dazzling, dizzying montage of slaying. Countless were the enemies that had fallen by her hand.

The moment passed.

Sitting in the darkness of her room, Thirianna felt relaxed and alert. The tension of the last cycles had drained away, replaced with energy and purpose, invigorated by the coming of the Avatar.

The enemy approached and Thirianna was ready to fight.

The seers had the best view of the opening stages of the war; better even than the captains and their crews aboard the starships gathering on the outer edges of the star system. The farseers came together in the Chamber of the Dawning World, a dark circular hall whose floor was inlaid with concentric circles of runes cast from precious metals that glowed with the power of the infinity circuit.

Each farseer had been ascribed a region of the skein to watch. Thirianna watched the unfolding fates of more than a dozen starships, from frigates to battleships, as they took station hidden in the gravity well of one of the outer planets.

The arrival of the humans was imminent and plain to see. Their ships bulled their way through the skein, casting long shadows on the warp that even the most inexperienced seer could detect. They were accompanied by a whispered moaning, their warp engines leaving torment and misery in their wake. Their rough passage formed eddies of power that made their direction and speed easy to calculate. Daemons and other predators trailed after them, drawn by the aura of life that leaked from within the crude warp shields protecting the human vessels.

The runes of the farseers danced around each other, combining together to form a picture of the star system as accurate to the seers' eyes as if they were gods looking down upon the dying star and its orbiting planets.

Yet this picture was not of the present but the future. It told a tale of what might be rather than what was. In the elaborate dance of fate, squadrons of attack craft whirled about each other while human strike cruisers and eldar destroyers duelled with laser and shell and torpedo.

The humans arrived, their warp engines splitting apart the aether, sending a shockwave ripping across the skein, momentarily blinding Thirianna and the others.

The first flotilla disengaged from the warp exactly where the council had predicted. The humans' backwards technology forced them to spread their fleet during entry, while crude scanners peered into the star system gathering data.

The outlying ships of Alaitoc were already moving, engines charged from their solar sails, drifting undetected from the cover of asteroid fields and gas clouds. The humans were still half-blind as their ships scoured the star system with laser and microwaves, and in their moment of weakness, the eldar struck the first blow.

Launching salvoes of torpedoes, the Alaitocii announced their presence. Waves of frigates made attack runs on the lead human ships, their laser batteries rippling along the energy shields encasing the armoured vessels.

Thirianna was impressed for a moment. The human ships were protected by warp-based technologies, their fields dissipating the energy of the fusillade into the alternate realm. With each barrage stopped came the scream of the warp, every failing shield a tiny pinprick break through the thin barrier between reality and the immaterial. She had not believed them capable of such technology, though it was still simplistic compared to the eldar mastery of the warp.

The humans struck back as best they could, launching flights of bombers and waves of torpedoes. Their clumsy cannons hurled plasma and huge explosive shells, but their tracking systems were unable to cope with the holofields hiding the eldar vessels. The frigates skipped away from the counter-attack, a few suffering minor damage from the sheer weight of fire furiously hurled out by the human guns.

The runes moved, growing brighter or darker as fortunes favoured one ship or another. Khaine's rune howled madly as a human ship exploded, consumed by its own reactor. At least half a dozen of the other vessels were severely damaged, their threads bleeding on the skein as they limped away from the eldar attack.

The main force of the invaders now appeared, arriving in small groups scattered around the edges of the star system. This also the seers had foretold, but the fleet of Alaitoc was not numerous enough to cover every approach. The farseers had located the flagships and the vessels with fates that would favour the humans and the autarchs had concentrated the efforts of the fleet towards them, determined to snuff out their potential before it could be realised.

The eldar attacks were fast and damaging, but could not be sustained against the immense firepower of the arriving ships. The autarchs had heeded the warning against a prolonged battle, and duly the fleet responded, melting away into the void before they suffered badly from the humans' retaliation.

The first phase was complete. There was no future in which the humans had been prevented from entering the system, but damage had been done. More importantly, doubt had been sown in the minds of the enemy commanders. Thirianna could see their threads wavering, splitting rapidly as they considered their course of action. A myriad scenarios filtered across the skein: the humans gathering into a single fleet and driving straight for Alaitoc; the enemy vessels dispersing, attempting to make their own way towards the craftworld before gathering for the attack; lighter vessels sent rapidly ahead to scout the way while the lumbering battle cruisers and battleships followed behind.

To confound the planning of the humans, eldar vessels continued to make hit-and-run attacks, directed towards lone and vulnerable vessels by the autarchs, who in turn were guided by the constant commentary from the seers.

'The *Finrairni Ano* and *Lasthetin* are the stalkers of the void, moving along the bloody crescent,' intoned Thirianna, her words spoken without thought as she concentrated on the visions filling her mind, channelling what she saw into a stream of description. 'A human light cruiser delays, suffering engine trouble in the shadow of the ninth world. The fiery blooms upon the arc of the stars wither the enemy, and in shadow we pass into light.'

A chorus of voices filled the chamber, the words and the images behind them directed through the infinity circuit to the waiting autarchs who passed on the messages to the admirals and captains of the fleet.

The ships themselves were part of the skein, their wraithbone hearts merged with the eternal matrix, forged from the infinity circuit of Alaitoc. No light or radio wave could travel as quickly as thought on the skein and every movement and action of the humans was almost instantaneously known to those aboard the craftworld.

The artful interplay of rune and fate was a graceful veneer atop the violence unleashed. Thirianna could feel every death brought about, played out in flickers of desperate struggle across the skein. Bodies froze in the void and burned in the fires of expelling gases. Mothers and fathers, sons and daughters perished, consumed by plasma and laser. Pain and fear flowed, feeding the rune of Khaine. Dread stalked the strands of fate, sapping the strength of the living, turning heroes to cowards. Blood was spilled, its taste lingering in Thirianna's mouth. Every thread that ended was a life lost, human or eldar.

The skein was awash with destruction, yet Thirianna drew on her war-mask to endure. She distanced herself from the struggle, seeing only sundered destinies and paths of hope. She did not let her anger come to the fore, instead she viewed the unfolding war with dispassionate eyes. To feel was to invite doubt and there could be no room for that.

The humans floundered for some time and Thirianna sensed discord flowing through their fate. Internal division, debate, was splitting asunder their threads. All the while the eldar continued to shadow the humans' ships, waiting for any opportunity to pounce, seizing on any moment of unwariness.

The second phase of the attack was a drawn-out affair. The invading fleet broke into three waves, much like an ancient column of advance with a vanguard, main force and rearguard. Picket ships were despatched by the human commanders to keep watch for the Alaitocii attacks, while several squadrons of the fastest starships broke ahead to secure the orbital area between the fourth and fifth planets.

Several times the enemy tried to lay traps, leaving vessels seemingly isolated and ripe for attack whilst in reality help remained near at hand. The skein revealed the blatant trickery behind these ploys and the eldar ignored the bait, instead launching raids against other parts of the enemy fleet.

For cycle after cycle the humans encroached on the space around Alaitoc. Having split their fleet, the enemy commanders ensured that no part was left too far away from the others, nor too close, and so their advance proceeded at the pace of their slow battleships and sluggish transports.

It was impossible to watch the skein for so long without pause, and the seers divided their labours so that some rested while the others watched for any new threat or opportunity. Like a choreographed performance in the Dome of a Thousand Shadows, the farseers passed on what they had seen to each other, their runes touching and parting, forming new patterns with each turning cycle, the collective far stronger than its individual parts.

The humans were direct but not hasty, and the skein was filled with images of the inevitable clash. As the seers had witnessed, there would be no stopping the humans from launching a direct attack.

Yet the delays of the humans provided some hope for the Alaitocii. The longer the invading fleet took to arrive, the more raids and passing attacks the craftworld's fleet could make.

The vanguard flotilla did its best to sweep away the waiting eldar ambushes, but their ships were too few and too slow to catch the elusive eldar vessels. Forewarned of any sudden changes in direction and speed of the enemy ships, the line of eldar vessels protecting the craftworld was able to quickly adjust, vanishing before retribution found them, stealing away to new hiding places.

As time passed, the Alaitocii were helped in other ways. More ships arrived through the webway, bringing back warriors and rangers who had been away from the craftworld. One particular arrival caused quite a stir on the skein.

On board were three of the greatest warriors of the eldar, the Phoenix Lords. They were the founders of the Aspect shrines, whose names were legend. Three founders of the Aspect shrines: The Cry of the Wind, Baharroth; The Harvester of Souls, Maugan Ra; The Shadow Hunter, Karandras.

Three Phoenix Lords, almost without precedent, had come to Alaitoc for a single purpose: war.

Thirianna marvelled at the threads of these remarkable beings. Their lives stretched back to the time of the Fall, where their fates had blossomed into life under the leadership of the First Exarch, Asurmen, yet their origins were hidden by the great shadow of She Who Thirsts. Their threads also stretched forwards into the impossibly distant future, to the final battle known as the Rhana Dandra, the Last Battle against Chaos.

Yet the threads were not a single thread, each was bound to dozens of other lives across their span. Other strands joined those of the Phoenix Lords, winding close about them before becoming part of the whole. Thirianna had seen something similar in the lives of the exarchs, their essence made up of a composite of eldar spirits. Examining them more closely, Thirianna saw that the initial appearance was deceptive. The lives were absorbed by the Phoenix Lords but the original thread continued on, bolstered by each new knot along its length.

As she was about to turn her attention elsewhere, Thirianna noticed something familiar about the thread that represented Karandras, the Shadow Hunter, Phoenix Lord of the Striking Scorpions. There would come a miniscule break in the near-future, but the splitting of fate, the ending of a life, was swiftly healed by the binding of another strand: Korlandril's. Thirianna was not sure what this presaged, but she did not have the time to investigate further.

Another rune threw itself to the fore, demanding attention from every seer.

The Wanderer rose high above the skein. Aradryan, unwitting instigator of this unfolding catastrophe, had returned to Alaitoc.

'You will not see him.' Kelamith's statement was definite, though it was an assertion rather than a prophecy. 'Your fate and his are too tightly bound for you to cause any more disruption.'

'How can you deny me?' argued Thirianna. 'Aradryan is my friend, I should speak with him. Am I not owed this small courtesy for my part in warning you of the peril that has beset us?'

'Your part in this remains unclear,' said Kelamith. 'The decision of the council is final. You will not see the renegade.'

'He is outcast, not renegade, there is a difference,' said Thirianna.

'That too will be for the council to decide,' said Kelamith. 'Aradryan's actions have brought untold disaster upon Alaitoc, whether he knew the danger or not. You have seen the skein, the uncertainty that surrounds your friend. He is a highly disruptive force and we do not yet know to what consequence his coming here will lead.'

'He brings reinforcements,' said Thirianna. 'Surely that will count in his favour. You see as well as I do the rune of the Laughing God. Harlequins accompany him, plus many outcasts of Alaitoc that wish to defend their home.'

'And that will be placed on the balance of judgement by the council,' said Kelamith. He made a short, chopping motion with his hand, a sign of irritation and an indication that the conversation was finished. 'Return to your duties and concentrate on your work.'

Thirianna held her tongue, knowing that to argue longer would achieve nothing and risk further admonishment from Kelamith. She glared at the farseer's back as he left the chamber, indignant at the council's decision to subject Aradryan to their judgement.

She made her way to the Chamber of the Orb, where the defence of Alaitoc had been moved. The divinations were becoming more intricate, as the human fleet massed again, barely three cycles' travel from Alaitoc. The humans appeared to have stalled, and were busily reorganising their ships; flurries of transports and communications were exchanged as they devised the final plan for their attack.

Half a dozen seers were immersed with the Orb of Elmarianin, keeping watch on the movements of the humans. Every ship had been brought back for the close defence of Alaitoc; the humans were gathered en masse and provided no easy target for attack. Perhaps, wondered Thirianna, they were hoping the eldar would foolishly try to confront them in a massed battle. Such a move would never happen. For the Alaitocii to surrender their advantages of speed and manoeuvrability would be a move of utter folly.

As the cycle passed into the night phase, Thirianna examined the humans with her companions, whilst allowing herself the occasional moment to look at the fate of Aradryan. The council's decision was in the balance, whether Aradryan was declared renegade and told to depart or if he would be welcomed back to the craftworld. His own temperament further complicated matters and several of his futures showed Aradryan leaving in anger or contempt at the council's behaviour, abandoning Alaitoc to its fate.

The humans had settled upon their course, the threads of fate coalescing once more, becoming a bright path that led directly to the rune of Alaitoc at the centre of Thirianna's thoughts. Out in the darkness of space, plasma engines were flaring into miniature suns, powering the Imperial vessels along that path.

* * *

Trails of fire criss-crossed the starry sky as missiles and torpedoes streaked across the firmament. The blinding flash of laser weapons flitted through the darkness, while blossoms of brief flame erupted in the void. Squadrons of graceful destroyers tacked effortlessly to bring their weapons to bear while battleships slid gently through the maelstrom, their batteries unleashing salvoes of destruction, open bays spewing wave after wave of darting fighter craft and wide-winged bombers.

On the skein, the threads of fate looped and coiled, colliding with each other as ships exchanged volleys of fire and torpedoes streaked through space. Within every strand were dozens of others: the lives of the eldar crews. Within the threads of the human fleet, the mass of fates entwined together was enormous, an impossible tangle of humanity in which it was impossible to tell who would live and who would die. Death was indiscriminate, laying low admiral and crewman alike, favouring none.

The seers had narrowed down the possible landing sites of the attack to three locations. The autarchs had arranged their forces accordingly, ready to respond as the course of destiny became clearer. Squads of Guardians and Aspect Warriors waited in their transports, spread across Alaitoc.

The infinity circuit was afire with the tension, the minds of all aboard the craftworld concentrated upon this single effort. Thirianna could feel expectation and fear from the many; anger and anticipation from the Avatar and the Aspect Warriors.

Breaking the cordon of eldar ships, an Imperial frigate approached the voidward rim of Alaitoc, heading towards the Dome of Crystal Seers. Thirianna could see the slab-sided, brutal vessel through the thousand eyes of Alaitoc's sensor batteries, encrusted with cornices and buttresses, its prow a giant golden ram shaped like an eagle's beak. Flashes rippled from bow to stern as it opened fire with deck after deck of guns, the flares cut through by the searing beams of laser turrets arranged along a crenulated dorsal deck.

Anger rippled through the craftworld and Alaitoc responded. Like a wounded beast, the craftworld lashed out at its attacker, sending a storm of lightning and laser leaping from defence turrets and anti-ship guns. The human frigate was enveloped by fire, shields scourged by the ire of Alaitoc. Under the torrential fusillade its hull quickly broke, sending plumes of burning air into the vacuum. The furious fire continued until the ship's plasma reactor was breached, turning it into a brief-lived miniature sun.

The breakthrough of the frigate was only the first foreseen by the seers. Thirianna saw more Imperial vessels smashing their way into range of Alaitoc. She spoke quickly, sending messages directly to the ships' commanders placed under her guidance, redirecting them so that they would be able to blunt the reckless human attacks.

The eldar ships glimmered with holofields, appearing as shimmering ghosts to open fire before disappearing against the star-filled backdrop.

Human void shields sputtered with blue and purple flares as they unleashed bursts of energy to shunt the attacks of the eldar into warp space.

Despite the efforts of Thirianna and her companions, the relentless ferocity of the humans would not be turned aside. The skein was awash with their hatred, their loathing of the eldar a unifying force that drew together disparate fates, focussing them upon a single goal: the destruction of Alaitoc.

The humans drew inexorably closer, their coming heralded by fresh waves of torpedoes and the glare of attack craft. Burning hulks drifted in their wake, both human and eldar, debris gently spiralling away from shattered wrecks. The humans seemed bent on their course, coming straight for Alaitoc like armoured comets, punching through the craftworld's fleet, heedless of the damage inflicted upon them.

There were too many converging destinies to keep track of them all and too late Thirianna saw a cruiser bursting past the burning remnants of one of the destroyers under her watch. She sent a warning to the captain but even his swift vessel did not have time to escape. Hundreds of explosions filled the void around the fleeing eldar ship, making a mockery of its holofields. Distraction and misdirection were no defence against the scattered bombardment unleashed by the human cruiser.

Broken in half, solar sail shredded, the eldar destroyer slowly disintegrated. Thirianna found painfully few threads of those aboard, the lives of a handful of crew who had reached the escape shuttles in time.

The cruiser ploughed on, intent on bringing its weapons to bear against Alaitoc. Thirianna reached into the infinity circuit, connecting with the minds of the gunners and urging them to concentrate their fire on the looming Imperial ship.

There were too many threats though, and her call was lost amidst the clamour of other farseers sending their own warnings.

Thirianna latched on to the thread of the human cruiser, flying ahead along its path to locate its destruction. She found nothing to give her hope, as she watched the long lines of armoured doors opening again to reveal bristling gun batteries.

At the last moment the weapons of Alaitoc heeded her call for attention. Laser fire converged on the cruiser and its shields rippled, dissipating the blasts with actinic flares. Its bow erupted with blossoms of orange and moments later the streak of torpedoes hurtled towards Alaitoc, breaking into hundreds of smaller missiles as they crashed into the craftworld.

Thirianna felt the impact in her spirit as well as in the trembling beneath her feet. It was as if her own body was pierced, and she recoiled from the infinity circuit as more salvoes from the cruiser's gun decks slammed into Alaitoc, crashing against the energy shields that protected the domes.

Forcing herself to endure the pain, Thirianna strove to unwind the coiling thread of fate that surrounded the cruiser. Transports were arriving in its wake. They could not be stopped. The barrage from the cruiser continued for some time and then fell silent, the flare of laser and shell replaced by the small pinpricks of assault craft engines.

Thirianna glanced ahead along the skein and saw human soldiers disgorged from the ramps of their drop-ships. She knew where the first boarding parties would land.

'Autarch Arhathain, the humans will come first to the Tower of Ascending Dreams.' She sent the message and turned her attention back to the skein, seeing the interplay of fates crystallising as the defenders of Alaitoc responded to the news.

'Come with me.' Kelamith broke Thirianna from her contemplation. She withdrew from the skein and found the farseer standing next to her, staff and sword in hand. He wore his jewel-lensed helmet, his voice carried to her across the skein.

Her own Witchblade thrummed into life at her belt, detecting imminent battle. Around her, the other farseers and warlocks were also readying for physical conflict, leaving those with no war-masks to continue to monitor the skein.

'We have done what we can from here,' said Kelamith. 'We set foot upon a new path. Now we must take a more direct role.'

By the time Thirianna had reached the arterial passageway adjoining the Chambers of the Seers, a Wave Serpent transport was already waiting for her, summoned by Kelamith. Two more of the sleek machines glided into view as the ramp in the back of the first opened to allow Thirianna to board.

Inside were ten Guardians, clad in armour made up of yellow polymer mesh overlaid with plates of deep blue. Ten helmeted heads turned towards Thirianna as she embarked and ten shuriken catapults were raised in deferential salute.

Kelamith's thoughts touched upon Thirianna's mind.

The Passing Spectacle. Stop the humans from reaching the Plaza of Shattered Memories.

She acknowledged the instruction and passed it on to the pilot of the Wave Serpent. The transport rose into the air as the ramp silently closed. Thirianna's last glimpse outside was of the two other Wave Serpents falling into formation behind.

As they sped along a cross-world highway, Thirianna slipped into the skein, focussing her mind on the spiralling pathway known as the Passing Spectacle. It acted as a bridge across a gorge-like split between two of the craftworld's domes, leading from the docks at the Tower of Ascending Dreams to the Plaza of Shattered Memories.

She foresaw human soldiers advancing quickly to the base of the pathway, three squads of them led by an officer in a heavy coat. They carried simple lasguns and their fear resonated along the thread of their fate; they had strayed too far from the other landing parties, misdirected by Alaitoc itself, and would be easy prey.

Thirianna followed this train of thought and glimpsed the humans being cut down in a crossfire of shurikens. She reached across the skein to the minds of Nathuriel and Unarian, the leaders of the two other guardian squads placed under her command.

'Depart at the Crescent of the Dawn and approach the Passing Spectacle from starwards. We will draw the enemy onto the bridge, allowing you to strike from behind.'

'Understood, Farseer Thirianna,' the two squad leaders replied.

The use of her honorific sent a brief thrill through Thirianna, but it was soon surpassed by a wave of anxiety. She looked again at the skein, going further into the future to locate the consequences of her plan.

All was well. The advance party of humans would be destroyed and the bottom of the Passing Spectacle secured. Several possibilities spawned from the act, all of them leading to fresh attacks against Thirianna and her warriors. She saw herself meeting another human officer blade-to-blade in one of the scenarios, her Witchblade matched against his chainsword. The farseer emerged victorious, though several of the Guardians would lose their lives defending the passageway.

There was another possible fate emerging. It was extremely vague, the hint of a possibility. Something was obscuring the skein, a presence she could not quite discern. With a thought, she tugged the Scorpion from her belt pouch and set her mind to the task of deciphering the riddle.

There was a figure cloaked in uncertainty, bound within the skein in a way Thirianna had not seen before. It troubled her that this person's actions were hidden. He was definitely human, his short, brutal fate tying a knot around the graceful arc of Thirianna's own thread. She could not see how the division came to pass, it was mired in circumstances beyond prediction, but on one path her life ended and on the other she killed the human.

A word from the Wave Serpent pilot informed her that they would soon be arriving at their destination. Thirianna took the last few moments to scour the skein for wider information.

The humans had forced a landing, several hundred of their soldiers breaking through the dock defences to create a safe zone for more dropships and shuttles to land. They were trying to unload their heavier weapons from the transports, but were being subjected to withering fire by several Guardian squads supported by heavy weapons on anti-grav platforms.

The grander scheme was unfurling as the autarchs had dictated. It was usual for the Aspect Warriors to bear the brunt of the fighting, with the militia of the Guardians acting as a reserve to counter-attack against enemy breakthroughs. However, the divining of the seer council had foreseen problems with this approach; some greater force of the humans was also held in reserve and once committed would sweep away all resistance. The source of this strength was unclear, but the autarchs had decided that the Guardians would bear the brunt of the early fighting, preserving the fighters of the Aspect shrines to confront this later threat.

The Wave Serpent slid to a halt, the ramp opening with a hiss of escaping pressurised air. Stepping out onto the pale grey of the Passing Spectacle, Thirianna realised that Alaitoc had drained the area of air, leaving only a thin atmosphere for the humans to breathe. With the aid of their helmets, the eldar had more than sufficient air to sustain them, another factor in their favour.

Thirianna and her squad took up position opposite an archway not far from where the Passing Spectacle blended with the lower levels of the dock. The humans would be entering soon and she warned her Guardians to be ready while she checked to make sure the other two squads were in position to strike.

The hallway in which they waited had a low, oval cross-section, flattened underfoot by a pathway of marble. Columns lined each side of the passageway, providing cover for Thirianna and her warriors.

'They are coming,' announced Thirianna, sensing a tremble on the skein caused by the approach of the humans.

The first soldier through the door seemed utterly unaware of his peril. Thirianna allowed a few more to enter before giving the order to open fire. Shurikens hissed down the passageway, slashing through the soldiers' grey uniforms, leaving arcs of blood spattered on the floor and walls.

Thirianna warned her Guardians to take cover a few moments before a sporadic blast of ruby-hued las-fire flared from the archway as the following soldiers opened fire. The Guardian nearest the door staggered out from behind a column, clutching the side of his helm. The name Temerill flashed through Thirianna's mind a moment before another las-bolt caught the Guardian in the chest, burning through the breastplate of this armour, sending him reeling to the floor.

His thread had ended.

Thirianna drew her shuriken pistol and fired back, her salvo joining with the fire of the others to cut down the three humans who were crouched in the archway. Sensing the moment for action, Thirianna stepped out into the corridor and ran forwards, her Witchblade flaring into life. She threw herself into the cover of a las-scarred column a heartbeat before another volley erupted from the outer hallway.

Thirianna glimpsed into her immediate future, judging whether to attack or stay in the sanctuary of her hiding place. She saw herself being struck by several las-bolts, but none penetrated the psychic field of her rune armour.

Witchblade levelled towards the arch, Thirianna stepped out from behind the pillar and focussed her mind. She filtered her psychic power through the anger of her war-mask, sending it coursing along the length of her weapon. Violet flames spewed along the passageway, roaring through the archway to engulf the soldiers beyond.

Thirianna felt four more lives flicker into nothingness.

'Fall back towards the ramp,' she told the others, noting the arrival of the human officer. He would lead the attack, the humans storming along the passageway with knives and bayonets. Thirianna saw that such a move would be most unwelcome at this moment in time and signalled again for the Guardians to retreat a few dozen paces to the archway behind them.

As the humans launched their fresh assault, Thirianna sent the call for the other two squads to make their move. The humans barrelled forwards into the fire of her Guardians, ignoring the several men that were cut down by the welcome of the eldar's shuriken catapults. The slow, clumsy humans wore ill-fitting suits of drab grey and black camouflage, stitched with skull and eagle insignias on their arms and chests, their helmets fitted with silvered visors that hid the upper part of their brutish faces.

Like the Guardians had done before, they took up positions behind the protection of the columns, lasguns propped against the burnt and chipped masonry. Thirianna saw the darker uniform of the officer striding through the gateway, his deep voice echoing along the passage as he bellowed at his troops and waved them forwards again.

Half of the humans let loose a volley of las-fire while the other half ran on, their breathing laboured, bayonets glinting in the light of the screaming las-bolts.

At the same moment, Unarian's warriors emerged from the far archway, weapons at the ready. Their burst of fire struck the enemy soldiers from behind, shurikens tearing through cloth uniforms and flesh.

Thirianna signalled for her squad to attack, and led the charge back into the corpse-choked corridor, her rune armour flaring with las-blasts. She singled out the human officer amongst the panicking soldiers, picking loose his thread from the tangle of the others. With a flick of her wrist, she sent a whining bolt of psychic energy into the ungainly crowd of humans. It struck the officer in the back of the head as he was turning to look at Unarian's warriors. Hair and skin charred instantly and with a high-pitched scream the officer toppled forwards, his pistol clattering across the floor as it fell from his grasp.

The men he had been leading lived for only a few moments longer. A few managed to snap off ragged shots, killing two of Unarian's Guardians, before they too were ripped to shreds by the coordinated shuriken volleys.

Thirianna checked the skein. Not a single human thread was left; all were dead.

More were approaching quickly, though not so fast that they would arrive before Thirianna had readied a fresh welcome for them. The passageway was too narrow for all three squads to defend, so she dispersed them through the surrounding rooms.

She looked down at the bodies of the dead humans, shocked and yet pleased by how easy it had been to outwit them. She cautioned herself against over-confidence. A momentary glance at the skein showed that her shadowy confrontation was becoming more likely. A circle of burning iron surrounded her rune, slowly constricting around her.

This was just the first skirmish in a battle and the first battle in a war that she had seen would last for several cycles. There was still a lot of fighting and killing to be done.

The infinity circuit was alive with reports of the humans' activities. The farseers passed on what they saw on the skein, their communications appearing to Thirianna alongside glimpsed images of the visions, while the autarchs issued their responses.

Alaitoc itself reacted to the presence of the invaders, reconfiguring walkways and passages, closing off domes and opening up new pathways for the eldar to encircle their foes. Air was expelled from some areas while others were flooded with noxious gases, suffocating the humans in their hundreds. Darkness enveloped other portions of the craftworld, allowing Striking Scorpions to attack from the shadows, slaying their foes unseen. The docks were subjected to barrages of flickering light to blind the humans, leaving them vulnerable to assault by Warp Spiders and Shining Spears. Sound was also used, to deafen the unprotected ears of the attackers, while their crude radio-based communications were easily blocked or subverted by the energies of the craftworld. The spirits of the infinity circuit were channelled to launch a massive psychic attack, driving the humans mad with visions of death and terror.

Thirianna and her Guardians had seen off two more assaults against the Passing Spectacle, though both had been lacklustre in their execution. A swift foray through the skein confirmed Thirianna's suspicion that these attacks were intended merely to keep her small force in place while the humans gathered numbers for a serious push forwards.

She highlighted this turn of events to the autarchs, who set in motion several more guardian squads and two squadrons of war walkers to come to Thirianna's aid. A breakthrough by the humans starward of Thirianna's position meant the reinforcements would not arrive until the next clash had begun.

'We must hold the bridge for as long as possible,' she told her warriors, who now numbered only twelve. If they tried to hold their ground in the teeth of the enemy attack, they would be surrounded and wiped out. 'Be ready to withdraw to the Passing Spectacle at my signal.'

It took some time for the humans to organise themselves for the renewed offensive. During the long pause, Thirianna studied the skein in more detail, trying to figure out the most likely routes of advance they would use. Her attention was drawn to the mysterious figure that was now appearing prominently through her own thread. Using the power of the Scorpion, Thirianna dug into the nature of this individual, and found herself touching upon another mind on the skein.

She recoiled in shock, her mind awash with images from the human psyker. His thoughts were anarchic, lacking the focus of an eldar seer, but the tendrils of his power stretched into many threads, drawing on a large reserve of energy. His mind was protected by a burning shield, which both warded away the prowling daemons but also acted as a beacon to them. If Thirianna's mind was a swift skiff skimming across the waves of the warp, eluding detection, the human was a loud and angry gunboat that bullied its way through the tides of energy.

The human psyker was not far away. Now that Thirianna had identified him, she could sense his location instinctively. Along with several armoured walkers, he had joined a force of nearly fifty humans preparing for the next assault. His presence was highly disruptive; the soldiers alongside the psyker were suspicious of his powers.

They were right to be worried. The psyker tapped into the warp without the benefit of runes, channelling the raw energy of Chaos. Though his mind was wrapped up in protective hymnals and armoured with bluntly fashioned talismans, if they failed he had no other defences against possession or psychic feedback.

The rattle of a large-calibre automatic weapon heralded the next assault. On awkward legs, a human war engine three times as tall as Thirianna stalked through the gloom, a multi-barrelled gun beneath its cockpit spewing fire. Fist-sized projectiles tore through the walls of the passageway and surrounding rooms.

Darting out of cover, the Guardians opened fire, but their shurikens inflicted little damage on the walker's armoured hull. Another followed, its rapid-firing laser strobing red beams down the passageway, scorching marks across the pillars and walls.

Behind the walkers advanced several squads of infantry, the psyker amongst them. He was easy to pick out, dressed in a long coat of purple and gold, with a high red-lined collar. His head was shaved bald and Thirianna could see the scars and bulges of implants inserted beneath his scalp. A wispy beard trailed from a narrow chin and his eyes were like beads of green glass. The psyker awkwardly held some form of laser pistol in one hand and a wand of curious design in the other. The rod was tipped with a crystal shaped like a skull and the glimmer of psychic energy surrounded it.

Two of the walkers and a third of the soldiers had come through the archway when Thirianna sent the signal to Alaitoc to close the doorway. The walls shifted, the petal-like plates of the door swishing into place in an instant; an unfortunate human was caught halfway through and was sheared in two by the closing portal.

At the same time, the light crystals blinked out, plunging the passage-way into utter darkness. The Guardians opened fire, able to see through the heat-sensing lenses of their helmets; Thirianna's helm had the same but her psychic eye highlighted the enemy even more clearly.

She leapt out of cover and ducked beneath a random cannonade of shells from the lead walker. Guided by her prescience she dodged to the right as the fire of her companions whickered through the darkness, cutting down a handful of humans. Three more steps took the farseer up to the first walking machine. Fire leaping from its edges, she swept her Witchblade towards the gun of the walker, slicing its barrel clean through.

She jumped back as the pilot tried to fire again. The cannon exploded as its shells jammed in the breech, sending flame and debris up through the floor of the cockpit to mangle and incinerate the pilot. The walker sagged to the left, crashing into a column in a shower of dust and sparks.

A bright light filled the passageway, gleaming from the wand of the psyker. Thirianna was caught in the open, facing the full force of the incoming volley of las-fire. She somersaulted behind the wreckage of the walker as red beams filled the corridor, her rune armour flaring with energy as several bolts found her.

'Avert your gaze,' she told her warriors as she sent another signal to the infinity circuit. If it was light the humans desired, it was light they would have.

Alaitoc flooded energy into the passageway, the walls themselves shin-ing with psychic power, harsh white light blazing into the eyes of the incoming humans. Thirianna vaulted over the downed walker, eyes closed, guided by her psychic sense. Fire streamed from her Witchblade, engulfing the next walker, lapping around the edges of the cockpit, lick-ing along hanging pipes and cables.

Fuel lines burst, spewing fire over the walls and ceiling as the machine erupted into a column of flame.

Thirianna continued her course, charging into the closest knot of humans. They were recovering from their blindness, but not quickly enough to see the farseer sprinting into their midst. Her Witchblade flashed left and then right, decapitating two of the soldiers.

As she parried a lunging bayonet, Thirianna directed her Guardians to the left. They opened fire at her urging, scything down more humans while she ducked under a heavily gloved fist and drove her Witchblade through the gut of another man.

Lightning poured down the passageway from the psyker's outstretched hand, leaping through three of the Guardians, cracking open armour, scorching flesh and snapping bones. Thirianna felt the pulse of energy along the skein as the psyker drew in another surge of power. She acted without thought, snaring the psyker's thread with her own, cutting off the supply of psychic energy.

The psyker choked and stumbled back with a howl of pain as Thirianna kicked aside one of his bodyguard. Blue energy enveloped Thirianna as the psyker flung out his wand, power coursing along the skein, engulfing the strand of Thirianna's life.

Her rune armour burned with white light for several heartbeats, absorbing the brunt of the attack. It was not enough to shield her from all damage though as the psychic blast throbbed through her thoughts, burning her mind from the inside.

Snarling away the pain, Thirianna unleashed the fury of her Witchblade, purple flames setting fire to the psyker's long coat. He flailed wildly, bolts of power erupting from his eyes as he stumbled backwards, his own attack swarming around him, consuming him from within.

Thirianna had no time to follow up the attack. The butt of a rifle struck her in the back. She rolled with the blow, rune armour clattering on the hard floor, and spun on her heel as she came back to her feet. The tip of her Witchblade found the human's chest, punching through breastbone into his heart.

The psyker's thread had come to a ragged end.

Aware of a pounding at the closed archway, Thirianna dipped into the future. The third walker was ramming itself against the door and cracks appeared where the artificial petals joined.

'Pull back to the Passing Spectacle,' she ordered, sending another sheet of violet flame into the humans, driving them back towards the archway.

The Guardians retreated, sending more shurikens down the corridor as they melted back towards the bridge.

Thirianna reached a psychic hand into the skein and snatched up the threads of the humans, crushing them together in an immaterial fist. The men around her stumbled into each other and groaned with pain, giving her the opening she needed to break free. Without a backwards glance, she dashed back down the corridor, reaching the safety of the next doorway just as the humans recovered and sent a barrage of red bolts after her.

Including the farseer, there were eight of them left, against at least twice that number of humans. A shuddering crash announced the collapse of the far portal and Thirianna corrected herself: at least four times that number of enemies.

The span of the Passing Spectacle was not without cover. Though it had no rail as it spiralled up over the interdome gulf, it was lined with high pedestals on which were set busts of renowned Alaitocii from the craftworld's long history.

Beneath the bridge stretched the expanse of the chasm, an expanse of gigantic interlocking crystals that formed the bedrock of the craftworld, their depth lost amidst a layer of glittering mist.

The humans advanced cautiously, allowing their remaining walker to take the lead. Thirianna and her squad kept just out of sight, pulling back each time the machine's laser tracked towards them.

They had completed three of the five loops of the spiral when Thirianna ordered them to hold their ground. The reinforcements were approaching rapidly, but the humans would reach the top of the Passing Spectacle before they arrived if they continued to advance at their current pace.

Settling into what cover they could find, the Guardians opened fire, sending a storm of shurikens towards the walker. Sparks flew from its armour, but it was not slowed. The marble-like surface of the bridge was scuffed and scratched by the walker's iron feet as it plodded forwards.

Its lascannon spat out a beam of red. A plinth shattered, sending shards of Neruenthia the Foreshadowed spraying into the Guardian behind. The eldar's bloodied remains toppled over the edge of the bridge and disappeared into the depths.

Thirianna searched the skein for the fate of the walker's pilot, seeking some means to bring about his death. She located it, a bright, burning strand, as the walker opened fire again, obliterating another of her Guardians. She cast about along the neighbouring threads and drew two together.

As the walker's lascannon swivelled towards its next target, a sleek shadow emerged from the fog of the chasm. Its holofields shimmering blue and yellow, the Wave Serpent rose above the Passing Spectacle. The holofields dimmed for a moment as its turret turned towards the walker. Twin trails rushed from its missile launchers and a few heartbeats later, the human war engine was wracked by two detonations, sending its mangled remains careening off the edge of the span.

More transports rushed from the depths, their turrets raking the advancing humans with shuriken cannon fire and stabs of blue plasma from their starcannons. Moving in from the base of the bridge, a trio of war walkers stopped the humans' retreat with a barrage of high-explosive missiles and scatter laser fire.

Rivulets of blood coursed down the Passing Spectacle, dripping over the edge into the misty chasm below. A few of the humans had survived, crawling into the cover of shattered plinths, their threads waning, their lives leaking away.

Thirianna did not pause to enjoy the moment of victory; the skein was alive with movement as more and more humans deployed onto the craftworld. Several hundred were pressing towards her position, far more than could be held.

Another force was heading towards a neighbouring bridge to rimwards, and they would cross into the next dome soon. Searching for some way to delay them while she redeployed her growing force, she found a stray squad of Striking Scorpions not too far away.

Her mind touched upon that of the exarch and she recognised

Morlaniath. His thoughts were immersed in shadows and death as his squad raced across Alaitoc aboard their Wave Serpent. Thirianna pushed through the chilling aura and sent him an image of the unfolding battle, allowing him to see the disposition of the squads and vehicles in the vicinity. She bound together several fates, addressing several dozen eldar with her thoughts.

'The enemy make progress along the Well of Disparate Fates. Walk the red path with them, drive them back to their landing craft.'

The runes were set in motion as the Alaitocii responded to her request. None were close enough to aid her at the Passing Spectacle and a swift survey of the unfolding future revealed that the bridge would not be held against the next attack, even if every eldar with her laid down their lives in its defence.

It was time to draw back to the next line. While she and others held where they could, a concerted counter-attack was being made to reclaim the landing grounds seized by the invaders.

Guided by Thirianna, her small force withdrew to the dome gates at the top of the spiralling bridge. The first humans were already at the base, streaming past the bodies of their dead compatriots, urged on by a bellowing officer whose mind was like an iron cage, impervious to Thirianna's scans.

She waited until the humans were halfway up the bridge before interfacing with the infinity circuit. She arrowed through the conduits of the Passing Spectacle, becoming one with the craftworld, closing off conduits and crystal pathways. With a last thought, she speared back along the bridge, detonating its wraithbone heart as she passed.

The Passing Spectacle erupted into shards from the base, falling in jagged lumps, pitching the advancing humans into the mists below, their screams swallowed by the swirling fog. Thirianna felt a spark of sorrow at the act but it did not last long; if Alaitoc was to be kept safe, much of it would have to be sacrificed for the ultimate victory.

With the humans' axis of advance cut off, Thirianna moved her troops back from the fighting, joining up with several Aspect Warriors squads, a pair of Falcon tanks and several Guardians crewing anti-grav support weapons. They moved as one along the Boulevard of Undimmed Glories, preparing for the next phase of the battle.

Something bright and powerful burned across the skein, spearing into the heart of Alaitoc's rune. Thirianna recognised it immediately and felt a shiver of apprehension. The hidden strength the seers had witnessed, the play of their deadly reserves, was unfolding. A red-and-white fist closed on the craftworld, smashing through hundreds of strands of fate.

Thirianna sped across the infinity circuit to the counter-attack against the landing site, seeing dozens of eldar lives shorn short by the reserves being committed. She saw giants, garbed in thick, powered armour. Their livery was a vivid red, their shoulder pads and insignia painted in stark white. Thirianna looked into their spirits and saw warriors hardened by lives of battle, their minds honed to sharp points, their existence directed towards the singular purpose of war.

She snatched what information she could, hearing devotional speeches directed to the spectre of their founder, and glimpsed a world where humans teemed like insects in gigantic cities that pierced polluted skies. She was overwhelmed by shadows of childhood memories of bitter fighting in dark, twisted tunnels, desperate struggles with sharpened metal splinters and home-made guns. They were killers raised from birth, their instinct for slaying honed since infancy in a world where the ruthless lived and the meek did not.

Yet all this was banded about by a willpower of steel, contained by the training of their masters and their dedication to their cause, forged into a cold fury, a righteous anger now directed at the eldar of Alaitoc. They were natural killers, who took joy in slaying, given the greatest armour and weapons the humans possessed, instilled with fervour for destruction like a war-mask that was never removed.

They were not human at all. An Aspect Warrior embraced the touch of Khaine and became a heartless killer, but he or she remained eldar in spirit, able to set aside their destructive impulses when not at war. These warriors had left behind concepts of mercy and desire for peace, and sought only conflict and bloodshed. They were more than human in many ways, yet to Thirianna's mind they were also less than the basest creatures, as crude as orks in their warlike desires, an affront to the galaxy, serving no part other than as harbingers of slaughter. That the self-declared Emperor of Mankind had desired them to be this way betrayed his barbaric nature.

Thirianna shuddered with fear at what she saw, momentarily gripped by panic.

The Sons of Orar, lauded and feared Space Marines of the Emperor, were about to commence their attack.

DESTINY

Alaitoc – Sword of Eldanesh. One of the first runes, Alaitoc signifies the cutting of ties, the sundering of past from present and present from future. For the seers of the craftworld that bears its name, Alaitoc is the hub about which all other runes are cast, determining the fate of the craftworld and its people. It is also a protective rune, which in dire circumstances can be used to cut through the skein, ensuring sanctuary from daemonic intrusion.

The battle for Alaitoc continued to rage. The attack of the Space Marines had bolstered the flagging invasion of the humans, sending the craftworld's defenders reeling back towards the central domes. Seizing control of several arterial routes, the attackers were advancing at speed, the charge led by the red-and-white-armoured warriors of the Sons of Orar. In their wake followed columns of infantry, tanks and artillery, ready to bring the full weight of the humans' strength to bear against the Alaitocii.

As had been agreed by the council before the invasion, parts of Alaitoc were surrendered without a fight. Force domes and energy shields were removed, exposing the advancing army to the ravages of open space. The great arches along the Way of Unerring Moonlight were sealed. The bridges across the Valley of Benign Modesty were cast down.

The humans were subjected to constant harassment from the swiftest eldar troops. Swooping Hawk Aspect Warriors flitted above the advancing lines, showering down las-fire and plasma grenades. Shining Spears darted from side tunnels, cutting swathes with shuriken fire and laser lance before dashing to safety. Warp Spiders teleported into the heart of the enemy, unleashing the monofilament webs of their deathspinners before withdrawing.

The eldar gave ground and counter-attacked with precise purpose. The enemy could not be halted, but they could be stalled and redirected. Every effort was made to divide the human forces, allowing isolated companies to be picked off by superior attacks. Tanks were led down dead-ends, forced to withdraw and advance again, only to find their new routes blocked to them.

The Space Marines were the toughest proposition. Individually and together they were a match for the Aspect Warriors. The only means to combat them was to bring them out into the open, where the Titans and other large war engines of Alaitoc could be brought to bear against the superhuman adversaries.

Thirianna received a message from Kelamith as she mustered several batteries of heavy weapons to meet an armoured thrust along the Starlit Causeway. Her fellow farseer requested that she met him in the Well of Silent Affection, a hall located close to the Chambers of the Seers at the core of Alaitoc.

She had known this time would come, but the thought still sent a shiver of trepidation through the farseer. There was only one reason to visit the Well of Silent Affection: to awaken the dead of Alaitoc.

The hall was well named, its strange acoustics absorbing every sound, muffling Thirianna's footfalls as she crossed the pale blue floor to join Kelamith. The walls were covered with a labyrinth of crystal cables, the infinity circuit laid bare. The energy conduits pulsed and flashed with light.

Kelamith had beside him a wraithbone chest, its lid open. Inside were several dozen waystones, each settled within its own niche within the interior. His expression was hidden behind his ghosthelm, but his voice betrayed his sombre mood.

'It is our duty to rouse the spirits of those passed, that they might fight for the future of generations to come,' said the farseer.

He plucked the first waystone from its nest and held it in its hand. It fitted snugly in his palm, a pale blue ovoid with a pearlescent sheen. Kelamith walked to the infinity circuit conduits, which were gathered in a spiral around a small aperture. He placed the waystone into the waiting hole.

Removing his glove, Kelamith took a sharp-edged rune from his belt: the symbol of Death. With this, he nicked the tip of his finger, allowing a single droplet of blood to emerge. The rune floated up from his fingers and hovered around the waystone as the farseer touched his finger to its cold surface.

The infinity circuit was set alight by the ceremony, psychic energy blazing through the pathways as Kelamith's blood seeped into the waystone.

A bright flash zoomed along the conduits, a spark of white fire, drawn by the farseer's tiny sacrifice. The speeding bolt followed the conduits around the waystone, circling swiftly before disappearing. A moment later the waystone gleamed with inner power, highlighting the farseer's helm and armour with a blue glow.

Kelamith plucked the spirit stone from its place. With measured stride, he crossed the hall to the other side. A wave of the hand drew back the veil of the thin walls, revealing a long line of alcoves. Within each stood a wraithbone form, each taller than an eldar. Their smooth, slender limbs were shaded in blue and yellow, the colours of Alaitoc. Domed heads like helms shone blackly in the light of the infinity circuit.

In their hands the immobile constructs held wraithcannons; Thirianna could feel the dormant warp cores of the weapons imprinting upon her thoughts.

As Kelamith approached the first artificial body, the helm-like head opened up, revealing a niche within for the spirit stone. The farseer placed the spirit stone in its receptacle and stepped back. The head closed down as psychic energy flared through the wraithbone, glowing from jewelled nodes fashioned within the artificial body and limbs. The black head paled, becoming white with inner light.

The wraithguard turned its head towards Kelamith and then moved its immortal gaze to Thirianna. She could sense its confusion, plucked from the eternal energy of the infinity circuit and placed in a new body. On the skein, a faint thread of fate glimmered into being, a life born anew, however fleetingly.

There is coldness. The ghosts walk amongst us.

The wraithguard's thoughts were confused, scattered. Thirianna felt Kelamith reaching out with his mind, linking his thread to that of the wraithguard, infusing it with his own purpose.

The construct raised its weapon and took a step towards the farseers.

Alaitoc in peril. War. I am ready.

At a signal from Kelamith, Thirianna accompanied him back to the box of waystones. She took one of the stones from the box and followed the same ritual as Kelamith. As her blood touched the waystone, she felt a flicker of connection between herself and the infinity circuit.

It was unlike any experience she had encountered before. She became a part of the infinity circuit in a way that was far deeper than her previous contact. She saw not the flow of psychic energy, but the spirits of the dead that generated it. No longer were its pulses and phases an abstract phenomenon; they were the spirits held within the circuit moving about the craftworld bringing their dormant consciousness to where it was needed.

She latched on to one of the passing spirits, feeling its distant, detached essence. It perceived her only vaguely but was lured by the connection, following the trail she had left on the infinity circuit.

She pulled back from the dead spirit a moment before it passed into the waystone, fearing that part of her would become trapped within it. Unformed questions nagged at Thirianna's thoughts as she took the spirit stone to the next waiting wraithguard.

Placing the stone within the core of the construct, Thirianna felt a name impressed upon her memories: Naetheriol. She had been a poet, a Dark Reaper, a pilot and a mother. A life full of experiences flashed through Thirianna as Naetheriol's spirit merged with the wraithbone of her new body.

Waking. Darkness.

Thirianna guided Naetheriol from her alcove, allowing her to glimpse the world through the seer's eyes, parting the misty veil of death that fogged the spirit's perceptions. Leaving a gleaming star of clarity in the dead eldar's thoughts, Thirianna turned back to the chest, ready to repeat the procedure.

When they were done, Thirianna and Kelamith had roused thirty wraithguard. It was not a large number, but they were formidable fighters. Their wraithcannons would be a match for the Space Marines' armour and their wraithbone bodies could withstand incredible amounts of damage.

Yet they would not be the deadliest weapons to be let free from the Well of Silent Affection.

Moving to the far end of the hall, Kelamith uncovered the bodies of the wraithlords. Though similar in design to the wraithguard, these constructs towered above the two seers, their long limbs carved with miniscule runes. Bright lances and missile launchers were fixed to mounts on their shoulders, scatter lasers and long power swords were gripped in massive fists.

Only the strongest spirits could power such constructs and Kelamith produced the rune of Khaine from his pouch as he returned to the waystones. Thirianna attached herself to his thoughts as the farseer delved into the infinity circuit searching for suitable candidates.

His psyche came upon the shrines of the Aspect Warriors. Every living exarch was already fighting, but there were several suits standing dormant in forgotten shrines. Kelamith opened up the wards that kept these war-like spirits away from the mass of the infinity circuit and Alaitoc shuddered with their rush of anger.

Vengeful, full of hatred, focussed on death and destruction, the spirits of the dead warriors screamed through the infinity circuit, seeking release. It was a simple matter to guide them along the conduits to the waiting wraithlords.

The first Thirianna recognised, albeit from a strange perspective. He was Kenainath, a Striking Scorpion exarch, the former mentor of Korlandril. His body had only recently succumbed to the weight of time and his spirit was almost fully formed; it had suffered little of the dissipation of essence that beset the wraithguard.

The exarch flowed into the wraithbone body that was chosen for him and raised twin fists that crackled with energy. A shuriken cannon on his shoulder moved in its mount as Kenainath spread out into the systems of his new-found body.

I serve Khaine again, sooner than expected; I shall bring ruin.

Three more wraithlords were given life, each fuelled by the spirit taken from a dormant exarch. Kelamith and Thirianna were joined by several other seers and each took five of the wraithguard to act as their warriors. They were sluggish to respond at first and Thirianna extended her thoughts into the wraithbone shells of the constructs, guiding them after her with her will.

The wraithlords, possessed of greater clarity, departed for council with the autarchs, leaving Thirianna with Kelamith.

'I see that your fate and that of Korlandril are as yet still closely entwined,' remarked Kelamith as he walked beside Thirianna, the ten wraithguard following with long strides behind them.

'Korlandril is no more, and Morlaniath who he has become has but a short fate remaining,' replied Thirianna.

'Yet it is fitting that you should share one last encounter, to complete the circle that was started,' said Kelamith.

'As you request,' said Thirianna.

The two of them parted company, boarding separate cloudskiffs with their immortal charges. Thirianna allowed the wraithguard to slumber while she searched the skein for Morlaniath. She found him in the Dome of Midnight Forests and directed the skiff pilot to take her there.

Only the ruddy glow of dying Mirianathir lit the sky of the dome. Beneath the ruddy shadows of the lianderin, the Alaitocii gathered. Grav-tanks prowled along the pathways while scores of Wave Serpents shuttled back and forth delivering squads to their positions. Here the eldar would make their next stand, able to rake fire across the wide clearings from the cover of the scattered woods. Every valley would become a killing field, every brook and meadow a graveyard for the invaders.

Disembarking from the skiff, Thirianna urged the wraithguard into motion. They followed her along a silvery pathway that cut through the lianderin trees as she followed the thread of fate towards Morlaniath. A Wave Serpent caught up with them as they crossed a bridge over a narrow stream, dropping off three warlocks: Methrain, Nenamin and Toladrissa. They accompanied Thirianna as she led the wraithguard into the trees again, heading for the centre of the dome.

She found the exarch and other Striking Scorpions in a clearing looking down on a long valley that stretched to the edge of the Dome of Midnight Forests. Morlaniath's squad was made up of the survivors of the Hidden Death, Deadly Shadow and Fall of Deadly Rain shrines. They had suffered badly in the Space Marine attack and Thirianna could sense apprehension amongst the Aspect Warriors, mixed with anger and a strong desire for vengeance.

Had it not been for her witch sight, Thirianna would have not known the Aspect Warriors were nearby, concealed in the shadows of the forest. The clearing was dominated by a Cobra tank, a massive war engine mounting a distortion cannon in its low turret. As with the wraith-cannons of her bodyguard, Thirianna could sense the warp core powering the weapon, though the rent it made in the skein was far larger. A pair of Vyper jetbikes circled through the trees around the clearing, keeping watch for approaching foes.

Thirianna allowed her mind to touch upon the strand of Morlaniath, attracting the exarch's attention. She raised her Witchblade in a salute to the ancient warrior.

'Our fates share the same path again for a while,' she said.

Is this coincidence, or a machination, brought about by your hand? The exarch's thoughts came as a chorus of voices, tainted with bitterness, an after-echo of Korlandril's past.

'I am not senior enough to influence the judgement of the autarchs,' replied Thirianna. 'Some have fates closely entwined. Others have strands that never touch. We are the former. Do you not remember where you are?'

Thirianna had recognised the place immediately, and with a deft thought looped back the thread of Korlandril's life, briefly laying it alongside that of the exarch. She felt a flash of recognition as the exarch's eyes fell upon a tall statue at the edge of the clearing, of an eldar warrior kneeling before the goddess Isha, catching her tears in a goblet.

'I present *The Gifts of Loving Isha*,' he announced with a smile.

There were a few gasps of enjoyment and a spontaneous ripple of applause from all present. Korlandril turned to look at his creation and allowed himself to admire his work fully for the first time since its completion.

Thirianna smiled at the memory shared, having never experienced Korlandril's pleasure at that moment. It was odd to her that such happiness would turn to such sadness swiftly after. With what she knew now, it was clear that Korlandril's psyche had been far from stable, his artistic temperament masking a deeper flaw.

I remember clearly, when disharmony reigned, when my spirit was split. This was my new birthplace, the path leading from here, which brought me full circle. It is no more than that, a place in a past life, of no special accord.

Korlandril had been consumed by this being, but his memory still lived on. She wanted to give that ghost of the friend she had known some comfort in the last moments of its existence. She had some time to search the skein, using the Wanderer to pull together disparate fates conjoined with the statue Korlandril had created.

She found what she had been hoping to see.

'Many new paths spring from this place,' said Thirianna. 'Some for good, others that lead to darker places. Your work began those paths, even if you did not intend it. We are all linked in the great web of destiny, the merest trembling on a silken thread sending tremors through the lives of countless others. Just a few cycles ago a child sat and stared at your creation and dreamed of Isha. He will be a poet and a warrior, a technician and a gardener. But it is as a sculptor that he will achieve great fame, and in turn will inspire others to create more works of beauty down the generations.'

I need no legacy, I am an undying, eternal warrior.

For most that would be true, but for Morlaniath, for the spirits that made him, that would not be so. Thirianna had seen his fate, to momentarily become one with Karandras the Phoenix Lord, imbuing his lifeless form with fresh energy and then dissipated upon the winds of the skein.

'No creature is eternal: not gods, not eldar, not humans or orks. Look above you and see a star dying. Even the universe is not immortal, though her life passes so slowly.'

What will become of me, have you divined my fate, looked upon my future?

The question unsettled Thirianna, both because of the answer and because the exarch was of the mind to ask such a thing. Clearly he detected something of the doom that was fast approaching, sensing his place on the skein though not appreciating it fully. It was better that he did not try to second-guess what would come to pass, but was focused on the battle to come.

She fell back on a trick that Kelamith had often employed when avoiding questions Thirianna had asked: enigmatic obfuscation. To seem wise and yet say nothing was an art she had been slowly studying since becoming a seer.

'We all have many fates, but only one comes to pass. It is not for me to meddle in the destiny of individuals, nor to look into our own futures. Trust that you shall die as you lived, and that it is not the True Death that awaits you, not for an age at least. Your passing will bring peace.'

I suffer many deaths, I remember each well, never is it peaceful.

Thirianna was bombarded by a succession of images as the exarch experienced his past deaths again. She broke off her contact with Morlaniath, sensing the skein swirling, new fates unveiled as the humans launched their next attack.

The Dome of Midnight Forests was rocked by a massive explosion. A plume of smoke billowed across the forests as the humans breached the dome to rimwards. Screeching and twittering, flocks of birds exploded from the canopy, flitting across the dark sky in their terror.

The crack of Space Marine bolters and the zip of lasers echoed in the distance.

The enemy are upon us! The infinity circuit carried the thoughts of Arhathain, bringing the autarch's words to every eldar on the craftworld. *The next battle begins. Do not sell your lives cheaply, nor forget the artistry with which we fight. They day has not yet come when the light of Alaitoc will be dimmed.*

Thirianna watched the slowly unfolding battle from afar, though the slaughter felt all too close as it shivered across the skein. The Space Marines spearheaded the next advance, punching through the thin line of eldar who had been set to defend the breach.

Support weapons and Falcon grav-tanks poured their fire into the advancing warriors of the Emperor, but they would not be stopped. The Space Marines overran the hills on which the batteries had been positioned, unleashing hails of explosive bolts from their weapons, driving off the grav-tanks with missile launchers and lascannons, chopping down the survivors of the crews with chainswords and knives.

The Imperial forces crept up the valley, their position given away by a trail of fire and explosions. Thirianna divided her attention three ways: keeping the wraithguard alert and ready to act; monitoring her own thread of fate seeking danger; following the thoughts of the seers and exarchs as the battle progressed.

Like a stain, the humans spread across the skein, their filthy lives polluting the bright eldar threads they touched. Blood flowed in their wake, of both sides, and Khaine was their constant companion.

Vampire bombers rained down sonic detonators and Swooping Hawks showered the advancing humans with plasma. The skein rippled with the warp jump generators of the Warp Spiders and shuddered from the carnage being unleashed.

The eldar forces moved under the direction of the autarchs, falling back, regrouping, attacking again. The beauty of their battle plan was laid out on the skein, a graceful, curving picture of ever-shifting momentum, drawn and re-drawn with each passing moment.

The humans, in contrast, were a blunt spear, cast towards the heart of Alaitoc without thought. They drove all before them, leaving the skein a tangled, rank mess. The Space Marines were the bright tip of the spear, death to all they touched, so that soon the eldar melted away before them, unwilling to lose more warriors in a vain attempt to halt the Sons of Orar.

Thirianna barely noticed as a squadron of war walkers passed by and headed down into the valley, so intent was she upon the diverging strands of destiny. Nothing had become clearer about Alaitoc's fate since the invasion had begun; the craftworld's future was mired in darkness and uncertainty.

Neither side weighed more heavily on the scales of fate and the future remained finely balanced, easily tipped one way or the other by a small act of heroism or cowardice, luck or ill fortune.

The humans continued their bloody advance, now unleashing the power of artillery guns dragged onto the slopes of the valley. The large cannons pounded the upper reaches of the valley, thinking they targeted the defenders of the craftworld. Nothing was further from the truth.

Forewarned of this development, the Alaitocii had pulled back out of the valley, leaving the artillery to hammer empty groves and destroy the cover that would have later protected the human advance. Thirianna was saddened by the smashed trees, each of which was immeasurably older than the creatures that destroyed them. The Dome of Midnight Forests was one of the most ancient parts of Alaitoc, created before the Fall to be the lungs of the original trade ship that would later become the vast craftworld.

She felt her anger duplicated across the skein. Runes of Isha wept as the bombardment continued and the rune of Khaine burned fiercely, brought to renewed life by the ire of the eldar. Thirianna assuaged her anguish with glimpses of the future, taking comfort in the scenes of dying humans she saw there, punished for the affront of their attack.

In the wake of the artillery barrage, the humans pushed on quickly, seeking to seize the head of the valley with a thrust of tanks and armoured personnel carriers. They brought with them a smog of exhaust fumes, their clattering, roaring engines echoing up the valley.

The Alaitocii responded, moving swiftly back into the positions they had abandoned. Falcon grav-tanks brought destruction on white beams of bright lance fire. Vyper jetbikes sped through the flames and smoke, missile launchers spitting trails of explosions.

As squads of grey-clad soldiers evacuated the burning wrecks of their transports, war walkers and jetbikes attacked, shuriken cannons and starcannons ripping through the survivors, painting the rucked mud red with the blood of the invaders. Warp Spiders materialised to engulf floundering human soldiers in webs of deadly monofilament that sliced through flesh and bone, dissecting the screaming soldiers within clouds of constricting mesh. These were joined by a battery of doomweavers that sent even larger swathes of the lethal fibres across the valley, engulfing whole companies.

As before, the humans looked to the Space Marines to fight back hardest. Thirianna was disconcerted by the seeming foresight of the humans. Whenever the eldar unleashed a backlash against the enemy, it always seemed to fall upon the regular soldiers and not the elite warriors.

Now they came on in their red-and-white tanks and transports, racing past the burning hulks of the other vehicles, their weapons spitting death at the eldar war engines. Vypers were brought down in hails of heavy bolter fire and Falcons turned to burning cinders by the shafts of lascannon beams.

The valley was lit up by plasma and laser as both sides exchanged furious volleys, each testing the resolve of the other. The Space Marines headed into the teeth of the storm unleashed by the Alaitocii, utterly heedless of the danger.

The farseers sensed trouble, Thirianna amongst them. She delved into the future and saw what would happen if the eldar tried to halt the attack with brute force: piles of dead Alaitocii and the dome in ruins.

The warnings sounded across the infinity circuit and the Alaitocii gave way, surrendering the slopes to the advancing Space Marines rather than suffer unsustainable casualties.

Into this newly-won ground the rest of the human army advanced again, shielded by the tanks and power armoured warriors from the Sons of Orar. Starshells were sent into the dark sky to illuminate the carnage and in the flickering white light of falling phosphor Thirianna could see hundreds, thousands of humans marching up the valley.

She spied an opportunity. The Space Marines were holding their ground in the open, allowing their less-armoured companions to seek the shelter of shattered tree trunks and deep craters. She let her mind touch upon the thoughts of the Cobra tank destroyer that lay waiting in the clearing, sending them a vision of the vulnerable Space Marines.

Spurred by Thirianna's instruction, the Cobra lifted effortlessly from the flattened grass, arcs of energy coruscating along its distortion cannon, throwing dancing shadows across the clearing. The skein bucked and twisted as the warp core opened, drawing in energy directly from the immaterial realm.

Images of the Chaos realms fluttered through Thirianna's thoughts; impossible vistas and baying calls filling her mind.

The lead Space Marine tanks were almost three-quarters of the way along the valley. Lascannon blasts stabbed from them into the darkness, setting fire to trees, gouging furrows in the ground as the enemy sought the elusive eldar.

With a thrum that set the ground shaking, the Cobra opened fire. The air itself screamed as the distortion cannon tore at its fabric, a rent appearing in the air above the closest Space Marine vehicle. Thirianna's head throbbed with the pressure of the energies unleashed, the skein itself shrieked as it was wrenched into the material universe.

The gap opened by the blast widened into a whirling hole framed with purple and green lightning, its depths a swirl of colours and reeling stars. Thirianna's spirit stone was hot upon her breast as she felt the pull of the warp, the lingering power of She Who Thirsts tugging at the edges of her essence. To open the realm of the Chaos gods was always risky, inviting terrible consequence, but the effect more than outweighed the dangers at this time.

A Space Marine tank lurching down the left slope was dragged to a stop by the implosive energies of the warphole, its tracks grinding vainly through the soil, smoke belching from its exhausts as the driver gunned the engine in an effort to maintain traction. With a drawn-out creak, the vehicle lifted from the ground, tipping backwards, stretching and contorting as the breach into warp space opened wider. Rivets sprang free and disappeared into the ravening hole, followed quickly by the tangled remains of the gun sponsons. An armoured figure was drawn out of the top hatch and spun crazily into the maw of the warp a moment before the tank slammed upwards and was sucked into the spiralling vortex.

Thirianna could feel the remnants of the tank and its crew lingering on the skein. They were not dead, not all of them. Their souls cried out in torment, subjected to the raw, ravaging energies of the warp, their minds exploding with the power of the immaterium flooding through their psyches.

She felt satisfaction at their deaths and stayed for a moment, relishing the after-echoes of doom that faded from the tattered ends of their threads.

With a crack like thunder the vortex closed, sending out a shockwave that sent a nearby Space Marine transport slamming into a tree with a shower of leaves.

The clearing fell still again as the Cobra's cannon recharged. Undaunted, the humans continued their advance, almost reckless in their haste to close. The humans had learnt from their earlier mistakes and the artillery opened fire again. Thirianna traced the shells across the skein, fearing that they would land close by. Instead they were directed to the outer slopes of the valley, where the eldar had been taking shelter from the advance.

Dozens of strands were cut short in the thunderous detonations. Fire spread along the valley, leaping from tree to tree, a pall of smoke blotting out the light of the descending starshells.

The Space Marines had pushed forwards again and one of their largest tanks had come within range of the clearing. Lascannon blasts seared through the darkness, shrieking off the Cobra's curved hull. The superheavy tank lifted again as more power surged along the length of its main gun. Again came the scream of tortured reality and the concussive blast of the warp vortex forming. More than a dozen armoured figures and a pair of troop transports were sucked into the energy maelstrom, their forms thinning and twisting before they disappeared from sight while raw psychic energy forked to the ground from the breach's undulating rim.

Wrecks and bodies littered the valley floor, but the Space Marines had gained the higher ground to either side and from their vantage point their tanks poured chattering fire into the treeline. Within this cordon, batteries of self-propelled guns lumbered into position, bringing them into range of the dome's heart. A least twenty tanks grumbled towards Thirianna's position, painted in the same grey as the soldiers' fatigues.

Four brightly coloured Space Marine transports charged ahead of the advance and would be at the edge of the clearing shortly.

Thirianna recognised the scale of the threat immediately, but as soon as she moved to the skein for a solution she found that help had already been despatched.

Hidden in the darkness by its holofields, a Phantom Titan carefully made its way through the trees. Thirianna soon heard the snap of branches under the towering war machine's tread and could feel the psychic power of the spirit stones bound within its wraithbone frame.

She allowed her mind to flow within the Titan's structure and for a short while shared in the vision of its crew.

From above the treetops the triplet crew looked down the valley, the dome canopy of their cockpit alive with runes highlighting the positions of friends and foes, the whispers of the spirits roaming through the wraithbone Titan constantly buzzing in their ears.

They guided the tread of their machine to avoid the Striking Scorpions hidden at the base of a statue, and stepped between them and the Cobra. They dimmed the power to the holofields and redirected it to the weapons as bright red symbols flashed across the view.

The shoulder-mounted missile launchers opened fire with a flurry of blazing trails that engulfed the lead tanks of the enemy. Hulls were split open by the armour-piercing warheads and engine blocks shattered by their detonations.

Acting in concert, the three eldar turned the Titan and swung its tremor cannon into position. They locked on to their target and plotted the most destructive arc of fire. Agreeing in unison, they unleashed the power of the tremor cannon's generator.

Protected within the head of the Titan, the crew were shielded from the throbbing violence of the sonic weapon. They watched with some satisfaction as the weapon traced an invisible path through the enemy vehicles. The air danced with agitated molecules, the weapon starting to tremble in its mounting as it unleashed a counter-harmonic, sending out a ground-shattering beam of sonic energy.

Where the line touched, the ground erupted, a huge gout of earth and rock rupturing into a widening crack that zigzagged along the hillside. Tanks shook themselves apart as the beam crossed over them; Space Marines were flattened inside their armour; unarmoured soldiers were torn limb from limb by the sonic energy coursing through their bodies.

The spirits of the Titan gave warnings that the weapon was overloading and the crew shut down the supply of power. While the tremor cannon recharged they launched another barrage of missiles into the infantry fleeing from the carnage they had wrought. Several tanks were still heading closer and so the crew turned their attention to the pulsar.

Lances of pure energy split the darkness of the Dome of Midnight

Forests, each pulse of light smashing into an enemy tank, splitting it apart with one hit. Ammunition set off secondary explosions inside the turret of one, while the engine of another detonated in a huge ball of fire and gas, a cloud of jagged debris scything down the humans nearby.

Thirianna withdrew from the Titan as the Cobra fired again and the valley descended into an anarchy of swirling vortexes, wailing sonic explosions and the steady strobe of the pulsar. Shells screamed in return, flashing past the wavering image of the Titan to crash into the trees beyond the clearing.

The farseer sensed the runes changing, moving away from the valley to another attack to starwards. She felt the request from another farseer for aid and passed this on to the two massive war engines. Together they departed, ready to lend their firepower to where it would do the most harm to the enemy.

Thirianna could feel the tension in the clearing was increasing; Morlaniath and his warriors were eager for battle, hungry to avenge their fallen. She sensed the exarch's growing excitement at the thought of imminent close-quarters combat.

'Arhathain is mustering forces for a counter-attack along this axis,' she told him, watching the developing manoeuvres through the lens of the skein. 'We wait for the reinforcements and then we will advance.'

Make ready your wargear, more warriors arrive, we shall be fighting soon, she heard the exarch tell his squad.

The battle continued, the greater part of its ferocity moving to other parts of the dome. In the valley, the Imperial troops secured their positions, digging crude entrenchments and piling up lines of earthworks. They seemed to be preparing for a counter-attack and she passed on this information to Arhathain, who was in the process of mounting just such an assault.

It seemed a rash move until Thirianna cast her gaze wider. She had been focussed primarily on the valley, and with only some thought to the wider dome. Now she looked across Alaitoc and saw that the humans were making advances elsewhere, four lines of fate converging on the centre of Alaitoc. They seemed to be heading directly for the Dome of Crystal Seers and the Chambers of the Seers, somehow knowing that the nerve centre of the craftworld lay in and around those places.

Not for the first time, Thirianna sensed a guiding hand directing the movements of the humans. There was someone else on the skein, someone not of Alaitoc.

Before she could investigate further, she was interrupted by an inquiring thought from Morlaniath, who wanted to know how the wider conflict progressed. She thought it was irrelevant at the moment, but she was not a lone commander and it was part of her role to pass on such information to the exarchs.

She decided to speak to the exarch in person, suddenly cautious of the enemy presence she had detected on the skein. She crossed the clearing quickly, leaving her wraithguard to protect the approach from the valley.

'We have abandoned the Dome of Lasting Vigilance, and the humans control more than a quarter of the access ways to Alaitoc's central region,' she told Morlaniath. She delivered the report without much enthusiasm, distracted by more personal concerns. 'We still hold the domes around the infinity circuit core. It is Arhathain's wish that we drive these humans from this dome so that we can mount an attack on the flank of their other forces, severing them from their landing zone in the docks.'

'The enemy prepare, waiting is a peril, how soon do we attack?' said Morlaniath.

Thirianna moved across the skein, touching on the minds of the other seers, anxious not to transmit her thoughts too far lest they be intercepted by malicious listening minds.

'The counter-attack is almost ready,' she said eventually. 'The humans' rough defences will be no obstacle. They think only of left and right, forwards and backwards. They still forget that we do not have to crawl along the groun–'

Fire burned across the skein. Fire and shadow, blood and death.

The farseer stopped and turned her gaze beyond Morlaniath and saw flickering light in the woods casting long shadows amongst the trees.

The Avatar was approaching.

Its presence joined the minds of the hundreds of eldar converging through the trees at the head of the valley, linking them together in one bloody purpose. Thirianna could feel hundreds of Guardians and Aspect Warriors advancing through the woods around her, all mustered around the burning incarnation of Khaine. Far above, Swooping Hawks circled in the thermals of the burning tanks while dagger-winged Vampire bombers cruised back and forth awaiting the order to strike.

A coldness seeped into Thirianna's heart and she looked across the clearing to find the Shadow Hunter, Karandras, in the darkness of the trees. There was a flicker of connection between his spirit and that of the Striking Scorpion exarch, a moment of contact and recognition.

She glanced at Morlaniath, knowing what was to come. She said nothing, leaving Korlandril's fate to run to its swift conclusion.

With the wraithguard behind them, Thirianna and the warlocks joined the force advancing with the Avatar. The presence of Khaine's incarnation drove the eldar forwards, filled with dreams of retribution, united in their cause to cleanse Alaitoc of the human presence that stained the craftworld.

'My attention is required elsewhere, trust the Avatar to lead.' Kelamith's presence was distant, moving to one of the other warzones. With a moment of misgiving, Thirianna realised that she was the last farseer left in the Dome of Midnight Forests. Her unease passed, burned away by the proximity of the Avatar.

She studied the skein, noting the patterns of advance that would be followed by the attacking eldar. Aerial and support weapon bombardment would herald the attack, while the ground forces slipped around the ends of the defensive lines and took the human army from the flanks.

They encountered the outlying forces quickly: squadrons of walkers and squads of Space Marines. Battle raged amongst the thinning trees as the Avatar led the attack down into the valley.

Thirianna found herself on the left flank, accompanied by Dire Avengers and Dark Reapers. Several squads of Space Marines waited ahead, their heavy weapons already firing on the advancing Alaitocii.

She despatched the Dark Reapers to a bluff overlooking the enemy positions and forged ahead with the Aspect Warriors and her wraithguard. Explosive bolts erupted from the Space Marines' positions behind rocks and splintered trees.

Drawing on the power of the skein, Thirianna swathed the fates of those around her with a maelstrom of energy, misdirecting the enemy fire, distracting the aim of the Space Marines so that they fired at shadows.

Not all of the Space Marines' fire went astray. Bolt rounds cracked from the bodies of the wraithguard. A ball of plasma flew up the ridge towards the Dark Reapers, sending charred bodies flying into the air.

Into this torrent of fire advanced the eldar, cloaked from view by Thirianna's psychic manipulations. Several of the Dire Avengers fell to the storm of bolts and missiles raging along the slope and a wraithguard collapsed in a heap as another plasma bolt caught it full in the chest; fewer casualties than they would have suffered without the farseer's protection.

Thirianna had done enough and the wraithguard were now within range. She poured consciousness into their half-dead minds, allowing them to see as she saw.

The wraithguard lifted their weapons and fired.

The warp rippled open through a cluster of multicoloured stars, ripping apart the armour of the Space Marines, tearing their spirits from their bodies. Thirianna winced at the psychic howling that swept across the skein but urged the wraithguard on, firing their weapons again and again.

The return fire from the Space Marines was lessening.

The Dark Reapers now added their missiles to the attack, blossoms of fire springing into life along the Space Marines' defences. The Dire Avengers sprinted forwards under the cover of this attack, their shuriken catapults slinging a hail of monomolecular-edged discs into the armoured giants confronting them.

Seeking the best angle of attack, Thirianna roamed across the skein as she advanced behind the wraithguard. Around her, the warlocks hurled bolts of fire and threw crackling spheres of psychic energy.

On the skein, Thirianna felt the touch of something alien in her thoughts. She ducked away but returned swiftly, seeking its source. Following the threads, she saw a second force of Space Marines readying to attack, a reserve that would throw back the eldar advance and drive them from the dome.

Every attack and counter-attack was being met by the Space Marines. Thirianna searched fervently for their seer, amazed that a human could be so gifted. She corrected herself; her foe was not human. She searched along the strands of the Space Marines' lives and located what she was looking for.

The Space Marine psyker was well hidden, shielded by centuries of discipline and dedication. His mind was almost as strong as an eldar's, yet it had been honed into a sharp weapon, capable of slicing through fate with a thought.

Yet for all his power, the Space Marine could not match Thirianna for prescience. He had not yet recognised the unfolding fates of the eldar attack; the Space Marines were not yet ready to respond.

If Thirianna could slay this psyker swiftly, his warning would not come, and the eldar attack would succeed.

She summoned her warriors to her and pressed on, searching the skein for a sign of her elusive foe. He could not wholly contain the power leaking from his mind and she found him with a squad of Space Marines a little further along the ridge, directing the actions of his followers.

Thirianna looked for other forces she could bring to bear, but they were all committed to the attack with the Avatar. Even if the Space Marine counter-attack was forestalled, Thirianna could see how closely-run the battle would be. She could not afford to withdraw any more forces to help her.

'Follow me,' she told the eldar around her, instilling purpose into the minds of the wraithguard.

Emerging from a shallow ravine, Thirianna found her foe: an armoured transport that looked more like a mobile bunker than a vehicle. Beside the huge tank stood a cluster of warriors in red-and-white armour, one amongst them marked out by his blue livery. As soon as Thirianna laid eyes on him, she knew what she faced. Librarians they were called by the Space Marines, and this one was ranked highly amongst them.

She drew on the Scorpion to slide close to his thoughts, slipping prompts and subtle images into his mind, seeking to direct his attention elsewhere. She was met with a wall of willpower that seemed forged of iron, rebounding her attempts at manipulation. Thirianna tried again and fared no better, unable to penetrate the solid shield of faith and devotion that protected the Space Marine.

She would have to end this physically.

The farseer and her warriors slipped along the slope as quickly as they could. The wraithguard were not so fleet of foot as the living eldar and Thirianna was forced to leave them behind, despatching Toladrissa to look over them.

The Dire Avengers and seers moved quickly down the valley, heading towards the bright searchlights of the Space Marine command vehicle. Thirianna could feel the Librarian's thoughts searching for her, alerted by her ill-considered attempt to infiltrate his thoughts. She drew a veil around her spirit, concealing herself behind the power of the Scorpion.

Time was running short. The Avatar and the main force were approaching the moment of commitment. Thirianna tried to warn the other seers, seeking aid from Kelamith, but they were occupied with their own problems and she realised she faced this task alone. If she failed, the Alaitocii counter-attack would fail. If that happened the Dome of Midnight Forests would fall to the enemy, allowing them to breach the infinity core that lay in the adjoining dome.

That could not be allowed to happen. For the final stage of Alaitoc's defence, the humans had to be kept in the ring of domes surrounding the core, allowed this close but no further.

The eldar leapt over the rocks and scrub, closing in on the jutting cliff where the Space Marines were stationed. The Dire Avengers opened fire as soon as the first enemy came into view.

The Space Marine fell, his thick armour scored by hundreds of shurikens, weaker joints and eye lenses shredded and shattered by the fusillade of discs. Almost immediately the other Space Marines returned fire, fiery bolts screaming back into the attacking eldar, three Dire Avengers smashed from their feet by bloody impacts.

Methrain and Nenamin cast their singing spears into the Space Marines, the triangular heads of the weapons gleaming with psychic energy. Both struck their targets, cutting through armour and fused ribcages to pierce vital organs. Thirianna let fly a ripple of lightning from her sword as she sprinted forwards, shattering the armour of another Space Marine.

The Librarian turned swiftly, instantly alert to the threat but, thanks to Thirianna, not psychically forewarned. Like the others he was clad in powered armour, of a deep blue, only his shoulder pads sharing the heraldry of his companions. His armour was scuffed and scored from fierce fighting and Thirianna sensed a wave of malicious intent. The Son of Orar held up a staff topped by an ornately carved rendition of a ram's head. The skein buckled as he summoned power, drawing in an immense swell of energy. Thirianna leapt to her right as a blast of pure white light erupted towards her, obliterating two of the Dire Avengers following behind the farseer.

Thirianna dodged back and forth as boltgun rounds split the air around her, runic wards blazing into life as some struck home. In moments she had closed the gap and was swinging her sword at the Space Marine's helmeted head. The Librarian met her Witchblade with the haft of his staff, smashing Thirianna to one side with his raw strength.

With his other hand he drew a shimmering sword, psychic energy playing along the crystalline seams threaded through the blade.

The Librarian swung at Thirianna's head as he tried to reach into her thoughts and shred her mind. She deflected the first with her Witchblade and the second with a deft turn of thought, sending the psychic blast back to where it came from.

The staff blazed again, hurling Thirianna from her feet as serpentine psychic energy crawled across her rune armour. She recovered swiftly, jumping to her feet to avoid a second blast. Fire raged from her sword, catching the Librarian in the shoulder, scorching paint and leaving a blackened sworl across the grey material beneath.

She saw his head was surrounded by a tracery of cables and wires and could feel the psychic power flowing along these conduits. She fired her shuriken pistol into the Space Marine's chest and he turned a shoulder towards her to catch the flying projectiles on his armoured pad.

The pistol shots had been a feint. The Space Marine was out of position as Thirianna spun past him, jumping up to lance the tip of her Witchblade into the gap between helm and the power plant of the Space Marine's backpack. Cables exploded with raw psychic power as the edge of Thirianna's weapon swept through the psychic wiring.

The Librarian lashed out with his staff, catching Thirianna in the back, sending her face-first into the dirt.

She did not need to see her foe to strike.

She snatched up the Librarian's thread of fate, now blazing and hot without the defences of his psychic hood. She sent a surge of power racing along its length, pouring all of her hatred and rage into the blast.

Rolling to her feet, Thirianna turned in time to see the Space Marine reeling back, his eyes burning through their lenses, staff and sword falling from his spasming hands. Thirianna could feel the iron shields of his mind closing down and knew she had only another moment to finish this.

She leapt, bringing down the Witchblade with all of her force, infusing the weapon with the last of her mental strength, turning it into a diamond-hard blade that split the Librarian's head from scalp to jaw.

Thirianna landed as the Space Marine's body crashed to the ground, brains and blood spilling from the fatal wound.

Desperately Thirianna returned to the skein to see if the Space Marines had been pulled back to reserve, ready to thwart the eldar assault.

Relief flooded through her as she saw the Avatar striding into the heart of the humans' defences, cutting down everything in its path. The Aspect Warriors tore into the Imperial army while aircraft raked them from above. The humans fled the assault, the Space Marines falling back to the edge of the dome, far from the infinity core.

Alaitoc's rune wavered, balanced between salvation and death once more.

The hawks circle. The time to strike is nigh.

Thirianna knew the meaning of the words sent to her by Kelamith. She reached to her belt to cast another rune: the Wanderer. Exhausted, she had enough strength left to spare for a moment of worry. For her whole life she had striven for control. She had laboured hard to manage her own affairs and choose her own direction. Her stomach sank at the thought of what she had to do, but there was no option, it had been agreed by the council.

The skein rippled as she poured what little remained of her willpower into the Wanderer, sending the signal for the final phase of the battle to begin. The infinity circuit blazed with the single rune and the skein became a maelstrom of energy, swirling all about the sigil.

The fate of Alaitoc was cast and Thirianna had left it in the hands of the selfish, capricious Aradryan.

It was now up to the outcast to bring peace to Alaitoc.

PATH OF THE OUTCAST

'Life is to us as the Maze of Linnian was to Ulthanesh, its mysterious corridors leading to wondrous vistas and nightmarish encounters in equal measure. Each of us must walk the maze alone, treading in the footsteps of those who came before but also forging new routes through the labyrinth of existence.

In times past we were drawn to the darkest secrets and ran wild about the maze, seeking to experience all that it had to offer. As individuals and as a civilisation, we lost our way, and in doing so created the means for our doom, our unfettered exploration leading to the darkness of the Fall.

In the emptiness that followed, a new way was revealed to us: the Path. Through the wisdom of the Path we spend our lives exploring the meaning of existence, moving from one part of the maze to another with discipline and guidance so that we never become lost again. On the Path we experience the full potential of love and hate, joy and woe, lust and purity, filling our lives with experience and fulfilment but never succumbing to the shadows that lurk within our thoughts.

But like all journeys, the Path is different for each of us. Some wander for a long while in one place; some spread their travels wide and visit many places for a short time while others remain for a long time to explore every nook and turn; some of us lose our way and leave the Path for a time or forever; and some of us find dead ends and become trapped.'

— Kysaduras the Anchorite, foreword to
Introspections upon Perfection

PROLOGUE

Death and rebirth played out across the heavens, every star a furnace of creation and an inferno of destruction. They stretched out in every direction, spiralling around the galactic core, seemingly timeless yet ultimately as mortal as any creature. Birth and demise, all of it cycling again and again, giving rise to life and civilisations, and destroying them as quickly as they appeared. Stability was an illusion. There was no stasis, just an everlasting dance of elements that would outlast any mind capable of comprehending it.

Opening his eyes, Aradryan surfaced slowly from the dream, feeling the weight of air upon him, the press of darkness on flesh as he lay still on the thin mattress of his bed, the silence suffusing every fibre of his being. It was utterly black in his chambers; not the least glimmer of light existed to intrude upon his thoughts.

The cosmic nature of the dream continued to spiral slowly in his thoughts as unconsciousness gave way to waking. Responding to his state, Aradryan's chambers suffused him with the barest glow of light, slowly brightening to bring him out of his mental submersion. Limbs tingling, the dreamer twitched his fingers and wriggled his toes, the first of several exercises that would enable him to lock his thoughts back to his physical body.

Aradryan sat up, his breathing becoming faster and shallower, his body reacting to the sudden influx of soft stimuli. Half sleeping, latched on to the core essence of the dream, Aradryan stood up slowly. He clothed himself without conscious effort, drawing on a long robe of dark blues and purples. Slipping his slender feet into a pair of knee-high boots, he left the dreaming room and went into the main chamber. Here the light was brighter still, though a fraction of its normal intensity, causing Aradryan to squint for a few moments while his eyes adjusted.

The after-images of the dream lingered still and he felt small and unimportant. The dream had shown him the vastness of the universe, and against that he was nothing, a tiny conglomeration of cells and thoughts that would be extinguished.

The chambers felt too constricting, so Aradryan left quickly, his heart yearning for something that would recapture the soaring majesty of the galaxy. Without conscious regard, he made his way to a skyrunner. Placing his hand upon the activation jewel, he let his desire pass into the machine's matrix, which in turn drew power from the infinity circuit: the psychic network of Alaitoc Craftworld.

The skyrunner interpreted his will as best it could, rising swiftly from the balcony-like docking bay to skim across the white grass fields that covered the floor of the Dome of Swift Longings. Realising that the sky-runner was taking him towards the dock towers on the craftworld rim, Aradryan chuckled to himself. The semi-sentient craft had felt his yearning for the wide galaxy and was taking him to the berths of the starships.

Aradryan's quiet laughter stilled. Perhaps the skyrunner was more intelligent than he was. He had experienced many dreams, but none had left an impression as strong as the one he had just woken from. Part of him was glad for that fact. The Path of Dreaming existed to tap into the power of the unconscious and subconscious, bringing forth fears and desires that it was impossible to recognise while awake. For nearly two passes he had trodden the Path of the Dreamer, alongside his friend Korlandril, and they had shared many special moments of pleasure and regret, their dream-bonds tighter than any ordinary friendship. Was this dream the Moment of Realisation? Had the dizzying vistas of the galaxy been the culmination of his searching for purpose?

Such thoughts, only partially constructed in his semi-fugue state, occupied Aradryan until the skyrunner arrived at its destination, furling its guiding sail to slip into a mooring at the Tower of Winding Destiny. Aradryan stepped from the craft and followed the passageway that led up to the heights of the docking spire. The few eldar that he encountered immediately recognised the half-alert state of a Dreamer and stepped nimbly out of his path, allowing him to follow his whims unimpeded, until they brought Aradryan to a broad expanse alongside one of the main quays.

It was hard to disassociate from the dream-images, but Aradryan was conscious of there being many other eldar around him. There was a ship docked at the quayside. It was massive, its hull towering above them, its stellar sail even higher still, stretching towards the glimmering force dome that held the ravening vacuum of space at bay.

Looking up, Aradryan saw the stars, scattered across the outer sky like diamonds on black velvet, enticing and bewitching.

Someone bumped into him, shaking him from the last vestiges of the dream's grip. A little disconcerted, Aradryan looked around and found himself in a large crowd thronging the dockside. More eldar were coming down the ramps that led from the open gateways of the starship.

Aradryan was aware of a solemn mood; he sensed it even before he heard the first sobs and saw the glistening tears in the eyes of those around him. He felt an emptiness, and when he looked again at the eldar disembarking from the ship he realised why.

The first to alight were Aspect Warriors. A wave of grim anger and deep hatred washed over Aradryan as Khaine's anointed killers strode down from the gangways, still armed and armoured. Striking Scorpions in heavily plated armour of greens and yellows bore three of their number amongst them, the corpses carried on floating biers, guided by the hands of the living. Dark Reapers in black and red followed, also accompanying their dead. And then came the Dire Avengers, so bright in their armour of blue, white and gold, yet so sinister with their faceless masks.

Aradryan wanted to back away, but there was someone behind him. The Aspect Warriors were apparitions of death to his half-dreaming mind, each an incarnation of the part of Khaine they represented. Howling Banshees filled his thoughts with screaming images of flashing death; Fire Dragons set his mind ablaze with an inferno of destruction.

It was almost too much to bear in his fragile state, but Aradryan stayed, morbid curiosity getting the better of him. From images glanced in the infinity circuit and snatches of conversation, he saw a blue sun and a yellow sun, gleaming down on a still lake. A white building, human-made, was wreathed in death and fire. The brightly-armoured Aspect Warriors stormed through doors and windows, cutting down the humans within without mercy.

After the Aspect Warriors, others came from the ship: Guardians and seers. These were not the grim-faced fighters that had come before, and it was their grief that suffused the crowd around him. The feeling of lament grew stronger and stronger as more of the dead and wounded were carried down to the dockside, each a life lost or damaged.

Aradryan stared at the blood-flecked blue and yellow armour of a Guardian. He could not say whether the blood was eldar or from their foes, but each glistening droplet, every ruddy stain, held within it some hidden secret of mortality.

The dream and the current surroundings melded in Aradryan's thoughts, forming a whole. Even the stars die, he thought.

Yet the eldar who had fallen were not yet wholly dead. Upon the chest of each glowed a spirit stone, containing the essence of each slain warrior. From here the stones would be taken into the depths of Alaitoc and placed upon the nodes of the infinity circuit. The spirits would flow free from the stones and mingle with the psychic energy of generations who had come before, becoming both the lifeblood and the nervous system of the craftworld.

The thought suddenly terrified Aradryan. To be trapped on Alaitoc for eternity, bodiless and voiceless, seemed to his dreaming mind a fate worse than death.

He stopped short, for there truly was a fate worse than death that awaited all eldar: She Who Thirsts. The creation of the eldar's depraved past hungered after their spirits, and would devour them all if given the chance. The spirit stones, the sanctuary of the infinity circuit, were the only defence against such a nightmare; the only bastion secure against an everlasting torment of spirit that terrified every eldar.

Yet even that fear could not fully cut through the sense of entrapment that had seized Aradryan. With glassy eyes he stared at the corpses as they floated past, body after body after body. Questions crammed into his thoughts, of who the slain had been and how they had died. Had there been pain? Had their lives been happy and complete, or had death taken them before their ambitions had been fulfilled, their desires sated? Would they linger ever after in the infinity circuit regretting the missed opportunities, now denied to them as much as the utter silence of true death?

'Save me...' Aradryan whispered, falling to his knees. Alaitoc was a prison, keeping him from a life amongst the stars. Worse than that, he realised. The craftworld was a place of the dead, fuelled by the spirits of the deceased, consuming their life force with a hunger every bit as ravenous as the Great Enemy's.

Aradryan surged to his feet and grabbed the nearest person, a maiden a little younger then himself with auburn hair that fell to her knees, and eyes of violet. She wore the robes of a healer, the white of death marked by handprints of dried blood.

'They cannot stay here!' snapped Aradryan. 'There is no more room. The dead, they are so many, we cannot have any more.'

'You are dream-touched,' said the healer, gently removing Aradryan's grasp. 'Leave me be.'

Aradryan staggered away, but wherever he looked there were more dead eldar. Each was a meaningless mote snuffed out of existence, and the thought threatened to tip him from his teetering state into the darkest abyss of madness.

A hand fell upon his shoulder, turning him. Aradryan looked into a pair of wise grey eyes and heard a soft voice.

'What is wrong?' said the other eldar, his face full of concern.

'I do not want to die here,' Aradryan replied simply. 'The stars call to me, and I do not want to die before I have seen them.'

'Then do not stay.' The eldar smiled and stroked his hand down Aradryan's arm, bringing a sense of stability and calm. 'This ship, she is called *Lacontiran*. She will leave again in four cycles' time, why not come aboard with me?'

'Come aboard?' Aradryan turned to look at the starship. Amongst all the blood and ugliness she was beautiful; sleek and purposeful.

'I am Nairnith, a steersman,' said the other eldar. 'It seems that you have dreamed enough. If you wish to see the stars, I will take you to them.'

'Yes, to see the stars,' said Aradryan, his panic fading into memory.

Part One

Steersman

FRIENDSHIP

The Endless Valley – There is a place, on the distant rim of the galaxy, where the darkness between stars stretches further than anywhere else. Beyond lies the gulf that separates galaxies, where the cold blackness seems to spread for eternity. It is here, in the Endless Valley, that the webway fades and the light of stars is nought but a glimmer. The Endless Valley is home to many secrets, of eldar and other, more sinister creatures, and empty save for the relics and ghosts of the distant past.

An aura of shimmering gold enveloped the *Lacontiran* as the starship passed out of the webway portal. The curving, spired mass of Alaitoc appeared in the spectral display that hovered in front of Aradryan, filling the steersman with mixed emotions. It was almost impossible to believe that twenty passes had turned since he had last seen the craftworld, but he had felt no homesickness on the long journey and seeing Alaitoc filled him with trepidation as much as familiarity.

Sitting in the rainbow glow of the pod-like steering chamber Aradryan moved his fingers lightly across the jewelled panel in front of him, trimming the aft sail to better catch the dying light of Mirianathir: the ruddy star about which Alaitoc slowly orbited, drinking in the rays of the huge orb. The star and the craftworld could be seen via a holo-projection that surrounded the steersmen, so that it seemed they floated in space, the unending firmament stretching out beneath and behind them even as Alaitoc grew larger beyond the undulating console of the controls. In a small sub-display at the heart of each eldar's controls the *Lacontiran*'s position was shown by a gleaming rune amidst an ever-changing web of four-dimensional telemetry. Beside Aradryan, Nairnith and Faethrunin adjusted the course of the *Lacontiran*, the three steersmen working in concert without spoken word, their minds subtly connected by the psychic skeleton of the starship.

The three of them guided the *Lacontiran* along the rim of Alaitoc, passing gracefully between arcing bridges and over glistening force domes through which could be seen vast plains and ranges of hills, artificial seas and twilit forest glades. Swarms of smaller craft moved aside for the starship as it glided down towards the docking spear of the Tower of Eternal Welcomes. Aradryan smiled at the name, and his unease dissipated a little; news of the vessel's arrival had been heralded for some time and he had received contact from Thirianna that she would be there to greet him. To see her again, and his dream-companion Korlandril, would ease the hurt that nestled deep in his heart. Part of him still felt as though he was returning to a prison, but the terror that had accompanied his departure had been assuaged by the voyage, with the aid of Faethrunin and Nairnith.

Passing through the rainbow field surrounding the dock, the *Lacontiran* slid alongside a curving quay, effortlessly coming to a halt under the urging of Aradryan and his companions. The stellar sails were furling themselves and already there was much activity aboard the ship: passengers moving to the gateways to disembark, the handful of crew ushering their charges through the passageways.

'We are back,' said Nairnith, the chief steersman, veteran of more than a score of voyages.

Aradryan met the old eldar's gaze and they shared a moment, their thoughts connecting across the membrane of the *Lacontiran*. Memories flashed past, of sights seen and encounters shared. There was something else present too: the vast psychic power of Alaitoc's infinity circuit merging with the spirit of the starship, drawing in its experiences, updating its semi-conscious essence of all that had transpired in its absence.

Aradryan ignored the influx of information and turned to Faethrunin. The other steersman extended a hand and the two of them lightly touched fingers in a gesture of parting. Almost immediately Aradryan felt a sense of loss as he drew his fingers away, knowing that he would miss Faethrunin's dry wit and easy words of encouragement.

Not willing to draw out the parting any longer, Aradryan stood and left the steering chamber. His bag was already packed, a few clothes and souvenirs picked up on his travels, but the real treasures he had gained were locked in his mind: sights of swirling nebulae and the spectacle of stars being born. It had been everything he had dreamed of and more, and as Aradryan joined the crowds filing out of the ship's dozen gateways, he knew that nothing would ever replace the majesty and wonder of the galaxy.

Bathed in the iridescent light spilling from *Lacontiran*, he walked down the gangway and was confronted by a wave of life; the quayside was filled with hundreds of eldar who had come to meet the ship, either because friends or loved ones were on board or simply to welcome the returning voyagers. Amongst the throng he caught a glimpse of Korlandril, though his friend's gaze passed over him initially. Beside Korlandril, Thirianna was stood on the tips of her toes to peer over the shoulders of those around her.

Seeing the two together as they were gave Aradryan a moment's pause and conflicted emotions raged inside him for a moment: happiness at seeing them, jealousy of what appeared to be a close relationship. When he had left, Thirianna had been a Dire Avenger, dedicated to the Path of the Warrior. Though always willing to share a joke or come on an excursion, there had been a coldness about her; yet that coldness had made the moments of warmth shared with her that much more special and intimate. Turning his attention to Korlandril, Aradryan saw nothing of the Dreamer he had left behind. There was no sign of the distant gaze of the dream-swept; instead Korlandril's eyes were in constant motion, taking in every movement and detail.

Aradryan realised that he must seem a strange sight, perhaps unrecognisable. His hair was cut short on the left side, almost to the scalp, and hung in unkempt waves to the right, neither bound nor styled. He had dark make-up upon his eyelids, giving him a sunken gaze, and he was dressed in deep blues and black, wrapped in long ribbons of twilight. His bright yellow waystone was worn as a brooch, mostly hidden by the folds of his robe.

He met Thirianna's gaze and smiled, and her expression of delight at seeing her friend returned momentarily expelled Aradryan's doubts about his homecoming. Aradryan waved a hand in greeting and made his way effortlessly through the crowd to stand in front of the pair.

'A felicitous return!' declared Korlandril, opening his arms in welcome, palms angled towards Aradryan's face. 'And a happy reunion.'

Thirianna dispensed with words altogether, brushing the back of her hand across Aradryan's cheek for a moment, lighting up his skin with her soft touch. She laid her slender fingers upon his shoulder, an exceptionally familiar gesture of welcome usually reserved for close family. Though taken aback by this display of familiarity, so at odds with the cool repose she had shown before, Aradryan returned the gesture, laying his fingers upon her shoulder.

The moment passed and Aradryan stepped away from Thirianna, laying his hands onto those of Korlandril, a wry smile on his lips.

'Well met, and many thanks for the welcome,' said Aradryan.

He looked at Korlandril as the other eldar kept his grip longer than was normal, perhaps seeking to reinforce the gesture with its duration. Looking into Korlandril's eyes, Aradryan saw that he was being scrutinised, not unkindly but openly, bordering on the impolite. With a slight smile to hide a quiver of discomfort, Aradryan withdrew his grasp and clasped his hands behind his back, raising his eyebrows inquisitively.

'Tell me, dearest and most happily-met of my friends, what have I missed?'

A feeling of unreality pervaded Aradryan's thoughts as he accompanied Thirianna and Korlandril, walking away from the docks. So different had the steersman's life been aboard the starship, it felt as if he was stepping back into a memory. He had spent the last cycles on Alaitoc in an almost constant dream state, and it was no wonder that he now felt that the craftworld was somehow half imagined. Korlandril offered to pilot a skiff to convey the trio back to the habitat domes, but Aradryan declined. He had sailed interstellar gulfs for a long time and until he felt Alaitoc beneath his feet, until he walked its boulevards and plazas, he would not truly believe that he was back.

So it was that they sauntered along the Avenue of Dreams, through a silver passageway that wound beneath a thousand crystal archways into the heart of Alaitoc. The dim light of Mirianathir was caught in the vaulted roof, captured and radiated by the intricately faceted crystal to shine down upon the pedestrians below, glowing with delicate oranges and pinks.

Korlandril was being garrulous, speaking at length about his works and his accomplishments. He could not help it; the mind of the Artist had no place for circumspection or self-awareness, only sensation and expression. Aradryan felt Thirianna looking at him occasionally and met her glance, sharing her patient amusement at their friend's talkativeness, while Korlandril continued to extol the virtues of his sculptures.

Aradryan was more curious about Thirianna's transformation than Korlandril's parroted profundities on artistic merit.

'I sense that you no longer walk in the shadow of Khaine,' said Aradryan, nodding in approval as he looked at Thirianna.

'It is true that the Path of the Warrior has ended for me,' she replied, For a moment she seemed distracted, and Aradryan saw a flicker of emotion, a hesitant moment of pain, mar her fair features. It was gone in an instant, but it was a sign of weakness, of vulnerability, which he had never seen in her face before; it speared into him with its delicacy, making Thirianna appear even more beautiful. 'The aspect of the Dire Avenger has sated my anger, enough for a hundred lifetimes. I write poetry, influenced by the Uriathillin school of verse. I find it has complexities that stimulate both the intellectual and the emotional in equal measure.'

'I would like to know Thirianna the Poet, and perhaps your verse will introduce me,' said Aradryan. Korlandril's change from Dreamer to Artist was not unexpected, but Thirianna was as different from the friend he had known as a warm star-rise was to a cold twilight. 'I would very much like to see a performance, as you see fit.'

'As would I,' laughed Korlandril. 'Thirianna refuses to share her work with me, though many times I have suggested that we collaborate on a piece that combines her words with my sculpture.'

'My verse is for myself, and no other. It is not for performance, nor for eyes that are not mine,' Thirianna said quietly. Aradryan noticed her cast a glance of irritation at the sculptor, suggesting that this was not the first time the subject had been broached, and rejected. 'While some create their art to express themselves to the world, my poems are inner secrets, for me to understand their meaning, to divine my own fears and wishes.'

Admonished, Korlandril fell silent for a moment and Aradryan felt a stab of pity for the Artist, who could not help but express every passing thought, such was the state of the Path he walked. He existed in the present, an ever-moving observer and creator, neither looking forwards nor glancing back.

'Have you come back to Alaitoc to stay?' asked Korlandril, his enthusiasm quickly returning. 'Is your time as a steersman complete, or will you be returning to *Lacontiran*?'

The question was hard for Aradryan, and it was not one that he wanted to – or could – answer so soon after arriving. Rather than show his discomfort, Aradryan decided on a shot of good-humoured retaliation for the indelicate question.

'I have only just arrived, are you so eager that I should leave once more?'

The look of shock and horror on Korlandril's face was worth the risk of offence. Realising that his friend was gently mocking him, and acknowledging that he had been deserving of such treatment, Korlandril bowed his head, accepting the joke. It was almost possible to forget the nightmarish moments that had nearly sent Aradryan spiralling into madness, taking him back to a time when he and Korlandril had cared not for a thing in all the craftworld, save to dream and joke and enjoy life.

'I do not yet know,' Aradryan continued, seeing that Thirianna was keen to hear a proper reply. How could he express the uncertainty that crowded his thoughts; would they be able to understand the dilemma he faced? 'I have learnt all that I can learn as a steersman and I feel complete. Gone is the turbulence that once plagued my thoughts. There is nothing like guiding a ship along the buffeting waves of a nebula, or along the swirling channels of the webway to foster control and focus. I have seen many great and wondrous things out in the stars, but I feel there is so much more out there to find, to touch and hear and experience. I may return to the starships, I may not. And, of course, I would like to spend a little time with my friends and family, to know again the life of Alaitoc, to see whether I wish to wander again or can be content here.'

Thirianna nodded with understanding, and Korlandril regarded Aradryan's reply with uncharacteristic silence and poise. Before the quiet became awkward, the Artist spoke again.

'Your return is most timely, Aradryan,' Korlandril said. 'My latest piece is nearing completion. In a few cycles' time I am hosting an unveiling. It would be a pleasure and an honour if both of you could attend.'

'I would have come even if you had not invited me!' laughed Thirianna. 'I hear your name mentioned quite often, and with much praise attached, and there are high expectations for this new work. It would not be seemly at all to miss such an event if one is to be considered as a person possessing any degree of taste.'

Korlandril's invitation sent a shiver of apprehension through Aradryan, but he masked it instantly. Amongst his fellow steersmen there had been few secrets, but each of them had mastered the means to withdraw their emotions, lest a rogue thought unsettle their companions during a delicate manoeuvre. It was this technique that Aradryan employed now, shielding his friends from his moment of fear. The thought of attending such a gathering unsettled Aradryan, as he was convinced there would be some there who remembered his near-collapse so many passes ago.

Korlandril looked earnest, and Thirianna seemed eager that Aradryan accompanied her, her body turned towards him, eyes wide with expectation and hope.

'Yes, I too would be delighted to attend,' Aradryan said eventually, trying to make the words sound natural. 'I am afraid that my tastes may have been left behind compared to yours, but I look forward to seeing what Korlandril the Sculptor has created in my absence.'

After they had become reacquainted, Aradryan parted from his friends and returned to the quarters where his family had lived before his departure. It had seemed odd to him that none of his family had come to meet him at the Tower of Eternal Welcomes – adding irony to the name – but the reason became clear as he arrived at the Spire of Wishes. All of Aradryan's extended family had gathered from across Alaitoc to welcome him back, including several half-sisters and cousins he had never met before, but his father had died while he had been away and his mother had left Alaitoc, travelling to Yme-Loc Craftworld to visit an old lover who was an autarch there.

The celebration was genuine and his family happy to see their wandering relation returned, but for Aradryan it was too much, too soon. The news of his father's death was a shock, though they had not been especially close. That his mother had left Alaitoc, perhaps for good, worried him more than he thought it would have done. He had thought more about returning to friends rather than family, but that was because, he realised, he had taken their presence for granted. Without his parents it seemed as if a foundation of his life, one that had sat comfortably unnoticed until now, had suddenly been pulled away.

He had grown accustomed to the peace and contemplation of shipboard life, and the sudden attention and activity taxed his endurance as well as his patience. He stayed at the festivities for as long as he could bear it and then made his excuses, fleeing the Spire of Wishes to seek solace in one of the garden domes.

His thoughts awhirl, Aradryan wandered the woods and riverbanks of the Dome of Subtle Rewards, which was kept in a permanent dawn-like state, the pre-day glow casting fire and gold upon the leaves and water. Even this beauty was a mockery of the genuine grandeur of nature, he thought. He had watched stars rise above worlds so pristine, no life had yet sprung up from their azure oceans. He had seen supernova consuming planets and listened to the strobing call of pulsars that had died before even the eldar had known sentience. It was impossible to reconcile such experiences with a simple miniature sun held in stasis like a cheap conjuror's trick.

Eventually, Aradryan's whimsical feet brought him to a platform at the foot of the Bridge of Yearning Sorrows. The massive field-clad arch rose high above Alaitoc, and as he stood looking up at the silver towers at its pinnacle, Aradryan's thoughts were flooded with memories. This was one of the most popular haunts of Dreamers, who could go to the transparent hab-spaces at the apex and fool themselves into thinking that they slept floating amongst the stars. Aradryan had spent many cycles there, and there was something about that illusion of freedom, no matter how false it was in reality, that lured him there again.

He summoned an open-topped carriage, which glided along the monorail from its hangar with barely a whisper to announce its presence. Stepping inside, Aradryan smirked to himself as he looked at the simple controls: three touch-sensitive gems of which one was the self-guidance activator. On the *Lacontiran* Aradryan had mastered a board of nearly seven hundred different controls. He laid a fingertip on the automatic drive and sat back, trying to relax.

The carriage accelerated quickly, encasing Aradryan in a dampening field so that the strengthening wind of its passage was dulled, allowing the steersman to feel the air through his hair and on his face as a pleasant breeze while beyond the bubble it sped past as a gale. From several other stations, more rails ascended towards the peak of the arc, coming together like the outer threads of a web to form an intricate, overlapping conjunction inside the lowest level of the apex tower.

A few eldar drifted about the terminal with the glazed look of the half-dreaming. Just coming here stirred memories and desires in Aradryan. He had spent many cycles here, lost in the wonder of his own subconscious, exploring the possibilities of imagination. Out of instinct he crossed the concourse and took a moving rampway to the next level.

Here there were open-fronted chambers where dreamers could

procure all manner of stimulants and tranquilisers to change their mood and alter their dreams. Little had changed since Aradryan had first come here, though as he walked along the parade of archways he saw no faces he recognised. It was the way of the Path, that an eldar delved into part of themselves for a time, but then moved on, broadening their experience and developing control of their fierce emotions.

Entering one of the dens, which Aradryan's memory told him served intoxicating beverages to bring about a lighter sleep to enable the blending of dreaming and reality, the steersman felt a sudden craving. It was not a physical need, for there were traps aplenty for a careless eldar without the snare of physiological addiction; it was an old yearning in his heart to step aside from the woes and cares of the world.

Aradryan fought the urge. Dreaming had brought him to an understanding of reality that could not be hidden from. His revelation amongst the dead and dying of Alaitoc had lain heavily on him ever since, and no amount of carefree fumes and liquors would expunge them.

There was nothing here for him, but as Aradryan turned back towards the central boulevard he spied a face he recognised. In the glow of a deep blue lamp, he saw one of the Dreamers, slouched upon a low seat, eyes half open, mouth pursed as if blowing a delicate kiss.

'Rhydathrin?' said Aradryan, crossing over to the somnolent figure. The other eldar's eyelids flickered and then opened. Unfocused eyes regarded Aradryan for a while before a slow smile crept across the lips of the Dreamer.

'It's Aradryan, is it not?' said Rhydathrin. He blinked slowly, surfacing from his half-sleep. 'Yes, it is. I thought you would never come back.'

'I took aboard a ship,' said Aradryan, sitting in the chair opposite his companion. He laid a hand on the other's arm as Rhydathrin tried to sit up. Aradryan knew well what his friend was experiencing: a fugue-like trance that was hard to break. 'It has been a long time, but I have returned.'

'The stars,' said Rhydathrin. 'The stars call to us all, do they not? I went to the stars too. I danced in the corona and swam in their hearts.'

'Yes, I remember,' said Aradryan. 'But that was just a dream. We dreamt that together, many times.'

'I was incinerated. So were you. I recall it precisely. Ash we became, blown away by the stellar winds.'

Aradryan shuddered, remembering the experience with a mixture of elation and horror. It had felt so peaceful yet terrifying, stripped away by one's own subconscious, the blaze of the imagined stars becoming a metaphor for self-revelation.

'I have been gone a long time, friend, but you are still here,' said Aradryan, suddenly concerned. 'Have you been Dreaming all of this time?'

'Of course not,' said Rhydathrin. He giggled and slumped to one side. 'Well, perhaps. It is hard to remember. Hard to remember what happened. Hard to... Didn't you go to the stars?'

'Yes, I have just told you that,' said Aradryan. He stood up, shaking his head gently. He had seen such a thing before, when an eldar became so enamoured of his dreams that his grip on reality was weakened almost to breaking. Time becomes meaningless, a cycle lasting an age or a moment, the present and the past no longer divided by the conscious mind.

There was little help that could be offered, and as he watched, Aradryan saw Rhydathrin slipping again into the half-sleep, his hand held up briefly in parting.

With swift steps, Aradryan left. There were no answers here, and coming to this place had served only as a reminder of the temptations he had overcome. Like the exarchs on the Warrior Path, or the bonesingers or farseers, the Everdreaming were trapped. Why could nobody else see how dangerous the Path was? For Aradryan it was clear. The Path was nothing more than an unending series of temptresses, each with her own lures, paraded through the life of an eldar until one snatched him up and held him captivated until death. It was a prison, no less so than the infinity circuit to which they were all destined to be sent. The tenets of discipline, obedience and focus were a sham, shackles invented to keep the eldar from being themselves.

Agitated, Aradryan left the Bridge of Yearning Sorrows and fled for the sanctuary of the docks at the Tower of Eternal Welcomes.

He could not stay on Alaitoc.

DISLOCATION

The Well of Harmonies – All things have a beginning, and for the webway that beginning took place at the Well of Harmonies. Some legends claim that this world was where Eldanesh first sired the eldar people, and where Khaine cast down his bloody spear to create the War in Heaven. There are some philosophers who say that the Well of Harmonies never existed, except as a metaphor, for everything is a cycle and begins nowhere, never ending. The truth may never be known, whether once there was a single place from which sprang the existence of the eldar empire, or if ever it was so, born into tragedy and reborn again and again in every subsequent generation.

The lower levels of the Tower of Eternal Welcomes gave a second meaning to the name. It was amongst these twilight corridors that the eldar of Alaitoc made fresh liaisons, most of a temporary nature. Starship crews from other craftworlds mingled with pleasure-seeking Alaitocii, while the young and the naive moved from drinking establishment to eateries to apartments seeking congress with like-minded spirits.

Aradryan had never been drawn to this place before, occupied as he had been by the more existential delights of the Dreamrooms, but he hoped to find someone from the *Lacontiran* that he would know. It was not entirely unpleasant to walk along the curving passageways and flame-lit balconies, just one stranger amongst many, as lost as the Ulthwénese, Saim-Hannian and Biel-Tani traders and crews who shared the space with him.

As he walked past the open doors of the tower's various concerns, Aradryan was greeted by a melange of different moods. Songs and poetry, laughter both delicate and uproarious, music and silence played out, accompanied by the smells of cooking and fine spirits, perfumes and incenses. If there was anywhere on Alaitoc where it was possible to feel free from the Path, this was it, but still its presence could be felt. Attendants who trod the Path of Service moved from patron to patron with trays of sweetmeats and wines, while those on the Path of the Merchant came to terms with their greed and materialism through hard haggling and double-dealing.

In just a short time, Aradryan saw dozens of different costumes and fashions, some old, some so new they had freshly arrived from other craftworlds. Colours in dazzling rainbows fought against bleak monochromes. Pale visages stared at him amongst crowds of highly painted faces, while all manner of exotic pets – feline gyrinx, sinuous silver-snakes, bipedal sconons and many others beside – purred and yowled and yapped as a backdrop to the constant conversation.

In contrast to the cloying crowd of his family, the throng of the Tower of Eternal Welcomes did not intimidate the steersman. Aradryan felt comfort in his anonymity, and with his courage bolstered by this, he ventured into a drinking hall. The interior was lit with a glow of bright neon blues and pinks, low couches forming broken circles around fountains encircled by constantly refreshing glasses.

Aradryan spied a gap at one of the drinking benches and crossed through the room to sit down. After inquiring with the eldar already seated whether the space was intended for an absent occupant, Aradryan was assured that it was truly available. He gingerly sat down, slightly embarrassed by his lack of experience at such things.

He looked at the glasses close at hand. They were like upended bells in shape, upon a belt that slowly but constantly travelled from one couch to the next. The silver liquid of the central fountain splashed into each glass, diluting the elixir already in the bottom, filling the glasses with blues and reds and oranges. Hesitantly, Aradryan snared a glass filled with an amber fluid and raised it to his nostrils. It smelt like burned honey, not altogether pleasant.

'I would avoid that one, if I were you,' said a voice to his right. He looked up and saw a female eldar sitting on the bench next to him. Her hair was black as night, save for a stripe of gold tucked behind her right ear. Golden too was the paint above her eyes, which were a piercing violet, and sable was the colour of her lips. Unlike many that Aradryan had seen since arriving, she eschewed colour on her cheeks, leaving her almost white skin unmarked. She was dressed in a high-necked robe, which clung tightly to the curves of her body as she leaned forwards and plucked the glass from Aradryan's trembling grasp. She replaced it with another, filled with a vermillion drink. Aradryan caught the scent of kaiberries and slightroot.

'This is my favourite,' the female eldar said, her dark lips forming a warm smile. 'Try it.'

Aradryan did as he was told, sipping the drink. It was sweet but not sickly, the liquid evaporating in his mouth as it was warmed by his breath, creating a swirl of flavour across his tongue. His eyes widened in appreciation and his companion laughed quietly.

'My name is Athelennil,' she said, touching her fingers to the back of Aradryan's hand. 'That is a good one, but do not drink it all, there are some other delights worth savouring.'

'I am not sure I should get intoxicated,' Aradryan said, feeling self-conscious. Athelennil smiled again.

'There is no fear of that here,' she said. 'Only taste and sensation from these drinks, nothing more. You can drink until you weep or your heart is contented, whichever you prefer.'

'Why would I weep?' Aradryan said sharply.

'I do not know, stranger,' Athelennil said pointedly. 'If we were to get to know each other, perhaps you would tell me.'

'My apologies, I have been very coarse. I am Aradryan, recently of *Lacontiran*.'

'A steersman, yes?' said Athelennil.

'Yes, how can you tell?'

The eldar waved a hand at Aradryan's hair and dark ensemble.

'The morose always feel drawn to steersmanship. It gives one a sense of control, yet brings untold wonders.'

'You speak as if out of experience.'

'Not of being a steersman. I was a navigator, though, for many passes.'

'And now?'

'Now? Now I am outcast,' said Athelennil. She grinned at Aradryan's shocked reaction. 'Of Biel-Tan, originally, though it has been some time since I trod upon the decks of my home. Do not look so shocked, Aradryan of *Lacontiran*. I would say a third of those around you are outcast, one way or another. There has been a bit of an impromptu gathering on Alaitoc in recent cycles.'

'Outcast tells me that you do not tread the Path,' said Aradryan, recovering his composure, 'but it does not tell me what you actually do with yourself, when not recommending drinks to strangers.'

'See? You can be charming when you try. I am mostly a ranger, my friend. I have spent the last three passes out amongst the Exodite worlds of the Falling Stair, learning about their ways.'

'An odd people, for sure,' said Aradryan. 'I myself have been along the Endless Valley, and so did not encounter Exodites, but all that I have heard marks them as a strange people.'

'The Alaitocii are a strange people,' said Athelennil, seeming to take no offence. 'When viewed from far enough away, that is.'

'Once I would have disagreed, but I have travelled enough to know that what you say is true,' said Aradryan. He took up a pale blue drink and offered it to Athelennil, before seizing a ruby mixture for himself. He held the rim of the glass to his lips in toast and then lifted it to eye level so that he looked at his companion through the translucent contents, turning her pale flesh scarlet and her eyes to deep purple. 'By our differences are we judged, by our shared heritage are we known.'

'A fine sentiment,' said Athelennil, one eyebrow raised in amusement. 'Though not one I feel you composed yourself.'

'I must confess the words belong to an old philosopher, called Kysaduras the Anchorite. You may have heard of him.'

'He is somewhat discredited on Biel-Tan, I must tell you,' said Athelennil. 'His *Introspections Upon Perfection* are sometimes dismissive of the role played by Asurmen in the forming of the Path. Biel-Tan has many Aspect Warriors, and they did not take kindly to such treatment.'

'You have been a Warrior?' asked Aradryan. He took a gulp of his drink when Athelennil nodded. It was delicately spiced, leaving a warm aftertaste that slowly seeped into his gums and down his throat. 'I have a friend who has also suffered the wrath of Khaine. She has moved on now, but perhaps it would be good for me to discuss it with her, do you think?'

'I would not,' Athelennil said, her mood becoming sombre. 'We don our war-mask for a reason. It is not wise to pry beyond that mask.'

The pair sat with that uncomfortable truth for a little while, until Athelennil raised a more humorous topic. Soon they were laughing as they shared old exploits and scrapes. Athelennil was a fount of tales from across the known galaxy, and there was a richness to her stories that intrigued Aradryan. He longed to know more about the life of the outcast, but Athelennil grew tired. To his surprise, she invited him back to her quarters.

To his further surprise, Aradryan accepted.

It was late in the cycle before Korlandril's grand unveiling of his latest masterpiece when Aradryan realised he had not been in contact with his friends since he had first arrived; nor his family, though that was of less concern. The previous few cycles had been a welcome distraction, spent in the company of Athelennil. They had shared a bed frequently, but also made a more telling acquaintance with each other in the establishments of the Tower of Eternal Welcomes and a few other well-chosen spots that Aradryan had used for romantic encounters prior to his departure.

He had remembered the unveiling as he had left Athelennil's apartment and a sudden guilt filled him at the thought. Firstly, he knew he should mention the event to Athelennil. It was, he had come to realise, something of a society occasion amongst the artistic circles of Alaitoc, and to be on good terms with a sculptor of Korlandril's renown was a matter of high regard. For all that she had shown him over the previous cycles concerning the underbelly of the Tower of Eternal Welcomes, Athelennil deserved an invite to this noteworthy celebration.

Secondly, he felt guilty because he knew he would never offer that invite; he would accompany Thirianna. Athelennil was vivacious and engaging, but on more than one occasion in her company Aradryan had caught himself wondering what it would be like to share a similar experience with Thirianna. As a Warrior she had intrigued him; as a Poet she enticed him. The time he had shared recently with Athelennil had reawakened in Aradryan a desire for closeness; not the harmonious friendship he shared with his fellow steersmen, but something of a less temporary nature, a bonding with a kindred spirit. Athelennil was good company, but Thirianna stirred his heart in a way he had not felt for a long time.

So it was that he left Athelennil's apartment as Alaitoc settled a false twilight over its inhabitants. Not far away was a node for the infinity circuit, as could be found all over Alaitoc. Aradryan had not yet interfaced with the psychic network of the craftworld, and remembering the brief contact he had felt when *Lacontiran* had docked, Aradryan approached the terminal with a little trepidation.

He placed his palm upon the gently pulsing gem, and at the instant of his touch the node came to life, glowing energy filling the crystal threads that ran up into the slender pedestal. Immediately Aradryan was connected to all of Alaitoc, and felt its immensity surrounding him. He blocked out the surge of signals, the chatter of countless eldar exchanging information, and settled himself, fearing to be overwhelmed by the rush of flowing data.

He concentrated, focusing on Thirianna. The infinity circuit responded, his thought rippling across the crystalline matrix. No more than two heartbeats later he felt a connection with the poet, though it was only a faint echo of her spirit, imprinted upon the psychic circuitry of her chambers. Still cautious of the wider network, Aradryan feared to search further for her and instead left an impression upon the matrix expressing his desire that they meet.

Taking his hand away, Aradryan broke the connection. He stepped back, wondering what to do next. It was still almost a full cycle until Korlandril's unveiling and he felt no desire to do anything in particular. It was tempting to return to the embrace of Athelennil, but he resisted the urge. Instead, he made his way up to the pinnacle of the Tower of Eternal Welcomes and from a viewing gallery there watched the procession of ships coming and going through the swirling webway gate that lay astern of Alaitoc, wondering where those vessels came from and where they were going.

Not long after mid-cycle, Aradryan entered the Dome of Silence Lost. He had never come here before, it being one of the smaller domes on

Alaitoc, situated away from the main habitation domes and thorough-fares. He was to meet Thirianna, who had responded to his message with the location of their rendezvous: the Bridge of Glimmering Sighs.

Most of the dome was made up of golden-grassed hillsides, the arti-ficial sky coloured as if lit by pale dawnlight. Slow-moving aerethirs glided on thermals rising from concealed vents, their four wings utterly still, craning long necks to the left and right as they snapped at high-flying insects with their slender beaks.

Bisecting the dome was a wide river, its banks steep and filled with fern fronds. As he made his way towards the gurgling water, Aradryan spied solitary figures elsewhere in the semi-wilderness: poets sitting or meandering in contemplation, seeking inspiration from the sigh of the wind and the flitting shadows that passed across the undulating hillsides.

At the heart of the parkland, a silver arc crossed over the ribbon of white-foamed water that cascaded through the Dome of Silence Lost, its span curving as it rose to the crest high above the river. Green and blue snapwings and red-crested meregulls trilled and squawked as they dived beneath the bridge and swept along the banks, skimming just above the water.

There were no other eldar nearby and no sign of Thirianna, so Aradryan walked up the Bridge of Glimmering Sighs, its surface reflect-ing the cloudy twilight above. There was no wall or rail on either side, but such protection was not needed by the sure-footed eldar. Aradryan reached the crest and took in a deep breath, catching the subtle fragrance of the winter grass far below.

He stepped to the edge of the bridge, leaving only his heels on the span. Looking down between his feet, Aradryan saw the swirling waters far below. Turquoise and azure, flecked with foam, the river sped past jagged rocks, the silver and gold of fish glinting beneath the surface.

All Aradryan had to do was step forwards.

He sneered at himself for the thought. There was no resolution here. In purely physical terms, Alaitoc would not allow him to be dashed upon the foam-sprayed boulders. The craftworld would act to save his life, dulling the artificial gravity or perhaps generating a buffer field to smooth his fall.

Even if that were not the case, to throw himself from the bridge would be a pointless act. His fate was the same, whichever way he died. His spirit would be absorbed by the waystone hanging on his chest and in turn would be interred into the infinity circuit, to be trapped in the limbo of undeath forever.

'Aradryan!'

He looked over his shoulder at the sound of Thirianna's voice. She was not far away, striding purposefully up the bridge. Her smile was enchant-ing and instantly dispelled his morbid thoughts. Though there was no sign that Thirianna had guessed his self-destructive intent, Aradryan felt like a child who had been caught doing something forbidden. He smiled and waved at Thirianna, disguising the knot of guilt that tightened around his stomach.

The gesture reminded him of the time when he had left. Korlandril had been unable to bear the thought of him leaving, so it had been Thirianna who had accompanied Aradryan to *Lacontiran*, waving him goodbye as he had boarded the starship, happy for him yet her eyes betraying concern. Now those eyes looked at him with a questioning gaze.

'A very pleasant location,' he said, stepping back from the edge of the bridge to face Thirianna. 'I do not recall coming here before.'

'We never came here,' Thirianna replied. 'It is a well-kept secret amongst the poets of Alaitoc, and I trust that you will keep it so.'

'Of course,' said Aradryan. He looked out over the edge again and the thought that he might simply step from the bridge returned. 'It reminds me a little of the gulfs of space, an endless depth to fall into.'

'I would prefer that you did not fall,' Thirianna said, reaching out a hand to Aradryan's arm to gently tug him back. 'You have only just come back, and we have much to talk about.'

'We do?' he said, delighted by the thought. 'Perhaps you have a verse or two you would like to share with me, now that Korlandril does not intrude upon us.'

'As Korlandril told you, I do not perform my poems.' Thirianna took her hand away from Aradryan's arm and cast her gaze into the distance. Aradryan did not know what she looked at, but her lips parted gently. Her face in profile was remarkable, as if drawn by an artist's hand.

'I thought perhaps they were written for a very select audience,' said Aradryan. 'It must be such a gift, to compose one's disparate thoughts – to embrace them and order them in such a way.'

'They have an audience of one,' said Thirianna, still not meeting Aradryan's gaze. 'That one is me, no other.'

'You know that we used to share everything,' said Aradryan. 'You can still trust me.'

'It is myself that I do not trust. I cannot allow any fear that my compositions might be seen by another to restrict my feelings and words. I would be mortified if my innermost thoughts were put on display to all-comers.'

'Is that what I am?' said Aradryan, hurt by her words. How could she not trust him? He reminded himself that she remembered him as a Dreamer, and knew nothing of the bond and mutual faith he had formed with his fellow steersmen. He took Thirianna by the arm and turned her towards him. 'One of many?'

'It is no slight against you, nor against Korlandril or any other,' explained Thirianna. 'I choose to share what I share. The rest is mine alone, for no other to know. Please appreciate that.'

'Such an attitude does not sit well aboard a starship,' said Aradryan. 'One is part of the many, and in confinement with others most of the time. It takes several to pilot such a vessel, and we must each trust the others implicitly. I have learnt that friendship is not the only thing that must be shared. Cooperation, the overlapping of lives in ways beneficial to all, is the key to understanding our place in the universe.'

'A grandiose conclusion,' laughed Thirianna. 'Perhaps there is something of the poet in you!'

Aradryan realised his words had been a bit pompous. He let go of her arm and glanced away, ashamed. She had not responded as he had hoped, and he could tell that there was nothing deeper than friendship between them. It seemed obvious that Korlandril had seen earlier what Aradryan had missed. Trying not to think about that, he looked at her again, hiding his feelings.

'Korlandril will not be entertaining us until the dusk of the cycle begins,' he said. 'If you will not grace me with your poems, perhaps you could suggest other entertainments that will divert us until the unveiling.'

Thirianna did not reply, but looked keenly at Aradryan, trying to penetrate the calm veneer he had assumed. Small twitches at the corner of her mouth and a slight narrowing of her eyes betrayed some internal dissent, but it passed in a moment and she forced a smile. Thirianna laid a palm upon the back of Aradryan's hand.

'The Weathering of the Nine takes place later today,' she said. She spoke of the carnival that took place aboard drifting sky barges, touring the nine great domes of inner Alaitoc. It was a haunt of adolescents and tourists. 'I have not been for many passes.'

'Nostalgia?' said Aradryan, smiling at the memories of the parade, an eyebrow rising in amusement.

'A return,' Thirianna replied. 'A return to a place we both know well.'

Aradryan considered the invitation for a moment, unsure whether it was wise to revisit old memories. If he declined, Athelennil would surely give him welcome instead. Yet that would be unfair on Thirianna. It was not her fault that she only sought friendship. It was the least Aradryan could do to attempt to enjoy some time with her.

'Yes, let us go back a while and revisit our youth,' Aradryan said. 'A return to happier times.'

'It is a truth that as we progress, our grief increases and our joys diminish,' said Thirianna.

The two of them started down the slope of the bridge towards the coreward bank. Thirianna's words seemed to be a general declaration rather than directed at him, but Aradryan felt them like a barb all the same. He could not allow his own depression to infect the happiness of a friend.

'It does not have to be so,' said Aradryan. 'The universe may have grief in plenty to heap upon us, but it is in our power to make our own joy.'

Thirianna looked to reply for a moment, but stayed silent, brow gently furrowed as she considered his words. They walked on a little further, close to each other but not intimately so.

'Yes, you are right,' said Thirianna, with a smile of genuine pleasure. 'Let us recapture the past and create some new happiness.'

The statue was bathed in a golden glow and tinged with sunset reds and purples from the dying star above. It depicted an impressionistic Isha in abstract, her body and limbs flowing from the trunk of a lianderin tree, her wave-like tresses entwined within yellow leaves in its upreaching branches. Her face was bowed, hidden in the shadow cast by tree and hair. From the darkness a slow trickle of silver liquid spilled from her eyes into a golden cup held aloft by an ancient eldar warrior kneeling at her feet: Eldanesh. Light glittered from the chalice on his alabaster face, his armour a stylised arrangement of organic geometry, his face blank except for a slender nose and the merest depression of eye sockets. From beneath him, a black-petalled rose coiled up Isha's legs and connected the two together in its thorny embrace.

'She is so serene,' Thirianna said. 'Such calm and beauty.'

Aradryan's fingers flicked in agitation at his companion's words, for he saw nothing of the sort. Korlandril's creation had the same ostentation as its creator. Its name was no more humble either: *The Gifts of Loving Isha*, it was called. Aradryan looked at the sculpture, which was perfectly executed, and felt nothing. The weaving of organic and inorganic was intriguing, and the lines were pleasing to the eye, but there was nothing new to stir the steersman's heart.

'It is self-referential,' Aradryan explained, his gaze moving from the statue to Thirianna. 'It is a work of remarkable skill and delicacy, certainly. Yet I find it somewhat... staid. It adds nothing to my experience of the myth, merely represents physically something that is felt. It is a metaphor in its most direct form. Beautiful, but merely reflecting back upon its maker rather than a wider truth.'

Aradryan found it hard to express himself. The words he sought did not come easily and by the look that passed briefly across Thirianna's face he realised she thought his opinion scornful. She took a deep breath before replying, obviously choosing her words with care.

'But is not that the point of art, to create representations for those thoughts, memories and emotions that cannot be conveyed directly?'

'Perhaps I am being unfair,' said Aradryan, speaking sincerely. He saw movement in the crowd behind Thirianna and out of the corner of his eye spied Korlandril advancing on them. His face was a mask of anger, and Aradryan realised his criticism had been overheard. And not taken well at all. He sought to temper his comments as Korlandril stormed closer. 'Out in the stars, I have seen such wondrous creations of nature that the artifices of mortals seem petty, even those that explore such momentous themes such as this.'

'Staid?' snapped Korlandril, stepping next to Thirianna, who turned with a look of shock which swiftly became one of guilt, as though she shared the blame for Aradryan's critique. 'Self-referential?'

Korlandril's childish outburst was embarrassing, but there was nothing Aradryan could do to take back the words; just as there was nothing to stop the Artist feeling the hurt he did. Aradryan tried to offer some advice.

'My words were not intended to cause offence, Korlandril,' he said, offering a placating palm towards his friend. 'They are but my opinion, and an ill-educated one at that. Perhaps you find my sentimentality gauche.'

Korlandril hesitated, blinking and glancing away in a moment of awkwardness. The pause lasted only the briefest heartbeat before his scowl returned.

'You are right to think your opinion ill-informed,' Korlandril said. 'While you gazed naively at glittering stars and swirling nebulae, I studied the works of Aethyril and Ildrintharir, learnt the disciplines of ghost stone weaving and inorganic symbiosis. If you have not the wit to extract the meaning from that which I have presented to you, perhaps you should consider your words more carefully.'

Korlandril's accusation was misplaced, and it irked Aradryan that he should be blamed for not being stirred by the Artist's pedestrian creation. The steersman noticed Thirianna stepping back as he crossed his arms and met Korlandril's glare with a stare of his own.

'And if you have not the skill to convey your meaning from your work, perhaps you need to continue studying,' Aradryan snarled. 'It is not from the past masters that you should learn your art but from the heavens and your heart. Your technique is flawless, but your message is parochial. How many statues of Isha might I see if I travelled across the craftworld? A dozen? More? How many more statues of Isha exist on other craftworlds? You have taken nothing from the Path save the ability to indulge yourself in this spectacle. You have learnt nothing of yourself, of the darkness and the light that battles within you. There is intellect alone in your work, and nothing of yourself. It might be that you should expand your terms of reference.'

The two of them had shared a bond of Dreamers, and had left imprints upon each other in ways that simple friends could not. Yet Korlandril had changed beyond recognition. His arrogance was towering, his self-importance colossal. The Artist's venomous words felt all the more like a deep betrayal because of the past they had shared.

'What do you mean by that?' said Korlandril, every syllable spat with anger.

'Get away from this place, from Alaitoc,' Aradryan said, trying to be patient, remembering that it was not Korlandril's fault; he had discarded all self-awareness when he had become the Artist. Aware of Thirianna's scrutiny, Aradryan made a show of seeking accord with Korlandril, for it did Aradryan no favours to appear the aggressor in the eyes of his would-be lover. 'Why stifle your art by seeking inspiration only from the halls and domes you have seen since childhood? Rather than trying to look upon old sights with fresh eyes, why not turn your old eyes upon fresh sights?'

Korlandril parted his lips for a moment, but then shut his mouth firmly. He directed a fierce glare at Aradryan, before stalking away through the blue grass, scattering guests in his flight.

Aradryan turned towards Thirianna, hands raised in apology, hoping that she did not attach any blame to him for Korlandril's tantrum.

'I am sorry, I d– ' he started, but Thirianna's scowl cut him off.

'It is not I that deserves your apology,' she said curtly, the words like barbs of guilt in Aradryan's gut. 'Perhaps such behaviour is tolerated on a starship, but you are back on Alaitoc. You are right, you have become gauche.'

With that parting remark, she left Aradryan, ignoring his call after her. As he watched her walking away, the steersman knew that he had made a grave error. His two closest friends had turned from him, and Alaitoc seemed even less like home than it did a few moments before.

FATE

The Deserts of Sain-Shelai – The black sands of Sain-Shelai spread to the horizon, lifeless and bleak. At their centre stands a solitary hill, and in that hill is the opening of a small cave. Inside that cave burns a small fire. The pall of its smoke spreads out across all of the desert, joining it as one with the flames. From the smoke comes the tale of what goes by, and so into the flames stares the one-eyed hag, Morai-heg. Seeing what passes, the crone weaves the skein of fate, choosing the length of the thread of life for each mortal, binding it to the destinies of others in the great pattern of existence. On occasion, a great storm will sweep the black sands and Morai-heg will be blinded. She throws her weavings upon the flames, casting fate adrift for those poor spirits, until the storms have passed and she can see once more.

Aradryan found Athelennil in one of the vapour lounges of the Tower of Eternal Welcomes. After his confrontation with Korlandril he was in no mood to relax, inhaling narcotic and hypnotic incenses and fumes. Taking note of his agitated disposition, Athelennil bid farewell to her companions and took Aradryan back to her quarters. Seeking some sense of release, the steersman took her arm and stepped towards the bed chamber but she twisted from his grip with a frown and pointed to the low couch that ran along one curved wall of the chamber.

'You misunderstand our relationship,' she said. 'I do not exist solely to salve your troubled thoughts. What we share must be mutual.'

'I am sorry,' said Aradryan, taking one of Athelennil's hands in his, bowing in apology. 'I meant no offence, my love.'

'My love?' her laugh was edged with bitterness. 'Love has nothing to do with what we have. Do not seek to woo me with false words.'

Aradryan was taken aback by her forthright denial and realised that he had said the words idly, without even considering them. She was right to rebuke him.

'I am disconcerted and dismayed,' Aradryan confessed. 'I have had a sorrowful parting with friends.'

'Not sorrowful,' said Athelennil. She took Aradryan by the arm and led him to the couch, pushing him to be seated. From an alcove in the wall she took up a crystal bottle and two glasses, pouring two measures of the lavender-coloured drink. 'Your agitation is not sorrow, it is something more than that.'

Knowing that the burden of the evening's events would stay upon him until he confided in another, Aradryan told the sorry tale of the unveiling, and confessed his regret for not taking Athelennil as his partner.

'Korlandril and I parted with angry words, and I fear I have also lost Thirianna,' he finished.

'Ah, sweet Thirianna,' said Athelennil. She held up a hand to Aradryan to silence his protest about her tone of voice, which was gently mocking. 'Do not think to deny that you have feelings for her. I say this not out of jealousy, but out of friendship. If you wish to be with her, you will have no complaint from me. I am due to leave Alaitoc in two cycles' time anyway, so it is irrelevant.'

'Two cycles?' Aradryan had known that Athelennil would leave at some point but he had not thought it would be so soon.

'I travel aboard *Irdiris*,' she said, sitting beside Aradryan.

'Bound for where?' he asked. 'Will you return?'

'I have no answer for either question, and I care for no answer.' Athelennil stretched an arm along the back of the couch and arched her back, her eyes never leaving Aradryan's 'That is the point of being outcast – to have no bonds to fetter one's travels.'

'I will come with you,' declared Aradryan.

'Will you?' replied Athelennil, assuming a pose of mock subservience. She flicked her hair from her face in annoyance. 'What if I do not want you to come with me?'

Aradryan had not thought of such a thing and slumped in the chair, shoulders sagging. He felt fingers on his knee and looked up to see Athelennil smiling at him.

'You are in such a sorry state, Aradryan.' She stroked a hand up his leg and then put her fingers to his cheek. 'Do not make a drama out of circumstance. I would be pleased if you chose to come with me, but be warned that we need no steersman. We are outcasts, not mentors, and if you leave on *Irdiris* you are choosing the Path of the Outcast too.'

'I am not so sure...'

Aradryan was changing his mind with every heartbeat. He wanted to see the galaxy, and to spend time with Athelennil; he also wanted to stay with Thirianna. Evidently the conflict was clear to Athelennil.

'I will take no umbrage if you wish to explore where the water flows,' she said, withdrawing her hand. 'Speak with Thirianna. Make inquiries of the other starships if you wish to continue to be a steersman.'

'There is no reason to contact Thirianna, save to give her fresh opportunity to share her scorn for me,' said Aradryan, standing up. 'You did not see the disdain in her face, disdain I deserved.'

'It is deserved if you think so little of your friends that they would judge you so harshly on a single episode.'

'You think she would speak with me?'

Athelennil waved a hand dismissively and looked away.

'It matters not what I think. If you fear further rebuke, then do not speak to her. If you have any courage at all, you will put aside your fear and seek her out.'

'Then I shall, if that is your feeling on the matter,' said Aradryan, heading for the door.

He hesitated a step but there was no further reply from Athelennil. Stung by the sentiment of her words, Aradryan headed to the infinity circuit node, seeking to link with Thirianna. As before, she was not to be easily found and so he left his imprint, conjoined with the desire for reconciliation.

Knowing that to return so swiftly to Athelennil would be an invitation for further mockery, Aradryan instead headed into Alaitoc, away from the dock towers and quay spires. The outcast's words accompanied him, though, distance no object to their pursuit. The offer to leave Alaitoc – properly leave as an outcast – preyed on his mind as he rode a spearcar from the Dome of Tranquil Reservations to the Boulevard of Split Moons.

The proposition filled him with fear for the most part, but in a way the fear added to the thrill of being outcast. It was safety that cloyed and coddled his thoughts, and so perhaps he needed to make the ultimate break from their safety, giving himself no refuge. If the Path was the trap he thought it to be, the only escape was to become outcast: to eschew the teachings of the Path altogether. It mattered nothing if he voyaged far from Alaitoc for the rest of his life if he did so on the ships of the craftworld, which though distant were still merely extensions; detached limbs of the same body.

Aradryan wandered the stalls that lined the Boulevard of Split Moons, named so for in shape the thoroughfare resembled two crescents backed onto each other. There were all manner of small trinkets on sale; gewgaws of pretty gems and polished jewels that caught the light in dazzling rainbows. The traders here were not mercantile in the true sense, but mostly artisans giving away their wares to make room for future projects. When one lived as long as an eldar, there was a great deal of clutter to be periodically cleared.

Some stalls had ancient artefacts that passed from generation to generation, some of them dating back hundreds of passes. Antiquity in itself held little value for the eldar, but some aesthetics, some designs had a timeless quality, and there were those who preferred to possess the purity of their original incarnations rather than objects created in the style of the old schools.

Also on display were clothes, of styles both fashionable and old. Aradryan had given little thought to his wardrobe of late and lingered awhile at these stands, studying the cut and cloth of loose robes and tight jackets, studded leggings and belted shirts. His own attire had earned him a few strange glances and a couple of admiring looks. He wore a wide-shouldered jacket of dark blue, flared at the hips, fastened by a line of tiny buckles from waist to neck and wrist to elbow. A heavy kilt of subtly blended greens and blacks covered his upper legs, above narrow boots studded with golden buttons. It was a style that had not been widely popular even before his departure, and now looked very out of place.

Thinking of how long he had been away aboard *Lacontiran*, it occurred to him that if he were to accept Athelennil's offer, he might never come back to Alaitoc.

Never.

He tried to summon up a little grief at the thought. He tried to imagine what it would be like never to come here again, but as Aradryan looked at the petty merchants and their meaningless wares he could find no enthusiasm for the place of his birth.

Into these thoughts came the apparition of Thirianna. At first, Aradryan thought that it was not strange that she should appear in his thoughts when he considered leaving the craftworld, but after a moment he realised that her appearance was not a creation of his imagination; she was touching upon his mind via the infinity circuit.

He was guarded at first, offering cordial greetings to his friend. In reply he received a wave of warmth, and sensed a desire to make amends and seek comfort. This was much to his liking, and Thirianna detected as such. She would come to him, he knew, and he would wait for her.

The connection dissipated, leaving Aradryan slightly out of touch with reality for a moment. He regained his senses, the lingering effect of the psychic connection ebbing away.

Aradryan did not have long to wait. Thirianna found him as he looked at a pair of plain golden earrings. Turning at the sound of her voice, Aradryan was stunned by the vision that appeared before him. Thirianna wore a tight bodysuit of glittering purple and silver. On her arms she wore several bejewelled torcs, with long white gloves up to the elbow.

Her boots were of the same material, and about her slender throat was wound a light scarf, which hung down to a wide belt studded with blazing blue gemstones. Her hair and eyes had been coloured a subtle jade green, matched by the colour of the small waistbag that hung at her hip.

Aradryan smiled broadly as she approached and held up the earrings, which were shaped vaguely like two leaping fish.

'Not really to my taste,' said Thirianna as they touched hands in greeting.

'Not for you, for me,' said Aradryan, nonplussed.

'I know,' said Thirianna, laughing softly. She took one of the earrings and held it up to the side of Aradryan's face. The curve of the jewellery matched well with his features and she nodded. 'Yes, they would look very good.'

'Then it is decided,' said Aradryan, recovering his composure. The steersman signalled his desire to take the jewellery to the stallholder, who nodded his head in appreciation of a choice well made and waved for the pair to continue on their way.

The two of them spoke little as they moved between the stalls and stores, examining gems and scarves, robes and headdresses. Thirianna's silence unnerved Aradryan and he found himself making inconsequential utterances to fill the quiet, yet the more he talked about the wares on display, the more distant she seemed to become. He tried to engage her with a commentary on the latest fashions, which were a trifle plain, boring by his standards, but she did not want to participate.

She was similarly quiet when he tried to hint at his dissatisfactions with craftworld life. He heard her sigh more than once, and the harder he tried to explain how distant he felt from life on Alaitoc, the more annoyed she became. Eventually it became too much for her.

'What is it about life here that chafes so badly that you must constantly gripe and find fault?' she snapped, taking Aradryan by the arm and guiding him to a small alleyway between two stores where they would not be overheard.

'I am sorry if I have broadened my view beyond the petty baubles on display here,' Aradryan replied, though he bit back a comment about the pettiness of spirit that pervaded the Alaitocii if they praised the baubles filling the market, realising that such a sentiment would include Thirianna. He paused and calmed himself. 'No, I am genuinely sorry. You say that life here chafes, and I can think of no better word to describe it. It rubs against my spirit, binding my thoughts like a cord around my limbs. Alaitoc is safe, and controlled, and suffocating. It offers comfort and dependability. I no longer desire these things.'

'So why did you return at all?' Thirianna asked, showing genuine concern. 'There must have been a reason to come back.'

Friendship had been the reason for his return, but his friends had gone by the time he got back, replaced by a Poet and an Artist. Love, of a deeper kind than he had felt for his friends, had grown in his heart when he had met Thirianna the Poet, but how could he tell her that? She had made it clear she did not feel the same, and so such a declaration was both selfish and pointless, serving to hurt both of them for no obvious gain. Aradryan clamped down on the emotions that raged through his breast, forcing himself to appear unperturbed though inside his thoughts were in tumult.

'My memories of Alaitoc were fonder than the reality,' said Aradryan. 'Or perhaps the reality has changed to one of which I am less fond.'

'You speak of Korlandril,' said Thirianna. The mention of the Artist's name caused a brief flicker of annoyance in Aradryan, which quickly turned to shame when he admitted to himself his part in angering the Artist.

'And you,' said Aradryan. He sighed and leaned back against the wall of the alley, crossing his arms over his chest. Though he could not confess all, there was something of his state of mind that he could share with Thirianna. Something she had to know if he was going to leave. 'I do not know my place here any longer.'

'It will take time, but you will adjust again and learn anew to find the delight in each moment that passes, and meaning in the things you now find trivial,' Thirianna assured him. 'Alaitoc is your home, Aradryan.'

'Is it?' he replied. 'I have no family left here, and my friends are not those I left behind. Why should I choose to stay here when all of the galaxy is open to me?'

'Though it would sadden me to see you leave again, I cannot argue against your desires,' said Thirianna, and her agreement served to dishearten Aradryan further.

'Is there some reason I should stay?' he asked. He made no attempt to hide his thoughts this time, directing a look of longing, of desire, at Thirianna. She was shocked and took a moment to reply.

'I have only my friendship to offer,' Thirianna said. Aradryan's disappointment was instant, showing as a furrowed brow and parted lips for a moment before the emotionless mask descended again.

'Friendship was once enough, but not now,' said Aradryan, his tone even and quiet. He directed a quick bow of the head to Thirianna, in deference to her feelings, eyes closed out of respect. The rejection hurt, but it was not unexpected. He had met her on a fool's errand. Perhaps Athelennil had known this all along, and so had forced him into confirming his fears rather than harbour baseless hope. 'It seems that even friendship is not possible with Korlandril. He has grown arrogant, I think, and he has no time for others. Thank you for your candour, Thirianna. I hope I have not caused you undue embarrassment or woe.'

His embarrassment growing, Aradryan fled, leaving Thirianna with quick strides. He stalked along the Boulevard of Split Moons, heading back to the transport that would take him to the Tower of Eternal

Welcomes. As he thought of joining Athelennil on her travels, his heart lightened a little and so too did his step.

Approaching the platform of the carriageway, Aradryan smiled, suddenly feeling free of the burden he had been carrying since he had seen Thirianna and Korlandril waiting for him beside *Lacontiran*. He owed them nothing. They had not waited for him, but had moved on with their lives, as they were right to do. Now he would move on with his life too. Thirianna was not unique, he told himself. If he spent more time with Athelennil the two of them would grow more alike. Freed from the constraints of the Path, Aradryan was sure he would become a more compatible companion.

It was better to leave Alaitoc. There really was nothing for him here.

The *Irdiris* was a small skiff, with a single stellar sail, her hull displaying a mottled green and black as Aradryan approached along the dockside. Cargo was being loaded into her hull, and a stepway arced up to an opening in her side not far from her slender nose. For all that she was considered small by starship standards, the *Irdiris* was still large enough to take some time to walk from tail to nose. Her golden sail stretched high between the beams of the docking wharf, on the outer edge of the Bay of Departing Sorrows.

The name meant nothing to Aradryan as he walked with Athelennil by his side. She was dressed in a tight bodysuit of yellow and blue, her hair coloured black and white in alternating stripes, tied into an elaborate braid that hung to the small of her back. Aradryan's eyes danced over the curve of her waist and hips, enjoying the spectacle.

'You have company,' murmured Athelennil, a moment before Aradryan heard a familiar voice calling his name. 'I will see you inside.'

Athelennil parted from him as he looked ahead, seeing Thirianna walking quickly along the dockside. His heart leapt at the sight, not with hope but with fear. He was so close to leaving now, he could not turn back. It did not bother him to disappoint Athelennil and her companions, if disappointed they would actually be, but he was on the brink of finally quitting Alaitoc and if Thirianna showed a change of heart he might never escape.

He stopped, hands on hips. Thirianna broke into a run. He heard a derisive snort from Athelennil moments before Thirianna reached him, before she turned up the boarding ramp.

'This is madness,' Thirianna said as she reached her friend. She reached out a hand to his arm but he stepped away, avoiding the contact.

'It is freedom,' he replied, glancing over his shoulder towards the open, iris-like door of the starship. He looked back at Thirianna and he realised that there was no need for his last words to her to be so harsh. 'I did not wish to be parted like this. It is too painful to say goodbye.'

'It does not have to be this way,' said Thirianna. 'Do not leave.'

'You wish me to stay?' said Aradryan, one eyebrow raised. He could tell from the way she held herself and the tone in her voice that she had not suddenly developed feelings for him. He was intrigued to hear what argument Thirianna would present. 'Would there be a purpose in remaining on Alaitoc?'

'There must be more to this than your desire to be with me,' she said. 'How can you hate Alaitoc, who has raised and nurtured you and given you so much?'

'I do not hate her. I am merely bored of her. Perhaps in time my thirst for new vistas and experiences will be sated and I will return.' A thought, half-formed, came to mind and Aradryan spoke it without hesitation; a solution to both of his problems. 'Would you come with me?'

'Be safe,' she said. 'See the stars and come back to us.'

'I will, Thirianna,' Aradryan replied. He strode close to her and laid his hands on her shoulders. 'Take care of Korlandril for me. I sense that he needs a good friend at the moment, if only to save him from himself.'

'And who is going to save you from yourself?' Thirianna asked, tears moistening her cheeks. She could not look at Aradryan and kept her gaze on the marble-like floor of the docking pier.

'Nobody,' Aradryan said. I do not need anybody, he told himself. He let go of her and stepped away, knowing that he had this one chance to do so. If he held her, if he comforted her, it would be too much and he would have to stay, to still the guilt that was even now stirring in his heart.

Luckily she did not look at him with her beautiful eyes, and he turned away, taking quick steps to the boarding gantry. He did not look back as the door hissed shut behind him, leaving him alone in a short passageway.

Like all eldar ships, the interior of the *Irdiris* was more organic than constructed. The vessel had been grown into being by the bonesingers and their choirs: first the wraithbone skeletal core and then the smooth weave of psycho-plastic that formed the hull, bulkheads and walls. The floor merged seamlessly with the walls, which merged seamlessly with the ceiling, forming a continuous enclosure of softly gleaming yellow and green. At regular intervals the walls bulged slightly around the internal rib-like bracing of the wraithbone skeleton.

The light from the walls was ample for the eldar to see by, suffusing the ship with a gentle, constant glow of dappled colour. Underfoot the floor was slightly soft and yielding to Aradryan's tread, and spaced between petal-like doorways were bulges and blisters of storage lockers, some small, others larger than Aradryan. Here and there were crystalline clusters set into the walls: interfaces with the ship's psychic matrix. The pulse of the energy network was a sensation in the spirit rather than heard or felt. Aradryan detected the telltale quickening of the wave passing from the ship's core along the hull, as the engines generated power to slip aside from Alaitoc's artificial gravity field.

* * *

Outside, lights sprang into life along the length of the *Irdiris*, bathing the dock in a warm aura of oranges and reds. With barely a sound, the breeze of its passing ruffling Thirianna's hair, the voidrunner lifted from the platform and tilted starwards. The forcefield enclosing the dock shimmered into silvery life as the *Irdiris* passed through it. *Irdiris* swiftly accelerated, diving towards the golden-edged circle of the webway gate swirling aft of Alaitoc. It became a shimmer against the stars as its holo-field activated, and then it was gone.

FREEDOM

The Exodite Worlds – First to escape the Fall were the Exodites. They saw the shadow that had fallen upon the hearts of the eldar and they took to their ships and fled the empire. To the newest worlds they travelled, seeded in recent generations, primordial and harsh. They tamed the reptilian beasts they found there, and named them dragons after the grand serpents of old. With them they took the secret of crystal networks and into the rock of their new homes they bound their world spirits, so that when the Fall came and She Who Thirsts came into being, their souls were captured by the crystal webs of their worlds and not devoured. Yet the world spirits that sustain the settlements of the Exodites are not without their own hunger, and into them must be passed the spirits of every generation sustained by their energy.

Though the *Irdiris* was not as large as *Lacontiran*, Aradryan was immediately familiar with the layout of the starship. Like all eldar vessels, she had been grown by the bonesingers from a central wraithbone core, resembling the spine and ribs of some large beast, though inverted. A dorsal passageway ran the length of the ship, with sizeable compartments to either side, the pastel blue psycho-plastic of the walls gently mottled with green. Curving bulkheads separated the chambers, extruded from thicker rib-like spars that bulged gently from the walls.

The structural core was also the power plant of the ship, suffused with psychic energy from Alaitoc's infinity circuit for transit in the webway, during which the stellar sail was furled and the mast retracted and lowered into the fuselage of the vessel. This energy matrix could be felt by Aradryan as *Irdiris* powered away from the craftworld, a gentle thrum throughout the ship that came to his mind rather than his other senses.

Athelennil waited from him in a small arched hallway at the end of the entry passage, near to the slender nose of the ship. She said nothing, but her expression showed a little surprise that he had joined them.

'There is nothing to keep me on Alaitoc,' Aradryan said as he joined her.

'It will always be your home, whatever happens,' said Athelennil. 'I have travelled to many worlds, but part of me still belongs to Biel-Tan. You cannot deny that.'

Aradryan shrugged dismissively and Athelennil took that, rightly, as a sign that he did not wish to continue with the topic of conversation.

'There is plenty of space, *Irdiris* is berthed for at least twenty, and there are only five aboard,' Athelennil told him. 'You are free to choose whichever space you prefer from those that are unoccupied. Come, I will show you the rest of the ship.'

Turning sternwards, she led Aradryan down the central corridor, which was broken by archways every dozen paces or so. Some were open and led into storage areas, curving ramps dropping down into the depths of the starship. Others were closed off by slit doorways. Athelennil stopped in front of one of these and it opened, responding to her mental command, revealing a communal eating area. An oval table dominated the room, supported on a wide leg that grew up from the floor, like green-veined marble in colour. On the far wall were crystal-fronted cabinets filled with dishes and utensils, many of which were unfamiliar to Aradryan.

'We all have to fend for ourselves here,' said Athelennil, noting his bemused expression. 'There is no Path of Service to tend to your needs.'

Aradryan nodded in understanding. It was not a consideration that had occurred to him, and this minor revelation made him realise just how different his life would be. Even aboard *Lacontiran* his lifestyle had not been much different from that experienced by the Alaitocii throughout their lives. As an outcast he would have to be all things: steersman, cook, warrior, navigator, messenger.

'Through there is the crop vale,' Athelennil said, interrupting his thoughts. She pointed at a doorway to their right. 'We have four bays set aside for growing food, and another with a freshwater pool. Everybody contributes their time.'

'Of course,' said Aradryan. He smiled faintly. 'You will have to teach me what to do.'

'And you best be a quick study, my friend. With only five of us, there is a lot of work to go around, even with the supplies we have in biostasis in the hold.'

She continued the tour, showing him several communal areas, all but one of which were bare save for low couches and tables. The fourth was furnished more fully, with an abstract tapestry hanging on one wall, its iridescent threads changing subtly in the breeze of the artificial air, creating a permanently shifting, wave-like pattern of greens and greys. Alcoves in the walls contained a few keepsakes and trophies: vases and small statuettes; crystal decanters containing a variety of glistening drinks; a child's animadoll which turned its doughy features towards Aradryan as he entered, its crude face scrutinising him without eyes.

On one of the couches was another eldar, dressed in a short robe of heavy black cloth. He eyed Aradryan with curiosity and stood up, his scarlet pantaloons billowing, tucked into short lizard-hide boots. Aradryan guessed him to be older by a generation.

'Jair Essinadith,' said the other eldar, raising a palm in greeting. His grey eyes never left Aradryan's and the former steersman met his stare without hesitation.

'Aradryan.'

'Of course you are,' said Jair. 'Athelennil has told us about you.'

'I hope she was flattering,' said Aradryan, glancing at his companion.

'Not really, my would-be vagabond,' said Jair. His tone was not overtly hostile, but Aradryan was in no doubt that he was entering a close-knit group and his arrival would cause disruption.

'And where do you hail from, originally?' Aradryan tried his best to be cordial. This was a new start for him, and if he was to make the most of the opportunity it would go well to be on friendly terms with his shipmates.

'Alaitoc, like you,' said Jair. 'Though I left many passes ago. I was once mentored by Naerithin Alaimana. The waterfalls in the Dome of Unintended Pleasures – I created them. Perhaps you know them?'

'A modern wonder, for sure,' said Aradryan. 'I spent three cycles dreaming on the viewing gallery there.'

'There will be plenty of time to exchange old tales, I am sure,' said Athelennil, taking Aradryan by the arm. 'You should meet the others first.'

Aradryan nodded his goodbye to Jair as he was gently guided from the room, receiving the same in return. When they were back in the main passageway, Athelennil slipped her arm under Aradryan's and leant closer.

'I do not think Jair will remain with us for much longer,' she said quietly as they headed aft. 'He speaks ever more about his past accomplishments, and the longing for Alaitoc's peace is growing stronger with every journey we take. His reminiscences are becoming repetitive, so it will be good for him to have another ear into which he can pour them.'

'I do not wish to hear of Alaitoc,' said Aradryan. 'It is to leave the craftworld behind that I have joined you. I fear constant reminder will only irritate me.'

'And so you must learn some patience. On the craftworld we can lose ourselves, for our entire lives if we wish, allowing petty grievances and grating encounters to pass us by. If you wish to remain on *Irdiris* you must accept the rest of us as we are.'

'I am not insensitive,' argued Aradryan. 'On *Lacontiran* I was in close proximity to many others and managed to make friends and remain civil.'

There was no reply from Athelennil, but in the absence of her voice Aradryan could hear the sound of music. The distinctive lilting notes of a summerflute drifted along the passageway from an open arch ahead.

'That is Lechthennian,' explained Athelennil, smiling as she tapped her fingers on Aradryan's arm in beat to the lively tune. 'He plays all manner of instruments, and composes his songs himself. He spends most of his time back here on his own, playing to himself or writing his music.'

Aradryan listened to the melody and could appreciate the complex harmonies that filled the corridor. The tune stirred his heart in a way that little else had done in the last few cycles, lifting his spirit, promising excitement and contentment in equal measure.

'Perhaps we should not disturb him,' Aradryan said. 'I would not like to intrude.'

'He will not mind,' Athelennil assured him. 'If we did not interrupt his playing, we would never get to speak to him. He is the oldest of us, by far. *Irdiris* has had many crews, changing over the passes, but as far as we can tell, Lechthennian has been here for at least two arcs.'

'He must be as old as the ship, almost,' exclaimed Aradryan. Even as he said the words, not far from the archway, he realised that the music had stopped.

'Not even close,' said a voice from the chamber beyond, soft and assured.

Aradryan and Athelennil stepped through the doorway to find Lechthennian standing by the wall, placing the arm-long summerflute into a purpose-shaped niche. There were other instruments on shelves, in alcoves and on stands upon the floor. Aradryan recognised some: a fourteen-stringed half-lyre, next to an arching holoharp; the red, white and black keys of a chime organ; a set of half a dozen lapdrums. Others were unknown to him, a variety of stringed, blown and percussion devices.

The eldar was barefoot, clad in loose trousers and a tight-fitting jacket of white that glimmered with a cross-thread of silver, which struck Aradryan as odd, for white was the colour of mourning and normally shunned by right-thinking folk. Lechthennian was old, to those who knew what to look for; the slight thinness of his hair and skin; the lines at the corners of his eyes; the flare of his nostrils and tapering of his ear tips. Yet none of these purely physical attributes betrayed his age as much as the weight of his gaze, which measured Aradryan in an instant.

'*Irdiris* is nearly as old as Alaitoc,' said Lechthennian, seating himself again on a stool to one side of the room. There were other plain chairs arranged facing him, set in a semicircle to the left of the archway. 'Her first voyage came just half an arc after the Fall.'

'I did not mean offence,' said Aradryan hastily.

'Why should I take offence, I am old, as you say,' replied Lechthennian. He waved a hand for the pair to seat themselves and produced a thin, whistle-like instrument from a pocket inside a robe. He tootled and tweeted for a few moments, the notes reminding Aradryan of a nursery tune from his childhood. Lechthennian then looked hard at Aradryan, the whistle spinning slowly between his fingers. 'Escape is not what you think it is.'

'I... I am not sure what you mean.'

'There is no need to be coy,' said Lechthennian. 'You are outcast now, and it is no cause of shame, just as my age is no cause of shame. You want to be away from Alaitoc, and that is no bad thing. Be careful, though, that in running from one trouble you do not pitch yourself headlong into another.'

'I am in no trouble,' said Aradryan. 'I do not know what Athelennil told you about me, but I came on board free of any dark cloud.'

'We both know that is not true, Aradryan,' said the aging eldar, his expression stern. 'I know only what I read in your eyes and I see that darkness comes with you, but it is not all doom and gloom.' He made another couple of toots on his whistle, like the call of the grasswitch frog, and grinned. 'You have good company, a fast ship and a desire to see the galaxy. There are worse fates.'

'You are an accomplished musician,' said Aradryan, glad for the opportunity to change the subject to his companion.

'No, I am not a musician,' said Lechthennian. 'As you would know it, a musician dedicates himself to the perfection of his composition and performance. I have simply had a long time to dabble and pick up a thing or two.'

'If you are not a musician, what are you?' said Aradryan. He felt Athelennil's fingers tighten on his arm, as though he had said something wrong, but Lechthennian continued to smile.

'I am a traveller, that is all,' he said. 'Welcome aboard *Irdiris*.'

The last member of the crew, Caolein, was also the pilot, and Aradryan did not see him for some time as he guided the ship through the webway, navigating the traffic of ships coming and going this close to Alaitoc. Younger even than Aradryan, Caolein sported blond and black hair to his waist, tied in three long locks that were bound with silver thread. He wore a pale grey steersman's suit studded with small gems of blue and purple, and flopped down with a sigh on the couch opposite Aradryan and Athelennil, who had been in the common area drinking sour whitenut tea and discussing the cooking arrangements.

'I'm glad that is done,' declared the pilot. He reached out and poured himself a cup of the white-nut tea from the steaming ewer. 'Out into the open webway, heading for the stars!'

'Towards Kha-alienni, like we discussed?' said Athelennil, eyes narrowing with suspicion.

'More or less,' Caolein replied defensively.

'Jair warned you about this before,' Athelennil snapped, standing up. She turned towards the door, and Aradryan was not sure whether he was meant to follow or not.

'Relax!' Caolein held out a hand. 'We are heading to Kha-alienni, for sure. I thought it might be nice to go by way of the Archer Cascades, that's all.'

Athelennil stopped and turned back in the archway.

'For truth? We do not need another of your wild detours, Caolein.'

'For truth. We have someone new on board, and I bet he has never seen the Archer Cascades.'

Aradryan shook his head.

'No, I do not think *Lacontiran* passed that way,' he said.

Caolein invited Aradryan to accompany him to the pilot's chamber, in a small blister just in front of the mast. Though smaller, with space only for two eldar, the control panel seemed similar to the one Aradryan had used on board the *Lacontiran*. In some ways it was simpler, there being only one stellar sail and the ship being smaller. In other ways, there was a lot more to think about, with various trim and attitude controls all being interconnected, rather than handled by separate pilots. For the moment, the spirit circuitry was piloting the vessel, guiding it along a straight, broad stretch of the webway. A display glowing from an oval crystal screen above the console showed a white tube stretching ahead and behind, rendered from the feedback the ship was receiving across the psychic connection with the webway.

'When we next have to manoeuvre, I'll let you practise,' promised Caolein.

Running his hand along the edge of the black console, feeling the slight thrum of the ship around him, Aradryan very much looked forward to that. A ship, guided by a single hand, capable of going anywhere in the galaxy... He looked at Caolein, who was grinning, and Aradryan found that he was smiling himself.

'Welcome to freedom, Aradryan.'

For several cycles, Aradryan immersed himself in the new routine of the ship. He picked fruit and cut down cereals in the bio-cabins, and learnt how to operate the cooking equipment in the galley. He spent a cycle tending to the freshwater system, marvelling at the miniscule fish that lived within the filtering pond and streams, feeding on contaminants.

At the end of each cycle, he would return to his bed chamber – or share Athelennil's – and would find sleep coming swiftly, brought about by a deep contentment. There was something therapeutic about fending for himself, of being himself and not a Dreamer or a Poet or an Artist; just Aradryan.

As time passed, Aradryan felt the harmony of ship-borne life soothing his concerns about mortality. There was no pressure here to prove himself, and he was no longer subjected to the overbearing presence of the infinity circuit. Alaitoc had a strong tradition of the Path, and since Aradryan had been born he had been lectured on its importance and his continual development. As an adolescent he had been drawn to the Path of Harmony, facilitating the callings of others. He had quickly bored of that, falling into the Path of the Dreamer, and when that had come to its abrupt end, it had been without thought or effort that he had changed to the Path of the Steersman. Now he was on no Path. He could do what he wanted, experience any emotions he wanted to feel, explore wherever his whim took him.

During a mid-cycle meal, Aradryan was in the company of Athelennil and Caolein, and he felt ready to confess his enthusiasm for the life of the outcast. He did not know his companions all that well, but in a way it did not matter; they had each experienced their own release and would understand how he felt.

Finishing his meal, Aradryan opened his mouth to say something but stopped. He had felt a shiver pass through his body: a faint tremble that set his teeth on edge. He had felt nothing like it before, and as he turned to Athelennil to ask the question he saw that she was already crossing the room, heading for the wraithbone interface terminal.

'You'll get used to it,' said Caolein, who saw Aradryan's confusion and continued to explain. 'You wouldn't have sensed it in something as big as *Lacontiran*, but here we're so close to the core, you can feel the pulse of the webway itself. It makes a joy out of flying, being there in the moment as we surge across from one web tunnel to the next, feeling the flow around you. Anyway, something's disturbing the webway, something quite significant.'

'It's bad,' said Athelennil, drawing her hand back from the terminal. 'Come feel for yourself.'

Caolein waved for Aradryan to precede him. Placing his fingertips onto the opalescent psychic node, Aradryan allowed his consciousness to touch upon the psychic core of *Irdiris*. As Caolein had warned, the ship was so much smaller, more compact then anything he had experienced before. The network upon *Lacontiran* had been interfacing with hundreds of spirits at any given moment, blocking out the background connection to the webway. Here the psychic network of the ship was flimsy, almost skittish in its spirit; agile and inquisitive.

Aradryan could feel where the boundaries of the warp and reality blurred, just beyond the rune gates and warding walls of the webway, bleeding into each other, forming the tunnels through which the eldar travelled. The network of the ship extended out into the void, psychically reaching for the webway material to find purchase; as a bird uses its wings to catch the breeze so *Irdiris* fastened on to the immaterial pulsing of the webway through its matrix.

The webway was rippling, recoiling strongly from sensations that emanated not far away. Sensations that filled Aradryan with a deep-seated dread.

All of this he took into himself in a moment, and before he could pull back he felt himself drawn along the webway, delving into the effect that had caused the ripple, iterated for him via the ship's psychic network.

He felt pain and loss, and his body spasmed at the magnitude of it. Thousands, hundreds of thousands, of spirits were in torment, their hurt and their misery sending shockwaves across the webway. The agony engulfed Aradryan, just for an instant, and he was witness to its cause.

Green-skinned beasts ravaged his body and slew his family. They crawled upon him like parasites, biting at his flesh, leaving welts and wounds in their wake. The towers of his cities toppled, falling into ruin, the bodies of the dead crushed beneath the white stone or hacked apart or burned on massive pyres that choked his air.

He was dying.

With a gasp, Aradryan pulled himself away from the node, his fingers tingling, mind reeling.

'Was that... Were they orks?' he said, his throat dry. Licking his lips, he looked at Athelennil. 'What was that?'

'That is the cry of an Exodite world spirit,' she said, a tear glistening in her eye. 'I know it well. Eileniliesh. The world is under attack.'

'Eileniliesh is only a few cycles from here,' said Caolein. 'Seven cycles at most.'

'We must speak to the others,' said Athelennil.

'We felt it,' said Lechthennian, standing at the doorway. He stepped through, Jair just behind.

'We have to help, don't we?' said Aradryan. 'I mean, we should, shouldn't we? If we're just seven cycles away?'

'It is not as simple as that,' said Jair. 'We are only five, we cannot turn an army of orks. That message was intended for Alaitoc, a cry for help. They will respond.'

'So what does that mean for us?' said Aradryan, turning his gaze from one companion to the next. 'We just ignore it?'

'No,' said Caolein. 'But we will have to meet with the others first, join forces with the crew of other ships.'

'What other ships?'

'There will be other outcasts adrift in the webway who will hear the distress of Eileniliesh and respond,' explained Jair. 'We will gather our strength and consult on the best course of action. But for you, I am afraid that means an early return.'

'A return to where?' said Aradryan, and then meaning dawned. 'The mustering, it will be on Alaitoc?'

'Yes,' said Athelennil, laying a hand on Aradryan's.

'I cannot go back, not so soon,' said Aradryan. 'I would look like a fool. No, I do not mean that.' A memory of the Exodite world spirit's message surged into his thoughts. 'Looking like a fool is nothing compared to the pain I felt in that call for aid. You have to go back to help, even if I cannot. I suppose I could just stay on the ship.'

'If that is what you wish,' said Lechthennian.

'We will be joining the ranger cadre,' said Athelennil, stepping away from Aradryan so that she was next to Jair. 'If you want to help the people of Eileniliesh, you might come with us.'

'Be a ranger?' Aradryan laughed. 'I know nothing of war or scoutcraft.'

'It was just an idea,' said Athelennil.

Aradryan could sense disapproval in the stance of the others, and knew that he was acting out of turn, but he could not see how he could help. Then he remembered Athelennil's earlier statement: everybody does what they have to for the needs of all. Aradryan sighed and smiled.

'Back to Alaitoc it is, I suppose,' he said. He looked at Jair and then Athelennil. 'Being a ranger, what does it entail?'

Behind the pilot's chamber a stairwell led down into the lower levels of *Irdiris*. With Athelennil leading the way into the hold area, Aradryan walked alongside Jair as the older eldar explained the principles of the ranger.

'It is the rangers that keep an eye out for threats to the craftworlds and Exodites,' said Jair. 'There is no duty, no oaths or vows, but we take it upon ourselves not to wholly abandon the rest of our kind. This attack, the ork invasion of Eileniliesh, is a call to arms.'

Aradryan was horrified by the idea of war and it must have shown in his face.

'I forget that you have never trodden the Path of the Warrior. I would say not to be afraid, but that is a lie. Fear is a great motivation that will help you to stay alive. Not all rangers confront the enemy directly, you do not have to fight if you do not wish. We will be consulting with the seers and autarchs of Alaitoc, to coordinate our efforts with those of the Aspect Warriors and fleet. What that might require, I cannot say, but if you stay by my side I will ensure you come to no harm.'

Aradryan was not sure Jair could guarantee his safety, not wholly, but he was reassured a little by the ranger's words.

'If I was to choose to fight,' Aradryan said quietly, 'how would that work? Where do we get weapons from?'

As if in answer, Athelennil stopped by one of the storage bay doors, which whispered open at her touch. Lights flickered into life, revealing the contents within.

The storage space was semicircular. Around the walls were hung coats and cloaks of curious design, each uniquely patterned with grey and white, matching the colour of the room. Beside each was a rifle, almost as long as Aradryan was tall, with a slender stock and complex sighting arrangement. There were shuriken pistols, long knives and slender swords also, holstered and scabbarded between the cloaks and coats. Knee-high boots, folded grey and black bodysuits and drab brown packbags were stowed on top of locker bins at the juncture of wall and floor, and hanging from the ceiling was more equipment: breathing masks and magnifying monocles; slender ropes and grapples; aquatic gear like artificial fins; furled airwings made of near-transparent thread.

Inscribed into the ceiling was an image of Kurnous, the Hunter God, once enemy of Khaine, consumed by She Who Thirsts like the rest of the ancient pantheon. Aradryan thought it a little superstitious to find such a picture here, celebrating a dead god, but said nothing.

'This is the gear of a ranger,' said Jair, waving a hand to encompass everything. 'Here is all that you need to survive, wherever we go, whatever we have to do.'

'I have never fired a gun nor swung a sword in my life,' said Aradryan. He stepped into the chamber and reached out, fingers stroking one of the cloaks. It shimmered, the cloth he touched taking on a pinkish hue to match his skin. 'So, this is cameleoline?'

'Yes,' said Athelennil. 'Do not be concerned about your military experience, or lack of it. It is irrelevant. The task of the ranger is to fight from a distance. We locate the enemy and guide the true warriors to their target. The longrifle is the preferred weapon. Remember that the foes we fight, be they orks, humans or whatever, are far less physically adept than we. With a little training you will be a match for their best marksmen, and your coat and cloak will hide you from retaliation.'

'I said I will keep you safe, and I will,' said Jair.

'It is not my life I fear for, only my sanity,' said Aradryan. 'I have never killed before, what if I cannot do it?'

'Whether you join us as a ranger or not, you will learn to kill,' said Jair. 'We will hunt for food, and you must slay what you wish to eat if you desire meat. The farm chambers can sustain us indefinitely, but you will grow bored eventually. That is when the fresh meat of a kill tastes the best! Life is but part of the cycle, and death its only end. You know this already.'

Aradryan accepted this with a silent nod. His hand moved from the coat to the rifle beside it. He picked it up, lifting the weapon from its hook. It was surprisingly light, easily hefted in one hand. Orange and red jewels set into the blister-like housing above the trigger glowed into life at his touch, and a faint purring signalled the energising of a powercell. Aradryan turned to Athelennil.

'Show me how it works,' he said.

* * *

The *Irdiris* was one of the first ranger ships to reach Alaitoc, having received the distress call from Eileniliesh not far from the craftworld. Jair and Athelennil were to meet with the ruling council of farseers and autarchs, who were no doubt already aware of the tumult coursing across the webway. Aradryan did not feel comfortable attending the meeting, and remained with Lechthennian and Caolein aboard the ship.

It was Caolein who convinced him to step out onto the craftworld again. The two of them sat on the couches of the common area, sipping iced juice.

'You left in pain, twice,' said the pilot.

'And why would I return to the source of that pain?'

'To rid the place of its power over you. You have a rare opportunity, Aradryan. The last time you departed Alaitoc, it was twenty passes before you returned and your friends had changed much. Now you have the chance, knowing that you have a chance for happiness, to see them and assure them you are well.'

'What if they do not care to see me?' said Aradryan, placing his goblet on the low table by his feet. 'The wound will reopen.'

'The wound may fester if not addressed,' replied Caolein. 'The worst that happens is that you come back to *Irdiris* without success. You do not have to see any of them ever again, and none aboard will think the less of you for the attempt.'

Thus reluctantly persuaded, Aradryan headed into Alaitoc once more, far sooner than he had expected. He did not trust himself to use the infinity circuit – and in a way did not wish to warn his former friends of his presence – and so he travelled directly to Thirianna's chambers. Here he was informed by the young family that now lived there that she had relocated, to quarters close to the Dome of Crystal Seers at the heart of the craftworld.

After making discreet inquiries, Aradryan located Thirianna's new abode and took a sky shuttle there. He stood outside the door for some time, summoning up the courage. When he was finally ready, though he did not know what he would say, the door detected his intent and signalled his presence with a long chime.

The door slid soundlessly open, revealing the main chamber of the apartment. Thirianna was standing in the middle of the room, putting something into a pouch at her belt.

'Aradryan!' she said, turning towards her visitor. 'This is unexpected.'

Not for the first time, Aradryan was aware that his appearance was somewhat irregular. Though he had not worn the cloak or coat, his ranger undersuit was a shifting pattern of holo-generated greens and blues, adopted from the sky and park beyond the balcony outside Thirianna's door.

'Hello, Thirianna,' said Aradryan, stepping into the apartment. He smiled and offered a palm in greeting. Thirianna laid her hand on his for a heartbeat, obviously nonplussed at his arrival. 'Sorry I could not warn you of my return.'

'I did not expect to see you again for much longer,' said Thirianna. She sat down and waved to a cushion for Aradryan to sit but he declined with a quick, single shake of the head.

'I cannot stay long,' he told her. In truth, just seeing her stirred up confusing emotions, and he was coming to the conclusion that Caolein had been wrong; this was a mistake. 'It seems my attempt to get far away from Alaitoc was destined to be thwarted. The *Irdiris* intercepted a transmission from Eileniliesh. It's an Exodite world that has been attacked by orks. We thought it wise to return to Alaitoc with the news.'

'Preparations are already under way for an expedition,' said Thirianna. 'Farseer Latheirin witnessed the impending attack several cycles ago.'

'Such is the way of farseers,' Aradryan said with a shrug. He laughed. 'Of course, you are becoming a seer now. Perhaps I should choose my words more carefully?'

'I do not take any offence,' replied Thirianna. 'They are an enigmatic group, that is sure. I have been around them for some time and I do not yet understand their ways.'

Aradryan did not know what else to say. He shifted his weight from one foot to the other and back again, unwilling to make small talk but uncertain of broaching any deeper subject.

'How have you fared?' Thirianna asked.

Aradryan shrugged again.

'There is not much yet to say,' he said. He gestured at his outfit. 'As you see, I have decided to join the rangers, but in truth I had not set foot off *Irdiris* before we had to return. On Eileniliesh we will fight the orks.'

'That would be unwise,' said Thirianna. 'You have never trodden the Path of the Warrior. You have no war-mask.'

'It is of no concern,' said Aradryan with a dismissive wave of the hand. 'My longrifle will keep me safe. It seems I have a natural talent for marksmanship.'

'It is not the physical danger that concerns me,' said Thirianna. She stood up and approached Aradryan. 'War corrupts us. The lure of Khaine can become irresistible.'

'There are many delights in the galaxy. Bloodshed is not one that appeals to me,' said Aradryan. He had expected his friend to be more supportive; it had been partly Thirianna's choices that had sent him from Alaitoc again. 'I never realised how blinkered you could be. You see the Path as the start and the end of existence. It is not.'

'It is,' said Thirianna. 'What you are doing, allowing your mind to run free, endangers not just you but those around you. You must show restraint. Korlandril, he has been touched by Khaine. His anger became too much.'

'He is an Aspect Warrior now?' said Aradryan, amused by the news. He could not suppress a laugh at the irony of the sculptor's last work being a testament to peaceful Isha whilst gripped by inner anger that had burst free. 'I did not realise my critique of his work was so harsh.'

Thirianna flicked her hair in annoyance, her fingertips pushing a stray lock behind one ear. Aradryan calmed himself, realising that he was the cause of her irritation.

'Why have you come here?' said Thirianna. 'What do you want from me?'

'Nothing,' said Aradryan. It seemed a self-centred question to ask. He had come to assure Thirianna that he was doing well, but she was clearly too involved with her new rune-casting to care about him. 'You made it very clear I should expect nothing from you. I came as a courtesy, nothing more. If I am not welcome, I shall leave.'

Weighing up her answer, Thirianna said nothing for a few moments, regarding Aradryan with a cool gaze. Her expression hardened.

'Yes, I think you should leave,' said Thirianna. Aradryan felt a stab of disappointment, anger even, but he nodded his acquiescence. Thirianna's harsh stare relented slightly. 'Please take care of yourself, Aradryan. I am pleased that you came to see me.'

Aradryan took a step towards the door, summarily dismissed, but Thirianna's last words fixed in his thoughts; she did care about him. Caolein had said that this was a second chance to part on better terms, but Aradryan had managed to squander the opportunity. Should he make amends, he thought? Did he need to tell her that he missed her?

'Goodbye,' he said, one hand on the edge of the open door. 'I do not expect us to meet again. Ever.'

Aradryan meant what he said. He wanted Thirianna to know that this was likely the last time she would see him. As a ranger he would travel far away, and he had no desire to come back. If he died, lost and forgotten on some distant world, he would be happy with such a fate.

'Goodbye,' Thirianna replied. 'Travel well and find contentment.'

With a sigh, Aradryan turned away and moved out of view. The door swished across the opening, and Aradryan headed along the balcony with a swift stride, annoyed with himself; for listening to Caolein and for letting Thirianna have the final say

As he was about to take the turn towards the stairwell, he heard Thirianna calling his name. His heart raced in his chest for a moment, but he kept his expression impassive as he turned to look over his shoulder at her.

'Please see Korlandril,' Thirianna called out to him. Aradryan nodded and raised a hand in acknowledgement. She was more concerned about Korlandril than him. So be it, thought Aradryan.

Perhaps it was egotism that prevented Aradryan returning directly to *Irdiris*; the thought of reporting his failure to Caolein nagged at him.

The encounter with Thirianna, while not an absolute disaster, had left Aradryan feeling a little raw and unable to face the questions Caolein would have for him if he came back without achieving at least some kind of understanding with his former friends. Also, he had promised, tacitly, to see Korlandril, and so to the ex-Sculptor's home Aradryan travelled next.

The door opened before Aradryan just in time to show Korlandril stepping into a side chamber. He waited for a moment, but there was no word of welcome, nor any call to leave.

'Things change again,' said Aradryan, calling out the first thing that came into his head in lieu of anything more profound. Korlandril stepped back into the main room, eyes widening with shock.

'Things change again,' agreed Korlandril. He stared at Aradryan for some time before gesturing for his guest to seat himself. The ranger declined with a slight shake of the head.

'I have come out of courtesy to the friendship we once shared,' said Aradryan. 'I thought it wrong to come back to Alaitoc and not see you.'

'I am glad that you have come,' said Korlandril. 'I owe you an apology for my behaviour the last time we met.'

Aradryan was taken aback by this outright confession. Of Thirianna and Korlandril, it was the latter Aradryan considered he had wronged the deepest, but his dreaming partner seemed sincere in his sorrow.

'It was never the case that we wronged each other intentionally,' replied Aradryan, feeling that he needed to meet honesty with honesty, 'and neither of us owes the other anything but respect.'

'I trust your travels have been fruitful?'

Aradryan smiled and nodded. And lied.

'I cannot describe the sights I have seen, the thrill of adventure that has coursed through my veins. The galaxy has been set out before me and I have experienced such a tiny fraction of the delights and darkness it has to offer.'

'I too have been on a journey,' said Korlandril, cleaning his hands with a cloth.

'I have heard this,' said Aradryan. Korlandril looked at him and raised his eyebrows in question. Aradryan was not quite sure how to bring up Korlandril's change of Path, and chose his words carefully. 'Thirianna. I met with her first. She told me that you are now an Aspect Warrior.'

'A Striking Scorpion of the Deadly Shadow shrine,' said Korlandril. He delicately rinsed his hands and dried them under a warm vent above the sink. 'It does not anger me that you saw Thirianna first. My parting from her is an event of the past, one with which I have wholly come to terms.'

Aradryan's eyes swept the living quarters, taking in the Isha statues arranged around the room. Each of them wore the face of Thirianna, or close representations of the same. Aradryan smiled and darted a doubtful look at Korlandril.

'Well, perhaps not *wholly*,' the warrior admitted with a short laugh. 'But I truly bear you no ill-will concerning your part, unwitting as it was, in the circumstances that engulfed me.'

'Have you seen her recently?'

Korlandril shook his head.

'It would serve no purpose. If I happen to cross her path, it will be well, but it is not my place to seek her company at this time. She and I travel to different places, and we make our own journeys.'

'Someone else?' suggested Aradryan.

Korlandril seemed confused for a moment, and then his lips parted silently in an expression of realisation.

'Aha!' laughed Aradryan.

'It is not like that,' Korlandril said hurriedly. 'She is a fellow warrior at the shrine, it would be entirely inappropriate for us to engage in any deeper relationship.'

Aradryan was aware of no such convention amongst Aspect Warriors and allowed Korlandril to see his doubt rather than say anything out loud. The two of them stood in silence, comfortable if not pleasant, before Aradryan realised that as a Striking Scorpion, Korlandril would be bound for Eileniliesh too. 'I have also come to give you advance warning that you will be shortly called to your shrine.'

'How might you know this?' asked Korlandril, frowning fiercely. 'Have you spoken to Kenainath?'

'I would not tread foot in an Aspect shrine! And your exarch does not venture forth. No, it is from first-hand knowledge that I am aware of this. I have just returned from Eileniliesh. It is an Exodite world not so far away. Orks have come to Eileniliesh and her people call on Alaitoc for help. I have come back as their messenger. Even now the autarchs and farseers debate the best course of action. There is no doubt in my mind that they will issue the call to war.'

'And I will be ready to answer it,' said Korlandril. At the mention of war, his whole posture had changed. His eyes had become hard as flint, his jaw set. It unsettled Aradryan, who had last seen that look just before Korlandril's outburst at the unveiling. The ranger thought it better to depart before the good grounds he had established with his friend were destroyed by some chance remark or perceived difference.

'I have my own preparations to make,' said Aradryan, taking a step towards the door. 'Other rangers are gathering here to share what they know of the enemy. I must join them.'

Korlandril nodded his understanding. Aradryan was at the door before Korlandril spoke again.

'I am glad that you are alive and well, my friend,' said the warrior, sincerity in every word.

'As am I of you, Korlandril.' Aradryan replied out of instinct but realised he meant it. The bonds of dreaming-partner went deep, deeper than ordinary friendship, and Korlandril had once meant a great deal to him. 'I do not know if I will see you on Eileniliesh or before we leave. If not, then I wish you good fortune and prosperity until our next meeting.'

'Good fortune and prosperity,' echoed Korlandril.

Aradryan stepped out of the apartment with a lighter step than he had entered. As the iris-door closed behind him, the ranger took a deep breath. Alaitoc would be in his past now. He would discover what the future held at Eileniliesh.

DISCOVERY

The Maze of Linnian – In the ancient days before Ulthanesh and Eldanesh were sundered from each other and Khaine wreaked his bloody vengeance during the War in Heaven, Eldanesh looked to the protection of his people while Ulthanesh turned his gaze out to the wider world. Intrigued, Ulthanesh left the house of his family and searched far and wide in the wilderness. It was slow work, though, for the winds were strong and the terrain harsh. Seeking shelter one night on the slopes of Mount Linnian, Ulthanesh came upon a golden gateway in a cave. At first he was afraid, and he left the cave, daring the cold twilight. The next night he came upon another golden gateway, behind a magnificent waterfall. Still Ulthanesh was too afraid to pass the portal. On the third night, when he saw a glimmering gateway atop a distant hill, Ulthanesh resolved to himself that he would not be frightened any more. He passed through the gateway, and found himself in another place: the Maze of Linnian. The labyrinth stretched across the world, above and beneath it, with many turning passages and dead-ends to frustrate Ulthanesh. There were hidden chambers where monsters and other perils awaited, and mighty were Ulthanesh's deeds to overcome these foes and obstacles. All was worthwhile, for the Maze of Linnian brought Ulthanesh unto glorious highlands and fertile hills, spanned the stars with rainbow bridges and delved into the sparkling depths beneath the world of the eldar. In time, Ulthanesh returned to the house of his family and gathered his followers. Now

*that he knew they were there, Ulthanesh saw the gleam of the golden
gates everywhere, and with his sons and grandsons he explored their
secrets.*

Overhead, the sun was hot, sending steam rising from the primordial forest. It was a real sun, and its real heat also touched the skin of Aradryan as he stepped from the docking ramp onto the soil of a real world. The first planet he had set foot on in his long life. He had been raised on Alaitoc and during his travels aboard *Lacontiran* he had never left the starship. As his boot sunk a little into the mud, he wondered why he had never done this before.

The wind tugged at his coat, his garments shifting to brown and green to blend with the surroundings, and it occurred to Aradryan that this wind was not generated by some hidden vent or artificially stirred by climatic engines, but the result of impossibly complex pressure and temperature interactions in the atmosphere of Eileniliesh. Far to his left, a dark smudge on the horizon could have been smoke, or perhaps storm clouds.

Covering his eyes against the glare of the sun, which on second consideration he decided would benefit greatly from being dimmed a little, Aradryan thought about the sky. There was no dome to hold it in place. The mass of the world and the physics of gravity bound the atmosphere to the planet, with no force shields required. It was a magnificent thing, and listening to the squeal and screech of birds – really, truly *wild* birds – sent a thrill through him.

'Ex-dreamers,' muttered Jair as he walked past. 'Always with their heads in the clouds.'

Aradryan turned to respond, but his harsh answer died in his throat as he saw the smile on the other ranger's face.

'I once actually had my head in a cloud,' Aradryan said, shifting the rifle slung over his shoulder into a more comfortable position. 'It was on the skybridge above the Gorge of Deep Regrets.'

'Fascinating,' said Jair. He pointed to a slender tower not far ahead, rising above the canopy of the trees surrounding the clearing where Caolein had set down *Irdiris*. The Exodite building was a light grey spear thrust into the indigo sky, widening to a disc-like platform pierced by arched windows not far below its narrow summit. The deep blue leaves of the forest fluttered in the wind around its base, showing their silvery undersides, their whisper drifting to Aradryan's ears.

'This is where we were told to meet the others?' said Aradryan.

'The Exodite elders will be speaking to all of the rangers in the first wave,' replied Jair.

'And when will Athelennil and the others arrive?'

The two of them started walking, passing into the shade of the immense trees. Having visited Eileniliesh before, Athelennil was amongst the outcasts who had remained with the craftworld army, to act as guides to the Aspect Warriors and seers. Aradryan missed her already, though Jair was proving to be a witty and informative companion.

'Tonight, I expect,' said Jair. 'The Alaitocii battleships are not so swift as our ranger craft, and the autarchs deemed a night attack to be the best course of action.'

'I am still not sure what I will be able to do,' said Aradryan. The soft mulch of leaves gave way slightly under his light tread and the not-unpleasant fragrance of gently rotting leaves surrounded him. It was autumn here, due to the planet's position in its orbit around the star and its particular axial tilt. Within the controlled climate of Alaitoc, seasons were a matter of whim or design, winter snows a marvel to be conjured up and then disposed of once the entertainment they provided grew wearisome.

'We have to find out where the orks are, and if they are on the move,' said Jair.

'How do they cope?' Aradryan asked. 'The Exodites, I mean.'

'Cope with what?'

'The randomness of their world,' explained Aradryan. 'A storm could sweep away their crops, or an earthquake could topple their towers and swallow their cities. How do they endure such unpredictability?'

'Some would say it is stubbornness,' said Jair. 'I think it is more deep-rooted than that. Once, before the Fall, our people commanded the stars and worlds were shaped to our whim. Like Alaitoc, there was nothing that we did not control. It was that laziness that allowed our bane to whisper in our ears, spreading the moral decline that brought about the Fall. The Exodites will never again trust themselves to be masters of their surrounds. Its capricious ways, the untamed weather and the vacillations of tectonic and volcanic activity, humble them and stave off the risk of idleness and ultimately a return to depravity.'

'A slightly masochistic temperament, by the sounds of it,' said Aradryan. They had come to another clearing, the solitary tower soaring into the sky above them, tall doorways open at its base. 'Why did they not simply adopt the Path as the craftworlds did?'

'You, who walk here as an outcast, ask that question?' Jair's laugh was of incredulity. 'The Exodites see the Path as a trap – an illusory control that masks an inner darkness. They think that there is purity in their hard lives, and that only constant denial of their emotions will eventually set them free from the taint of... Well, you know.'

'The Great Enemy? She Who Thirsts? The Prince of Pleasure? We both know to what you refer, why so suddenly coy?'

'Even those names are best left unsaid, Aradryan,' said Jair, stopping to take hold of his arm. 'You are not behind the wards of Alaitoc, protected by the warp spiders and barriers of the infinity circuit. It is not wise to tempt the gaze of that power, especially in jest.'

Aradryan was suddenly scared by Jair's earnest warning and stepped back, pulling his arm free. For a brief heartbeat he thought his waystone glowed a little brighter in its golden setting, a moment of warmth touching his chest. It was probably imagined, but Aradryan glanced around nonetheless, disturbed by the sensation.

'The trees are glowing!' he exclaimed, thoughts of the Great Enemy dispersed by this sudden revelation.

It was perhaps an overstatement, but there was a light from the trees around the tower, an aura strongest at the roots, gleaming between the folds of the bark, glimmering along the serrated edges of leaves. Now that his attention was drawn to it, Aradryan noticed the faint light elsewhere, similar to the silver glow that came from the uppermost storeys of the tower. Crossing to one of the trees, Aradryan knelt down and examined its roots. There was a miniscule vein of crystal running along the wood.

'Careful, that is the world spirit,' Jair said when he noticed what Aradryan was doing. 'This tower must be some kind of node point, where the crystal matrix is close to the surface.'

'And it delves into the ground, going deeper?'

'A world spirit makes the infinity circuit of Alaitoc look small,' said Jair, crouching to run his hand through the dirt. 'It stretches across the whole planet, seeping into the cracks between rocks, like the rootlets of a plant.'

Concentrating, Aradryan tried to feel the presence of the world spirit, as he would a ship network on the infinity circuit. He felt nothing, expect perhaps the slightest background awareness. Closing his eyes, he tried to home in on the spirit, opening his thoughts to it, but there was nothing to hear but the sighing of the wind. Aradryan remembered the moment of contact he had felt aboard *Irdiris*, but that shared experience created no connection here.

'A matrix that size, that could send that message across the webway, must be powerful indeed, but I cannot sense it at all,' he said, opening his eyes.

'The world spirit is vast in size, but its potency is exceptionally diffuse,' said Jair. He motioned that they should continue across the glade to the tower. 'Originally, perhaps less than a thousand Exodites fled to this world. Even after generations, the energy that has been stored within from their dying spirits is a fraction of the millions of spirits contained by Alaitoc. Like all Exodite creations, it is a basic, rudimentary thing, which serves its purpose as a sanctuary for their departing spirits but nothing more.'

A figure, clothed in red and white, appeared at an archway ahead. Her hair reached to her knees, braided tightly and tied with plain thongs. A belt of reptilian hide held the eldar's robes in place. In her right hand she carried a staff of knotted, twisted wood, its top entwined about an irregularly-shaped green crystal.

'Well met, visitors,' said the stranger, opening her free hand in greeting.

'Well met, host,' replied Jair with a formal bow of his head. Aradryan copied his companion, keeping his eyes on the figure. 'Are you Saryengith?'

'I am Rijaliss Saryengith Naiad, the Pandita of Hirith-Hreslain. Please, come inside and join the others.'

Saryengith spent some time explaining what had happened to the seventeen rangers who had arrived ahead of the Alaitoc fleet. The orks had come to the maiden world thirty cycles before – Aradryan had a strange thought that the length of the cycles here were as fixed as the seasons – and while Alaitoc and the outcasts had readied their response, the settlement of Hirith-Hreslain had been overrun.

The Exodites of Eileniliesh were few in number, and not disposed to conflict. What armaments they possessed, and the warriors capable of wielding them, were sufficient to keep at bay carnosaurs and razordons that menaced their herds, but the orks had crashed down onto the planet with bikes and buggies, cannons and tanks: a horde of battle-hungry beasts bred for battle in an age long past.

Hirith-Hreslain had been invaded four cycles ago, and though Saryengith and her fellow elders had evacuated the town before the wrath of the orks had fallen upon it, there had been many of the warrior sects too stubborn to retreat. They had been slaughtered defending the town, rather than waiting the extra time for reinforcements to arrive from other settlements and nearby Alaitoc. From what little the scouts of the Exodites had seen, the orks were keeping themselves occupied and amused by looting and smashing up the ancient buildings; there were guarded whispers that some of the Exodite knights had been taken alive too. No party had been sent in the last cycle, though, so whether the orks had tired of their sport and started another rampage into the forest or not, was not known. What little that could be gleaned from the pain of the world spirit indicated the orks were still in Hirith-Hreslain in some numbers, but it was impossible to say if they had split their force.

Hirith-Hreslain was a paired-town located on a wide river, Hresh on one side of a connecting bridge, Selain on the other. After a quarter of a cycle with Saryengith and her scouts, discussing the best approach to the overrun town, it was down this water course that the rangers ventured, split into three bands. Dusk was some time away still, they had been assured, leaving them plenty of opportunity to reach Hirith-Hreslain and return.

Running effortlessly along the river path, Aradryan and the rest of his group covered the distance quickly. Though he enjoyed stretching his legs and the openness of the limitless sky above, the trek seemed a little pointless to him.

'Why do we not just take *Irdiris* and fly to Hirith-Hreslain?' he asked

Naomilith, a female ranger who was running beside him to the right. 'Or one of the other ships, perhaps?'

'It is best that the enemy remain ignorant of our presence,' replied Naomilith. 'They must have arrived by starship, and so if we wish to destroy them we should give them no cause to return to their vessel.'

'How long have you been a ranger?' Aradryan asked. He glanced at Naomilith, admiring the way the shade and light of the tree branches overhead played across the delicate features of her face.

'Long enough to know when to keep quiet,' she replied with a cold smile.

Silenced by this retort, Aradryan ran on. Ahead, the smudge he had thought might be a storm cloud was revealed to be a column of smoke; several smaller columns in fact, merging into one cloud that lingered over the burning forest. They approached from upwind, and so the smell of the burning was absent, but the sight filled Aradryan with foreboding. It was obvious that Hirith-Hreslain had been set ablaze, and he was not sure how he would cope with the evidence of such destruction. What if he saw bodies? Would he be rendered almost incapable, as he had been all that time ago, before he had left aboard *Lacontiran*?

His apprehension increased as they neared the settlement. The roar of crude fossil fuel engines and raucous shouts and laughter announced from a distance that the orks had not left the town.

'That's that question answered,' Aradryan said to Naomilith. 'We can report now, yes?'

He was only half-joking, but the withering stare from Naomilith silenced further comment before it was made. A whistle from across the river attracted the attention of the rangers, and Aradryan looked over the waters to his left and saw another group beneath the eaves of the forest on the far side. He raised a hand in greeting, just as the communicator he wore as a piercing in his right ear tingled into life.

'Gahian is leading the third group around to the left, to come upon Hirith-Hreslain from the opposite direction,' reported Khannihain, the most experienced ranger in the group upon the far bank. 'I suggest that you move away from the river to explore the remnants of Selain, while we go into Hresh.'

All of the rangers had heard Khannihain's words and they looked at each other, seeking consensus.

'Seems a reasonable plan to me,' said Jair.

'I concur,' said Lithalian, from just behind Aradryan.

'Are there any objections?' asked Naomilith. She looked at the rangers in turn, each shaking his or her head, until Naomilith's gaze fell upon Aradryan.

'How would I know whether it is a good plan or not?' Aradryan said with a quiet, self-conscious laugh.

'Your voice is equal,' said Naomilith, 'despite your lack of experience.'

'What if I do not like this plan?' said Aradryan, bemused by the situation.

'If you have a counter-proposal, let us hear it,' said Jair, impatiently. 'If not, you are free to come with us or leave and follow your own course.'

'That does not sound sensible, I think I will stay with you.'

'So you are in agreement with Khannihain's suggestions? You will come with us into Selain?' said Naomilith.

'If that is what Jair or Khannihain say we should do.'

Naomilith let out a short hiss and shook her head in exasperation. She stalked away from Aradryan and whispered something to Jair as she passed. The older ranger approached Aradryan.

'I hope that you genuinely do not understand the proposition, and our situation,' said Jair, talking softly as he placed a hand on the younger eldar's shoulder and led Aradryan a short distance from the others. 'Naomilith wants to be sure that you are acting of your own will.'

'So I could really just leave now and do whatever I want?' said Aradryan.

'We hope you would not pursue a course of action that would endanger the rest of us,' said Jair. The other eldar frowned with thought as Aradryan stared blankly at him, still not quite comprehending why the others were so agitated about getting his approval. 'Let me see if I can make you understand. To be outcast is to make a choice, and to continue making choices without the guidance or the restraints of the Path. We are each free – free in a way that perhaps you still do not picture. We are free from everything. We are free from hierarchy, from any authority we do not choose for ourselves, free from orders and doctrine. Every spirit is equal as an outcast, there can be no coercion or subjugation.'

'Why is there such a delay? What are you discussing?' Khannihain asked over the communicator.

'I am sorry for the misunderstanding,' said Aradryan. He touched a finger to the ring at his ear, so that he could transmit. 'We are in accord with you, Khannihain. Explore Hresh while we see what there is to find in Selain.'

'Very well, it is advisable to reconvene here at dusk,' said Khannihain.

There came a chorus of affirmatives from the other rangers, and Aradryan added his own consent to the replies.

'Ready your weapon,' said Jair, turning away. 'We will be getting close to the orks.'

His fingers trembling just a little at this thought, Aradryan slung the rifle from his shoulder and carried it in both hands. The wind was turning and he tasted ash on the air, reminding him of the slaughter that the orks had already perpetrated. Licking his lips, which had become quite dry in the last few moments, he glanced around and then headed after the other rangers, whose coats were quickly disappearing into the scrub ahead.

* * *

The river curved sharply, and as Aradryan's group rounded the bend, the settlement of Hirith-Hreslain came into view. The town spread from both river banks, linked by a long bridge. On the far bank, the part known as Hresh rose up as a group of towers and elevated walkways from amongst the trees themselves. Selain was more open, and the buildings generally of fewer storeys.

Even from this distance the destruction wrought by the orks was plain to see. Some of the white buildings were marked with soot and burn marks, their shattered windows reflecting low flames still burning in the settlement. Smoke choked the air.

A splash drew Aradryan's attention to the river. Something long and grey, like a giant finned eel, slid through the water just below the surface. There were other things in the water too: corpses. The dead of Hirith-Hreslain floated amongst the reeds, bodies bobbing on the gentle waves.

Aradryan wanted to look away, but he could not. Morbidly, he watched as the river beast rose to the surface, jaws opening to reveal rows of small serrated teeth. It clamped around the arm of a floating corpse and turned, plunging into the water to drag its meal into the murky depths.

Hissing his breath through gritted teeth, Aradryan looked along the river towards the bridge. He could not tell how many dead eldar were in the water, but there were a lot of them. Many were caught in the foam that broke against the piles of the span, turning over and around in the current.

Disgust welled up in the ranger, tainted with anger. It was the first time he had felt such deep revulsion, not of the dead but of their killers. The orks were still in the settlement, their raucous cries and guttural laughter easy to hear on the light breeze.

'Careful,' said Jair, laying a hand on Aradryan's wrist.

Aradryan realised that he had slipped his finger into the trigger guard, his grip on the longrifle tight. Noticing the alarm in Jair's eyes, Aradryan relaxed his fingers and nodded.

'Later,' said Jair. 'Later the orks will be punished for what they have done.'

The group moved on, slipping from the waterside into the forest surrounding Selain. They came upon an outbuilding, its windows and red-tiled roof still intact though the wooden doors had been broken in. Stealing inside, the rangers found the place had been ransacked. It was bare save for a few broken pieces of furniture and scattered shards of pottery.

Aradryan was intrigued by the construction of the building. He ran his hand over the walls, and could feel the slight joins between large blocks.

'What is it made of?' he asked.

'Stone,' said Jair, confused by the obvious question.

'Yes, but what type? Ghost stone? Firestone? W–'

'Stone, from the ground,' snapped Naomilith. 'Blocks quarried and shaped and assembled. The Exodites fashion all of their settlements in the traditional ways.'

'Would it not be easier to grow their structures, as we do on the craftworlds?'

'I refer you to our earlier conversation,' said Jair. 'The Exodites eschew the easy path, especially those deeds we accomplish with our psychic abilities. They work with the physical, the labour of their works occupying their minds and keeping them from the temptations of flesh and spirit.'

'We waste time,' said Caloth, who was about the same age as Aradryan, though she had been a ranger for nearly two passes. A scar ran from the side of her nose to her right ear, a disturbing affectation that could have easily been remedied in any craftworld's Halls of Healing. 'We should enter Selain proper so that we can assess the strength of the enemy.'

That sounded like a dangerous prospect, but Aradryan kept his thoughts to himself, fearing more scorn from Naomilith, who had no qualms about displaying her dislike of him.

Reaching the outskirts of the town proved to be easy; the orks had set no patrols or sentries to guard against observation. In fact, the greenskins seemed wholly unconcerned by the possibility of attack. Aradryan thought that perhaps the aliens considered the eldar defeated, or perhaps too cowardly to return to their sacked town. If so, their error of judgement would be bloodily corrected that coming night.

'We should split into pairs,' suggested Jair. 'I will go with Aradryan, and head in the direction of the river.'

This received assent from the others, and the six rangers divided, heading in different directions to investigate the situation in Selain. Aradryan was happy to go with Jair, who had at least shown some patience with his questions and inexperience.

'I know that I said we have no leaders, and no hierarchy, but please do what I tell you,' said Jair as they cut through the trees towards a tower on the edge of the main clearing. 'I would rather we were not discovered.'

'Have no fear, I shall follow in your footsteps and do exactly as you bid,' replied Aradryan.

The sun was still some time from setting, but the shadows were lengthening. Jair and Aradryan flitted from the trees into the shade of an arched doorway. Aradryan tried the door but it was barred from the inside. A shattered window further along the wall provided ingress and the two rangers slipped over the sill. Inside was much like the first building. They ascended quickly to the top of the tower, coming to a bedchamber where blood had been daubed on the walls and spilled in sticky pools on the bare boards of the floor.

Ignoring the smell, Aradryan followed Jair as he stepped through the broken remnants of the windows onto a balcony. They crouched at the ledge and peered over, but could see little beyond the surrounding towers. Judging by the clamour of the orks – harsh shouts and the revving of combustion engines – the majority of the aliens were somewhere in the heart of the settlement.

They crept through the streets, heading in the direction of the river, occasionally searching the buildings they passed. They found no bodies, which worried Aradryan, and caused a thought to cross his mind.

'Do you think they have taken prisoners?' he asked. 'Should we try to rescue them if we find them?'

'I do not think they have prisoners,' Jair replied with a grim expression.

'How can you tell?'

'I do not hear any screams.'

With a shudder, Aradryan continued after Jair, who was moving more swiftly. The streets grew narrower and the buildings to either side were linked by skybridges and walkways in their upper levels. Once or twice Jair froze in place and Aradryan did likewise, pressing against the smooth walls as a brutish, hunched figure or two would pass along one of these aerial paths.

When they next paused, Aradryan could hear the gurgle of the river in the distance, even through the increasing noise of the ork occupiers. Jair signalled for Aradryan to join him where a high wall turned sharply around the edge of a garden. From here, the rangers could see into the open space at the centre of the town: a plaza that opened out from one end of the bridge.

'We need to go up,' said Jair, jabbing a thumb skywards.

The other ranger surprised Aradryan when he leapt onto the wall, pulling himself up to its top. With a glance back at Aradryan, Jair then sidled along the wall to the building adjoining it. Another jump and lift took him onto the small roof of a jutting turret. Aradryan realised he was meant to follow. Ensuring that his rifle was properly on his shoulder, he repeated Jair's actions, finding the climb easier than he had imagined.

From the turret roof, they leapt across an alley to a deserted balcony opposite. Checking inside, they found the room within empty. From there, they located a staircase winding up to a roof terrace at the summit of the tower. There was a pool at the centre of the garden, an arm floating amongst the lily pads, nibbled by the black-and-white fish. Putting this to the back of his mind, where all manner of unpleasant images were now hidden, Aradryan scurried across to the walled lip of the terrace. It was not very high, forcing the two rangers to sink to their bellies and slink along like serpents.

The plaza stretched below them, a massive pyre at its centre. On huge tripods and spits, chunks of a megasaur roasted noisily. The huge reptilian creatures were the staple herd of the Exodites, kept both to feed the local eldar and to trade with the craftworlds in exchange for goods and devices they could not manufacture themselves. Tatters of its scaled hide were being used as awnings on several of the ork vehicles, and covered a rough enclosure at one end of the plaza.

Around the fires the orks clustered, some of them exceptionally large, easily half again as tall as an eldar. Smaller orks lounged further from the centre. All were being attended to by a swarm of little creatures with pinched faces, large ears and shrieking voices. The servant aliens lugged crates and sacks, brought food and polished guns and boots. They were subjected to a constant barrage of growls, shouts and fists, and seemed equally eager to squabble amongst themselves as they were to see to their larger cousins' needs.

Disgust welled up inside Aradryan, masking the fear he had felt since entering the settlement. From birth he had been taught about the barbarous greenskins – worst amongst all of the lesser races – but to confront their nature personally was an affront to everything he was as an eldar. He listened to their crudes barks, grunts and howls, and knew that such a language could never conceive of the higher philosophies of life; it was a language for commands and subjugation and nothing more. That they destroyed what they did not desire, and desired little except war, was evidence of their base nature.

In an instant it was easy to understand the orks and their society. The larger creatures bullied the smaller, which bullied the even smaller. In just one glance at the plaza, Aradryan saw this social system played out a dozen times, will enforced by physical brutality and nothing else. There was cunning here, he knew from old tales, but no intellect. Though the orks walked on two legs and constructed vehicles and guns, that did not hide the fact that they were beasts in heart and mind.

Appalled at what the unthinking brutes had done to the settlement of the Exodites, Aradryan brought his rifle from his shoulder. He had never wanted to kill anything before – out of anger or sport – but deep down he knew there was no way to negotiate with the orks, or wait for them to pass on and rebuild. Unlike other natural cataclysms, the arrival of the orks could only be stopped with one means – to meet violence with a greater, more directed violence. Aradryan knew that he should not take pleasure in a cull, any more than one took pleasure in a firegull eating sandgrubs, but he could not stop feeling that an injustice needed to be addressed.

And there would be vengeance. It was not enough that the ork invaders were slain. Bitter experience had taught the eldar in times past that the greatest menace of an ork invasion was not the warriors. Orks alive or dead shed spores to breed and once these spores had a grip on a world, especially a young, burgeoning planet like Eileniliesh, they were almost impossible to root out. The only way to be rid of the green beasts was swift and utter annihilation. So it was that Alaitoc had mustered what strength it could and even the Avatar had roused itself from its dormancy to bring battle to Hirith-Hreslain. If just one ork was to escape into the forests, a few short orbits from now Eileniliesh might be overrun by a new green horde and be lost forever. The autarchs and farseers had not responded to make battle with the orks, for orks thrived on war as other creatures thrive on food and drink; the Alaitocii had come to exterminate them.

'Look over there,' said Jair. He had removed the sighting array from his rifle and was using it as a telescope. Aradryan followed suit and turned his gaze across the plaza in the direction his companion had indicated.

The buildings were in a far more ruinous state here, in the direction away from the river and away from the sunset. Many had collapsed, whether from bombardment or deliberate demolition he could not say. Rubble choked some of the streets and broken roof tiles, cracked balustrades and toppled walls littered the town. It was not this that Jair had noticed, though.

In the gardens of one of the towers were several crude-looking cannons, hidden in the shadow of a porch roof. They were crewed by the smaller greenskins under the watchful eye of an ork with a cruelly barbed whip, the former stacking shells against the garden wall; a lot of shells.

Aradryan remembered that he was not just here for his own edification. Using the gunsight, he scanned the surrounding streets and buildings, noting where barricades had been built and guns emplaced. There was some kind of vehicle pool at the far end of the plaza, and he set about counting up the buggies, open-backed trucks, large battlewagons and half-tracked bikes he could see.

Under the direction of Jair, he examined the defences on the bridge. This did not take long, as there were none that he could see. He also cast his gaze along the river banks, but this also revealed that the orks were taking no particular precaution to guard themselves against attack from along the waterway.

When they had seen all there was to be seen from their vantage point, Jair signalled for Aradryan to lead the way back down to the lower levels. This time they took one of the skybridges across the street to the next tower, moving from the shadow of one column to the next so as not to be seen from below.

They descended to street level, but had taken no more than a few strides from the door when Jair suddenly stepped back, moving against the wall. The sun was quite low by now, and the long shadows of a group of the smaller greenskins appeared at the end of the alley.

Though they were diminutive, no taller than Aradryan's waist, the ranger felt a sudden panic gripping him at the thought of confrontation. They may be small, he thought, but they had vicious claws and fangs, and were used to fighting. He noticed that Jair had slipped his knife from his belt and unholstered his shuriken pistol; Aradryan had forgotten he carried such weapons.

The instinct to run tried to sweep away Aradryan's rational thoughts and his breaths became short and shallow as his body responded to the imminent threat. Jair must have detected something of his dread, for the other ranger turned around with a concerned expression and raised a finger to his lips.

Trying to remain calm, Aradryan pushed himself back against the wall as the shadows crept closer.

He could hear a smattering of high-pitched conversation growing louder. He couldn't move as the patter of bare feet on the paving stones came closer and closer, yet at the same time his brain was screaming at him that if he did not turn and run now it would be too late. Locked in stasis between the instinct to fight or flee, Aradryan gritted his teeth, his hands making fists at his sides.

Aradryan could smell them now, filthy and pungent. There was blood and smoke and rotting meat on the air, and he could imagine dirt-encrusted nails scratching at his flesh while jagged teeth sawed through his skin. His gut writhed at the thought, cramping painfully, but he kept his lips clamped shut despite the sudden ache in his stomach.

The greenskins came into view, four of them. They had beady red eyes. Their ragged ears and bulbous noses were pierced with studs and rings. Two wore nothing more than stained loincloths, the other two, ever so slightly larger, wore jerkins and boots of untreated animal hide, which added to their stink. One of them had a revolver-style pistol thrust into its rope belt, the others carried sharpened metal spikes to serve as daggers.

It was impossible to discern what they were saying, or to guess their mood from their nasal whining. They jostled each other and snarled, paying no attention to what was around them. Glancing to his left, Aradryan saw that Jair had his hood pulled across his face, his cloak drawn close about him. Moving gradually, Aradryan copied his companion, swathing himself with the cameleoline material.

Almost within arm's reach, the small goblin-like creatures walked past, oblivious to the presence of the two rangers. Aradryan dared not to breathe lest his gasps be heard, though the greenskins patrol, for such he guessed it to be, was making more than enough noise with its chattering to mask any such sound.

Then they turned out of sight, heading into a street that led back to the plaza. Aradryan almost collapsed with relief.

'Let's go,' hissed Jair, gesturing with his knife. 'We'll head back via the river.'

For a moment, Aradryan could not walk. He sank to his haunches, back against the wall, and took several deep breaths, eyes closed.

It was hard for him to believe that he was still alive. Aradryan chuckled, the sound coming unbidden from deep within him. The relief was so profound that he had to laugh to let it out.

Jair appeared over him, scowling. The other ranger grabbed Aradryan's coat and dragged him to his feet, clamping a hand over his mouth as more laughter threatened to erupt from his lungs.

'Control yourself,' Jair whispered. 'Remember where we are.'

Aradryan could not help it; his body was shaking, his mind overflowing with gratitude at still being alive.

'I will abandon you here, if you do not calm yourself,' warned Jair, stepping away.

The thought of being left alone in this ork-infested town sobered Aradryan immediately. He opened his mouth to say sorry, but Jair cut him off with a swipe of his hand.

'Apologise later,' said the ranger. He pointed to the sky, which was streaked red and purple by the dusk sun. 'We must regroup with the others.'

The forest took on a different air as night fell. Swooping winged beasts with long, toothed beaks screeched from the treetops. The roar of predatory carnosaurs broke the still night and the wind in the trees sounded like the whisper of dead gods as Aradryan waited in the darkness.

The sky glimpsed between the swaying canopy looked like brushed steel, the stars hidden by cloud and the smog of Hirith-Hreslain burning. The moons, of which two were currently creeping over the horizon, lit everything with a bluish gleam.

The other rangers had headed back into Hirith-Hreslain, to place webway beacons for the waiting fleet to fix on to. On the frigates and battleships waiting off-world, wayseers would detect these hidden markers and delve temporary passages into the heart of the town, allowing some of Alaitoc's warriors to attack from within the ork force.

Jair would signal to Aradryan when it was time for him to enter the town and assist in the attack with his longrifle. Alone in a small dell where the river was a half-seen silver sliver through the trees, the ranger considered his extreme reaction earlier in the day.

He was embarrassed by it now, but at the time he had been so certain of being discovered, and his subsequent butchery at the hands of the orks, that it had seemed miraculous to survive. Now it seemed so stupid, viewed with the benefit of hindsight. Had the greenskin sentries located them, there would have been ample opportunity to escape, even if Aradryan and Jair had been incapable of slaying them. The small creatures would have had no chance of keeping pace, and any resultant hue and cry would have been left far behind by the swift eldar.

It had been fear that had ensnared Aradryan: a true and deep terror that he had never felt before. The dread he had experienced on the quayside by the *Lacontiran* had been an intellectual, existential dread of being. The fear he had felt at the thought of dying, or worse being captured, had been a barbaric, instinctual response, as primordial as the world he was on.

Aradryan hoped that having gone through the experience once

already, he would be better prepared for it next time – if there was a next time. If he was fortunate, he would never feel again that desperate moment and the frustration of inaction that had paralysed him. If the sensation did grip him again he was sure he would master himself and keep control. None of the other rangers had said it, but there was a name for his deepest fear: coward.

Jair's voice in his ear broke Aradryan's contemplation. He was on his feet and heading towards Hirith-Hreslain before Jair had finished speaking.

'I am with Assintahil, Loaekhi, Naomilith and Estrellian, in the building where we spied upon the orks. Can you remember the way?'

As he jogged, Aradryan filtered back through his memories, skimming past the trauma of their near-discovery, and found that the route was straightforward. One of the benefits of Dreaming was the honing of access to unconscious memories, so that dreams could be recalled. Those who persisted on the Path of Dreaming were able to relive past experiences, whether real or imagined, in minute detail, with a heightened reality when compared to the original experience. These memedreams were the greatest lure of the Path of Dreaming, allowing an eldar to constantly revisit past glories, loves and happiness without ever experiencing woe or setbacks.

In a way, Aradryan's experience on the *Lacontiran* had snapped him from a potentially dangerous journey into imaginary, wishful self-fulfilment.

'Yes, I know the way,' he replied, realising that he had been running through the trees for some time, on the brink of half-dream as he had examined his memories. 'I shall signal you when I am at the base of the building. Please do not shoot me by mistake.'

'Hurry up, if you wish to see something truly memorable,' urged Jair.

The sounds of the orks had been constant for some time, but Aradryan realised there was other noise too, and that the bellows of the greenskins and the roar of their engines had changed in pitch. The boom of a gun made him realise that the Alaitocii had begun their attack already!

He sprinted through the forest, quickly reaching the buildings. Without pausing, he dashed through the streets, eyes and ears alert to the slightest sign of any alien foe in the shadows of the buildings. The firelight lit the sky above, ruddily dappling the clouds of oily smoke from the engines of the ork vehicles.

'I am almost with you,' Aradryan told the others as he leapt onto the wall from which he could access the secondary turret that granted access to the rangers' vantage point. He nimbly sprang from perch to perch, his muscles remembering the feat from earlier without conscious prompting.

Rather than cut through the tower, he continued up the wall, finding hand- and footholds on window sills and balcony balustrades. If he lost his grip, he would be dashed to a bloody pulp on the ground far below, but he moved without hesitation. This was a danger he could master, and he felt nothing but exhilaration as he climbed spider-like up the last section of wall and then swung himself over the parapet of the roof terrace, his coat and cloak fluttering.

'There!' Loaekhi was standing up, pointing directly across the plaza. His face was thin, cheeks hollow, eyes sunken, and his black hair waved in unruly wisps from beneath his hood. The rest of him was almost impossible to see, his cameleoline coat and hood blue and grey against the sky. From the ground he would have been impossible to see.

Aradryan looked across Selain and saw that the orks had been stirred; like daggerwasps roused from their nest they were gathering against the eldar attack. Already on the far side of the river there was fierce fighting, the sky torn apart by lasers and the trail of missiles. Below the rangers, the orks were assembling around the largest of the beasts: their warlord. The creature was clad in slabs of thick armour and in one hand carried an immense cleaver-like blade and in the other a gun that must have weighed as much as Aradryan. Clanking transports billowing choking exhaust smoke pulled up beside the hulking greenskins and they clambered aboard before the armoured battle trucks sped off towards the bridge in a cloud of oily smoke and dust.

It was not this that Loaekhi had seen.

In an alleyway on the far side of the main square, a glimmer of gold and blue lit the pale walls. Aradryan knew it immediately, for he had seen webway portals many times on his travels aboard *Lacontiran*. In a few moments more, a squad of ten Dire Avengers were heading into the ruins of a low building behind the orks, their exarch's azure-and-gold gonfalon flowing from the banner pole upon his back.

'I see something far more deadly,' whispered Naomilith. 'Look beneath the bridge. You will need your telesights.'

Intrigued, Aradryan raised the sight to his eye. It automatically enhanced his view, multiplying the dim light of the moons so that the image that Aradryan saw was as though it were midday. Directing his gaze towards the bridge, he saw nothing at first. As he increased the magnification and became accustomed to the bubble of water around the piles, he saw unmoving shapes, half-crouched in the shallow waters. Like statues they waited, their chainswords and pistols held above the water, no more visible than solidified shadows. They were Aspect Warriors lying in ambush: Striking Scorpions.

'I wonder if Korlandril is down there,' said Aradryan. He shrugged, it was impossible to see any markings that would identify any particular shrine, and Aradryan did not know to which his friend belonged.

Turning his attention back to the streets leading to the plaza beneath him, Aradryan saw that other Aspect Warriors were gathering – more Dire Avengers waiting in the darkness, while on the rooftops opposite he spied Dark Reapers moving into position.

'Take out the gun crews,' whispered Jair. 'The ones we saw earlier today.'

Aradryan nodded and found the garden in which they had spied the first battery of cannons. Through the shattered remnants of a gatehouse, the ork guns would be able to fire across the bridge, directly into the plaza on the opposite side.

He raised his rifle to his shoulder, easing the stock into place, trying to stay relaxed though his heart was beginning to race. He remembered what Jair and Athelennil had taught him as they had returned to Alaitoc, and put into practice the routine he had repeated hundreds of times when they had left the craftworld to come to Eileniliesh.

The movement felt natural, not forced, as he snapped the sight back into place on its magnetic lock and tilted his head to peer down its length. Taking a breath, he moved the red-lit image until he could see the small alien creatures scurrying around their weapons. They were loading shells into the breeches of their cannons, somewhat poorly judging by the number of times their ork overseer cracked his whip. Shells were dropped and picked up, and fingers caught in the slamming breech lock.

Two of the silhouetted figures in his gunsight fell down. After a moment, he realised they had been shot by the others. There was more panicked movement, but he sighted on one of the smaller creatures kneeling near to the closest cannon, a trigger-rope clutched in its fist. The resolution of the night sight meant that he could see nothing of the creature's features, only its outline, and the faintest brighter patch of its open mouth as it exhaled into the cold night.

He had never killed anything before, he thought, as he touched his finger to the trigger of his longrifle. Earlier, when he had seen Jair pull his pistol and knife to the ready, he had been horrified by the proposition. This was a different matter entirely. All he had to do was apply a little more pressure through his index finger and the creature directly in the middle of his sight would be no more.

There was a slight hiss and the delicate whine of a powercell. An invisible laser bolt shot across the plaza, just a hair's-breadth in front a needle-thin crystalline projectile laden with toxins that would slay most creatures in moments.

Aradryan only realised he had fired when the figure in his sights suddenly reared up, one hand snatching at its shoulder. It spun once with flailing arms, somewhat melodramatically Aradryan thought, and then collapsed to the ground like a grotesque marionette that had snapped its strings.

He sighted again, smiling at how easy it was. He tried for a slightly harder shot, choosing a small alien that was crawling between two crates.

His shot took it in the head, felling the greenskin instantly.

Again and again he fired, hearing the telltale whine of his fellow rangers' rifles spitting death across the divide. The ork gangmaster was stomping to and fro, trying in vain to rouse its dying underlings. Aradryan missed a shot at the beast, the merest twitch in his arm causing his aim to go wide. Concentrating again, he fired once more, but the ork still did not go down.

'I'm sure I hit it,' Aradryan muttered.

'The ork?' said Naomilith. 'They're tough beasts. You might not have even penetrated the skin. Try again, and next time aim for the eyes.'

'The eyes?' replied Aradryan.

'Like this.'

Aradryan was not even sure where the creature's eyes were, until he saw the tiniest puff of droplets erupting from the line of its heavy brow, a heartbeat before the ork fell backwards, crashing into a stack of shells. The unstable ammunition spilled across the garden, and a moment before he pulled his eye away from the sight Aradryan saw a spark of ignition.

A series of explosions rocked the ork battery, blowing apart the garden wall and hurling stone blocks into the air. The front of the building, already weakened by previous impacts, toppled sideways, tearing away from supporting beams in a cloud of dust and rubble, burying the bodies and guns beneath a heap of broken debris.

Aradryan laughed, captivated by the destruction. The smoke and dust billowed across the square, and in the darkness he spied the Aspect Warriors moving forwards, readying to attack the orks from behind as they set off towards the river.

Turning his gaze that way, there was not much to see, save for the flicker of missiles, the muzzle flare of ork guns and the bright flash of lasers. He could not tell if the battle was going well or badly, but there was nothing he could do to affect the fighting on the far side of the bridge.

Returning his attention to enemies closer at hand, he lifted his rifle again and picked out an ork amongst a large group that were running towards the plaza, heading after the vehicles of the warlord. His first shot struck the ork in the shoulder. It stumbled, falling to one knee, and then rose up again, shaking its head as the nerve toxins coursed through its system. Aradryan's next shot missed as the ork bent to retrieve its dropped pistol. The third shot caught it in the leg, just above the knee, and this time the poison proved too much, the ork pitching face-first into the ground.

The plaza was filled with furious action as the Dark Reapers and Dire Avengers opened fire together, ripping into the ork mobs with a barrage of rockets and a storm of shuriken catapult volleys. A dozen orks were torn apart in moments, as many again losing limbs or suffering grievous wounds that would have felled lesser creatures.

A one-armed ork staggered from the throng, slumping against the burning remnants of a half-tracked vehicle. Aradryan could see its head through the twisted metal frame of the transport and took aim. His shot hit home just behind the ork's ear and the alien slid from view.

'Our task is done here,' said Jair.

Aradryan ignored him, taking aim once more to target another wounded ork limping past the body of the one he had just slain. Aradryan caressed the trigger of his rifle and the ork fell, its head bouncing off the chassis of the wreck as it spun to the ground.

'We have another mission,' Jair said, more insistent. The ranger laid his hand on Aradryan's arm, pulling his rifle to one side.

'There are plenty of targets still,' Aradryan said, snatching his arm away from Jair's grip.

'There are others that can deal with them,' said Jair, speaking calmly, though his eyes betrayed agitation in the flickering light of the battle. 'We have to move closer to the river, the Exodites will be arriving and we must ensure their path is clear.'

With some effort, Aradryan dragged his eyes away from the battle raging below. He nodded, some measure of clarity returning to his thoughts. Jair and the others headed to the stairwell and Aradryan followed reluctantly.

'Do you know why the Aspect Warriors must wear a war-mask?' Jair asked as the group descended the stairs, moving quickly to the lower floors.

'So that the grief and distress of battle does not consume them,' replied Aradryan. 'Do not worry about me, the death of these beasts is nothing. This is a cull, nothing more.'

'You are wrong,' said Jair. He stopped at the next floor and stared intently at Aradryan. 'The war-mask allows the Aspect Warriors to shed blood in the name of Khaine, but when they remove their wargear they can forget the thrill of killing. The elation you are feeling, it is the touch of Khaine, and you must be wary of its grasp. To hold life and death in your hand is a powerful thing, and it can become addictive.'

Aradryan did not reply, but as he followed Jair down to the street, he realised that the other ranger spoke the truth. It was a sobering moment as he looked back at the joy that had filled him with the death of each ork. The sensation he felt as the group made their way through the moon- and fire-lit streets was different to the relief he had experienced following his first encounter with the aliens. There was a cold calculation about the death he brought, which in itself heightened his sense of superiority.

A shouted warning from Naomilith had all five rangers reaching for their weapons. Three orks came lurching around a corner ahead, no doubt fleeing from the slaughter unleashed by the Aspect Warriors. Unlike before, Aradryan did not freeze. His shuriken pistol was in his hand before he even thought about it.

The orks raised their crude guns as the rangers opened fire. The hiss of shurikens split the air, slicing into the alien trio, Aradryan's shots amongst the fusillade. His heart raced again as the monomolecular discs sliced into the nearest of the enemy, shredding the ork's jerkin and lacerating green flesh.

One of the alien beasts fell immediately, throat slit amongst scores of wounds, and another stumbled backwards, roaring in pain. The third ork unleashed a blaze of bullets, the noise of its gun thunderous in the narrow street, the flare of the muzzle almost blinding. Estrellian was flung back, his flailing arms masked by the camouflage effect of his cloak, blood spraying into the air. Bullet impacts cracked from the wall to Aradryan's right as he fired his pistol again, teeth gritted.

The ork that had killed Estrellian staggered and collapsed, leaking thick blood from across its face and body, gun falling from its spasmodic grip. The creature that had been wounded recovered its footing, but only for an instant; Jair and Naomilith's pistols spat another hail of shurikens, sending the ork thrashing to the ground. It convulsed for a few moments and then fell still.

Loaekhi stooped over Estrellian, shaking his head. The numbness of shock welled up from Aradryan's stomach, but he took a deep breath and stepped up to stand beside the dead ranger. He looked at Estrellian's blood-spattered face, realisation dawning that the battle was far closer than he had thought.

'That could have been any of us,' Aradryan whispered. He swallowed hard, mastering his fear.

'Stay alert,' Jair said.

'We cannot leave him here,' said Aradryan, his gaze drawn to the waystone half visible inside Estrellian's coat. It glowed with a warm blue light, pulsing softly. The four surviving eldar exchanged a look, and Aradryan was reassured by the composure of his companions. Loaekhi and Naomilith stowed their pistols and picked up Estrellian's corpse. The cameleoline masked the body still, so that it looked as though the pair of rangers were carrying nothing but distorted air, a disembodied face and hand floating between them.

'The two of us will have to meet the Exodites,' said Jair, as the other rangers disappeared into the darkness, bearing away the body of their fallen comrade. 'The orks are not yet defeated.'

Appearing very different in her battlegear, Saryengith met Aradryan and Jair at the appointed place, in a clearing not far from the outskirts of Hirith-Hreslain. She was dressed in armour made of scaled hide, her head encased in a helm fashioned from the skull of one of Eileniliesh's giant reptiles. She had a laser lance couched in her right hand, a silver-faced shield in her left. The elder sat astride a dragon: a winged creature covered in red and purple scales that was more than five times the height of an eldar in length. Its tail ended in a diamond-shaped mace, its long, leathery wings folded back against its flanks for the moment, revealing the broad straps of the dark wooden riding throne in which the Exodite leader was seated.

Saryengith was not alone. There were more than a dozen other dragon riders, their mounts basking in the moonlight at the centre of the clearing. Several scores of Exodites were close by, riding on bipedal reptiles with harnesses studded by slivers of precious metal and flashing gems. Like Saryengith they carried shields and laser lances, though several had rifles too, similar to those carried by the rangers.

There were other creatures still, in the darkness of the forest: megasaurs. On their huge backs were howdahs similar in design to the towers of Hirith-Hreslain. Crewed by dozens of Exodites, the behemoths had armoured plates on their chests and hanging down their flanks. Upon galleries surrounding the howdah were several large laser cannons, each directed by two eldar dressed in the distinctive scaled robes of Exodite armour.

Aradryan's previous experience of megasaurs had been sliced on a platter, and he had never encountered a dragon before. The air in the clearing was thick with the smell of dung and oiled harnesses, which whilst powerful was not totally unpleasant. The beasts made all manner of rumbles, growls, clicks, hoots and hollers, some of them muted, some of them ringing out across the forest in challenge. Some had long necks for reaching up to the trees, their legs as thick as trunks. Several had horny crests or bony frills to protect their heads and necks, and spiralling or curving horns jutting from nose and brow. All of them were larger than anything the orks had built.

Standing next to Saryengith, Aradryan was a little uneasy. Her reptilian mount leered at him with a black eye, ropes of saliva dripping from exposed fangs almost as long as his knife. The moonlight glistened on the creature's scales, green and yellow, and its claws were sheathed with silvery metal studded with sharp jags of red and black gems, so that they appeared like serrated, jewelled carving knives. Its bulk was enough to intimidate Aradryan, who had seen cloud-whales in the gaseous domes of Alaitoc, but only ever from a considerable distance. The creature almost within reach was a mass of scaled muscle and tendon, its ferocious temperament only held in check by the chains of its reins in Saryengith's gloved hands.

She wore a half-mask beneath her hood, shielding her eyes and the bridge of her nose. It was enamelled in red and black, the lenses made to look like flaming, daemonic eyes. A saddle pack was stowed across the back of her mount, just behind her throne-like seat. A longrifle was within reach, and a slender-barrelled fusion pistol hung amongst the baggage. Looking at the packs, Aradryan realised that everything that the pandita owned was in those bags; she would have lost home and possessions when the orks had overrun Hirith-Hreslain. For those on the craftworld, personal possessions were of little value except sentimental; lost or broken belongings were easy to replace, and fashions came and went quicker than seasons on Eileniliesh. For Saryengith, it would take considerable time and effort to fashion or purchase replacements for everything that had been destroyed or taken.

'What word from the battle?' asked Saryengith.

'Selain is almost empty of foes, their dead piled high in the streets,' Jair told her. Aradryan was content to allow his companion to speak. The journey back through the forest – after a hectic sweep of the streets close to the river to confirm that few, if any, orks had escaped – had been made in silence. Jair had seemed unwilling to talk about what had happened to Estrellian, and Aradryan thought that no good would come from forcing the issue.

The death of the ranger had brought about mixed emotions in Aradryan. He was sad to have witnessed another eldar die, especially at the hands of the brutish orks. Yet he did not feel as shocked or miserable as he thought he should; the fact that he was still alive outweighed his grief. As he had made his way between the trees, following Jair without conscious effort, Aradryan had relived the moment of Estrellian's death several times. Etched into Aradryan's memory was the cruel, angry glare of the ork and the brightness of the ranger's blood as it had erupted from the flapping folds of his cloak. The rattle of bullets beside Aradryan had been no more than an arm's-length away. If he had not stopped to speak with Jair on the stairwell, Aradryan might have been standing where Estrellian had died. Had the ork that shot Estrellian been the closest of the group, it would have been slain by the ranger's pistols and the creature in front of Aradryan might have opened fire.

In such situations, it was the narrowest of margins, the most fickle circumstances of chance, which made the difference between life and death. The thought should have terrified Aradryan, to realise that he had been so close to death. His actual state of mind was the opposite. The forest around him was alive with sounds and smells and sights, teeming with life that still flowed through his body. His first encounter with an enemy had frozen Aradryan; his latest had let him free.

Aradryan was drifting back into a memedream of the event when he realised Jair was speaking to him.

'The Exodites will ride out immediately, to push the advantage,' the other ranger was saying.

Looking around, Aradryan saw that the host of Hirith-Hreslain, less than a hundred who had survived the initial attack, was moving out of the clearing. The ground shuddered beneath the tread of the megasaurs, each footfall sending reverberations that fluttered the leaves of the trees.

'We can return to *Irdiris* if you wish,' said Jair, watching the Exodites depart.

'Not yet,' replied Aradryan. 'Let us see the battle to its end.'

'Are you sure?'

'Never more so.' Aradryan needed to return to Hirith-Hreslain, to see the orks destroyed. The town had been home to a vivid awakening for him, and he had to see how things would end. More than that, he needed to take part in that conclusion, to be an agent of the orks' defeat. If he left now, he might never find any meaning in the things he had witnessed and experienced. 'There are still orks to be killed.'

They followed the Exodites along the road as the dragon riders took to the night skies. The timing of their arrival was vital to the success of the plan laid out by the seers and autarchs. The Alaitocii and such rangers that had travelled on their battleships had slain the orks in Selain and were encircling the enemy left in Hresh. Through careful manoeuvring, the orks were being pushed back onto one of the main thoroughfares through the settlement, with only one seeming escape route. It was here that the Exodites would close the encirclement, dooming any orks that remained. If the warriors of Hirith-Hreslain arrived too early, the orks would realise their peril and try to break out into other parts of their town; come too late and the aliens would be able to escape into the forests.

Aradryan marvelled at his companions and their scaled mounts. The Exodites looked like other eldar, perhaps a little shorter and broader than the Alaitocii, but still possessed of the same slender build, sloping eyes and pointed ears. It was in their dress and mannerisms that they were most different. Aradryan could see the delicate stitching on their robes, made by hand, and the polished scale armour and shields that protected them had similarly been fashioned by manual labour. They bore spears and swords in addition to their rifles and laser lances: weapons of honed metal, chased with inscribed runes but with no energy source for a power field or whirling chainblade teeth.

The Exodites wore knee-high boots, heavily strapped with buckles, and their hands and forearms were clad in gloves of the same heavy hide-like material, knuckles and fingertips reinforced with dark grey metal. Some wore surplices, bound with wide belts and pierced by metal rings. Their helms were tall and pointed, like those of a Guardian, with open faces. Many wore long, elaborately embroidered scarves around their necks and across their mouths.

As they approached Hirith-Hreslain, the sights and sounds of fighting stirred Aradryan from a half-reverie. He could see nothing of the battle from where he was, but the flare of guns and missile launchers punctuated the silhouetted landscape in front, and the wind carried the bark of guns and the whine of shurikens.

One of the Exodites at the front of the column rose up in his stirrups, standing high with his laser lance held aloft. He turned to look back at the following warriors.

'The enemy are cornered and their fate awaits them!' he cried out. 'The time to attack is upon us. Ready your weapons and steel your hearts. Slay those that must be slain, but take no pleasure in it. Guard against the lusts of Khaine, for they are no more than an iron voice giving word to the lies of She Who Thirsts. All desire is a trap, so kill without joy and strike down the vermin that have despoiled our homes. We will triumph and we will rebuild.'

'Hirith-Hreslain!' The Exodites raised their weapons in salute.

No sooner had the speech been made than ear-splitting screeches split the night air. Monstrous winged shapes dropped down from the clouds, silhouetted against the setting moons. Blasts of multicoloured lasers stabbed into the orks as the Exodite dragon riders plunged into the attack.

With a chorus of ground-shaking bellows and rasping cries, the Exodites' war-beasts entered the battle. Surging along the main road, the megasaurs and lithodons charged into the orks retreating from the attacks of the Alaitocii. There was nothing the orks could do against this new threat, though some turned their crude guns on the gigantic forces of nature bearing down upon them.

Jair and Aradryan followed as swiftly as they could, occasionally pausing to snap off shots at orks that were trying to lurk amongst the ruins, shouting warnings up to the crew of a nearby megasaur to direct their fire against alien mobs skulking in the shattered buildings. Lascannon and scatter laser and fusion lance fire erupted from the howdahs of the enormous beasts, screaming down like lightning from a storm of wrath.

Clearing the street and surrounding buildings with their first thrust, the Exodites pressed on, driving the orks back into the guns and blades of the pursuing Aspect Warriors. With laser lances and fusion pikes, the Exodites closed, determined to exact revenge for the destruction of the town and the deaths of their kin.

It was fitting that the autarchs and farseers had granted the warriors of Hirith-Hreslain the opportunity to deliver the killing blow to the occupiers of their town. They settled the bloody score with grim faces and dispassionate eyes.

Pulses of white fire and burning lasers strobed through the orks, cutting down a score in one salvo. The dragons soared above, their riders raining down more las-fire and showers of plasma grenades. Against the fury of the Exodites, the orks did not survive for long. They were cut down in short order, the wounded crushed beneath the feet of the advancing behemoths.

Dawn found Jair and Aradryan picking through the ruins, searching for wounded eldar and surviving orks with the rest of the rangers and squads of Aspect Warriors. They met up again with Athelennil, and Aradryan was pleased to see her, though he realised with some guilt that he had not thought about his lover throughout the battle. On reflection, his lack of thought concerning her wellbeing had been to his advantage, for he did not know if he would have been able to cope worrying about her life as well as his own.

Here and there they would find a casualty of one side or the other; the eldar were taken to the healers, the orks despatched with pinpoint shots.

'You know that Thirianna fought here,' Athelennil told Aradryan as the two of them climbed down a broken wall from a ruined upper storey, having assured themselves that it was empty.

'And I trust that she is unharmed,' said Aradryan.

'That is all?'

Aradryan dropped down to the street, landing next to the sprawled body of an ork, one of its arms missing, bite and claw marks across its back.

'What else would I think? Thirianna and I are friends, if that.'

'So, you have no urge to return to Alaitoc with her?' Athelennil wrinkled her lip upon seeing the dead ork. 'Are you sure this is the life you wish to choose?'

Aradryan looked around. There were alien bodies everywhere, and smoke rising from dozens of fires. The stink of fumes and orks was all-pervading, and the glare of Eileniliesh's sun was harsh. Death hung like a shroud over Hirith-Hreslain, but it was not death that occupied his thoughts.

'It was fear of death that drove me to *Lacontiran*,' he said, grasping Athelennil's hand. 'I cannot let that fear rule my life. I have learnt here that death will come to us all, so it is in life that we must pursue our dreams and chart our own course. I cannot return to Alaitoc, for Thirianna or any other reason. There is no life there. Where there is no risk of death, life has no meaning.'

'Yet, death is so much closer out here,' said Athelennil. She reached out with her other hand and prodded a gloved finger against Aradryan's spirit stone. 'All that you are could be ended, far from home and friends.'

'If I am to die, it will be out here,' said Aradryan. 'Out amongst the stars where I belong.'

BEGINNINGS

The Black Library of Chaos – Deep in the weft and folds of the webway is a craftworld unlike any other. It was to here that the Laughing God, Cegorach, first travelled when he escaped the clutches of She Who Thirsts. The scholars who dwelt upon the craftworld were surprised to see the god appearing amongst them, but he stilled their excitement and related to them his tale, and that of what had happened to the other gods. The Laughing God finished his narrative and disappeared, instructing the scholars and their protectors not to forget what he had told them. Thus was the Black Library founded, and the first of the Harlequins created. From the Black Library the followers of Cegorach travel far and wide, searching for all knowledge of the power of Chaos and the manner of the dark gods of the Othersea. Artefacts of Chaos are brought here, for study and destruction, and within thousands of grimoires and tomes and volumes and tracts has been gathered an unprecedented literature concerning the warp and its denizens.

'Madness!' said Aradryan, his gaze moving from one companion to the next, unable to believe what he had heard.

They were barely ten cycles out from Eileniliesh, where the hunt for orks in the wilderness still continued; Aradryan had left with some reluctance. Of all the places he would have chosen for their next destination, the Chasm of Desires would have been last. The thought was horrifying. At one moment he had been considering the boundless possibilities of his new life, the experiences he could seek out; at the next, his shipmates had announced that they intended to delve into the heart of the Great Enemy itself.

'It is not madness,' said Caolein. 'Other outcast ships have done it before.'

'Where do you think that came from,' said Jair, jabbing a finger at the waystone brooch on Aradryan's chest. 'The Tears of Isha fell only upon the crone worlds.'

'But why now?' said Aradryan. 'What about the winterfalls? The Mosaic of Kadion? Another Exodite world, perhaps? There are others who will throw away their lives for the Tears of Isha, we do not have to be numbered among them.'

'We do not even know if it can be done,' said Athelennil. 'It is an idea, nothing more.'

'It's a suicidal whim, that is what it is!' Aradryan folded his arms defiantly. 'There is a reason it is called the Well of Sins, the Gulf of Utter Darkness, the Void of Eternal Damnation.'

'And despite those titles, it is also where the greatest rangers have gone before, to bring back the Tears of Isha so that future generations can avoid the hunger of She Who Thirsts. You wanted adventure, Aradryan. What greater adventure could we set upon?'

'I think I am prepared to aim a little lower, this early in my life as an outcast,' said Aradryan. He turned to Lechthennian, who had said nothing since Caolein had announced his intent to dare the Eye of Terror. 'What do you think of this insanity?'

Lechthennian had a lap-harp, which he strummed distractedly. He looked up at the mention of his name, shaking his head.

'I travel with the ship, nothing more,' he said. 'I do not choose its course.'

'You do not care where you go?' said Aradryan, frowning at the answer he had received. 'It has been suggested that we venture into the greatest warp storm in the galaxy, the physical embodiment of the bane of our entire people, and you don't have an opinion?'

His fingers picking out a jaunty four-note refrain, Lechthennian shook his head.

'We are not committed yet,' said Jair, reaching out a placating hand towards Aradryan. 'It may be impossible, or too difficult at least, as you say. We will not know until we reach Khai-dazaar. When we are there, you will be able to choose what you wish to do.'

'Khai-dazaar? I have never heard of it. What will I have to decide there?'

Athelennil sat down next to Aradryan, but he leaned away from her, disappointed that she would argue against him.

'Khai-dazaar is an interspace in the webway, where we can find those who would guide us to the crone worlds. If we are successful, you can always choose to remain there, or perhaps leave with another ship.'

'Leave? Would it come to that?'

'If we wish to go, we are not beholden to your view,' said Jair. 'There will be others willing to come with us, your presence is not required. Do not think like a Path-wrapped. Your destiny is no more attached to this ship than any other. *Irdiris* is but a vessel, its crews coming and going as they wish. It is not special, we are not special, and neither are you. You are outcast now, enjoy the freedom of choice that is laid before you.'

'From a maiden world to a crone world,' Aradryan murmured. 'Or abandoned to fend for myself. Madness.'

Sitting at the piloting console next to Caolein, Aradryan laid his hands upon the semicircular arrangement of jewel-like interfaces. It was not the first time he had steered the *Irdiris* since coming aboard, but he still felt a thrill as his fingers lightly touched the guide-gems. The contact brought a moment of communion with the energy of the ship's psychic network: formless sentience derived from the spirits of past eldar. Aradryan allowed himself a moment to settle, attuning his thoughts to the rhythm and flow of the vessel's pulse.

The display sphere in front of him showed the webway tunnel curving gently down and to the right, realised in the glowing globe as an ethereal passageway of gold and silver. The *Irdiris* was quite capable of navigating the stretch on its own, so Aradryan sat back, feeling the control vanes of the starship adjusting to take in the sweep of the curve.

'Not far now,' said Caolein. 'Are you sure you're ready?'

'This might be the only chance I have to do this,' replied Aradryan. 'If you are intent on leaving me here.'

Ahead, the webway opened out into the interspace of Khai-dazaar. Dozens of webway passages intersected, forming a near-globular arrangement more than three times the size of Alaitoc's largest domes. The settlement that had grown up on the interspace looked like an inverted city, spires rising up from the artificial fieldwalls that kept the interspace together, pointing towards a glowing false sun at the centre. Bridges and concourses criss-crossed Khai-dazaar, forming a maze of quays and walkways, arcing over and looping around the turrets and towers that soared like gigantic stalactites. Lights of every hue shone from slender windows, and guiding lanterns blinked red and blue to form rainbow causeways between the labyrinth of structures.

A craftworld had landing protocols and the guiding hand of its infinity circuit to steer an arriving ship to its correct berth; Khai-dazaar was a free-for-all of ships coming and going, steering about each other on seemingly random courses. Small skyrunners cut past stately liners, while silver-hulled sky barges floated serenely from tower to tower.

Aradryan took in a deep breath, trying to figure out a way through the sprawling maze of arches and traffic.

'We should head to the Spire of Discontented Bliss,' suggested Caolein. Aradryan felt the other pilot merging with him on the guidance matrix, their spirits coalescing briefly as Caolein highlighted a route towards their destination. On the display in front of them, a gleaming silver ribbon appeared, turning beneath a wide gantry before spiralling down towards one of the lower docks about a third of the way around the rim of the interspace.

Nudging *Irdiris* into line with the proposed trajectory, Aradryan enjoyed the sensation of movement afforded by the view of the city. In the webway, it was often the case that there was no sense of momentum, but as bright windows flashed past and roadways speared overhead he could feel the ship racing into Khai-dazaar. In fact, he felt they were going too fast and directed *Irdiris* to slow down, which required another course correction to keep them from heading into the higher levels of a spire.

Concentrating intensely, Aradryan was soon lost in the task of guiding the ship safely to its destination; always Caolein's presence was there with him to take over should he make a mistake. Determined not to embarrass himself, Aradryan pictured the elegant sapphiretails of the Dome of Enchanted Declarations, and in doing so *Irdiris* swooped gracefully down into the lower depths of the city, passing through the shadow of an immense battleship marked with tiger stripes of black and purple.

'Commorraghans?' he said in surprise, recognising the blade-like design of the energy arrays and steering fins.

'There are eldar of all kindreds here,' said Caolein. 'Rangers, corsairs, Commorraghans, traders from the craftworlds. And, of course, Harlequins, White Seers and others.'

Slowing the ship to a sedate glide, Aradryan made final adjustments towards the sweeping arc of the dock portal highlighted in the display. There were black stone runes embedded in the white stone of the gateway: 'Of all the Fates that Morai-heg wove, none was so damned as the life of Narai-tethor.' The reference was lost on Aradryan; a myth-tale he had not heard. He glanced at Caolein, who sensed his desire for explanation over the piloting interface.

'I have no idea,' laughed the pilot with a shrug. 'I think it might be from Saim-Hann, or maybe Thelth-adris. The city has been built by people from every craftworld and beyond, each leaving their own mark and stories.'

A guidance beacon sprang into glittering life as they flew into the opening of the dock, connecting with the *Irdiris*. Aradryan latched on to this wave of psychic energy and allowed the ship to slowly slew sideways, adjustor vanes angled steeply to kill the rest of its momentum. With barely a shudder to indicate they had touched down, *Irdiris* extended her landing feet and settled on the concourse between two pearl-sailed pleasure yachts.

'Stylish,' said Caolein, leaning back from the controls with a smile.

Aradryan shut down the piloting controls and directed his thoughts through the psychic matrix, informing the others that they had arrived. He felt a flutter of excitement emanating from the rest of the crew, and it was infectious. The viewing sphere enlarged, showing a real-light view of their surroundings. Aradryan could not see any other eldar on the broad apron, but the matrix of *Irdiris* buzzed with the life of the city.

'So this is Khai-dazaar,' he said, thoughts awash with the possibilities.

The webway pocket realm was initially bewildering. Every street was home to crafty-eyed hawkers selling wares ranging from cloaks and robes to ancient texts and supposed artefacts of the old eldar empire. Far from the polite traders on the Boulevard of Split Moons, these eldar haggled and competed, vying for the attention and patronage of visitors and each other. There seemed to be as many deals being struck between the merchants as with the other eldar who slowly wound their way between the stalls.

The goods put any craftworld trader to shame. Fine art pieces, some of them genuinely ancient, sat alongside processed ship stores. Exotic animals – mammalian, reptile, avian and indeterminate – lay in cages or blinkered or leashed, howling, yammering and hooting, while others watched the procession of potential owners with placid, intelligent eyes. Materials of every weave and colour and design were on show, together with jewellery of precious metals and ghost stone and cinderclay and shaped mineral; gems and semi-precious stones of every hue and shape, both natural and fashioned; statuettes and busts, ceramic tiles and beaten metal dishes. Aradryan saw treatises of philosophers next to popular poetry collections and political tracts; artists painting flattering portraits and not-so-flattering caricatures; plants and grasses, blossoms and bulbs, buds and petals from hundreds of worlds and craftworlds; animal hides and furs, treated skins and preserved horns, ground bones and polished skulls.

The open-fronted establishments behind the stalls were more reminiscent of the Bridge of Yearning Sorrows than anywhere else. Keeping close to Athelennil, who seemed to have a particular destination in mind, Aradryan passed narcotics dens and drinking houses, lyrical recitals and debating chambers, tattooists and bodypainters, dreamers and singers, ghost stone sculptors and flesh designers. The latter were a Commorraghan influence, offering their services for free in exchange for the opportunity to turn living eldar into works of art. Aradryan saw one old female wearing a sash marked by the runes of Biel-Tan sitting in a chair while a skeletal flesh designer fused bright blue feathers into her scalp, replacing her hair with an extravagant crest. Next to the eldar was an infant male, her son most likely, the skin of his exposed arms being redrafted with mottled snake scales.

'Not there,' said Athelennil, dragging Aradryan by the arm. 'If that is something you are interested in, I know a far more accomplished flesh-worker over in the Crimson Galleries.'

'Not just now,' said Aradryan, pulling his eyes away from the bizarre vision, nose wrinkled in distaste.

'There is nothing wrong with expressing yourself through a little body modification,' said Athelennil. She waggled the fingers of her free hand in Aradryan's face. 'I had talons for a few passes, if you can believe that.'

'Whatever for?' asked Aradryan, appalled rather than amused by the idea. 'And is that not very impractical?'

'I did not have them *for* anything,' said Athelennil. 'I had them because I could. Also, my consort at the time rather liked a little scratching in his lovemaking.'

'I really did not need to know that.' Looking around, Aradryan felt a twinge of concern. The contrast between Khai-dazaar and Eileniliesh was stark. He could see the Exodites' point of view; this was just the sort of behaviour that could lead to obsession and depravity.

'Do not be prudish,' warned Athelennil, mistaking his expression of apprehension for disgust. 'It is not for you to judge what others do with their lives.'

'It is just a shock, that is all,' said Aradryan, forcing a smile. He pulled Athelennil closer. 'I am still adjusting to life away from the Path. Does it not worry you? How do you maintain perspective and control?'

They continued along the street, passing underneath gaudy bunting strung between the balconies of the upper storeys. Aradryan swerved to avoid two scantily clad eldar in a heated discussion, whose melodramatic gesticulations were a hazard to those trying to pass too close. His last moment course correction forced Athelennil to duck beneath a low hanging garland of purple and white flowers.

'Control is definitely an area you need to work on,' she laughed, pushing Aradryan in retaliation for his bump. She stopped, her smile fading. 'The Path deludes us, teaching that we must curb our natural enthusiasm, blind our senses to the reality of our lives. To be outcast and wander from the Path is to accept yourself and to be free from the tyranny of self-perfection. The founders of the Path laid down an ideal, but it has become more than a goal to strive for – it has become a prison for our spirits.'

'The tales of the Fall, of the coming of the Great Enemy, are not simple propaganda,' replied Aradryan, with more vehemence than he expected. Though the prospect of a post-life existence in an infinity circuit depressed him, the thought of being consumed by She Who Thirsts was a genuine terror. His recent brush with indulgence during the fighting at Hirith-Hreslain had been a timely warning. 'We were possessed by our passions and it led to the destruction of our civilisation. Can we truly trust ourselves not to repeat the past?'

'Abstinence is a false philosophy, no better than the puritanical beliefs of the Exodites,' argued Athelennil. At Aradryan's nod the two of them continued on their way, side-by-side but not touching each other. 'With every generation, more become trapped. The society of the craftworlds survives because of those who fail on the Path. Seers, and exarchs, and Waywardens, all of them needed to pass on the lessons that they failed to learn. When does self-deprivation become an obsession in its own right? Must we wait until there are only teachers left and no pupils before we realise that the Path condemns us to stasis? It grants us no future.'

Aradryan was taken aback by the passion of Athelennil's argument. He had never asked why she had decided to become outcast, and she had not volunteered the information. Now was not the time to inquire, he sensed, as Athelennil gestured for the pair to turn right into an alley lit by strings of blue and green parchment lanterns. Something bounded across in front of them: a small, white-furred primate of a species Aradryan had not encountered before. It leapt up onto one of the lantern ropes and swung away, moments before an eldar child came sprinting after it, shouting curses.

Stooping beneath the lamplines, Aradryan found himself coming out into a walled courtyard where glowing coal braziers and chairs of woven reed were arranged around a central fountain. Two eldar, garbed head to foot in heavy robes of scarlet, their faces and heads covered with scarves of the same, stood beside a doorway. The lounge area was otherwise empty. Ruddy light glowed through a slit window in the door between the two eldar, but the wall in which it was set was otherwise blank white.

'The Passage of Sunken Fears,' declared Athelennil. 'Let us not go in straight away.'

She reclined on one of the benches, close to the fountain. Aradryan lay down near to her, finding that the light sprinkling of water combined pleasantly with the ambient heat of the braziers. The coals smoked with sweet-smelling incense, while the water that fell on his lips had a tang of salt. He closed his eyes, trying to relax. He wore his ranger bodysuit, finding it more comfortable and practical than his old clothes, and the arms and legs shrank away from his skin to create a vest-like costume, responding to his desire to feel the heat and water on his limbs.

'The mistake of the Path is that it enables those upon it to dwell too long upon one aspect of themselves,' said Athelennil. Her quiet voice was hard to hear over the splashing of the fountain, and Aradryan realised he had quickly been slipping into a semi- slumber. He opened his eyes, experiencing a moment of vertigo as he stared up at Khai-dazaar's artificial sun, surrounded by a corona of jagged building peaks and curving skywalks.

'What is to stop the same happening to an outcast?' said Aradryan, pushing himself up on one elbow.

'The galaxy itself,' replied Athelennil. 'Away from the security and sanctity of the craftworlds is a dangerous, testing place. There can be little indulgence when you have to keep your eyes and ears open.'

'You are mistaken,' said Aradryan. 'I could slip into a memedream here and spend my life indulging in fantasy and phantasm. What is to stop me?'

'Thirst and hunger, for a start. You think that the people here will give you food and drink out of the goodness of their hearts? There is nobody on the Path of the Creator, none treading the Path of Service to bring it to your lap. And there are some very unsavoury types here. If you want to dream, you best not do it without someone to stand guard over you, unless you want to awake in the fleshpits or fighting arenas of Commorragh. Or somewhere worse.'

'I see what you mean...' said Aradryan, casting an eye towards the pair of eldar standing as sentries by the doorway.

'Them?' Athelennil laughed, cocking her head to look at the silent Guardians. 'They would never harm us.'

'Why are we here?' asked Aradryan. 'Who are they?'

'We are here to see Estrathain Unair, to see if a Harlequin troupe is currently in Khai-dazaar. They are the door wardens, who are here to greet visitors and inquire as to their purpose in coming.'

'Did you send word already?'

'That was not necessary,' said Athelennil. 'Estrathain knew my intent as soon as we arrived.'

'Indeed I did.'

Aradryan sat up abruptly as three figures stepped out of the doorway, garbed in the same all-enclosing clothes as the door wardens. They had spoken in unison, and as the trio advanced towards the fountain Aradryan noticed that they did so in step with each other.

'I am Estrathain Unair, mediator of Khai-dazaar.' The three figures stopped just short of Aradryan and raised their right hands, palms outwards and thumbs folded in greeting. The way that all three eldar spoke together was disconcerting, their voices exactly the same as each other. 'You must be very confused, Aradryan. Please come inside, have refreshments and allow me to explain.'

'Of course, I am your guest,' said Aradryan. He watched the red-swathed figures closely, noticing that there was something disturbing about their eyes. The ranger saw himself reflected in the black orbs and realised he was looking into gemstones, not organic visual organs.

'Please do not be disturbed by my kami, they cannot harm you,' said Estrathain, the three figures parting, hands directing Aradryan and Athelennil towards the now-open archway.

Beyond the plain wall was a short corridor, which led into another open space, almost exactly like the first, except that the incense on the braziers was more delicate and fruity, and the water that splashed from the fountain a pale shade of pink. There were seven identical arched doorways leading from the courtyard, and two more of the red-robed 'kami'. One of the doors opened and a third kami came into view, holding a tray on which was a pitcher of dark green liquid and two goblets, set beside a small platter holding a variety of confectionary treats.

'Welcome to Khai-dazaar, my home,' said Estrathain. Only one of the kami spoke, as it sat down and gestured for the rangers to do the same, voice slightly muffled by its scarf.

'Are you the real Estrathain?' asked Aradryan. He peered under the headscarf and saw the same glimmering lenses as before.

'We are all the "real" Estrathain,' said all of the constructs in unison. The single kami that had sat continued on its own. 'Only one of us will speak, to avoid further confusion. As I said earlier, I am the mediator of Khai-dazaar, and I know of your intent to dare the secrets of the crone worlds.'

'Do you rule Khai-dazaar?' asked Aradryan. He plucked a goblet from the tray held by the motionless kami. 'Do we have to seek your permission or make tribute?'

'You mistake me for a Commorraghan overlord, Aradryan,' said Estrathain. 'I am no archon, be assured. As it appears that Athelennil has not furnished you with the nature of my existence, with her permission I shall digress from the immediate matter to enlighten you.'

All six kami looked at Athelennil, who laughed and nodded.

'Of course, please tell Aradryan your story,' she said. 'I forget how polite you always are.'

'Thank you,' said Estrathain, the attention of the kami returning to Aradryan. 'I do not rule Khai-dazaar. No individual or group has control of Khai-dazaar, and while I exist none ever shall. I founded this place, you see, and intended it to be a coming together of our disparate kindreds. Harlequins and folks of the craftworlds, Commorraghans and Exodites. Of course, the Exodites never came, but I invited them.'

The kami leaned back, its scarf slipping a little to reveal a plainly featured face fashioned from an off-white psycho-plastic. As Estrathain continued, Aradryan realised what had alerted him earlier to the unnatural nature of the kami: their mouths and eyes did not move when they spoke. In fact, their faces were simply masks, close approximations of an eldar visage but immobile.

'I was no bonesinger, and so my fledgling realm of equality and peace had no matrix, no equivalent to an infinity circuit. Instead, I possessed a considerable psychic talent of my own, furnished by a lengthy walk upon the Path of the Seer before I dispossessed myself from Ulthwé. I became the spine, the nervous system of Khai-dazaar, in a manner of speaking, putting myself at the service of those who wished to communicate, create and explore.'

'So you are somewhere else, controlling these mannequins?' said Aradryan. 'A very good way to hide from those who might want to exert influence over you. It sounds as if you are powerful here, I would not condemn your paranoia.'

'That is amusing,' said Estrathain, raising a hand in demonstration. 'If the kami could laugh, I would. Alas, they are not capable. You must understand something about the nature of what we are. Those who have been seers understand the separation of mind, thought and form. Normally all are encompassed together, but not always so.'

The kami sat forwards and pointed a scarlet-gloved finger at Aradryan's chest, indicating his waystone.

'When your body is no more, your mind and thought persist,' Estrathain explained. 'Very shortly after, thought also dissipates, for it requires the physical form to operate. This leaves only the pure mind, the essence of each of us. It is our spirit, if you would accept such a term. It is mind alone that transfers to the infinity circuit of a craftworld. If given form again, the mind can give rise to thought once more, though often in limited fashion and of a temporary nature.'

'Of course,' said Aradryan. 'That form might be a starship or a skycutter, or a wraith-construct. Did you die, then? Is that why you have several forms?'

'I did not die, I was in the prime of my life when I became the kami.'

The puppet-thing swung its legs onto the couch and leaned back, hands behind its head. It seemed such a natural movement, but the unfeeling eyes and unmoving features twisted the familiarity into something much more disturbing. The other kami, except for the one that was standing at Aradryan's side holding the drinks tray, had departed; moving off on their other business, Aradryan assumed.

'Khai-dazaar started as a single ship, locked into the webway at this interspace,' Estrathain continued. 'I would send news to passing ships. Some of those ships remained, seeing the value of placing themselves at this intercourse between the stars. Traders came, and I brokered deals between the ships' crews, acting as an initiator and a confidant. Khai-dazaar grew, as ships became towers and gangways became docks. I could not be everywhere at once, and the demands on my time grew too great. So it was that I had the idea of the kami.'

'I understand,' said Aradryan, lifting up his goblet for it to be refilled. 'These are semi-autonomous creations, allowing you to be in more than one place.'

'You do not quite understand. They are fully sentient and autonomous.' The kami on the couch sat up and pulled back the front of its robe, revealing smooth artificial skin. In the centre of its chest glowed a spirit stone, blinking with tiny starlight, indicating that there was an eldar essence within. 'There were adventurers who were willing to trade Tears of Isha for information, contacts and berthing spaces. Over many passes, I assembled a score of waystones. With the flesh sculptors, my own psychic power and the aid of a self-exiled bonesinger, I became the kami. Each of them is me. We are all Estrathain.'

Aradryan laughed in shock, not quite sure he could comprehend what he had been told. He looked at the kami with the tray, scrutinising it closely. It tilted its head slightly and nodded. When Estrathain next spoke, it was through this body.

'Each of them is me, and I am all of them. One divided, and several as a whole. My disparate forms can act in concert or separately as we require. There are many of us now, all across Khai-dazaar.'

'And the answer to what you seek can be found in the Channelways of Saim Khat,' said the reclining kami.

'That is where we can find a Harlequin troupe?' said Athelennil, excited. She glanced at Aradryan. 'There are no others that can guide us to the crone world.'

'You are aware of my price,' said both kami.

'Three Tears of Isha, when we return,' said Athelennil, nodding in acknowledgement. 'We have an agreement.'

'You barter for waystones?' Aradryan was confused. 'Yet you said there was no infinity circuit here.'

'The kami are semi-organic and not immortal, and ever there are more demands upon me, so my numbers must continue to increase,' replied the kami with the tray.

'How many of you are there?' asked Aradryan. He stood up, placed his goblet on the tray and took up a piece of fruit-based confectionary.

'We do not know, we have not counted for some time,' said the kami on the couch. 'Several dozen, at least.'

'If the Harlequins agree to your request, I will be accompanying you,' said another kami, appearing in a doorway to Aradryan's left.

'You can leave Khai-dazaar?' It was Athelennil's turn to be surprised. 'I never knew that.'

'We are quite independent of each other,' said the tray holder. 'There is not a particular bond to this place. We have never travelled to the crone worlds and we are intrigued.'

'You realise that it is dangerous,' Aradryan said to the kami. 'You might not return.'

'It is a loss we can bear,' replied Estrathain. 'That is the advantage of being multiply incarnated.'

'But as an individual, you must be afraid of your death,' Aradryan said, laying a hand on the thick sleeve of the kami who had just entered. 'If you are each autonomous, the Estrathain that I am touching risks the end of its existence.'

'That is true,' the kami replied, laying a hand on Aradryan's as if to comfort him. 'All things die, and I wish to see the Abyss of Shadows before this vessel is of no more use. It is an opportunity that few eldar will ever have.'

'I told you!' said Athelennil, looking at Aradryan. 'You are leaving behind a great chance if you do not come with us.'

'I sensed your hesitancy when you arrived, but in your mind you know that your fears do not outweigh your intrigue,' said the kami that was sitting down.

'It is true,' confessed Aradryan, looking at Athelennil. 'The more I have thought about it, the more the thought of the danger entices me. Perhaps it is just hubris, but there is a strong part of me that desires to truly claim to have seen the crone worlds and returned.'

'You wish to brag about it?' laughed Athelennil. 'That is why you will come with us?'

'If one is to brag, make it something worth bragging about,' replied Aradryan, indignant. 'We are getting ahead of ourselves. The Harlequins have not agreed to take us there.'

'And we will need to find others who will join us,' said Estrathain.

Both rangers looked at the kami who had spoken; the one with the drinks.

'Others?' said Athelennil. 'What others?'

'We are going to the crone worlds,' said Estrathain. 'A troupe of Harlequins, five outcasts and I are not sufficient for such an expedition. There will be considerable dangers and foes to overcome. Go to the Channelways and seek out Findelsith, Great Harlequin. If he consents, you will find a Commorraghan exile called Maensith Drakar Alkhask. She has a ship and warrior company that is sufficient for the venture.'

'You seem to know exactly what we need,' said Aradryan, growing suspicious of the mediator's motives.

'I facilitate the existence of Khai-dazaar,' replied Estrathain. 'At this moment, at least a handful of my other selves will be brokering similar deals for others, matching sellers to buyers, suppliers to markets, crews to ships, followers to leaders. It is our purpose to know these things and bring together interested parties in mutually-beneficial accommodations. Maensith desires a contract, one that will pay well, and a journey to the crone worlds will not intimidate her. You desire to go to the crone worlds, and so there is harmony. The unknown factor rests with the Harlequins. Findelsith and his kind are unpredictable and I know nothing of their intentions while they are here.'

'Then our next task is obvious,' said Athelennil. 'We must head to the Channelways. Please could you inform the other members of our ship's company that we will meet them there.'

'As you wish, I shall pass the word,' said all three kami. 'One of me will also join with your rendezvous, to help in the approach to Findelsith.'

'That is settled then,' said Aradryan, with a short, nervous laugh.

He had become accustomed to the idea of going to the crone worlds in no small part because he had thought the expedition unlikely to begin. Now it seemed there was an increasing chance that he might actually be setting out for the Eye of Terror and his uncertainty returned. He consoled himself with the notion that the whole venture relied upon the cooperation of some Harlequins, who were notoriously fickle in their loyalties and capricious in their schemes. This thought settled his nerves a little as he followed Athelennil out of Estrathain's chambers. The Harlequins would very likely turn down their petition.

After all, they probably had much better things to do than plunge into the nightmarish heart of She Who Thirsts.

The audience waited with hushed expectation, standing in small groups in front of the stage. The performance was to take place in one of Khaidazaar's recital halls, where usually poets and singers and musicians would entertain the eldar of the city in exchange for gifts, passage or simple accommodation from appreciative onlookers. Black drapes hung over the windows, blocking out the light of Khai-dazaar's ever-present artificial star, and in the gloom of ruddy lamps, Aradryan and the rest of *Irdiris*'s crew stood to the right of the stage. As in the rest of the city, there were all manner of eldar in the crowd, including one of Estrathain's kami, who watched over the proceedings from a small dais at the back of the shadowed room.

The lights dimmed almost to darkness as a single figure walked out onto the stage. She moved with measured steps, the diamond patterning of her tight leggings and long hooded jacket difficult to see in the gloom. Under her raised hood, there was no sign of a face, only a bare silver mask that reflected the ruddy glow of the lamps, looking like distant nebulae. Streamers fluttered from her broad belt, twirling lazily in her wake as she came to a stop a little off centre stage. On her back she wore an elaborate device, sprouting two elegant funnels that rose above each shoulder, gems twinkling on its surface.

A whisper rippled through the audience, murmuring a single word: Shadowseer.

Poised, one foot crossed against the other, the Shadowseer bowed, and as she did so, a plume of glittering green and silver issued from her backpack, spreading quickly across the crowd. The sparkling fog drifted over Aradryan, tiny stars dancing in his eyes, the scent of fresh flowers carried on the breeze, filling him with a sense of peace.

Distracted by this, he had not seen a dozen figures appearing on stage. They wore brightly patterned bodysuits, decorated with diamonds and lozenges, stripes and whorls of rainbow colours. For the moment they were frozen in plateau, each holding a different instrument.

From the Shadowseer issued more light, a golden glow that illuminated the stage, bathing the Harlequins in its warm aura. Each wore a comic mask or half-mask with exaggerated features, gem-like tears and painted lips, and garish beading, while scarves, bejewelled bangles and headbands swayed and tinkled and twirled. Their heads were topped with vibrant multicoloured crests that fluttered gently as the dance began. As the gold fell upon each performer, he or she came to life, plucking at strings, tapping on small drums, slowly starting to twist and turn, moving about each other with effortless steps. From offstage came the sound of pipes and flutes, whimsical and mellow, causing Aradryan to relax further.

In his mind he pictured the World as Was, the eldar from before the Fall living in harmony and peace with themselves. For some time the music continued, breathing contentment, while the stars and mists swirled about the stage and audience, growing thicker and brighter.

Another handful of Harlequins entered with quick steps; they moved as a group through the musicians, passing effortlessly between them, showers of red sparks trailing from fingertips as they skipped and ran, surrounding the other performers with a maelstrom of colour. The music was quickening, Aradryan's pulse increasing with the tempo. The musicians separated, whirling away from each other, leaving one alone at the centre. She plucked the strings of her half-lyre with a gloved hand, while the Harlequins looked on appreciatively.

Then, with a discordant rasp, a windharp player stepped forwards, melodramatically thrusting the lyrist aside, the deposed musician falling gracefully to the stage with an arm outstretched in woe. The new musician took up the tune, fingers moving faster, while the drum beats grew louder. The dancers returned, spilling more red upon the players as the harpist was himself pushed away, tumbling head over heels to lie sprawling on the far end of the stage. The pair that had ousted him struck up a duet, their fingers becoming a blur as they faced each other, plucking and strumming faster and faster in an effort to outdo each other.

The other musicians brought up their instruments again as the Shadowseer's cloud turned to a darker mist, billowing heavily across stage and spectator alike, swathing the motes of silver and gold that remained. Aradryan looked at the Shadowseer and was shocked to see his own face beneath her hood, lips twisted in a cruel smile, eyes wide and fierce. It was a discomfiting sight; he glanced at the others around him, realising from their apprehension that each was seeing himself or herself mirrored in the Shadowseer's mask.

A sinking feeling took root in Aradryan's gut as the darkness descended. Foreboding filled him as he watched the musicians circling about each other, each now striking up his own tune. Where there had been harmony, now there was discord. Notes screeched against each other and the pipes had become a mournful dirge, weighing down Aradryan's mood even further. He felt as helpless as he had been on his first encounter at Hirith-Hreslain, rooted to the spot while the performers competed with each other; the music grew harsh and loud while the dancers flipped and rolled and spun, showing off their acrobatic prowess in extravagant style.

Two more performers had appeared unnoticed, cloaked and hooded with subtle pinks and pastel blues, their masked faces covered with silken purple scarves. Amidst the clashing notes and whirling dancers, they moved from Harlequin to Harlequin, stealthy and sinister, pausing to whisper in the ears of the other performers. Each Harlequin thus contacted paused for a moment, before renewing their efforts with even greater vigour. The cloaked mimes made great show of being amused and pleased by their interference; they laughed silently, pointing at the frenzied Harlequins as they skirled and danced and spun about each other, so fast it was hard for Aradryan to keep track, the display becoming a movement of light and darkness, colour and sound without figures or meaning.

Feeling dizzied and yet uplifted by the remarkable performance, Aradryan was rapt, unaware of anything else in the room. He realised he too was swaying with the music, his movements slightly jerky as he responded first to one tune and then another, his limbs twitching in rhythm to the different dancers.

A crash of drums and utter blackness set his heart racing. While the noise rolled away, echoing far longer than it should have done in the small hall, white light blazed from the Shadowseer, nearly blinding Aradryan. Narrowing his eyes against the glare, he saw a figure in black rising up at the centre of the stage as ominous notes flowed from the unseen pipes, low and beating like the pulse of some gigantic beast.

The figure was a Death Jester, her mask a bony visage, her suit studded with silver skulls. In her hands she held a miniature scythe, which she spun and twirled, its keen edge gleaming in the light cast by the Shadowseer. Aradryan wanted to cry out, knowing what was to come. Fear gripped him as that scythe-edge flashed around the other Harlequins, passing within a hair's-breadth of every performer as the Death Jester stalked and skulked, picking her first victim. The warning died in his throat and there was frightened, wordless breaths from those around him, barely heard by the ranger.

Finally Aradryan did cry out as the Death Jester's blade slashed across the throat of a moonharp player. There were other panicked calls from the audience as crimson specks marred the white light and the slain Harlequin collapsed, his instrument clattering to the stage. The Death Jester raised up her arms in triumph, and then spun on her heel, scythe flashing across the chest of a cartwheeling dancer. More red seeped into the whiteness, spraying up from the lethally wounded performer.

Again and again the Death Jester struck, until the stage was bathed with crimson, the musicians and dancers piled upon each other, entwined in their last throes, thrashing and wailing. Tears were streaming down Aradryan's face, his lips parted in horror. His whole body was trembling as he witnessed the carnage, while the cloaked mimes danced with glee, snatching up the bodies of the fallen, dragging them off the stage one-by-one as they died.

All fell to blackness and silence once more, making Aradryan's stomach lurch, his ears ringing from the cacophony that had been raised, the salt of his tears on his lips.

Gentle silver light prevailed again, revealing the Shadowseer alone on the stage once more. Aradryan had heard no patter or step of departing performers. The sound of weeping was all around Aradryan, and he realised that Athelennil was clutching his arm, her fingers painfully tight on his flesh.

With arms outstretched to either side, the Shadowseer bowed low, giving Aradryan one last glimpse of his own face as the hood fell, a wry smile on his image's lips as it gave him a wink.

He didn't know whether to applaud, shout, laugh or cry. He could feel his body shaking with expended energy, and was as fatigued as if he had been performing himself, every muscle clenched tight, his nerves jangling.

With silent steps, the Shadowseer left and the lights returned, revealing the numb crowd. Conversation, some heated, some subdued, erupted almost immediately, the sudden life and vitality of the audience making the display of the Harlequins seem even more ethereal and unreal, like a dream half-forgotten.

Findelsith joined them clothed in his full performance regalia. He had not taken part in the piece, as his role as the Laughing God was not required. His garb was an even more outlandish and extravagant motley than those worn by his troupe. His crest went through every colour of the spectrum, standing high from his scalpcap and cascading in streamers of increasing length to his waist. Precious metals glittered in the weave of his bodysuit, which was worn underneath a jacket with gem-glistening collar and cuffs. His mask was blank black on one side, save for a cross-shaped eye-lens behind which the Great Harlequin's deep red eyes glittered with mischievous intent. The right side was a blue face with a dagger-like pointed nose and upcurving chin, almost making a half-moon in shape. Red painted eyebrows and lips completed the face's features.

A kami stood close at hand. Estrathain had made the initial introductions, having fetched Findelsith from the backstage area, and now remained on hand to assist if needed. It was Jair who had been nominated to speak for the group, and he welcomed the Great Harlequin to the group with a bow.

'Thank you for the performance,' said Jair. 'For some of us, it is the first opportunity we have encountered to witness such a spectacle.'

'Your attendance is pleasing to the troupe,' said Findelsith, his deep voice resonant with a poetic cadence, 'and I am happy to listen to you. From Estrathain we learnt of your bold plans, I tell you now that we will not help you.'

'What?' blurted Athelennil, immediately disregarding the ban they had agreed on anyone but Jair speaking. 'How can you reply so quickly when we have not even told you our intentions?'

'Intentions are always the same, I find, and why should I not think the same of you? Waystones it is, every single time, always the same, and it is so boring. What performance is there for us to play that we have not yet played a hundred times?'

'We bore you?' Caolein took a step forwards; shoulders hunching. The Great Harlequin did not move, save to turn his head slowly and regard Caolein with that half-smirking mask.

'Do not play his games,' said Aradryan, laying a hand on Caolein's shoulder. 'He is the clown, he is meant to amuse us, so do not indulge him.'

Findelsith raised a gloved hand and pointed at Aradryan whilst still looking at Caolein.

'You I like, you have something special inside you, but even to you the answer is no.'

'I never thought I would see the cycle when a Harlequin dared not into the gut of the Great Enemy,' said Lechthennian, the other outcasts stepping out of his way as the elderly traveller approached. 'A poor excuse it is, to quote boredom and repetition, when one has the chance to be one with the Laughing God. Dare her lair, and laugh in his face. If it is not to tweak the nose of She Who Thirsts, what is it to be a Harlequin?'

Tilting his head in surprise, Findelsith stood up abruptly. He looked at each of the outcasts, lingering for just a heartbeat, before his gaze finished on Lechthennian, as inscrutable as ever.

'A chance challenge you lay upon my spirit, and a charge I cannot well deny,' said the Great Harlequin, turning away with an airy wave of his hand. 'You, friend, have the best of the argument, and you are welcome to it, I might say.'

'Tarry just for one more moment, and hear my debate, and you and I will be in accord, I grant you,' said Lechthennian, stepping quickly after the departing Findelsith.

The Great Harlequin paused a moment, allowing the outcast to catch him. Lechthennian's next words were softly spoken, and Aradryan could not hear them, nor see Lechthennian's lips nor read his expression. Aradryan looked at the others and their intrigued faces told him that they were as mystified as he.

There seemed to be a short debate, during which Lechthennian made imploring gestures several times, elbows tucked into his ribs, hands splayed out with a shallow bow. Aradryan was about to go over and ask the aging traveller to cease embarrassing himself, but before he took a stride he saw Findelsith take a step back and nod his head once in agreement. Lechthennian smiled briefly, bowed once more and returned to bring back the happy news.

'He seemed so adamant,' said Jair.

'How did you change his mind?' asked Caolein. 'He did change his mind, yes? We did see that?'

'All I had to do was employ a bit of flattery and dangle a proposition too exciting for him to decline,' replied Lechthennian. He motioned them to head towards the door. 'In part we can thank Estrathain for his agreement, as he was most intrigued by the idea of journeying with the kami.'

'And what else?' said Aradryan, thinking Lechthennian's account a little vague and unconvincing. 'You are not an agile liar, your concealment of something is plain to see.'

'I confess, I am reluctant to share,' said the musician. 'I dared Findelsith, you see, and now that we are committed, I fear I might have overstepped my bounds.'

'What dare?' said Athelennil, glaring daggers at Lechthennian.

'I challenged him to lead us somewhere he had never been before, to a world that caused even him a deep dread,' said Lechthennian. 'If he admits to fear, he cannot truly be an avatar of the Laughing God, for Cegorach laughs in the face of death and danger. To prove to himself that he is not truly afraid, he must take us to the place for which he holds the deepest fear, or give up his position as Great Harlequin.'

'We are going to journey to a world in the bosom of She Who Thirsts, at the heart of the Abyss of Despair, to a world so bad that a Great Harlequin of the Laughing God is afraid to go there?' said Aradryan, uttering the words slowly, unable to believe them himself. He sighed, and shrugged. 'Perfect. That is just perfect.'

ADVENTURE

The crone worlds – When the ancient empire stretched across the stars, the heart of civilisation was located at the Wheel of Destiny, our first world where Eldanesh was born at the hub. It was from the Wheel of Destiny that Morai-heg spun that fate of the eldar race, and about that wheel all things revolved, for good or ill. Populous were the worlds of the Wheel, and their art and fashions were considered the height of society. As with everything else, it was from the Wheel of Destiny that the strand of the Great Enemy was spun. The first of the sects and cults were created here, and from the Wheel of Destiny that poison spread through the empire. When the Fall came and the Great Enemy was born, it was Morai-heg that was consumed first, the Wheel of Destiny absorbed into the body of She Who Thirsts. Ever they have belonged to her and so now those worlds, once the heart of civilisation and now the heart of the Eye of Terror, are known as the crone worlds.

Aradryan left the business of organising the expedition to the more experienced members of *Irdiris*'s crew, and spent the time exploring some of the arcades and dens of Khai-dazaar. When the preparations were complete, he met with Athelennil, Jair and the others at the quayside where the starship was docked. From here, Caolein guided the *Irdiris* to the large battleship they had passed on their arrival: the *Fae Taeruth*.

The Harlequins had preceded them on board, their gaily coloured webskimmer inside the *Fae Taeruth*'s sizeable docking bay when the outcasts landed. They were met by the captain, the female exiled Commorraghan Maensith. She was not at all what Aradryan had been expecting. The tales of the dark kin of Commorragh had left an image in his mind of cruel, sneering, whip-wielding torturers. While the reputation was well-deserved, his first impression of Maensith was of a cultured, polite starship captain.

She and her crew were dressed in black and purple and dark blues, it was true, but devoid of their armour they seemed like any other ship's complement in Khai-dazaar. Maensith had white hair, swept back from her face with a band of emerald-studded metal, the gems matching the colour of her eyes.

Most remarkably, Maensith wore no waystone. This realisation brought out a mix of dread and awe in Aradryan, who instinctively touched his fingertips to the brooch at his breast to reassure himself that his waystone was there. The thought of going through life exposed to the predation of She Who Thirsts horrified him, and he tried not to stare at his host.

Maensith might have noticed his gaze; she glanced at Aradryan for a moment, meeting his eye. There was a hardness to her that silently spoke of grim experiences, but the ship captain's smile was also quick and infectious as she introduced the notable officers from her two hundred-strong complement.

Aradryan had been warned by Estrathain not to inquire too deeply into her past, so he held his tongue despite the obvious questions that nagged him as Maensith explained the running of the ship and its layout. Of the *Fae Taeruth*, the only thing that marked it as significantly different from *Lacontiran* were the weapons bays and blisters. Running for most of the ship's length in the middle decks, the weapons batteries consisted of several dozen high-powered laser turrets, supplemented by shorter-ranged rocket batteries for anti-boarding defence. The crew that they passed on the tour, which took place as the *Fae Taeruth* slipped her moorings and headed into the webway, nodded deference to their commander and her guests, which was something that Aradryan had not encountered before, either on Alaitoc or further abroad.

'Do all of your crew hail from Commorragh?' he asked, slightly nervous of the company. They had returned to the landing bay to retrieve their belongings, and would be quartered with the officers of the mercenary company close to the ship's command bridge.

'Only a handful,' replied Maensith. 'Most are simply outcasts like yourselves, seeking some excitement and meaning in their lives. It is never wise to have too many kabalites in your crew if you are no longer in service to an archon.'

'Kabalites?' Aradryan had not heard the term before.

'If you wish, I could tell you more of the Commorraghan kabals, the wych cults and incubi of the Dark City, but that can wait for the moment,' said Maensith. 'My pilots and I need to speak to Findelsith regarding our journey.'

'This is your first foray into the Dark Abyss?' asked Jair.

'It is, though I have been close to its outer reaches in the past,' said Maensith. She lay a reassuring hand on the arm of Aradryan, noticing his apprehension at this revelation. 'I would say not to be afraid, but that would be a lie. Where we are going is dangerous, and I will not pretend otherwise. However, my crew and I have experienced battle and peril many times, and you are in good hands.'

With a nod of farewell, Maensith turned away. She stopped at the archway that led from the flight deck and turned.

'We are all going to profit well from this excursion, mark my words!'

When she had left, the outcasts boarded *Irdiris* to take up their possessions. Athelennil caught Aradryan by the arm when they were in the main passageway.

'Do not be tricked by pretty eyes and a welcoming smile,' she warned. Aradryan could not help but consider some of this to be due to jealousy on Athelennil's part, despite her prior declarations to hold no romantic claim to Aradryan or any other.

'I judge as I find,' Aradryan replied, laying his hand onto hers. 'It is good to know that you still watch out for my wellbeing.'

'Remember that, when we are in the heart of the Great Enemy,' said Athelennil. 'We all need to stand together if we are to return.'

Aradryan nodded, the warning reminding him of the course they were setting and the hellish destination at its end.

The *Fae Taeruth* made swift progress, keeping to the main arterial passages of the webway, heading towards the Eye of Terror. During the journey, the disparate groups that made up the expedition mingled little, so that Aradryan saw little of the Harlequins or mercenaries. On his forays from the cabin he shared with Athelennil, he was struck by something: all of the starship's crew went about their duties armed. Every mercenary he passed had a pistol and blade at his or her waist.

When he and the others were invited to be guests at a meal with Maensith, he raised this observation with the mercenary captain. Jair, Caolein and Athelennil were amongst the complement who joined Maensith and her handful of lieutenants in a dining area that more closely resembled a ballroom on Alaitoc than a mess hall on a battleship. Crystals glowed overhead, dappling the diners with red and gold and purple, and underfoot was a thick carpet, woven with a pattern of black roses on powder blue, their jade stems entwining to form mesmerising geometries.

The fare on offer was also better than he had experienced on either *Irdiris* or *Lacontiran*. There were meats cured in delicate spices, fresh fruit and cereals, lightly baked, sweet-tasting breads and bowls of pungent broth. All was laid out on an oval table that would have comfortably sat twice as many guests, laden with silver and golden platters, amongst which delicate ceramic dishes steamed while carafes of wines and juices were freely passed amongst the eldar.

'It is a necessary precaution in our lives,' Maensith explained. 'It is better to be accustomed to the weight of a sword at your hip, and to have your weapons to hand if you need them. The webway is not safe, whatever your experiences in the past may be, and where we are going it is far from a sanctuary.'

'Do you think we should be armed?' Aradryan asked. He took a sip of a particularly azure wine from a crystal goblet edged with delicate white gold. The ranger had realised as soon as he had sat down that much of his surroundings and what was on offer were no doubt the proceeds of piracy, or at least payment for less-than-moral deeds, but the notion had not dampened his appetite or thirst, which had been whetted by the festivities he had enjoyed in Khai-dazaar.

'A ranger longrifle is of little use in a ship action,' laughed Maensith. 'I am sure no one will take offence if you choose to wear your pistols from here on.'

'I do not think I shall be of much assistance, if that is the case,' said Aradryan, shaking his head. 'I am comfortable with a longrifle, but encounters at closer quarters have not gone so well for me.'

'Nonsense,' said Jair, who was on his second jug of wine already. 'When we ran into the orks on the way to the Exodites, you showed no hesitation.'

'I fear that I did, perhaps for an instant,' said Aradryan. He shuddered as he remembered the red-eyed orks and the gush of blood from Estrellian's mortal wounds. 'I may have cost Estrellian his life in that brief moment.'

'Regret is as harmful as fear,' said Maensith. Her words were sharply spoken, the first time Aradryan had detected any harshness in her voice. 'To linger in the past invites doubt, and doubt eats away at the spirit.'

'And what of learning from the mistakes of the past?' asked Caolein. The question seemed innocent enough, but there was something about the pilot's words that hinted at accusation, and Aradryan, who was sat at Maensith's right hand, felt the captain stiffen slightly. He had almost forgotten that she hailed originally from the Dark City, so pleasant and convivial was the feast and its attendants. Why Caolein chose to ask such a barbed question of their congenial host was a mystery to Aradryan.

'The past cannot be changed,' said Maensith, keeping her tone even, though her eyes narrowed slightly. 'It is equally dangerous to cast one's gaze too far ahead, perhaps longing for something that will never come, missing the opportunities of the moment.'

'To experience the moment, and be nothing more?' Caolein asked, eyebrows raised.

'Just so,' said Maensith. Her fingers tapped a beat on the tabletop for a moment, before she reached out and grasped the stem of a golden goblet. She raised it a fraction and tipped the cup towards Caolein, before lifting it higher in toast to all present.

'Let us wish for a fruitful and uneventful expedition,' said the captain. 'The prize to those who dare!'

This last sentiment was echoed by her officers, and Aradryan murmured a late echo in response. There was an awkward silence, which was broken by the hiss of the door and the arrival of Estrathain's kami. The artificial being was clothed as always in its scarlet robes and scarves, and entered the feasting hall with quick steps.

'Apologies for the intrusion, my captain, but I come direct from the chambers of Findelsith,' announced the kami. 'This branch of the webway has almost taken us as far as it can, and we must make preparations for a transference to the material world. He must speak with you about the next stage of our journey.'

'Of course,' said Maensith. She set down her goblet as she stood and dipped her head to each of the diners in turn, finishing with a lingering look at Aradryan that he could not quite decipher. Her next words were almost a whisper, directed at the ranger. 'Come to see me, and I shall instruct you in the basics of swordcraft, Aradryan. You will feel the more confident for the lesson.'

With that she left, taking Estrathain with her. One by one, the mercenary lieutenants offered their apologies and excused themselves, claiming duties to attend, until only those of *Irdiris* remained. Aradryan noticed an absent member of their complement and wondered why he had not seen him earlier.

'What of Lechthennian?' he asked.

'I do not know where he is,' said Athelennil. There was a quiet rebuke in her next words, which Aradryan knew were meant for him. 'I think he is more discerning of the company he keeps.'

Despite Athelennil's misgivings, Aradryan contacted Maensith during the following cycle. He arranged to meet the mercenary captain in one of the empty storage holds in the lower decks, and chose not to mention the rendezvous to Athelennil to head off any further chiding.

Maensith met him in her full battle gear. Over a black bodysuit she wore a shaped breastplate of silvered ceramic material, which fitted her body as snugly as the bodyglove. She had tassets and ailettes of the same design on her shoulders and thighs, edged with sharply tapered edges. About her waist was a skirt of purple laminar, split at the front to allow her to move with freedom. Her gloves went up to her elbows, and were lined with serrated blades on the outside of the hand and forearm, her fingers and thumbs protected with segmented armour. She also wore a helm that protected her skull and cheeks, with an aventail of scale. The armour shimmered like the carapace of a beetle or slick of oil, rainbows playing on the curved surfaces beneath the white strip lights of the cargo bay.

A pistol hung at Maensith's right hip, and on her left was a curved sword in a long scabbard. She held another blade of the same design in her hand, and proffered it to Aradryan without any word as he entered. He took the sheathed sword, feeling its weight approvingly. The scabbard was plainly decorated with a line of four red gems, the lower part bound with overlapping white cord.

'Wear it like this,' said Maensith. She stepped behind Aradryan and took the sword from him, releasing two lengths of binding. He was aware of her right next to him, the blades of her armour less than a hand's breadth from his flesh. She crouched, passing the thongs around his waist, looping them through ringlets on the scabbard before tying a firm but decorative knot. She tugged the sheath a little towards his thigh, settling its weight better on his hip. 'Now draw it.'

Aradryan reached across with his right hand as Maensith circled to stand in front of him, weight on one leg, finger held to her chin as she made her critique. The ranger grabbed the sword and tugged it free. His arm felt awkward, his elbow jutting at an odd angle, as he pulled the blade fully from its scabbard.

'Not like that,' said Maensith, stepping forwards with a purposeful look. She again stood behind him, reaching around so that her hand was on his wrist, fingers slightly splayed. 'Like this. Do not make a fist around the hilt, make the blade an extension of your arm.'

Aradryan did as he was told, keenly aware of her breath on the side of his neck. She had a peculiar presence, both disturbing and exciting at the same time. He could sense wildness kept in check by this veneer of civility. The sword certainly felt more natural after he had adjusted his grip.

'A little lower, towards the pommel, so that the weight balances easily,' Maensith continued. She stepped next to him, drawing her own sword, showing him the proper form. 'This is a slashing blade, used for cutting more than stabbing. Though if you find yourself in a tight fix, ramming the pointy part into your enemies might suffice.'

Her laughter was edged with just a hint of unkindness, which gave Aradryan pause. He turned to look at her.

'Why are you doing this?' he asked.

'Circumstance has thrown us together, my friend,' Maensith replied, swishing her blade back and forth a few times, stepping lightly from one foot to the other. 'It may come to pass that you and I must fight side-by-side. I would rather you did more damage to our enemies than to me.'

'Surely it would be better to leave me to fend for myself in that event,' said Aradryan, laughing at his own suggestion. Maensith did not laugh with him, but instead fixed him with a curious stare.

'Would you abandon me so swiftly?' she asked, her voice a soft purr. 'And I thought we had an understanding.'

'Oh no, you shall not trick me so easily,' Aradryan said, wagging a finger in mock disapproval. 'I know what you Commorraghans are like, and how fickle your loyalties can be.'

He regretted the words almost immediately, seeing the genuine hurt on Maensith's face. She sheathed her sword and turned away, shoulders tense.

'If that is all you see in me, a dirty Commorraghan, then perhaps I should just leave you to die,' she snapped, stalking towards the wide bay door. 'One less clueless Alaitocii to get in my way.'

'No regrets, you said!' Aradryan called after her, his voice echoing quietly around the empty hold. 'Am I allowed to apologise?'

Maensith stopped but did not turn around or look back.

'You can admit to making a mistake, if you want,' she said, relaxing.

'I do not just see a filthy Commorraghan,' Aradryan said. 'Please, I need you to teach me how to at least defend myself. You never know, if I stay alive a little longer it might give you more time to get away.'

Turning with a half-smile on her lips, Maensith eyed him for some time, gauging him from head to toe. She evidently liked what she saw and rejoined him, sword in hand.

'There are four basic parries.' And so the lessons began.

For another sixty-eight cycles the *Fae Taeruth* forged across the galaxy, sometimes hopping across realspace from webway portal to webway portal, heading towards the Eye of Terror. In that time, Aradryan learnt swordplay with Maensith, spending whole cycles in the lower decks practising parry and cut, dodge and riposte. Maensith proved herself a capable teacher, though prone to toying with him during their sparring sessions. She had perfected her bladecraft over a long lifetime and he was but the barest novice; often he ended a session panting with exertion while she appeared unruffled.

Disapproving of his growing attachment to the ex-Commorraghan, Athelennil found quarters for herself, so that Aradryan slept alone. He and his fellow outcasts spent some time together, playing games of chance with the mercenary officers, and on two occasions they hosted a performance of storytelling, swapping exploits and anecdotes with some of those they had befriended amongst the *Fae Taeruth*'s company; none of them Commorraghans. Aradryan could see that they distrusted any kin of the Dark City on reputation alone, but knew better than to argue against this bias; the dark eldar were on the whole depraved and loathsome cousins to the Exodites and eldar of the craftworlds. It was perhaps his own yearning for a change in his life that guided Aradryan towards Maensith, who had been forced from her home and had adapted to life outside of Commorraghan society.

He saw Lechthennian little and the Harlequins even less. Occasionally he would hear the trill of a lip-flute or thrum of a mourning harp from the bowels of the ship, and once or twice he spied his fellow outcast out-side his cabin, humming or whistling to himself, sitting in the corridor. He seemed utterly unconcerned by their current quest, though as time passed and they came closer and closer to the Maw of Eternity, the others in the company showed signs of increasing nervousness.

When Aradryan was not with Maensith, most of his time was spent with the kami of Estrathain. The half-living creation seemed to have inherited a disproportionate amount of his creator's curiosity, and asked endless questions on Alaitoc and *Lacontiran* that Aradryan was happy to answer. The kami's experience was all second-hand, but he regaled Aradryan and others with stories of those who had passed through Khai-dazaar during his life, and despite assurances of confidentiality to the contrary, shared a small amount of gossip and salacious tales of the more humorous and colourful disputes into which he had been brought for mediation.

On the sixty-eighth cycle, as the lights were dimmed for sleep, Aradryan was called from his chambers by Taelisieth, one of Maensith's lieutenants. Along with Maensith and her senior officers, the outcasts, Lechthennian included, were greeted in the navigational hall by Find-elsith and his Shadowseer, Rhoinithiel. The whole chamber seemed to float in space, the walls, floor and ceiling covered with a psychogrammic projection of their location and the surrounding star systems. Opposite the door pulsed a seething wound of purple and crimson: the Eye of Terror.

'We come to the hem, the blurring of worlds,' said Findelsith, as the other eldar gathered in a circle around the two Harlequins. As he spoke, the view changed, coiling tubes of the webway overlapping the stars. Aradryan realised that the illusion was created by Rhoinithiel, the Shad-owseer blending her abilities with the projections of the *Fae Taeruth*'s navigational network. 'Into the Womb of Destruction we pass, if on this course our hearts and minds are set. The webway corrodes, falling to nothing, and the raw bleeding of the warp remains. This is the Great Enemy before us, not just of legend but in form made real. Our goal lies within that maelstrom of woe, into the heart of the Prince of Pleas-ure. Speak now and be mindful of your desires, for even here She Who Thirsts can know you.'

It was odd the way Findelsith spoke this last sentence, indicating that he considered himself and his troupe apart from the other eldar in this regard. Aradryan wondered what made the Great Harlequin so sure that his own mind was free of the doom of the eldar. He put such thoughts aside and considered the matter at hand. He had tried not to dwell on the prospect of entering the Eye of Terror, and in a way it had become secondary to the journey he had been making. It had not occurred to him that they might come this far and yet be baulked by the last effort, and so he had resigned himself to the quest with some misgiving.

Having already spoken his mind at the outset and been overruled, he felt no desire to regurgitate old arguments. Instead, if one of the others was having doubts, let them be the first to raise it and he would support them.

The discussion was swift, though, and there were none amongst the outcasts nor the mercenaries who was of a mind to retreat from the task before them. In the fashion of outcasts, Aradryan was asked directly by Jair if he wanted to continue. If he desired, he offered Aradryan *Irdiris* to make the journey back to Khai-dazaar, or to wherever his wishes would take him.

It was a tempting offer, to have a ship and the freedom to go across the stars guided by only whim, and Aradryan was on the verge of accepting. He stopped himself, realising that a few swordcraft lessons and one battle with a longrifle was a woeful lack of preparation for life alone as an outcast. He might well make it back to Khai-dazaar, but if he was to leave now he would not only be abandoning his companions, he would be passing by an opportunity that might never come again.

Steeling himself to the decision, he declined the command of *Irdiris* and confirmed himself to the quest for the Tears of Isha. There was some amusement, misplaced to Aradryan's mind, in Findelsith's acknowledgement of this.

'So all are settled on the matter now, who will be undertaking this journey, to fetch the prize of Isha's Tears and in doing earn themselves high reward. Be silent and listen to my warning, for it shall be delivered only once. When we cross the veil we must take good care, so that not one of us is all alone. My troupe will watch over you for the time and so ensure that none are tainted. Many are the wiles of your greatest doom, heed not to any whispers of desire, for if not they shall be your undoing, and perhaps in your fall you doom us all.'

As Findelsith had promised, so it was. The Harlequins divided amongst the crew of the *Fae Taeruth* as the ship emerged from the webway and delved into the swirling vortex that was the incarnation of She Who Thirsts. In those first few moments, Aradryan felt something like panic gripping him, though it went deeper than just the fear of their environs. He became quickly convinced that he was not strong enough to resist the temptations and snares that the Great Enemy would surely set for him, and the warning of Findelsith rang loudly in his mind's ear, reverberating around his head.

Along with the others of *Irdiris*, he sat on a couch in one of the gathering areas above the starboard weapons batteries. With them was Taenemeth, one of the Harlequin masque's three Death Jesters, complete with bone-laden costume and skull-mask. The vision of death had said nothing since he had arrived, and his presence was more unsettling than it was reassuring. Thinking of death being amongst his companions sent

Aradryan's train of thought careening into more self-doubt.

He was weak, selfish and cowardly, and had no place in such company. He would be the undoing of them all; the perpetrator of some chance act or remark that would open the way for She Who Thirsts to devour the entire complement of the *Fae Taeruth*.

All of these thoughts clustered into his brain at once, clamouring for his attention. He imagined the lurid whispers of the Great Enemy's daemonic servants, and wondered if he would be able to recognise them as such. Again and again his fingers fluttered to the waystone at his chest, seeking comfort in its presence, though its surface had turned icy cold to the touch. And then another fear took him: what if his dread was simply the whisperings of some daemonic voice, and not his own?

Circular fears whirled about, reinforcing his desire to be away from this place. He stood up, desperate to be on his own, where he could do no harm.

'I could kill you now if it would help out,' said a voice close to Aradryan's ear, mocking him. 'Such a cure might be considered drastic. But if that is what you truly desire, I will make your demise look fantastic.'

Spinning about, Aradryan came face to face with the death's head visage of Taenemeth. The Death Jester titled his head sideways, waiting for a response.

'Leave me alone,' muttered Aradryan, stepping to one side to move past the Harlequin. Taenemeth moved to bar his path, shaking his head and wagging his finger.

'A shame it would be to leave you a ghost,' said the Death Jester, 'that is the tree of the seed you have sown. But you do not have to fear such a fate, if not by my hand then surely your own.'

What the Death Jester said was verging on nonsense, but Aradryan could not ignore the kernel of truth at its heart; it was in the company of the others that he was safest. There was no point running away from this, he had to endure whatever torments assailed his thoughts, for to be alone with such dark passions running through him would be to invite murder or suicide.

Taenemeth took a step aside, allowing Aradryan to sit down next to Lechthennian. Noticing his agitation, the musician winked and pulled a thumb whistle from his pocket. He passed it to Aradryan, who held it in his hands like it was a serpent.

'Just put the narrow end in your mouth and blow,' suggested Lechthennian. 'It will take your mind from other matters. If you want to get adventurous, there are three holes in the back you can cover with your thumb to make different notes.'

Aradryan laughed at the absurdity of it; Lechthennian's jibe on top of Taenemeth's morbid joking. He brought up the thumb whistle and blew a hesitant note. It warbled quickly and died away. The others were looking at him, but he could not feel ashamed, not now. He realised how ridiculous the whole situation was, and how close he had come to falling prey to his own fears. He tootled a few more notes and laughed again, looking up at the skull face of the Death Jester. He thought he understood, just a little bit, how the Harlequin felt, and what it must be like to be touched by the Laughing God. There was nothing he could do at the moment to preserve his fate, so if he died right now it might just as well be with a whistle on his lips as a frown on his brow.

Into the storm that was the incarnation of She Who Thirsts plunged the *Fae Taeruth*. Aradryan did not suffer a repeat of the episode that had beset him on their first entry, but he was acutely aware of everything that passed. It was as if his life had been brought into a sharper focus, so that every word uttered by his comrades, every thought that entered his mind, was loaded with meaning, both obvious and hidden. His senses felt acute, so that the touch of his sheets at night was a lover's caress and the gentlest throbbing of the starship's engines felt like rumbling thunder. He was aware of the stares of the crew as they passed, and every eldar aboard seemed to be touched by a vague paranoia. The ranger felt his temper fraying, as were his nerves, but always when he thought he was about to burst with the tension there was a Harlequin nearby, distracting him with a quip, brief poetic recital or an improvised dance that burst the bubble of his agitation.

During the night cycle, his dreams were vivid and took him to scenes both remembered and imagined, and often both, so that he awoke with a start, unsure whether what he had felt was a real experience or just unconscious fantasy. He had expected nightmares, to be assailed by the visions of the Great Enemy, but the opposite was true. Aradryan's dreams were awash with romance and love, filled with happiness and belonging.

Sometimes he dreamed he was a bird, and would climb to the highest pinnacle of a tower that speared into a violet sky. There was no fear in him as he leapt from the parapet, and his wishes bore him aloft like wings, to soar amongst the purple clouds. Other times he was a fish, swimming with the shoal, one of many glittering bodies, enjoying the surge of current around him, drawn to the dappling light upon the surface of the raging river.

There were much more intimate dreams too, of Thirianna and Maensith and Athelennil and past amours, as well as associates of his own creation. Sometimes these were gentle encounters, other times wild and carefree.

Always after the dreams he was left with a slight melancholy, a sense of longing that was not wholly unpleasant. He spent much time in his cabin, seeking the dreams he had experienced, but despite his training he was unable to recapture them, their reincarnations never quite as satisfying as the originals. A sense of unreality crept into his waking life, coupled with the heightened sense of his surroundings, so that as he ate and talked and practised with pistol and sword he would feel dislocated from himself at times, only to be brought back to the dullness of reality with a jolt, bringing a short but profound sadness.

He saw nothing of Maensith in that time, and he assumed she was kept busy with the piloting and navigation of the ship. Thrice he had made inquiries after her, driven to distraction by the lingering moments of a remembered dream, seeking release from the gentle torment of dreamt promises, but she was incommunicado and he would return to his chambers with his ardour unchecked.

Once, and once only, he took himself to the viewing gallery on the highest deck, to look upon the Womb of Destruction for himself. The long, domed chamber was empty except for Findelsith, who sat on a stool by the arched windows staring into the abyss. He did not have his mask on, revealing a face that was younger than Aradryan had expected. The eyes were different too, with none of the playfulness that glittered behind the ornate mask. Findelsith's gaze was tired, and filled with woe. The red teardrop tattooed upon his cheek, the tiniest of rubies sparkling at its heart, summed up the Great Harlequin's demeanour.

Findelsith ignored Aradryan, so the ranger crossed to the other side of the narrow gallery and looked out. What he saw drew forth a choked gasp.

He had been expecting a field of stars, perhaps, but what he saw was a blend of both the real universe and the energy of the warp. Everything was shimmering, and stars burned with every colour, some of them seemingly so close that their coronal ejections of green and orange and blue must surely incinerate the vessel. As though he peered through the magnifying sight of his longrifle, wherever he looked came into stark focus, seemingly just out of reach.

He could see worlds circling around the flaming orbs, shadows passing across the light. Some appeared normal, simple globes or gaseous giants, some ringed, others with circling moon systems. Many were utterly strange: triangular pyramids or straight-sided cubes, or dual and triple worlds that spun crazily about each other while leering faces made storm clouds in their skies. Dozens of lancing flames erupted from one world to his right, streaming into the haze of the space between stars.

All seemed impossibly compressed, like a child's interpretation of the galaxy rendered in holographic form, so that it could be rotated and manipulated, allowing Aradryan to look behind stars and into the whirling nebulae that painted images of lurid congress or swept past as flocks of celestial birds that darted through the heavens.

Feeling dizzy and sick, Aradryan stepped back and looked away, fixing his gaze upon the toes of his boots to give himself a point of reference for reality and stability. It did not work, and he staggered to one side, losing his footing as the deck seemed to buckle and ripple beneath him.

'To stare into the void is no delight, and but a few have eyes for such a sight.' Aradryan looked up from all fours, seeing that Findelsith had replaced his mask and was coming towards him, a hand outstretched to help Aradryan to his feet. 'It is too much for mortals to behold, to see nature's end where the warp unfolds. Such are the dark whims of a mad god's dreams, where once our towers rose and cities gleamed.'

Swallowing hard, Aradryan stood up with Findelsith's aid, keeping his eyes away from the windows, focused on the mask of the Great Harlequin. He nodded his thanks and stumbled towards the door, unable to speak of what he had seen.

Having witnessed the madness of the Chaos realm, Aradryan was consumed by trepidation when the announcement came via Estrathain that they were shortly to disembark. They had come upon their destination, the crone world of Miarisillion, somewhere in the depths of the Eye of Terror. The journey had not been without some tribulations – the Womb of Destruction was home not just to immaterial foes but also enemies of flesh such as the Space Marine Legions that had turned traitor against the will of the human Emperor. With speed sometimes, and with caution at others, the expedition had avoided these threats, moving into the depths of the Eye of Terror, always ready to turn and run lest they encounter some force or obstacle too great for them.

It was a harrowing time, made all the worse by the ever-present pressure of She Who Thirsts bearing down upon Aradryan's spirit. The *Fae Taeruth* was too large to enter the atmosphere of the planet, and so the expedition divided between *Irdiris* and the nameless vessel of the Harlequins. It was Aradryan's duty to take his place beside Caolein at the controls of the ship, and he entered the piloting chamber just as his companion was guiding the starship from the bay of the *Fae Taeruth*.

Miarisillion almost filled the navigational display, which was showing a true view of the vista ahead. Between grey scrapes of cloud Aradryan saw blue seas and white land. It looked like a frozen world, the landmasses encased in ice. Caolein shrugged at this suggestion, no wiser to the truth that Aradryan.

Entering the upper atmosphere, *Irdiris* swooped down on the tail of the red-and-green diamond-patterned Harlequin vessel. It was some time before they entered the cloud canopy, and Aradryan switched the spherical imager to a rendered version of their surroundings, the Harlequin ship appearing as a pulsing rune not far ahead.

Breaking out of the cloud at hypersonic speed, the two starships levelled, cruising above a wild ocean flecked with white crests of crashing waves. Daylight sparkled on the waters, though Aradryan could see no star to cast the light. Despite this, from the high altitude it was possible to see the terminator of night in the far distance, retreating towards the horizon.

It was some time before Aradryan sighted land, as Caolein guided the ship down in a decelerating glide. A high cliff of dark stone rose up at the edge of his vision, marked at this distance only by the massive fountains of surf that crashed upon its rocky foundations. As they swept closer, Aradryan could see the remains of a building along the summit of the cliff. Pillars and piles of masonry jutted from the waves, brought tumbling into the seas by an age of erosion.

The half-broken building continued along the cliff to the left and right, showing a remarkable cross-section of many-storeyed towers, stairwells and cellars. Aradryan could see the floors separating each level, linked by ramps and shafts, in places a maze of small chambers, in others becoming broad corridors and hallways.

Beyond the edge of the sea, the building continued; wherever it was that Aradryan looked he saw endless white stone, which from orbit he had mistaken for permafrost. Every scrap of land as far as he could see was covered with domes and bridges, towers and halls. Long and winding open staircases ascended solid pilasters that stretched into the sky, tipped with circular balconies, while curving roadways scythed between colonnaded forums and statue-filled plazas in elaborate loops and geometric swirls.

The whole edifice, save for that crumbled by the breaking cliffside, looked remarkably intact. Aradryan had been expecting a ruin, laid waste by the great tumult of the Fall, but the city looked no more damaged or decayed than if its occupants had simply departed peacefully a few cycles earlier. Pennants of grey and green snapped in the wind atop high banner poles.

'Look there,' said Caolein, pointing.

Aradryan had not been completely correct. The building did not enclose every last piece of earth, for off to the right a forest of blue-leaved trees broke the undulating white of tiled roofs and flagged terraces. It too seemed untouched by the ravages of time; an arrangement of circular lawns, spiralling towards a centre point, each a little smaller than the outer clearing, was clearly visible amongst the broad ring of trees.

There were other gardens, on the roofs and in gorge-like gaps between soaring halls. There were thousands of arched windows still glinting with panes, and doorways narrow and wide that led from hexagonally paved courtyards into the dark interior. Ponds and pools broke the monotony of the whiteness, some seemingly inaccessible except from the air. There were sculpture parks, their subjects too small to see even with the magnification of *Irdiris*'s viewer; streets were lined with much larger creations too, depicting naive interpretations of the eldar gods.

'This city must have been teeming with people in its prime,' said Aradryan.

'Not at all,' said Lechthennian. Aradryan had been so engrossed in the vista that he had not noticed the traveller coming into the piloting suite. Just behind him stood Estrathain. The kami's head slowly turned left and right, taking in the magnificent view with gem eyes. 'Only four thousand dwelt here. It is a palace, not a city.'

'That is fewer inhabitants than one of Alaitoc's habitation towers,' replied Aradryan, frowning. 'What of the other dwellings? How many lived outside the palace.'

'There is only the palace,' said Lechthennian, standing with his hands on the back of Aradryan's chair as he looked up into the display overhead. 'The whole world is the palace, every continent and island built to the design of one person.'

'To think that we had so many worlds that such vanity was possible,' said Estrathain. 'From such bounty and plenty come indolence and disaster.'

'It is unusual, even by the excesses of the empire in its greatest pomp,' said Lechthennian, eyes half closed as if in remembrance. 'There were those who built worlds in the webway, but for the creator of Miarisillion it was the dominance of the physical realm that stoked his pride.'

'How can you know this?' asked Caolein, twisting in his seat to look at the musician. 'Where did you learn such a tale?'

Lechthennian did not answer immediately, but looked at Caolein with a half-smile. The traveller shrugged, as if deciding that there was no secret to keep.

'How do the Harlequins know that it is here? In the Black Library, where all of our knowledge of the ancient empire and the Fall is kept, there are maps and atlases and charts aplenty, and journals both written and recorded survive from before the coming of She Who Thirsts.'

As Lechthennian mentioned the name of the eldar's doom, Aradryan felt a shiver run through him. He did not know whether it was a simple reaction to the use of the title, or whether the dark god that had destroyed the eldar could sense its name being spoken inside itself, even when only spoken in euphemism. The others had fallen quiet and Aradryan guessed he had not been alone in the sensation.

'You have been to the Black Library?' said Estrathain finally, turning his sculpted face towards Lechthennian. 'A most remarkable achievement, and one that can be claimed by even fewer than those who have come to the crone worlds.'

'It was a long time ago, and I am sure I do not remember the way,' said Lechthennian, still with the wry smile he had worn since raising the subject. 'If we survive this adventure, perhaps you could persuade Findelsith to take you there.'

'Looks like we will be landing nearby,' said Aradryan, as he noticed the Harlequin ship had begun a descending spiral towards the palace, bleeding off speed in preparation for touchdown.

Caolein returned his attention to the controls, guiding the ship along the vortex of a vapour trail left by the preceding craft. After a time-consuming descent, they eventually saw the Harlequins landing in a wide courtyard, lined with silver-barked trees with bright red leaves. Not far away was a massive dome, almost as large as one of Alaitoc's, though constructed of stone rather than an energy field, its contents concealed from view.

There was plenty of space to set *Irdiris* down beside the Harlequins, and as Aradryan let the engines decrease to idle, Caolein opened up the entry hatch and activated the boarding ramp. Aradryan took a last look at the view outside, noticing there were no birds or insects despite the mild clime and temperate conditions.

'I think we are the only creatures on this world,' said Aradryan, pushing himself from the reclining seat.

'Let us hope that things remain that way,' replied Caolein.

PERIL

The Womb of Destruction – When She Who Thirsts came into being, roused from dormancy by the depravity of the old civilisation, the god's body took form where the ancient empire had been at its strongest. So powerful was the birth-scream of the Great Enemy, it tore open reality, fusing the warp and the material universe together, creating a vast warp storm that has raged to this day. This rift has many names, for it is the most important feature in the galaxy. The Womb of Destruction it was called at first, for it was in the depths of this bleeding wound that the eldar doom was born. Some refer to it as the Abyss of Magic, as it is the Realm of Chaos given physical property, a well of psychic power. Another name there is; unusually it is a theft-phrase taken in translation from the mon-keigh, but it summarises the sense of despair one feels when thinking of the warp rupture through which the Dark Prince still jealously watches us: the Eye of Terror.

The expedition mustered under the branches of the trees. Aradryan had brought his longrifle, pistol and the sword gifted to him by Maensith, and was not surprised to see the mercenaries more heavily armed with rifles, shuriken cannons, brightlances and other weapons that he could not identify. Slightly more revealing were the Harlequins, who sported all manner of blades and pistols. Findelsith carried an axe with a long, elegant blade across his back, and his wrists were sheathed in bladed cuffs that glimmered with energy fields.

The Death Jesters carried shrieker cannons, black-painted versions of the shuriken weapons possessed by Maensith's company, while several of the troupe were armed with the tubular, glove-like harlequin's kiss, which Aradryan had heard about from Jair. The older ranger had claimed that when the harlequin's kiss was punched into a foe, it released a long, molecule-thick wire into their innards, slicing them apart from within. If true, it was a grisly weapon for such gaily-appointed warriors.

The entrance into the palace interior was formed by two trees at one end of the courtyard, the boughs of which formed an arched, glassed gateway. Findelsith led the way with Rhoinithiel the Shadowseer by his side and a cadre of Harlequins not far behind. Maensith followed with Aradryan and the others close by, flanked by the mercenaries, while the rest of the Harlequins brought up the rear. Passing into the glass-ceilinged entranceway, the padding of their feet echoed along the corridor, disturbing a silence that had persisted since the Fall.

Coming to a corridor that seemed to stretch into the distance to the left and right, the expedition split into two groups, each a mix of outcasts and Harlequins. Aradryan and the others were in the group led by Findelsith, while Maensith took leadership of the other. Before they each went their separate way, Findelsith had a warning for them.

'Baubles and treasures aplenty there are, to turn a mind or hand to their taking. You must resist such plundering urges, for in this place there can be no desire. Take nothing but the Tears that you did not bring with you, and leave nothing that we bring to this place. Feel no yearning and lust for another, for through these things the Great Enemy strikes. He can feel us but he does not see us – give her no pause to turn her gaze this way.'

Another shudder gripped Aradryan at the reminder that despite the relative normality of their surroundings – as normal as a planet-spanning palace built by the arrogance of a single ruler could be – they were in fact on a crone world, steeped in warp energy, sustained by the psychic power of She Who Thirsts, who had fed upon the eldar since her birth during the Fall.

Aradryan paused, thinking that he heard whispering, but dismissed the noise as the breeze on the windows above. He felt as though they were being watched, but put the feeling down to the tapestries that hung on the walls, each a larger-than-life-size depiction of a noble-looking eldar with a narrow nose and high brow. In the closest, his white hair hung in braids across each shoulder, and around his neck was a tight choker studded with diamonds fashioned as tiny skulls. Aradryan sneered at the embroidered portrait, as if in accusation that it was spying upon him.

Turning, Aradryan realised that he recognised the face from a bust he had seen on a pedestal opposite where the entrance hall met the passageway. Examining the tapestries to the left and right, he saw that they all depicted the same person; though his hair and clothes and environs changed, the haughty features were unmistakable.

'A testament to aggrandisement and ego,' said Lechthennian. 'A whole world dedicated to the hubris of one, who doomed his family and friends to share in this self-inflicted confinement of pride.'

They continued to explore, finding several bedchambers and dining halls along the length of the corridor. As with the exterior, the inside of the palace was immaculate, with not a speck of dust, nor scratch or stain. The furnishings – portraits, sculptures, busts, tapestries and all showing the same overbearing face – were intact, with not a weave or stitch out of place in the carpets and chairs, the dark wood of the tables and mantels gleaming with polish.

It was impossible to explore the widening maze of rooms as one group, so one at a time, and in pairs, the band dispersed through the chambers. Aradryan did not know what he was looking for, if anything at all, and he found himself leaving Lechthennian in contemplation of an ornate fireplace, the mantel and surround of which was carved from green marble, forming intertwining figures and animals, with spears and bows in evidence. Yet whether they were hunting or doing something far less desirable was unclear to Aradryan, given the interconnectedness of the participants, and he looked away hurriedly, content to leave the musician to answer the question for himself.

Through various side passages, short stairwells and doorways Aradryan continued, always keeping a picture in his mind of where he was in relation to where he had come from, so that he could head back immediately if he needed to rejoin the others. This task was made more confusing by the abundance of mirrors he encountered. There seemed to be one every other room, and several in each passageway. Some were so large that at first he mistook them for branching corridors or additional chambers. The portraits at least had given way to this new form of vanity, but glimpsing himself every few steps, or seeing movement out of the corner of his eye, did nothing to help Aradryan relax.

He was sure that when he was not quite looking directly at them, his reflections pulled different expressions. Figures flitted where they should not, though in truth they were probably reflections of reflections. On the whole, it was a most unsettling experience, but there was nothing to do except to push on in the hopes of finding something significant to report.

The whispering seemed to have grown louder too, but Aradryan was almost used to it by now, it becoming a part of the background noise along with the pad of his feet on tile or hardwood floor, or the scrape of his scabbard as it caught on the corner of a table or shelf that he passed.

Aradryan found an answer to the riddle of the whispering in the next room. It was another arena-size bedchamber, the bed itself almost lost at the heart of a carpeted red sea and crimson hangings. Through a massive window he saw a seascape just a stone's throw from the palace, at the foot of a black-sanded beach. The waves seemed almost purple, and Aradryan realised with surprise that twilight was coming, the distant horizon darkening as he watched. The way the sea lapped, the sussurant hissing of the water, set his mind at ease. It was a comforting whisper, not a conspiratorial one.

Senses dulled by the mesmeric washing of the waves, Aradryan felt the need to sit down for just a moment. He had been searching for quite a time, and if he could just rest for a little while he would be rejuvenated to continue the search. He looked around but the vast chamber had no chairs or stools or chests, only the large bed at its centre.

Before he even realised what he was doing, Aradryan was beside the bed, stroking a hand across the silk-like covers. He did not need to sleep, he told himself as he turned and sat down on the edge of the bed. He would just sit here for a few moments, recharging his strength. He could see why such a place had been constructed; from the bed the sea seemed to come right up to the window, its wordless voice urging him to close his eyes and relax.

Aradryan most definitely did not sleep. He did not even close his eyes, and stayed sat on the edge of the bed staring out at the alien sea. Despite being very obviously awake, the ranger started to notice that things were becoming decidedly dream-like. For a start, his waystone was gleaming gold and hot to the touch when he lifted his fingers to it. On top of that, he was not alone on the bed. He did not dare turn around, but he could feel the presence of someone else behind him, their weight on the mattress.

Delicate music tinkled in the distance, soothing and quiet, echoing along the empty corridors and across abandoned rooms. Except the corridors and rooms were not empty and abandoned. The figures of eldar moved around the apartment, several of them gathering by the window in front of Aradryan, holding hands with each other as they looked out across the waves as darkness descended. They were a family, two small girls with their mother and father. The person behind Aradryan called out a series of names and the family turned with smiles, the children breaking free to run to the bed. One of them leapt onto the mattress, passing straight through Aradryan.

Bolting to his feet, Aradryan turned to look at the ghosts. The eldar from the portraits, eyes lined with greater age, lay beneath the covers, which were rucked back to reveal his thin shoulders and shallow chest.

The music had stopped, and the small girl who had leapt onto the bed was not smiling any more. Her tiny hands were at the old noble's throat, and there were shouts and rings of metal from across the palace grounds. Old scores were being settled, the extended families dividing into factions, sectarian violence erupting between them to decide who should inherit the luxurious planet-manse.

'Come with us.'

Aradryan turned to see a beautiful eldar female in an elegant blue gown, the white of her thigh showing through a slit, her arms bare but covered in rings and torcs. Her black hair was heaped up upon her head, fixed by many jewelled pins. Her lips pouted at him and her eyelids fluttered ever so slightly as she sighed. He felt the light touch of her breath upon his cheek and smelt the fragrance of her perfume.

'It has been so long since we had visitors,' she said, her hand moving to Aradryan's arm. He could not feel her through his undersuit, but her fingers lay upon his forearm as if they were real. Behind the aristocratic-looking eldar, the girl on the bed had finished strangling the old noble and was pulling the heavy rings from his fingers, while her sister had joined her and was using a knife to cut his hair, pulling free gemstones from the bindings thus freed.

They were ghosts, Aradryan knew, but there was something alluring about the invitation that he could not shake. He knew in his heart that he could be content here. To live for eternity by the dying light across the sea was not such a bad fate. It was peaceful, nothing like the anarchy that had reigned elsewhere when the elderly ruler had drawn his last breath. It might have been coincidence, the birth scream of She Who Thirsts ripping apart the galaxy just moments after the self-proclaimed regent had perished, but the ghosts liked to think that their immortality was reward for the actions in bringing about the eruption of the Great Enemy.

'We will make you comfortable here,' she said, stroking Aradryan's arm. 'You will never hunger nor know thirst, and you shan't tire or be lonely. The children will play games forever, and you will never grow old either. Stay with us. Stay in our home by the sea.'

A screeching noise tore through Aradryan's thoughts. The ghosts snarled and fluttered away, becoming mist and then nothing. Aradryan was still sitting on the bed and he looked to where the noise had come from, seeing Lechthennian standing at the door with his finger upon the string of a half-lyre.

The screams of the dying eldar echoed in Aradryan's thoughts, carried by the after-echoes of that harsh note. It was not just those in the palace who had perished. Billions of eldar died, consumed by the god of the warp that had been created by their hedonism. Aradryan felt the tiniest fraction of their demise, his body quaking with reaction as the universe imploded around him, bringing into being She Who Thirsts, embodied by a storm thousands of light years wide that devoured the heart of the ancient eldar empire.

'Now is not the time to tarry with ghosts, Aradryan,' said Lechthennian, hanging his instrument from his belt. 'It is no pleasant fate to spend eternity trapped between worlds, lingering on the precipice between life and death.'

'What are they?' asked Aradryan. As he crossed the room back to the door, the shadowy figures were coalescing around him once more. Their whispering returned, almost beyond hearing, imploring and cajoling with soft words.

'They are the unfortunate ones who were trapped in damnation, their spirits remaining to be taunted by a life they can never have again, their torment a source of titillation to She Who Thirsts.' Lechthennian waved Aradryan through the doorway. 'Come, the time is nigh for the Witch Time and we will not have long. The others are waiting for us in the garden dome.'

Aradryan did not have any idea what Lechthennian was talking about, but followed the itinerant musician as he hurried through halls and chambers. The ghostly after-images of the damned eldar flowed around them, young and old, male and female. Aradryan caught snatches of invitation and threat, but now there was no melancholy in the disembodied voices, only menacing hisses and snarled reproach.

The pair caught up with Maensith and the rest of the expedition by a grand gatehouse linking the residential wing with the massive dome Aradryan had seen earlier. The ghosts here were much in evidence, seeming more substantial though still semi-transparent, dozens of them drifting into the dome with agitated chattering.

'Where are the Tears of Isha?' asked Maensith. She had her blade in hand, and many of her warriors had their weapons ready also, perturbed by the apparitions that glided onto the carefully-trimmed blue lawns that covered the dome, a tree-lined road cutting from the entrance hall across the far side of the gardens.

Looking around, Aradryan saw more families, sitting beneath the boughs, while lovers stood hand in hand gazing at their reflections in ponds and pools. The small figures of children laughed shrilly as they chased about the trees and hid behind hedges and bushes, the noise bringing no joy to the ranger but putting his nerves on edge.

'It comes upon us, the Time of Witching,' said Findelsith, pointing towards the top of the dome. 'We must be quick, the Tears of Isha fall.'

Far above in the artificial cloud of the dome, a golden light shimmered. Like rain, the light descended and in its aura the ghosts of the doomed eldar grew bright, becoming auric silhouettes. They stopped and gazed upwards, reaching out with imploring hands as the light fell upon them.

The screams began at the far side of the dome, unearthly and distant but terrifying all the same. Aradryan gritted his teeth as the unnatural shrieking of the ghosts filled the air, the faces of the apparitions contorting with agony and despair as though the light burned them. Collapsing to their knees, the ghastly host's wails reached a deafening crescendo, their bodiless pleas for mercy echoing from the trees and dome wall, reverberating inside Aradryan's skull so that he felt as if it was his body that was disintegrating.

The first of the ghosts fell to the ground on a path not far to Aradryan's left, curling up in a foetal position, twitching and wailing. It shook the ranger to the core as others collapsed, like a cluster of dolls knocked over by a violent gale. Writhing and flailing, clasping immaterial hands to immaterial faces, the doomed eldar relived the moment of ecstatic torture that was the Fall.

The golden light was almost as bright as a sun now, and Aradryan could see little of what happened next. Each ghost wavered and shrank, losing shape and focus, becoming smaller and smaller until only a flickering star of gold was left. And then the light dimmed, leaving dozens of smooth, pearlescent stones lying about the dome.

'Be swift and sure and take your prizes now!' Findelsith declared, sweeping an arm to encompass the gardens. Even as Aradryan started towards the closest Tear, where a robed young female had been standing a few moments before, he saw that the stones were shimmering, becoming as ethereal as the ghosts they had been.

The Tear of Isha was warm to the touch, its heat felt through the fabric of Aradryan's gloves. He lifted up the Tear and in the dancing patterns on its surface thought for a heartbeat that he saw the face of the dead eldar from whom it had been created. It felt wrong to take such a thing, but as his own waystone pulsed strongly at his chest he knew that it was a necessary task to protect the spirits of generations to come. The Tear would be gifted to an eldar infant, becoming their guardian from birth, attuning itself to their essence so that when later they passed from the mortal life, their spirit would be safeguarded from the hunger of the Great Enemy. Not until now had Aradryan known that the Tears of Isha were formed of the spirits of those who had been consumed by the Fall, and he could see why such knowledge was kept secret. It wrenched his heart to think of the unfortunates who had perished in this place, and to know that they relived that hateful moment again and again for the amusement of the Great Enemy brought a choking sob to his throat. It was a release he was giving the damned, to take them from this place.

In his hand the Tear was cooling, its surface solidifying into something more closely resembling the waystone it would become. He slipped it into a pouch at his belt and looked around for another. Spying the glint of a Tear in a thicket of grass beside a pond, he stooped to retrieve it. It had almost disappeared but became solid at his touch. It followed the first into the pouch.

No more than twenty heartbeats had passed when the Tears of Isha faded from existence. There were cries of dismay from some of the others, for they had managed to gather less than a quarter of the stones that had materialised. The suggestion was made that they should remain for the Time of the Witch to return, so that more Tears could be claimed, but Findelsith shook his head and pointed back to the way they had entered.

'With daring we have entered the foe's lair, but she is not blind to us forever,' warned the Great Harlequin. 'The purity of the Tears protects yet we cannot remain here for too long. The eye of She Who Thirsts will turn this way, bringing retort from he who we steal from.'

This timely cautioning did not fall on deaf ears. Maensith quickly gathered her warriors and, forming up into two groups, they made one last search of the nearby dells and copses, but no more Tears were to be found. Findelsith and his troupe were already moving back towards the entranceway, and Aradryan followed close behind them.

'Remarkable,' said Estrathain, falling into step beside the ranger. 'This body cannot shed tears, but if it could I fear I would drown in them.'

Aradryan said nothing, unable to put into words the feelings stirred by the vista of misery that had surrounded him.

After the events inside the dome, the journey back to the courtyard where the expedition had landed was conducted in silence. The ring of the mercenaries' boots echoed hollowly along the passageways and Aradryan's thoughts seemed loud in his head. Gone was the disturbing background whisper, but the utter absence of noise in its stead was just as unsettling. This was truly a dead place, where the living had no right to trespass.

The Harlequins led the way back to the ships, unerringly moving through the seemingly identical chambers and hallways. Aradryan found himself towards the back of the group, walking alongside Estrathain. The kami stared straight ahead, paying no heed to the artworks and furnishings, but Aradryan was again convinced that he saw flurries of movement in mirrors and window panes and silver decorations, movements that were not reflections of the eldar but possessed a life of their own.

He heard a scratching sound, for the briefest of moments and stopped, glancing back. There was a slight tremor in a curtained archway he had just passed. Aradryan would have dismissed it as a draught except that the air was still. Through the windows high in the walls of the corridor they were following the sky had turned to twilight, as he had first seen in the chamber by the sea. It should not have mattered whether it was night or day, but on a world with no sun the coming of dusk might portend something far more sinister.

Chiding himself for his paranoia, Aradryan took a few hasty steps to catch up with Estrathain. As he came level with the kami the ranger glanced to his left. He gasped, thinking he saw a pair of jet black eyes peering at him from the shadow of an alcove holding a silver statue with arms upraised. Looking more closely, Aradryan saw that there was nothing concealed behind the sculpture, but he could not shake the feeling of being observed.

They were not far from the entranceway that led to the courtyard where the ships had been left; Aradryan recognised some of the tapestries that covered the walls. It was with a sense of relief that he spied the glitter of the glass-ceilinged entrance hall some distance ahead, and he allowed himself a smile.

It was then that he heard the scratching again, and a distinctive click-clack, like a snapping twig. Some of the mercenaries ahead turned at the sound, so the ranger knew he had not imagined it. Maensith noticed the commotion and headed back.

'Why have you all stopped?' she demanded, glaring at her warriors. 'We must be gone swiftly.'

Before there was any reply, the skittering, scratching noise sounded again, like something running through the walls and ceiling. Aradryan caught a half-glimpse of something pale pink flittering across an arch-way ahead. He gave a shout and pointed, but the doorway was empty as the others turned.

'It is just the ghosts returning,' snapped Maensith, waving her pistol to move the group on.

Findelsith had now returned with some of the Harlequins to investigate the cause of the delay. The Great Harlequin was tense, his weapons in hand, his masked face turning left and right as he scanned the corridors and archways. Aradryan yelped as he thought he felt something brush against his back. Spinning on his heel, he yanked out his sword and took a step backwards towards the others, the point of his blade making circles in front of him.

'Not all is as it once appeared to be,' said Findelsith, whipping around to stare at one of Maensith's officers, Thyarsion. The Great Harlequin extended his arm and tapped a finger to a sapphire-studded pendant hanging around the mercenary's neck. 'Your throat was not adorned with this trinket. Did you not heed the warning that I gave?'

'Where did you get this?' snarled Maensith, ripping the jewellery from Thyarsion, the silver chain parting with a scatter of glinting links.

'It was wasted, lying unwanted in a drawer,' said Thyarsion. He made to take back the necklace but Maensith snatched away her hand.

'Who else has broken the ban of thievery?' she demanded, holding the pilfered jewel aloft. There were muttered confessions from several of the mercenaries, and a variety of gems and artworks were revealed, stuffed into pouches, bags and pockets.

'Nobody will miss them, there is nobody here,' said one offender.

'Tis fools who steal the treasures of this place!' said Findelsith, striding through the gathered warriors to confront the individual who had spoken. 'Your greed is like a beacon blazing bright, did you not heed my words of dire warning? They will be coming to reclaim their gilt. This trove is not for mortals to ransack, it is the vault of the Prince of Pleasure.'

There were angry retorts and exclamations as the Harlequins moved through the throng, demanding the treasures from those who had taken them. Aradryan looked horrified as some of the mercenaries raised their blades and pistols to defend their ill-gotten prizes. Through the clamour of raised voices, Aradryan heard Lechthennian beside him speaking, but the words were lost.

A piercing screech from the musician's half-lyre silenced the arguments.

'Run,' he said, pointing to the windows ahead of the group, his voice cold and calm. 'We are discovered.'

Aradryan looked down the corridor and his blood froze and his skin prickled with a chill of utter dread. At the arched windows stood dozens – hundreds – of pale-skinned figures. They had androgynous faces and single-breasted bodies, with eyes like polished coal that stared at the eldar with rapt hunger. Forked tongues slithered in anticipation over needle-thin teeth. They were bereft of clothes save for bangles and loops of beads, and each sported a crest of hair of purple or red or dark blue, splaying dramatically from their scalps. Instead of hands they had elongated claws, like some monstrous lobster, and these they tapped against the window panes while narrow faces snarled and grinned and leered.

Aradryan's waystone was like a nail being driven into his heart, piercing hot as it burned through his chest. A chorus of voices sang in his head, beautiful and terrible, alluring and yet filling him with disgust. Though he had never laid eyes on the creatures before, he had heard tales from his earliest memories and knew in his gut, in the deepest pit of his spirit, the nature of the apparitions that confronted him: servants of the Great Enemy, daemonettes of dread Slaanesh.

With a splintering crash, the horde of daemons burst into the palace, laughing and screeching, taloned feet rattling on the tiled floor, claws snapping. A warning shout caused Aradryan to turn, just in time to see more daemonettes scuttling from the archways behind, scalp-fronds waving madly as they ran down the corridor.

Remembering Lechthennian's words, Aradryan thought to run, but the way towards the ships was barred by the enemy. Maensith and her warriors opened fire with las-bolts and shuriken, filling the passageway with glittering discs and actinic blasts. The hiss of shuriken cannons and crack of fusion pistols added to the noise.

'Move on,' said Estrathain, gently pushing Aradryan aside as the kami stepped forwards, one arm raised towards the daemonettes rushing from the back. 'It has been some time, but I have a little of my power left.'

A blaze of white light burst from the kami's upraised palm spreading to become a burning coruscation that shrieked through the approaching daemonettes. Where the flames touched, the daemons turned to crystal and shattered, spraying shards that sliced down more of their kind. Estrathain was thrown back by the strength of the blast, staggering into Lechthennian. The kami held up his hand in surprise, blackened scraps of red cloth falling from the charred remnants of his glove. Smoke wisps rose from his ceramic fingers, the artificial flesh dis-coloured by burned whorls.

'We are at the heart of the Gulf of Magic,' said Lechthennian, supporting Estrathain as he straightened. 'It would not be wise to open up your mind again.'

'I miscalculated, but it is not a calamity,' said the kami. He threw off his scarf and discarded his robe and gloves, revealing a white form, which looked like liquid stone, flowing and rippling as he stepped forwards again. Hundreds of tiny silver runes glowed in his artificial skin, crackling with psychic power. 'I have not served Khai-dazaar for so long as its spirit conduit without taking some precautions.'

Though the daemonettes had been thrown back by the kami's first assault, they had gathered again, even more numerous than before, and came hurtling down the passageway. Gone were the expressions of cruel delight and covetousness, replaced with glares of deepest hatred.

Lightning forked along the corridor from Estrathain's fingers, leaping from one daemon to the next, turning every foe touched into a shower of ebon sparks. The psychic storm was not enough to keep every enemy at bay, and the daemonettes raced swiftly closer, claws opening and closing with excitement.

Glancing over his shoulder to see if passage to the ship had been cleared, Aradryan saw that the rest of the company fared little better. Maensith and her warriors had managed to band together into three groups, their rifles and pistols enough to keep most of the daemonettes at bay. Amongst them, Jair, Caolein and Athelennil fought on, though Aradryan felt a moment of concern as he saw blood dripping from a cut across the cheek of his former lover.

Those daemonettes that survived the fire of the mercenaries and outcasts had to contend with the dazzling skills of the Harlequins. Just as he had been at the performance in Khai-dazaar, Aradryan was momentarily transfixed by their display. Somersaulting, cartwheeling and pirouetting, the warrior-troupers danced around the daemonettes, dodging and ducking snapping claws, their chainblades and power swords licking out to cut away limbs and sever necks. That such carnage was wrought by the brightly-dressed performers, their faces covered with grinning and snarling masks, added to the surrealism of the scene. The skull-faced Death Jesters swept and twirled their shrieker cannons like batons, powered blades on the stocks and muzzles flashing, slicing apart the foe, giving themselves room to unleash hails of shurikens.

At the centre of the Harlequins stood Findelsith and his Shadowseer, shouting commands in his their sing-song tones like joint conductors of a lethal orchestra. Now and then Findelsith would level his pistol to shoot into the face of a pouncing daemonette.

The display was fascinating, but Aradryan forced himself to turn away, concluding that there would be no retreat just yet. He returned his attention to the daemonettes closing down the corridor. Shurikens and laser fire sprayed past him from some of Maensith's warriors, but the daemons were almost upon the ranger and kami. Aradryan was aware of Lechthennian just behind him, and could not recall seeing any weapons on the musician. He was defenceless, unless a quick skirl of his half-lyre could banish the daemonettes.

Estrathain leapt forwards, fists blazing with energy, to meet the dae-monettes head on. Protective wards flared into life as their claws sparked from his artificial body. Aradryan had no attention to spare for his com-panion as lightning flared from his hands, for the daemonettes would be upon the ranger in moments.

Aradryan tried to remain as calm as if he were in the bay of the *Fae Taeruth*, sparring with Maensith. He took a shallow breath and raised his blade in readiness for the first attack. Looking at the daemonettes, he was shocked, his blade trembling in his hand as he saw in their pale faces glimpses of likenesses of his loved ones. The glaring black eyes were the same, but there was something in the tilt of the head and cheeks of a daemon to his right that put him in mind of Thirianna, while a creature pulling back its claw to swipe at him reminded Aradryan of Maensith; here and there he saw lovers of his past, including Athelennil.

And then he saw the face of his mother.

With a scream of rage, Aradryan lashed out at the daemon that dared to wear the face of his mother, slashing his sword across its throat. As its incorporeal body shimmered into a cloud of pastel blue mist, Aradryan stepped up to catch the claw of another on the edge of his blade, deflecting the blow aside. He whipped the tip back-handed across the daemonette's chest, opening up a wound that bled silver across its single breast. Spitting, the creature fell back, giving Aradryan space to lunge forwards beneath the claws of another daemon, pulling his sword up to slice through the leg of his attacker.

He felt a hand grabbing his arm and he staggered back a step, glancing to see Lechthennian pulling him away from the fight. Beyond the musi-cian, the passageway was clear for the moment and, without waiting for their rearguard, the mercenaries were heading back to the courtyard.

'What about Estrathain?' said Aradryan, but his worries were unfounded. A white sheet of fire exploded from the kami, hurling back the daemonettes that had been surrounding the psyker.

'Run!' said Lechthennian, pushing Aradryan towards the others.

The ranger needed no second invitation and sprinted down the cor-ridor with long strides, Estrathain at his heels. The enemy were not totally destroyed ahead; a glance through the broken windows showed more and more of them spilling from other palace wings, converging on the ships in the courtyard. There were other creatures coming too: six-limbed fiends with lashing tongues stalked towards the pair, coming between them and the remains of the entryway.

'Shortcut,' said Aradryan, leaping over the sill of a shattered window to land in a shrub-filled border. Estrathain followed him out into the court-yard and the two of them cut across a lawn, heading directly for *Irdiris*.

They were halfway towards the ships, the mercenaries not far ahead plunging over flagstones and grass, when something burst from the pal-ace to Aradryan's left. Masonry and glass erupted as a gigantic daemon exploded into the courtyard.

Aradryan staggered, his waystone flaring with white light, his mind and body awhirl with dislocation. The ranger was not the only one affected; mercenaries tripped and fell, some of them crying out in pain at the daemon's appearance. Those that stayed on their feet clutched hands to heads and waystones, moaning and snarling. Only the Harle-quins were unaffected, forming a ring around the stricken warriors and outcasts.

The creature towered above the eldar, two of its arms ending in larger versions of the claws of the daemonettes, while another two ended in slender-fingered hands that grasped scimitars as long as Aradryan was tall. Its unnatural flesh was pierced with rings, and chains of gold and silver hung with runes and pendants that glittered hypnotically. Into its incorporeal hide were sunk gems of every colour, which Aradryan realised with horror were the spirit stones of dead eldar, scores of them. The stolen spirit stones gleamed with dark light, eldar essences trapped within. Its face was elongated, with razor teeth, looking oddly bovine except for its eyes; these were many-faceted orbs of black that reflected back Aradryan's face a dozen different ways. Spiralled horns, two above each eye, arched back from its brow, and two more curved around its pointed ears from the back of its head.

The creature was surrounded by an aura like the golden rain that had fallen during the Time of the Witch, only denser, more cloying. The air around the greater daemon shimmered with its power, and the ground under its tread cracked and sparked with Chaotic magic. Aradryan could hear his name being called, over and over, sometimes in a mocking voice, sometimes enticing.

'A Bride of Perversion,' hissed Estrathain, though Aradryan did not need to be told the title of the monstrosity that was charging towards the starships, swords flashing. The greater daemon was a monstrous embodiment of the Prince of Pleasure's power, known by many names in the craftworld myths: a Warden of Spirits, King of Hearts and Deca-dent Lord amongst others. 'Run for your ship!'

Before Aradryan could grab Estrathain, guessing his intent and know-ing the folly of confrontation with the greater daemon, the kami broke into a run, heading directly for the Decadent Lord. The kami's body blazed with psychic fire as he sprinted across the courtyard with sparks trailing from his fingertips. The greater daemon turned at the kami's defiant shout, raising up its twin scimitars as it rounded on Estrathain.

A shining shield of silver sprang up around the kami as he held an arm up towards the Decadent Lord. The greater daemon laughed, a high-pitched, chilling sound that froze Aradryan to the spot despite the kami's instruction to run. The two daemonic swords swept down, turning Estrathain's shield into falling shards like a broken mirror. The blades continued on their course, slicing into the shoulders of the kami, spraying silver blood-like fluid as they quartered him from neck to waist, the body parts sent spinning through the air.

Claws snapping, blades weaving a complex pattern through the air, the Decadent Lord advanced on the other eldar, its pale skin spattered with the silver of Estrathain's vital fluid. The greater daemon stopped for a moment to extend a long, thin tongue, which flicked along its swords, tasting the essence of the dead kami. Hissing in distaste, the Decadent Lord reached out a clawed hand towards the Harlequins, who were massing behind Findelsith, their weapons ready. The creature beckoned to them with its claw, laughing again.

'Do as he said, my companion bold.' Aradryan heard Lechthennian right behind him. The voice was unmistakeably that of the musician, though the meter of his words was more poetic than normal. 'Run swift now and let the old tale unfold.'

'I thought you had been caught,' replied the ranger, turning. His next words remained unsaid, as he saw the manner of the person who had spoken.

Lechthennian was dressed in the garb of the Harlequins, in a manner. A hood and cowl covered his head and shoulders, chequered with red and black. He had discarded his robes, revealing a bodysuit of purple and white and yellow, patterned with stripes and dots and banding. His face was hidden by a plain mask, totally blank and black except for a single rune in red upon one cheek: the symbol of Cegorach the Laughing God.

'I was caught, a long time ago, my friend,' said Lechthennian. There was jest in his tone. 'Yet I wriggled free and here I am still. The friendless and lonely traveller, fell guardian of the Black Library, webway wanderer without a sprit – my life hostage to the Great Enemy. I am Solitaire.'

A bellow of anger, terrible and long, reverberated around the courtyard. The Decadent Lord sensed the presence of the Solitaire and turned, clashing its swords together in challenge.

'Cometh unto me, thee pretty prancer,' called out the greater daemon, in a voice deep and luxurious. The words were ancient eldar, the language spoken before the Fall. 'Cometh unto me and dance the dance of eternity. Your spirit is ours already.'

Lechthennian stepped past Aradryan, two golden daggers seeming to appear in his hands as he broke into a run towards the Decadent Lord.

'We shall whirl and twirl and see who is best,' Lechthennian replied, performing a flip over a line of bushes. 'There is nought of true heart in your foul breast.'

The greater daemon pounded over paving and through hedgerows in a headlong charge, its roar of ancient hatred still echoing from the broken walls of the palace. Seeing that it was intent upon Lechthennian, Aradryan was able to run too, circling around the gardens towards the rest of the expedition, who were being shepherded towards *Irdiris* and the Harlequins' vessel.

As he ran, Aradryan cast glances back towards the Decadent Lord and Lechthennian, thinking that despite the tales he had heard concerning the Harlequin Solitaire, a single eldar would last only moments against the greater daemon of She Who Thirsts; the shockingly swift demise of Estrathain was proof of that.

The Decadent Lord skidded to a stop, its clawed feet throwing up splinters of stone from the ground. Lechthennian dived beneath its right-hand blade, the sorcerous weapon missing the Solitaire by the tiniest of margins. Leaping to one side, Lechthennian dodged the claw that swept out towards his gut, hand-springing away as the Decadent Lord turned and lashed out with its other blade.

Reaching the Harlequins, Aradryan came to a stop beside Maensith and Findelsith. It was impossible to see what the Great Harlequin thought of the unfolding confrontation, and Maensith looked on with wide-eyed fascination.

'We have to help Lechthennian,' said Aradryan, pointing his sword back at the greater daemon. As he did so, Lechthennian somersaulted over a clawed foot aimed at his head. His daggers flashed, drawing a slender line across the greater daemon's clawed right arm.

'It is not our purpose to interfere, it was for this that he wanted to come,' replied Findelsith, holstering his pistol. 'This dance has been danced for a long, long time. The Solitaire always dances alone, for he has been taken by She Who Thirsts. The Laughing God will watch over our friend, watch and you will see that I am not wrong.'

Aradryan and the other eldar were not the only audience to the dramatic fight unfolding in the courtyard. The lesser daemons and beasts were gathering at the periphery, watching the duel between the Solitaire and Decadent Lord. There were hundreds of daemonettes and fiends and beasts, and like the Harlequins they did not intervene. Aradryan assumed that the moment the greater daemon or Lechthennian was slain the immaterial host would descend upon the surviving eldar, and he edged towards *Irdiris* as he watched the unfolding scene.

The Decadent Lord and Lechthennian moved with fluid grace, weaving about each other, sometimes so fast their weapons were a blur. It was like the performance of the Death Jesters on the stage, weapons whirling close but never quite touching, like an elaborately choreographed dance. The greater daemon was at least four times Lechthennian's height, its reach far longer, but the more agile Solitaire nimbly spun and ducked and dodged its attacks, nipping close to the greater daemon with his daggers ready, only to be sent somersaulting or cartwheeling away before he could land a telling blow. The four arms of the Decadent Lord were in constant motion, claws and swords slashing and swinging, while its tongue lashed out, cracking like a whip.

Aradryan watched transfixed, the interplay of the two fighters creating a mesmeric scene. The golden cloud that surrounded the greater daemon trailed in its wake as the two moved from lawn to patio to pathway, the ground churning beneath the tread of the greater daemon, the Solitaire's acrobatics leaving spiralling trails in the creature's misty aura.

As the two moved back and forth, Aradryan realised that Lechthennian did have a plan. Slowly, subtly, the Solitaire was luring the Decadent Lord towards a copse of trees. Beneath the boughs of silver branches, the greater daemon would be disadvantaged.

As Aradryan had guessed, so the fight unfolded, with Lechthennian retreating towards the cover of the silver-barked trees. Turning, he ran the rest of the short distance, running straight up the closest trunk into the lower branches, leaping through the blue leaves from limb to limb. The Decadent Lord followed, sending up a shower of leaves and splintered wood as it slashed both swords after the Solitaire.

Though the woods gave Lechthennian some cover, his ascent into the branches brought him up to a level where the greater daemon's horns could be used. The Decadent Lord flung its head at the Solitaire as he jumped past its shoulder, catching the Harlequin in the leg. Aradryan gave a cry of dismay as Lechthennian lost his footing and tumbled, spinning at the last moment to land awkwardly on his feet.

With a triumphant shout, the Decadent Lord thrust out its right sword, seeking to skewer Lechthennian. The bellow was answered by a laugh, as the Solitaire's ploy played out. Flipping out of the blade's path, the Solitaire avoided death by a hair's-breadth. The point of the sword passed into the trunk of the tree that had been behind Lechthennian and stuck fast for a moment.

It was all the hesitation Lechthennian needed. Using the Decadent Lord's outstretched arm as a step, the Solitaire skipped from the ground to the greater daemon's shoulder, ducking beneath its swiping claw. Twisting in mid-air, the Harlequin jumped up and hooked a leg around one of the daemon's horns, swinging across its face.

The Solitaire's daggers blazed as he plunged them into the eyes of the Decadent Lord. The daemon howled in pain, letting go of its sword to flail at the Solitaire, who leapt free into the treetop again, escaping retribution.

Aradryan ran again, turning his back as the demented screeches of the greater daemon and its servants swept across the courtyard. He dared not look back, and joined a throng of mercenaries speeding up the ramp of

Irdiris. It was not designed for so many to embark swiftly, and Aradryan was forced to wait at the foot of the ramp. Caolein had already boarded and the ship's engines whined in preparation for take-off as Aradryan darted one last look back at the host of Slaanesh.

Lechthennian sprinted back towards the ships, the still-twitching form of the greater daemon lying beneath the trees behind him. The daemon horde raced after the fleeing Solitaire, his laughter goading them into enraged screams and wails.

'Come on!' Maensith grabbed the sleeve of Aradryan's coat as she sped past, dragging him up into *Irdiris*. Lechthennian was heading for the Harlequin ship and so Aradryan was the last to board. He sent a message to *Irdiris* to close the entryway, and looked out to see the ground already dropping away as a tide of pink and red and purple spilled over the lawns and pavement below. A daemonette leapt up, claw seeking to grab a purchase on the lifting ship, but the ramp was withdrawing too quickly and the daemon fell back into the mass below. A sea of faces – the devilish likeness of Aradryan's family and friends amongst them – stared back at the ranger.

And then the door iris closed, cutting off the view, and *Irdiris* sped away from Miarisillion, the crone world, Planet of the Pleasure Palace.

CRAVINGS

Commorragh – When the Fall consumed the eldar and the Vortex of Misery engulfed the ancient empire, those who had not departed with the Exodites or craftworlds were forced to flee into the webway. For long generations the webway had been expanded and great palaces, beautiful estates and entire cities had been birthed in the links between dimensions. The most wicked and depraved of the Fall's survivors took over these interspaces and pocket worlds, and in time the twisted kin of the dark eldar built a city to rival their pride and evil: Commorragh. Here the worst excesses and most depraved practices of the ancient days continue, and the sects that once tore apart eldar civilisation grew into the mighty kabals that now rule the Dark City with intimidation and incessant violence.

The journey departing the Eye of Terror was strangely more peaceful than the expedition's entry, though Aradryan would have expected the Great Enemy to have plagued the eldar with nightmares and pursuit now that they had revealed themselves. Instead, a quiet air of contemplation settled upon the starship. Perhaps it was in this self-reflection that the Great Enemy sought to do the most damage, leaving her victims free to consider their own dooms and desires, the seed having been sown in aeons past.

For the first few cycles back aboard the *Fae Taeruth*, Aradryan spent time alone in his cabin, relieved and drained in equal measure. Nothing he had been expecting or had previously experienced could have prepared him for the episode on the crone world, and the heart-chilling encounter with the daemonettes and Decadent Lord would linger in his dreams for as long as he could sleep.

Yet for all the fear and desperation that had clutched at his spirit in those moments, Aradryan had been invigorated by the venture. As with the battle with the orks, his sense of freedom, his appreciation of life, was enhanced by the trauma of Miarisillion. In comparison to the deadly foes of the crone worlds, the brutish greenskins that had invaded Hirith-Hreslain seemed laughable. It was as if Aradryan had passed through fire and not been burned, and the latest blaze had been hottest of all and yet had left him physically unscathed.

In purely material terms, the expedition had also been a qualified success. They had recovered nearly two hundred waystones, though Maensith had lost sixteen of her warriors to the daemonic attack. Efforts had been made to bring their spirit stones back, but four had been left behind in the final rush for the ships, no doubt to suffer torment in the grasp of the Great Enemy. One of those who had fallen had been a Commorraghan, who had possessed no waystone, his spirit most likely enduring untold tortures at the hands of the daemonettes.

Two Harlequins had perished also, one the Death Jester Taenemeth, and for some reason the loss of these warrior-dancers struck Aradryan as particularly sad, for they had brought joy and awe to him in their performance and would never dance again. Findelsith was sanguine about the losses, and assured Aradryan that the spirits of the fallen Harlequins were safe, sneaked away from the Great Enemy by the Laughing God they had served and emulated in life.

And there was the loss of Estrathain too, torn asunder by the greater daemon. In a sense, the kami was but a single facet of Estrathain, who would continue to live, but the experience the divided eldar spirit had sought had been lost on the crone world, and all the memory therein, and so while the other kami would endure, they would be lessened by the loss.

To think about those who had not survived was perversely encouraging to Aradryan. It reinforced his belief that the manner of one's death was unimportant, it was the life that one led beforehand that was defining; not to others but to he who was living the life. All things passed, even the greatest and longest legacies would eventually fail and be forgotten. Aradryan thought of what Maensith had said about regrets, and realised that despite the horror and death and his misgivings before setting out, he did not regret the adventure. He had survived and the experience had enriched his life; if he had died it would no longer matter as he would be in no position to be aware of the loss.

After breaking back into the webway, the Harlequins took their leave of the *Fae Taeruth*. Lechthennian had chosen to go with them, and so the outcasts of the *Irdiris* gathered on the launch deck to say goodbye to their companion. Lechthennian was dressed in his normal travelling clothes, his Harlequin suit and mask concealed once more amongst his belongings. The musician seemed happy, and when he had been questioned on the fight with the Decadent Lord he had simply shrugged and laughed away the encounter.

'You could stay with us,' said Athelennil, holding a hand to Lechthennian's chest in a sign of deep friendship. '*Irdiris* is your home.'

'It is not the nature of the Solitaire to have a home,' Lechthennian replied, patting the ranger on her shoulder. 'I shall spend some time with Findelsith's troupe, and we shall perhaps go to Ulthwé to perform the Dance without End, for it is the first and perhaps only time Findelsith will have a Solitaire in his masque.'

Aradryan felt his skin crawl at the thought of watching the Dance without End. He had only heard and read about it, for not in his lifetime had a Solitaire travelled to Alaitoc to perform the dance – at least not to Aradryan's knowledge, for now that he had seen the way that Lechthennian had kept his true identity hidden, the ranger wondered if any of the other eldar he had met or known were Solitaires in disguise. The performance in Khai-dazaar, as shocking and disturbing as it had been, was only an overture, a preamble to the true Dance without End, in which the Great Harlequin took the role of the Laughing God and the Solitaire played the part of She Who Thirsts.

'We could meet you again in Khai-dazaar,' suggested Caolein. '*Irdiris* is not the same without Lechthennian.'

'Lechthennian will be no more, when I set foot from this ship,' said the Solitaire. 'I am the Laughing God and I am the Great Enemy, and I travel where fate wills me. My true persona cannot be known, for I would become a lodestone of temptation, luring those around me to share my dark fate. *Irdiris* will find new stories to tell.'

Aradryan had not known the musician as long as the others and so did not feel quite the sense of loss that they did, though he was aware that Lechthennian's departure did represent something of the end of an era for the ship.

'Thank you, for your wisdom and protection,' said Aradryan, raising a hand in appreciation. Lechthennian nodded in acknowledgement but did not smile. He leaned close and whispered so that only Aradryan could hear.

'Each of us dances to the tune he hears, played out in our hopes, ambitions and fears. Some of us are bold, some of us meek, where one sees strength, another seems weak. Whether you fight or whether you run, She Who Thirsts calls out the beat of the drum.'

With that perplexing riddle delivered, Lechthennian stepped away, bowed with a sweeping arm and trotted up the winding boarding gantry to the door of the Harlequin's starship. He turned at the last moment and something silver flashed in the air, spinning down from the Solitaire. By instinct, Aradryan caught it: the silver thumb whistle. By the time he looked back to say thank you, Lechthennian was gone from sight and the door of the ship was closing fast.

Maensith came to Aradryan after a few days of the *Fae Taeruth* being back in the webway proper. She was her relaxed, playful self again, in stark contrast to the state in which she had been during the descent into the crone worlds. Though her words were as teasing as ever, her actions were more forthright than before the expedition, and Aradryan found himself a guest in her chambers often over the coming cycles. After one such liaison he came across Athelennil, who gave him a look of disdain but made no outright accusation. It was easy to attribute her behaviour to jealousy, and Athelennil's mood was probably all the more depressed following the departure of Lechthennian, so Aradryan ignored the slight and left his former lover in the companionway aft of the officer's quarters.

Ten cycles from Khai-dazaar, Maensith had the *Fae Taeruth* break into realspace, exiting from the webway via an oval portal of shimmering white. They had entered a star system called Assain-alei-Nemech, which was on the rim of a swirling nebula that Maensith referred to as the Lake of Sorrows. Aradryan was with the mercenary commander in the viewing deck when Jair and Athelennil entered, seeking the ship's captain.

'Why have we come here?' asked Jair, who darted a disapproving look towards Aradryan. 'We should be returning to Khai-dazaar with the waystones.'

'What is there for us in this place?' said Athelennil. She looked out of the row of broad windows, seeing a few gas giants orbiting a pale blue star. 'It looks like a dead system.'

'If my dallying here delays you, feel free to depart whenever you wish,' replied Maensith. 'I am here to add a little extra to the spoils for the markets in Khai-dazaar. You may enjoy the company of outcasts who are willing to share in the burden and cost of ship life, but I have a complement that demand a fair reward for the risk of their lives and labours. The waystones we took, our share of it, are not sufficient compensation for the resources we have expended so far.'

'Piracy?' Aradryan had harboured suspicions since he had first come aboard the *Fae Taeruth* but had not broached the subject with Maensith. She laughed at the shock in his voice.

'Where do you think all of this pretty finery comes from?' she asked, her waved hand encapsulating the ornate chairs and couches, low tables and cabinets that furnished the observation deck.

'I am not so naive as you think,' said Aradryan, scowling at the flippancy of the answer. 'I am just surprised that you would bring us here so soon after risking your life in the crone worlds. Would it not be better to recuperate before embarking on more conflict?'

'We do not have that luxury, my dear Aradryan,' said Maensith. 'If we wish to berth at Khai-dazaar, and compensate Estrathain for the loss of his kami, our profits are severely cut. Besides, compared to the company we have been keeping recently, a few haugri-alim will hardly be any threat at all.'

'The haugri-alim?' It was Jair who asked the question before Aradryan had the chance. 'An alien species? Is that what you wish to find here?'

'More than wish, we will find them here. In fact, we will not have to wait at all,' said Maensith. Touching her hand to a plate beneath one of the windows, she magnified the view. The sliding display brought into focus a starship unlike anything Aradryan had seen before – and he realised that seeing sights for the first time was becoming something of a theme since he had become outcast.

The name of the haugri-alim Aradryan guessed to be a play on haugrilim, a race from the oldest myths who had dwelt at the bottom of the seas and were tricked by Eldanesh into revealing the secrets of how to breathe water. Their craft was a simple cylindrical shape, with an outer ring supported by long spars on which its engines were located. Though it was still quite small in the magnified image, Aradryan could see blocky structures arranged in rings around the central superstructure, which he assumed to be weapons of some kind.

'Their ships pass through this system on nearly every journey,' explained Maensith. 'They are gas-dwellers, and have a holy site in the clouds of the world below. It is sort of a pilgrimage, or an homage or something. I do not quite understand it myself, but it makes them terribly predictable and vulnerable.'

'We will take you up on the offer to depart,' said Jair. Athelennil nodded her agreement and the two rangers looked at Aradryan expectantly. 'To be an outcast does not force one to become a corsair.'

'No, but it makes life a lot more comfortable if you do,' said Maensith. The ship captain also turned her gaze on Aradryan, an eyebrow lifted in query.

'This is not a life you will want,' said Jair, shaking his head sadly.

'This Commorraghan fascinates you, but there will be sights and experiences of unimaginable beauty and power if you come with us,' said Athelennil. 'Do not become a pirate, Aradryan, it is a pointless, repetitive existence.'

Aradryan thought about it for a few moments. There would likely be more safety aboard the *Irdiris* and, despite recent divisions, he liked Jair and Caolein, and still had fond thoughts for Athelennil. He did not wholly trust Maensith; he did not trust her in the slightest if he was being honest with himself. His new company would be corsairs and Commorraghans, who were not known for their loyalty. It was a life of danger, of strife and fighting, and it was likely to be shorter as a pirate than a ranger. As the latter he could visit Exodite worlds and distant craftworlds, explore alien planets and seek out new experiences.

But would it be worthwhile? Would he have the satisfaction he had felt on their successful escape from the crone worlds. Life on board the *Fae Taeruth* would be more exciting, the contrast between life and death brought into sharp relief. Aradryan did not feel particularly bloodthirsty, but on the other hand it was battle that had given him his greatest thrill, and nothing else he had ever experienced, no dream or journey, came close to filling him with the same heady mixture of excitement and fear.

'I do not think I will be as welcome as you say,' Aradryan told the rangers, an apologetic expression on his face. 'And I feel that you will be more content without me in your company. That is, if Maensith wishes me to stay.'

'You are more than welcome to join the crew of the *Fae Taeruth*,' said the captain. 'I will offer you the same deal as everybody else aboard. Stay for a cycle, stay for a thousand, as your heart desires, no onus is placed upon you and no oath binds you to this ship. Fight for me and earn equal share. Protect your companions and they will protect you. I will ask nothing of you that I would not do myself, and if you have any complaint you can bring it to me openly. I spent half of my life in a kabal, watching for the dagger of an ally aimed between my shoulder blades, kicking those beneath me to keep them down whilst reaching up with one hand to grasp the ankles of those who climbed above me. That is not the life I want on the *Fae Taeruth*.'

'I shall stay aboard, for a cycle or a thousand,' said Aradryan. He turned back to Athelennil and Jair. There was sadness on their faces, genuine and deep. Aradryan smiled to lighten the mood of their departure. 'You look as if you mourn for me, but I am not dead yet. I promise I will see you again, and I owe you a debt that cannot be easily repaid. Athelennil, you took me from Alaitoc and showed me what was possible. Jair, you watched over me when I took those first steps, guiding me away from the structure of the Path into a universe of possibilities. I cannot thank you enough for what you have done, but I hope that it does not seem disloyal of me to seek a future that will allow me to spread my wings ever further.'

'Take care,' said Athelennil. Then, taking Aradryan by surprise, she took a few steps and embraced him, pulling him tight to her body. He wrapped an arm around her shoulders and squeezed back. When she stepped back, Athelennil glared at Maensith. 'If you wrong him, I will find you and make you pay, Commorraghan.'

Maensith's laugh was short and harsh but she said nothing as she strode from the room, leaving Aradryan with his former companions.

'Good fortune and prosperity,' Aradryan said to the other rangers, and left them to follow Maensith.

Ghosting close under the mask of its holofields, the *Fae Taeruth* manoeuvred behind the haugri-alim ship as the alien vessel turned into the gravity well of its destination planet. Maensith had tackled several such targets when she had been a kabalite officer operating out of Commorragh, and she ran her ship with smooth efficiency.

Some rogue scanner flicker or stray sensor return spooked the haugri-alim, and their engines flared into full fury as they tried to run for the safety of the gas giant's upper atmosphere. Swinging after the fleeing vessel, the stellar sail of the *Fae Taeruth* catching the full force of the system's stellar winds to speed them after their quarry, the eldar closed quickly, outpacing their lumbering prey by a considerable margin.

The control deck of the warship was different to that of *Lacontiran*. On the merchant cruiser there was only a small weapons station, and her scanning array was far less sophisticated. Aradryan and the other pilots had been situated in an isolated compartment high in the ship and communication took place over the psychic network. On the *Fae Taeruth*, the crew were all located in one large space, subdivided into a rosette of decks surrounding a central command pod; engines, piloting, navigation, weapons, sensors and damage control were all within sight of each other so that Maensith and her officers could monitor the situation with sight and hearing as well as feedback over the internal matrix.

Like the ship she pursued, the majority of the *Fae Taeruth*'s weapons systems were to port and starboard, with a single high-powered, long-ranged laser turret directed from the bow. Aradryan watched with fascination as Maensith summoned a floating display in front of her, created by glittering projectors located in the floor beneath the command pod. Her left hand rested on a glowing network interface, while the fingers of her right danced across the runes of a projected holo-pad. The main holographic display was centred on the target ship, dark against the swirl of orange and red of the gas giant's atmosphere. Runes danced across the image, highlighting various systems on the fleeing ship detected by the scanning team. Maensith guided aiming reticules into position; glowing red diamonds flashed as target trajectories and ranges were laid in by the eldar manning the weapons consoles. The ship's captain provided a narration for the benefit of Aradryan.

'A ship of this size will be carrying more than a thousand haugri-alim,' she explained. 'Coupled with their dense and gravity-heavy artificial environment, that makes it virtually impossible for us to successfully board. This is a fight we must win from a distance.'

'Why do they not turn and attack?' asked Aradryan.

'Instinct, I suppose.' Maensith shrugged and manipulated the image in front of her, magnifying the view of the vessel's engine housings. More target runes sprang into life. 'Some of us are predators and some of us are prey. Haugri-alim are the latter.'

Maensith fell silent for a moment, communing across the network with other officers. A few moments later a startling burst of white beams sprang from the bow turret, flashing across the gulf between the ships in an instant. Red energy flared where they struck – defensive shields. Maensith hissed in annoyance.

'Most of these traders forego shield generators for more hold space,' she said.

'Is that a problem?'

'Not of the kind you are thinking,' replied Maensith. She made some adjustments to the target matrix, focusing on a jutting piece of super-structure above and forward of the engines. The laser lance fired again. This time the red spark of the shields was less intense and several of the beams broke through, burning into the targeted area of the enemy ship. Clouds of molten metal glittered and the next salvo met no resistance, tearing through the shield mast and the hull around it. Maensith turned with a wry smile. 'It just means less cargo for us to take.'

With its shields compromised, the haugri-alim ship finally began to turn, trying to bring its weapon batteries to bear on its pursuer. The *Fae Taeruth* was too swift to be caught so easy, sliding to port as the enemy turned to starboard, staying in the wake of its quarry's engines. Another flash of laser beams cut through the engines of the desperately turning ship, causing plasma explosions to ripple through the circular section. Crippled, the cylindrical vessel started to spin while fitful plumes of escaping gas caused the ship to yaw back and forth, creating a sporadic spiral of trailing debris.

With her prey crippled, Maensith and the crew guided the *Fae Taeruth* closer, matching their target's erratic course as best they could whilst bringing the broadside weapon batteries to bear. Laser and plasma sprayed from the gun decks, converging at three points along the top of the haugri-alim ship, burrowing through armour plate and reinforced bulkheads.

'The haugri-alim are as good at engineering as they are at fighting,' said Maensith as Aradryan watched more glowing slag jettisoned from breaks in the damaged ship's metal carcass. 'Another couple of salvoes and we will...'

As she spoke, the enemy ship started to crack open, sending spin-ning fragments into space, chasm-like tears opening up along one side of its hull. There seemed to be dust or mist venting into the vacuum, until Maensith increased the magnification of the view and Aradryan saw many-limbed, squid-like shapes drifting out within the escaping artificial atmosphere; distance and scale had made them appear no larger than floating motes of debris. The haugri-alim were clad in silvery, banded suits that allowed their dozens of flailing tentacles free move-ment. Their torsos were protected within heavily reinforced domes of transparent material, allowing them a view in every direction.

'Each is three times as tall as you or me,' said Maensith, shaking her head. 'They favour microwave-based weapons. Very nasty at close range.

Anyway, they will not be posing any further threat. We will take our time before we board, to ensure that they have all been blown out or asphyxiated. The last thing we need is to run into a few survivors. When that is done, we can go down and take what we like.'

'And what do they have that we want?' asked Aradryan. 'They seem so crude, I cannot believe anybody would want anything made by these creatures.'

'They have access to many valuable ores and elements that are difficult to acquire by other means,' said Maensith. She stepped out of the command pod, signalling to one of her lieutenants to take charge now that the enemy had been dealt a fatal blow. 'Also, you will be surprised at the items that generate interest in markets like Khai-dazaar. Haugri-alim skin is very tough, and there are some in Commorragh who swear that there is no material as thick yet flexible, ideal for working with to make undersuits and armour joints. Some of their digestive organs are also rich in certain rare minerals. It is a shame that we have to waste so many.'

Aradryan said nothing as he watched the corpses of the haugri-alim dispersing through the void, their tattered suits and cracked protective domes glinting in the light of the distant star. He was not sure how he felt about their deaths. From so far away it was easy to dismiss such casual slaughter. It had been almost laughably easy to defeat them, and Aradryan wondered if he had made the wrong choice. He had stayed with Maensith for the promise of excitement and life-defining battle, but all he had witnessed so far was a cold, calculated massacre.

Perhaps it would not all be like this, he told himself. It was probably better to think of the haugri-alim bodies drifting away from their ship in the same way as the others on board the *Fae Taeruth*: lost profit.

ALLIANCES

The Winter Gulf – There was a time when the lands of Eldanesh and Ulthanesh were sundered from each other. A torrent as wide as an ocean divided the Houses of the great founders, and so it was that they would never come to meet. However, seeing that her children would forever be divided, the Goddess Isha gave thanks to Mighty Asuryan the All-seeing and asked that he part the rapids and allow the folk of Eldanesh and the folk of Ulthanesh to meet. This the Great Pillar of the Heavens did not do, for he was of the opinion that by their own efforts should Ulthanesh and Eldanesh come upon each other. Yet he tempered his judgement with a cooling breath, with which he stilled the waters of the Winter Gulf for a time. The torrent froze and the people of the two Houses were able to cross over. At times the waters thawed and they were divided of people and purpose, but at times they were united and the Winter Gulf served as a union between Eldanesh and Ulthanesh, as well as a barrier.

The attack on the haugri-alim was only the first of several raids by the *Fae Taeruth*. After exchanging their spoils for more supplies at Khai-dazaar, Maensith took the ship out to a stretch of star systems along the arm of a nebula known as the Winter Gulf. Some of these engagements were won from afar, as had been the case with the haugri-alim, but on two occasions Aradryan was amongst the boarding crew. With each encounter his confidence grew; the humans who provided such easy pickings were slow and clumsy, with weapons as crude as their wielders. After the sheer terror of his daemonic encounter, Aradryan viewed these combats as little more than a chance to practise his marksmanship and swordcraft.

Even though the challenge posed by these untrained adversaries was slim, the hack-and-slash of mortal combat was still exhilarating. Aradryan grew accustomed to the excitement of coming conflict as the *Fae Taeruth* would close in on her crippled prey, boarding boats sent screaming across the void to swiftly finish any survivors from the precision strikes of the weapon batteries. After each raid, he would return to the ship and the welcoming embrace of Maensith, temporarily sated but soon expectant of further excitement.

His favoured position with Maensith did not earn him many friends amongst the ship's officers, all of whom had served on the *Fae Taeruth* for a considerable time. Although bound together in battle, the company of the corsair vessel were not averse to veiled insults and threats; a very different atmosphere than aboard *Lacontiran* and *Irdiris*. Knowing that he could not rely upon the capricious whim of Maensith to protect him against all harm, Aradryan gathered about him a complement of self-interested eldar, freely lavishing his own share of the spoils upon them to guarantee their loyalty. Amongst the regular mercenaries such generosity was welcomed, and when others amongst the officers saw his popularity they wisely chose to align themselves with the up-and-coming corsair. Aradryan had never been one to bear grudges or ill wish and found it easy to accept such allegiances, his magnanimous attitude earning yet further influence. Such precautions meant that he had yet to be forced to bare a blade against a rival, and long he hoped that situation would prevail; he could face a party of humans without qualm but there were some amongst the *Fae Taeruth's* crew who far surpassed Aradryan in swordsense and fighting experience.

The successes enjoyed by the corsairs quickly healed any divisions, and Maensith was keen to have a lieutenant like Aradryan. A Commorraghan by birth, she was feared and respected by her crew but rarely liked, despite her easy-going disposition towards them. Aided by Aradryan's quick wit, she was able to keep her fractious underlings from falling out too often and it was agreed across the company that they could expect fine and profitable times ahead.

Such was the optimism aboard the *Fae Taeruth* as they headed for another foray into human space. The webway gave the eldar the advantage over their foes; humans were forced to traverse the astronomical distances between stars using the perilous, untamed warp. Only able to travel a relatively few light years at a time, hopping from system to system, the human merchants who plied their trade along the rim of the Winter Gulf were easily found and run down.

Moving through the webway in preparation for a convoy raid into a system known as Naimh-neilith, the *Fae Taeruth* came upon an extraordinary gathering of ships. Summoned to the observation gallery,

Aradryan met Maensith. Several holo-displays showed a vast interspace at the confluence of two arterial webway tunnels, and in that juncture a fleet was assembling.

Aradryan counted eight other ships, three as large as the *Fae Taeruth*, the others being smaller frigate- and destroyer-sized vessels. Two of the other cruisers, menacingly black and midnight blue, clearly bore the markings of Commorragh, which Maensith quickly identified as coming from the same kabal – the Ascendant Spear. The rest were displaying a variety of bold and colourful patterns, tiger-striped and mottled with blues and whites and oranges. The matrix of the webway was thrumming with communication, and the *Fae Taeruth* was hailed as soon as she appeared.

One of the holo-images changed at Maensith's command, switching from a view of the largest corsair ship to show a tall eldar dressed in a long coat of shimmering gold over a bodysuit of purple and white. His hair was raven-black, styled in a high crest that cascaded past his shoulders. There was a scar on his upper lip that twisted his mouth into what resembled a permanent sneer, an expression that was matched by the look in his eyes.

'It seems we have an uninvited guest,' said the eldar. 'Perhaps you catch the scent of the scraps we will leave you.'

'I am Maensith of the *Fae Taeruth*.' The captain kept her calm despite the insult. 'Please do me the courtesy of naming yourself.'

'Saidar Yrithain, Prince-Commander of the Azure Flame,' said the other with a mocking bow. 'My ship is the *Sathaisun*. I am sure you have heard of me.'

'I have now,' said Maensith. 'I have raided the Winter Gulf for a dozen passes, but I do not recall the fleet of the Azure Flame.'

Before Yrithain could retort, another holo-figure shimmered into existence. The armour-clad figure immediately put Aradryan in mind of Maensith in her full battledress; he wore black, bladed plates over golden mesh, segmented gauntlets sheathing long-fingered hands. The newcomer's face was gaunt and pale, his eyes dark and piercing, and his head was bald except for a white scalplock threaded with silver skull-shaped beads.

'Maensith of the Crimson Talon is known to me,' said the Commorraghan.

'And Khiadysis, Hierarch of the Ascendant Spear needs no introduction to me,' replied Maensith, touching the fingertips of her right hand to her left shoulder with a quick nod of the head. Though the captain kept a passive face and calmly clasped her hands behind her back, Aradryan sensed a sudden nervousness in the mannerisms of his lover. 'It has been a long time since I laid claim to any membership of the Crimson Talon.'

'Your self-exile is a matter of little remark any more,' said Khiadysis. 'You were one of the most promising dracons, but memories can be cruelly short in Commorragh.'

'Success in the kabals breeds its own kind of peril, hierarch. I did not expect to meet with such a lord of Commorragh so far from the Dark City. I hope that it is good fortune, as it would be a great inconvenience to locate new raiding territories.'

Khiadysis laughed, short and sharp, and waved a benevolent hand in Maensith's direction.

'I understand your worry. It would not serve any purpose to disclose our meeting to your former kabalites, so harbour no concerns on that account. Your present location shall remain unspoken to those in the Crimson Talon who might desire to know it.'

'You have my thanks.' Maensith nodded again, though she did not relax.

'Perhaps the two of you could reminisce at your pleasure when we have concluded our purpose here,' cut in Yrithain. His holo-image turned towards Maensith. 'Your timing is unfortunate, and if you sought to conduct some action at Naimh-neilith you must re-evaluate your plans.'

'Nonsense, Yrithain,' said Khiadysis. 'Another ship of the *Fae Taeruth*'s size, which I am sure is more than ably commanded by Maensith, would be a notable addition to our firepower.'

Yrithain glowered at the kabalite but did not argue. Aradryan watched the exchange in silence, unsure of the comparative authority and agendas of the two commanders. At a guess, he thought that Khiadysis held the upper hand in the conversation, though his ships were outnumbered by the corsairs. The arrival of the *Fae Taeruth* may have altered the power balance in the ad-hoc fleet, and they would do well to keep both Yrithain and Khiadysis happy.

'If that is to be the case, we must adapt our strategy,' said the prince-commander. 'Maensith, please ready your ship for communion with the *Sathaisun* and we shall be able to locate a role for you and your vessel.'

'Of course, Yrithain. And what is the purpose of this gathering? Is there a convoy en route?'

'Nothing so dull,' said Khiadysis. 'I have not come all of this way for a few ships. We will be raiding Naimh-neilith itself.'

'Attacking the planet?' said Aradryan, his surprise getting the better of him. His outburst was not seen by the others – his form was not part of the holo-projection from the *Fae Taeruth* – but he earned himself a scowl from Maensith. The captain turned back to the others with a sly smile.

'It is good fortune indeed that brings us here at this time,' she said. 'I shall begin the communion shortly.'

With nods of parting, the images of the other two commanders flickered into nothing. Maensith looked at Aradryan, her displeasure dissipating.

'You, my lover, are about to experience the greatest thrill this life can offer,' she said.

* * *

Laser fire strobed across the ether, ripping livid wounds of flame and debris across the armour of the human's orbital station. Missiles flared from the battlestation's defence turrets, sweeping past the voidcutter piloted by Aradryan, targeted at the larger eldar ships behind the flotilla of boarding craft. Aradryan did his best to focus on the controls of the small single-sailed vessel, but it was impossible to totally ignore the mayhem that was going on around the boarding parties.

The wreckage of system defence ships drifted across his view, billowing gas and fire as they were drawn into the gravity well of the planet below. The shimmering shape of an eldar frigate enclosed by holofields stole around the periphery of the battle, its laser batteries intercepting a swarm of bombers launching from a dock set high in the battlestation's superstructure. The tracery of laser fire and blossoms of explosion lit the huge orbiting platform, highlighting the cave-like opening that was the pirates' point of attack.

The station looked like an inverted, four-storeyed ziggurat in general shape, with a single command tower extending far beneath its shadowed bulk, navigation lights and sensor arrays jutting from the shaft of the control spire. Stubby defence emplacements dotted its surface and the space around it shimmered red with powerfields overloading as the fire of the eldar fleet converged on the platform.

Shockwaves of energy rippled past the voidcutter, but Aradryan dealt with each successive buffering with practised control, riding through the expanding clouds of radiation and glittering particles.

Maensith had been right: this was one of the most beautiful and terrifying acts Aradryan had performed. The interplay of the fleet, the web of laser fire lancing from turrets and gun decks, created mesmerising patterns against the dark circle of the world, with the station a glittering ruby at their centre. As when he had been at Hirith-Hreslain and the raid on the haugri-alim, Aradryan felt detachment, and had the time and space to admire and be awed by the spectacle of war. Yet there was also the danger of the encounter with the orks and the flight from the daemonettes, for there was genuine peril as laser beams seared across the cockpit display and missiles as large as the voidcutter powered past. And at the end was the promise of the close-fighting that Aradryan found so thrilling.

The *Fae Taeruth* had been added to the part of the fleet tasked with silencing the battlestation, so that the Commorraghans and Yrithain's cruiser could close to low orbit and launch their raid on the planet itself. The orbital platform was more than a tactical objective; it housed weapons magazines and extensive storage holds full of potential plunder. Yrithain had assured Maensith that he already had a party interested in the acquisition of these items, and delivery of the guns, ammunition and food packs would ensure the *Fae Taeruth*'s crew would share in their allotment of the spoils.

Along with a dozen other voidcutters and star-runners, Aradryan's craft arrowed through the emerging streams of laser fire. As the range to the battlestation closed, shell-firing cannons opened up, their high-explosive rounds filling the vacuum with spinning shrapnel. Their holofields as effective against the crude human sensors as they were the naked eye, the assault boats sped through the furious defensive fire, trusting to speed to keep them ahead of the enemy's targeting matrices.

The opening that Aradryan was aiming for grew larger and larger on the display. With enough power in the voidcutter's engines to continue the mission, Aradryan furled the stellar sail and outriggers as the flotilla passed beyond the minimum range of the defence turrets. White light blazed from the open bay, from which a squadron of fighters had launched at the first sign of attack. Those craft had been dealt with by the initial eldar wave of Nightwing fighters, and the way was clear for the boarding parties to land.

Guiding the voidcutter on a curving path beneath the upper levels of the platform, Aradryan steered towards the bay opening. As the craft plunged into the bright docking lights within, the landing area could be clearly seen. Several dozen humans were in the bay, dressed in white trousers and long blue coats. They wore no helmets, their shaven heads glinting in the glare of the lights, but they had rebreather masks on, connected by ribbed piping to air tanks on their backs. Aradryan's second-in-command on the mission, Taelisieth, activated the twin brightlances mounted in the nose of the voidcutter. From the other attack boats spewed more laser fire, joined by the flare of blue plasma stars. The combined fire scythed through the waiting humans as the station's defenders opened fire with their lasguns and crude automatic rifles. Miniature warp vortexes, no wider than Aradryan's outstretched arms, appeared in the midst of the humans; the distort cannons on two of the raiders had been activated. The defenders caught in the grip of these pocket warp gates were pulled apart by the crashing forces, some sucked directly into the warp. Aradryan had no time to contemplate the hideous fate of those unfortunate enough to survive the transition into warp space; their torment would not last long.

Braking heavily, brightlances still spitting beams of blue energy across the dock, Aradryan brought the voidcutter to a sharp stop, dropping to the bay floor. Even as the craft settled down, the main door was opening and he was rising from his seat. He snatched his sword from the console and clipped the scabbard to his belt as he hurried down the voidcutter's central passageway.

Emerging into the landing bay, nose and mouth covered with a lightweight breathing mask, Aradryan found that there were no survivors of the assault boats' barrage of fire. To his right, several corsairs were guiding an anti-grav dais down the ramp of their star-runner, another distort cannon mounted on the floating platform. Other groups were heading to secure the entry routes into the bay – two of them – ensuring that the humans could not counter-attack.

Under Aradryan's direction, the distort cannon was steered across the bay and aimed towards the wall to the left. The weapon opened fire at the wall, its metal and rock-like substance engulfed by a whirling sphere of flickering energy. The small portal collapsed after a few moments, leaving a perfect circle burrowed through the thick bulkhead, leading into an access corridor not directly connected to the launch bay.

Aradryan drew his sword and pistol and waved for his team of forty warriors to move through the newly created opening, the d-cannon gliding under the control of its gunners. With a last glance to assure himself that the rearguard were set to defend the voidcutters and star-runners, Aradryan stepped through the bulkhead, calling for his raiders to head to the right.

On the last leg through the webway Aradryan had memorised the internal layout of the station – he had not asked how Yrithain had come by such information – and knew the allotted roles of the corsairs aboard his vessel and the others to the finest detail. Surprise and timing were key if they were to be successful; the larger ships would be making their run to orbit at a precise time and the battlestation's main weapons had to be rendered ineffective by then or the whole raid would have to be abandoned. Knowing that Yrithain's patience had already been tested by the *Fae Taeruth*'s arrival, and that the favour of Khiadysis would be fickle, Aradryan had no doubts regarding the price of failure.

Plotting a route through the station's interior, Aradryan was struck by the inelegance and artificiality that formed the basis of the humans' sense of space and architecture. There was nothing of nature in the design, no flow or grace to the simple grid layout; it was purely functional. The doorways and arches passed by the corsairs were broad and low, often marked with red and yellow stripes to denote hazards, indecipherable stencilled lettering on the walls beside them.

Using the d-cannon, Aradryan and his party were able to bypass the worst chokepoints and defensive bottlenecks, moving from one line of attack to another in a few heartbeats, so that the humans were easily outflanked and cut down. The masked soldiers would form a line ahead of the advancing eldar, ready to defend a junction or crossing. Aradryan would have a handful of his warriors engage the humans from the front for long enough for him to devise another route of advance. Sometimes the eldar would simply disengage from the defenders, having slipped into a secondary access tunnel, or dropped or climbed up a level. Most of the times, though, Aradryan led his corsairs on the attack, striking the defenders from the side or rear while their attention was drawn by those left behind.

The humans' communications systems and command structure

seemed woefully inadequate in the face of such a threat. Aradryan was surprised by the continued success of this tactic, as he slashed his sword across the throat of a human officer defending a stairwell that led to the innermost decks of the battlestation. Ducking beneath a pistol swung as a club, Aradryan kicked out at his attacker's knee, sending the man sprawling to the floor. The gleaming edge of Aradryan's blade bit into the side of the human's head, stilling his resistance.

Firing a flurry of shurikens from his pistol into the throat of another foe, Aradryan stepped over the corpses of the fallen and glanced down the stairwell. There appeared to be no defenders on the level below, but he was not about to take any chances.

As the last of the humans died, a gurgling rasp emerging from his shuriken-ripped throat, Aradryan parted his company with gestures from his sword. The d-cannon crew understood his intent, and pointed their machine at the landing at the top of the stairs.

Aradryan's skin crawled and his hair rose up with static energy as the distort cannon opened fire, punching a hole between reality and the warp. Part of the landing collapsed, sending a slide of broken masonry and twisted metal reinforcing rods plummeting down into the floor below. There were a few cries of shock and pain amongst the rumble of the tumbling landing.

Leaping down into the hole with his followers close behind, Aradryan landed on top of another human, who had been crawling across a tipped slab of flooring. Losing his footing, Aradryan rolled to one side, his pistol spitting discs that shredded the fallen man's jerkin, droplets of blood spraying through the cloud of dust that surrounded Aradryan. In the gloom, Aradryan saw shapes moving – too slow and cumbersome to be his companions. He slashed at the disorientated soldiers with his sword, cutting down three enemies in quick succession.

As the dust cloud dispersed, the corsairs came leaping through the hole and Aradryan regained his bearings. The d-cannon floated down last, its gunners standing on the anti-grav platform. Aradryan double-checked their current position against his mental map, fixing the junction ahead in relation to the image in his mind. A left turn would bring them to where they needed to be.

Suited men came running around the corner ahead, no doubt responding to the noise of the collapsing stairwell. They were taken una-wares as Aradryan and the rest of the corsairs opened fire, sending out a hail of shurikens and las-bolts. Sword held ready, Aradryan sprinted to the junction with Taelisieth at his shoulder. The passages to the left and right were clear for the moment, so Aradryan sent his lieutenant to the end of the corridor on the left, to secure the distant archway with a handful of corsairs. Turning his attention to the right, Aradryan sent another party to the far end of the passageway, where an armoured door had descended across the hall; he did not know whether the door could be raised again and it was best to assume the worst.

The walls and floor gently vibrated, set to a faint tremor by hidden power cabling. The passage and its surrounds were atop the power plant of the station: a crude plasma chamber that held an artificial star in check with magnetic fields and ceramic walls. The thrum that resonated around Aradryan was a lifeless, mechanical vibration, with none of the potency of an infinity circuit or world spirit. It was purely electrical energy, converted from the plasma reactor and sent along metal wires to distant gun posts and laser arrays. As basic as the system was, the electromagnetic flux created by the plasma chamber was enough to distort the scanners of the eldar warships, making its exact location impossible to fix.

This was where Aradryan and his team came into the plan. Bringing forth a trio of beacons similar to those the rangers used at Hirith-Hreslain, the corsairs looked to Aradryan for guidance on their placement. He paced out the required distance along the corridor and, as he had expected, there was a door to his left, hung on hinges that creaked a little as he pushed open the rudimentary portal.

'One in there,' Aradryan told one of the beacon-holders, nodding towards the doorway. 'Another at the sealed archway ahead. Bring the third.'

A little further from the junction was a small access panel. It came off to Aradryan's prising fingers easily enough, revealing a circular cableway just about wide enough for an eldar to crawl into. Aradryan crouched and looked into the hole. There was a metal band holding a cluster of cables in place at roughly the right place, and he pointed out this feature to the corsair with the beacon. There was no need to be absolutely precise; Yrithain's instructions had left some margin for error.

Ushering his companions back to the junction, Aradryan heard a commotion from the direction of Taelisieth and he saw fighting had broken out at the far end of the corridor. He sent reinforcements to his second-in-command as red las-blasts seared the walls around the eldar, two of the corsairs falling back from the passage junction with cries of pain. It seemed the humans were aware of the corsairs' location and were about to launch a concerted assault. The enemy could not have any idea what the eldar planned – Aradryan had been astounded and amused by the suggestion – but the timing of the counter-attack was inconvenient.

Activating the beacons remotely, all Aradryan could do next was wait and hope that Maensith had been able to manoeuvre the *Fae Taeruth* into position. Like the group that had delved into the heart of the battle-station, the corsair's leader had been put into the risky but pivotal lead position of the second wave. She would have to rely on skill and speed to outpace the fully operational cannons of the orbital platform.

Once in position, and this was the ingenuity of Yrithain's plan, Maensith would activate the cruiser's webway portal, burrowing a tubular breach through realspace to create a temporary extension of the webway. Normally such a thing would have no impact on the material universe and would pass unnoticed through solid matter. With a small modification in the webway's flux, and the target of the beacons, the web passage could be used to isolate the station's plasma generator. If Aradryan had tried a conventional attack against the plasma reactor – assuming he and his companions had been able to fight their way through the massed layers of security blockades and hundreds of soldiers, and been able to penetrate the thick walls surrounding it with something like a distort cannon – any breach of the chamber would have resulted in a catastrophic feedback and meltdown event.

As if coming to a cue on a script, a shimmering wall bisected the tunnel behind Aradryan; streaming, half-seen energy cascaded at a slight diagonal to the angle of the walls. He knew from vast experience that he was looking at a webway manifestation, though the speed of its pulsing and partially temporal nature were new to him. Almost immediately, the webway tunnel appeared and raucous klaxons sounded along the passage, deafeningly loud.

Everything plunged into blackness, and all went still and silent.

Somewhere in the plane between realspace and the warp, a star blossomed into life and died in a heartbeat as the breached plasma chamber ran riot for an instant before being snuffed out by the impossible physics of the webway.

Aradryan stood absolutely still, knowing that in the moment that the plasma generator had been spirited into the alternate dimension, all of the major systems of the platform would have crashed. Along with the all-important weapons systems, environmental controls would be compromised too. Soon the air would be growing staler and the temperature was already slowly dropping, gradually being leeched out through the structure of the battlestation. Artificial gravity had ceased, hence Aradryan's immobility for the moment, and all lights had been extinguished.

The battlestation, to all intents and purposes, was dead.

The sudden loss of power had interrupted the fighting between Taelisieth and the humans, neither side sure of what to do next. Aradryan blinked three times in rapid succession, activating the artificial lenses over his eyes. They were not as powerful as a proper visor, but there was enough reflected heat from the eldar and the cables within the walls to create a fuzzy image of Aradryan's surrounds, while his fellow corsairs stood out like yellow silhouettes.

Kicking lightly off the floor, Aradryan did a slow cartwheel until his feet touched the ceiling. Rebounding towards the floor, he twisted again, splaying his arms to slow his descent. Touching down lightly, he stepped again, and in this way he made safe progress along the passageway towards Taelisieth.

The silence had not lasted more than few heartbeats before the shouted panic and the curt snarl of commands echoed along the corridor. Taelisieth reacted swiftly, leading his warriors against the humans in the darkness, making the most of their fear and confusion. Like ghosts, the bright images of the eldar pirates floated out of sight around the corner.

'Onwards, the enemy will be converging,' Aradryan told his warriors, pointing after Taelisieth. Turning to plant a foot on a wall, Aradryan pushed himself around the junction.

Ahead, the flash of laspistols and the whirr of shurikens punctuated the fight between eldar and human. Propelling himself down the corridor as fast as he could, Aradryan reached Taelisieth and the others as a sprawling melee broke out. Using his momentum, blade held out in front of him like a lance, Aradryan threw himself into the humans. The tip of his sword scored across the neck of a man struggling to gain his footing, the strap of his rifle tangling his arms. Blood jetted slowly from the wound, painting Aradryan's arm red as his mass carried him past the dying soldier.

Twisting to avoid a swinging rifle aimed at his head, Aradryan found himself spinning out of control towards the floor. He punched down and turned, correcting his fall. Pulling up his knees, he was able to get his feet under himself and push up, leaping over the human who was pulling back his rifle for another swing. Aradryan lashed out with his sword, severing the man's wrist. As the human fell back, pain wracking his features, Aradryan stretched out a leg, catching the wall with enough force to spin him towards the ceiling feet-first. Landing cat-like on the tiles above the two sides, Aradryan looked down on the unfolding fight.

The humans were utterly unable to deal with the change in conditions; they could not react quickly enough to prevent themselves colliding with walls, floor or ceiling, nor were they supple or dextrous enough to use their weapons whilst in mid-air. The eldar were like a flock of predatory birds, moving though their enemies with pistols and blades, shooting and cutting at leisure while their victims flailed helplessly in response. The cries of the wounded and dying humans formed a bass foundation to the light and lilting laughter of their superiors.

Aradryan spied a human trying to get away, using the lip of a ventilation cover for purchase as he pulled himself along the wall. With a turn and a kick, Aradryan somersaulted down to the floor just ahead of the fleeing soldier. The eldar drove his sword point between the shoulder blades of the human, the force of the blow sending Aradryan back to the ceiling once more. Using light fittings as hand- and footholds, Aradryan sped along the ceiling to the next junction. Checking to the left and right, he assured himself there were no further reinforcements coming for the moment.

Glancing back, he saw Taelisieth and his party binding a number of humans with gossamer-like fibres, made more difficult because their prisoner's struggles caused human and eldar alike to spin through the air.

'What are you doing?' Aradryan demanded, somer-saulting back down the corridor to confront the lieutenant.

'Maensith's command,' replied Taelisieth. There was a hint of humour in his voice. 'Did you not hear?'

'I did not,' said Aradryan. 'They will only slow us down. We have to get to the weapons lockers as quickly as possible.'

'No need to worry about carrying all of that bulky stuff, when you can plunder something that moves under its own power,' said Taelisieth. He placed a foot against the wall to brace himself as he hauled a bound human to his feet and pushed the man down the corridor. The human wiggled helplessly as he floated along the passageway. Taelisieth took a step after, but was stopped by Aradryan's hand on his arm, causing the two of them to begin to slowly turn head over heels.

'And what use are prisoners going to be when it comes to getting our share of the spoils? You heard Yrithain the same as I did. He has already arranged payment for the stores of the battlestation. What is Maensith's game?'

'You should ask her,' said Taelisieth, his shrug causing him to turn away from Aradryan. 'I thought you were the one she confided in. You are her favourite, after all.'

Aradryan said nothing, pushing himself away from his second. If Maensith had a plan, it was better to keep to it than cause further delay and disruption. The battlestation had no secondary systems of any import – why would it when normally the loss of its reactor would also be the cause of its destruction – but the corsairs were still outnumbered by several thousand humans. It was clear the way back to the ships would not be easy, even though the loss of light and gravity no doubt favoured the raiders.

'So be it, we shall see what we can do,' said Aradryan. He lifted a finger to the communicator stud in the lobe of his ear. 'For those who have not yet been informed, we will be taking prisoners if possible. Do not risk your lives for them, but if you can take any enemies alive, then do so. There will be no attack on the upper storage levels; we head back as a group to the landing craft.'

As the party set off once more, half a dozen captured humans in tow, Aradryan considered Maensith's instruction, and wondered why she had not chosen to share her orders, or her rationale, with him. There was only one reason Aradryan could think of for Maensith to refuse Yrithain's wishes, only one group of people that were interested in live prisoners: the Commorraghans.

The corsairs had a running battle back to their landing craft, and though they lost nearly a quarter of their number, Aradryan and his company managed to capture several scores of humans for whatever bargain Maensith had struck with the Commorraghans. In the zero gravity and darkness, such encounters were harsh, brief affairs of flashing laser and shuriken volleys, sweeping swords against bayonets, power mauls and knives. The eldar brought their dead with them, taking their spirit stones into safekeeping before forcing the captives to pull the lifeless remains.

Corridor by corridor, hallway by hallway, Aradryan guided his warriors back to the ships. The d-cannon had been destroyed, its anti-grav platform rendered inoperative after the loss of the station's artificial gravity field; Aradryan would not leave such technology to be studied by the humans and so the workings of the cannon had been melted with a fusion charge.

Without the means to create their own shortcuts and doorways, the corsairs were harder pressed to outmanoeuvre the human soldiers, who had managed to recover some of the organisation and structure they had lost following the destruction of the power network. Even so, they were poorly equipped to deal with the conditions, and though the losses of the corsairs were growing in number, they did not encounter irresistible odds.

Approaching the docking area where the void-cutters and star-runners were located, Aradryan signalled the parties he had left defending the ships. As he expected, they had faced fierce counter-attacks and had been forced to withdraw to the craft, using the ship's weapons to destroy the occasional forays from the human forces. They reported that no attack had been made since the plasma chamber's destruction, but the ships' sensors detected large bodies of troops guarding the approaches to the landing bay, waiting for the pirates to return to their vessels.

It was a tricky situation, but one that Maensith and Aradryan had considered. After receiving as much information as was available concerning the positions of the humans, Aradryan devised a plan of attack. It was not necessary to destroy all of the defenders; the corsairs merely had to punch a hole through the cordon and withdraw under the cover of their vessel's guns. As with their initial response to attack, the humans displayed a short-sightedness in their deployment, and gave no consideration to the possibility that their attackers might choose not to follow the routes already dictated by the architecture of the station.

Sending a group of a dozen corsairs to scout the path ahead, Aradryan contacted the warriors on the ships. Since the removal of the plasma core, the pirates had been circling back to the dock from the opposite direction to their departure. This put them in an ideal position to make a last run for sanctuary, with only one guard outpost in their path. Aradryan called on the ships' crews to target their weapons at two particular points in the wall to their right, on the other side of the bay from the hole created by the d-cannon. The first was the rear wall of a defensive emplacement guarding an access conduit; the second was a junction with that conduit.

When the scouting party returned to report that there were no enemy between the pirates and the junction, Aradryan gave the order to his warriors. Setting off at speed, pushing and dragging lines of bound humans tied together with hair-thin polymer strands, Aradryan and the corsairs made their final dash.

On coming within sight of the junction, Aradryan told the ships' crews to open fire. A combination of brightlances, scatter lasers and d-cannon blasts smashed into the dividing bulkhead, ripping a new opening through the wall. The way was not yet clear, however, and as the pirates reached the smoke-filled juncture of corridors, heavy las-fire erupted from the manned posts to their right. Chunks of debris glided along the corridor away from the previous fusillade, but not enough to provide significant cover against the lascannons and lasguns of the defenders.

As Aradryan had hoped, the humans were too cautious and had drawn their men into an embrasure overlooking the passageway. Gun slits and murder holes pierced the walls, and anyone trying to make it across to the breach in the bulkhead would be cut down in moments.

'Fire again, second position,' said Aradryan, peeking a look around the corner of the junction. His infrareceptor lenses picked out the body heat of several dozen humans clustered in the bunker-like rooms either side of the corridor. A moment later he saw the clashing, ravening sphere of a d-cannon detonation tearing out a portion of the bulkhead, sucking half a dozen defenders into the maw of its warp vortex. Through the newly-created gap erupted a storm of fire from the other ships' guns, and in that first moment of anarchy, as humans were cut down by the searing lances of laser and hails of shuriken cannon fire, Aradryan signalled for his warriors to make the run across to the blasted hole in the bulkhead.

A few humans were competent enough to snap off las-shots from their fortification, but their aim was poor and Aradryan made it across to the opening without so much as risking a near-miss. He ducked into the landing bay through the gouge in the wall, to see that some of the other pirates had emerged from the ships, lasrifles and shuriken catapults ready to cut down any defenders entering the dock; thread-like tethers held them to the ships in the zero gravity.

Not waiting to see how the others fared, Aradryan backed up against the wall and then kicked himself forwards, sailing through the air towards his voidcutter. The air coming through his rebreather mask was already beginning to taste stale and he knew that the atmospheric quality was dropping rapidly. For a moment he considered the possibility that the human prisoners were the lucky few; their comrades would suffocate to death in the following hours, with perhaps only a few fortunate commanders and upper echelon officers having access to emergency air supplies. Aradryan soon dismissed the notion, knowing that even a lingering, dreadful death by asphyxiation was probably better than whatever fate the prisoners faced at the hands of the Commorraghans.

Aradryan had misjudged his course slightly and was forced to reach out to grasp the hand of a pirate standing at the top of the voidcutter's boarding ramp. Grabbing the other eldar's wrist, Aradryan pulled himself down into the opening. As soon as he was within the grip of the vessel's smaller artificial field, weight returned, catching him by surprise. He managed to land on his feet, but his awkward fall jarred his sword from his grip, which clattered to the deck, accompanied by a laugh from the pirate on the gangway. Ignoring his embarrassment and retrieving his weapon, Aradryan picked his way to the piloting chamber and made ready to take off as the other crews soared across the landing bay, trailing lines of prisoners like squirming serpent tails.

When Aradryan received word that all were aboard the voidcutter, he sealed the doorway and guided the craft into the air. Just as with their arrival, humans were heading into the dock, bringing with them heavy weapons that spat missiles and laser pulses after the departing pirates. Under Aradryan's deft fingers, the voidcutter jinked to the left and right, making itself an impossible target as the stellar sail unfurled and the holofield shimmered.

Passing out of the docking bay, Aradryan turned the viewsphere to the rear, so that he could see the *Fae Taeruth* and other ships converging on the planet below. They had already attained low orbit, pulses of laser fire spewing from their lance turrets towards the surface. A cloud of tiny stars was pouring from the Commorraghan warships: fleets of attack craft plunging into the atmosphere of the world intent on loot and prisoners.

Aradryan turned the voidcutter out-system, trimming the sail to catch what he could of the stellar winds, recharging the engines of the ship. Behind him the dark shape of the battlestation was silhouetted against the star's light creeping around the edge of the world, hanging lifeless in the void.

As with his previous encounters and fights, Aradryan felt enormous relief and satisfaction. The audacity of the attack, the cunning and ruthlessness employed in its execution, was stronger than any drug or dream he could remember. Even the revelation of Maensith's double-cross of Yrithain partway through and the rapid change of plans only added to the drama after the event. Laughing, Aradryan leaned back in his chair and closed his eyes, reliving the moments of near-death, the clash of sword on rifle and the flicker of las-fire across his vision. There would be a time when Morai-heg would cut his thread and seal his fate, but that time had not yet come and while he lived, Aradryan was determined to enjoy everything his life offered him.

A ruddy light suffused the landing bay, bathing the voidcutter with scarlet. Stepping down the craft's ramp, Aradryan felt like he was striding into permanent twilight. He and Maensith were aboard Khiadysis's flagship to attend a captains' council convened at the insistence of the

Commorraghan hierarch; Khiadysis had refused to conduct the meeting by holo-communication but had not mentioned the nature of the discussion he desired.

Since the raid on the battlestation, the *Fae Taeruth* had joined forces with the corsairs of the Azure Flame and the Commorraghans of Hierarch Khiadysis for three more attacks. Each had gone well enough, but it became increasingly obvious with each raid that the target of the attacks were not the ships but their crews, and after each attack the Commorraghans took their share in aliens and left the corsairs to squabble over the meagre remains of the spoils. Maensith's support of Khiadysis had firmly swung the balance of power within the fleet towards the Commorraghans, and though he did not express his nervousness to his captain, Aradryan believed this to be a mistake. As untrustworthy and arrogant as Yrithain was, he was still born of the craftworlds. The Commorraghans were not just outcasts, they were barbaric and savage, and allying himself to their cause, even through the proxy of Maensith, made Aradryan shudder more than once.

For all that, Maensith had been able to manage her relationships with both Khiadysis and Yrithain to the advantage of the *Fae Taeruth* and Aradryan knew that now was not the time to withdraw from the pirate fleet to set out alone again – Khiadysis had made it clear he expected Maensith's support for some time to come. Less clear, but suspected by Aradryan, was an underlying threat; any attempt by Maensith to turn on Khiadysis or otherwise leave would result in her former kabal swiftly learning her whereabouts. Though the pirate captain never spoke to Aradryan of those times, it was painfully clear that she had fled Commorragh in less-than-ideal circumstances and had hidden away for good reason.

Aradryan hoped that the coming meeting would reveal the hierarch's greater intent – for it was obvious that he had one, and the raids they had been conducting were building up to another large expedition. With that completed, Aradryan hoped to persuade Maensith to leave the fleet and forge a lone fate; he was tired of answering to the whims of a soulless predator even if the cost was the risk of retribution from the past, and the thought of becoming one of Yrithain's followers threatened to be just as bad.

'Why does it have to be so dark?' asked Aradryan. Six armed Commorraghans fell in behind the pair as they left the voidcutter, saying nothing. Ahead, a door hissed open and a robed, bald-headed eldar appeared. He bowed and beckoned for Maensith and Aradryan to approach.

'This is captured light from the tame star at the heart of Commorragh,' said Maensith. She walked with long, nonchalant strides, but like Aradryan she was armed with pistol and sword at her waist and her eyes were constantly moving, alert to all around her. In the glow, her skin was tinged with red, her eyes glittering with the same. 'It is not called the

Dark City simply because of its inhabitants' lifestyles.'

'Dracon Maensith,' said the dark eldar at the door, bowing again, his expression slightly leering as he regarded the shapely captain. 'I must ask that you submit your weapons to me.'

'Never,' snapped Maensith. 'Step away from me, casket-born. Convey me to Khiadysis Hierarch immediately. And I am no longer dracon, you can dispense with the flattery.'

Cowed, the attendant nodded and headed out of the door. Following, their escort a few steps behind, Aradryan and Maensith were led to an elevating chamber. During the short walk, Aradryan noticed that there was something other than the lighting that lent a mood of oppressiveness to the atmosphere. On Alaitoc or a ship, he was used to the ever-present warmth and energy of the infinity circuit. Even at Hirith-Hreslain there had been the unconscious touch of the world spirit. On the Commorraghan ship there was nothing. A glance at their guide and the warriors behind reaffirmed Aradryan's initial observation that none of them were wearing waystones.

Apart from the coldness emanating from the lack of a psychic network, there was another sensation that dragged at Aradryan's spirit as the group boarded the ascending chamber, which rose soundlessly up through the levels of the ship. The Commorraghans deliberately cultivated an air of malice about them. There was an undercurrent of misery, which lingered on the edge of perception like a half-heard scream of torment. The whole ship was steeped in torture and agony, and its stench dripped like oily sweat from the dark eldar around Aradryan. He felt unclean just standing this close to them. Their presence tainted the air and he wanted to choke, suddenly able to taste pain and depravity in his mouth, cloying in his throat and filling his lungs.

He felt a movement close to him and relaxed, feeling Maensith's hand brush against his for the briefest moment.

There was none of the depraved filth about her, though once she had been hailed as a leader amongst the Commorraghans. Aradryan harboured no illusions about his lover's past; she had undoubtedly committed acts of evil and taken part in perverse rites that would turn the stomach of any sane eldar. Yet now, as Aradryan considered her amongst her former kin, he realised that she was no longer one of them. She had spoken the truth when she had claimed to have left behind the double-dealing and predatory behaviour of her birthplace. Even though she would ever be a pirate and a mercenary, she had somehow managed to cleanse the taint of her history.

Without a sound, the conveyance slid to a halt and the doors opened, revealing an opulently decorated and furnished hall. The Commorraghan functionary bowed and waved for Maensith to exit. Aradryan followed after her, and glanced back to see the doors closing, in a moment becoming invisible behind velvet curtains.

The escort of kabalite warriors had been left behind but Aradryan felt no more secure. On a gilded throne at the far end of the hall sat Khiadysis, and the Commorraghan lord was flanked by a dozen white-helmed warriors with lyrate horns twisting from their crests. Each bodyguard wielded a dual-handed blade almost as tall as an eldar and was garbed with heavy plates of dark armour painted with small Commorraghan runes. Though he had never seen them before, Aradryan guessed that these were the deadly incubi, believed by some to be the followers of the Fallen Phoenix, Arhra, who had founded the Striking Scorpion Shrine of Aspect Warriors. To see so many of the sinister mercenaries aboard Khiadysis's ship was testament to the wealth and power of the hierarch.

The incubi were not alone in attending the kabalite commander. Sitting on a stool at his feet was a female eldar, dressed in a black robe banded with silver rings, her hands and forearms sheathed in silken gloves. Aradryan noticed the glint of partially concealed blades on fingers and within the folds of the courtesan's dress.

'Lhamaean,' said Maensith, her voice barely a breath. 'Poisoners without equal. Do not get too close. And look, in the shadows to your right. Ur-ghuls from the depths of Commorragh.'

Aradryan glanced as directed and saw indistinct, grey-skinned shapes in the ruddy darkness between the huge rib-like columns that lined the hall's wall and ceiling. The things crouched in the shadows, turning eyeless heads in his direction as he passed.

On a long couch on a lower step in front of the Commorraghan hierarch sat Yrithain. With him were two of his captains. The self-proclaimed Prince-Commander of the Azure Flame looked less than comfortable, and he fidgeted with the collar of his blue robe with a hand heavy with rings, his wrist clasped by a silver torc. The pirate prince glanced often towards the incubi standing silent sentry around their employer.

'Come in, my guests, come in,' said Khiadysis, lifting a hand in greeting. His words emerged from hidden speakers around the hall, so that he did not have to raise his voice yet it was heard across the large chamber.

A raised path ran the length of the hall towards the throne dais, and it was along this thickly-carpeted runway that Maensith led Aradryan. To either side were deeper enclosures, some of them fitted with cushions and sheets where naked eldar were locked together in passionate contortions; others were barred and dank, and Aradryan heard whimpering and mewls from the prisoners kept within.

Stopping for a moment, he looked down into one of the cages. A round, human face stared up at him, blood matting her hair, her forehead and cheeks scarred with dozens of tiny scratches. She opened her mouth, pleading, revealing the ragged stub of a tongue shorn away. Nailless, broken-fingered hands reached out in supplication. Despite her obvious pain, the human had dry eyes, and Aradryan remarked upon this to Maensith as they continued towards the dais.

'The haemonculi will have removed the tear ducts first,' replied Maensith, keeping her gaze on Khiadysis, her tone deliberately devoid of emotion. 'Lack of lubrication will eventually blind her, and she cannot cry.'

Ignoring the displays to either side, Maensith strode up the aisle towards the platform on which Khiadysis's throne was situated, Aradryan following close behind her, keeping his gaze ahead. As much as he did not have to look, he could not block out the sounds of pleasure and pain that surrounded him. More than just the noise, the hall seethed with passion and punishment, making Aradryan's skin crawl with its slick touch, even as Khiadysis luxuriated in it. The hierarch's eyes were half closed, his lips trembling gently with pleasure as his gaze followed the pair from the *Fae Taeruth*.

Sitting opposite Yrithain, Maensith directed a satisfied glance at the prince-commander. The look Aradryan shared with the lesser officers of the Azure Flame was not so assured. Still, Aradryan was confident that Maensith knew what she was doing, and obviously she had judged it to be in their better interests to lend support to Khiadysis rather than Yrithain.

As he seated himself, Aradryan caught a glimpse of a serpentine face staring at him from a curtained alcove behind the throne. The bright red-scaled visage disappeared almost immediately, but it had been unmistakeable. Some of the sounds issuing from the cages under the hall were definitely not eldar or human in origin, and it was with some effort that Aradryan forced himself to listen to Khiadysis.

'I am pleased with the outcome of my latest adventure,' said the hierarch. He lifted up a hand and a small, smoking dish was placed in his palm. Inhaling the fumes deeply, Khiadysis's eyes opened wide, the pupils shrinking into tiny black dots in twin pools of green. Veins darkened beneath his pale skin, sketching a pale blue web across throat and face.

'We are not so pleased,' said Yrithain, folding his arms and darting an angry glance at Maensith. 'I have made promises that will go unfulfilled.'

'Ah yes, your deal with Commander De'vaque,' said Khiadysis. The title and name was unfamiliar to Aradryan, but to his surprise they sounded human. 'I would not worry about him any more. In fact, that is why I have brought you here, to discuss an attack on Daethronin.'

'Out of the question,' said Yrithain, standing up. His officers followed suit, more uncertain than their leader. 'The deal I have brokered with Commander De'vaque is both profitable and stable. I see no need to risk antagonising the Imperial commander with a raid on his home system.'

'You have become his lackey, Yrithain,' said Khiadysis. The words were spoken in a matter-of-fact tone, devoid of malice or accusation. 'He takes half of your spoils, in return for what?'

'Without the information we were given by De'vaque, we would not have enjoyed our recent success. The safe harbour he provides at Daethronin shields us from the attention of Imperial Navy patrols, and the targets he has guided us to have been weakly protected.'

'Yes, it is all very safe, isn't it?' Khiadysis looked at Maensith. 'Safe and sound, nice and friendly. These are not concepts that are common amongst my people. We take what we want, without the permission of others. You were a hound, Yrithain, hunting the game of the humans. De'vaque feared you and has managed to leash you with these agreements and pacts. Now you hunt the prey he chooses, and you have forgotten what it was like to run free.'

Yrithain did not argue, but his face was a war of emotions as he sought to counter what the hierarch had said, but knew that there was truth to the accusation. Instead, the prince-commander turned his anger on Maensith.

'I brought you into my plans, offered you a part to play and a share of the spoils, and this is how you repay me?'

'It was Khiadysis Hierarch that brought me into the raid,' Maensith replied calmly, meeting Yrithain's accusing glare. 'I do not owe you any loyalty.'

'And so you support this half-witted scheme to attack Daethronin? You think to turn the tables on my ally?'

'I know nothing of your allies, or of Daethronin,' said Maensith. 'Khiadysis Hierarch simply asked for a tribute from me as a sign of my gratitude.'

'Tribute?' Yrithain almost spat the word, and Aradryan empathised with him. Handing over the prisoners they had taken to the hierarch was tantamount to paying their own ransom. Aradryan kept his lips tightly sealed, however, wishing to show no discord with his captain.

The argument continued, to little end, and Aradryan started to entertain different thoughts to those he had enjoyed before, namely whether he had been right to join with Maensith. For certain he had benefitted from the relationship, and the unconstrained life of a corsair suited him better than the half-duty of the rangers. Conversely, that freedom was always at the behest of another, whether that had been Maensith or Khiadysis. Ambition – insomuch as it related to the imposition of his will over others – had never been part of Aradryan's goals, and life growing up on a craftworld eradicated most desires along such lines, emphasising the qualities of cooperation over competition.

With that in mind, the freedom to do as he wished was strong in Aradryan, and that freedom could be ensured with a ship and crew to follow his will. He had been fortunate so far in finding sponsors such as Athelennil and Maensith, but if he was ultimately to take control of his own fate, Aradryan needed to literally take control too. He glanced at Yrithain and wondered if the corsair prince would be vulnerable to a newcomer taking his place. After all, it was Yrithain who had brokered the first deal with the Commorraghans, which had now gone so badly wrong for the Azure Flame.

Aradryan did not want to betray Maensith, it was not in his character to be treacherous, but perhaps some kind of joint-leadership could be arranged. He was virtually co-commander of the *Fae Taeruth* already, so it would not be so much of a leap as might be imagined.

Turning his attention back to the ongoing debate, Aradryan reminded himself to be patient and to develop his plans one step at a time. There was no point in expending too much effort or thought on Yrithain just yet – Khiadysis was the immediate concern. As he listened to the conversation, Aradryan heard that the hierarch had been able to bring Yrithain on board with a plan to attack Daethronin, wherever that was; the three pirate commanders were arguing over the exact detail of the assault.

'I think it may be useful for a neutral party to be the first to make contact,' said Aradryan, sensing an opportunity. If he could somehow get *Fae Taeruth* separated from the rest of the fleet without violence, he and Maensith could consider their options. Khiadysis turned a questioning look on Aradryan, and he suppressed a shiver at being the subject of the cold-hearted stare.

'Prince Yrithain has already had dealings with this De'vaque person,' Aradryan continued, smiling apologetically at the commander of the Azure Flame. 'Far be it from me, being just a humble officer of the *Fae Taeruth*, to cast doubt on the character of my superiors, but it would seem unwise to me, hierarch, to allow Yrithain to approach De'vaque without monitor.'

'You think I would concoct some kind of double-deal?' Yrithain's lip trembled with anger at the proposition.

'I would no sooner let you out of my sight than turn my back on my dracons,' said Khiadysis, darting a murderous look at the prince-commander before returning his steady gaze to Aradryan. 'Why can we not travel to Daethronin together?'

'That is a perfectly sound strategy for attack,' said Aradryan, looking at the others. 'However, the longer and greater the surprise of our coming, the better it will be for all of us. The *Fae Taeruth* can act as scout and messenger, travelling to Daethronin just a few cycles before the rest of the fleet. We can bring back word of the enemy strength, if anything has changed since the Azure Flame last travelled there, and if encountered by the humans we can rightfully claim to be emissaries of Prince Yrithain. In fact, I would seek out such contact, to lure the humans into a misplaced sense of familiarity.'

'That might work,' said Khiadysis, rubbing the side of his nose with a bony finger. Yrithain caught something of Aradryan's brief look, and his eyes narrowed with suspicion for a moment. Aradryan thought that perhaps the pirate prince would say something to the hierarch, but instead Yrithain's lips twisted in a lopsided smile.

'That is a far better plan, Khiadysis Hierarch,' said Yrithain. 'The *Fae Taeruth* can arrive first and make contact with Commander De'vaque on my behalf. The humans will prepare their port facilities for the incoming cargo, making them vulnerable. I will then travel to Daethronin under the guise of bringing the commander his share of our latest spoils. The Azure Flame and the *Fae Taeruth* will be in position to attack the enemy immediately when your ships break from the webway as the third phase.'

Maensith watched the exchange impassively, eyes flicking between the prince and the hierarch before glancing at Aradryan. She licked her lips quickly, and was about to speak when Khiadysis cut her off.

'I did not rise to the position of hierarch, nor have I maintained it for so long, by allowing myself to be lured into potential ambushes.' Aradryan's chest tightened around his heart and he fought the urge to glance at the incubi spread across the stage. If Khiadysis deemed it more to his advantage to kill his allies now, all the hierarch had to do was give the word to his hired slayers. There was little he or Maensith or Yrithain could do to prevent their deaths in a few heartbeats; it was why they had been allowed into the throne chamber even though they were still armed.

'There is no need to suspect such a thing,' said Maensith. 'To ensure that nothing is amiss, the *Fae Taeruth* will leave Daethronin as soon as the Azure Flame arrive. The greater strength of the fleet will still be with you, hierarch.'

Khiadysis considered this as Aradryan tried to keep his breaths regular and calm. He wondered if the hierarch would speak, or whether a simple gesture would be sufficient to bring down the wrath of the incubi. Perhaps even that would not be needed; the mercenaries may have some other means of discerning their master's wishes.

'I concur,' said the hierarch, nodding briskly. 'The burden of risk will lie with Prince Yrithain.'

Yrithain murmured a few protests at this conclusion, though whether out of genuine concern or simply so as not to appear too happy with the outcome of the meeting, Aradryan could not tell. The pirate prince took his leave soon after. Maensith rose to accompany him but was stayed by a gesture from Khiadysis.

'Remain with me for a little while longer, child,' he said. 'Forgive my paranoia, but I would prefer it if you and the good prince do not engage in any discussions without me present. I will be monitoring the holo-network to assuage my anxiety and do not expect you nor any of your representatives to meet with any of the Azure Flame. Is that agreeable?'

'I am glad that we have an opportunity to discuss the future without Yrithain present,' said Maensith, sitting down again, leaning ever so slightly closer to the hierarch than she had been previously. She looked with narrowed eyes at the back of Yrithain as he stepped from the hall. 'It seems to me that we have an opportunity to not only take what we wish from Daethronin, but also rid ourselves of some dead weight.'

ASCENSION

The True Stars – There is a band of star systems, a great swathe of the galaxy, that lies between the Eye of Terror and the ring of the Exodite worlds. Many of these star systems were once home to eldar planets before the Fall. The inhabitants of these worlds perished when She Who Thirsts was born screaming into the galaxy, but their cities and technologies still survive. These places are known as the True Stars: the last remaining evidence of the Empire That Was. Great are the treasures hidden on these worlds, and powerful are some of the weapons that still defend them. Some True Stars have fallen to alien invasion, inhabited by humans, orks and others. Some are wildernesses, never to be found again. Many harbour treasure troves and vaults from the time before the Fall, and rangers from the craftworlds, Commorraghan expeditions and alien explorers often seek out these ancient and majestic worlds.

As Aradryan prepared to shift the *Fae Taeruth* from the webway into realspace, he ran over the plan in his head, endeavouring to find any flaw or missed opportunity. In theory, the scheme he had concocted with Maensith was simple enough: forewarn the humans of the attack and aid in the destruction of the Commorraghans. With Khiadysis and his ilk disposed of, the *Fae Taeruth* would be free to stay with the Azure Flame or leave as the corsairs saw fit. The complications came when one considered the humans. They were a fickle race at best, and downright stubborn and contrary at worst. There was every chance that Commander

De'vaque would try to imprison or kill Maensith and her crew.

It was to forestall any negative reaction that the *Fae Taeruth* was exiting the webway far out-system from Daethronin's star. The ship would coast in at cruising speed without holofields, hailing the humans from the outset. Maensith's hope was that there would be no surprises on either side. Once the peaceful intent of the eldar was established, a meaningful discourse could be held with the Imperial governor.

In discussions with Yrithain, at which Khiadysis had been present, Aradryan had learnt that Commander De'vaque ruled Daethronin in the name of the Emperor; the humans called the system Carasto. From a previous, fortuitous encounter, Yrithain had run afoul of the Imperial commander's starships, but had been able to broker a deal with the human. In return for safe berths and information about nearby Imperial convoys and transports, Yrithain gave a proportion of his spoils to the Imperial commander and left alone fleets and vessels leaving and destined for Daethronin. In this way, Commander De'vaque grew in power over his Imperial neighbours while the Azure Flame corsairs were given free rein to attack other star systems and merchant flotillas.

Aradryan wondered if there was some deeper reason behind Khiadysis's desire to attack Daethronin. As one of the True Stars, it had once been part of the great eldar empire before the Fall. There were many Commorraghans that still harked back to those glory days, seeing themselves as the true inheritors of the old empire. It would not be a stretch of the imagination to believe that Khiadysis wished to strike back at the humans, who had built their Imperium on the ruins of the eldar civilisation.

With this in mind, Aradryan slipped the *Fae Taeruth* across the veil that separated the physical galaxy from the webway. Half distracted by thoughts of True Stars and whether there was a way in which Yrithain could be deposed from his position in charge of the Azure Flame, Aradryan was shocked when his sensor bank came alive with readings. He had been sure the *Fae Taeruth* would emerge a good distance from the orbit of Daethronin's primary world, but as soon as the ship had broken into realspace the scanning arrays detected five human ships all within half a cycle's travel of the cruiser.

There was no need to relay this information to Maensith. Via the psychic conduits running the length and breadth of the ship she was aware of the situation as soon as Aradryan. Contrary to instinct, Maensith ordered the crew to remain steady and did not order the holofields to be raised or the weapon batteries armed; she stayed true to the guise of an Azure Flame raider returning to its home. To this end, the *Fae Taeruth* had recoloured its hull to blue and black tiger stripes, and at Maensith's insistence began broadcasting several crude human ciphers and hails passed on by Yrithain.

The simple radio wave messages took some time to be detected and for responses to be broadcast; time during which the *Fae Taeruth* came to a stop and allowed the human ships to form a cordon around her. There did not seem to be much urgency about the humans' manoeuvres and Aradryan shared Maensith's confidence that the *Fae Taeruth* was being treated as an unexpected but not unwelcome visitor.

Eventually the responses to the eldar's transmissions were picked up. It took moments to run the garble of noises through the translator banks, which revealed a demand for the *Fae Taeruth* to meet the flagship of the human flotilla at a designated coordinate. There was no hint of suspicion in the message received, which was undersigned by a human calling himself Darson De'vaque. The repetition of the surname, Maensith explained, indicated that it was likely that the human fleet was under the command of a genetic relation of Commander De'vaque, though Yrithain had not furnished her with any information regarding siblings, parents or children.

Routing a brief acknowledgement through the translators and transmission systems, Maensith ordered the *Fae Taeruth* onto her new course, to rendezvous with the humans in one-quarter of a cycle. Aradryan was intrigued and excited. This would be the first time he had met a human without trying to kill or capture it; the prospect of a fresh experience raised him from the gentle lethargy that had plagued him during the last few raids.

The human ship stank.

Aradryan had always been aware of the stench during raids and boarding actions, but he had never really considered it having been occupied with more pressing matters of life and death. Though not tinged by the ozone of laser fire or the iron of spilled blood, the small frigate onto which he had been brought – along with Maensith and Iriakhin, one of Khiadysis's warriors – was filled with a disgusting array of aromas. There was the filthy perspiration of the humans themselves, mingling with the smell of fossil-based lubricants. Metal and corrosion assaulted Aradryan's sensitive nostrils alongside human effluent, unsubtly and ineffectively masked by olfactory-scouring antibacterial chemicals and artificially-scented detergent surfactants.

As if the stench was not enough to make Aradryan dizzy, the ship was in a state of constant vibration, both gentle and strong. Every corridor they passed along was abuzz with electrical charges from cabling within the walls, while crude light fittings fizzed with power. A more deep-seated resonation shook the ship from its plasma engines, creating an ever-present rumbling that unsettled Aradryan's stomach. The thump of their escort's heavy boots on bare metal decking pounded in the eldar's ears, as did the rasping breaths of the 'armsmen' that had met the corsairs' shuttle.

To complete the sensory assault, the artificial light flickered at a painfully slow frequency, so that to Aradryan and his companions' eyes they seemed to strobe rather than provide the constant glow afforded by the more advanced, organic lighting used on craftworlds and the eldar's ships. The contrast of glaring light and sharp shadow made strange, harsh angles out of the undecorated bulkheads they passed.

Without the distraction of deadly combat, Aradryan noticed all of these unpleasant sensations and more. They were conveyed to a primitive mechanical elevation chamber that clanked and clattered on chains as they ascended through the ship, the clunk of each passing level ringing through Aradryan's ears. He focused on the humans, who wore ill-fitting pressure suits and bore short-barrelled, chemically-powered laser carbines; he could smell the laughably inefficient acidic compounds used in the weapons' power packs. The men did not have helms or hats, but all were shaven-headed, bearing tattoos on their scalps akin to clan or House markings; their meaning was lost on the corsair.

At least a head shorter than the eldar, the soldiers of Darson De'vaque had flat faces and noses, their mouths wide, their eyes small and porcine. They glared with barely repressed anger at the eldar, their faces screwed up in clownish grimaces and sneers, but in their eyes Aradryan could see the touch of fear as well. The humans hated their eldar charges because they feared them, and they feared them because they did not understand them. Aradryan smiled at one of the humans in an attempt to alleviate his discontent, but the change of expression was misinterpreted and the soldier raised his gun a little higher, the comically deep frown creasing his forehead becoming even more contorted.

Amongst the stink and the clatter, it was not surprising that humans could barely think, Aradryan realised. It was almost impossible for him to concentrate for more than a few moments with such distractions. As if being short-lived was not curse enough for the people of the Emperor... It was no surprise that they had reverted to such barbarous ways, in the absence of genuine philosophy and culture.

Eventually they reached their destination, somewhere in the heart of the Imperial frigate. Other than a perfunctory welcome issued by Darson De'vaque upon the *Fae Taeruth*'s arrival at the rendezvous, they had heard no message of importance from their host. It seemed unlikely that hostilities would ensue, considering the dispositions of the other human ships in the vicinity, and Aradryan was hopeful of a cordial if not enriching experience.

They were brought to a low-ceilinged room lit by burning wax lamps. The effect of the lighting was not entirely unpleasant, in a prehistoric sort of way, and the lack of illumination was of no concern to the eldar, who could see far more clearly in the dim light than their human companions. At a long table that ran lengthways along the room sat Darson De'vaque, or so Aradryan presumed. He was a slender person, in comparison to the stocky guards that had formed their escort, and a little taller than the average human Aradryan had encountered. There was a softness to his face that indicated he was better fed than his subordinates, and his carefully trimmed facial hair also indicated a slightly higher standard of personal hygiene. Some flowery fragrance, overpowering in its own way, had been used in an attempt to obliterate the man's inherent smell, and Aradryan detected the sheen of perfumed oil in De'vaque's slicked, shoulder-length hair.

The man was dressed in a formal-looking blue frock coat with high collars around his neck, hemmed and braided with golden thread. There was a piercing in the side of his nose, of a small human rune made from silver, which connected by a slender chain of the same metal to a ring in his lower lip. His hands were bare – a pair of black gloves were laid on the table in front of De'vaque – and his hands showed signs of care and attention, with neatly cut and buffed nails that glistened with a dark red polish. On seeing this, Aradryan examined the man's face again and detected a powdery cosmetic that had been applied to smooth away some of the blemishes and discolorations that marked his skin; it had not been immediately apparent in the dim lighting.

De'vaque had bright blue eyes, surprisingly engaging and alert for one of his species. Blubbery lips turned upwards in an exaggerated parody of a smile as those eyes moved from Aradryan to Iriakhin to Maensith. The human stood up and raised a hand to his chest, presumably in a gesture of greeting, and then spoke. Aradryan knew enough of the human language to understand De'vaque's words – though the human tongue was incredibly disparate and diverse across the galaxy, its underlying principles and sounds were easily learnt in comparison to the complexities of the Eldar language – but like his companions Aradryan had a translator device fitted to his shoulder. It was better that the humans believed that their 'guests' could not understand them without the devices.

'Welcome aboard the *Invigorating Glory*, my allies,' said De'vaque. Aradryan wondered whether the translator had worked properly, having indicated the name was that of the starship. It seemed a pompous title for such a small vessel. 'I am Darson De'vaque, Viceroy of Carasto, Rogue Trader of the Chartist Captains and heir to the Imperial command of this star system.'

Quickly deciphering the meanings of the titles, Aradryan realised that Darson was the eldest son of Imperial commander De'vaque. Though no expert in human physiology, he guessed Darson to be of middle age, if not a little older, and surmised that his father would be entering his final span of life shortly, if he had bred at the usual age for humans. While that much was clear, the concept of 'rogue trader', if the translation had been correct, was lost on Aradryan.

'We accept your welcome,' said the eldar pirate. It had been decided that he would act as spokesperson for the *Fae Taeruth*, which the humans would mistake for seniority, thus affording Maensith a degree of protection should matters turn sour. The translator spat out a few guttural syllables before Aradryan continued. 'I am Aradryan, of the *Fae Taeruth*, lately of the Azure Flame corsairs with whom I believe you are already acquainted. It is a pleasant surprise to encounter you in these circumstances.'

De'vaque listened to the translation with his fixed idiotic smile and then nodded.

'Please, be seated while I send for refreshments and food,' said De'vaque, waving a hand towards the seats opposite him.

The odour rising from the plates and cups that were subsequently brought forth was nauseating in the extreme. Even the clear liquid that on casual inspection might be mistaken for water had a chemical taint to it, and despite such anti-microbial efforts was somewhat cloudy in the crudely-cut crystal bottle. Aradryan offered thanks for the repast, but did not eat or drink anything that was offered.

What followed was a drawn out and increasingly tedious conversation, made all the more painful by the subterfuge of waiting for the translator; Aradryan was forced to listen to each meaningless platitude twice before replying while Darson had to genuinely wait for the device to render Aradryan's lyric replies into his crude language. Try as he might to subtly indicate through word and posture that all was not well with De'vaque's allies, the garbled nonsense spewed from the speaker of Aradryan's device conveyed nothing of his implicit warnings.

With Iriakhin listening to everything that was being said, it was impossible for Aradryan to be more overt in his cautioning. Khiadysis's minion would have to be waylaid or otherwise removed for a short period in order to be blunt with Darson De'vaque, in such a way that Iriakhin would not suspect that anything was amiss.

As Darson's inquiries regarding the business of the *Fae Taeruth* became more insistent, Aradryan was at a loss to parry the human's questions with meaningless pleasantries. There were few enough goods on board to offer as trade – due to the change of plans on the orbital station – and without Commander De'vaque's cut of the spoils there was no reason to come to Daethronin.

Struck by the genius of desperation, Aradryan picked up one of the curious cubes of food that had been left in a platter on the table close at hand. Not pausing to think what he might be consuming, Aradryan popped the morsel into his mouth. As he had feared, it was horribly overspiced and barely cooked, so that when he feigned a choking fit he was not far from genuinely retching.

Doubling up, one hand slapping the tabletop, Aradryan imitated a paroxysm of suffocation, holding his breath until he felt quite dizzy. The humans clustered around him, Maensith and Iriakhin stood protectively over him. Out of instinct, Aradryan took a proffered cup, the near-stagnant water he almost gulped down throwing him into a new and entirely unplanned bout of choking. Eyes streaming, Aradryan forced himself to his feet for a few moments. In doing so, he managed to turn his back to Iriakhin and meet Maensith's gaze. The moment their eyes met there was a flash of understanding between the two eldar.

'What is the nature of this food?' the pirate captain demanded through her translator. 'Are you trying to poison us?'

Catching the theme and thinking that some human plot was unfolding, Iriakhin snarled accusations at Darson, who was quite taken aback by the turn of events, though he remained seated throughout. In his remonstrations, Iriakhin became highly animated, forcing the human guards to intervene, their weapons pointed at the eldar.

'Calm yourself, we cannot cause an incident,' Maensith told Iriakhin in their own tongue, while Aradryan continued to hack in fraudulent asphyxiation. 'Let us quickly reappraise the situation before we lose control.'

Lulled by her calming words, Iriakhin allowed himself to be backed towards the door by Maensith. As a wall of men surrounded the two retreating eldar, Aradryan leaned across the table. With a thought, he muted his translator before hissing his words directly at Darson, low enough to be inaudible to Iriakhin.

'Say nothing, we are spied upon. When Yrithain comes, he will be followed by others who are not friends. Have your ships ready to strike. We will assist.'

The man's eyes widened with shock, though whether at hearing his own language rolling from the tongue of the eldar or the message given was unclear. He nodded quickly in understanding as Aradryan flopped back into his chair, still coughing. The eldar reactivated his translator and said a few words between gasping breaths, directing them towards Iriakhin.

'It is no heinous conspiracy, companions,' he said, holding up a hand. 'The human food was not to the liking of my palate, and nothing more sinister. I am recovered now, I assure you.'

'Clear away this mess,' said De'vaque, waving at the attendants who had gathered around Aradryan. Within a few moments the plates and goblets were gone, leaving the wooden table bare save for a single cup in front of Darson. 'My most humble apologies. Please, return to your starship immediately, to seek assurance that your health has not been affected. Thank you for bringing word of Prince Yrithain's arrival, I will ensure that my father greets your coming ships in a suitable manner.'

Listening to these words, Aradryan did not know whether his warning had been understood or not. He had to believe that the warning had been delivered.

Nodding, Aradryan turned to the other two eldar. Maensith came forwards, offering her shoulder for Aradryan to support himself. Iriakhin darted Aradryan an annoyed glance, but irritation was preferable to suspicion. Aradryan allowed himself a moment of satisfaction; that he had managed to warn Darson of the Commorraghan attack and fooled Iriakhin into thinking no such thing had happened.

When the *Fae Taeruth* rejoined the rest of the pirate fleet, there was time only for a brief conference with Yrithain and Khiadysis, to confirm that the humans were expecting the eldar's arrival. There was no means to convey to Yrithain that a warning had been sent, and as the ships of the Azure Flame disappeared along the webway, Aradryan was left with a feeling of unease.

Iriakhin left to report to Khiadysis on the events aboard the *Fae Taeruth*, leaving Aradryan free to voice his doubts to Maensith. The two of them spoke in one of the sub-chambers adjoining the command hall, furnished with a circle of armchairs around a low table, the walls lined with crystal-fronted cabinets holding a variety of drinks decanters and trophy pieces taken from raided vessels. Maensith sat, while Aradryan took a short-bladed, bone-hilted knife from one of the cupboards, idly twisting the dagger between his fingers.

'We have overlooked a possibility,' said Aradryan. 'In all our concern for what Khiadysis might do, and our efforts to allay any suspicions he may harbour, we have neglected to fully consider the options open to Yrithain.'

'Yrithain is under the same constraints as we are,' said Maensith. 'If he turns on us as well as Khiadysis he will be outgunned.'

'Not now, with the humans as his allies,' Aradryan said quietly.

Maensith's lips parted and then closed again, her argument dismissed. She shook her head slightly, brow creasing gently.

'Do you think Yrithain will have the humans turn on us as well?'

'If we were in the same position as Yrithain, would we not sense an opportunity to rid ourselves of *all* our rivals? It would be prudent to expect Yrithain will convince the humans to attack all of the vessels in the second wave, including ours.'

'We cannot warn Khiadysis about the humans' forewarning without implicating ourselves in the treachery. What are we to do, Aradryan? It was your idea to caution the humans against our plans, and now we are caught again between Khiadysis and Yrithain.'

'I do not know what to do!' snapped Aradryan, slamming the tip of the knife into the deep red wood of a cabinet top. He took a deep breath. 'We have half a cycle before the rest of the fleet moves to Daethronin. That is not much time for the humans to prepare; their ships are very slow. We must think of something in that time.'

'Or we can hope that Yrithain remains true to our common goal of dispensing with Khiadysis's alliance, without any action against ourselves.'

'I would prefer we took hold of our own threads of fate than leave them to dangle in the grip of Yrithain. I cannot believe we are utterly trapped with no third option.'

'You are right.' Maensith stood up and crossed the chamber to lay a hand on Aradryan's cheek. Her skin was cool to the touch, but the softness of her fingers sent a flare of pleasure through Aradryan. Since the chance meeting with the Azure Flame and the Commorraghans, Maensith had been much preoccupied, and the two of them had enjoyed little intimacy. 'Between us we will find a solution, I am sure of it. Maybe, if we take our minds from our immediate problems, an answer will present itself.'

Aradryan smiled, a moment before Maensith's lips met his.

Everything at Daethronin was as agreed between the pirate commanders. Yrithain and the Azure Flame were in position behind the escort of small human ships that came out-system to greet the *Fae Taeruth* and the Commorraghans. The handful of destroyers were little match for the weaponry of the three eldar cruisers and the journey towards Daethronin's primary world was uneventful.

For all that Aradryan could see, the humans were ripe for the ambush and had taken no precautions at all against attack, despite the warning given. The timing of the Commorraghans' arrival had been determined to ensure the humans would be caught between the two waves of eldar ships. When the flotilla arrived above the human world, the *Fae Taeruth* and Khiadysis's ships would attack, driving the human escorts against the fleet of the Azure Flame.

It would take at least five cycles to reach the prime world, probably more when accounting for the ponderous nature of the human vessels. Aradryan was not looking forward to such a tense time, wondering when they would receive the order from Khiadysis; at the moment it looked like there was nothing the humans could do to defend themselves, which would effectively leave the battle to Yrithain and Maensith against the Commorraghans. The odds were too close in that event, which was why the aid of the humans had been required in the first place. Not only that, the *Fae Taeruth* was in the most dangerous position, situated between the two dark eldar cruisers. In the event of the Azure Flame turning their guns on the Commorraghans, the most prudent course of action would be to side with Khiadysis.

As soon as the second wave slipped into realspace, Aradryan left his position in the piloting chamber and joined Maensith in the main control hall. At a nod from her, he relieved Taelisieth at the main gunnery controls; to ensure security, neither of them had shared their plans and doubts with the rest of the crew and immediate action would be required whatever circumstances arose.

After a series of customary hails had been exchanged, the combined human and eldar fleet started towards the heart of Daethronin. As the *Fae Taeruth* unfurled her stellar sails and turned gracefully in-system, Aradryan noticed that none of the scanner returns of the human ships corresponded to Darson De'vaque's vessel. In fact, comparing the sensor sweep with those retained in the ship's matrix indicated half a dozen ships were now unaccounted for.

Aradryan sent this information across the matrix to Maensith, but the reason for the discrepancy became immediately obvious. Warning tones chimed across the control chamber, indicating multiple warp breaches. Maensith brought up the visual display, the globe of stars circling slowly above her command pod. Kaleidoscopic whorls broke the fabric of space-time as raw warp energy poured into the material universe. Aradryan counted six rifts opening, and from each emerged one of the missing human ships, directly behind the *Fae Taeruth* and Khiadysis's cruisers.

As the warp breaches closed, the holo-images of Khiadysis and Yrithain burst into view on the main chamber floor. It was the hierarch who spoke first.

'We are surrounded,' snarled the Commorraghan leader. 'It is of little advantage to the humans. Their reinforcements are out of range at the moment. We will obliterate those close at hand first, and then turn our guns on the new arrivals. They cannot match us for speed and firepower.'

'Those reinforcements are merely the lid on the trap,' said Yrithain. In the revolving system display, the Azure Flame vessels were tacking hard, turning across the stellar winds towards the Commorraghans. Plasma flared as the human ships also reduced speed for tight manoeuvres, though far more laboriously than the eldar vessels.

'Traitor!' rasped the hierarch. 'We will see you destroyed first!'

Maensith said nothing, but looked across the chamber at Aradryan. He nodded in reply and activated both weapon batteries, locking on to the Commorraghan cruisers to either side even as Maensith sent the commands that would pull up the *Fae Taeruth*.

Aradryan's fingers danced across the gems of the console, unleashing a barrage of laser and missile fire into the neighbouring cruisers. The aftsail of Khiadysis's cruiser turned into golden shreds flittering across the firmament, while the gun decks of the other erupted with fire and debris. Aradryan's heart raced as he expected a destructive reply, but none came, such was the surprise with which the opening blow had been struck. The *Fae Taeruth* dipped sharply at the prow and rolled to starboard, giving Aradryan one last salvo at Khiadysis's flagship before the weapon batteries could no longer bear upon their targets.

Turning from the weapons controls, Aradryan fixed his gaze on the display, anxious to see what their new enemies would do. The view in the sensor sphere spun rapidly to keep the two cruisers in view as the *Fae Taeruth* turned sharply away from both the Commorraghans and the humans. Yrithain was far from the fight, and his loyalty questionable when he was able to intervene, and if Khiadysis was set on retaliation, the *Fae Taeruth* had little chance against two adversaries. It had been a desperate plan Aradryan and Maensith had concocted during their second voyage to Daethronin and whether it had been successful or not was far from established.

The Commorraghans had been trimming their sails to counter the approach of the Azure Flame, and the attack from the *Fae Taeruth* left them caught between two courses of action. Khiadysis's ship, with its damaged stellar sail, stayed on its course change towards Yrithain's ships; the other stuttered mid-manoeuvre as its captain sought to turn onto the tail of the fleeing *Fae Taeruth*.

The holo-image of Khiadysis disappeared with a howl of rage. Yrithain's apparition remained, arms crossed, his expression a little agitated.

'Well done,' said the prince of the Azure Flame, his smile mocking rather than good humoured. 'I had told Darson De'vaque that you might not be trustworthy, but making the first strike has ensured he will not turn his guns against you. I commend your ingenuity and courage.'

'And do not forget that it was we that first issued warning of the attack, not you,' said Maensith. 'I am sure the Imperial commander and his son will take that into account when the negotiations begin.'

Aradryan briefly returned his attention to the scanner globe. Despite his threat of retribution, Khiadysis was breaking away from the combat as quickly as possible, abandoning his second cruiser, which was now continuing a sweeping turn away from the *Fae Taeruth*; her commander had no doubt realised that his damaged ship was outgunned by the other cruiser without the aid of the hierarch.

The human ships did their best to take up intercepting courses, but there was little doubt the Commorraghans would escape the trap unless the Azure Flame gave chase. Yrithain must have noticed the same, judging by his next question to Maensith.

'Are you going to let them escape? I would not like to list Khiadysis amongst my enemies.'

'He will not return,' said Maensith. 'He is far from Commorragh already, and there is no guarantee we will be here still when he has affected his repairs. Regardless of any hurt he might feel, he also cannot return to the kabal and admit he was the victim of such a simple trick. No, he will return with a tale of overwhelming odds barely escaped, and keep to a life within the towering spires conniving against his archon and stepping on the lives of his underlings, as most hierarchs are content to do.'

'What did you mean by negotiations, which you mentioned a moment ago?' said Yrithain.

'Is it not obvious?' said Maensith. 'Your arrangement with Commander De'vaque is compromised. You brought an enemy to his star system, and you cannot be trusted. We will have to make a new offer, a much more generous offer, on behalf of the Azure Flame to ensure we are welcome at Daethronin.'

'There is no reason to assume the commander will conclude I was complicit in any attack,' said Yrithain.

'Believe me,' Maensith said with a smile, 'that is exactly what I will endeavour to make him conclude.'

She broke the holo-link, isolating the ship's network to prevent Yrithain establishing any further contact without permission.

'Yrithain was right, in part,' said Aradryan, gesturing for Taelisieth to take command of the gunnery console again. When the officer was at his station once more, Aradryan crossed the floor of the command chamber and took the hand of Maensith.

'How was Yrithain right?' she asked.

'The threat that Khiadysis held over you still exists. He will tell your old kabal where to find you, and I fear that will not go well.'

'It is true that I parted from the Crimson Talon as a thief and a fugitive, but there is no reason to be concerned for my future,' replied the captain. She lifted her hand, still gripped in Aradryan's fingers, and kissed the inside of his wrist. 'Let us set course to intercept Darson De'vaque's ship before Yrithain has a chance to get a step ahead of us again.'

With a swagger in his step, Aradryan strode down the carpeted aisle of the Imperial commander's reception chamber. It was located aboard a pleasure yacht of some kind – a stubby, plasma-powered tugboat in comparison to any eldar ship worthy of that name – located in high orbit over the principle world of Daethronin, which the humans insisted on calling Carasto.

Aradryan was feeling supremely confident, despite the rows of soldiers that stood to attention to his left and right, and the small company of marksmen he had spied stationed amongst the metal beams that held aloft the high-arched ceiling. He felt their magnified sights upon him like evil eyes, as once he had looked from afar through his ranger longrifle.

As well as the men-under-arms, Imperial commander De'vaque had a mass of advisers, scribes and heralds loitering in the audience chamber. Their whispering was as clear to Aradryan as if he was in conversation with them, but their exclamations and utterances were entirely dull and revolved mainly around Aradryan's appearance – both his being aboard the yacht and his mode of dress.

This latter was indeed remarkable, for Aradryan had taken some time over his clothes for such an important meeting. Yrithain had seen fit to depart rather than risk the displeasure of the humans, and the remaining ships of the Azure Flame had been keen to broadcast their thanks and loyalty to the warriors of the *Fae Taeruth*. It had become clear soon after that Yrithain had not been a popular leader, and the increasing demands made by Commander De'vaque had stretched the patience and fealty of his underlings almost to breaking point. The arrival of the

Commorraghans had provided a common adversary to rally against, but with that particular problem solved, the other corsairs were happy to join Maensith and Aradryan, once more promised fair division of spoils and a voice in any debate.

Aradryan had suggested to Maensith that they maintain the fallacy of his command, protecting her from any double-dealing De'vaque might contemplate, and so he came to the court of the Imperial commander in his finest regalia, as befitted a prince of the corsairs. He wore a skin-tight undersuit of purple and gold, beneath a knee-length black coat that flared wide at the hips, the shoulders studded with tiny stars of wintersilver. The wide lapels were edged with more silver and hung with fine chains of the same material, stretching across Aradryan's chest in refined mockery of the gold braiding and frogging that was heaped upon De'vaque's uniform. Boots drawn up to his thighs, of supple dawn-leopard skin in black, red and yellow, completed the ensemble, along with numerous rings, bracelets and an elongated skull-shaped piercing in the side of his brow. Aradryan had drawn his hair up into a high crest, further emphasising his height over the stunted humans, and his face was subtly painted to accentuate the shape of his eyes, which were wide and bright compared to the sunken orbs of his host.

The Imperial commander stood next to a high-backed chair, the man as solid as the wood and velvet throne on which he leaned. His cheeks and upper lip were hidden by a bush of thick, greying hair, his chin clear of the growth to display three slender scars. De'vaque wore a peaked cap, of dark blue, the same as his dress coat, its visor coming down over straggling eyebrows. A flat nose and mauled ears betrayed a history of physical conflict – probably recreational, Aradryan guessed, judging the scars on the man's chin to be from some kind of slender duelling sword – and the man's hands were balled into fists with rough knuckles, thumbs tucked into a broad belt that was hung with a pistol on one hip and a tapering, curved sword on the other.

Aradryan was armed also, pistol and sword like the commander, but only for display; if he was required to use his weapons his plan would have failed and he'd be swiftly slain by the several dozen men with guns trained upon him. Well aware of the dashing figure he must pose to the gangling, awkward humans, Aradryan gracefully progressed along the black and gold carpet towards the Imperial commander, timing his strides so that he covered the ground at a sedate but purposeful pace.

The chamber itself was furnished with a heavily-grained wood lacquered with deep red. Various eagles and other Imperial insignia adorned the banners that hung from the ceiling every twenty or so paces. The floor was tiled with intricate mosaic, though from his position Aradryan could not tell whether it was simply a patterned design or some more illustrative image; there was a balcony above the throne stage from which the view would undoubtedly be more suited.

Stopping some ten paces from the throne, Aradryan cast his gaze above the crowd of gaudily-dressed human males and females clustered to his right; courtiers, family and other hangers-on, the eldar pirate surmised.

'Forgive my lack of introduction,' said Aradryan, once more speaking through the face-like translator brooch upon his breast; his spirit stone was mounted in a gold sunburst on the other side. 'Your herald, as willing as he was to accommodate me, was quite unable to pronounce my name. The mangled sounds he made reminded me of a bovine animal in distress. Thus, I must present myself. I am Prince-Commander Aradryan Iadhsuan Adiarrin Naio of the Azure Flame, Admiral of the Winter Gulf.'

'It is customary for petitioners to bow in recognition of the Imperial commander's rank.'

This rebuke came from a younger human standing just behind De'vaque. He was a little taller than the commander, and much slighter of build. Aradryan could see no family resemblance between the two and categorised the man who had spoken as some kind of functionary. He turned his eyes – purposefully coloured a startling violet for the encounter – back on the Imperial commander.

'Your pet appears to be squawking out of turn,' said Aradryan. 'Please silence it.'

'I am Antoine Nallim, Chief Steward of Carasto, and you will not treat me with disrespect, pirate scum.'

Aradryan turned slightly and allowed his gaze to roam across the other people in the hall. In the civilian men he saw the odd cut on brow and cheek, and amongst the officers of the soldiers he saw the same, reinforcing his opinion that duelling was an acceptable sport on this world. Turning his attention back to De'vaque, who had remained grumpily silent so far, Aradryan smiled thinly.

'Am I correct in the belief that duelling with blades is regarded as a suitable means for settling dispute?'

'We duel, yes,' said De'vaque, folding his arms across his chest. 'What makes you think I will allow you the honour of duelling with my chief steward?'

'If your culture believes it is appropriate to establish superiority through violence, surely you must allow me the opportunity to seek redress against the insult I have suffered from the words of your underling?'

'I'll give this arrogant thief a scar to remind him of his manners,' said Nallim, unbuttoning his coat. The man beneath was athletically built, by human standards. Rolling up the sleeves of his undershirt, Nallim drew a sword from its sheath at his hip, exactly the same in design as the one worn by the Imperial commander.

'Would it be allowed for me to use my own weapon, or must I use one of those flimsy skewers you call swords?' asked Aradryan.

'You may use whichever blade you feel best suits you,' said De'vaque. His jaw was clenched tight, and he clearly did not feel that his chief steward's challenge had been wise. Nonetheless, he held his tongue; it was probably bad manners for him to intervene on either side's behalf.

'Feel free to remove your coat, pirate,' said Nallim, bounding across to the carpeted aisle, his booted feet slapping on the tiles. 'You should not encumber yourself unnecessarily.'

'Style before purpose, I am afraid,' Aradryan said as he slowly drew his sword. He looked at De'vaque and tried to find the human words for what he wanted to say. 'Is there some official start to the violence, or do we just start swinging?'

'Raise your blade to your brow in salute, and then you may begin,' replied the Imperial commander. Aradryan noticed that De'vaque's eyes had not left him throughout the exchange. For a human, he was very focused and attentive.

Aradryan did as he was bid, bringing the flat of his sword to touch his forehead just above the bridge of his nose. Nallim did likewise, and the two stood as still as statues for a heartbeat, staring at each other.

Aradryan noticed the tiny dilation in Nallim's eyes as he thought about the strike he would make. The skin of his knuckles paled a fraction more and there was a twitch of a tendon in his wrist. It was a signal as clear as day to Aradryan that his opponent was about to attack.

Bringing his sword down to a straight lunge, Aradryan took a long stride forwards. So swift was the strike that Nallim's sabre was barely a finger's width from his face when the point of Aradryan's sword lanced through the human's throat, twisting slightly to avoid the blade being chipped on the man's vertebrae before the point erupted form the back of his neck.

What seemed like an age later, there were shouts and screams from the gathered men and women. De'vaque was bellowing madly for his men to hold their fire, while several of the courtesans fainted to the ground, eyes rolling in their sockets as blood sprayed over the carpet and tiles.

'A duel is only to first blood!' roared De'vaque, turning towards Aradryan with balled fists, his face reddening.

Aradryan let go of his sword, so that Nallim's body crumpled to the ground, the blood spurting from the wound creating rivulets in the gaps between the mosaic pieces.

'He is certainly bleeding,' said Aradryan, clasping one hand in the other at his waist.

'I should have you killed here and now, and your ships blown out of the stars,' continued the Imperial commander, but Aradryan knew the threat was empty; why would De'vaque stop his men from shooting if he wished the pirate commander dead?

'It would be unwise to try such a thing, Commander De'vaque,' said Aradryan. He stepped over Nallim's twitching corpse and took three more strides, his height advantage over De'vaque becoming even more pronounced in such close proximity.

'What do you want?' De'vaque backed away and slumped into his chair while a squad of soldiers picked up Nallim and carried him from the hall, trailing a spattered line of crimson. 'The same agreement as Irrithan?'

Aradryan suppressed a wince at the mangling of the name, and shook his head.

'There will be no further arrangements with the Azure Flame,' said the eldar, earning a scowl, but he continued. 'The Azure Flame will no longer take sanctuary in Daethronin, nor will the ships that pass through this system be vouched any safe passage. Any relationship between you and Yrithain is over. You will allow me and my fleet to depart this star system unmolested. We will no longer be your tamed hounds, Imperial commander.'

'You think to double-cross me again?' De'vaque's jowls shook and he spat the next words. 'I'll see you gutted and skinned before I let you out of here.'

'I would reconsider, commander, if I were you,' said Aradryan. He reached out his right hand, activating the holo-projector set into the ruby ring on his index finger. A ruddy vignette sprang into life between him and De'vaque, of Maensith and Darson sitting at a table together. The two of them were tasting long strands of confectionary and sipping gently effervescing wine from crystal goblets. 'You see, I was kind enough to invite your son on board my ship before I departed. As you can see, he is being looked after. For the moment. He will continue to enjoy our hospitality until we are ready to leave this place.'

'Darson, you idiot!' bellowed De'vaque, shaking a fist at the image. 'What do you think you are doing?'

'It is only an image, commander, there is no audio relay,' explained Aradryan.

'Trickery. Any fool can conjure up a moving hololith.'

'Please make whatever inquiries you require to confirm my statement, Imperial commander De'vaque. The officers of your son's ship will inform you that he is aboard my vessel, as are several of his bodyguard. Trust me, the guards will not prove very useful if you choose to act against us.'

'Why? Why did you not just leave? What was the point of coming here, to see me, if all you wanted to do was leave safely?'

'It is not in my nature to slip away like vermin in the night, commander, especially in the face of a lesser species,' Aradryan said. 'I want you to know that it is only by my will that you are still alive today. Had it not been for my actions, my twisted kin would have attacked your world and exacted a far more agonising retribution for your occupation of it. They take unkindly to upstart barbarian-apes squatting on one of our planets, you see. I am less troubled by the past, and you are welcome to stay at Daethronin as long as you wish. I thought you might appreciate my permission on the matter.'

'Your... permission?' A vein was throbbing dangerously in De'vaque's forehead as he squeezed the two words between gritted teeth. The man inhaled deeply and flexed his fingers, forcing himself to visibly relax. 'I will make sure you pay for this poisonous act, pirate. You will not get away with this.'

'Oh, but I will, Imperial commander De'vaque,' said Aradryan, smiling broadly. 'In fact, I already have.'

Saying the words made the feeling a reality. It had been as much to gratify himself as to arrange a ceasefire that Aradryan had answered the Imperial commander's summons. Here he was, standing in the middle of De'vaque's domain, surrounded by men who would kill him as soon as blink, and there was nothing they could do about the situation. He had known from the outset that Darson would be the man's weakness; despite their prolific breeding, humans of status set great value on their heirs and to have one taken in such cavalier manner would be a massive loss of prestige and honour. The moment was to be savoured, and Aradryan enjoyed the looks of dismay and fury on the humans as he stepped lightly back towards the hall's doors.

Stepping through the open portal, Aradryan laughed, leaving a lilting echo in the hall behind him.

When the *Fae Taeruth* and the other ships of the Azure Flame were safely away from Daethronin and the breaches into the webway were prepared, Darson De'vaque and his guards were escorted back to their shuttle. Aradryan stood at the gunnery controls and watched the small craft jet away from the cruiser.

'I am sure that Imperial commander De'vaque will not take kindly to this treatment,' said Maensith, her voice coming from the command pod at the heart of the chamber.

'He should know his place in the galaxy better,' said Aradryan. 'He may rule a world in the name of the human Emperor, but he is but a speck of grit – no, a tiniest fragment of a miniscule particle – in the grand design of the galaxy. Commander De'vaque should be taught that ultimately he is powerless and worthless, and that he should not underestimate us.'

Aradryan looked over his shoulder and saw that Maensith was smiling, her lips twisted in a cruel expression. It was not quite as intimidating as the half-insane grimaces of Khiadysis, but it was a reminder that Maensith had been brought up with a very different view of the universe.

'You have something in mind, my dear?' asked the ship's captain.

In reply, Aradryan returned his attention to the console and activated one of the laser cannon batteries. He locked on to the targeting network to the signature of the departing shuttle.

'De'vaque would have hunted us down like wild animals,' said Aradryan, remembering the look on the Imperial commander's face as he had watched Aradryan cut down his chief steward. He had wanted to control the pirates, at one and the same time desiring their loyalty yet thinking of them as expendable tools. Aradryan's finger hovered over the firing gem as he looked again at his captain. 'He knew that we were of no more use to him and would have thrown us to his allies in order to benefit himself. Such treachery should not go unrewarded.'

Maensith nodded once and Aradryan fired the laser cannons. In the spherical display at the centre of the chamber, the human shuttle exploded into a ball of fire and gas, utterly obliterated.

'Make shift to the webway, as swift as you can,' Maensith declared, transmitting her message to the rest of the fleet. 'The leash is off, and wolves must hunt!'

THEFT

The Forge of Vaul – At the heart of the galaxy lies the Forge of Vaul, where the stars and planets and nebulae were brought into being upon the anvil of the Smith God. Here, the hottest furnaces of the oldest stars burn to fuel the fires of the Forge. Starmetal and sunbronze are the materials with which Vaul worked, and mighty were the artefacts he created. It was here that Vaul was chained by Khaine to labour in atonement for freeing Isha and Kurnus, and it was in the Forge of Vaul that the Godslayer, the Sword of Khaine, deadliest weapon in all the worlds, was created. When Khaine was torn apart in the duel between She Who Thirsts and the Lord of War, it is said that the Widowmaker flew from his hand and returned to the place of its birth. It waits there now, biding the long aeons until a hand worthy of wielding it pulls it from the anvil in which it rests.

Following their departure from Daethronin, the Azure Flame, now under the joint command of Maensith and Aradryan, found great sport and spoils across the star systems of the Winter Gulf. Having been held back by their agreements with De'vaque, some of the captains of the Azure Flame delighted in targeting ships coming to and from the Imperial commander's star system. It was not only around Daethronin that the pirates made their presence felt. From Eldaseth to Taerinnin, a stretch of nearly three thousand light years, the Azure Flame swooped upon lone merchant ships and isolated outposts, dared the guns of convoy escorts and the cannons of orbital platforms.

Aradryan earned himself a reputation amongst the corsairs as a brazen, daring adventurer. He could barely believe the transformation in himself, from the weak-willed, terrified ranger who had cowered at the approach of a diminutive orkoid, to the carefree and courageous pirate prince he had become. Despite Aradryan's popularity amongst most of the Azure Flame fleet, there were some aboard the *Fae Taeruth* who were not so indulgent. Chief amongst his critics was Taelisieth, who missed no opportunity to raise objections and doubts about Aradryan's leadership, decisions and motives with Maensith. Such an argument came to a head aboard the *Fae Taeruth* as the three eldar discussed an upcoming raid on a convoy mustering point.

The three of them were in the observation gallery, surrounded by the glowing fabric of the webway shimmering beyond the window interfaces. Aradryan saw a curving wall of purple and blue held aloft by white columns that burned with ember-like runes. The *Fae Taeruth* had travelled this part of the Winter Gulf frequently, and Aradryan had dubbed this particular weave of tunnels the Golden Gate due to its proximity to a number of warp routes used frequently by the human Imperium. There were rich pickings indeed to be had, if one did not mind risking the Imperial Navy patrols.

'It is too reckless, for little reward,' protested Taelisieth. 'We have already drawn too much attention to ourselves in this area, we need to move on.'

'But the convoy staging area is nearby, in Laesithanan,' replied Aradryan. 'It is ripe for us. Darson De'vaque spoke of it before his departure.'

'The more dangerous, the better for you,' snarled Taelisieth. 'I know what drives you, Aradryan. This system, it will be well-guarded, and you want to spite the humans by taking their ships from under their noses. It is not worth the risk, not for your further aggrandisement.'

'My aggrandisement?' laughed Aradryan. He turned to Maensith, laying a hand on her arm. 'Who was it that led the attack at Niemesh? It was me! Who saw the opportunity to outwit that battlecruiser commander at Caelosis? Me! If it was not for my wit, this fleet would have seen half as much action.'

'And the *Laethrin* and *Naeghli Atun* would both still be with us,' countered Taelisieth. 'Yrithain never lost a single ship, and you have lost two in less than a hundred cycles. The captains follow you still because they are excited, but their patience will wear thin soon enough. This convoy, it carries nothing of importance – weapons for some human warzone far away. Without De'vaque to take them, what use are they? Will you find another corrupt Imperial governor willing to trade for them? And for what?'

'We will be taking prisoners,' said Aradryan, earning himself sharp looks from both Maensith and Taelisieth. He enjoyed their surprise, but suppressed his smile. 'It is just an idea of mine, but hear me out. It is only a matter of time before the Crimson Talon seek revenge on Maensith, now that Khiadysis is bound to have told them of her whereabouts.'

'You think to pay them off with prisoners?' said Maensith.

'I am sure we could find an intermediary at Khai-dazaar who will be able to negotiate on our behalf,' said Aradryan. 'I know that it might not be easy, but it is worth considering.'

Maensith's face showed that she was considering the idea, and at some length. Her expression changed subtly from doubt to interest to thoughtfulness, and back again several times as she weighed up the possibilities. Her gaze fell upon Aradryan and they locked eyes, sharing a moment of common purpose and understanding. The hint of a smile twitched the corners of Maensith's mouth.

'And the rest of the fleet, what do they gain from this attack?' said Taelisieth, holding out his hands.

'By which you mean the rest of the crew,' said Aradryan, breaking his stare from Maensith's bewitching gaze to turn it upon Taelisieth. The lieutenant did not blink to show any sign of shame at the accusation.

'All get equal share that is the rule. I have no use for clumsy humans, do you? If you wish to offer a love gift to our captain, feel free to do so with your own share, but do not empty our pockets for your gesture.'

'I would have thought you owed our captain a little more respect and loyalty, considering all that she has given you, and how far she has carried you,' said Aradryan.

Taelisieth snapped to his feet, eyes wide with anger.

'Carried me?' he shouted. 'You have been nothing but a chain around our necks since your arrival, Aradryan of Alaitoc. If you are so magnificent, perhaps you would deign to repeat your performance of De'vaque's court?'

One hand on the hilt of his sword, Taelisieth stepped back and gestured for Aradryan to rise. Aradryan was about to comply, filled with indignation, but Taelisieth continued his tirade and gave Aradryan pause to reconsider drawing his weapon.

'It is one thing to puncture a sluggish lump of a human, it is quite another challenge to match your sword against one of our kind. Do you dare that?'

'My skill at arms is not the subject of debate,' Aradryan said slowly, keeping his gaze fixed on Taelisieth's sword hand. The moment the pirate looked to draw his weapon Aradryan was ready to leap aside. His words were spoken calmly, trying to defuse the irate lieutenant's mood. 'If it is my leadership you doubt, then give us an alternative.'

'Have you a more profitable suggestion, perhaps?' said Maensith. 'One that is better than this convoy?'

'The Gallows Stars, near Khebuin, where anasoloi traders make a dash from the Indiras Gap to reach the safety of the Naeirth cluster.' Taelisieth said the words quickly, as if he had been rehearsing them repeatedly. 'We can be there in three cycles, and back with a prize within ten.'

'Lone anasoloi traders?' Aradryan's laugh was sharp and short. 'What challenge is that?'

'Easy pickings, captain,' insisted Taelisieth. He took his hand from his sword and knelt on one knee beside Maensith, eyes fixed earnestly on her face. 'Think of what they might be carrying – Cthellan spheres, cudbear hides or perhaps even Anasaloi devil-wyrds. All can be bargained at great profit at Khai-dazaar. We are corsairs, not Commorraghan arena fighters. We do not need a challenge to prosper or prove ourselves.'

Maensith stroked her chin and looked between Aradryan and Maensith. Aradryan gave her hand an encouraging squeeze, but she drew it away and stood up.

'We shall see who is the better leader, not by deciding here but by a test in truth,' said the captain. She smoothed her long black robe with pale fingers and smiled thinly. 'My cherished Aradryan, I shall leave you in command of the *Fae Taeruth*. Taelisieth and I will transfer to the *Haenamor*, under his command. Whichever of the other ships' captains you can persuade to your cause will accompany each endeavour. In ten cycles' time we will return to the Cradle of Moons to see who is worthy of commanding the Azure Flame with me.'

'And what happens to the loser?' asked Taelisieth.

'What do you suggest?' Maensith asked.

'Winning will be reward enough,' said Aradryan. 'Taelisieth's shame will be sufficient punishment for the wrongs he has spoken against me.'

'And I will see you humbled, for my part,' said Taelisieth. 'Should I bring back the larger prize, you will never set foot again on the command deck of a ship.'

'So be it,' said Maensith as she strode from the room, leaving Aradryan alone with Taelisieth. The lieutenant smiled coldly.

'You have gone too far this time, Aradryan.' Standing up, Taelisieth patted Aradryan on the shoulder in condescending fashion. 'This is exactly what I wanted. Without Maensith and me to protect you from your rash impulses, I do not expect you to return. It is a shame that we might lose the *Fae Taeruth*, but at least you will have a grand tomb for your corpse.'

'If I lose the *Fae Taeruth*, I will gladly step aside for you,' said Aradryan. He ran a finger down Taelisieth's cheek and winked. 'Have fun popping anasolois for cudbear hides. When I have finished humiliating you in front of the whole fleet, you can wrap yourself up in them for comfort.'

Three ships of the Azure Flame slid from the webway not far behind the cluster of human ships gathering in high orbit over the fifth world of the system. Alongside Aradryan on the *Fae Taeruth* were *Naestro*, under the leadership of Kharias Elthirin, and Namianis aboard the *Kaeden Durith*.

With the three most powerful ships of the Azure Flame under his command, Aradryan was confident that the gaggle of merchantmen would be little threat.

Though he longed to prove himself against a foe more challenging, the initial sensor sweeps indicated only a single warship to protect the flotilla; by its size it would be outgunned by the eldar cruisers.

'I came looking for sport, but it appears we shall have little of that,' Aradryan said, turning to smile at his second-in-command, Laellin. She nodded but said nothing, her focus set on the gunnery panel. Aradryan allowed a sliver of his consciousness to slip into the *Fae Taeruth*'s matrix. It was an empowering feeling, to be at the heart of so many systems. Beforehand he had only interfaced with the piloting networks, but now he had access to every component of the cruiser. His thoughts touched briefly upon those manning the various stations around the command hall, acknowledging them one by one.

Establishing a contact with Aerissan at the sensor controls, Aradryan felt for a moment as though he looked through the *Fae Taeruth*'s eyes. It was a bewildering experience, momentary but intoxicating. Aerissan guided Aradryan's attention to the scanner readings. The warship they had detected was attached to one of the cargo ships, although its plasma reactor, weapons and shields showed a spike in energy output as they were brought up to full strength.

With a thought of thanks to Aerissan, Aradryan slipped from the sensory banks into the communications suite. Immediately his holo-image appeared in the control chambers of the other two ships, while the slightly translucent ghosts of Kharias and Namianis materialised on the deck of the *Fae Taeruth*.

'Morai-heg has seen fit to spin us a rich thread, my friends,' declared Aradryan. 'Eight ships to be plundered and only a single worthy adversary to protect them. We shall split, so that the escort cannot protect the fleet from one direction. Avoid engaging the enemy, for as small as it is, I expect this guard dog's bite to be fierce. There is no need to be hasty, we can pick off the prizes in turn, after all.'

As the Azure Flame closed in, the freighter commanders tried to make a run for freedom. There was no coherent plan as cargo haulers, gas carriers, bulk transporters and superlifters split from each other in a flurry of blazing plasma trails, falling back on the ancient survival instinct of the herd: the predators cannot catch us all. The human warship broke its docking and turned towards the incoming eldar ships, forcing the *Naestro* to break away her attack, but leaving the *Fae Taeruth* and *Kaeden Durith* a clear run into the heart of the spreading flotilla.

As the *Fae Taeruth* overhauled the closest ship, Laellin targeted its aft sections with the starboard lasers, scoring a flurry of hits across its engine housings.

'Careful,' warned Aradryan, focusing the scanner sphere on the stricken ship. 'These human ships have fragile plasma drives. We do not wish to detonate our prize, do we?'

The *Kaeden Durith* swept ahead, gravity nets extending towards the crippled freighter. Aradryan did not mind the audacity of Namianis in taking the first prize; his goal was the much larger vessel at the heart of the convoy. The enemy warship was staying close to the biggest freighter, and three other ships of the convoy had decided that the guns of the light cruiser were a better defence than open space. They were wrong, Aradryan told himself in triumph. There was no way a single ship could protect every vessel in the convoy, especially against much swifter foes.

It was not long before the commander of the human escort came to the same conclusion and brought his ship onto a bearing that cut between the eldar and the ships trying to escape out-system. It was a wise move, forcing both the *Fae Taeruth* and *Naestro* to abort runs toward the fleeing vessels. However, it did mean that the cluster of four ships it had been protecting were now vulnerable.

Despite the urge to plunge in for the kill, Aradryan held himself and the *Naestro* in check for the time being. There was something about the way the warship had suddenly abandoned its charges that made Aradryan suspicious. There was also the unanswered question of why it had been docked with the large cargo ship when the eldar had arrived.

The four ships that had been left to their own protection were clustered together. They would be armed, no doubt, and although their weapons were little match for the holofields of the *Fae Taeruth*, in order to board their prize, the eldar would have to slow down, increasing the chances of being successfully targeted. There was safety in numbers for the moment, and though Aradryan desperately wanted the largest ship for himself, he remembered the mockery of Taelisieth. Only a fool would take on four vessels with a lone ship, no matter how poorly armed the more numerous vessels were. If he had wanted to destroy the cargo haulers, it would be easy enough, but he had to take them intact. Even more than that, Aradryan needed to capture as many of them as possible if he was to offer the kabal of the Crimson Talon sufficient pay-off to forget Maensith's past indiscretions. Aradryan held his tempestuous mood in check and resolved that he would not be caught out by making rash decisions.

Turning his attention back to the ships that had scattered, Aradryan used the infinity network to plot the intercept routes required to catch them. With the position taken up by the escort, there was a good chance that the portion of the convoy that had held together would be able to flee in-system before the *Fae Taeruth* could disable the scattering ships and return.

With a grimace of frustration, Aradryan looked back and forth across the display globe, trying to decide between the two options. Then, as if Morai-heg had not granted him enough fortune, he saw the largest ship suddenly expelling a cloud of plasma from emergency exhausts along its starboard flank. Yawing violently away from its companions, the ship started to fall behind, its engines flaring and dying fitfully, leaving scattered blooms of expanding plasma in its wake.

'That is our first prize!' Aradryan declared in triumph.

Chasing the running cargo haulers for a while longer, Aradryan drew the escort further and further out of position. When he was confident that he could outrun the warship back to the stuttering freighter, he ordered the *Fae Taeruth* to come about. Though the route back to the largest vessel was more circuitous, the higher speed of the eldar ship would give Aradryan plenty of time to affect an attack. To ensure that he and his crew were not disturbed, he ordered the *Naestro* to close towards weapons range of the human light cruiser, to dissuade the enemy captain from turning after the *Fae Taeruth*.

It was soon clear that the strategy had worked. Sails glittering gold in the stellar winds, the *Fae Taeruth* sped towards her prey.

Pulling along the starboard flank of the erratically powered freighter, the *Fae Taeruth* extended her gravity nets, binding herself to the larger ship. Half a dozen boarding tunnels latched on to the hull of the target vessel, high-powered lascutters in their tips melting through the outer shell to allow the boarding parties to dash aboard.

Normally Aradryan would have been at the forefront of the attack, leading the corsairs into deadly combat. This time he would not take part in the hack and thrust of the fighting; he was a leader not a warrior now. The initial parties reported minimal resistance – a couple of dozen humans swept away by the impetus of the attack. Securing a foothold across several decks, the pirates brought on reinforcements, Aradryan moving across to the human ship with them.

There were two main objectives – the control bridge and the storage holds. Dividing his force into three, Aradryan sent the greater part forwards to look for the captain and officers. Another descended the stairwells to the lower decks, seeking the cargo containers. Aradryan remained where he was, with twenty more pirates to guard the route back to the *Fae Taeruth*.

Through the communications stud in his ear, Aradryan monitored the progress of the boarding parties. They were under instruction to take prisoners wherever possible and soon there was a steady flow of unconscious or wounded humans being brought back to the staging area. The attack was progressing smoothly, although no sign could be found of the ship's captain; Aradryan knew things would go more smoothly if he could arrange an orderly surrender.

It was then that things started to go wrong. Naphiliar, who had been leading the search for the command crew, reported that his party had encountered heavily armoured warriors. They were being cut down by devastating firepower and had to fall back towards the boarding area.

'Armoured warriors?' replied Aradryan. 'What sort of armour? What weapons do they have? Tell me more!'

In response Aradryan heard his lieutenant panting heavily, punctuated by groans. Evidently he had been wounded. Over the open feed of the communicator, Aradryan heard sharp cracks and thunderous detonations. Something heavy thudded on the decking close to Naphiliar.

'This one is still alive.' The voice was deep, tainted by artificial modulation. Aradryan could hear a dull hissing, which was suddenly blotted out by the horrendous roar of a crude engine. Naphiliar screamed, his voice drowned out by the rasp of a chainsword and the snap of shattering bones.

'Praise the Emperor and abhor the alien.'

The tone of the voice was unmistakeable, as was the heavy tread that receded into the distance. Aradryan had heard many horror stories of the Emperor's Space Marines, but had thankfully never encountered the physically-enhanced warriors of the Imperium. On board *Lacontiran* he had talked to warriors who had seen the genetically-altered soldiers and been fortunate enough to survive. Their presence was a shock, and a hard blow against Aradryan's desires to prove himself superior to Taelisieth. A ship-borne combat suited the Space Marines perfectly, and Aradryan suddenly realised that the escort ship had to be a Space Marine vessel. With that being the case, there was no telling how many more of them there might be; his corsairs were poorly matched for the coming battle.

Their presence changed everything, and Aradryan filtered through the tales of the Space Marines from memory, trying to find something that would give him an advantage. Everything he recalled merely emphasised what a terrible proposition they were to face in combat. The Space Marines would fight to the death rather than allow the ship to be taken, that was certain. In his ear-piece he could hear more reports of the deadly warriors' counter-attack, and he knew he had to react quickly to avert a disaster.

Aradryan quickly told the rest of his corsairs about the nature of their foes, and ordered them to avoid direct confrontation if possible. Evasion and ambush would be the best tactic against the hulking Space Marines – Aradryan's warriors possessed a few fusion pistols and powered blades capable of penetrating their armour, but they would have to bring across some heavier weaponry from the *Fae Taeruth* if they were to wipe out the Emperor's elite.

There were more encounters with the Space Marines by the parties moving aftwards, working through the hold space. Forewarned, these groups were able to swiftly retreat from their heavily armoured adversaries before any fighting broke out. To make matters worse for the raiders, the crew were still roving randomly across the ship, running into bands of corsairs as they tried to lay in wait for the Space Marines or retreat from their counter-attacks.

The situation was rapidly becoming confused, and Aradryan had only the scantest information regarding his enemies and the layout of the ship. With the *Fae Taeruth* grappled alongside, the cruiser was too close to perform anything but the most basic sensor sweeps of the vessel. What these told Aradryan was not encouraging – the Space Marines seemed to be gathering in strength in the lower decks towards the prow, most likely to push up to the corsair's landing area. There was nothing Aradryan could do against a determined attack except to fall back to the *Fae Taeruth* and disengage. He paced back and forth along the metal corridor beside the boarding tunnel entrances, trying to think of some way to outwit his foes. The sound of fighting – the distinctive noise of the Space Marine's boltguns and the detonation of grenades – echoed up the stairwells and along the passages. It was difficult to tell exactly where the noises were coming from, but they seemed to be getting closer. Aradryan tried to gather reports from his warriors over the communicator but their replies were fragmentary and hurried.

'Look at this!' Aradryan turned to see Laellin hurrying along the corridor, dragging something behind her. It was one of the crew, a large and bloodied hole in his chest. Before Aradryan could ask her what was so important about a dead human, Aerissan contacted him from the *Fae Taeruth*.

'We have detected significant warp breaches at the system limits. Human ships breaking from warp space, I would say. Nearly a dozen of them.'

'The escort for the convoy or more freighters?' Aradryan asked, gesturing for Laellin to wait before speaking. His second dropped the corpse on the deck and folded her arms impatiently.

'Too distant to say for certain, but warships would be my assumption,' replied Aerissan.

'What is it?' Aradryan demanded, distracted by Laellin's agitated fidgeting next to him.

'Look,' said his second-in-command, pointing at the dead crewman's chest. Aradryan looked into the ragged hole, seeing ribs splayed outwards, the internal organs turned to a mush.

'It is a dead – very dead – human,' said Aradryan. 'There will be more of them around if you want to start a collection. Now, I have something important to attend to.'

'Do you think a lasgun or shuriken did this?' snapped Laellin, grabbing Aradryan's arm, forcing him to look at the opened carcass again. 'This wound was blown open from the inside by a small explosion.'

'So what could cause such an injury, if it was not one of our weapons?'

'A Space Marine's boltgun, of course,' said Laellin, clenching her fists in exasperation.

'Why...' The question faltered on Aradryan's lips as he reached an answer for himself. 'Take me to see these Space Marines. Quickly now!'

Aradryan followed Laellin as she turned and sprinted back up the corridor. They passed a handful of corsairs guarding the open bulkhead at the end of the passage and stepped out into a narrow landing. Turning right, Laellin headed up the open stairwell, her light tread barely making a sound on the metal mesh of the steps. She turned through a small doorway that led into a thin conduit barely wide enough for the eldar to run along. The air was humid and hot here, pipes running along the floor sprinkled with droplets of condensation.

'I think this is one of their artificial atmosphere exchanges,' explained Laellin as she ducked beneath another pipe running across the corridor at chest height. She stopped above a grate and glanced down. Her lip twisted in consternation. 'They were here before. They must have moved down a level.'

She pulled out her laspistol and fired at the bolts securing the grating. It fell with a loud clang on the deck below. Aradryan jumped through first, hand moving to the hilt of his sword as he landed. He could hear the thump of the Space Marines' boots close at hand. Landing lightly next to him, Laellin pointed towards a stairwell to their left.

Moving swiftly and silently, Aradryan ran to the top of the stairs. He glanced over the rail and then stepped back immediately, seeing a mass of blackened armour at the bottom of the steps. As quick as it had been, the brief look had confirmed what he had suspected. He moved back to where Laellin was keeping watch in the corridor.

'Pull everybody back, half to protect the boarding tunnels, the rest to somewhere spacious,' he told his lieutenant.

'There is some kind of communal mess three decks up. Will that suit?'

'Perfect,' said Aradryan, 'I shall come with you.'

'What are you thinking?' Laellin asked when she had disseminated the necessary information via her communicator.

'The Space Marine I saw had black armour, hastily and badly painted,' explained Aradryan as they moved silently up the stairwell, leaving the Space Marines behind. 'There was a crude motto written on his shoulder guard, and no icons. I think we are dealing with renegades.'

'Ah, renegades,' said Laellin, with a smile. 'So, they are protecting the convoy for themselves? They would not like to be caught here by the real escort any more than we would.'

'Exactly,' said Aradryan.

It took them a little while to reach the mess hall Laellin had mentioned. More than fifty corsairs were already there and a few more were entering from the doorway at the opposite end of the long room. The mess hall was a wide open space, divided by long tables and benches riveted to the floor. Hatchways and doors to the kitchen lined one wall, and lighting was provided by four strips that ran the length of the room, flickering and fizzing in an annoying fashion.

'Please give me your communicator,' said Aradryan, reaching out to Laellin.

Laellin complied, pulling the stud from her ear to pass it over. Aradryan used a fingernail to pry open the tiny cover, splitting the device like a pea. A minuscule reflective panel glistened inside and he pressed the device between thumb and forefinger. A quiet but high-pitched tone sounded from the device as it began to scan the different frequencies, seeking a signal. It was only a few moments before static hissed and then Aradryan could hear gruff voices.

'Heynke, use the auspex.'

The following words were accompanied by short bursts of static, which Aradryan guessed to be interference from some kind of scanning device.

'Most have reached the upper decks,' said a different voice. 'Too much interference from the superstructure for an accura... Hold on, something strange.'

'What is it?'

Aradryan reassembled the communicator and held it up to the translator face he had affixed to his coat. He smiled at his warriors, and held a finger to his lips to hush their chatter.

'I think this conversation is too dull,' said Aradryan. 'Let us give these fools something worth talking about.'

'Look for yourself.'

'What do you think they are up to?'

'Commander of the Space Marines,' Aradryan said, the communicator picking up the harsh words from the translator. 'I am monitoring your transmissions. Listen carefully to me. This loss of life is senseless and is not of benefit to myself or to you. It occurs to me that we do not need to fight. I detect your simple scanner and know that you can find me. I know something that would be valuable to you. Meet me where we can hold conference and we will discuss this matter like civilised creatures.'

'Was that...?' said a third human voice. 'Did that bastard override our comm-frequency?'

There was laughter from the corsairs as the translation echoed from Aradryan's device.

'How?'

'Forget how, did you hear what he said?' another voice cut in. 'He wants a truce!'

Hearing the clump of boots outside the far doors, Aradryan leaned back against the end of a table and waited for the Space Marines to enter. Around him several dozen eldar waited, some of them with weapons ready, most of them lounging across the tables and seats. Aradryan caught a glimpse of himself in the scuffed metal of a cabinet. He was dressed in a long coat of green and red diamond patches, which reached to his booted ankles. A ruff of white and blue feathers jutted from the high collar, acting as a wispy halo for his narrow, sharp-cheeked face. His skin was almost white, his hair black and pulled back in a single braid plaited with shining thread. Aradryan smiled at what he saw, but grew serious as the doors hissed open in front of him.

The two creatures that entered were as tall as Aradryan, and more than twice as broad in chest and shoulder. Both were clad shoulder to foot in thick plates of powered armour, daubed black in the same manner as the Space Marine Aradryan had spied earlier. One held a heavy-looking, double-barrelled weapon in one hand, its outer casing inlaid with golden decoration against a blue enamel. The other had no helm and his face was flat, his chin wide and his brow heavy. His head showed a thin layer of blond stubble. He carried a crystalline sword in his huge gauntleted hand, and a pistol in the other. There was something about the bare-headed Space Marine that unnerved Aradryan, but he could not identify what it was as the two hulking warriors stomped up the mess hall.

They stopped a dozen paces from Aradryan, weapons held easily. The pirate captain moved his eyes to meet the red-lensed gaze of the first Space Marine. He stood a fraction taller than the other, holding himself more upright, and was several paces closer than his companion. Aradryan assumed he was in charge.

'What is the name of he who has the honour of addressing Aradryan, Admiral of the Winter Gulf?' Aradryan barely made a sound as he spoke; the hard-edged tone of his speaking-brooch sent the words across the mess hall.

'Gessart,' said the helmeted Space Marine. 'Is that a translator?'

'I understand your crude language, but will not sully my lips with its barbaric grunts,' replied Aradryan.

The helmetless Space Marine moved up next to Gessart and Aradryan saw clearly what it was that had disturbed him before. The Space Marine's eyes were flecked with churning gold. He had psychic power, of that much Aradryan was certain. There was something about that golden light in his eyes that reminded Aradryan of the Master of Magic, the most manipulative of the Chaos Gods. It was ever-changing, like the Grand Mutator, flickering with azure and violet shadows. There was something unnatural; even more unnatural than psychic power. The resonance it left in Aradryan's mind reminded him of the Gulf of Despair, where he had faced the daemonettes. That was it, Aradryan realised. The second Space Marine was touched by the presence of a daemon!

Aradryan looked at Gessart with a furrowed brow, disturbed that he seemed to be parleying with devotees of the Dark Gods. Strangely, Aradryan did not catch the same scent of corruption from Gessart, but that did not settle his fear.

'That you consort with this sort of creature is ample evidence that you are no longer in service to the Emperor of Mankind,' Aradryan said, wishing to swiftly conclude his business here. Alaitoc had a long history, and the memory of the eldar stretched back to the dawn of the human's

Imperium when half of the Emperor's warriors had been tainted by Chaos. 'We have encountered other renegades like yourselves in the past. My assumptions are proven correct.'

'Zacherys is one of us,' said Gessart with a glance towards the psyker. 'What do you mean?'

'Can you not see that which dwells within him?' Aradryan could not believe that Gessart was oblivious to the creature possessing his companion. There was far more to this situation than appeared, but Aradryan did not want to get drawn into whatever was going on with the Space Marines.

'What do you want?' demanded Gessart.

'To save needless loss for both of us,' Aradryan replied, opening his hands in a placating gesture. 'You will soon be aware that those whose duty it is to protect these vessels are close at hand. If we engage in this pointless fighting they will come upon us both. This does not serve my purpose or yours. I propose that we settle our differences in a peaceful way. I am certain that we can come to an agreement that accommodates the desires of both parties.'

'A truce? We divide the spoils of the convoy?' It was hard to tell Gessart's mood through the mechanical modulation of his helmet's speakers. Aradryan thought he detected hope rather than incredulity.

'It brings happiness to my spirit to find that you understand my intent. I feared greatly that you would respond to my entreaty with the blind ignorance that blights so many of your species.'

'I have become a recent acquaintance of compromise,' said Gessart. 'I find it makes better company than the alternatives. What agreement do you propose?'

'There is time enough for us both to take what we wish before these new arrivals can intervene in our affairs. We have no interest in the clumsy weapons and goods these vessels carry. You may take as much as you wish.'

'If you don't want the cargo, what is your half of the deal?' Gessart looked at the assembled pirates, finger twitching on the trigger of his weapon.

'Everything else,' said Aradryan with a sly smile.

'He means the crews,' whispered Zacherys.

'That is correct, tainted one,' said Aradryan. The eldar pirate fixed his eyes on Gessart, pleased that he detected a note of agreement although the Space Marine was hesitant, perhaps not trusting Aradryan's intent. The pirate leader sought to encourage Gessart to the right conclusion. 'Do you accede to these demands, or do you wish that we expend more energy killing one another in a pointless display of pride? You must know that I am aware of how few warriors you have should you choose to fight.'

'How long before the escort arrives?' Gessart asked Zacherys.

'Two days at most.'

'You have enough time to unload whatever you wish and will not be hampered by my ships or my warriors. You have my assurance that you will be unmolested if you offer me the same.'

Gessart stared at Aradryan for some time, but it was impossible to discern the alien's thoughts behind his helmet. Aradryan kept his own expression impassive, giving nothing away though inside he was rejoicing at the chance to sweep up the crews of the ships without undue aggravation.

'The terms are agreed,' said Gessart. 'I will order my warriors to suspend fighting. I have no control over the crews of the convoy.'

'We are capable of dealing with such problems in our own way,' said Aradryan. Indeed, Maensith had taught her warriors many techniques for subduing recalcitrant foes, having learnt from the best slavemasters of Commorragh. 'Be thankful that this day you have found me in a generous mood.'

Gessart hefted his weapon and fixed the eldar pirate with the cold, red stare. As Gessart spoke, Aradryan saw himself reflected in the helm lenses, one hand raised expressively, lips almost forming a sneer.

'Don't give me an excuse to change my mind.'

The *Fae Taeruth* built up speed, turning towards the last of the freighters to be boarded. Gessart's ship was powering away from the vessel, the renegade Space Marines having completed their own pillaging. Aradryan watched the strike cruiser through the holo-orb, thoughts touching lightly upon the psychic matrix to monitor the *Fae Taeruth*'s manoeuvre.

A sudden panic gripped Aradryan, flowing into him from the cruiser. The *Fae Taeruth* roared in alarm, sending a psychic shockwave rippling across her decks. Aradryan felt the semi-sentience of the ship spearing into his thoughts, his mind awash with scanner readings. The passing Space Marine vessel had targeted the *Fae Taeruth* with a variety of high-density sensors emanating from its weapon batteries: its guns were locked on!

The distress of the cruiser was matched by Aradryan's own dread as he saw gun ports sliding open along the starboard side of the strike cruiser. There was no time to activate the holofield, no space in which to manoeuvre away from the worst of the coming bombardment.

Laser, shell and plasma flared from the gun batteries of Gessart's ship, pounding the flank and mast of the *Fae Taeruth*. Still enmeshed with the infinity matrix, Aradryan felt every blow as a faint wound on himself, an ache spreading up his spine as the pounding continued, smashing the mast of the primary stellar sail. Secondary flares of pain registered in Aradryan's mind as gun decks exploded and holds filled with human prisoners were breached, belching atmosphere and corpses into the void.

Reeling, Aradryan staggered from the command pod, gasping heavily. The lights in the chamber had dimmed as the *Fae Taeruth* struggled to redirect her available power to maintaining the integrity of her compromised hull. Warning chimes and voices sounded a barrage of alerts.

Everything went dark and the ship plunged into silence. Somewhere, on a deck below, Aradryan could hear prisoners distantly shrieking in terror. He staggered back to the interface and laid his hand upon the dull gems. Nothing happened.

'She is dead,' muttered Aradryan, numbed by the realisation. '*Fae Taeruth* is dead.'

ESCAPE

The World of Blood and Tears – When the End of the Universe comes, there shall be a great battle to decide the fate of the spirits of the eldar. The Rhana Dandra will see the might of the eldar pitted against the Great Enemy, the Final Battle against Chaos, and all shall perish. The Herald of the Death, Fuegan the Burning Lance, agent of the Rhana Dandra, will call together the Phoenix Lords who forged the Path on which all eldar tread, and they shall be brought as one to Haranshemash, the World of Blood and Tears. Here they will fight their last battle, and the universe shall know peace once more.

Gessart's parting gesture, a bitter repeat of Aradryan's slaying of Darson De'vaque, had not quite slain the ship as Aradryan had feared. Minimal life support and the barest vestiges of the psychic matrix were still operational. Communication was compromised – only Kharias's voice could be heard as the captain of the *Naestro* offered assistance.

'Sensors report that the Imperial escort ships are less than a cycle away,' reported Kharias. 'Do you wish us to take your survivors on board?'

'No, we can manage,' Aradryan snarled in reply. He refused to accept that the *Fae Taeruth* was finished. 'There is still time to affect repairs. If we can bring the webway slipstream back to life, the human ships will not be able to follow us.'

'Such repairs would require many cycles and full dock facilities.' Kharias spoke patiently, but Aradryan knew that his fellow captain would not

677

remain too long to offer assistance. The risk of being caught by the vengeful human ships increased the longer they remained. 'See sense, Aradryan.'

Still feeling soreness in his body from the psychosomatic connection he had shared with the ship when it had been damaged, Aradryan was in no mood to back down. He could remember clearly the words of Taelisieth; to return without the *Fae Taeruth* would be the deepest humiliation.

'Come alongside to take possession of the prisoners,' he snapped. Aradryan addressed the other eldar in the dim light of the command hall. 'We are not abandoning ship. There is time enough to repair the webway slipstream, I am sure of it.'

He saw several of the other officers shaking their heads despondently. 'Kharias is right,' said Laellin, stepping away from her console. 'There is nothing to be salvaged here. Our prisoners outnumber us by four to one. If any of the holds have been breached internally, they will attack us. We cannot stay.'

'Nonsense!' Aradryan looked for support from some of the others, but in the twilight he saw only sad faces and shaking heads. 'I can't...'

With a heavy sigh, Aradryan slumped to the floor of the command pod, his back against the main console. He could feel the tiniest tendrils of the *Fae Taeruth*'s energy circuits stroking gently at his thoughts. Tears filled Aradryan's eyes; not for himself but for the ship that he had lost. For generations she had survived and it had been his hubris that had destroyed her.

Aradryan tried to speak, but the words stuck against the lump in his throat. He swallowed hard as tears ran down his cheeks. His voice was barely a whisper.

'Take the survivors aboard, Kharias. Ready weapons batteries to destroy the *Fae Taeruth*. We will not abandon her to the scavenging grasp of the humans.'

As Aradryan watched the hull of the *Fae Taeruth* breaking apart under the laser cannonade, part of him wished that he had stayed aboard. He had been tempted, but at the last moment he had crossed the boarding bridge to the *Naestro*, driven by an instinct to survive that was deeper and stronger than his desire to avoid the humiliation that awaited him when they returned to the rest of the Azure Flame.

Not only had he failed to bring back the *Fae Taeruth*, nearly a thousand prisoners had been lost with the ship; there was neither the room nor the supplies to keep them on board the remaining two vessels. Aradryan had not been so callous as to leave the humans on board the cruiser during its destruction. Drugged so as not to risk any trouble, they had been ferried back to their ships and left to the attention of their arriving allies. With so many to be abandoned from the *Fae Taeruth*, it had been pointless taking the others on the *Naestro* and they too had been deposited unconscious on their vessels.

Leaving the viewing gallery, he headed back to his cabin. There were stares of disgust and pity from the eldar that he passed; disgust from former crewmates and pity from those who served aboard the *Naestro* and *Kaeden Durith*. Regardless of whatever retribution Taelisieth decided to impose upon Aradryan, the loss of reputation was absolute, and without it Aradryan knew he was worthless to himself and Maensith.

Aradryan took to his cabin, sealing the door with a mumbled word before he lowered himself onto his bed. On the floor beside him was a small shoulder bag, containing the few possessions he had decided to salvage from the *Fae Taeruth*. Reaching inside, he brought out a folded packet of dried purple leaves: dreamleaf. He had not dreamed since he had joined *Irdiris* and for a moment the scent of the narcotic was unfamiliar and frightening. The fear passed as old memories surfaced, of dreams and remembrances filled with joy and wonder.

Licking his fingertip, Aradryan dabbed at the dreamleaf and brought it up to his mouth. He smelt it again, this time the fragrance reminding him of soaring amongst dream-woven clouds and looking upon galaxies of blinding stars. It was dreaming that had set him on the road to where he was now, he thought. A road that had ended in ruin and despair. He took the dried leaf from his finger with the tip of his tongue and laid back, head against the hard surface of the mattress.

The dreamleaf did its job, flowing through his body, relaxing his muscles and dulling his mind. Closing his eyes, Aradryan blocked out external sensation, quietly speaking the mantras he had learnt to disassociate his senses from the rest of his body. It was as if darkness and silence cocooned him, but not in a frightening, cold way. The numbness was a warm embrace, allowing him to slip into the deep meta-sleep of the memedream.

Laughing at noonsparrows courting in the bushes, sat with Korlandril on the flower-decked hillsides of Etherian Tor in the Dome of Magnificent Tribulations.

The look of resignation on Thirianna's face as she said goodbye, and the warmth of Athelennil beside him.

The touch of Maensith on the first night he had been welcomed aboard the *Fae Taeruth*. Her joy did not last long; blood started to weep from Maensith's eyes, forcing Aradryan to retreat, seeking sanctuary in pure fantasy.

A volcanic eruption spewed glittering green fire into the heavens, bearing Aradryan up as ash on the superheated winds. Nothing more than a mote of dust in the raging storm, the winds howling around him, he was borne higher and higher, until the fiery plains spread out beneath him.

He fluttered for a long time, flicked from one wind to the next, never falling, always carried upwards until the ground itself disappeared and the stars surrounded him.

Now the stellar winds took hold of his immaterial form, swishing him from star to star, sliding his incorporeal body along the clouds of nebulae and through the rings of supernovae. He became starlight itself, as fast and light as thought, and then became nothing; a part of the fabric of the ether that bound together the universe.

And here was peace and freedom.

Sometimes Aradryan ate, and sometimes he drank, though such intermittent breaks in his dreaming barely registered. When wakefulness threatened to hinder his return to the meta-sleep – true waking prompted by physical needs – he returned to the dreamleaf again, forcing back the conscious world so that he could continue to explore the depths and heights of his unconscious. Here he could evade the pain of failure. In the world of the dreams, there was no laughter from Taelisieth. Beyond the veil of consciousness, Aradryan could turn away from the horror and the hurt in Maensith's eyes when she asked what had become of her ship.

He fled, cycle after cycle, into the dull embrace of the memedreams. Some kind spirit – perhaps ordered by Maensith or perhaps not – left food and drink by his cabin door. Aradryan never turned on the lights, but ate in darkness and silence, his last dreams and his next imagining drifting together, turning every meal into a potential banquet, every glass of water and juice into lavish wine.

It was better this way, he told himself in the few lucid moments between doses of dreamleaf. He was of no use to anybody, least of all himself, too afraid to die and too pointless to live.

He laughed at his own moroseness and enjoyed the sadness that gripped his heart. His dreams became vistas of Alaitoc's infinity circuit, trapping him between life and death. He was nothing but a spark of energy in the great craftworld, and it nothing but a glimmer of lights in the galaxy.

Commander De'vaque's face returned to haunt him, rage incarnate, throwing back Aradryan's taunts that he was nothing to the universe. Now Aradryan could see that all of life was for nothing. There was no purpose other than to exist, to continue on until the end came, touching briefly upon other lives but leaving no lasting impression on the great turning of the universe.

Aradryan's dreams became more evocative and less rooted in reality. He knew that he should not indulge any longer, that the dreaming and the dreamleaf would break apart his thoughts. Faces from the past swam together. He saw Rhydathrin as he had been during that last meeting on the Bridge of Yearning Sorrows. Yet Rhydathrin shared Aradryan's face, and he realised that it was not Rhydathrin at all, but the mirrored mask of the Shadowseer Rhoinithiel. The laughter came then, so hard and loud that Aradryan thought he would rip apart his stomach and chest.

And so he did, pulling apart ribcage to expose his beating heart. Except his heart was no longer there. In his dream, he followed the trail of bloody droplets, and found that his heart was being fought over by tiny figures: Thirianna and Korlandril, Athelennil and Maensith. They bit and clawed at each other, pulling and ripping at Aradryan's heart with minute hands, their fingers digging into the red flesh.

With a wet popping noise, the heart split asunder, showering Aradryan with sweet nectar.

On the ground where his heart had been lay his waystone, pulsing slowly. He tried to pick it up, to force the stone back into his chest to fill the void left by his missing heart, but his fingers passed through the waystone.

Childish giggling sounded from the shadows of the room, and half-seen, androgynous figures crept in the darkness, their black eyes fixed on Aradryan.

The chamber was huge, as Aradryan found himself asleep on the bed by the sea, in the ancient haunted palace. There were pictures everywhere, images from his life, his friends and family and strangers and enemies; every face he had ever seen. He bounded across the immense room with sudden energy, to lift a silver-framed image from the floor.

'I am several and one,' said the picture of Estrathain. The kami's blank face filled every image around Aradryan, thousands of eyeless, noseless visages staring down at him from the walls and ceiling, glaring up at him with accusation from the tiled floor.

In the distance Aradryan could hear the tootle of Lechthennian's flute and the strum of his half-lyre, but the Solitaire was becoming quieter, moving away. He was not coming to help.

The dreams came and went, and Aradryan did not care for the real world.

The dreams changed more over time. Aradryan went back again and again to his liaisons with Athelennil. Only he did not spend those moments of passion with Athelennil but with Thirianna. All else was the same, the places and the mood, the laughter and the heat, but Thirianna played the part of his lover in a way that she had never done so in fact.

'They are coming to kill us,' Thirianna whispered as she lay next to Aradryan. The heat of her body warmed his arms as she lay cradled against his chest. 'We will all burn.'

'I do not understand,' replied Aradryan, sitting up.

* * *

He could hear screams; distant shouts of pain and terror echoed around the room. Aradryan was sure he was awake. The effect of his last dose of dreamleaf had worn off. The dream persisted, though, leaving the stench of burning in his nostrils.

He looked down at the dreamleaf pouch, now only half-full. It did not matter, he told himself. Most dreams meant nothing. He reached for another pinch of dreamleaf, and was soon swept away on a silver cloud of pleasure, Thirianna laughing by his side.

'They are coming to kill us,' Thirianna whispered as she lay next to Aradryan. The heat of her body warmed his side as she lay cradled against his chest. 'We will all burn.'

Sitting up, Aradryan found himself on Alaitoc. It was the Dome of Crystal Seers. Around Aradryan were the glittering statues of seers past, their bodies turned from flesh to glassy immobility. Every face was the same, and the lips of all the seers moved. Every single one had become Thirianna and they all issued the same warning.

'They are coming to kill us. We will all burn.'

Aradryan reached for the dreamleaf with a shaking hand. No matter how much he took, or how many exercises and mantras he put himself through, he could not rid himself of the nightmares. Whatever venue he took himself to in his dreams, Thirianna was there, with the same message every time.

Fingers touching the pouch, Aradryan stopped himself and rolled back onto the mattress. He stared up at the slowly shifting purple and red that dappled the ceiling. Once he would have been able to turn the shapes into the foundation of any landscape he desired, channelling the gently changing patterns into mountains and seas, cities and forests. Now they just reminded him of burning.

He pushed himself to his feet, trying hard to focus. He had been dreaming for a long time – how long he was not sure, but many cycles. Reality was hard to grasp and he stumbled, his legs weak from inactivity. Bracing himself against the wall with one hand, he arched his back, taking in three deep breaths.

Slowly, painfully, a degree of clarity returned. The light hurt his eyes and the touch of the air on his skin was rasping and cold. He embraced the sensation, drawing it into himself to drive out the vestiges of the dreaming.

Still he heard Thirianna's warning, a whisper in the air around him.

'They are coming to kill us. We will all burn.'

Making his way out into the passage, Aradryan took slow steps, acclimatising himself to his waking state. His head throbbed and his gut ached. The taste of dreamleaf was acrid in his mouth and his skin felt stiff and dry. With aching eyes, he peered down the corridor.

'Wait,' he croaked, reaching out a hand as a shape flittered from one archway to another ahead of him. The figure stopped and turned in surprise.

'Aradryan? I thought you lost forever to the dreams.'

The voice was familiar, but Aradryan could not place it. He took a few steps closer, the other eldar's facing resolving into the gaunt features of Nasimieth. The gunnery captain was frowning, more from confusion than anger.

'Where is Maensith,' Aradryan said, forcing the words to form with dead lips and thick tongue. 'I must speak with her.'

'I do not think she wishes to see you,' said Nasimieth. Aradryan straightened as best he could, forcing himself to concentrate on Nasimieth's face.

'I can find her through the matrix,' said Aradryan, stepping past the other eldar.

'Not in that state.' Nasimieth held out an arm to stop Aradryan. He laid a hand on his shoulder. 'She is in her chambers.'

It seemed as if Nasimieth whispered something else – 'They are coming to kill us. We will all burn.'

Shaking his head, Aradryan stumbled on.

Maensith's chambers were a suite of rooms situated above the command deck, adjoining the observation gallery. Aradryan recovered some of his composure and sense as he walked the length of the *Naestro*, which had become the new flagship of the Azure Flame. The ship was quiet, the stillness filtering through his dilapidated mind.

It was the stillness of pre-battle tension.

The door to Maensith's chamber opened to his approach, revealing a circular common area. The captain, Taelisieth and several other lieutenants were sat in the collection of chairs and couches set upon a thick rug that dominated the room. All eyes turned to Aradryan as he entered, apathy in some, outright hostility in others.

'You should not be here,' said Taelisieth, getting to his feet. 'Crawl back to your dreams, cursed one.'

Ignoring the jibe, Aradryan focused on Maensith. She looked on impassively as Aradryan stiffly walked across the carpet and stood before her.

'We need to speak,' said Aradryan. 'In private.'

'Now is not the time, Aradryan.' Maensith's tone was stern rather than cruel. She shook her head softly. 'You are in no state for any conversation, and we are about to embark on an attack.'

'You look like a corpse,' remarked another of the officers, Sayian.

Picking up a silver plate from one of the tables, Aradryan looked at himself. His eyes were shrunken in dark sockets, all life leached from them to leave them bloodshot and red-rimmed. His skin was like creased and cracked parchment, flaking away as he lifted a finger tip to prod at his stiff flesh. His fingernail was half-chewed and bloody, and his knuckles prominent and rubbed raw. His hair sat in a tangled mess upon his head, the natural black colour coming through, the white ends still showing artificial pigment.

He felt as bad as he looked. Aradryan's spine ached as though the bones had fused together from so much time spent lying down. His breath wheezed in and out of his dry mouth and down a raw throat into shrivelled lungs. His spirit stone was a grey oval on his chest, with the barest flicker of light. Every joint flared with pain as he stooped to place the plate back where he had lifted it from, the dish falling onto the tabletop with a clatter from his numb fingers.

'An attack? Where?' He asked, turning his bleary look on to Maensith. The words were little more than a wisp of breath from shrivelled lips.

'It is none of your concern,' said Taelisieth, shoving Aradryan. The former steersman had no strength to resist and tottered awkwardly backwards for half a dozen steps. 'You do not belong here.'

'I have to go back to Alaitoc,' said Aradryan, clumsily dodging Taelisieth's next thrust, pain flaring through the muscles of his legs and back. 'Please, a moment of your time is all I ask.'

'When the raid is finished,' said Maensith. 'Whatever you have to say can wait until then.'

Dizziness struck Aradryan and he staggered to his left, almost colliding with Taelisieth. The officer struck Aradryan in the chest with an elbow, sending him sprawling onto a couch. Aradryan lay there, only half aware of what was going on. Thirianna's warning whispered in his ears.

'They are coming to kill us. We will all burn.'

'Leave him for the moment,' he heard Maensith say. The looming shadow of Taelisieth withdrew. Aradryan lay still, breathing quickly. He dimly heard the conversation continuing, but could not make any sense of it.

A name struck him, heard amongst talk of strategy and manoeuvres: Nathai-athil. It was a star system not far from where he had lost the *Fae Taeruth*. Through the fugue of his exhaustion, he recalled that it was a dead system, of no interest at all.

'Why Nathai-athil?' he asked, pushing himself upright. 'There is nothing there.'

'It is a new convoy mustering point,' said Maensith, waving for Taelisieth to silence his protest.

Aradryan absorbed this without comment, slumping to one side, head pounding. The conversation continued around him. Something nagged at him, trying to pierce his thoughts through the constant whispering that threatened doom and fire. There was something about Nathai-athil that unsettled him.

'There is nothing there,' he said, straightening once more.

'You are babbling, cretinous wretch,' said Taelisieth. 'Please, Maensith, let me eject this wreck.'

'Wait a moment,' said Aradryan, fending away Taelisieth's grasping arm, focus returning. 'How did you learn of this place?'

'We captured a fast freighter moving out of Daethronin three cycles ago,' said Maensith, again waving for Taelisieth to halt. 'Its systems showed a rendezvous at Nathai-athil. Seven ships, poorly escorted.'

'Nathai-athil is a terrible mustering point,' said Aradryan. 'It is nothing but dust clouds, gas and asteroid fields. There are no navigation markers or landmarks. The humans will find it difficult to gather there.'

'But it is an ideal place to hide if you do not want to be caught,' said Maensith. 'You do not know this, but we have continued to reap great success in your absence. The humans will try anything to avoid or catch us.'

'Anything?' said Aradryan. 'Would they sacrifice a ship for that?'

'An ideal place to hide...' muttered Taelisieth. He looked with narrowed eyes at Aradryan, but some of the aggression had gone, replaced with curiosity. 'You think we are being lured into an ambush?'

Aradryan shrugged. The effort of staying coherent amidst the afterimages and echoes of the long dreaming was becoming more and more taxing.

'We cannot simply turn away,' said Maensith, her gaze moving across her officers. 'If it is not a trap, we waste a great opportunity.'

There were no replies from the others. Maensith shook her head in irritation, darting an angry glance at Aradryan.

'A dream- and drug-addled fool, you are, and paranoid too,' she said. 'A doom-monger no less.'

'Yet we should act with caution,' said Taelisieth. 'Send the *Kaeden Durith* to investigate first.'

'And risk warning the flotilla and escorts of attack?' Maensith was scornful. 'They would scatter into the clouds and be lost.'

'We do not have to separate the fleet,' said Taelisieth. 'Just send a ship first before committing full strength from the safety of the webway.'

Aradryan could barely hear what was said next. The dreaming was beckoning to him, dragging him back from reality. He remembered why he had come here, and fought against the lure of the dreaming. His body was almost dead, the exhaustion dragging him down into dark, cold depths. Aradryan managed to summon the energy to pass on the warning.

'I need to go back to Alaitoc,' he said. 'They are coming to kill us. We will all burn.'

Aradryan woke up feeling more refreshed than before, though his throat and lips were still dry and there was an ache in the back of his head that pulsed dully down his spine. He found himself lying on one of the couches in Maensith's chamber – the same seat on which he had passed out, he recalled with some difficulty. His mind was blurred, as was his vision, and it was hard to remember what had happened. He was left with a recurring thought, as of a half-dream.

'They are coming to kill us. We will all burn.'

Sitting up, Aradryan was relieved that there was no fit of dizziness. He found a carafe of water on the floor next to him, and a small crystal tumbler. As he reached out for the drink, he noticed the yellowish stains on his fingertips and wondered at the amount of dreamleaf he had consumed over the cycles following his humiliation by Taelisieth. It was no wonder he had lost sense of himself. Despite his slightly improved physical condition, he was still ashamed to his core at his recent failures; his indulgences with the Dreaming would have done nothing to repair his shattered reputation.

Swinging himself around to sit properly on the couch, Aradryan leaned forwards, hands on knees. There was a tingle in his mouth, an itch of craving for dreamleaf that was easy to ignore. Less accommodating was the nagging whisper in his ears. If he paid attention, Aradryan would swear it sounded like Thirianna's voice.

Recalling the mix of dream and nightmare, the presence of Thirianna and the dread warnings she brought with her, Aradryan's head swam again. He squeezed his knees tight and stamped his foot on the floor, trying to assure himself that he was not dreaming again. It was impossible to tell, of course. With so much dreamleaf and his long expertise, any dream he underwent could well be indistinguishable from reality. For all that he knew, this was a memedream that he was experiencing, and not a new awakening at all. He tried hard to remember if he had woken before and subsequently returned to the dreaming, but he could not tell.

Such thoughts threatened to send him down into a spiral of insanity. He drank a tumblerful of water, savouring the liquid as it slipped over his swollen tongue and down his parched throat. If this was not reality, his imagination was doing him proud, he thought.

'More coherent this time, I hope.' Aradryan looked towards the door and saw that Maensith had returned. She wore her battle armour, her weapons hanging from her belt. Seeing her sent flashes of recollection through Aradryan's skull.

'Did I...' He did not know how to ask the question. 'Have I dreamt long?'

'Thirty cycles and more, with barely a mouthful to eat and drink every cycle,' said Maensith, her face showing pity rather than sympathy. Her look sent barbs into Aradryan's pride and he straightened up and looked her in the eye.

'And what else did I do?'

'Nothing much,' said Maensith. 'You asked me to return to Alaitoc. You did not say why, but it seemed very important to you. Who is Thirianna?'

'They are coming to kill us. We will all burn.' Aradryan spoke the words without thought, letting them free from where they had been fluttering around inside his head.

'That is what you kept saying as you dreamt,' said Maensith, her face now showing genuine concern. She sat beside him. 'What have you seen?'

'Alaitoc aflame,' replied Aradryan. He shuddered as images from the dreaming floated through his thoughts: images of death and burning and misery. He could not shake the feeling that it was somehow his fault. He looked at Maensith, a deep dread gripping his heart. 'It is a warning, I am sure.'

'We shall see soon enough,' said Maensith, standing up. 'In seven more cycles we shall be there.'

'What do you mean?' Aradryan stood also. 'We are returning to Alaitoc?'

'Yes, we are, which is why you need to bring yourself back to a state that at least vaguely resembles sanity and hygiene. There are still some of your clothes in my bedchambers, if you wish to change.'

Maensith took three steps towards the door before Aradryan spoke her name and stopped her.

'Why are we going to Alaitoc? This is not because of me, is it?'

'Yes, in more ways than one,' Maensith replied. 'Even in your dream-woven state you saw something was wrong with our attack at Nathai-athil. Taelisieth went first with the *Kaeden Durith* and found more than a dozen Imperial ships waiting for us. It seems we have agitated the humans enough for the moment, so I decided we should leave the Winter Gulf. Between your babbling about fires and Thirianna, and my desire to seek out somewhere a bit safer than open space to collect myself, Alaitoc seemed the natural choice.'

'I do not want to go back, not now.'

'It is not your choice, Aradryan. Morai-heg cast a loose thread for you, and now it is unravelling. You have already lost me one flagship, the ship I stole from my kabal to earn my freedom, and you are not welcome on this one. The crew speak out against you, and I must listen. Even the passion I once shared with you does not turn me to your cause any more. I will be returning you to Alaitoc, or setting you on a small moon somewhere. It is your choice as long as you do not stay aboard.'

Aradryan flopped back onto the couch, limbs limp. Maensith twitched her head in irritation and left him to his dark thoughts.

When he slept, Aradryan did not dream. It was better to fall into the utter blankness of unconsciousness than to risk the return of the nightmarish Thirianna and her whispered warnings. Aradryan slept and woke, and regained something of his strength and dignity, if not his pride.

When he awoke again he felt a strange tension in the air. The chambers were empty still, but a note thrummed through the ship, keening across its fabric and along the crystal lines of its psychic network. It was this that had roused him from his deep slumber and it took a moment for Aradryan to realise what the sensation was. The *Naestro* was at full stretch, every part of her engines running at the highest power. Aradryan's nerves resonated with the force flowing through the matrix, sending the ship speeding through the webway.

Leaving Maensith's chambers, Aradryan headed for the control hall. The doors opened for him – he had wondered if there had been a psychic bar put in place – and he stepped inside. Maensith was in the command pod, her face screwed up in intense concentration. Taelisieth glanced up from the weapons console. A frown creased his brow when he recognised who had entered, but he said nothing, nodding his head towards the display sphere at the heart of the hall.

The holo-image showed the webway behind the *Naestro*. It looked like they were rushing up a gleaming silver tunnel towards the surface, a black lattice of rune-carved wraithbone keeping the walls of the webway in place. Two dark shapes stood out against the streaming silver fabric, their hulls mottled midnight blue and black, their prows studded with curving sensor blades, hulls jutting with barb-like cannons: Commorraghans. The livid white marks along the lengths of their hulls spoke of recent repairs and Aradryan's gut shrivelled into a tight knot.

'Khiadysis,' he muttered.

'It was not just the humans waiting for us at Nathai-athil,' said Taelisieth. 'Khiadysis must have heard something of the trap being laid. They were waiting for us to bolt back to the webway, but we spotted them two cycles ago. They have been following us ever since.'

'Where is the rest of the fleet?' asked Aradryan. 'We have two cruisers outgunned.'

'The cowards scattered as soon as the Commorraghans appeared,' Maensith snarled from the centre of the chamber. Aradryan looked at her, but her eyes were focused on the console gems. 'Our only hope is the sanctuary of Alaitoc. Even Khiadysis will hesitate to attack us there.'

'And how long before we reach Alaitoc?' asked Aradryan. He started towards the stairway leading up to the piloting suite, but Taelisieth broke from his console to stop him.

'You are not a pilot or officer,' said the corsair, eyes narrowed. 'It is no small fault of yours that we are pursued.'

'We will be at Alaitoc shortly,' replied Maensith.

Aradryan felt impotent as he watched the dark shapes of the Commorraghan cruisers closing slowly with the *Naestro*. Forward gun turrets extended from the prow of the ship, revealed by lines of sliding shutters that opened up like the gills of some monstrous shark.

'Baring their teeth for nothing. They are still out of weapons range,' announced Taelisieth.

'Keep them out,' snapped Maensith.

In the holo-display two small stars appeared, each deep red in colour, jettisoned into the wake of the *Naestro*. Aradryan realised they were some kind of munitions, but was not sure of what type. The pursuing pair of cruisers had time and space to avoid a direct contact with the two stars, though they lost some momentum doing so. When the lead cruiser – it looked like Khiadysis's own ship to Aradryan – was level with the closest star, Taelisieth gave a satisfied growl and manipulated a control on his console.

The star expanded into a ball of red lightning, flaring from one side of the webway to the other. The detonation caught the second star in its arcs of energy, causing a secondary explosion. The tubular passage of the webway was filled with a storm of power that sped along the walls and rippled along the hull of the Commorraghan cruiser. The energy wave expanded, catching up with the *Naestro* in a few moments.

Aradryan felt the shock of the webway's shuddering through the psychic network, a moment before the ship physically shuddered, causing him to sway on his feet. Looking back at the display, he saw that both Commorraghan cruisers had ploughed on through the psychic storm, the flares of energy dripping from their hulls like water off the oiled skin of a marine beast. Taelisieth cursed loudly and looked over to Jain Anirith at the sensor controls.

'Some kind of psychic shielding,' Jain reported. 'No lasting damage detected.'

The chase continued endlessly. Aradryan was rooted to the spot, unable to tear his gaze away from the holo-display. He was not sure if it was reality or his imagination, but he thought he could see the Commorraghans eating up the gap between the ships. He did not know how they could move faster than the *Naestro*, which was one of the most efficient ships he had ever been on, but somehow they did. Aradryan sensed the Commorraghans getting closer and closer, creeping up on him like a slow death. Eventually their forecannons would come into range and the chase would rapidly end.

'Sending warning to Alaitoc of our approach,' announced Maensith. 'We will be coming out of the portal at full speed.'

'Let us hope that there is no ship trying to come back in,' said Aradryan. Maensith scowled at him for pointing out the obvious danger.

Aradryan could not bear the tension – both in his body and the fraught psychic power being channelled through the ship. As much as it pained him to stay and not be able to do anything, he could not leave and simply wait for the outcome. He lived every moment, etching the sight of those two black predators into his memory like nothing else.

This is vengeance, he thought, as he looked at the Commorraghan vessels. This is the payment I make for the decisions I have made. It would all catch up with him in the end, he knew that. Ever since

Hirith-Hreslain he had stayed one step ahead of his doom, trying his best to outwit fate. Now it was not up to him. He would perish or live by the actions of Maensith and the others.

Looking back he realised he had craved freedom but had enjoyed none. Always had he been in the thrall of someone or something else. First it had been his fear of death, and then his lust for Athelennil. His desire for danger had mingled with Maensith's passion to create an intoxicating and addictive combination that had steered his life for a while. And then his shame had been his prison, locking him into his fears as much as the dreamleaf.

'Freedom is a myth,' he said, to nobody in particular.

He was startled when he realised that the ships in the holo-display were getting smaller. Suddenly they were replaced by the snarling face of Khiadysis.

'Run, you pathetic worms, run!' growled the hierarch. His right eye twitched with a tic that Aradryan had not noticed before. 'You cannot stay at Alaitoc forever, you conniving bitch. I will find you, or the Crimson Talon will.'

That image disappeared to be replaced by a golden wheel of energy, the brightness of the webway gate causing Aradryan to put his hand in front of his eyes, blinking hard. When he could see again, the soaring towers of Alaitoc were racing past, silhouetted against the slowly turning disc of the craftworld's webway portal. The *Naestro* swept over domes and bridges, almost brushing the forcefields and gravity nets that covered Alaitoc. It was a view of the craftworld that Aradryan had never experienced before, seeing her racing past in all of her glory; he had previously been too occupied with piloting to notice the size and grandeur.

'I am back,' he whispered and he realised he was crying.

RESOLUTION

Alaitoc – One of the major craftworlds that survived the Fall, Alaitoc is known for the strength of its inhabitants' adherence to the Path. This strict regime can be too much for some, and so many depart Alaitoc seeking the life of the Outcast, and thus it has a large diaspora of rangers, corsairs and other adventurers across the galaxy and other craftworlds. The name of the craftworld derives from the legend of Khaine and means 'Sword of the Heavens'.

The council of Alaitoc sat on the stepped seats of the amphitheatre-like Hall of Communing. It was a column-lined dome set close to the rim of Alaitoc, and Aradryan felt very small as he stood at its centre, surrounded by nothing but a transparent force dome and the stars of the galaxy. The council consisted of the seers and autarchs of Alaitoc, joined by a few other select individuals of exceptional wisdom or age.

Farseer Anatharan Alaitin had been nominated as spokesman, though in truth the eldest councillor's role had been more of inter-rogator than mouthpiece. There were shining motes of crystal in the ancient farseer's skin and eyes, and his hair was as white as snow. Aradryan had been questioned for several cycles, pausing only for refreshment, concerning his exploits since he had left the craftworld. He was still not sure why everybody was so concerned with his busi-ness, and as the fourth cycle of questioning began his exasperation became vocal.

'What do you want from me?' he demanded, turning a circle to look at the assembled councillors. 'I feel as if I am on trial for some charge that has not yet been levelled.'

'In a way, you are.' This came from one of the eldar sat on the lowest step of the hall. Aradryan recalled the lengthy introductions that had preceded the inquisition and brought up a name: Kelamith. 'Purposefully or unwittingly, your actions have brought about great destruction to Alaitoc. We are here to divine the nature of that threat and whether you are complicit in its arrival or simply a victim.'

'Destruction?' Aradryan looked around, hands spread wide in innocent appeal. 'I see no destruction. What have I done?'

'The humans are coming,' said Alaitin. 'Soon, we fear. They bring war with them.'

'And what has that to do with me?'

'This Imperial commander, De'vaque, tell us more about him,' said Kelamith. 'We see your thread and his tightly bound together. On the skein we have seen that the bloodshed stems from your line, but there are too many fates to count at the moment. We need your help, Aradryan, to avert disaster for our craftworld.'

Taken aback by the farseer's humble tone, Aradryan nodded. He felt ashamed of what had happened with De'vaque, realising that his pride and self-opinion had fuelled his confrontation with the governor more than sense or desire for freedom. He carefully explained the circumstances that brought him into De'vaque's circle, firmly placing the emphasis on the existing relationship created by Yrithain. Alaitin delved deeper, demanding to know what happened at Daethronin. With some chagrin, Aradryan related the encounter on the Imperial commander's yacht. There were whispers and mutters amongst the councillors, who felt that they were now hearing something that would explain how such a doom was being brought down upon Alaitoc.

'And so you held his son hostage until you were free, yes?' said Alaitin. 'That was the last you saw of the Imperial commander?'

Aradryan swallowed hard, painfully recalling his actions that had followed. He looked at Alaitin, who regarded him sternly with slate-grey eyes.

'That is not what happened,' said Aradryan. At that moment, he desperately wanted to wake up. This dream had gone on long enough, it was beyond tiresome and had now becoming frightening.

'What happened, Aradryan?' Alaitin's question was like a blade slicing into Aradryan's heart, through flesh and bone into the core of his being. Aradryan remembered a cloud of exploding plasma and gas. In his heart he felt the galaxy trembling with the affront he had done to De'vaque. He could not believe his own callousness, and his head swam at the recollection.

'What did you do, Aradryan?' Alaitin was relentless, his eyes boring into Aradryan.

'We killed them,' he replied softly, meeting the gaze of some in the assembled audience. As he spoke, Aradryan saw dismay and disgust written on their faces. '*I* killed them: De'vaque's son and bodyguards. I blasted their shuttle apart and scattered their ashes into the ether. It was unnecessary and cruel, and the greatest hurt I could have inflicted on Commander De'vaque.'

Silence more condemning than any shouted accusations swallowed Aradryan. He felt the scorn of the councillors washing over him, stripping away the last tattered vestiges of his dignity. Their silent charge echoed over and over in his mind: cold-blooded murderer.

'So now we perhaps come to understand the why,' said Kelamith. He laid a hand on Aradryan's shoulder, eyes soft with pity. 'Thank you.'

'There is as yet no explanation as to the how.' This came from a tall, well-built figure who had been sitting opposite Kelamith. His robes were dark and light blue, threaded with white, and his face was narrow with flared nostrils and bright blue eyes. Aradryan knew who he was – everybody on Alaitoc knew Arhathain, chief amongst the autarchs. He stood up now and approached Aradryan, fixing him with that pale stare.

'Commander De'vaque knows nothing of your connection to Alaitoc, nor where the craftworld might be found?'

'That is correct, autarch,' said Aradryan. He wanted to flee from that piercing glare, but was pinned to the spot by its intensity. 'My place of birth never arose in conversation with him or his son, and Alaitoc is far from the eyes of the humans. I cannot see how he...'

Aradryan's voice died away as he thought about the question. His heart sank even further, though he had thought it impossible. Even his confession about Darson De'vaque paled in comparison to the revelation that was coursing through his thoughts. Panic gripped him as he looked into the uncaring eyes that regarded him from every direction, dozens of them judging him silently.

'The Commorraghans.' Aradryan squarely met Arhathain's. 'They had been waiting in the webway for the Azure Flame to flee from the ambush at Nathai-athil. We thought it was simply opportunism, but...'

He let them draw their own conclusion, unable to voice it himself. It was Kelamith who spoke next. When Aradryan turned in the direction of the farseer, the psyker's eyes were ablaze with energy.

'Bitter and spiteful, filled with hatred for the betrayal against him, Khiadysis Hierarch will lead Commander De'vaque after the one he despises.' The farseer's unnatural gaze fell upon Aradryan. 'The Imperial commander brings allies with him, for he has persuaded others that Alaitoc is a nest of pirates that has been plaguing their star systems of late. A fleet he brings, and soldiers of the Emperor's army. And with them comes another, a titan of a man who leads a Chapter of the Emperor's Space Marines. He is called Achol Nadeus and it will be by his hand and his word that Alaitoc will be doomed.'

Aradryan shuddered at the prophecy, remembering the dreams of fire and Thirianna's warning. He felt a tremble, not from within but from Alaitoc itself. It was as if a great drum had pounded in the depths of the craftworld and reverberated to its outer edge in moments. The sensation brought with it a quickening of Aradryan's heart. His pulse raced and an image flickered in his vision; a memory from Hirith-Hreslain, of a giant of fire and wrath that wrought carnage wherever it trod.

The Avatar of Khaine was awakening and war was coming to Alaitoc.

The Dome of Crystal Seers was bathed in twilight from the dying star that Alaitoc was orbiting. The orange light glinted from the faces of past farseers, their flesh absorbed by the infinity circuit of the craftworld, so that now they stood as crystalline statues, dozens of them across the dome, set into sweeping, beautiful parklands of silver and blue.

Aradryan flexed his fingers, trying to work off some of the tension that gripped his body. Every joint felt stiff, every nerve taut. His mind buzzed with what might come to pass. And all he could do for the moment was wait.

'You may like to know that Thirianna is doing well,' said Alaitin, who waited with him. The two sat on a curving white marble bench, their backs to a glittering pool of black. Alaitin was garbed in battle dress, his robes covered with rune armour, his head encased in a jewelled helm that hid his face. He was unarmed, as was Aradryan. The farseer had explained several times that this was essential, but Aradryan felt naked without his sword and pistol. He wished he still had his longrifle. For one who had not known battle for so long, he realised he had swiftly become accustomed to its accoutrements.

'It will not be long now,' said the farseer. He turned his head away for a moment.

Earlier Aradryan had watched the fire and strife of the space battle unfolding through the dome. Las-fire and plasma had flickered across the firmament and ships like cathedrals and swans had duelled against the stars. The humans had not been stopped – could not be stopped – and they had boarded at the docks two cycles ago. Since then, they had been pushing steadily towards the core of the craftworld, the spearpoint of their attack formed by the Sons of Orar Space Marines led by Achol Nadeus.

'What of Maensith and the *Naestro*?' asked Aradryan. 'She told me they would stay to help in the fight against their starships.'

'The *Naestro*... survives for the moment,' replied Alaitin. 'She was badly damaged in a duel with an enemy frigate, but the ship and her captain are still with us.'

Aradryan nodded, relieved by the news. Whatever happened to him – to Alaitoc – the ships would be able to escape. There was a little comfort in knowing that.

The silence that followed was not quite complete. Aradryan could hear the distant sound of shells and explosions. Now and then a tremor would ripple through the infinity circuit. Here, in the Dome of the Crystal Seers, that ripple was magnified, and it seemed that the ancient farseers would whisper amongst themselves for a moment as the wind stirred around them. The rustling was no more than a breeze in the trees, Aradryan told himself, but it was no less disturbing to hear.

He found himself listening for the next sussurant exchange, but instead he heard something entirely unexpected. It was jolly, chirping notes, though no bird made its home here. His hand strayed to his pocket, and there he found a thin, silver tube – the thumb whistle Lechthennian had given him. It had been amongst the possessions he had taken from the *Fae Taeruth*, and throughout his adventures Aradryan had never once thought about it before now.

He lifted the thumb whistle to his lips and blew a few stuttering notes. A flurry of a reply sounded to his right and he stood up, playing a little more. Sat on the edge of a fountain not far away Aradryan saw a figure garbed in outlandish colours and patterns, his face hidden behind a blank mask beneath a diamond-studded hood. Something silver glinted in his gloved hand.

'Lechthennian!' Aradryan cried out the name and ran over to the Solitaire. Mischievous eyes glinted in the dark beneath his hood, looking at Aradryan through the lenses of the mask.

'Not just I, my wayward companion,' said the Solitaire, pointing with his thumb whistle. 'The stone you cast has rippled far and wide.'

Aradryan recognised Findelsith's motley costume immediately, and with him were his troupe, leaping acrobatically from two skyrunners. The Harlequins bounded lithely across the grey turf and formed a group behind their leader. Findelsith pointed dramatically at Aradryan and shook his head. His finger then moved to Lechthennian, and the Great Harlequin gave an exaggerated, resigned shrug.

'For you I would not cross the voids of space,' Findelsith said in his sing-song way. 'Yet the Solitaire has brought me to you, and to you I must now pledge my service. In his company his debt is now mine, and the Laughing God will not be denied.'

'What debt?' asked Aradryan, looking at Lechthennian. 'You do not owe me anything.'

'Not knowing me, you defended my back, when we fought the daemons of She Who Thirsts,' explained the Solitaire. 'You were a brighter spirit at that time, it is a woe to see the darkness now.'

'I have travelled many dark paths since we parted, and I have none but myself to blame for taking them.'

'For Alaitoc we will fight our battle,' declared Findelsith. 'The humans will be our clumsy partners in the Dance of the Bloody and the Bold.'

Sensing someone behind him, Aradryan looked over his shoulder to see that Alaitin had joined him.

'Did you know they were coming?' Aradryan asked the farseer, who shook his head. The Harlequins returned to their skyrunners, Lechthennian waving a farewell as he bounded aboard the open-topped skimmer. The two vehicles rose into the air and hissed past, heading towards the rimward side of the dome.

'The Laughing God prances lightly up the skein, and it is a rare seer that can follow his trajectory. I count us amongst the blessed that Cegorach's servants have come, but they step lightly and will not alter our fate for the better or for the worse. There are, however, some others who have come who are known to you. The *Irdiris* arrived ten cycles ago and her rangers even now lure the humans into our trap in the Dome of Midnight Forests.'

'Athelennil is on Alaitoc? Can I see her?'

'There is not time,' replied Alaitin. He raised his head, as if looking at the stars above. 'Thirianna has done well indeed. The attack in the Dome of Midnight Forests is halted, and so the next and final blow will come here, to the Dome of Crystal Seers. All is in motion as we predicted.'

'And my part?' asked Aradryan, mouth becoming dry as he contemplated the fate the seers had decreed for him.

'It will be as we explained.' Alaitin took Aradryan by the elbow and led him back to the bench, but the outcast could not sit down. He was too agitated to stay in one place and started to pace back and forth across the paved area surrounding the dark pool.

'You cannot be certain we will succeed,' said Aradryan.

'Nothing is ever certain, but this course grants us the greatest chance of success. It is too late now to avert what must be done. Since your arrival events have been set into motion that must be guided to a satisfactory conclusion. You cannot escape your fate any more than we can guarantee it.'

'So all I can do is wait?' said Aradryan.

'Yes,' said Alaitin. 'But you will not have to wait long.'

Aradryan forced himself to sit down, pulling his coat tight around him though the air was warm enough. He looked at generations of seers around him, their cold crystal bodies gleaming in the light of a dying star, and felt utterly alone. It had been pleasant to see Lechthennian, who still held some measure of regard for Aradryan, but there was nobody else in his life who would spare him a moment's thought. The only reason he was still on Alaitoc, and not formally banished, was because the craftworld needed him. He was the centre of this catastrophe and it would only be through him that final oblivion could be averted.

'There is a moment of imbalance,' announced Alaitin, his tone worried. Aradryan shot a look at the farseer next to him.

'What sort of imbalance?'

'A human psyker, one of the Space Marines, has been protecting the enemy against our interference, masking his part on the skein.'

'You mean that something has been hidden from us all along?' Aradryan swallowed hard. 'There is not time to change the plan now!'

'Do not be afraid,' said Alaitin. 'Thirianna sees the threat and moves to thwart it. The attack across the Dome of Midnight Forests can still be halted, forcing the enemy here.'

'Thirianna? She has no experience, how can she possibly prevail where others have failed?'

'Through her love of her friends and her duty to Alaitoc,' the farseer replied, regaining his air of equilibrium.

Time seemed to pass slowly, and Aradryan's skin crawled as he thought of all the plans of the autarchs and seers going awry, sent off course by the actions of one Space Marine. It was too late to change now, though; the fate of the craftworld had been set in motion the moment Aradryan had been told what he must do by the council.

'Thirianna prevails,' said Alaitin. Although the farseer had waited as calmly as the immobile statues around the pair, there was a hint of relief in his voice.

Aradryan gazed morosely at the blue moss creeping through the cracks between the paving slabs under his feet, still not convinced that all would proceed as the farseers had predicted. There was much still that could go wrong and doom him to a painful death, and see Alaitoc destroyed.

He felt a tremor of energy course through the infinity circuit. The whispering of the farseers started again, but this time it did not quieten within a few moments. He thought he caught words amongst the gentle murmuring.

'The wanderer returns.'

'The wanderer returns.'

'The wanderer returns.'

Over and over the phrase echoed through Aradryan's thoughts.

'Thirianna has cast the rune and sent the signal,' said Alaitin, sitting next to Aradryan, hands in the lap of his seer's robe. Rune-incised rings glinted on his fingers. Aradryan twitched as an explosion rolled across the dome, from somewhere to his right. He looked and saw a pall of black smoke rising towards the stars. Alaitin did not react at all. 'The humans have been halted and their new offensive brings them here, seeking the core of Alaitoc. Sensing victory, Achol Nadeus will lead the attack. Our doom approaches.'

Las-fire scorched across the plaza, blasting fragments from the surrounds of the ponds and fountains. Aradryan sat rooted to his spot on the bench, hands white from clenching the edge of the seat as a hail of shuriken fire whistled in front of him, ripping apart the arm and shoulder of a human soldier, his grey uniform torn to thin tatters.

Aradryan repeated to himself the assurance that Alaitin had given him moments before the first humans had crested the hill behind them – they cannot see us.

Lechthennian somersaulted over the head of another human, his harlequin's kiss punching into the back of a second. The pierced soldier spasmed, near-invisible tendrils of wire erupting from his mouth, ears and eyes, scattering bloody mist for a moment before they were drawn back into the Solitaire's weapon.

'They cannot see us,' Aradryan whispered to himself, flinching as a Death Jester's shrieker cannon fired behind him. A human fell to one knee, a gaping wound in his thigh. His pained expression turned to one of horror as his skin reddened, the accelerating toxins in the shrieker round spreading through his system. Veins and eyes bulging, the man somehow staggered to his feet, his lasrifle dropping from his bloating fingers.

The human exploded, the detonation fuelled by his own biochemistry, shards of bone slicing into the other humans around him. Aghast at their companions' deaths, the squad of warriors started to fall back from the plaza, only to be caught by a hail of shuriken fire from a squadron of jetbikes arriving behind them.

The battle had spread across the dome, which was lit by fires and laslight, plasma and human flare shells. Aradryan had been in many raids and boarding actions, but nothing compared to the terrifying thunder and roar of the human assault. Big guns pounded in the distance and the wind brought the stench of tank engines; Aradryan was reminded of his first encounter with the orks at Hirith-Hreslain.

Alaitin had said nothing since the humans had broken into the dome. He might be concentrating on concealing their location, Aradryan guessed, or he might just as likely be asleep. It was impossible to tell either way.

Their engines humming, a trio of Vyper jetbikes sped past, their gunners directing the fire of their scatter lasers against a company of soldiers advancing from Aradryan's right. As shells started to create a line of fiery blossoms along a hillside not far away, the thought occurred to Aradryan that artillery could fall anywhere: it did not have to see him to kill him.

'They come,' said Alaitin.

Aradryan did not know what the farseer was talking about at first, and then he heard a different timbre of engines approaching. Miniature rockets screamed across the plaza and he saw boxy troop transports rearing over the surrounding hills, painted in quartered swathes of red and white. Spewing smoke from quad-exhausts, their tracks clacking and clanking and grinding in an awful cacophony, three of the slab-sided, unwieldy troop carriers hove over a nearby crest like armoured whales beaching themselves. Each had an open cupola in the roof manned by a Space Marine clad in armour of the same colours: the Sons of Orar.

Further away, there were other variations of the crudely angled tanks ploughing across lawns, crushing crystal statues under their garish bulk: some with slope-armoured turrets and side sponsons, others with multiple-missile racks on their roofs and two with single, large-bore cannons mounted in their frontal armour. If the Falcon grav-tank was so named for its swooping grace, effortless speed and streamlined hull, the Space Marines' vehicles were wheeled and tracked blocks that bulled their way across the ground, smashing through any obstacle with brute force.

Aradryan glanced at his companion, to see if he reacted at all to the incoming attack, but Alaitin was as placid as if the two of them were merely enjoying the landscape of the dome. The eldar fell back from the Space Marines' assault; the Harlequins leapt upon their skyrunners and were away swiftly, followed by a stream of jetbikes darting away into the maze of bridges and silver streams. Wave Serpents carrying Guardians and Aspect Warriors pulled back enclosed within the glimmer of their protective shields.

Slabs cracking beneath their weight, the Space Marine vehicles rumbled between the pools, their gunners tacking left and right, searching for targets. After them came an even larger tank, which seemed more like a mobile bunker than a vehicle. Sponsons on its sides mounted a plethora of heavy weapons, while the lenses of artificial eyes gleamed from sensor arrays mounted atop its back.

With a wheeze of hydraulics and a puff of air that washed over Aradryan and caused his hair to flutter, the front of the vehicle opened up, spilling red light from its interior. A single warrior walked down the ramp that was dropping to the ground, as the other part of the hull lifted up to create an opening taller than an eldar.

The warrior's armour was even heavier than that of the other Space Marines, his heraldry augmented by rubies and scrolls carved from white marble. He wore no helm, revealing close-cropped black hair that topped a heavily tanned face criss-crossed and puckered with pale scar tissue. Slate-grey eyes swept the plaza and then turned to stare across the dome, towards the hub of Alaitoc. His shoulder pads were adorned with gold script, and from the powerpack on his back rose a pole from which a long rectangular pennant flew, embroidered with more human writing in red on black, the edges bound with gold thread.

Chapter Master Achol Nadeus of the Sons of Orar; the man who held the doom of Alaitoc in his grip.

A squad of Space Marines from one of the other transports assembled on their leader. Aradryan detected a faint buzz of communicators activating but he could not hear what was being said. The Space Marines divided into two groups of five, one of them returning to their vehicle, the other remaining with the Chapter Master.

As one, Nadeus and his warriors turned towards Aradryan. The Space Marines had their weapons raised, and there was a look of shock on the face of the Chapter Master. Cupolas and sponsons on the vehicles whirred in Aradryan's direction, the glimmer of sighting arrays appearing as a collection of multicoloured dots on his chest.

'They can see me now?' said Aradryan.

'Yes,' replied Alaitin. 'They can see you now.'

'Peace, peace!' Aradryan called out in the human tongue, flinging his arms out and slipping to his knees. 'I have no weapons.'

Within a few moments filled with the crunch of heavy boots and whine of armour, he was surrounded by the Space Marines, their boltguns and other weapons pointed directly at him. That they had not opened fire on instinct was surprising enough.

'Do you understand me?' said Aradryan, a note of pleading in his voice. He had known this was the part he hated, but the seers had assured him there was no other option. They had traced the thread of his life and this route, contrary to appearances, offered Aradryan and the craftworld the best chance of survival. Outright resistance would not prevail against the might of the human forces, and so Aradryan was left with only this humiliating salvation. 'Please, I have no weapons.'

There was another buzz of communication. Nadeus towered over Aradryan, like a colossal statue silhouetted against a ruddy sky filled with the light of the dying star.

'Speak, xenos, and quickly,' said the Chapter Master. Aradryan was not sure what 'xenos' meant, but from the tone employed by Nadeus he assumed it was not an honorific.

'I have important news and an offer of peace,' said Aradryan. He resisted the urge to glance at where he could see Alaitin sitting out of the corner of his eye but still invisible to the Space Marines. The farseer stared at him through unblinking crystal lenses. Aradryan took a breath, long and deep.

'You are being tricked, Chapter Master. Your enemies have placed you exactly where they want you. I must speak with Imperial commander De'vaque in person, or we are all dead.'

Nadeus reached down and grabbed the front of Aradryan's robe, easily lifting the eldar to his feet with one arm.

'What do you know of De'vaque?' asked the Chapter Master.

'Tell him it is Aradryan! Aradryan! I know him, and I am repaying the debt I owe him.'

Holding his breath, Aradryan studied the Space Marine's face. There was disbelief written there, and anger. The Chapter Master's grip tightened, almost crushing Aradryan inside his robe. Aradryan was convinced Nadeus was going to kill him that moment, and closed his eyes.

'Please, Chapter Master, you have to tell De'vaque it is Aradryan.' It was the most demeaning thing Aradryan had ever done, grovelling to this murderous barbarian, but he wanted to live so badly he would do anything. 'He knows me. Do not kill me, please. Do not kill me.'

'Keep this filth secure,' said Nadeus, hauling Aradryan from his feet to pass him to one of his warriors. Fingers stronger than a vice gripped Aradryan's arms as he was lifted away, but he breathed a sigh of relief as he saw the Chapter Master striding back to his command vehicle.

The battle for the Dome of Crystal Seers continued to rage and Aradryan feared that he had been too slow or that the farseers had made a mistake. Airburst detonations left clouds of smoke in the upper air, showering shrapnel on the eldar Guardians below. Grasslands older than the Imperium of Mankind were churned to filth beneath the treads of tank columns, and the remains of seers who had guided Alaitoc to safety for generations before any of the humans had been born were shattered by shell strikes and lascannons. Aradryan wanted to weep, but he kept his emotions in check. Despite his protestations and begging, his mind was alert and clear; if he was to come out of this encounter alive he needed all of his wits about him.

Chapter Master Nadeus had returned after making his inquiries, and stood silently in front of Aradryan, boring holes through the eldar's skull with his stare. There was little doubt that he would kill Aradryan without hesitation. For his part, Aradryan hung his head and avoided the commander's gaze as much as possible.

De'vaque's arrival was heralded by a squadron of four tri-rotor aircraft soaring across the dome. Bubble-like gun mounts dotted their underbellies, twin-barrelled cannons swivelling to survey the scene below. Behind them came a smaller craft with a single rotor, flitting left and right as it evaded possible anti-aircraft fire. A blue blazon was painted on the nose of the craft and Aradryan saw that it was a leaping fish leaving a trail of sparkling diamonds. Seeing this, Aradryan realised that the design was the same as the mosaic that had been on the floor of De'vaque's yacht: a personal symbol or family heraldry.

De'vaque's craft landed amidst much wind and whirling dust, as the other four aircraft kept watch for attack above. When the Imperial commander was safely deposited, the patrolling aircraft spread out, lifting higher into the air. De'vaque stomped across the plaza, gaze immediately drawn to Aradryan, who was being held between two Sons of Orar.

It was hard to follow the emotions that swept across the commander's face. First there was surprise and then anger. His scowl intensified as he came closer, but then was replaced by a twitching of the lips and the hint of a triumphant smile.

Unprompted, Aradryan fell to his knees again, hands lifted towards the Imperial commander in supplication.

'Lord De'vaque, thank the stars!' cried Aradryan.

'Kill it!' snarled the governor, his hand resting on the pommel of the sword at his waist.

'I have a warning,' said Aradryan, desperation making his voice almost a screech. 'You are being tricked, Imperial commander. I know I have wronged you harshly, but I swear for atonement and my life that you must listen to me!'

'It is a cowardly, treacherous wretch,' said De'vaque, directing his words to Nadeus. 'Nothing it says can be of value.'

Aradryan felt an armoured gauntlet on his shoulder, about to pull him to his feet. He wriggled from its grip before the fingers closed, prostrating himself on the cracked slabs in front of De'vaque.

'I am so sorry for the death of your son,' squealed Aradryan, eyes fixed on De'vaque's face. The words were truthful, though used now in guile. 'Darson was killed by my hand, and it should not have been.'

De'vaque's eyes opened wider into a murderous glare and he bared his teeth, spittle erupting from his mouth. Drawing his sword form its scabbard. the Imperial commander stepped forwards.

'Halt your men, Nadeus, I shall kill this filth myself.'

'That would be a mistake, Master Nadeus,' said Aradryan, turning his imploring gaze to the Space Marine leader. 'I have vital information.'

'Wait,' said Nadeus, putting a hand to De'vaque's chest to stop him. 'I still do not understand how this creature knows you, Imperial commander.'

'He is a captain of the pirates we are here to destroy, Nadeus,' replied De'vaque. 'I almost had him before, but he escaped.'

De'vaque stepped around the Chapter Master's outstretched arm, sword raised for the killing blow.

'There are more ships coming!' yelped Aradryan, flinching away from the sword.

Nadeus's fingers enveloped the wrist of the Imperial commander as the blade descended, stopping the sword before it hit Aradryan. The former pirate breathed out in relief, but the moment was short-lived as the Chapter Master turned his stare back to Aradryan.

'What ships? Where?'

'We are almost victorious,' said De'vaque, trying unsuccessfully to shake free from the Space Marine's grasp. 'We need to slay this creature and press on. The infinity core is not far from here.'

'What ships?' Nadeus demanded again. He plucked De'vaque's sword from his trembling grasp, the thin duelling blade looking like a piece of cutlery in the Chapter Master's huge fist. 'Tell me or I will kill you here and now.'

Aradryan did not have to reply. Nadeus tilted his head to one side as the communicator bead in his ear rattled into life. The Chapter Master looked up, through the dome above their heads.

'How many?' he growled.

'Just kill him!' snarled De'vaque. 'He betrayed me! He killed my son!'

The Imperial commander lunged for his sword and was knocked to his backside by a swipe from Nadeus's free hand. The point of the blade was only the length of a finger from Aradryan's face, unwaveringly directed towards his right eye. He swallowed to moisten his throat.

'One moment, please, Chapter Master.'

Aradryan felt the surge of power beneath him, coursing along the matrix of the infinity circuit. Alaitoc trembled with energy and it sent a surge of strength through Aradryan's fatigued body.

The Dome of Crystal Seers burst into brilliant white light. Every statuesque seer was glowing with psychic power and the floor itself gleamed with them. Traceries of the infinity circuit could be seen like veins throughout the dome, connecting and interconnecting the seers with their craftworld.

As his eyes swiftly adjusted to the light, Aradryan noticed something else: the silence.

There was not a crack of gunshot, shout of anger or blast of shell. The entire dome was quiet. Looking up, Aradryan saw the streak of laser and the flare of missile frozen in the air. Like a lightshow, beams and tracer rounds criss-crossed the dome, an immobile rainbow of violence.

Aradryan stood up as Nadeus looked around in disbelief. The entire battle had frozen. Jetbikes hung in the air above some trees to their left, while a squad of Space Marines were in mid-charge down a slope to the right, the flare of their bolters held in stasis. The white light of Alaitoc's power penetrated everything.

'Look up,' said a voice behind Aradryan.

Out of instinct, Nadeus did so, as did Aradryan. Against the backdrop of the stars he could see the plasma flares of spaceships stuck against the firmament. Bombers and fighters were locked together in a twirling dance, looking like the frozen plateau of a painting.

'The stasis will not remain for long,' said Alaitin, stepping up beside Aradryan. 'We must conclude this business swiftly or all be killed.'

'Slay them, Nadeus,' barked De'vaque, pushing himself to his feet. 'They are an affront to the Emperor. Do your duty, Chapter Master.'

'Ships from a dozen craftworlds have exited our webway portal, Chapter Master,' said Alaitin. 'At the moment they are held in stasis with your fleet. When I draw this veil back and time resumes, they will destroy your fleet utterly.'

'Do not think that Alaitoc stands alone,' Aradryan snarled at De'vaque. 'You cannot bring war to one craftworld without threatening it against all others. Your miserable army will not leave this star system unless we decree it.'

'Mutual annihilation,' said Alaitin.

'I am comfortable with that,' replied Nadeus. 'To rid the universe of this abomination would be reward enough.'

'A tainted reward, and ultimately driven by the vanity of one man,' said Alaitin. The farseer pointed at De'vaque, who stepped back, aghast, expecting some psychic bolt to strike him down. 'There is no justice or honour to be found here, Chapter Master.'

'Everybody knows that the eldar are liars and thieves,' said the Imperial commander. 'They are trying to fool you. Attack now and we shall have victory and glory!'

'When our ships have finished destroying your fleet, Alaitoc will kill herself,' Alaitin continued. 'She will implode her webway portal and consume us all in one conflagration that will briefly outshine the star we currently orbit.'

'But not before our surviving ships have departed,' added Aradryan, still staring at De'vaque. 'They know where there are weapons that can scorch entire worlds in moments and extinguish stars. Destroy Alaitoc and the whole eldar race will respond, and a hundred human worlds will die.'

'More lies,' growled De'vaque. 'Empty threats.'

'If you are so much of a threat, why should I not destroy you now while I have the chance?' asked Nadeus.

'You would perish in vain and for vanity,' said Aradryan. 'Ask the Imperial commander who Yrithain is. Or perhaps he will tell you of his dealings with Khiadysis? Go ahead, ask him.'

Nadeus looked at the Imperial commander, who suddenly had lost much of his bravado.

'Meaningless gibberish,' said De'vaque.

'Names of his conspirators,' said Aradryan. 'If you wish further proof, I can tell you the places and times when attacks took place, not only sanctioned by this traitor, but only made possible by his collusion. He seeks me for killing his son, I cannot deny that. Are you to be the instrument of his personal vendetta, Chapter Master? Will your Sons of Orar perish for the pride of this weak-willed hypocrite?'

'Pirate filth!' roared De'vaque. He tried to snatch a boltgun from the grip of one of the stasis-bound Space Marines, but it would not move.

'Stand back, Imperial commander,' said Nadeus. The Chapter Master's bolt pistol was in his hand and pointed at De'vaque's chest. 'Tell me that these are more lies. Let me see your face when you do it. And tell me how you came to find this place, or how this pirate came to know your name?'

'They cannot turn you against the Emperor's will,' said De'vaque, holding his hands out in front of him as a barrier to the pistol.

'How many thousands have died already?' whispered Alaitin. 'How many of your warriors have fallen to clean the blood from this man's hands, Chapter Master?'

The boom of the pistol caused Aradryan to jump. De'vaque's head disappeared in a cloud of blood and bone and his headless corpse collapsed to the pavement.

'Too many,' snarled the Chapter Master. 'Call off your ships and I will cease the attack.'

EPILOGUE

There were thousands of dead, too many for the Dome of Everlasting Stillness. Those Aspect Warriors who had fallen were laid to rest in the catacombs of their shrines until the Guardians and civilians had been conducted through the ceremony of internment. Only seven of Alaitoc's spiritseers had survived the battle, and so they were aided by the others of the Path of the Seer. They moved silently along the long rows of the dead, followed by floating caskets into which they placed the glowing spirit stones of the fallen. There was not time to give thanks and bear witness to the passing of every individual – to do so would take hundreds of cycles.

Aradryan drew up the hood of his white robe and stepped across the threshold of the dome. Just as there were too few spiritseers to conduct the dead to the infinity circuit, there were not enough Mourners for there to be one for every fallen eldar.

When the humans had eventually left, four cycles after the showdown in the Dome of Crystal Seers, Aradryan had been faced with the awful truth of what had happened. There was no way to extinguish the guilt; it was so great it would crush the greatest of minds and the most patient of philosophers. He had known, as he had watched the first of the bodies being lifted from the blood-slicked field, that he would tread the Path of Grieving. There was no other way to deal with the loss and the hurt that was created by the knowledge that so many had been slain because of his actions.

It was easy to cry. Tears rolled down his cheeks in a constant stream, every droplet shed in memory of a lost life. The magnitude of what he had perpetrated threatened to overwhelm him, and his tears became choking sobs. To Mourn came easily; he trod the Path of Grieving to learn how he might eventually stop.

Nearly a third of Alaitoc lay in ruins, from rim to core, the swathe cut by the Imperial troops a scar that would take generations to heal. Some domes would never recover. They would be let free from the base of the craftworld and sent into the fiery heart of dying Mirianathir, to be reborn one day as particles that would fuel the craftworld again.

He thought of so many spirits to be absorbed by the infinity circuit. The thought had horrified him before, and sent him into the stars to seek escape from his own mortality. The irony was not lost on him; of how everything had come full cycle and here he was again surrounded by corpses. This time he was not afraid. He had come to terms with death, and though he could not end his own life without atoning for what he had done, he would welcome the release when it eventually came.

'We must all bear a heavy burden.'

Aradryan stopped and turned to find Thirianna following him along the path between the lines of the dead. Her seer robes were overlaid with a belt and sash of white, and after her came one of the spirit-caskets.

'There are not enough tears in the universe to wash away the guilt of what I have done,' said Aradryan, choking back his sobs. 'Not just those here, but the blood that I spilled by my own hand, and the lives that were taken by my words. The fallen will never have justice.'

'There is no justice, just fate,' said Thirianna, 'and I have found that even fate is not so immutable as we might think. I must share the blame for this cataclysm, for I have been guilty of one of the grossest crimes of the seer.'

'I do not understand,' said Aradryan. He motioned Thirianna to a bench and the pair of them sat down, heads bowed. They did not look at each other.

'It may have been your actions that set in motion events that would bring down the hatred of Commander De'vaque, but it was my actions that ensured those events culminated in the disaster that befell our home. Without my intervention, Alaitoc would have been safe.'

'I am still unclear what you mean,' said Aradryan. He produced a square of linen from a pocket inside his sleeve, its corners embroidered with runes of comfort, and dabbed at his eyes. He pushed a wisp of white-coloured hair back inside his hood. 'If you think that you could have made me stay on Alaitoc, then that is just foolishness. You cannot feel guilty for that – you take no responsibility for my subsequent actions.'

'It was not that of which I am guilty, though thank you for reminding me,' Thirianna replied with a soft laugh. 'When you became involved with Yrithain, confrontation with De'vaque became a distinct possibility. I glimpsed the narrowest of futures, possible only by the most complex chain of events, and hence far more unlikely to happen than likely. Yet for my own selfishness, I manipulated people and fate to satisfy my curiosity and sate my fear, and in doing so I brought about the very catastrophe I sought to avoid.'

'There must be some kind of seer's logic in your words, because I do not know what it is you have done.'

'I manipulated Korlandril, and through him Arhathain, to make the council of seers investigate my glimpse of Alaitoc's doom. From that moment, a sequence of thread came together which turned a remote possibility into a self-fulfilling prophecy. The more we looked, the more we were likely to bring it about, because as soon as we found the danger and saw your part in the doom that would come, I sent warning to you, across the gulf of space through the eternal matrix that underpins the webway.'

'My dreams... They are coming for us. We will all burn. Such nightmares I have never known.'

Thirianna stared at him, hand lifted to her mouth in shock.

'I meant to warn you, not to torment you.'

'Yet it is still not such a grave transgression as I have committed,' said Aradryan. 'If it were not for that warning, I would not have been on Alaitoc, and present to intervene against De'vaque. Without me, our people might never have stopped the humans. And that brings to mind a question I have not yet been given clear answer to. Why is it that I could not tell the tale of De'vaque's treachery to Nadeus earlier? If he had known from the outset what a venal creature he was allied with, the attack might never have taken place.'

'You heard it from the lips of De'vaque: our words cannot be trusted. De'vaque had to betray himself, to show his guilt to Nadeus, in order that the Chapter Master would be convinced. We tried many threads to bring about that fate, but the only one that had any measure of success was to draw the human forces on, to allow them to sear into the heart of Alaitoc. Only at the moment of apparent victory would De'vaque himself come to the craftworld, and only by placing him alongside the thread of Nadeus and yours could we bring about the conclusion we so desired.'

'And so it was well that you sent me warning,' said Aradryan, standing up. He offered a hand to Thirianna and helped her to her feet. 'Many have died, but annihilation has been averted.'

'Had I not implanted that psychic message in your dreams, you would not have woken from the Dreaming that gripped you,' Thirianna whispered, laying her head against his shoulder. 'I did not realise this at the time, but that act brought grave consequences, and I should have known not to interfere in such a delicate matter. Had you been Dreaming when the *Naestro* came to Nathai-athil the fleet would have been caught in the ambush laid by De'vaque and Khiadysis.'

'Wait,' said Aradryan, stepping away from Thirianna. 'You mean we would have been killed there? If that is the case, I owe you my life!'

'When you survived Nathai-athil you were set on a course, driven by my dream-borne warnings, to return to Alaitoc. With your return to Alaitoc you brought Khiadysis to the craftworld.' Aradryan followed the logic and a sickness began to well up in his stomach as he realised the import of Thirianna's words. 'Once Khiadysis knew you were at Alaitoc, he passed this to De'vaque and the human warriors who had been mobilised to hunt you down came here also.

'I became a seer to know what would happen to my friends, and I doomed us all. Korlandril was taken by his anger and consumed by the Phoenix Lord Karandras. You might never overcome the grief and guilt of what you are responsible for. And me... I saved your life, yes, but almost at the cost of Alaitoc...'

There was no comfort for Aradryan to offer his friend. Each in his way, he and Thirianna and Korlandril had been victims of their own nature. The Path and all its protections could only offer a means by which they might survive themselves. Whatever calling, whether of Commorragh or the maiden worlds, on the Path or Outcast, no eldar could fully escape himself or herself. They had been the seed of their own doom, and thus would it be until the Rhana Dandra and the end of all things.

Aradryan stood up and could not look at his friend. He looked at the lines of the dead that had been the victims of their mistakes, and walked away.

'The greatest truth about the Path is the simplest to say and yet the hardest to comprehend. In this profound moment comes a realisation of the genius of the Asuryas, and the flaw in their genius.

There is only one Path, and it binds all of us together.

We seers may pick apart the strands, until we reach the infinitesimally small details, but their presence is a distraction to the overall flow of the skein. Be you Poet or Dreamer or Mourner, Warrior or Seer or Outcast, as the events in your life are but threads in the cord of your fate, so your whole life is but a thread in the cord of the fate of the eldar. We all walk the Path as a single species, and as a collective we must learn to control our passions and our fears together, or face destruction from one and the same.'

– Kysaduras the Anchorite, afterword to
Introspections upon Perfection

THE CURSE OF SHAA-DOM

On a dry, savage world, Elemenath felt the Alaitocii unleash slaughter upon the humans who had found the Jade Scarab of Neimenh. The white seer's mind was ice, hardened to the constant whispering that tried in vain to enter his thoughts from the infernal artefact, but he could not block out the death screams of the humans, nor the exultation of violence that pealed like a thousand bells from the minds of the Aspect Warriors.

It was a sad but necessary cull. The humans who dwelt within the fortress had come into contact with the Jade Scarab and had become corrupted, even if they did not realise it. They had to be exterminated to prevent the taint of the Great Enemy spreading. When the dying was over, Elemenath and his five fellow white seers brought forth the null-coffin from their ship and escorted it to the place where the Jade Scarab had been found.

The wraithbone sarcophagus – a long ovoid of pale psychoplastic inscribed with protective runes – floated between the white seers as they made their way up the flights of stairs to the top of the tower, passing the bloodied corpses of the humans. The Alaitocii autarch waited for them at the uppermost storey, with him a farseer and a young warlock. Elemenath paid little heed to the other seers, his mind focussed on blanking out the impassioned pleading that emanated from the Jade Scarab. It cajoled and threatened, begging to be freed from the small box that contained it.

Not for the white seers the barrier of runes that shielded the Alaitocii seers from the pervasive effects of the Jade Scarab. Each had sought a purer path, dedicating their lives to the sole purpose of thwarting the designs of the Great Enemy and the other Chaos powers. In the Black Library, they had spent their lives learning the rituals of defiance that allowed them to look upon the realm of the Chaos gods and yet not be drawn into the abyss. They did not seek revelation in the future, nor did they harbour the desire to wield the power of the warp for their own ends. Theirs was a path of denial, their psychic gifts turned towards the sole purpose of containing the potential of others and suppressing the corrupting influence of artefacts like the Jade Scarab.

The infernal piece was placed within the null-coffin, its haranguing and whining almost blotted out by the counter-seals and wards crafted into the wraithbone container. Without further word, the white seers left the Alaitocii and returned to their ship.

The ship was a strange craft, even more out of place floating amongst the ruin of the compound's courtyard, surrounded by the dead. Its main hull was dart-like in shape, swirling gold and blue in colour, surrounded by a circle of six curving tail fins of shimmering black that swept forward almost to the pointed prow. It was just large enough to accommodate a dozen eldar, the bulk of its length taken up by the warp-resonating vanes that gave rise to its name: a skeinrunner.

The null-coffin was sealed into a compartment that extruded from the bottom of the hull and, satisfied that all was in order, the white seers gathered in a circle to commune. Their minds touched upon each other, no words spoken.

It is not necessary for all of us to accompany this cargo, thought Nemerian, the most senior of the white seers.

We are a short journey from Biel-Tanigh, agreed Khetherim, second in age. *Only one of us should suffice.*

I nominate Elemenath to the task, continued Eidoriar. *He has yet to make the journey to the sanctuary.*

I am honoured, but I do not think I am ready yet for such a responsibility, replied Elemenath. He was the youngest of the six and had never visited Biel-Tanigh alone.

It will be of no great peril, said Nemerian. *You may take the hirelings with you. We shall accompany one of the Alaitocii vessels back to Neir-Saman and you will rejoin us there.*

It is agreed, chorused the others, leaving Elemenath feeling privileged but apprehensive.

He was left alone with Nemerian as the rest of the white seers drifted back towards the tower.

There is no cause for concern. Nemerian laid a comforting hand on the wrist of Elemenath. *The journey is swift and without undue obstacles. You know what must be done. Deliver the cargo and your task is complete.*

Elemenath bowed his head in acknowledgement of the other's

wisdom, then strode up the ramp into the skeinrunner. He had barely crossed the threshold when the ramp slid up behind him and the hull sealed.

Inside were four other eldar, sitting on low couches that segued smoothly with the floor and wall of the spherical chamber. Two were garbed in the ever-distorting robes and coats of rangers, their cameleoline attire currently blending in with the deep red interior of the ship. The first was Anithei. She had joined the servants of the Black Library before Elemenath, having left ill-fated Morwhe-Sheno only a short time before it had been consumed by the Great Enemy's mortal followers. The other ranger was Khai-lian of Biel-tan, an aging eldar who had finally grown bored of craftworld life after treading many paths, finding new purpose in service to the Guardians of the Black Library.

Sprawled on the bench opposite was Syllion. He had been a pirate for most of his life and his clothes and demeanour celebrated his notorious reputation. His white hair was cut in a scalplock, the bald skin tattooed with winding red dragons. The adventurer's thin face sported a scar from right eye to top lip; an affectation that was well within the technology of the eldar to remove. He wore a baggy shirt of black and silver, fastened with a broad belt chased with sworls of tiny sapphires and diamonds. Silver-studded leggings became boots below his knees, of a deep blue that gave his lower half the appearance of a twilight sky broken by stars.

The last member of the team was sitting a little apart from the others on a small stool, his head covered with a white cowl and mask that left only his deep blue eyes on show. He wore a single piece bodysuit of woven gold and red, which shimmered like the scales of a fish as he twisted towards the white seer. He was the pilot, Zain Jalir, and it was to him that Elemenath turned.

'Take us to Biel-Tanigh.'

The skeinrunner lifted silently from the ground and rose up above the human compound. Within, Elemenath seated himself in a small cubicle behind the main chamber, his robe gathered up as he lowered himself onto the ornately patterned rug on the floor. Golden sigils joined by thin traceries of crystal marked the walls and ceiling, and as the white seer extended his mind they came alive with the glint of psychic energy.

'Ready to engage the portal,' announced Zain Jalir.

There came a whine that was felt in the mind more than the ears, the enormous crystal of the skeinrunner ghost engine flaring with psychic life. Elemenath drew in the power of the crystal, shaping it into a faceted bubble surrounding the craft. With another thought, he instructed Zain Jalir to engage the portal.

The air around the skeinrunner was wreathed with energy. Flares of every colour danced across the invisible outline of the psychic barrier as a whirling hole appeared in reality at the nose of the craft. The vortex grew wider, spinning faster and faster. A few heartbeats later, the skeinrunner slipped forwards into the tear, propelled by the thoughts of Elemenath.

Unlike other eldar craft, the skeinrunner was not restricted to existing strands and tunnels of the webway. It burrowed through the gap between the material universe and the warp; opening up its own passageway before it, the walls of the delving collapsing behind as the craft passed on.

Elemenath was in control for the moment, his mind linked to the swirling energies of warpspace, looking at them as no other could; not even a farseer could witness the warp in its raw form. The white seer saw clashing energies, waves and tides of pure emotion and psychic power crashing against each other. Through the maelstrom of colours and textures he located the slender fibres of the nearby webway and steered the ship towards them.

For the shortest moment, the skeinrunner had to pass into the pure immaterium, allowing it to bypass the shielding walls of the webway under the white seer's guidance. Elemenath felt a freezing sensation, the spirit stone at his breast throbbing hot as he hardened the psychic shell around the ship during its brief translation. His mind and body ached as he felt his life essence leeching away, just for an instant, held in the grip of She Who Thirsts.

For an eternally long heartbeat, all that kept at bay the ravaging hunger of the god created by the eldar was the willpower of the white seer. He had performed this act several times before in the company of the others, but it was his first solo foray and he attended to every detail with precise preparation. His mind was encased by a white wall of denial, blocked of all thought that might attract attention, his actions performed on an unthinking, instinctual level.

With a flash of psychic expulsion, the transfer was complete.

Now hidden within the undulating passages of the webway, secured against attack by immaterial walls erected before the Fall, Elemenath could relax slightly. The webway's wardings were not a guaranteed defence though and he kept his mind alert to any sign of damage in the protective layers encompassing the tunnel.

Within the webway, Zain Jalir was able to take over, piloting the craft as he would any other ship, its engine siphoning power from the raw stuff of the warp. Turning down a side passage, the skeinrunner continued towards the vault of Biel-Tanigh.

The maze of tunnels surrounding Biel-Tanigh was too convoluted and small for the skeinrunner; leaving Zain Jalir with the craft, Elemenath led the others on foot. Unlike the interstellar branches they had just traversed, these passageways were made of solid material, shaped from the colliding energies of the real and unreal. To the normal eye, the pastel-blue and cream-coloured passage appeared to be a vaulted arch in cross-section, curving slowly, joined by many others at star-shaped junctions. To the psychic sense of Elemenath, it barely existed except as a shimmering barrier of force keeping the ravening energies of the warp at bay. At least it provided greater comfort to the white seer than the unshuttered warp and he was able to block out what residual noise emanated from around him.

Guided by an inner compass taught to him by the Harlequins of the Laughing God, Elemenath sensed the ebb and flow of power through the webway itself. Biel-Tanigh was close, weighing heavily on the fabric of the warp-realspace construct. After passing dozens of seemingly identical star-junctions, Elemenath turned left, passed a few more, turned right and continued on for some time.

It was here that the webway took on a different appearance, simulating its great antiquity in a way that mortal minds could comprehend. Gone were the gleaming, identical corridors of colour and light. In their place the eldar found themselves walking along twilit streets, the sky overhead utterly black and starless, the crumbling walls to either side that guided their course moss-covered, wreathed with thorny vines that slowly moved with a life of their own.

The air became dry, filled with fine dust like a desert wind. Drifts of ancient debris gathered against the sloping walls and encrusted the nooks between worn stones. The sighing of the breeze echoed from arched courtyards that appeared now and then in the walls, giving brief glimpses of ancient villas and decaying estates.

The wind brought with it sad voices, and set the thorn-vines rasping and rattling so that it appeared as if they spoke. The whisperthorns spoke of ancient days of glory, when Biel-Tanigh had been a place of learning and scholarly pursuit. The husky voices lamented the collegiate conflicts that had engulfed the campus as the various factions within sought to pursue ever more esoteric and illuminating lines of thought at the expense of other sects. Logic and reason, the voices cried, had given away to dogma and ritual, and Biel-Tanigh became a place of death and perversion, where study became a religion and investigation was conducted through blade and flame upon the bodies of innocents.

We are dead, dead by our own folly, whispered the spirits trapped within the thorns. Let the living learn from dry Biel-Tanigh, for we can learn no more for ourselves.

Shuddering, Elemenath pushed on through the dilapidation, his mind barred against the intrusive fingers of the dead spirits that sought to claw into his thoughts with their freezing touch.

One further turn, which almost took them back to where they had begun but approaching from the correct direction now, brought the small group of eldar to an impressive gateway. In appearance it seemed wrought of iron and gold, its main structure a dark, forbidding metal decorated by curling eldar runes in glittering yellow that declared its name: Biel-Tanigh. A complex interweaving arrangement of bars and levers could be seen through the gate; its ornate silver locking mechanism was covered with runes no bigger than pinheads.

The gate hung from a no-less imposing pair of pillars that flanked the passageway, of red-veined marble carved with dire warnings and warding glyphs. The red was the colour of blood and seemed to throb as if fluid passed along them.

Or so the eye saw. Elemenath had been trained to rely on less deceptive senses. He observed a swirling-yet-solid barrier of psychic energy, a small rune of pure white at its centre, beyond which nothing could pass.

There was no bell-pull nor rune nor any other device by which the party could make their presence known, short of shouting, which they were all loathe to do in this benighted place. Elemenath counselled his companions to patience, for on all his previous visits the denizens of Biel-Tanigh had been well aware of their visitors and attended to them in their own time.

The four eldar amused and occupied themselves, each to their own mind. Elemenath recited protective mantras to keep his thoughts busy. The two rangers set to investigating their surroundings – though not moving out of sight of the gate – and inspecting the slowly writhing whispervine and the flaking stonework. Syllion sat with his back to one of the gateposts, a small, white memestone in his hand, lips barely moving as he whispered his secret tale to its memory. Elemenath cared not to think of the things the pirate had done in the past and was pleased that his psychic strength had been directed towards the protection of his own mind rather than the invasion of others', for the temptation to look at the past and fate of such a character was considerable.

Eventually a dismal chime sounded from beyond the gate. The whispervine was thrown into a quivering of anticipation as its black leaves and dead-skin-pale flowers fluttered towards the gateway, straining to enter.

Dim, dark shapes could be seen through the bars of the gate, moving back and forth without haste. The lock mechanism spun and ratcheted and slid, while the psychic wards that Elemenath could see were peeled away, layer by layer, revealing the webway beyond.

The gates swung silently outwards, revealing four figures; Elemenath had noticed before that the number of Guardians that greeted visitors always numbered the same as those who came to Biel-Tanigh, like dark reflections.

The four eldar were clad in black and grey, their bodies wreathed about by trailing creepers barbed with hooks and dripping thorns. Their emaciated forms were thin even for eldar, their shadow-hidden faces giving glimpses of almost skull-like gauntness. Dark eyes stared solemnly from sunken sockets, their black gazes pinning Elemenath and the others with their intensity.

Behind the thorn-clad Guardians could be seen the dim shapes of warrior-constructs against a bland crimson sky, their many gangling blade-limbs glinting in the light of a flickering silver star. The cracked pavement under the feet of the dark keepers writhed with more thorny growths, whose barbs dripped foul-smelling venom onto the crazily broken flags.

With a gesture, Elemenath brought forward the null coffin. Biel-Tanigh's Guardians moved their disconcerting stares to the wraithbone casket, straightening sharply with hissing intakes of breath; from apprehension or excitement Elemenath was not sure.

'Long we have sought this infernal device.' It was not clear which of the figures had spoken. The voice seemed to come from none of them. 'The Jade Scarab of Neimenh. A treasure indeed for the dead scholars.'

'It is powerful,' said Elemenath, feeling that a warning was necessary. The fate of the scarab had been discussed by the group before they had joined the Alaitocii attack. 'The white seers feel that it should be destroyed immediately.'

'The white seers do not decide what happens within the boundaries of Biel-Tanigh. Do not fear. There is no lure left that can tempt the dead scholars into corruption. Their dreams have withered like a drop of water in a desert. Their desires have been burnt like a butterfly's wings before a sun. Their physical needs no longer vex them, for they have departed into the immortality of spirit. The Jade Scarab comes from the Time Before, and was once used to shape the very tunnels in which you have passed. It was taken from us by those who were the most perverse, steeped in the wakening power of She Who Thirsts, binding it to the will of the Great Enemy. Rest assured that it will be destroyed, in time, when its secrets have been prised from its depths.'

The gates started to swing shut and the figures turned away. Elemenath realised that the null coffin was still next to him, though it had returned to its milky white, neutral state; how the Jade Scarab had been removed was a mystery to him.

'That was... different,' said Syllion. 'I have never known them to be so talkative.'

'Let's just get back to the skeinrunner,' said Khai-lian. 'The sooner we are away from here, the better.'

Elemenath concurred with his companion's assessment and signalled for them to leave.

They had travelled almost halfway back to the ship, leaving behind the dismal surrounds of Biel-Tanigh, when Anithei pulled up quickly, Syllion following behind almost walking into her back.

'Watch what you are doing,' snapped Syllion, stepping around the ranger.

'Did you not hear that?' Anithei asked. She turned slowly on the spot, head cocked to one side. 'Can you not feel that?'

'Feel what?' asked Khai-lian, stepping up beside his fellow ranger, eyes narrowed.

'Singing,' said Anithei. 'A dirge, such a sorrowful dirge.'

Elemenath opened up his psychic sense, searching for some break in the webway that might explain the sensation Anithei was experiencing. He saw nothing wrong with the immediate webway, but there was certainly a damaged section close by. The warp was permeating the fabric of the webway, seeping through a break between the wards. It was not a serious breach yet but warranted investigation.

'Take us to the singing,' said the white seer.

The patch of webway was oddly narrow and transparent, the nothingness of the warp beyond its walls hinted at through the insubstantial enclosure. Here and there, actual tears in the fabric of the webway offered up brain-churning glances of the raw void, a maddening vista of impossibility hinted at but not fully seen.

The air itself seemed cold and thin. Microscopically narrow tendrils of gossamer matter floated in it. The eldar avoided the floating ghost-filaments, knowing that they were the ephemeral leavings of daemonic intrusion, the lingering desires and dreams sown by She Who Thirsts given form, waiting to ensnare the unwary.

'It is safe, the daemons have fled from my presence,' said the white seer.

With a hand gloved in white silk and his mind armoured with ritual chants, Elemenath gathered up the psychofibres, cleaning the air of their taint as he rolled them into an impossibly delicate ball and placed them in a rune-buttoned pouch at his belt. Anithei watched the white seer crouch before one of the cracks in the wall, studying the damage, but she felt her attention pulled elsewhere.

The singing had waxed and waned since she had first heard it, intoxicating yet dread-inspiring, like a sweet-smelling unguent that will bring burning pain. There was deep beauty in the lament, a sorrow of ages that touched upon her heart like nothing had done so before. It was a memory of a song, an echo of a dream she could not remember.

'Where are you going?' asked Khai-lian, grabbing Anithei's arm and breaking her from the bewitching trance.

As she recovered her senses, she glimpsed something nestling in a shadowy corner: the tip of a boot.

She pointed out this discovery to the others and they gathered around to investigate. They came upon a corpse, shrouded in the ghost filaments like a spider's prey cocooned in silk. Elemenath carefully parted the fibres, revealing what appeared to be a slumbering eldar, save that her skin was as dry as parchment, her open eyes filmed over with dark mist. The body was garbed in armour that was the colour of smoke, the ghost-filaments clinging to a hooded cloak that sucked in the light, appearing as deep shadow. She was clearly a warrior of some kind, her skinsuit holding sheaths, holsters and pouches for many knives, long pistols and other weapons.

'Kin of Commoragh,' muttered Khai-lian, glancing around nervously, eyes wide and alert for danger.

'She passed some time ago,' said Elemenath, pulling the long hood over the dead eldar to conceal her face. 'Her spirit has long departed.'

He began a whispered incantation to seal the body against possession.

Anithei watched all of this with only passing interest. The singing was stronger here and did not come from the body, nor did it emanate from the rip in the webway fabric not far away. Here and there, the walls of the webway had been broken, literally shattered so that shards of psychoplastic were scattered all around.

The singing was coming from behind Anithei, close and insistent. With a glance at the others, she confirmed that they were all concentrated upon the examination of the corpse. She sidled away, drawn by the dirge, needing to hear more, to listen to every sad verse.

Her toe touched something amongst the debris. Glancing down, she saw an opal-coloured gem about the size of her closed fist. With another check to ensure she was unseen, Anithei stooped swiftly, swept up the opal, and placed it in the pocket of her long coat.

Her body throbbed momentarily at the touch of the jewel, the chorus in her mind reaching a crescendo that lit along her nerves and burrowed into her memories, bringing forth recollections of loss and pain; the loss and pain of a whole city condemned to damnation by their enemies.

'There is nothing to be learned here,' announced Elemenath, standing up. 'I shall let the others know of the damage, though I fear it is too far progressed to be repaired. Another passageway that must be sealed and lost to us forever.'

'So, back to the skeinrunner?' said Syllion. The adventurer turned and saw Anithei a little apart from the rest. 'Spooked by the dead, ranger?'

She blinked and pushed aside the singing that had enraptured her.

'There are too many dead,' she replied, trying to focus, her words echoing the choir in her mind.

Feeling a presence at the doorway to her chambers, Anithei quickly slipped the stone into her bag and tossed the knapsack behind her low bed. She lay down upon the covers and called for her visitor to enter. It was Elemenath. The white seer had discarded his heavy robe of office and wore a flimsy tunic and leggings, padding barefooted into the room. His expression was stern.

'I did not wish to embarrass you in front of the others,' said Elemenath, 'but I know that you found something in the webway. Did you think that just because I did not look at you, you could keep this secret from me? Please, let me see your hidden treasure.'

Hesitantly, Aneithei rolled over and took up the bag from the floor. She reached inside and her fingers closed about the stone. She stopped, suddenly concerned.

'Why?' she asked.

'I wish to ensure it is of no danger to you,' said the white seer. Anithei saw concern on Elemenath's face, but it could have been feigned. Perhaps the white seer heard the singing too and wished to take the stone for himself.

'That would not be right,' said the ranger. 'It is mine. I found it.'

'I feel its weight upon your thoughts,' said Elemenath. He stepped forward and thrust his hand out insistently. 'Give it to me.'

Jealousy and anger flared through Anithei. The white seer hungered for her prize, but he would not have it. She brought out the opal but, as quick as a serpent, she lashed out, smashing the heavy stone into the side of the white seer's head, cracking open his skull in an instant. He fell without a cry.

The touch of Elemenath's blood set the stone's chorus singing loudly, lamenting his demise yet glorifying the act at the same time. Anithei put the stone down and dragged Elemenath's body fully into the chamber, hiding it behind the bed.

She sat down, unperturbed by what she had done, and picked up the opal again.

'I will take you home,' she said, stroking a finger across its cool surface. 'What's this?'

Anithei looked up, startled to see Syllion standing in the doorway. The former pirate's eyes narrowed and moved between Anithei, the opal and the white figure of Elemenath's body, poorly concealed behind her. 'What have you done?'

'It is mine!' hissed Anithei, pulling a knife from her bag. She lunged, but Syllion was expecting the attack, grabbing her wrist to turn the blow aside. His other hand whipped a curved dagger from his belt and in one fluid movement slashed the ranger across the throat.

The opal tumbled from Anithei's dying grasp but Syllion moved instantly, letting go of her wrist to catch the stone before it hit the ground. He smiled as the music in his mind resumed, congratulating himself on seizing possession of the prize he had desired since hearing its call moments earlier. He had only just seen the stone, but felt as if he had wanted to hold it for his entire life.

A choir of ghostly shadows sung a long, low lament in Khai-lian's dreams. A thousand times a thousand voices rose up in sorrow and rage, telling of how they had been betrayed. He felt their sense of loss a hundredfold and murmured in his sleep, tossing and turning with disquiet. The spirits had to be released, had to be set free to wreak their vengeance on the dark traitors who had slain them.

Khai-lian awoke, a fevered sweat on his brow. The key was close, he could feel its presence. There was something else too: another spirit close by.

Opening his eyes a slit, he saw a figure silhouetted at the doorway. He recognised Syllion's topknot immediately and sensed danger. Pretending to slumber, he rolled over, closer to the holster belt hanging beside the bed, one hand moving towards it under the pillow.

'What are you doing?' the ranger mumbled, pretending to wake.

'It is ours.' Syllion's voice had changed. He spoke as many, the syllables echoing strangely around the bedchamber.

Khai-lian made a grab for the pistol, but its grip was barely in his hand when Syllion struck, the pirate's knife plunging into the base of Khai-lian's skull. The ranger died wordlessly, blood seeping into the bed clothes as Syllion pulled free his blade.

There was only one left, and then the key would be his alone. Syllion left the aft chambers and entered the main compartment, heading for the passageway to the pilot's room.

He was only a few steps from the door to the cockpit when he stumbled. His head was spinning, dizziness throwing him off balance. Arms and legs weakening by the moment, Syllion floundered into the wall and then fell heavily, knife dropping from his numb grasp though he clutched the stone to his chest as if it were his life. The pirate's breath was heavy in his lungs, every inhalation sending a quiver of pain through his chest.

He lay there for some time, shuddering and gasping, his vision blurred. After a while, light broke from ahead, sending agony down his optic nerve and into the rest of his body. A shadow loomed over him and Syllion heard mocking laughter through the rushing of blood in his ears.

'I see you have already despatched the others for me,' said Zain Jalir. 'No matter, the toxin that poisons you would have dealt with them as well. You have something that belongs to me.'

Syllion could do nothing as his last ragged breaths whispered from his lips and the pilot crouched beside him, pulling the opal from the pirate's twitching fingers. Another surge of pain wracked Syllion's body before he died, his spirit filled with the sadness of those trapped within the stone.

Pressing deeper into the shadow of the archway, Zain Jalir listened as the hum of the passing skiff receded into the distance. He knew he was being hunted and had dared the dangers of the underspur to journey back to his lair. The bribes at the portway would not have been enough to stop all remarks concerning his return and he had expected to draw some attention, hence his furtive passage through the dark underbelly of the city. As he waited for the sound to pass away, his hand moved to the pouch at his waist that contained the key to Shaa-dom. He felt a moment of pride, knowing that the liberation of his kin was one step closer.

He had learned that the key had been taken from Biel-Tanigh and had left the Dark City to search for it, joining the white seers under the guise of an outcast. It had been a stroke of fortune to find the key in the manner he had, but everything else that would put in motion the freeing of Shaa-dom had been meticulously planned since he had been born. The spirit stones of the others – the white seer's in particular – would be enough to hire dozens of mercenaries, and with them he would join with the other scions of Shaa-dom to bring about the return of the old empire.

A nearby hiss snapped Zain Jalir from his moment of reverie. It was a sound he knew all too well, and his heart hammered in his chest. Spinning to his right, he snatched up his pistol as the ur-ghul pounced from the top of the archway. The volley of poisoned splinters took the creature full in the chest, ripping apart its half-rotted flesh.

Too late he heard other noises. He glanced over his shoulder to see four more of the bestial creatures, their scent-pits flaring in the gloomy night. He had been a fool to come this way; of all the perils to face, the hideous fugitives of Shaa-dom should have been avoided. The irony of dying to the atavistic escapees of Shaa-dom was bitter in Zain Jalir's thoughts.

His blade met the next ur-ghul in the throat, but the claws of the third and the fourth slashed across his limbs and body. Zain Jalir collapsed and the ur-ghuls fell upon him, shredding and eviscerating as the air was broken with a cacophony of triumphant shrieks.

From the bloodied tatters of skin and muscle and cloth, the key to Shaa-dom was ripped free, sent into the shadows by an uncaring claw. It came to rest in a twisted patch of blood briar, which constricted quickly around the crimson-speckled stone.

There it would remain, ignored by the ur-ghuls, to await its next victim.

THE REWARDS OF TOLERANCE

Encased in a flickering Geller field, the *Vengeful* slid through the psychic tides of the warp. The field flared intermittently as it crossed the path of itinerant warp denizens, becoming a shell of writhing, fanged faces and swirling colours. In the turmoil of its wake, dark shapes gathered in a flitting shoal; occasionally a creature would speed forwards and hurl itself at the strike cruiser, seeking the life force of those within. Each time the unreal predators were hurled back by a flash of psychic force.

Sitting in the Navigator's cockpit Zacherys, former Librarian of the Avenging Sons, gazed out into the warp through eyes ablaze with blue energy. Sparks crackled from the pinpricks of his pupils and thick beads of sweat rolled down his cheeks. With a trembling hand, he reached out to the comm-unit and switched to the command frequency.

'I can hear them whispering,' he growled.

There was a hiss of static before the reply came through the speakers.

'Hold them as long as you can,' said Gessart, the ship's captain. Once master of an Avenging Sons company, he now led a small renegade band only two dozen strong. 'We'll reach safe exit distance in less than an hour.'

The comm buzzed for a few seconds more and fell silent. Left alone in the quiet, Zacherys could not help but listen to the voices pawing at the edge of his hearing. Most were gibberish, some snarled threats, others begged Zacherys to let down his guard. A mellifluous voice cut through, silencing them with its authority.

I can take you to safety, it said. *Listen to me, Zacherys. I can protect you.*

All I ask is a small favour. Just let me help you. Open your thoughts to me. Let me see your mind and I will grant your desires.

The sensation of claws prising at the sides of Zacherys's thoughts suddenly disappeared, like a great pressure released by an opening airlock. The chittering stopped and the Geller field stabilised, becoming a placid oily-sheened bubble once more.

Zacherys relaxed his fingers, loosening his fist on the arm of the Navigator's chair, indentations left in the metal from his fierce grip. He took a deep breath and closed his eyes. When he opened them, they had returned to normal, the burst of psychic energy drawn back into his mind.

Thank you, he thought.

You are welcome, replied the voice.

What do I call you? Zacherys asked.

Call me Messenger, it said.

What are you? A daemon?

I am Messenger. I am the one that will open your mind to your true power. I will show you the full scope of your abilities. Together we will grow stronger. We will both be pupil and teacher.

We need to break out of warp space, thought Zacherys. I cannot resist another attack.

Allow me, said Messenger. *Call to me when you return. I will be waiting.*

The streaming rivers of psychic energy surrounding the *Vengeful* bucked and spiralled, turning upon themselves until they split into an immaterial whirlpool. Through the widening hole, Zacherys could see the blue glow of a star.

Fingers moving gently across the steering panel, he guided the *Vengeful* towards the opening. The strike cruiser burst out of the immaterium with a flash of multi-coloured light. The rift behind fluttered for a moment and disappeared. Silence followed; the emptiness of space. Zacherys looked around and saw a dense swathe of stars: the northern arm of the galactic spiral spread out before him. He smiled with relief and prodded the automatic telemetry systems into action. It was time to find out where they were.

The renegade Space Marines gathered in the briefing hall. The twenty-four warriors barely filled a quarter of the large chamber, which was designed to house a whole Space Marine company. Gessart looked down from the briefing podium and marvelled at how quickly his followers had asserted their individuality. After decades of loyal service to their Chapter – centuries in the case of some – the Space Marines were rediscovering their true selves, throwing off millennia of tradition and dogma.

All of them wore armour blackened with thick paint, their old livery and symbols obliterated. Some had gone further, taking their gear down to the armoury to chisel off Imperial insignia and weld plates over aquilas and other icons of the Imperium. A few had painted new mottos across the black to replace the devotional texts that had been removed. In a neat script, Willusch had written 'The Peace of Death' along the rim of his left shoulder pad. Lehenhart, with his customary humour, had daubed a white skull across the face of his helm, a ragged bullet hole painted in the centre of its forehead. Nicz, Gessart's self-appointed second-in-command, sat with a chainsword across his lap, a thin brush in his left hand, putting the finishing touches to his own design: 'The Truth Hurts', written in red paint to resemble smeared blood.

Zacherys was the last to attend. The psyker nodded to Gessart as he sat down, confirming the location estimate he had passed on earlier. Gessart smiled.

'It seems that though the Emperor looks over us no more, we have not yet been abandoned by the galaxy,' he announced. 'Helmabad is more than a dozen light years behind us. That's the only good news. We are dangerously low on supplies, despite what we salvaged from Helmabad. We are six thousand light years away from safety – a considerable distance. If we are to complete our journey to sanctuary in the Eye of Terror, we will need more weapons and equipment, as well as food.'

Gessart rasped a hand across the thick stubble on his chin. The Space Marines all looked at him attentively, faces impassive as they received this news. Some habits were harder to break than others and they waited in silence for their leader to continue.

'Whether by luck, fate or some other power, our half-blind flight through the warp has brought us within a hundred light years of the Geddan system. The system is virtually lifeless, but it's a chartist captains' convoy meeting point. Merchant ships from across the sector converge there to make the run down past the ork territories towards Rhodus. We'll take what we need from the merchantmen.'

'Those convoys have Imperial Navy escorts,' said Heynke.

'Usually nothing more than a few frigates and destroyers,' said Nicz before Gessart could answer. 'Not too much for a strike cruiser to overcome.'

'If this were a fully-manned ship, I'd agree,' said Gessart. 'But it isn't. If there's a light escort we'll try to cut out a cargo ship or two and avoid confrontation. If there's a more sizeable Imperial Navy presence we cannot risk an open battle. The task is to gather more supplies, not expend what little we have.'

Nicz conceded the point with a shrug.

'You're in charge,' the Space Marine muttered.

Gessart ignored the slight and turned his attention to Zacherys.

'Can you guide us to Geddan in a single jump?'

The psyker looked away for a moment, obviously unsure.

'I think I can manage that,' he said eventually.

'Can you, or can't you?' snapped Gessart. 'I don't want to drop into the middle of something we aren't expecting.'

Zacherys nodded, uncertainly at first and then with greater conviction. 'Yes, I have a way to do it,' the psyker said. 'I can take us to Geddan.'

'Good. There is another issue that needs to be resolved before we leave,' said Gessart. He looked directly at Nicz, who glanced to either side, surprised by his commander's attention.

'Something I've done?' said Nicz.

'Not yet,' replied Gessart. 'The menial crew are still loyal to us, but they do not know the full facts of what happened on Helmabad. If we have to fight at Geddan, there can be no hesitation. I want you to ensure that they will open fire on command, even against an Imperial vessel. I want every weapon system overseen by one of us, and dispose of any crew that may prove problematic.'

'Dispose?' said Nicz. 'You mean kill?'

'Don't get carried away, we cannot run the ship without them. But leave them with no doubt that we are still their masters and they will follow our instructions without question.'

'I'll see that it is done,' said Nicz, patting his chainsword.

'Are there any questions?' Gessart asked the rest of the Space Marines. They exchanged glances and shook their heads until Lehenhart stood up.

'What happens when we reach the Eye of Terror?' he asked.

Gessart considered his reply carefully.

'I don't know. We'll have to go there and find out. At the moment, nobody knows what we have done. I'd rather keep it that way.'

'What if Rykhel somehow survived on Helmabad?' asked Heynke. 'What if he contacts the rest of the Avenging Sons?'

'Between the rebels and the daemons, Rykhel is dead,' said Nicz.

'But what if he isn't?' insisted Heynke.

'Then our former battle-brothers will attempt to live up to their name,' said Gessart. 'That's why we're going to the Eye of Terror. Nobody would dare follow us into that nightmare. Once we attack the convoy word will spread about what we have done. We have one chance to do this right. If we fail, the Emperor's servants will be looking for us, and getting to the Cadian Gate will be all the harder for it.'

'So let's not mess it up,' said Lehenhart.

Zacherys's hand hesitated over the warp engine activation rune on the console beside his Navigator's chair. He glanced at the panel above it, looking at the fluctuating lines of green fading into orange and then surging with power into green again. Although the warp engine was not fully active, the psyker could feel the boundaries of reality thinning around the *Vengeful*. Through the canopy around him, he saw the stars wavering, the darkness between them glowing occasionally with rainbows of psychic energy.

He had promised Gessart that he would get the ship to Geddan, thinking he would use the daemon Messenger to do so. He was having second thoughts, but could not back down. Not only would Zacherys face the scorn of the others, the ship was stranded in wilderness space. At some point they would have to re-enter the warp or simply stay here and eventually die from starvation – a prospect even more harrowing for a Space Marine than a normal man. Doubtless they would kill each other before that fate overtook them.

Taking a deep breath, Zacherys touched the rune. From the *Vengeful*'s innards a deep rumbling reverberated through the ship, increasing to a rapid vibration that whined in Zacherys's ears.

The starfield around the *Vengeful* wavered and spun, engulfing the starship with a whirl of colours: the eye of a kaleidoscopic storm of the material and immaterial. Zacherys engaged the drive and the strike cruiser lurched into the warp; not a physical strain of inertia but a stretching of the mind, filled with momentary flashes of memory and dizziness. For the psyker, the transition welled up at the base of his skull, suffusing his thoughts with pressure as synapses flared randomly for a heartbeat.

It was over in a moment. The *Vengeful* was sliding along the psychic current, Geller field sparkling around it. Zacherys opened his mind up to the power of the warp and felt the shifting energies around him. He could sense the ebb and flow of the immaterium, but he was no Navigator; he lacked true warp-sight. Though he could feel the titanic psychic power surging around the ship, he could see only a little along their route, enough to avoid the swirls and plunging currents that would hurl them off-course, but little more.

Messenger? he thought. There was no reply and Zacherys became fearful that the creature had tricked him back into warp space, to drift on the tides until the Geller field finally failed and they were set upon by the daemons and other denizens that hungered after their souls.

'Foolish,' Zacherys muttered to himself.

The ship was buffeted by a wave of energy and Zacherys's focus turned to the steering controls as he attempted to ride the surge. As with the warp jump itself, he felt this not in the pit of his stomach like a man upon an ordinary sea, but as crests and troughs of sensation behind his eyes, along every nerve.

He regained some control, moving the *Vengeful* into a calmer stream of power. He was making a huge mistake.

Zacherys's hand hovered over the emergency disengage rune, which would rip open the fabric of real/warp space and dump the *Vengeful* back into the material galaxy. There was no telling what damage would be done to the warp engines, or those on board, and Zacherys would have to confess all to Gessart.

It seemed such an ignominious end. So soon after taking the first steps on the road to freedom. It made a mockery of Zacherys's aspirations; his hopes to understand the nature of his abilities and his place between the real and unreal. The bright path leading from Helmabad he had seen in his visions was guttering and dying, swallowed by the formless energy of the void.

I am here.

Zacherys let out an explosive breath of relief.

I need your help, he thought.

Of course you do, replied Messenger. *Look how perilous your situation has become, flinging yourselves into our domain without heed to the dangers.*

I need a guide, thought Zacherys. Can you show me the way ahead?

As I told you before, you must lower your defences and allow me to enter your mind. I must see with your eyes to guide you. Do not worry – I will protect you from the others.

Zacherys's hand was shaking as he leaned over towards the Geller field controls. It would be a rash act, dooming not just the psyker but every soul on board the *Vengeful*. What option did he have?

Indeed, said Messenger. *You have cast yourselves upon the whims of cruel fate. Yet, there is no need to succumb to despair. You can still control your destiny, with me beside you.*

What do you get as your part of the bargain? asked Zacherys. Why should I trust you?

I get your mind, my friend. And your loyalty. We need each other, you and I. In this world you are at my mercy, but I have no reach into your world other than with your hands. We shall help each other, and both shall benefit.

You could destroy the ship, thought Zacherys.

What would I gain? A momentary gratification, a brief peak of power and nothing more. Do not mistake me for the mindless soul-eaters that flock after your ship. I too have my ambitions and desires, and a mind and body such as yours can take me closer to them.

You will possess me, drive me from my own flesh!

You know that I cannot. Your armour against me is your will, strengthened over your whole life. We would wage war against each other constantly, neither victorious. You are no normal mortal – you are a Space Marine still, with all the power that entails.

Klaxons screeched across the *Vengeful* as Zacherys punched in the first cipher to unlock the Geller field controls. Within moments, Gessart was on the comm.

'What is it? Warp breach?' the warband leader demanded.

'There is nothing to fear,' said Zacherys, convincing himself as much as the commander. The blaring was joined by a host of flashing red lights on the display board as Zacherys keyed in the next sequence. 'Everything is under control.'

He tapped out the last digits and pressed the deactivation rune. With a screech that could only be heard inside his head, Zacherys cut the Geller field. The bubble of psychic energy around the starship imploded, the full pressure of the warp rushing into and through the *Vengeful*.

Zacherys felt cold, a freezing chill of the void that encrusted every cell of his being. With gritted teeth, he put his head back against the chair.

'The moment of truth,' he whispered. 'I am at your mercy, Messenger. Prove me right or wrong.'

The bitter cold vanished, replaced by warmth that glowed through Zacherys's limbs. He felt the heat expanding outwards, engulfing the rest of the ship. The energy of the warp remained, not pushed back like it was with the Geller field, but the *Vengeful* settled in an oasis of calm, resting gently upon the stilled psychic tide.

Zacherys opened his eyes. Other than the tingling in his nerves, the psyker felt no different. He flexed his fingers and looked around until he was confident that he was in full control of his faculties. He laughed, buoyed up by a sudden feeling of ecstasy that suffused his body.

And then he felt it.

It was indistinct, like the tendrils of a light fog, spreading through his mind, dribbling along the course of his thoughts. It was a dark web, an alien cancer latching on to all of his emotions, every hope and fear, dream and disappointment, suckling upon his centuries of experience. Zacherys sensed satisfaction seeping through him, leeched from his new companion.

Such delights we have to offer one another. But for another time. Tell me, my friend: where do you wish to go?

Gessart paced the command bridge as he waited for the results of the initial sensor sweep. Zacherys had done an admirable job, dropping the ship out of warp space just outside the orbit of Geddan's fourth world. Gessart wondered how the psyker had overcome the graviometric problems that normally prevented ships from emerging so close to a celestial body, but decided against asking for details; the former Librarian's strangely contented expression and the incident with the collapsing Geller field warned Gessart that there was something odd happening, but he could not afford the distraction for the moment.

'Seven signatures on response, captain,' announced Kholich Beyne, the head of the *Vengeful*'s non-Space Marine crew. The young man checked something on the data-slab in his hands. 'No military channels in use.'

'Confirm that,' said Gessart. 'Are there any Imperial Navy vessels?'

Kholich headed over to the sensor technicians and conferred briefly with each. He turned back to Gessart with a solemn expression.

'Confirm that there are no Imperial Navy vessels in the system, captain. The convoy is assembling around the fifth planet. From their comms chatter, they are expecting to receive their escort in the next day or two.'

'Defences in that grid?' Gessart stopped his pacing and knotted his hands behind his back, trying to stay calm.

'We're not picking up any orbital defences, captain. It seems unlikely that the convoy would gather without some form of protection.'

'Surface-to-orbit weapons, most likely,' said Gessart. 'Nothing that can attack us if we get amongst the convoy before they start opening fire.'

He rounded on the comms team.

'Transmit our identifier to the convoy ships. Tell them we will be approaching.'

'If they require an explanation, captain?' asked Kholich. 'What do we tell them?'

'Nothing,' replied Gessart, heading towards the bridge doors. 'Find out who the civilian convoy captain is and inform him that I'll be boarding his vessel and speaking to him in person.'

'Very well, captain,' said Kholich as the armoured doors slid open with a rumble. 'I'll inform you of any developments.'

Though not considered a large vessel by Imperial standards, the *Vengeful* dwarfed the merchantman carrying Sebanius Loil, the man who had identified himself as the merchant commander of the convoy. Following a terse conversation, during which Gessart had done most of the talking, the trader had acquiesced to the Space Marine's demand to be allowed on board. Now Gessart and his warriors were fully armoured and crossing the few hundred kilometres between the strike cruiser and the *Lady Bountiful* aboard their last surviving Thunderhawk gunship.

Gessart looked at the merchantman through the cockpit canopy, noticing the three defence turrets clustered around her midsection: short-ranged weapons that might fend off a lone pirate but which would be hard-pressed to overload even one of the *Vengeful*'s void shields. Beyond the *Lady Bountiful* was the rest of the convoy, visible only as returns on the Thunderhawk's scanners, separated from each other by several thousand kilometres of vacuum. Four were of similar size, but two of the ships were immense transports, three times the size of the *Vengeful*. Fortunately they were empty, destined to pick up their cargo of an Imperial Guard regiment en route to the warzone in Rhodus.

Bright light streamed from an opening that stretched a quarter of the length of the *Lady Bountiful* as the ship slid back its loading bay doors to allow the Thunderhawk to land. Nicz eased the gunship into a course and speed parallel with the merchantship and then fired the landing thrusters to guide them into the bay.

A lone man waited for Gessart as the Thunderhawk's ramp lowered to the deck, smoke and steam billowing across the bare rockcrete floor. He was stocky, clad in a heavy fur-lined coat with puffed shoulders slashed with red. Sebanius Loil warily watched the Space Marines with one good eye and an augmetic device riveted into his face in place of the other. Lenses clacked as the merchant focussed on Gessart. A servo whined as

Loil lifted his right hand in welcome, the sleeve of the coat falling back to reveal a three-clawed metal hand.

'Welcome aboard the *Lady Bountiful*, captain,' said Loil. His voice was a hoarse whisper and through the ruff of the coat Gessart could see more bionics; an artificial larynx bobbed up and down at Loil's throat.

Gessart did not return the greeting. He looked at his warriors over his shoulder and signalled them to spread out around the docking bay.

'I'm taking your cargo,' he said.

Loil did not seem surprised by this pronouncement. He lowered his cybernetic arm with a whirr and held out his good hand towards Gessart.

'You know that I cannot allow that, captain,' said the merchant. 'My cargo is destined for Imperial forces fighting at Rhodus. I have an agreement with the Departmento Munitorum.'

The bionic hand delved into a deep pocket and produced a datacrystal. Loil offered it towards Gessart as proof of his contract.

'You have no choice in the matter,' said Gessart as he thrust Loil aside. 'Your compliance will be for your own good.'

'You cannot seriously threaten us with force,' said Loil, following Gessart as the Space Marine stalked across the bay towards the main doors. Gessart darted the man a look that confirmed he could very well make such a threat. Loil paled and his artificial eye buzzed erratically. 'This is intolerable! I will…'

The trader's words petered away as Zacherys thudded down the ramp. The psyker's eyes were orbs of golden energy. Zacherys turned that infernal gaze upon Loil, who recoiled in horror, holding up his hands in front of his ravaged face. The merchant whimpered and fell to his knees, tears coursing down his scarred cheeks. Zacherys stood over the man for a moment, looking down, lips pursed in contemplation.

'Where is the main cargo hold?' asked Gessart.

Zacherys looked up, broken from his thoughts by Gessart's questions.

'Aft,' said the former Librarian. 'Four bays, all filled with crates. Too much for the Thunderhawk, we will have to bring the *Vengeful* alongside and dock directly.'

Zacherys held out a hand above Loil's head. He twitched his armoured fingers and the merchant looked up, meeting the psyker's gaze. The gold of Zacherys's eyes spread down his right arm and engulfed the head of the merchant before disappearing. Zacherys smiled and lifted his hand further. The ship's captain rose jerkily to his feet, swaying slightly.

'Lead me to the bridge,' said Zacherys.

Loil's first steps were faltering as he resisted the control of the psyker, scraping his feet across the floor. Zacherys twisted his wrist a fraction and Loil mewled like a wounded animal, knees buckling. The merchant righted himself and stumbled on, Zacherys following with long, slow strides.

The double doors hissed open, revealing a cluster of crew members holding an assortment of weapons: shotguns, autoguns, lasrifles. They stared in disbelief as their captain shuffled through the open doors, Zacherys and Gessart close behind. On their heels, the rest of the Space Marines hefted their bolters meaningfully.

'What do we do, Captain Loil?' asked one of the men, lasgun trembling in his grip.

'Wh-whatever they say,' hissed the merchant. 'Do whatever they say.'

The men looked uncertain. Gessart towered over them, fists clenched.

'Make ready to unload your cargo to our vessel,' he said slowly. 'Comply and no harm will come to you. Disobey and you will be killed. Put down your weapons.'

Most of them did as they were told, their guns clattering on the deck. One, face twisted with indignation, raised his shotgun. He didn't have time to pull the trigger. Gessart's fist slammed into his face, snapping the crewman's neck and hurling him across the corridor.

'Pass the word to your crewmates,' said Gessart. 'Unloading will begin in ten minutes.'

Zacherys made Loil cut the comm-link and then released his psychic grip on the merchant. The man swooned to the floor, head banging loudly against the deck. Blood oozed from a gash in the captain's scalp. It didn't matter; he had served his purpose. The rest of the convoy would be gathering on the *Lady Bountiful* to await boarding and 'inspection' by the Space Marines.

I think I pushed him too far, thought Zacherys as he noticed blood leaking from Loil's ears and nose.

It does not matter, replied Messenger. *There are more of his kind, weak and pathetic, than there are stars in your galaxy. Did you feel how easy it was to control his feeble mind?*

I did, replied Zacherys. The thrill of using the man as a puppet ebbed away, leaving Zacherys strangely empty. What else can I do?

Whatever you desire. You power will no longer be chained by the dogma of weaklings. The full force of γ– Wait! Did you feel that?

I felt nothing, thought Zacherys. What is it?

Let me show you.

Zacherys felt the daemon shifting inside him, pulling back its tendrils from his limbs, coalescing its power in his brain. His witchsight flared into life – the psychic sense that allowed Zacherys to feel the thoughts of others, sense their emotions and locate the spark of their minds in the warp. Zacherys's golden eyes did not see the cramped bridge of the merchantman or the bloodied bodies of the three officers lying crumpled by the door. His thoughts expanded through the ship and beyond, touching on the moon below, sensing the minds of the crew aboard the *Vengeful* alongside. Out and out his mind stretched, reaching through the veil that separated reality from the warp.

And then he felt them.

They were indistinct, faint reflections of presence like shadows in darkness. They were not in the warp; even before his pact with Messenger, Zacherys could tell the approach of a ship by its wake in the immaterium. They were somewhere else.

What are they, he asked? Where are they?

Between here and there, in their little tunnels burrowed through dimensions. The children of the Dark Prince – you call them eldar.

Zacherys strained to focus on their location, but could not fix upon them. They were close, within the system. He broke off the search and forced himself back to his mortal senses.

'Gessart, we might have a problem,' he barked over the comm.

Out of glimmering stars of silver, the eldar ships emerged into real space, a little over twenty thousand kilometres away on the starboard bow. Gessart cursed the rudimentary scanner arrays of the *Lady Bountiful*, which were painfully short-ranged and slow. He opened up a channel to the *Vengeful*.

'Kholich, I'm transmitting coordinates. Give me a full augur sweep of that area. Three eldar ships detected. I want to know course, speed and type in two minutes.'

Gessart's fingers danced over the transmitter controls as he sent the information to the strike cruiser.

'We have to assume they are hostile,' he said as he stabbed the transmit rune. Zacherys, Nicz, Lehenhart and Ustrekh were with him in the bridge while the others oversaw the transfer of the cargo containers from the hold to the bays of the *Vengeful*. 'How much longer until we have what we need?'

'Not long enough,' replied Nicz. 'Assuming they come for us as quick as they can.'

'They will,' said Zacherys. 'They are predators and they are hunting. I feel their desire for the kill.'

Gessart flexed his gauntleted fingers with agitation.

'If we cut and run now, we might get away,' he muttered, more to himself than his companions. 'But then we will have to find more supplies before we reach the Eye. Yet, we have no idea of their strength or intent. A stiff warning may force them to break off. They cannot know our numbers either.'

'I say we fight,' said Ustrekh. 'They've come here looking for easy pickings. They'll have little stomach for a real battle.'

Gessart turned to Lehenhart, knowing the veteran would have his own thoughts on the matter.

'It won't take them long to get here,' said Lehenhart. 'Whatever we're going to do, we have to decide quickly. If we leave it too late to run, their ships can easily overhaul a strike cruiser. If we're going to fight, we had best start preparing our defences.'

Gessart sighed. That observation didn't make the choice any easier. The comm chimed in his ear before he could say anything else.

'This is *Vengeful*,' came Kholich's tinny voice. 'Confirm three vessels on a closing course. Warships, cruiser-class. We're beating to orders, arming weapon batteries and setting plasma reactors to battle readiness. Do you wish us to break from docking?'

Gessart glared at the main screen, searching for a sign of the attackers but they were still too far away to be seen against the darkness of space. On the scanner, he could see the merchant ships closest to the eldar turning away, scattering in all directions like sheep before wolves.

'Remain docked,' said Gessart.

'Captain, we will not have battle manoeuvrability whilst attached to the *Lady Bountiful*.'

'Do not question my orders! Continue loading until the enemy are ten thousand kilometres away and then break docking. Take up escort position on the *Lady Bountiful*. We will remain aboard the trader. Signal the civilian fleet to maintain formation and make best speed to our location.'

'Understood, captain.'

The link crackled and fell silent. With a sub-vocal order, he switched the comm to his command channel, addressing the Space Marines of his force.

'Arm the crew,' he said. 'Let them fight for their vessel alongside us. If nothing else, they will be a distraction to the enemy. Remember that we do not fight for the Emperor, nor to protect these people and their ships. This is a battle we must win because our survival depends upon it. Fail here and we are doomed. Better to die in battle now than to eke out a worthless existence drifting the stars. Our destiny is in our hands and though we are no longer slaves to the Imperium, we are still Space Marines!'

The eldar were not dissuaded from their attack by the presence of the *Vengeful*. The three warships swooped in for the kill, sleek, fast and deadly. On the *Lady Bountiful*'s flickering scanner, Gessart watched the pirates circling around one of the other merchantmen.

'Detect laser weaponry fire,' Kholich reported from the strike cruiser. 'They are targeting the engines of the *Valdiatius Five*. Shall we move to intercept, captain?'

Gessart quickly assessed the situation on the scanner. As well as the *Lady Bountiful*, three other ships were already within range of the *Vengeful*'s batteries. The rest of the convoy were making slow progress and the eldar would fall upon each in turn without having to risk a confrontation with the strike cruiser if it maintained its current position.

'Put yourself between the raiders and the rest of the convoy,' he told Kholich. 'Force them towards our position.'

'Affirmative, captain, moving to intercept,' replied Kholich.

'Engage at long range only,' Gessart added. It was unlikely the eldar would risk boarding a Space Marine vessel, but he didn't want to risk losing the strike cruiser. He turned to Nicz, who was at the helm and engine controls. 'Can you manoeuvre this piece of scrap?'

'Engines and control systems responding well,' replied Nicz without looking up. 'The ship's a mess on the outside, but Loil kept the important functions well maintained.'

'Can you simulate thruster difficulties?'

Nicz glanced at Gessart, guessing his intent.

'I can set them up with intermittent firing,' he said. 'We'll fall behind the rest of the ships and make ourselves an easy target.'

'Do it,' said Gessart, returning his attention to the scanner screen.

As he had hoped, the eldar were unwilling to tackle the strike cruiser directly, despite having more ships. As the *Vengeful* cut through the scattered ships of the convoy, the pirates broke away from their attack and retreated, putting several thousand kilometres between themselves and the escort.

The *Lady Bountiful* trembled violently as Nicz misfired the engines. His armour was bathed with an orange glow as warning lights flickered across the panel in front of him.

'Venting plasma,' he announced.

The ship shook again and rocked to starboard as a plume of super-heated gas exploded from emergency exhausts along the portside stern. Nicz was deliberately clumsy in his attempts to correct their course, causing the ship to list sideways for several minutes while the main engines stuttered with flaring blasts of fire. Another glance at the scanner confirmed to Gessart that the three other merchant ships close to the *Lady Bountiful* were pulling away, heading directly from the eldar attack.

'Come on, take the bait,' Gessart muttered. 'Look at us, we're crippled. Come and get us!'

His attention was fixed on the scanner display, but the vague blobs of green that represented the eldar ships were too inaccurate to track any heading changes. He growled with frustration and fought the urge to slam his fist through the useless piece of equipment.

'Kholich, report!' he snapped. 'What are the enemy doing?'

'They've altered course towards you, captain,' Kholich reported. 'Not at full speed. They seem cautious.'

'They're waiting to see what you are going to do,' Nicz cut in across the comm. 'Move further away from our position.'

'Captain?' Kholich was uncertain, surprised by the break in protocol.

'Move out of weapons range of the *Lady Bountiful*,' Gessart said. 'But stand ready to come about and make full speed to our position if needed. Keep me informed of the eldar's movement, these scanners are worthless.'

'Affirmative, captain.'

Gessart broke the link and rounded on Nicz, stalking across the bridge to slam an open hand into the Space Marine's armoured chest.

'Stay off the command channel!' Gessart growled. 'I am still in charge.'

Nicz knocked away his leader's hand and stepped forwards, the grille of his helm a few centimetres from Gessart's.

'You're just guessing,' Nicz replied calmly. 'You haven't any more idea what to do than the rest of us. We should be aboard the *Vengeful*, chasing down these scum.'

'They would run rings around us, and you know it,' snapped Gessart. 'If they split up, we'll have no chance of catching any of them. We need to draw them in, convince them to board. That's when we'll have the advantage.'

Nicz stepped back and his shock was clear in his voice.

'You intend to counter-board one of their ships?'

'If possible. We will have to see how badly they want to fight.'

Nicz said nothing but a shake of the head made it clear what he thought of Gessart's plan. Gessart turned away and returned to his place at the command controls. His fingers drummed the side of the scanner display as he waited to find out what the eldar would do next.

'They're using cutters on the starboard bow!' Lehenhart reported. 'Decks six and seven.'

'Meet me at Lehenhart's position,' Gessart told his warriors. One of the eldar warships had snared the *Lady Bountiful* in a gravity net and had pulled her alongside to board. The other two raiders had taken up a position a few thousand kilometres away to block the path of the *Vengeful* if it tried to intervene.

Gessart swung around to face Nicz. 'Can I trust you to keep an eye on the other two ships?'

'I'll tell you if either of them tries to board,' the Space Marine replied.

Gessart nodded and ran out of the bridge. He pounded along the uppermost deck until he came to a stairwell. Ducking sideways to fit his bulk through the low door, he hurled himself down the metal steps three at a time, the mesh buckling slightly under the impact of his boots. Three decks down, he squeezed into a narrow passageway flanked by rows of small cabins. Turning to his left he headed towards the bow of the ship. After a few hundred metres the corridor split to the left and right. Bolter fire ran along the bare metal walls from starboard.

Unslinging his storm bolter, Gessart slowed to a jog, eyes scanning the open doorways ahead. He saw nothing until Lehenhart advanced into view along the gallery at the end of the passage, his bionic right hand holding his bolter in a firing position, serrated combat knife in the left. Bright blue lances of laser light erupted from ahead of the Space Marine, zipping past him as he shifted to his left and returned fire, his bolter blazing three times, the roar of each round echoing along the corridor around Gessart.

Glancing over his shoulder at the thump of booted feet, Gessart saw Willusch, Gerhart and Johun a few dozen strides behind him. Over the comm, he heard the reports of others closing in from aft.

Lehenhart had moved out of sight; as Gessart turned into the starboard gallery he saw the Space Marine holding a landing ahead, firing down the stairwell. Five eldar bodies lay sprawled on the decking. Gessart paused for a moment to examine the dead aliens.

Each was as tall as a Space Marine, though far slighter of build. They had thin, angular faces, their almond-shaped eyes wide with the gaze of the dead, ears slightly pointed, brows high and arched. They appeared to have no uniform, though all five wore close-fitting tunics of iridescent scales. One was swathed in the ragged remains of a long red cloak, half his chest missing from a bolt detonation; another was sprawled across the corridor face-down, two holes in the back of his high-collared, dark blue coat. Two of the others were female, their hair wound in elaborate blonde braids spattered with bright red blood, skin-tight suits of black and white beneath their mesh armour; the last half-sat against the wall, narrow chin on chest, head shaven but for a blue scalplock, wearing a broad-shouldered black jacket studded with glistening gems, his legs naked but for knee-high boots.

Long-barrelled lasrifles lay on the floor next to each body, of similar design but each decorated with different coloured gemstones and swirling golden filigrees. Gessart picked up one of the weapons and examined it. It was elegant, powered by some form of crystal cell in the thin stock of the weapon. It crumpled easily as he tightened his grip, no sturdier than the creature that had wielded it.

Reaching Lehenhart, Gessart leaned over the balustrade and saw lithe figures darting from cover to cover on the landing below. He snatched two fragmentation grenades from his belt, thumbed the activation studs and dropped them over the edge. The stairwell rang with twin detonations; shrapnel and smoke filled the enclosed space, a lingering scream signalling that he had found at least one target.

'Do we wait, or go to them?' asked Lehenhart.

Gessart dragged up his memory of the ship's layout; he had to assume the eldar had scanned the vessel and knew something of its configuration as well. The upper four decks only extended for a third of the ship and did not connect to the hold directly. If the eldar were after the cargo – which was no longer aboard – they would have to go down to the lower six decks. With only twenty-five Space Marines to cover the hold, loading bays, docking areas and crew quarters, it would be hard to concentrate any resistance.

'Counter-attack!' Gessart told his warriors. 'Make them pay in blood for ever setting foot on this ship!'

A fusillade of bright blasts and blurring discs filled the stairwell. Gessart recognised shuriken catapult fire amongst the laser shots. He leaned over the railing and unleashed a hail of fire from his storm bolter, the explosive ammunition ripping a trail of splintering metal across the landing below. Slender shapes darted from the shadows and he was engulfed by a hail of razor-sharp projectiles. Pushing himself back, he glanced down at his armour and saw a row of barbed discs embedded across his chest plastron.

'With me,' he growled, pounding down the steps. He heard Lehenhart and the others close behind.

The railing buckled as Gessart grabbed a hold to swing around a turn in the steps. Enemy fire stormed up to meet him; las-bolts seared the paint from his armour while more shurikens sliced through his left arm and leg.

With a leap, he crashed to the landing. There were more than a dozen eldar taking cover in the two doorways; they were dressed in the same strange mix of coats, cloaks and armour he had seen on the bodies above. Quicker than a heartbeat, some of the alien warriors leapt to attack, wielding chainswords with glittering teeth and long blades that gleamed with energy.

Gessart let loose with another burst of fire, shredding an eldar directly in front of him. Before he could adjust his aim, two more were upon him, the teeth of their chainswords shrieking as they skittered across his right shoulder pad and backpack. He swung the storm bolter like a club, aiming for the head of one of his attackers. The eldar dropped cat-like to all fours and then leapt past, dragging her chainsword across the side of Gessart's helm. He took a step back, trying to keep both assailants in view.

Lehenhart arrived at a run, smashing his fist into the back of one of the eldar. The alien bent awkwardly and flopped to the ground, limbs twitching. Gessart had no time to spare a further glance for his warriors coming in behind him as more eldar appeared at the doorway ahead, pistols and swords gripped by slender fingers.

Gessart turned his right shoulder towards them and charged with a roar. Most of the eldar scattered quickly from his path but one was caught with nowhere to go; he was smashed bloodily into the wall by the headlong rush. A warning siren sounded in Gessart's ears as blades bit deep into his backpack and legs, the eldar like a swarm of wasps, darting in to strike before swiftly retreating out of reach.

The Space Marine swung a booted foot at the closest, looking to sweep away the pirate's legs. The eldar nimbly somersaulted over Gessart's attack and landed with sure-footed grace to fire his pistol directly into Gessart's face.

Gessart's finger tightened instinctively on the trigger as he reeled back. Through the cracked lenses of his helm he saw the alien bisected by bolts, sheared through by detonations across his scale-armoured stomach.

Detecting the patter of feet behind him, Gessart swung around to confront a new attacker, but found only empty air. The eldar were falling back, disappearing quickly along both passageways. Willusch and Lehenhart set off after them but Gessart called them back.

'They'll pick each of us off if we split up,' he said. 'Let's not run into an ambush.'

He quickly took stock of the scene. Two of his warriors lay still on the steps, their armour and flesh cut through to the bone in dozens of places. Another three were bleeding heavily from wounds to their arms and legs.

'Report in!' he barked over the comm.

The replies painted a complicated picture. Some of his Space Marines had fended off an eldar advance along the portside, causing significant casualties for no losses. Another group had been caught out on their way to support Gessart and two of their number had fallen in moments before the eldar had swiftly withdrawn. Those who had been stationed by the aft holds were still making their way towards the bow and had yet to encounter any foes.

Unfortunately the *Lady Bountiful* had no internal scanners to keep track of the pirates. Gessart looked for Heynke, who had the force's only functional auspex. The Space Marine was at the top of the flight of steps, bolter in his hands, guarding the approach from above. His armour appeared undamaged, in stark contrast to the others, who all showed signs of the brief but fierce fight.

'Heynke, use the auspex,' Gessart said, checking the ammunition counter on his storm bolter. Seventeen rounds left. He had two more magazines at his belt. More than enough for the moment.

Heynke hooked his bolter to his belt and unslung the scanning device. His armoured fingers coaxed the machine into life, his helm reflecting the pale yellow of the display. Heynke moved the auspex around, trying to get a fix on the lifesigns of the eldar.

'Most have reached the upper decks,' he reported. 'Too much interference from the superstructure for an accura... Hold on, something strange.'

'What is it?' demanded Gessart leaping up the steps to stand beside Heynke.

'Look for yourself,' the Space Marine said, holding the auspex towards Gessart.

The semi-circular screen was filled with bright lines – the power conduits running through the walls of the ship. The eldar showed as fainter traces, little more than pale yellow smudges. The largest concentration was two decks above in the crew mess hall. They were not moving.

'What do you think they are up to?' asked Heynke.

Gessart did not know and any speculation he might offer was abruptly stopped by a buzzing over the comm. The static lasted for a few moments, scaling higher in pitch, and then stopped. There was a pause before he heard a voice, the words slightly stilted with a mechanical edge to them.

'Commander of the Space Marines,' it said. 'I have found the air upon which you speak. Heed the wisdom of my words. This loss of life is senseless and is not of benefit to myself or to you. I have become aware that we should not be adversaries. I detect the eyes that see far and know that you are aware of where I am. I have knowledge that you would wish I share with you. Meet me where we can hold conference and we will discuss this matter like civilised creatures.'

The link crackled again and fell silent.

'Was that…?' said Lehenhart. 'Did that bastard override our comm-frequency?'

'How?' said Heynke.

'Forget how, did you hear what he said?' This was from Freichz. 'He wants a truce!'

Gessart's comm chimed again, signalling a switch to the private channel. He bit back a snarl of frustration at this fresh interruption.

'Yes?' he snapped.

'Gessart, we have a serious problem,' replied Zacherys. 'Ships have broken through the warp boundary. I believe it is the Imperial Navy escort for the convoy.'

'Did you hear the pirate commander?'

'I did. I believe this is the information he wished to pass to us. Somehow he knows that we are protecting the fleet for ourselves. I would recommend that you hear what he has to say.'

'Agreed. Meet me at the aft entrance to the mess hall.' Gessart switched to general transmission. 'Take up guard positions around the mess hall but do not enter. This may be some kind of trick, so stay alert.'

He snapped off more precise orders and instructed Tylo, the Apothecary, to set up an aid station in one of the holds so that the wounded could be tended. With these preparations made, Gessart headed up the stairwell, uncertain what to expect.

Zacherys met Gessart outside the mess hall. There was bright eldar blood splashed across the psyker's armour, some of it still steaming and bubbling. Gessart decided it would be better not to ask. The main doors of the mess hall slid open in front of them and they stepped inside, weapons in hand.

The mess hall was a wide open space, divided by long tables and benches riveted to the floor. At the centre several dozen eldar waited, some of them with weapons ready, most of them lounging across the tables and seats. Gessart's eye was immediately drawn to the one at the centre of the group, who leaned against the end of a table with his legs casually crossed, arms folded. He was dressed in a long coat of green and red diamond patches, which reached to his booted ankles. A ruff of white and blue feathers jutted from the high collar, acting as a wispy halo for his narrow, sharp-cheeked face. His skin was almost white, his hair black and pulled back in a single braid plaited with shining thread. Dark eyes fixed on Gessart as the Space Marine stomped across the metal floor and stopped about ten metres away.

The eldar straightened and his lips moved faintly. The words that echoed across the hall came not from his mouth, but from a brooch upon his lapel, shaped like a thin, stylised skull.

'What is the name of he who has the honour of addressing Aradryan, Admiral of the Winter Gulf?'

'Gessart. Is that a translator?'

'I understand your crude language, but will not sully my lips with its barbaric grunts,' came the metallic reply.

Zacherys moved up next to Gessart and Aradryan's eyes widened with shock and fear. He looked at Gessart with a furrowed brow.

'That you consort with this sort of creature is ample evidence that you are no longer in service to the Emperor of Mankind. We have encountered other renegades like yourselves in the past. My assumptions are proven correct.'

'Zacherys is one of us,' said Gessart with a glance towards the psyker. 'What do you mean?'

'Can you not see that which dwells within him?' The machine spoke in a flat tone but Aradryan's incredulity was clear.

'What do you want?' demanded Gessart.

'To save needless loss for both of us,' Aradryan replied, opening his hands in a placating gesture. 'You will soon be aware that those whose duty it is to protect these vessels are close at hand. If we engage in this pointless fighting they will come upon us both. This does not serve my purpose or yours. I propose that we settle our differences in a peaceful way. I am certain that we can come to an agreement that accommodates the desires of both parties.'

'A truce? We divide the spoils of the convoy?'

'It brings happiness to my spirit to find that you understand my intent. I feared greatly that you would respond to my entreaty with the blind ignorance that blights so many of your species.'

'I have become a recent acquaintance of compromise,' said Gessart. 'I find it makes better company than the alternatives. What agreement do you propose?'

'There is time enough for us both to take what we wish before these new arrivals can intervene in our affairs. We have no interest in the clumsy weapons and goods these vessels carry. You may take as much as you wish.'

'If you don't want the cargo, what is your half of the deal?'

'Everything else,' said Aradryan with a sly smile.

'He means the crews,' whispered Zacherys.

'That is correct, tainted one,' said Aradryan. The eldar pirate fixed his large eyes on Gessart, the hint of a smile twisting his thin lips. 'Do you accede to these demands, or do you wish that we expend more energy killing one another in a pointless display of pride? You must know that I am aware of how few warriors you have should you choose to fight.'

'How long before the escort arrives?' Gessart asked Zacherys.

'Two days at the most.'

'You have enough time to unload whatever you wish and will not be hampered by my ships or my warriors. You have my assurance that you will be unmolested if you offer me the same.'

Gessart stared at Aradryan for some time, but it was impossible to discern the alien's thoughts from his expression. He knew that he could no more trust an eldar than he could take his eye off Nicz, but there seemed little choice. He suppressed a sigh, wondering what it was that he had done to deserve a succession of impossible decisions lately: between protecting innocents and killing the enemy on Archimedon, between millions of rebels and a host of daemons at Helmabad, and now he had to make a bargain with an alien or risk being destroyed by those he had once fought alongside.

'The terms are agreed,' said Gessart. 'I will order my warriors to suspend fighting. I have no control over the crews of the convoy.'

'We are capable of dealing with such problems in our own way,' said Aradryan. 'Be thankful that this day you have found me in a generous mood.'

Gessart hefted his storm bolter and fixed the eldar pirate with a cold stare.

'Don't give me an excuse to change my mind.'

All available space aboard the *Vengeful* was packed with pillaged supplies. Crates filled the hangars that had berthed lost Thunderhawks; ammunition boxes were piled high in the chapel and Reclusiam; crew quarters that would never again house battle-brothers were used as storage for medical wares and maintenance parts. Gessart was exceptionally pleased with the haul; they had enough to survive for several years if necessary.

He stood on the bridge of the strike cruiser as it broke dock from the civilian transport. It had taken more than a day to ferry everything across, and two of the convoy's ships had been left untouched: there simply wasn't room to take on board anything else. As the *Vengeful* powered away one of the eldar cruisers slipped past, the swirl of its gravity nets hooking onto the cargo hauler. The alien ship glided serenely on, its yellow hull fluctuating with black tiger stripes, its solar sails shimmering gold.

'Are we ready to jump?' Gessart asked Zacherys.

'At your command,' came the reply.

Gessart caught Nicz staring at him.

'Don't tell me that you disapprove,' said Gessart.

'Not at all, quite the opposite,' replied Nicz. 'I wondered if Helmabad was a unique moment, but I see that I might be wrong.'

'Let me convince you,' said Gessart, striding to the gunnery control panel.

The systems had been at full power since their first arrival so he knew the eldar would not detect a spike in power. The lock-on was another matter. His fingers danced over the controls as gun ports slid open along the starboard side of the strike cruiser. The eldar ship was only a few hundred kilometres away and the targeting metriculators found their range within seconds.

'What are you doing?' said Nicz.

'Leaving the Imperial Navy something to play with,' Gessart replied with a smile.

Gessart tapped in the command for a single salvo and pressed the firing rune. The *Vengeful* shook as the ship unleashed a full broadside at the eldar cruiser. On the main screen explosions blossomed around the alien ship, snapping the main sail mast and rippling along the hull. Flames billowed from exploding gases, the pressure of their release causing the cruiser to yaw violently.

'Zacherys, take us into the warp.'

DARK SON

A giant of iron and fire lit the shrine, bathing the walls with flickers of orange and red. Its eyes were dark embers, its flesh flame beneath cracked metal skin. Seven figures stood bathed in the light; armoured in plates of dark blue and black, heads covered with ornately horned helms. In gauntleted hands they held their long, broad blades, the edges of their klaives gleaming in the ruddy glare. Behind them in the shadows lurked others, pale flesh and flashing eyes half-glimpsed in the darkness.

Another entered. She was clad as the others, though her armour was more ornate, her chosen weapons a pair of curving demi-klaives that glittered with energy.

'Fear,' said the klaivex, her voice issuing as a low whisper from her helm.

The word hung in the air as she paced back and forth in front of the immobile warriors. Seven pairs of eyes followed the klaivex as she strode from one end of the line to the other. They watched for any pause, for any moment of hesitation, fingers curling on the hafts of their weapons.

'Fear drives us. Our entire existence is now predicated on a dread so utterly damning that we cannot name it. Our scattered kindred, each are driven by this fear, even those who live in the Dark City below.'

The klaivex, Naremun, stopped at the centre of the line, three strides away from seven deadly fighters seeking the merest moment of weakness. She was directly in front of Kolidaran, staring straight at him. Her words seem directed at him and he wondered if she knew of the ambition in his heart. Of course she knew, for it had been her own ambition and was shared by any that became incubi.

'We do not refuse fear. We cannot forget our fear any more than we can forget to breathe the air. It is part of us.'

Naremun started to pace again, almost but not quite turning her back on her incubi followers. Kolidaran sensed Jurathi beside him tense but the warrior made no move. Like Kolidaran, Jurathi knew that the time was not yet right. Naremun was not truly unaware; she was simply testing them, teasing them. Three strides was a short distance, but not great enough to attack and strike a clean blow uncontested.

And it would take a single killing blow to defeat Naremun.

Kolidaran had seen her fight, as had the others. He had seen the way she had cut down Siamnath and Laghinuir and Norrianar. He had seen the klaivex butcher her way through orks and humans and fellow eldar.

There would be no second strike.

He could wait. Life amongst the incubi taught nothing if not patience. The time would come when Naremun was truly vulnerable and then he would make his move. Not before.

'To face fear is true strength.' The klaivex faced her followers once more, her tone conveying disappointment at their inaction. 'We must embrace the fear and become one with it. An age ago our ancestors created a terror so profound the galaxy still shakes in dread. The faithless, the cowards, ran from that terror and hid themselves away on their craftworlds. Our kin in the Dark City cower no less, using the pain and dread of others to mask their own.'

She paused again, silhouetted against the burning idol of Khaine. For a moment her dark outline was swallowed up by the flames and smoke, seeming to become invested with the image of the war-god.

'We do not shirk from our fear. Let the misguided seek to shackle the gifts Khaine gave to us. We do not shy away from our fear: the fear that we are creatures of deep hate and irresistible anger. This is not our dread. Our dread is to be meaningless. What we fear is the passing of a life without achievement, without import. To die and be consumed by that terror we created, without first making a mark upon the universe, that is failure. That is fear.'

Naremun stepped away from the idol, her demi-klaives still raised to the guard position.

'None of you are worthy,' she snapped. 'None of you dare to challenge me. Your fear of death overpowers you. It makes you weak.'

'To die on your blades is failure,' said Aneathuin. 'Wasteful.'

'Yet if you are to succeed, if you are to become klaivex and gain your place and glory, you must dare it. Success cannot be gained without risking failure. Victory is the twin maiden of defeat. Death is the father of life.'

The klaivex shook her head and her blades lowered a fraction. When she spoke again, Kolidaran thought she sounded tired but knew this was also a ruse, a feigned show of weakness.

'Is there none who would dare to step forward? Do you not feel the hunger?' Her voice became a rasping shout. 'Do you not hate me enough?'

Empty questions, Kolidaran knew. They all wanted to be klaivex. They all felt the hunger gnawing inside them, the source of that existential fear that Naremun spoke of. And they certainly hated her. Her berating, her bullying, her sarcasm and loathing were enough to wake hatred hot enough to burn like the idol of Khaine. Her barbs to the pride of her warriors were a constant agony. But as the deaths of Siamnath and Laghinuir and Norrianar had demonstrated, Khaine did not reward those who struck out in blind fury.

Amongst the flame and smoke, Khaine's heart was ice. The Bloody-Handed demanded the slaying to be cold and calculating. Kolidaran would die no other way.

'Embrace the fear and make it your own. Become the terror. Step into th–'

Something struck Kolidaran in the back of the head.

He rolled with the blow, tumbling forward and turning at the same time. His attacker leapt forward and Kolidaran caught a glimpse of Khissareth's face beneath the hood of his acolyte's cowl, the fire lighting up his snarling face and wide eyes. Khissareth kicked out, aiming not for Kolidaran but the haft of his klaive.

The weapon flew from the incubi's grasp and spun above his head. Kolidaran jumped to his feet, but too slow. The acolyte snatched the spinning blade out of the air. With quick steps Kolidaran retreated a few paces, staying on the balls of his feet, ready to move again.

'I have your weapon,' crowed Khissareth. He brought the klaive up to the attack position, elbows out, right foot forward. 'Now I am incubi.'

'You have it,' said Kolidaran. 'Can you keep it?'

Incensed, Khissareth lashed out: a wild blow that Kolidaran easily ducked. The acolyte stabbed towards Kolidaran's midriff but the veteran warrior had expected the attack and sidestepped with a laugh.

'You should not have wasted your victory with gloating,' said the incubi.

'I shall be the last who laughs,' snapped Khissareth, lunging again.

Kolidaran backtracked, dodging the tip of the klaive by a hair's-breadth. He cartwheeled to his left as Khissareth came again. Stab and sweep and thrust all missed their mark by the finest margins, Kolidaran always a moment ahead of his attacker. The clatter of Kolidaran's boots and Khissareth's grunts were the only sounds to break the stillness.

Eyes fixed on his opponent, the incubi lowered his left shoulder as if about to move in that direction. A momentary look of triumph gleamed in Khissareth's gaze as he swung the klaive to intercept the dodge. It was a feint, a simple one at that, and Kolidaran shifted his weight and span to the right, moving past the end of the blade.

He arrowed his straightened fingers into Khissareth's throat. As the acolyte gave a choked cry and stepped back, Kolidaran followed, grabbing hold of the klaive's haft in his left hand. The incubi drove an armoured knee into Khissareth's gut and brought his foot down into the side of his foe's knee in one motion, wrenching the klaive from Khissareth's grasp as he fell.

Another kick sent the would-be-incubi sprawling to his back.

'Fear drove you to act in haste,' said Kolidaran. He relaxed, the klaive held to one side. 'The fear that no opportunity would come forced your hand too early. The klaivex's words bit deep, did they not?'

'I regret nothing,' said Khissareth but his expression made his defiant words hollow. His eyes shone with tears as they fixed on Kolidaran's blade and his jaw trembled as he spoke. 'No success without failure. Just end it.'

'Not so easy, not for you,' said Kolidaran. 'You are the first to try to take my klaive since I pulled it from Nathrikh's dead hands. May you be the last.'

He looked at the other acolytes who were still hiding in the shadows. Turning, he handed Jurathi the klaive – there was no incentive for his fellow incubi to take advantage of his disarmed state, the klaivex was the object of their ambitions.

Further words would only cheapen the lesson, so Kolidaran advanced on Khissareth in silence. The acolyte tried to turn and run but his shattered knee failed him. Kolidaran stooped over his fallen foe, driving his fists into the acolyte's back, breaking ribs and bruising organs.

Snatching up Khissareth by his robe, Kolidaran turned the youth to face him. With a few simple moves the challenger was sent to the floor again, wailing, his broken arms trembling uselessly. Another flash of hands and Khissareth's right eye was gone, a bloody hole in its place.

The acolyte's screams echoed harshly around the chamber.

'Take him,' snarled Kolidaran, pointing towards the door. His anger was not directed at Khissareth, not now that he had been punished. Kolidaran's ire was reserved for himself; for appearing vulnerable to the acolyte. 'Dump him in the undercity where the ur-ghuls will make sport of his flesh.'

A trio of acolytes emerged from the darkness and dragged away the screaming youth.

Kolidaran retrieved his klaive and turned to Naremun. He raised the blade briefly to his face and then bowed. As he straightened up he did not raise the tip of his klaive, but left it pointing at Naremun.

He looked straight at her and though it was impossible to see his expression his intent was clear enough. She knew open challenge would never be made, and because he had stated his purpose – though the statement was silently made – she would have to be on her guard. It could be so tiring, waiting for that moment when another's ambition overcame fear, and she would make a mistake.

Kolidaran was patient. He could wait.

'Apologies for the interruption, klaivex. You were labouring some point about fear, I believe. Please feel free to continue.'

The grand hall of the starship *Astheakh* rang with raucous laughter and terrified screams. From his vantage point at the head of the stairs leading to Shyadysis Hierarch's chambers Kolidaran watched the warriors from the Kabal of the Ascendant Spear making sport of their slaves. Some were made to fight for the pleasure of their captors, chained together and armed only with blunted knives to prolong the combat. Others suffered the attentions of Likha, Shyadysis's haemonculus; she was busy inserting slivers of metal beneath acid-scarred flesh atop a bloodstained table at the centre of the chamber. The least sophisticated simply beat and whipped their living possessions, creating a chorus of wails and howls with their blows.

To Kolidaran's left, while the incubi ensured no interloper could enter the private rooms at the top of the stair, Shyadysis watched the proceedings from a throne made of bones and black marble, his favoured courtiers sat on the steps that led up to his dais. The hierarch was dressed in a long robe of dark blue, hung with charms and jewellery made from the same materials as his chair. Shyadysis regarded the spectacles being put on for his benefit with an affected smile, his thin lips coloured black against pale skin, eyes rimmed with kohl. His eyes never stopped moving, though whether he was keeping vigil for signs of treachery or was merely distracted by the numerous displays Kolidaran could not tell.

At the right shoulder of the hierarch stood Naremun, head turning slowly from one end of the hall to the other as she kept watch, her demi-klaives in her hands ready to counter any attack. Few were allowed drawn weapons in the presence of the hierarch but the incubi were above the squabbles and politics of the kabal.

The crack of whips, the moans of the slaves, the jeers and cheers of the audience was a pale reflection of the torment being inflicted. Kolidaran could feel the real pain and fear and desperation of the slaves like a slick beneath his skin; a palpable, slithering aura of agony. Here in the webway, just a dream's sliver away from the raw Chaos of the warp, the pulsating energy amplified the sensation, making the incubi's flesh tingle gently.

'Do you miss partaking in such entertainments?' asked Jurathi, standing on the opposite side of the sweeping stairs. 'The raw joy of pain and death?'

'No,' said Kolidaran, keeping alert for any untoward movement below.

'Not even a little?'

'No.'

'Sometimes I wonder what life would have held for me if I had not come to the shrine. Perhaps I would be a hierarch by now.'

'You would most likely be dead, or some fawning minion in the lesser ranks.' Kolidaran looked at the mass below and sneered inside his helm. 'I detest them. They are no better than the beasts that they torture. Look at them, Jurathi. See them for what they really are. They are animals, driven by their base instincts, masquerading as eldar. Strip away the veneer of civilisation, the ranks and customs of the kabal, and they are simply low creatures vying for scraps, debasing themselves to survive.'

'I can see why you left your kabal, if you think so little of life in the Dark City.'

'I had no kabal,' Kolidaran replied softly. 'Not even the scraps from an archon's table to feed upon. My first memories are of Low Commorragh when my mother, a slave-bitch who escaped from the Corespur, gave her life to protect me from a prowling ur-ghul. I strived, Jurathi, and fought tooth and claw just to elevate myself to the slums of Sec Maegra. I feasted on the decayed fruit of Khaides to survive.'

'Such an able fighter would surely have found swift acceptance by a kabal,' said his companion. 'Many recruit from the fighting dens of Sec Maegra.'

'What do I want for the charity of some hierarch or archon? Pets, nothing more, even those that call themselves warriors. No, I wanted no part of that life. I crept and killed my way through Sec Maegra and dared the territories of the hellions in the Middle Darkness looking for something with more purpose.'

'Then why did you not seek sanctuary in the Wych Cults of the Bone Middens? A natural fighter such as yourself would have quickly risen in reputation and power. You could be a wolf of a hekatrix now rather than a cur snapping at the heels of Naremun.'

'I considered it only briefly,' admitted Kolidaran. 'I feel no shame to confess that the dire shadows of Aelindrach threatened too much of a hazard, and so I moved up through the city and came upon the shrine. Perhaps it called to me.'

'Your climb has stalled of late, Kolidaran.'

'Nor have I seen you show the slightest inclination to challenge the klaivex. Neither of us is a fool.'

'But it burns you, does it not? To be told by another where and for whom we will fight? To see Naremun stand beside an archon as bodyguard? I see now why you took Nathrikh's klaive so readily. We all have ambition, but you have something else to prove. You are gutter scum, Kolidaran, acting the part of warrior. It does not matter how far you stretch, your reach will never extend beyond such lowly birth.'

'Better to outreach one's means than be a contented, ignorant slave. And look, here comes another.'

Kolidaran had noticed a slender female emerge from a small door behind the throne. It was the *Astheakh*'s commander, Neastra Daemuis. Naremun raised her blades in the blink of an eye, but the ship's captain lowered to one knee some distance from the hierarch.

Words were exchanged, too quiet for Kolidaran to hear. He did see the sharp look of delight that crossed Shyadysis's face, though. Even as the hierarch stood up and held out his hands for the attention of his subjects, Naremun's voice came from the communicator in the incubi's helm.

'An Alaitocii warship approaches,' warned the klaivex. 'Our employer wishes to attack. Ready yourselves at the hierarch's chambers. We will lead the assault.'

In one of the wider branches of the webway the *Astheakh* came upon the vessel of the craftworld eldar. There was a brief exchange of gunfire, its effects much reduced by the strange conditions of the webway, before the *Astheakh* closed to within range, launching forth barb-like boarding spines to fix the enemy ship in place. While flights of attack craft carried other warriors towards the rear quarters the incubi formed a vanguard piercing the main decks of the craftworld starship like the point of a blade. Behind came the hierarch and his kabalite warriors, adding weight to the precision of the incubi attack.

As the incubi formed the sword-point of the whole force, so did Naremun lead her fighters from the front. It was not unknown for a klaivex to be set upon by one of his or her followers mid-battle but it was rare; close combat was fraught enough without slaying one's own warriors in its midst.

Kolidaran had no mind to usurp the klaivex at this time and focused his efforts on slaying the eldar of Alaitoc that crewed the starship. The craftworld warship had been taken by surprise by Shyadysis's attack and the hastily-armed foe was little threat.

Fighting just behind and to the right of Naremun, Jurathi further still to his right, Kolidaran cut down those who evaded the attention of the klaivex. They were few in the confines of the gun chamber where the boarding had started, but enough to wet Kolidaran's blade. He stepped to his left as a crew member aimed a laser pistol at him, the blast of white searing past the incubi's shoulder. The craftworlder did not get a second shot; Kolidaran's klaive cut the head from the Alaitocii with a single sweep.

They breached the corridor beyond the gun deck and turned left while kabalites spilled to the right. The high walls of the corridor were topped with narrow windows beyond which could be seen the swirling rivulets of the webway. The mournful wail of a warning alarm echoed around Kolidaran as he and the other incubi advanced towards the prow of the starship.

The alarm faded but the silence lasted only a moment. Fighting had broken out behind the incubi; raucous shouts from the kabalites alerted Kolidaran to a craftworlder counter-attack.

'We return to the fight, follow me!' snapped Naremun, pushing back through her group of warriors. Close behind, Kolidaran followed back down the corridor to where half-clad wyches were cutting their way through a press of Alaitocii crew, the hierarch's kabalites fanning out through the surrounding rooms and galleries around them.

Past the swirl of swords and half-naked flesh Kolidaran saw a sight that sent a shudder of pleasant expectation flooding through him. Warriors were assaulting the wych cultists, armoured in overlapping plates of dark green, purring chainswords cutting, shuriken pistols rending. Striking Scorpions, Aspect Warriors of Khaine who followed the teachings of the coward Karandras.

Here was a true test of Kolidaran's martial skills and a chance to prove himself worthy in the eyes of his companions. Kolidaran could see the prize he sought on the chest of each warrior; a precious spirit stone that would absorb the essence of the Striking Scorpion when he or she was slain. Kolidaran would take the soulstone of one of the dead Aspect Warriors for himself, break it and corrupt it to create his Tormentor and secure himself true rank and position within the incubi.

Cutting down the last of the Alaitocii crew around him Kolidaran chose his prey. An Aspect Warrior caught his eye as the craftworlder met sword-to-sword with one of the wyches, catching her twin daggers on the flat of his chainsword. She fought more swiftly, but his armour bore the brunt of her strikes, sparks of energy flying from her blades as they struck. He brought up his pistol to her face and she ducked, to be met by the rising point of his chainsword. Her face split in twain, the wych fell to the ground, her beautiful features now a gory mess.

'Death comes for you, little scorpion!' Kolidaran snarled as he launched himself at the Aspect Warrior, seeking to cut him down before he recovered from his duel with the wych. Before he could strike, the Striking Scorpion saw Kolidaran coming and threw himself at the incubi with equal determination.

The Aspect Warrior's chainsword plunged towards Kolidaran's head. The incubi swayed back, his klaive rising to deflect the attack. Spinning, Kolidaran delivered a kick to the Striking Scorpion's midriff, sending him staggering. His foe's chainsword flashed up to ward away a strike towards the chest, sending the klaive's gleaming head screaming past his shoulder.

The pair parted and circled, feinting and jabbing with their weapons. The Aspect Warrior's eye lenses glinted red as if filled with rage as he launched another flurry of attacks, the mandiblasters mounted on the sides of his helm spitting las-shots, chainsword weaving left and right. Kolidaran dodged the mandiblaster attack, ducked and swerved aside from each blow, the tip of his klaive carving figures of eight in front of him.

His chance for a swift kill had passed and Kolidaran's frustration grew. He parried each incoming strike, waiting for his moment to despatch his enemy with a decapitation blow but no opening presented. Kolidaran's patience snapped and he risked a hasty lunge, only for a chance salvo from the Striking Scorpion's pistol to catch him in the thigh. As Kolidaran's leg buckled the craftworlder followed up with a blistering series of strikes towards head and throat, forcing Kolidaran to catch the rasping teeth of the chainsword on the haft of his klaive, razor-bladed fangs spitting sparks from the metal.

Kolidaran saw the Striking Scorpion's right shoulder dipping. Ignoring the pain in his leg, he straightened to bring down his klaive in the killing blow, seeking to part the warrior's neck.

A sudden change of direction and a twist to the left sent the klaive stroke wide. It was the same move Kolidaran had employed against Khissareth.

His surprise turned to horror a moment later as the Aspect Warrior's chainsword bit into Kolidaran's lower back, slivers of torn armour spraying to the floor.

Hissing in pain, Kolidaran lurched to one side only to be caught by a backward sweep that struck a glancing blow to the side of the head, shearing away part of his armour, splintering the eye lens on the left side of his face. He staggered and fell, the klaive falling from his numbed grasp, a gasp ripped from his lips.

Kolidaran looked up at the looming Aspect Warrior with a knot of terror in his gut. The Striking Scorpion drew back his chainsword, ready for the killing blow. There was no defence but Kolidaran threw up a warding hand out of raw instinct.

The Striking Scorpion had no time for the death-blow; Naremun attacked from the right, her demi-klaives sending the Aspect Warrior reeling back as the incubi and kabalites pushed onwards. Red tinged the edge of Kolidaran's vision, the scene becoming darker as he watched the melee moving away, leaving him helpless amongst the dead and wounded, his legs devoid of strength, his klaive out of reach.

Moving in and out of consciousness, Kolidaran only dimly viewed what was happening. The fighting around him dissipated, the counterattack of the Aspect Warriors driving the hierarch's warriors back to their boarding craft. A figure appeared to his left, a long two-handed chainsword in its hands. Fear returned as the apparition loomed over him and the incubi recognised the heavier armour and trappings of the Striking Scorpion Exarch, poised to attack.

Kolidaran closed his eyes, awaiting the blow.

After several agonising heartbeats Kolidaran opened his eyes to see the exarch still waiting.

'You face, at my hand, a choice.' The exarch's voice had a steady tempo and rhythm to it, the language not dissimilar to the ancient tongues spoken in Commorragh. The Striking Scorpion raised his blade, assuming a more defensive stance. 'Without prejudice, free from threat, an offer. Choose life, surrender your will, or death.'

Not quite believing what he heard, Kolidaran blinked back tears of dread and pain and squinted up at the exarch.

'For truth?' He laughed, slightly manic. 'You stand with blade ready and claim no coercion? What conditions do you place upon my capitulation?'

'Your life, and your fate, to me. Your blade, and your loyalty, to Alaitoc. Your rage, and your hate, to Khaine. Natural warriors, such as you, are rare. More yet, you will learn, from me. A promise, upon my word, of peace. No fear, no more doubts, no doom.'

Kolidaran pondered the meaning of the words for a moment, trying to unravel the exarch's intent from the florid phrases.

'You offer to bring me into your shrine? To abandon my Path for yours?'

'Just so, it will be done, without prejudice.'

The fear brought on a sharp pang of the hunger that ate at Kolidaran's spirit. The ebbing away of his essence, combined with the pain of his wounds, made him feel dizzy. He could feel his heart beating hard in his chest, but growing weaker. As his pulse slowed, the hunger grew. She Who Thirsts waited for his spirit and was but a breath away from claiming her prize. The terror of that thought leant strength to Kolidaran's words.

Survival outshone pride or loyalty every time.

'I accept! Save me from this eternal doom, my life and spirit in your hands.'

Waking, feeling warm sheets beneath and upon him, Kolidaran kept his eyes closed, enjoying the comfort of half-sleep. He could not remember when he had slumbered so deeply. The moment passed quickly, giving way to vulnerability. He was without armour or weapon – they had been taken from him before he had been brought to the starship's halls of healing – and instinct of a life spent under threat made him yearn for such protections. In the incubi shrine he would not have survived without such measures.

A quiet voice, female, spoke close by.

'Rest easily, you are safe.'

Something rested on his arm beneath the sheet and Kolidaran opened his eyes to see the healer, Naroami, standing over him. Her left hand was upon him, and in her right she held an amulet studded with four diamond-like jewels. A tiny star of blue glowed in the heart of each gem.

They were in a small room – isolated from the crew Kolidaran had noted – with the single bed and a low cabinet topped with a marble-like counter. Various crystals of different sizes, colours and shapes were arranged on a rack atop the cupboard and there was a tray of medical implements beside them.

'Your body responds well to your will,' she said. 'You have a strong spirit.'

'It has been honed by long adversity.'

'And how do you feel?'

Kolidaran moved slightly, flexing muscles. He grimaced as pain flared up his spine.

'Stiffness everywhere,' he said through gritted teeth, 'and my back feels as though it is on fire.'

'You misunderstand the question. I am fully cogent of your body's ailments. Your physical injuries will heal. It is your spirit, your thoughts, which I seek to understand. How do you *feel*?'

'Why?'

A slight frown of confusion wrinkled Naroami's brow, the healer surprised by the question.

'Tissue can be knitted together, fractures set, but the damage to your spirit is beyond simply reconstruction. If you are not well of spirit, the healing of the body is pointless.'

'Typical craftworlder drivel! You said yourself that my spirit is strong. I have endured worse in my life.'

Naroami looked long at Kolidaran, and he sneered at the compassion that filled her eyes. He met her gaze with a hard stare.

'I do not desire your sympathy and your pity is offensive.'

Naroami looked away, distracting herself with the crystal device in her hand. She did not look up when she spoke.

'Bitterness is to be expected. You have been touched by such darkness and you do not understand the full extent of your peril.'

'Peril? It would be pointless to heal me and then slay me; even craftworlders are not that stupid. When my body is repaired, what is your intent?'

'I have no intent. Nor does any other. The bleak lens through which you view the universe taints your perception, seeing enemies that do not exist.'

'The exarch, he said my fate would belong to him. That would be intent.'

'Kenainath, exarch of the Hidden Death. He brought you to me, naked as you are now, and said nothing of how you came to him nor of any bargain made.'

'Then his words ring hollow. He promises me peace and then abandons me.'

'He can do nothing for you as you are, but now I understand his meaning. As an Aspect Warrior you can learn to control the anger and hate that defines you. You are Commorraghan, that much is clear from your speech and attitude. Why Kenainath spared you, I do not know, but it is not under the auspices of an exarch that you will begin to find peace.'

'If I understand right, do not craftworlders excise their Khaine-given rage in the Aspect Temples? It would seem Kenainath would do the same for me.'

'You cannot become an Aspect Warrior. You are not ready.'

'I assure you that my skill is beyond question, and you must know that I have slain many foes before. My whole life has prepared me for battle.'

Naroami shook her head, saddened. She turned her back on Kolidaran for a moment; when she returned her gaze to him her expression had hardened, her face set.

'You are damned. Even now, the Great Enemy lays claim to your spirit. One such as you can never find peace while the fear of She Who Thirsts and the hunger of that grip consume you.'

'So what am I to do? Am I prisoner here?'

'Not by force, but by circumstance. We return to Alaitoc, but you are free to leave at any time. No constraint is placed upon you. Yet, where would you go?'

Kolidaran thought of the matter for a few moments.

'I cannot return to Commorragh,' he said, scowling. 'My position at the shrine is forfeit and I would not crawl begging to the kabals.'

'It would be a terrible waste of the opportunity that fate has presented you. Guided by whatever hand, Kenainath has granted you a moment to pause and reflect, to see the paths laid out for you to follow. Simply to return to your previous existence would be unwise.'

'Fate?' Kolidaran laughed cruelly. 'I will tell you what fate means. It means facing the fear every moment of your life, knowing that one day all will fall to doom. Fate does not decree the path I take, only my own will.'

'And what does your will tell you?'

'There are other employments for one trained in the craft of battle.' There was disappointment in Naroami's expression, almost the pity she had shown before. It pierced Kolidaran's bravado and he deflated, shamed though he did not understand why. 'I am a death-dealer, not a healer. I kill or I am killed. Do you think I would be content within your craftworld? Shunned, perhaps despised, though your kind oft-claim not to hate us as much as we hate you. My spirit is awash with the blood of innocents, you cannot cleanse it. You cannot change what I am.'

'You are right.' Naroami smiled and once more laid her hand on Kolidaran's arm. She squeezed gently. 'I can do nothing. You... You have the power to be whatever you desire, if you could shed the darkness that fills you.'

'And what would you do to free me from the doom that waits for me? Would the Alaitocii send armies into the Womb of Catastrophe to destroy the Great Enemy for me? Is that how you would see me free?'

'Always it is battle you turn to, but you might consider an alternative.'

'Become a Harlequin, perhaps? Yes, I could swear my life to Cegorach and hope that the Laughing God chooses to snatch my spirit from She Who Thirsts when the time comes. But alas, my singing voice is poor and I have no liking for dance.'

The healer's hand moved to the silver chain of a pendant and pulled forth an oval ruby-coloured gem from within her robe. Kolidaran sensed warmth and protection emanating from the jewel.

'You proudly display your spirit stone, as if that could give me reassurance. You mock me, surely? To show me a shield I can never bear. Yes, you might think yourself safe from cruel attentions after death, but it is too late for me. No such comfort for such as me. A pirate, a mercenary, that will be my fate. You were bonded to that stone at birth.'

'It is our way,' said Naroami. 'The best way. But it is not the only way.'

Seeing the earnestness in the healer's eyes, Kolidaran was intrigued. More than intrigued, he felt a brief glimmer of hope birthed within the hunger of his spirit; a tiny star amidst a universe of darkness.

'Another way? I could have a spirit stone? Do not give false promise, or I will kill you now and seal my doom without regret.'

'It is not a simple thing, for it requires you to be reborn. For one who has lived a life such as yours the experience will be painful, and the pain might madden you past all reason.'

'Insanity? It seems little risk, for if I am to go mad I will not know what has befallen me.'

'If the rebirth takes such a toll, there is only one outcome. For your own sake you would be euthanised.'

'And finally here comes the threat. You would kill me if I fail?'

'It would be a mercy, believe me.'

Kolidaran did believe her, such was the sincerity that radiated from the healer.

'The choice is wholly yours to make. I offer only an option, not a sure cure.'

Kolidaran's lip twisted in scorn, but it was more for show than keenly felt. The choice the craftworlders offered, what Kenainath must have known would be presented, was tempting. More than tempting, it offered salvation and the thought of it grew in Kolidaran's mind, growing stronger, and in growing it soothed the hunger in a way that his cold ambition had never achieved.

'Insanity and death on the one hand,' he said. 'On the other, a violent life doomed to end with damnation and my spirit devoured for endless torment.'

The fear returned as he spoke, like a chilling fog that crept out of his heart and caused his limbs to tremble. If he was to attempt the rebirth and fail, he would hasten eternal agony. But if he risked that...

Suddenly, he understood his terror in a different way. The lectures of his former klaivex returned to thought. Even as he had sought standing and greatness it had merely been distraction from the dread in his heart. He realised how shallow, how empty, his existence as an incubi had been. He had learnt to survive, but in doing so had given up any chance to truly live.

'Better a slim chance than none. I accept your offer, healer.'

The arrival at Alaitoc had been inconspicuous. Naroami had taken him to the exarch, Kenainath, after the other warriors and crew had left. In the company of the shrine-leader he had been brought before a small kabal of other Striking Scorpion exarchs. The debate had been short and to the point.

'He must be accepted, pupils are not turned away – it is not a choice.' Kenainath stood in the Chamber of Autarchs with the five other Striking Scorpion exarchs. Beside the Deadly Shadow exarch stood the former incubi, eyes downcast, demure and silent. He wore a plain white robe from the Halls of Healing, several spirit-aligning gems hung about his person to aid his recovery.

'He is the enemy, one of the dark kin. He cannot be one of us!' The exarch, introduced as Kadonil, was vehement.

'This is no debate, I have made my final choice, I will not change it.'

'What you say, it is true, he is yours,' said the female called Liruieth, her voice quiet but firm. 'Watch him close, tell no one, work him hard.'

'He will be silent, none but us shall ever know, a Scorpion's secret,' Kenainath assured them.

Kadonil whirled away in disgust. Aranahra stalked off without a word. The remaining exarchs nodded in compliance, and departed.

'That went well,' said Kolidaran.

'You will be silent, speaking to no other but me, until we are done,' the exarch said sternly. Kenainath turned away. Kolidaran took a step to follow and the exarch stopped to look back at him.

'You will remain here, another will come to you soon, prepare for rebirth.'

With an exasperated exhalation, Kolidaran sat on a bench and watched Kenainath depart. He looked around, his annoyance quickly dissipated by interest in his surroundings. The craftworld, like the starship, was utterly unlike Commorragh. Here there was light everywhere, sometimes dim and pale, but ever present. There were no shadows, he noticed. No dark places where mandrake or ur-ghul might lurk.

The chamber was not large, a small hall with arching ribs that formed a dome above him. Hemispheres set into the spars spilled their yellow light upon him, gently dappled to oranges and white that slowly moved and split and coalesced.

It was quite calming, in a way, but the feeling of naked vulnerability returned as Kolidaran awaited the arrival of his next captor.

He did not have to wait long before the portal sighed open and a heavily robed figure stood in the doorway. She wore many rune-talismans on necklaces and bracelets over her dark red robes, green-and-white tinted hair drawn back in an elaborate topknot to show a face that was slightly too narrow, the cheekbones too high to be considered beautiful even by Commorraghan standards.

Kolidaran stood up as the seer entered, for such she clearly was.

'I am Shyladuril, I will be your guide for the rebirth.'

Kolidaran nodded in acceptance of this fact.

'You have no words of greeting for me?'

'The exarch bade me speak to no one.'

'A wise precaution, but you will speak with me, for I know already who and what you are.'

'You are a farseer?' The possibility intrigued Kolidaran. The psyker could see the threads of fate and would be able to tell him whether his rebirth was an attempt at folly.

'Your fate is uncertain,' said Shyladuril, answering the question before it formed on his lips. 'Many are the knots on our threads when the future is yet unfolding. The decision is made but the outcome not set.'

'You have no guidance for me? I thought farseers were meant to be advisors.'

'I offer no words or encouragement, but I have no words of warning either. Both you have heard, from others and within your thoughts. I will ask you, at this time and place, as we stand upon a branching destiny, is it your will, alone and without coercion, that you wish to do this thing?'

'Without coercion?' Kolidaran laughed, bitterness adding a sharp edge to his humour. 'The horror unleashed by our forebears coerces me. The fate sealed for all of us when the first temples fell and the Great Enemy screamed his triumph motivates me upon this course.'

'You are astute, and your fear is not without just cause. It was your misfortune that fate placed your spirit into a body born into the darkness of Commorragh. Rare is the second chance fate has given you, and rarer still those who can accept it. Almost unique are those who survive to enjoy its full benefits.'

'Others? Commorraghans who have been bonded to spirit stones? It really is possible!'

'Of the kin of Commorragh, I do not know. Perhaps they live on other craftworlds – there are none like you on Alaitoc. I speak of those eldar born beyond the craftworld, unexpectedly or in secret, not to be blessed with the spirit stone at their birth. If we get them as children, it is not so difficult. As adults...'

Kolidaran did not like the silence that followed.

'I will do it, nevertheless. Cast what runes you must and let us begin.'

'Haste will see you doomed, so first temper your impatience.'

Shyladuril produced an oval grey stone from one of the pouches at her belt. Compared to those he had seen bonded to the craftworlders it seemed dull and inert, lacking the spark of life at its core. The farseer held it out on her palm. 'Take it.'

Hesitantly, Kolidaran reached out. He jerked back his fingers a moment before they touched, fearing what contact might bring.

'Take it, it cannot harm you. Simple possession of a Tear of Isha does not begin the process.'

Emboldened by Shyladuril's words, Kolidaran plucked the spirit stone from her hand. It was cold to the touch, the surface as smooth as silk. He held it up, watching as amber light reflected from its curve.

'Where did it come from? I hear that the Tears of Isha can only be recovered from the crone worlds at the heart of the Womb of Destruction.'

'Even in Commorragh there are some truths. This tear was wept upon Naimashamenth.'

The name meant World of Glittering Falls.

'I have not heard of it,' confessed Kolidaran. The stone was warmer now, though whether from his touch or some inner energy he could not tell.

'It does not matter. Regard the stone. It will become part of you. It will become you. See it. Hear it. Smell it. Feel it.'

'Smell it?' Kolidaran chuckled as he lifted it to his nose, doubtful. At first he detected nothing. 'Stone does not smell.'

'Open up your senses to your spirit, for that is what you must seek. Do not sense the stone as it is, but as it will be.'

Vexed, Kolidaran sniffed once more, closing his eyes to focus on his sense of smell. Again, at first, there was nothing. As he was about to give up he caught a scent: the unmistakable fragrance of fresh blood. As he absorbed this a distant sound came to his ears, of cries of pain and blades clashing. He started to tremble, moved by the recollection of battle. The spirit stone grew warmer and then pulsed.

Such was his shock, he almost dropped it.

When he opened his eyes, he found that he was alone in the chamber, the lights dimmed to twilight. He did not know whether he had spent a moment or an age with the stone, but it was there still, gently throbbing between his fingertips.

Kolidaran moved across the chamber to lay on one of the benches, his surrounds slightly dream-like and unfocussed. Resting his head against the unyielding seat gave him a sense of place, of solid reality. He closed his eyes and brought the spirit stone up to this chest, resting his hands one on the other on top of it.

The blood smell came back, stronger than before. The noise of war and weapons grew to a clamour. The spirit stone pulsed quickly, his heart racing in time with it.

* * *

The first memory is little more than a flash. A chainsword lashes against the side of his head. Terror fills him, wrenching out his heart and freezing his mind. Death is certain. The hunger consumes him, burning up his existence from within like a flame crawling along paper, leaving the ashes of damnation.

Another battle. Humans scream and shout as the incubi break into their hovel. He leads the attack, cutting the head from the first woman and gutting the second. Too old and weak to be any sport for the hierarch desiring prisoners for the fighting pits. The children are left for the kabalites that follow in the wake of the shrine-warriors. A male adult wearing the oil-stained clothes of a labourer swings a bulky metal tool at his head. He swerves from its slow arc, the blade of his klaive slicing through the wrist of the man. He smashes the butt into the human's throat, knocking him to the floor, gasping and coughing. An armoured boot to the side of the head silences the man's choking.

The incubi sell their skills for the goals of others, but it is unsatisfying to subdue rather than kill. He wants to see the splash of crimson that signals the swift, efficient kill. He wants to witness that moment where life becomes death, when animate becomes inanimate. This battle is empty, only the panic of the humans providing a momentary cessation of the gnawing feeling in the base of his skull.

Another has found an arcane-looking pistol and fires. A solid slug of metal ricochets from his armour, and cracks into the low, poorly plastered ceiling, showering motes of dust. The human hastily reloads, cracking open the breach of the pistol, fumbling with clumsy hands at the bullets in his pocket.

He wants to kill. The man is armed; it would be justified. He holds back, his bloodthirsty spirit raging against the colder, higher functions that turn the killing blow into a sweep that topples the man from his feet, the pistol spinning from his grasp. Klaive held in one hand, he activates the shred-net launcher attached to his forearm. Clinging, thorned tendrils envelop the scrabbling human. The prey tries to writhe free but his movements only make the shred-net constrict. Soon the barbs digging into the man's flesh, tipped with paralysing toxins, cause him to fall still rather than suffer more pain.

He moves through the household, but it is empty of more prey. Disappointed, he breaks a window at the rear, climbing into an alley. Above him a pall of smoke spreads across the night-shrouded sky, blotting out the stars.

Faster and faster come the memories, of old battles and midnight raids. His is a life awash with blood, of lives ended to the symphony of crackling blades, breaking bones and screams cut short. They come so fast they become a blur, a nauseating strobe of violence and mayhem.

* * *

Nathrikh is lax, paying more attention to Asanakit than to him. Asanakit has been too obvious of late, prowling like a caged animal, watching every move of their incubi masters with starved eyes. Nathrikh turns her back to him to keep an eye on Asanakit while the other acolyte polishes the trophy badges hanging from the ceiling on strips of tanned alien skin.

He strikes, using the moment of vulnerability to ram a spike of bone into the back of Nathrikh's right knee. Just as he planned while he sharpened the stolen femur in his cell, thinking and dreaming and waiting patiently, Nathrikh buckles. In a moment he has his arm around her throat, wedged tight between chestplate and helm. With his free hand he catches the haft of her klaive as Nathrikh tries to swing it over her shoulder. A kick to her injured leg causes her to fall further and he twists, wrenching the weapon from her hands even as his arm tightens on her throat.

He jerks her head to one side, feeling vertebrae cracking, her windpipe collapsing. Letting go, he steps back to watch her die. Out of the corner of his eye he sees Asanakit take a step, but the other acolyte is too slow; the tip of the klaive rises towards him and Asanakit retreats into the shadows.

Fingers clawing at the stone floor, Nathrikh tries to crawl towards him, hacking and retching inside her helm, limbs weak and trembling from the damage to her spine.

It is taking too long. Though the ebb of despair that flows from the defeated incubi is like a gentle, cooling breeze soothing the hunger within, he wants that moment of death. With a casual flick of the klaive, he parts the artery at the side of her neck and watches as rich blood spurts onto the floor he had been scrubbing only moments before.

He raises the klaive above his head in triumph. He will clean floors no more. He is a slayer. He is incubi.

The archway is forbidding, but no greater obstacle than those he has already overcome. Inside is sanctuary. The ancient runes above the portal mean nothing to him; he cannot read or write. Yet there is something in the other designs, the blades and flames and burning skulls, that makes it clear that sanctuary will not be granted easily.

He crosses the threshold, the pain in his gut, the gnawing and churning of the hunger like acid in his veins.

He is swallowed by shadow for a moment and presses on. Three steps more, he forces himself out into a broad courtyard. Three hooded and cloaked youths confront him.

'You are not welcome,' says one.

'This is a hall of pain,' says another.

'Turn back,' says the third.

'No,' he manages to whisper through cracked lips, his tongue and gums as dry as ash.

He can do nothing as fists and feet pummel him to the ground, pounding into flesh, bruising and breaking. All he has to do to make it stop is crawl out into the archway again.

He cannot. He will not.

The beating stops after an eternity of mind-numbing pain.

A shadow falls over him and he looks up to see the klaivex, her blades drawn. She smiles, the expression more sinister than anything he has ever encountered before. She steps aside and points one of her demi-klaives towards the door on the other side of the courtyard; a silent welcome.

The gnawing of starvation in his gut is nothing compared to the wrenching abyss within his spirit, but he must eat. The sluggish waters of the Khaides gurgle past, swirling into eddies beneath the piles of the bridge. From the darkness he sees what he needs washing along on the current. It catches on the line he has strung beneath the span and gently turns in the water, coming to rest against one of the ornate pillars holding up the bridge.

He waits, checking the darkness with ears and nose as much as sight. Ur-ghuls frequent these parts.

There is nothing. He steals from his lair and drags the corpse out of the water. It is good. A human, body marked by lash and brand, tossed from the heights of the towers above the black river. He cannot light a fire to cook it without drawing attention and such is his famished state he cannot wait to drag the body to a safer den.

He sinks his teeth into the raw flesh.

And finally a single tableau etched deep into his memory, buried so far beneath the blood and pain it had never before surfaced.

His mother stands over him, her knife rammed into the mouth of the rearing ur-ghul. The creature's scent-pits flare while dark blood cascades across her pale skin. From her back jut three sword-like claws and her life-fluid sprays down upon him.

It is here that the fear begins. It is here that the pit in his essence opens up, revealing the doom that awaits. Death. Damnation.

There is no innocence lost, for he was condemned at the moment of his birth.

With recollection comes a haunting feeling, worse even than the starvation of spirit that has plagued his life. It is like a thousand daggers in his mind, a thousand razor edges slicing his thoughts, a thousand despicable deeds reflected in each shining blade.

Despair. Hate. Anger. Lust. All are washed away as his life flows from the wounds to be replaced by an excruciating ache.

Guilt.

* * *

White, brilliant light blinds him. The daggers turn to shards of crystal in his spirit, their touch like the frozen wastes of the void.

Like a healer drawing venom, the crystal splinters soak up the guilt and the pain. And the fear.

But the pain is too much. He is lost. Without the hunger, without the dread, he is nothing. He does not want to be obliterated but the crystalline hooks in his essence will not release him. Like the shred-net they grow tighter the more he struggles.

He pauses, gathering his strength for one last effort, to rip himself free from the terrifying claws that rend him. In that moment he finds clarity. There is more than war and hate and pain. There can be peace.

He must surrender to it.

He has never surrendered in all of his hard life. To live is to fight, to exist is to know agony. He cannot succumb, but he must.

He feels sorrow. A sorrow so deep it would drown worlds. The Tears of Isha, raining down upon a doomed civilisation. A goddess mourns for the loss of an entire race, her children dragged into damnation by their own greed and desires and selfishness.

It is then that he understands. He knows why a she-bitch of a slave would give her life for a mewling infant that is more burden than boon. He knows why the hunger can never be sated by blood and why the pain will never remove the stings of his doom.

And then he gives up, setting his mind free, letting his spirit soar into the light, allowing himself to relinquish the fight. He capitulates entirely, trusting to the love of a mother and a goddess.

Opening his eyes, Kolidaran found that the chamber was filled with light again.

The stone upon his breast was warm to the touch, filled with a deep blue light that gently waxed and waned with the beating of his heart. And then he felt it; or rather did not feel it. The emptiness, the hunger and pain had gone.

He cradled his spirit stone like a child and wept.

When Shyladuril returned, Kolidaran was sat with the spirit stone in his lap, entranced by its ever-shifting patterns. He was rapt by the thought that this stone could protect him from the hunger, from the doom of the eldar.

'You are whole and sane, I see,' said the farseer.

'Your sight is not in error.'

'How do you feel?'

Kolidaran had to think for a moment.

'Content, but strangely restless.'

'The rebirth is only the beginning of your new journey. That which we have practised since childhood, the control of memory and emotion, the exercise of discipline and order, will have to be learnt. But it is a good start.'

The farseer sat next to Kolidaran and handed him a silver brooch, the centre inset to take his spirit stone. He accepted the gift without word, slipped the stone into place and pinned the brooch upon the breast of his robe.

'From here you will go to the Shrine of the Hidden Death, and receive teaching from Kenainath to take power over your hate and anger. When you have trodden the Path for the first time you will be truly of the craft-worlds and this life will begin anew, refreshed with each new Path you tread.' The seer gave him an intent look. 'Your past life is gone, and your Commorraghan name with it. The individual that you were is no more. You need a name by which you will be known on Alaitoc.'

He had already considered this. Kolidaran was a creature of his memories, another person entirely, though they shared a past. Yet something of that Commorraghan love of irony remained and influenced his choice. He had heard Naroami use it several times while he had been convalescing. It meant Spirit on the Wind, and was a craftworlder term for those that died without a spirit stone to guard them.

'I shall be Bechareth,' he said.

Kenainath had been very specific: Bechareth was not to leave the Shrine of the Hidden Death. Until he had learnt properly to don his 'war-mask' the ex-incubi was considered a threat to the craftworlders. His silence was similarly enforced even with those of the Hidden Death. He had spoken at length with Shyladuril about this matter, but she had been adamant. If his history became widely known he would no longer be welcomed by the Alaitocii, for all their espoused tolerance and love of harmony.

It was difficult to think of himself as one of the Alaitocii yet. Their life, the concept of the Path, was so very different. However, he had been born again, gifted a fresh start that few ever had. His memories, the blood-soaked past that he had ignored for so long, were still there, but his rebirth had washed away all association with them. It was if he looked upon another when he delved into his recollections; watched some other gutter-child drag himself up from the filth to become a savage killer.

The disassociation was not total, so he had been warned. His hate, his anger, the things that had shaped Kolidaran still drove Bechareth, though his detachment now allowed him to see their influence and the destruction they had wrought upon his spirit.

Yet such emotions still had their uses and when the Hidden Death had been called to war, Bechareth had been called with them. So it was that he found himself again in the midst of strife and death. Clad in new armour he now stalked the galleries of a human ship, killing all in his path as he had done countless times before. Now he fought alongside Kenainath and the Hidden Death, a member of a team not a group of individuals, and it felt good to share in the slaying.

It seemed strange, to wield the chainsword and pistol of the Striking Scorpion rather than his klaive, but many of Kenainath's lessons in battle-craft had echoed sentiments first delivered by Naremun: the swift attack and quick kill; the superiority of feints and misdirection; the supremacy of the hidden strike. All that was required was to master the same techniques with these new weapons.

The humans were unwittingly transporting worshippers of the Dark Gods, he had been told, and posed a threat to the future of Alaitoc. As he slashed his chainsword across the face of a flat-nosed crewman Bechareth did not care for the reasons why he was here, only that he could give vent to the nascent hate that still resided within.

He had feared that the spirit stone would have robbed him of his zeal for slaughter, but now he was given free rein, to unleash the bloodlust with the full force of something he had never felt before: righteousness.

As he cut down another human he knew that he was far from finding peace, but at least there was no more fear.

ABOUT THE AUTHOR

Gav Thorpe is the *New York Times* bestselling author of 'The Lion', a novella in the collection *The Primarchs*. He has written many other Black Library books, including the Horus Heresy novel *Deliverance Lost* and audio drama *Raven's Flight* as well as fan-favourite Warhammer 40,000 novel *Angels of Darkness* and the epic Time of Legends trilogy, *The Sundering*. He is currently working on a new Dark Angels series, *The Legacy of Caliban*. Gav hails from Nottingham, where he shares his hideout with the evil genius that is Dennis, the mechanical hamster.